# THE EDINBURGH SEER TRILOGY

*Complete Trilogy*

ALISHA KLAPHEKE

USA Today Bestselling Author
# ALISHA KLAPHEKE

# the Edinburgh Seer

EDINBURGH SEER BOOK ONE

This is a work of fiction. All events, dialogue, and characters are products of the author's imagination. In all respects, any resemblance to persons living or dead is entirely coincidental.

Text copyright © 2017 by Alisha Klapheke
Cover art copyright © 2017 by Damonza

All rights reserved.
Visit Alisha on the web! http://www.alishaklapheke.com

Library of Congress Cataloging-in-Publication Data
Klapheke, Alisha
The Edinburgh Seer Complete Trilogy/Alisha Klapheke. —First Edition.
Summary: A candymaker's daughter conceals her sixth sense to avoid the firing squad until her father is kidnapped and she must use her ability to track him through a trail of ancient artifacts.
ISBN 9781987488913
[1. Fantasy. 2. Magic—Fiction.] I. Title.

Printed in the United States of America
10 9 8 7 6 5 4 3 2 1
First Edition

ISBN: 978-0-9987379-7-3

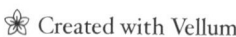 Created with Vellum

*To my Uncommon Crew and my Reading Rebels*
*May the goats be with you*

CHAPTER 1
CANDYMAKER'S DAUGHTER

Summer, 2017, Fifteenth Year of John III's Reign

THE MORNING SUN HAD JUST MANAGED TO PAINT A PALE yellow light over Edinburgh's Old Town, and, as usual, Aini MacGregor had already run three errands and set up her father's candy lab for the day's work. Pots, scrubbed and warmed, on the stove. Measuring spoons shined to make the morning sun jealous. Bags of powdered sugar and vials of hormones and chemicals standing in place like disciplined kingsmen. Everything was exactly where it needed to be.

The tower was chilly this time of day and goosebumps hurried over Aini's skin as she unscrewed a jar and shifted the newly purchased cinnamon into its tidy home. She inhaled the lovely scent. Tears burned her eyes—not because of the many spices she had at her fingertips, but because of the rasping voice carried on the wind through the cracked, leaded window above her head—the voice of Nathair Campbell, the very powerful man who would shoot her dead if he knew what she was.

A sixth-senser.

Demanding her skittering heart to quit distracting her, Aini continued about her work. Today would be a great one for her father, Lewis MacGregor, crafter of the nobility's beloved sweets. Together, with the apprentices' help, they shaped goodies that not only tasted divine, but gave the eater certain short-term abilities usually enjoyed by birds or insects, or only dreamed up by wild imaginations. They'd been a hit at the king's last birthday party. The British king was a terrible man—Aini couldn't change that—but at least his parties helped with business. With the vision-inducing gum they were about to craft and test, the MacGregor business, Enliven, was poised to rule the boutique sweets market. If only the stupid thugs, the Campbells, would leave well enough alone.

Clan Campbell worked for the king, maintaining his rules here in Scotland. But lately...they seemed to have become very full of themselves and were taking on projects that Aini was certain the king himself knew nothing about.

"Who is shouting to wake the dead in the Grassmarket?" Neve demanded in place of a *Good Morning*. Father's female apprentice padded into the room. When she wasn't working in the lab, Neve took tourists around Scotland with Caledonia Tours. She knew her history, that was for sure.

With quick fingers and a smile, the Edinburgh native pulled her hair into two high buns and secured them with pins. All the girls here wore their hair like that. Aini tugged at one of her own heavy, black locks. It refused to be tied up, but even though it made her stand out—not many half Balinese girls in Scotland— she couldn't hate it. It reminded her of her mom, a woman who hadn't been perfect, but who'd loved her completely.

Aini straightened her lab coat and eyed the king's rules hanging on the wall. An identical list of "Scottish citizens cannot do this" and "All citizens and colonials must do that" were posted in every pub, home, and store in the entire British Empire. Even across the pond in the rebellious Dominion of New England colonies. Aini wondered if they'd ever get over their 18th century loss. They were nearly as bad as the Scottish rebels here.

Blinking, she remembered Neve's earlier question. "Nathair Campbell is down there, dirtying the morning."

Neve made a Scottish sound of disgust in the back of her throat. Aini couldn't have agreed more. "I'm excited about that new gum recipe," Neve said.

Perfectly on time—because Aini perfectly timed it—the gum base started to bubble on the stove.

"Your white pepper idea for the gum is going to work. I can feel it." Aini wiped her hands on a towel, breathing in the sweet smells. "I really think it'll trigger the chewer's schema for fire."

Neve grinned, and Aini realized her Dominion of New England accent was blazing again.

Thane loped into the lab, and Aini's heart whirred like a broken taffy puller and pushed every other thought out of her head. At six-foot-four, the Scotsman dominated the room, all broad shoulders, gray flashing eyes, and downturned mouth. He pulled his glasses out of his messy, honey-colored hair and headed toward his lab coat on the far hook. Mud caked the toes of his boots, and a silver necklace winked from his collarbone.

Because of who Aini was, and *what* Aini was, Thane with his late nights and penchant for whisky was the very definition of *Look, but don't touch.* She had to be careful. Do nothing dangerous. Never break any rules.

"Good morning, Thane."

Just because he wasn't for her didn't mean she had to be rude. After all, he was Father's favorite, besides herself, of course. Thane had developed the original formula for the vision gum. Aini wished she had half the brains he did.

"We're almost ready to mix," she said.

His gaze slid over her fingers and up her arms, and he gave her a nod.

As Neve measured out the pepper, Aini held a hand toward the bubbling broiler. "A little help?" she asked Thane. Her face heated. Why did her cheeks have to flush so easily?

"Aye. Course." Thane's thick, West Scots accent wrapped around every O and tripped over each R beautifully.

Tugging his coat on, Thane slid his glasses onto his slightly overlarge nose. Tattoos of chemical formulas snaked down his fingers in black letters, tiny numbers, and mathematical symbols. Aini leaned forward a little. NaCl was salt. Another finger had a $V$ over a $t$ and—*oh*—it was the formula for viscosity. But the other markings? She could never quite get a good look at them.

Father walked in, wearing his usual style—all black under his lab coat, and every item ironed into full submission. He winked before readying the powdered sugar at the lab's silver table. He still wore his wedding ring, though the divorce happened long before Aini's mother died two years ago. She sighed, wishing she could do something about that pain.

"I was thinking," Father said to Thane, "if we used a pressure cooker to force the Maillard reaction in tomorrow's Dulce de Leche recipe…"

Thane's face brightened. "We could decrease the cooking time by perhaps six times." Thane lifted the pot as Aini stirred. His arm brushed hers and she swallowed. "Genius, Mr. MacGregor," Thane said.

"Will you never stop with the Mr. MacGregor? Just Lewis, please."

Thane smiled at Father like he was his own, like Father could somehow heal the hurt that clouded the uni student's eyes. But it was all right. She wasn't jealous. Aini knew Father was good at providing a stable life, a simple and scheduled way of living, something maybe Thane hadn't experienced before apprenticing here.

"Neve, will you please warm up the mixer?" Father wiped a spot of sugar off his nose and set his planner on the desk near the far end of the lab. The green and blue sugar, in the jars he'd mounted on the whitewashed wall, sparkled. He frowned like there was something unpleasant about them. Aini touched her chin. She'd always wondered why he displayed the jars like that. They'd never used those colored sugars and surely it would be better to have them with the other ingredients, organized by the lab table. She'd look into it later.

Father shook his head and went to help Thane pour the steaming gum base into the powdered sugar.

The lab's landline rang and Aini picked up. A familiar, rough voice asked for Lewis MacGregor. Aini gritted her teeth. Not *them* again. Her grip on the phone tightened.

"Hold please." She looked to Father. "It's for you."

He stared at the ceiling, eyes pressed closed, before finally taking the call.

While Neve dealt with the mixer's perpetually moody switch across the room—all while humming a song loved by Father's other male apprentice, Myles—Aini took Father's place beside Thane.

Plunging her hands into the gum blend, she kneaded the sticky stuff. The mix was ready for flavor. The powdered sage, white pepper, and smoky nutmeg did nothing to improve the color of the chewing gum, but she was pretty sure Neve was on to something with this flavor choice. The herbs and spices, along with the medieval art packaging that Myles had drawn up, might just get people seeing ancient castles and feasts in great halls. Chemistry crossed with suggestion. It was how the human brain worked.

"No." Father's knuckles whitened as he squeezed the phone. "I'm not going to weaponize my products. Not until I see the royal approval. I'm finished talking about this." He punched a button and threw the phone to his desk where it banged against his laptop. "Campbells. Pushing and pushing. Playing both sides, and I know very well I'm not going to be the winner no matter how..." Muttering, he stalked back to the table. "I need to get something from my downstairs office. Give me a shout when we're ready to test." He disappeared down the staircase, growling about being left in peace.

The Campbells made up the majority of kingsmen stationed in Edinburgh. Normally, they were the law, acting as the king's agents, along with the other kingsmen. But since that public execution of those rebels last month, things had been different. Nathair Campbell had executed Scottish subjects without a trial of any kind. The king had excused him, blaming overzealous loyalty to the crown, but Aini wasn't so sure. Clan Campbell was less an arm of the king and more of a criminal gang these days. Aini couldn't believe they were pressuring Father to develop products that could covertly paralyze and poison without the king's seal of approval. Even if it was to fight the rebels. It was unfathomable.

Thane breathed hard through his nose like an angry horse.

She eyed the gum, looking for dry spots or uneven spicing. "What is it? What's off?"

Vine-like muscles twisted below Thane's rolled coat sleeves.

He dusted his hands off and pushed his glasses into his hair. "If your father would agree to aid the Campbells, he'd be helping Scotland fight the rebels."

"He doesn't want to twist our craft into something sick and evil." She put her hands on her hips and powdered sugar puffed like little clouds. Flushing, she brushed herself off. "He's worked long and hard to establish Enliven. It's a boutique candy supplier. Not a government laboratory. Besides that, why can't the Campbells go through the official channels and find their own chemists if they're so set on this?"

Neve gathered the pre-blended gum mix. "Because Mr. MacGregor is the best chemist in the empire and they know it."

"Well, we're going to follow the official rules." Aini crossed her arms. "The king could shut us down and you know it."

Neve opened her mouth and closed it again. She hurried to the mixer and dropped her bundle into the metal bowl.

Aini chewed the inside of her cheek. She didn't want to be hard on Neve, but the rules were the rules.

"The Campbells and the king have the same goal, don't they?" Thane frowned. "What difference does fussing about with royal seals make?"

"If my father skirts the law like the Campbells want him to do, the Campbells might get away with it, but I seriously doubt he will."

An image flashed through her memory—an executed sixth-senser.

The woman had been about her mother's age. Aini remembered the lady's wispy, auburn hair. The black band across her eyes. Her body jerking as the bullet hit her chest. The red blood against her striped dress. Her clothing said native Edinburgh, the style Aini tried to imitate. But even fitting in hadn't saved her.

If Aini was found out, the Campbells would assume Father knew about her ability, which he didn't. She squeezed her hands together. She couldn't even think about him rotting in a dark cell.

When the gum was mixed and cooled, Thane cut the ropes into small pieces and Aini called her father back up to the lab. It was time to see if the gum really worked.

THE LIGHT THROUGH THE LAB'S WINDOWS CAST A NET OF GOLD around Aini's father as he peered at his watch. He handed Aini the clipboard of notes they'd destroy as soon as the trial was complete. They couldn't let anyone outside of Enliven get a hold of the information. The competition would leap at the chance to outdo them. Because of this, Aini and the rest had become very, very good at remembering recipes.

Neve and Aini found seats and Thane took a stool, ready to try the gum.

"Where is Myles anyway?" Neve asked.

Aini was actually glad Father's second male apprentice wasn't here. "Buying new paints for his adverts." Myles was great fun, but he could really be a distraction during tests like this.

Father stared at Thane. "I want to know the very minute—the exact moment—you see something." He started the timer on his watch.

"Aye," Thane popped the gum between his lips and chewed, rubbing a hand over his sharp chin.

"How's it taste, then?" Neve scooted forward on her stool.

"A bit fiery."

"Fiery?" Aini asked, pen poised over the clipboard. "Be more specific. We need details for the investors."

"Any visions yet?" Father inched closer to Thane.

Stumbling back, Thane's mouth dropped open, the gum on his tongue.

Aini laughed.

Father practically hopped on Thane. "What do you see, lad?" He normally hid his accent, wanting to please his many English clients, but excitement drew it right out of him.

Staring at the ceiling beams, Thane paled. "Translucent wings. About ten feet long. He's...he's..." The uni student ducked and laughed once, his Adam's apple bobbing in his throat. "He's breathing fire." He shoved his hands through his hair and knocked his glasses to the floor.

Neve hugged herself. "A dragon."

Father lifted his feet in a little jig and grabbed Aini's arm, pulling her into his dance. Heart light, she did a spin, then squeezed him, feeling safe and loved, as if everything was going to be okay.

"I can't believe it," Thane whispered.

Neve grinned. "I knew that white pepper would do the trick."

"Couldn't have done it without you, my wee squirrel," Father said to Aini. "The king will reward us handsomely, what with his birthday celebration coming up. We might get a tax exemption."

"And the elite will want it at their parties if the king has it at his," she said.

Father shouted, "Huzzah!" and zipped over to his desk to write something up.

Aini couldn't stop smiling. Another candy for their impressive inventory. Another building block for Father's beloved business. Somehow, she had to thank the apprentices for all their hard work. Maybe a special dinner or a big night out. This vision-inducing gum was another reason she loved having all of them here, a part of the family.

Neve peppered Thane with questions about the formula. Over Neve's head, Thane met Aini's gaze. A shadow passed over his face. He was a melancholy sort, but this was more. Something...darker. Aini's smile faded. He had nothing to be upset about today. What could be bothering him? Surely not all this stuff about the Campbells. It would pass. Wouldn't it?

Father tugged Aini into another jubilant hug, and her smile returned. She could maintain this happiness. She would maintain it. No matter what. She just had to keep her sixth sense concealed. Because visions prompted by chewing gum earned money, but visions of another sort only led to death.

CHAPTER 2

LIVING IN THE DARKNESS

In Mr. MacGregor's townhouse common room, Thane pulled a book off a shelf. It was a mystery set in the Dominion of New England, where Aini had lived with her mother, then her grandmother after her mother passed on.

Now Aini and her father were settling in for their nightly poetry nonsense by the stone fireplace, and Thane wanted to give them room. Deep inside, Thane knew their ritual was anything but nonsensical, but he didn't want to think on that. He had to stay cold, stay focused.

"Robert Burns again tonight, squirrel?" Lewis said to Aini as he crossed his legs and opened a book on his lap.

The light scrape of a turning page followed the click of the lamp. Aini sat opposite Lewis, her foot pointed as she drew an imaginary circle on the floor with her toe like a ballet dancer. Thane's neck grew a little too warm. He turned away.

"Care to join us, Thane?" Aini asked, her red lips plump and lovely in the lamplight.

"No. Thank you though."

His heart pulled at his chest as he bid them goodnight and went to the room he shared with Myles. The time Thane spent with his own father was minimal and perfunctory, more about drilling loyalty to the clan into him than any kind of bonding.

Thane pushed the bedroom door open, and the glare of the overhead made him squint. A quilt—stitched with the leaf logo of Myles's favorite band, Mint—lay half on, half off the guy's bed. Myles was still upstairs working on his advert with Neve. At least there'd be an hour or so of quiet before the colonial tossed himself into bed to snore like a Highland cow.

Thane switched the overhead off and lit a wide candle on his nightstand. When in the lab, focusing on chemistry and his mission, bright light was key to staying alert, focused. Alternatively, the golden shadows of a candle told Thane's brain to relax.

Using a paperclip, Thane popped his phone open, revealing the electronic guts. He picked out the small square that fed his calls to Campbell headquarters, set it near the candle, and dialed his mother's number.

She answered on the first ring, as always, her strong voice softened by anxiety. "Thane?"

"Yes, Mother. And how are you today?"

"Oh, it's a joy to hear your voice. How's all with you?"

"All right."

"Liar," she said. "You know I don't sleep at night, thinking about the orders they give you."

He rubbed his face roughly. "Can we *not* talk about that for a bit, aye? How is your new gardener working out, then?"

She made a huffing noise over the line. "I had to let him go." Her voice was sad, but then it lifted and sparked. "The man had no sense of what I wanted."

Thane smiled. "Too much trimming?"

"Exactly that. He wanted it like an English garden."

"Well, that wouldn't do, would it?"

"Certainly not," she said, a laugh in her voice. "I can't stand feeling like I'm in someone's parlor when I'm enjoying a walk." She broke off, coughing.

"Are you sick?" he asked.

"No." There was a sound like she'd switched the phone to her other ear. "I'm..."

"He hasn't hurt you again, has he? Just leave, Mother. Please."

"You know he would find me. Find us."

Thane let the silence speak for a beat. It was an old argument. There was no answer for either of them.

"I should have something to please the clan soon," he said tightly. "It's something to do with my mission here."

"Don't fret over me, Son. I've been managing that man since long before you were a twinkle in his eye."

Managing. Enduring abuse is what she did. Thane pressed the corner of the phone into his forehead until the pain cleared away his anger.

"I'll ring you again soon," he said. "All right?"

With her blessing, he clicked the phone off.

He could picture her folding her arms over herself, the phone tucked under an elbow. She was probably standing beside her bedroom window, looking out on the green gardens she loved so well and wearing her favorite cashmere sweater. Though her hair had gone prematurely white, she stood tall, nearly as tall as he, and her shoulders only slightly bent against the life she lived. She'd tug on her perfectly plucked eyebrow as she planned how next to handle her husband, how to best cover the yellowing bruise on her cheek. If there was a woman who could survive under these circumstances, it was her.

If only Thane could help her get away. But the network of

Campbell relatives, operatives, and kingsman, both related and not, was too thick and far-reaching. No one could find their way out. Especially not Thane.

He couldn't truly think of leaving Scotland. He'd been to Paris, Rome, even the colonies and parts of Asia, but no place gave him the same feeling as his own home country. He wondered if others—maybe those who were also descendants of the country's most ancient families—felt the same way. It was like Scotland was a living, breathing being. A person to come home to, who laughed at your jokes and gave you rest when you needed it. The high slopes of the bens, the peat-brown waters, the smell of the air, his feisty people. Scotland beat in his chest like a second heart. It'd kill him to turn his back on the homeland, and he hoped with everything in him he'd never have to do it.

He leaned back on the bed to start on the mystery, but his book sat in his hands, ignored, as Lewis's reaction to the clan's pressure flickered through his mind.

So Lewis thought he could simply say *No*. That Nathair Campbell needed royal approval to actually force him to create sweets that were anything but sweet. Until a month ago, Thane would've agreed his father would wait for the king's go-ahead to pursue this route. But when Nathair ordered those rebels and sixth-sensers shot down in public last month, he'd turned a page in the story of his growing madness. The king had excused Nathair's disregard for following proper execution mandates, saying his head of security was simply overcome with loyalty to king and crown.

Thane knew better.

Nathair wasn't overcome with loyalty; the scarred and vicious leader of Clan Campbell, Thane's own terrible father, lusted for more power.

Unable to read, Thane blew out the candle and pretended to sleep when Myles came in, smelling like paint.

"Good night, sleeping beauty," Myles said, comic sarcasm dripping from his southern colonial accent.

Thane rolled his eyes in the dark. He turned over and began the long wait for a short sleep. He wondered if he'd sleep better if he had a different life to wake up to. Working in the lab was a sick sort of tease. Having Lewis MacGregor as a mentor—such a master chemist and a good man all around. Sharing work space with the others who knew nothing about Thane's real life. It was a dream that would end all too soon, and in a bang, if the past had taught him anything.

THANE WOKE ABRUPTLY, HEART RUMBLING AND STUTTERING. He sat up. The clock on his nightstand said five in the morning. He'd had that strange dream again. The one that had haunted him since childhood.

It began with him simply looking down at his palm. The focus narrowed onto one of his fingers, zooming in, closer, deeper. He seemed to race through the ridges and lines of his own fingerprint. They towered over him like walls of a great valley. Their flesh tone faded. The curves and patterns of his fingerprint grew black as he seemed to rush backward. The sound bothered Thane most. In this last part of the recurring dream, the air reverberated with a shattering boom that made him feel as if his eyes might pop from their sockets.

He'd never told a soul about the dream. When he was young, he didn't want to tell his mother. Running to Mummy was something only wee bairns did. Now, the dream smacked of a sixth sense, so he ignored it as best he could.

One of Myles's ear-cracking snores broke the silence in the dark room, and Thane forced his tired legs out of bed, fumbling for his glasses. Leaving Myles to his dreams, he slipped out of the room, through the warm kitchen, and up the winding, stone steps to the tower lab.

At the low, wide stove, he poured ingredients for Lewis's golden taffy into a huge copper pot. Aini had edged the color enhancing sweet into the day's schedule after she pre-sold a batch to the Earl of Lincoln. With that boiling, and the automatic wooden spoon spinning in the pot, Thane moved on to his real project. If anyone was out of bed this early and surprised him, he could simply point to the taffy as his reason for being here.

The mortar and pestle were still where he'd stored them, behind the blocks of wax they sometimes used for molds. Henbane and nightshade, the dried anticholinergic herbs he'd researched and gathered, hid under the mortar. After setting all this on the table, Thane pulled a vial from his boot.

The small glass container held the substance he'd developed during his first week here. He'd drawn the basics of it from Lewis's aphrodisiac cherry drops. The way Thane distilled the substance increased the paralyzing effect ninety-seven percent and would hopefully, with today's mix, draw the herbal additions through the victim's tongue and into the body.

Dropping the ingredients into the mortar, he ground them until they made a fine powder he had to be sure not to inhale.

The taffy was ready on the stove, so he added the sparkling golden color and orange flavoring, then pulled it off the heat. The mix cooled, and Thane added one tablespoon of Lewis's photoreceptor enhancer, Cone5, into the mix. Those who ate this golden taffy would see the world in an array of colors usually reserved for the Chinese yellow swallowtail butterfly, *Papilio xuthus.* Twenty minutes after consuming, candy-eaters' eyes would be flooded with two extra types of rods that allowed ultraviolet and violet color vision. Thane had never tried it, but it sounded fairly interesting.

Pouring the hot taffy onto a baking sheet and placing it in the lab's oven on two hundred degrees, he'd keep it warm enough to put on the puller when he'd finished his secret project—the altered, intensified cherry drops.

Now for the dangerous drops' flavor—the project for his clan to possibly use on the rebels.

It had to be something unique, not simply cherry. Something that would make any daft fool want to give it a go. Setting the pestle down, he eyed the shelves and jars. What flavor would cover the foul taste the higher levels of the chemical produced?

Above him on a high open shelf, a tall glass container held a cloudy liquid. Coconut extract. He poured two teaspoons into the mortar, his brain latching onto the scent and throwing out mental images of Aini. Ebony hair knotted high and showing off her slim neck. Her ruby lips. That sweet, painfully innocent smile.

"What are you working on?" Aini's voice carried across the lab.

Heart rate increasing, Thane smiled casually, quickly setting the coconut extract on the table and turning to take the warm taffy from the oven.

"Just the taffy you had on schedule."

He laid the baking sheet near the extract, the orange of the taffy rising and combining with the island scent.

Aini gave him a quick smile, then eyed the coconut oil. "And what's this for?"

As she turned, he slipped the mortar and the secret herbs onto the shelf below the table. "I was thinking about a twist on your father's cherry drop recipe. Adding coconut." A little truth turned lies to gold.

"Did you fill out the form for the flavor addition?" Aini touched the mound of taffy on the table, wincing a bit at the heat. With a metal scraper, she began folding the taffy to ready it for the puller. "The king can shut us down for not following procedures." Her hand went to her hip and her eyebrow quirked into a vicious slant.

"Give me the form then. I'm not here to ruin anything." The words stuck a bit in his throat. He certainly wasn't there to make things all rosy.

Lewis walked in, his gaze raging over the lab. "Why is the coconut extract out? Where's the mortar?" He took a breath and looked at Aini, who was ringing her hands. "Can you tidy this place up a bit? I'm shutting the lab down for today. I have to go to the kingsmen's office and have a chat about the Campbells." Lewis's gaze strayed to the battered ring on his left hand.

Thane fisted his hands, his nails cutting into his palms.

"At least I've readied the King's Ointment they ordered..." Lewis pointed to a crate of vials nestled in packing paper. The stuff could heal almost any wound. Expensive and time-consuming to craft though. "Thane, will you take it downstairs?"

"Aye. No bother, Mr. MacGregor."

Pushing the tall bottle of coconut extract over—on purpose —with his elbow, Thane apologized. As Aini and Lewis rushed to clean the mess, Thane bent and cupped the mortar. With the substance behind his back, he retreated, then rounded the table, heading for the vials of King's Ointment. Cloaking his movements with his body, Thane tucked the mortar and herbs into the crate.

His secret concoction hidden, he grabbed a towel and helped with the cleanup.

"Never knew you to be clumsy," Lewis said, frowning at him.

"Didn't sleep much I guess."

Again, Aini raised that eyebrow. She screwed the cap onto the oil. "Did you go out last night?"

"No. Just...my brain would not shut down."

She smiled then, looking sorry for accusing him of sneaking out. It made Thane feel even worse. "That, I understand," she said.

Lewis clapped a hand on his shoulder. "I'm sorry I was so abrupt. I'm a bit...stressed. Please remember, I require dedication, lad, but not more than your mind and body can handle. Why don't you go have a lie down?"

Thane swallowed and his eyes burned. The man was far kinder than any he'd ever known. "I thank you, but no. I'll do."

"All right then."

"Father, why don't we let Thane finish up here," Aini said. "I'll make some oatmeal downstairs and you can be on your way."

Lewis started to pick up the crate of King's Ointment.

"Don't," Thane said. "I'll take it. Don't worry."

Aini looped her arm through her father's and they disappeared down the stairs.

With them gone, Thane had a moment to turn the powder in the mortar into something he could use. After finding a jar of petroleum jelly, he snapped on a pair of latex gloves from his lab coat pocket and lifted the tiny container of healing ointment from its nest. He smeared a nice glob of jelly into the mortar, mixed it, and scooped it into a vial.

It wasn't a clever candy recipe, not what he'd been ordered to work on, but the paralyzing ointment might be enough to please his fool cousin for the time being.

## CHAPTER 3
## GONE

*T*o do list:

1. *buy apples*
2. *look for deals on spices/herbs*
3. *purchase the bread Father likes with his stew*

Since her father had deemed the lab closed, and it was Williamsday, Aini herded the apprentices to the weekly market. If she let them stay home, they'd lie around eating and watching television.

Her mother had been like that; throwing time away as if it wasn't already designated as work hours by the oily man who managed their dance troupe. During their off weeks, Aini tried to get her mom to teach her Balinese or even Scottish history, the story of Lewis's homeland, where Aini had been born. But her mother would only smile condescendingly and claim she needed rest. Aini would retreat to her cot and simmer, frustrated at her mother's nature and the fact that she'd broken up the family for a reason she'd never share.

Visits to Edinburgh were the opposite of Aini's changeable, painfully lackadaisical days in the colonies. With her father's penchant for order, Aini slipped into his type of life happily. He was like her. A goal, a list, the rules—and they were off, conquering.

At the market, the hot and determined sun washed the gathering clouds, whitening their edges and deepening the gray-blue of their heavy middles.

"It amazes me that the days are named after the king now," Myles said, joining everyone under a produce man's tarp and picking up the thread of Neve's conversation about the days of the week.

Aini added another shiny apple to the bag Neve held.

"It shouldn't." Neve used group funds to pay the man.

Thane took the proffered bag of red fruit from Aini, his head brushing the tarp.

"The king can do as he likes." Aini checked off the first chore on the list and enjoyed the momentary shade.

Myles brushed imagined dirt off his purposefully ripped, designer T-shirt. "I know. But I thought I was the only soul arrogant enough to do something like that."

Aini elbowed him. "Quiet." He needed to be careful. Kingsmen patrolled the streets, occasionally stopping people and studying their Subject Identification Cards. "Seriously. Hush."

Myles frowned and pulled at two clumps of his green-dyed hair, lengthening them to resemble horns. Incorrigible. A lot of boys from the plantations of the southern American colonies wore the same style because of that banjo and drum band, Mint. Aini wondered how many of them talked bad about the king like Myles.

"God, look at those poor kids over there." Myles shook his head. "Sucks."

Aini squinted into the sunny marketplace. Children wove around their parents. And yes, they were thinner than she remembered them being. In the colonies, everyone was thin, but Edinburgh had always seemed immune. Until now. The king's new taxes were obviously having a marked effect on those who didn't have a lucrative business like Father's.

The group left the shady produce spot, tall Thane ducking to escape the tarp.

"Give me two of those apples, Neve," Aini said. She slipped away and handed the fruit to one of the scrawny children. It wasn't against the king's rules or the law. They grinned up at her, eyes bright, and ran back to their parents as her heart pinched. If only she could buy them all apples. Even if she had the means, the kingsmen wouldn't like it.

Myles was doing a ridiculous dance, all elbows and raised knees, when she returned. In the craziness of the market, only Neve had noticed her little errand.

"There's that fool with those fancy measuring spoons you like, Aini." Thane pointed across the crowd.

"He's selling cider too, looks like," Neve said, and with a quick smile, she took off.

The merchant accepted money from a foreign woman who'd apparently bought a set of spoons as another tourist reached over her to grab a cutting board made in the shape of Edinburgh Castle. Why people felt the need to buy such silly things was beyond Aini. At least the tourists brought money in. Too bad

Scots were forced to give most of it to the Campbells and the king.

Sweat drizzled down Aini's chest as she trailed Thane and Myles. "This isn't next on our list. I only brought enough money for—"

At the booth, Thane twisted and shoved a cold bottle of cider into her hands. He smiled, his gaze going to her lips. He blinked and looked away. "Hurry. Go on," he hissed at the group.

He'd stolen the cider. Aini blinked, shocked.

As they passed a row of postcard displays, Myles took another bottle from Thane and drank.

Neve looked at the one Aini held. "May I have a bit? It's rough in this sun."

Aini couldn't believe it. Thane had stolen things and right in front of some kingsmen. "But...but we didn't buy these. We can't," Aini lowered her voice, "steal."

She could just imagine what would happen if a kingsman questioned her. If she touched anything sentimental to him—a ring, a bracelet, anything—the memories, they'd swamp her, and it'd be obvious she wasn't normal. It'd all be over for her, for Enliven, for Father.

Thane put a hand behind her back and gently pushed her forward. "Last week you paid eight pounds for one bottle. There's the real crime in this. The man's prices are three times what they should be."

She spun and headed back toward the man's booth. She wasn't about to break the law for some free cider. Ridiculous. She peeked over her shoulder. Thane smiled a little as Neve and Myles finished their stolen treat. This was yet another of the many reasons she couldn't get her head around Thane. It almost seemed like he lived to bend the rules.

With the to-do list complete, they set off for the townhouse, holding their market buys: a bag of apples, a loaf of delicious-smelling fresh bread, a new dress Aini had bought for Neve as a birthday gift (not planned but a good buy nonetheless), a tub of honey, and some dried lavender, which was cheaper than Aini had seen it in a while.

Patting the honey crock, Myles wiggled his dark eyebrows at Neve. "In the past, some ladies have dubbed me their little tub of honey."

Pink patches rose on Neve's neck.

Thane pretended to vomit. "You're pure giving me the boak."

A laugh bubbled out of Aini and she took an apple from the bag. "If you'd cook when it's your turn, Myles, instead of talking that girl down the road into doing it, Neve might consider calling you something nicer. Doubt it'll involve food stuffs, but you can hope."

Neve pulled an edge off the loaf of bread. "She has a point, colonial."

Myles raised his hands to heaven dramatically. "*Colonial.* She got that from you, Thane. Now every time she refers to me, she'll be thinking of your handsome arse."

"Only because you've mentioned it," Thane said.

Myles leaned back to view the subject of the conversation. He whistled low at Thane's backside. "It's only my jealousy talking." He twisted to look at his own rear and shook his head sadly.

Laughing, Aini threw an apple core at him, knowing the tourists' carriage horses would enjoy the treat. Thane palmed Myles's head and shoved him away playfully.

A shriek tore at the morning.

Three kingsmen—not Campbells as they didn't wear the tartan—herded a family of four toward the back of a black van. The smallest, a boy missing most of his front teeth, yanked at the kingsman's grip, crying out. Tears ran freely down his parents' dirty cheeks.

"Let him go." Aini was beside the nearest kingsman before she even realized what she was doing. Her body began to tremble. If they questioned her...

The kingsman's ruddy face pinched into an ugly frown. "Their Subject Identification Cards are expired."

"We don't have the money to renew them," the mother said. "Not after the new tax. Maybe if we—"

The kingsman cut her off. "No maybes. You and yours are going in as punishment for your crime."

"But the children..." Neve started forward, pale. She was probably imagining how this could happen to her little brothers.

Aini took Neve's arm and raised her chin, willing herself not to cow to these men.

"The wee ones will be cared for," the kingsman said. "By the courts. Now move on or you'll be the next taken in." He made to push Aini away.

Heart drumming, watching the kingsman's ring, Aini jerked back, bumping up against Thane who swore quietly and stared the kingsmen down. If that man's ring had touched her, she'd have seen something and it would've all come down on her and Father. There was nothing she could do here and not risk her own family. The wee ones wouldn't be properly cared for. They'd be slaves in all but name, cleaning for the courts and never having someone to look after them. But there was nothing she could do without seriously endangering Father's life. She hated her selfishness, but it was what it was. She couldn't risk Father just to argue with these kingsmen only to lose the fight.

"L-let's go," she said shakily to the group.

The boy's crying leaked through the city's sounds of cars honking, sea birds cawing out, and the hum of market crowds.

None of them spoke as a misty rain started and they rounded the corner, nearing home.

The townhouse, as old as everything else in this area, reached toward the sky and endured the squeeze of the neighboring structures. Greyfriars Cemetery with its tombstone labyrinth and lurking ghosts were only steps away. Aini pulled the three keys to the front door's massive locks from her purse.

Neve touched the door. It swung open. "Aini..."

A prickly sensation climbed over Aini. Palms sweating, she pushed inside. "Father?"

Myles and Thane eased past her and Neve.

"Mr. MacGregor?" Myles called out. "Maybe he just forgot to lock it."

"Doubt it," Thane said, his voice very deep and almost...threatening.

The only sound in the house was the refrigerator's hum in the kitchen and the buzz of the computer in the glass-walled office. Shadows hung around the room; day never really lit the place. An odd smell—tangy, metallic—grabbed Aini's nose. The hairs on the back of her neck lifted.

The carved walking stick she'd bought Father on one of his birthday trips to Ireland sat in the umbrella bin beside the door. She picked it up and stalked farther inside, Thane beside her, as she made her way toward the office. Neve and Myles branched out into the sitting room.

"Should I go check the lab?" Neve asked.

The office door's knob was sticky. Her heart in her ears, Aini brought a hand to her nose.

*Blood.*

Her lungs solidified.

Raising the walking stick over her head, she looked right, left, down, searching the office for more, that prickling sensation running wild over her skin.

"Father!"

Myles ran in. "What is it?"

Reaching up on the wall, Thane flipped the switch, lighting the empty office. A spatter of blood on the edge of the tasseled rug. Three drops of red on the wall. A line across the desk.

The room pulled away, like Aini was suddenly very, very small.

She tore out of the office and toward his bedroom. Pounding through the hallway, into the kitchen, and stopping at the well-worn threshold of his room, she tried to breathe. No air would come.

His room had been ransacked.

The others' jumbled voices ghosted down the hallway.

"I'll go to the local police..." Myles was saying.

"The Campbells own them and you know it," Neve said. "That's who has done this. After all that yelling over the phone and—"

Something crashed and Thane yelled in Gaelic.

"Don't punch the wall. You'll break your hand!" Tears clouded Neve's voice.

Aini pressed hands over her ears, shoulder pressing into Father's doorframe. In the room, his black coverlet tangled around scientific journals thrown from his bedside table. The doors of the armoire hung open to show clothes pulled from their shelves and socks yanked from their drawers to litter the floor. A crack marred the framed photo of Aini and her mother in traditional yellow and red Balinese dancer costumes, taken a month after the divorce.

She started toward it, hands shaking, and her toe caught on something. Father's diary. The cover, what was left of it, was covered in blood.

Her heart was a runaway train. Her vision went blurry.

She spun and ran directly into Thane's hard chest. Her fingers curled into his shirt.

"They've taken him," she said. "There's...there's blood." Her hand, feeling separate from the rest of her, swung in rickety circles at the broken diary and toward the hallway.

"I know. Just—" He started to pull away, but she held to his jacket, her lungs tight, burning.

"What am I supposed to do?" She pressed fisted hands into his chest as the hallway tilted.

"Shh." He pulled her into the warmth of his arms. He ran a hand over her back, his fingers hot. But even though his skin and words were warm, his tone was cold. "You're strong, Aini. Smart. You'll go on."

She jerked away. His nostrils flared and his mouth pinched up.

"Go on?" The door hit the back of her head as she reared away.

Her mind wouldn't work. It couldn't be. Father couldn't be gone. The walls crowded her, choking, smothering. She had to get out of the townhouse, away, away, out, out, out. Away from the smell of blood.

She twisted away from them all and tore out of the townhouse and down Candlemaker Row, her flats slapping the cobblestones, throwing sounds off the stone walls of Ivy's Food and Photography Emporium, where she and Father had eaten steaming bowls of onion noodles in a room with changing walls of Japanese landscape photos. Sucking air, she passed the red glass windows of the perfumery, where they'd hashed out which scents brought forth which memories, leading to the theory about the vision-inducing gum.

She imagined his kind eyes squeezed shut in pain. Someone hitting him. Strangers dragging his slumped body out of the townhouse and into a waiting truck.

*Father. Father. Father.*

Outside the iron scrollwork of Greyfriars Cemetery, she dropped to her knees and put her hands to her chest, trying to force air into her lungs. Her throat convulsed, and the musky air of Father's homeland finally poured into her.

Then Neve, Myles, and even Thane, were there, helping her up.

"I'm fine. It's fine," she said.

But they wouldn't let go, their voices kind and close to her ears. Her hands automatically tucked themselves under her folded arms to avoid touching anything that might hold a memory.

## CHAPTER 4
## WITHOUT

Hot water morphed into clouds of steam in the bathroom attached to Aini and Neve's room. Aini opened the shower door and stepped inside. With the glass casing, she was a caterpillar in a cocoon. But instead of emerging with strong wings and a new life, she'd leave this escape only to find a home without a father. A lab without a leader. A life without the one person left alive who'd known and loved her since childhood. Mother had died two years ago. Grandmother Wayan had followed three months ago. All she had was her father.

And he was gone.

The blood under her fingernails didn't come off easily under the bristles of a scrub brush. It hung on, clinging there and in the creases between her fingers. She pictured Father's laughing eyes, his jig in the lab, and last night with their Robert Burns poetry. Her heart clenched and sputtered, every beat a jagged spike of pain. The images of Father blurred.

The Campbells were the law. What did you do when lawkeepers broke the law? She'd thought abiding by the rules would give Father a peaceful life, a life he deserved. Mother had broken something inside him when she ended their relationship. Aini wanted to fix it with steady days of predictability, just enough excitement to keep things fun, but not dangerous—not too much risk.

Three months. They'd had only three months of peace.

Before all this, Aini's mother had moved her around so much in the colonies. Her dancing troupe toured almost continually, and they'd slept in a different bed every night during those trips, waking to new faces, working to say the right things and entertain the crowd and the ones who'd hired them. It'd been exhausting. They'd never quite fit in anywhere. Not with other colonists. Not with people born and raised in Bali, like her grandmother. And then she'd visit Father and never fit in here either. But at least when she visited him, she slept in the same bed, woke to him every morning.

A sudden thought of a kingsman's fist smashing into Father's bearded chin attacked her mind. The awful sound that would come out of him. Rough. Ugly. Not a sound Father should ever, ever have to make. Tears stormed from her eyes and she fell against the hard shower wall, slumped to the tub floor, and disappeared into pain, hurt, and wild disbelief.

## CHAPTER 5
## THE BLUEFOOT

Once Aini settled into her room with Neve, the scant amount of blood was scrubbed from the office and bedroom, and the authorities were called, Thane raged out the front door. What a joke. The authorities. As if they weren't ordered about by the very ones who'd taken him—Thane's own clan, the Campbells.

The mist outside had morphed into a wet, evening fog that cloaked Thane's face and made his shirt and trousers cling to him. He pulled his glasses off and swiped a hand over his head, sluicing cold water from his hair. He wished he could clean the Campbell from his flesh as easily.

Because they shouldn't have taken Lewis.

He was a good man. Not a rebel. Just a man who didn't want to get caught up in vicious politics.

An empty beer bottle nearly tripped Thane. He kicked it, and the glass shattered against the opposite curb. A group of younger guys laughed and pointed.

Stalking down the slate-colored road, Thane passed the

graveyard's towering stone wall and the unseen spirits who called it home. His thoughts rushed through one side of his mind to the other, his heart tugging at each worry, every consideration. For most of his life, it'd been fine serving his clan and the king. It wasn't a pretty job, full of morally gray duties that felt wrong, but led to good ends—keeping the country safe from rebels and under the protective thumb of his family.

But lately? Lately his father, Nathair—head of the clan and Earl of Argyll—made being a Campbell less of a noble duty and more of a horror show. He'd publicly executed those sixth-sensers and rebels without so much as a trial. Claimed they'd attacked the kingsmen during arrest. A lie. The rebels had hung the banned Scottish flag—the blue Saltire Thane couldn't help but love—over the king's residence at Holyrood Palace, but that was it. This time, the rebels hadn't killed anyone or sacrificed themselves in a bombing like they'd done in the past. It'd been a peaceful protest and one Thane might even see himself doing were he someone else. They'd called for a repeal of the king's rough new tax on factory workers throughout the Empire.

The tax would see more people on the street, homeless, but what did Thane know of what the king needed? Surely there was a safe, political way to battle the new tax. Something that didn't involve breaking the king's laws and incurring the wrath of the Campbells.

And the two sixth-sensers with the rebels? Well, it didn't matter what they'd done or not done. The king ordered them arrested and questioned just for having their strange abilities to see visions or talk to ghosts or whatever the skill happened to be—there were as many different senses as there were Campbells at the king's court. Thane supposed the king hated the sixth-sensers for what they could do for enemies—intel and all that. But he called them abominations. That wasn't right. It wasn't the sensers' fault. They were born with the sixth sense. It wasn't as if they chose it. So why did the king insult them so? Was there more to the king's hatred of sixth-sensers? Probably. But the old man wasn't talking of it to anyone, including the Campbells as far as Thane knew. He only passed on his hate and Thane's father ate it up and spit it back onto the Scottish people. Why did the right side feel so much like the wrong side? There was no right side. Not truly. Thane rubbed his face roughly, his mind whirring like a broken mixer.

The road in front of Thane opened into a courtyard called the Grassmarket, where farmers used to sell animals and crops. The moon shrouded the square of age-nibbled buildings in white light. Thane felt he himself was a ghost, seeing through insubstantial eyes. Anger burned through him, but he couldn't do a thing about it. He had no power to influence his clan's actions. None. His quiet swearing disappeared, worthless, into the growing dark. He could at least make it known Lewis acted as a good subject of the king. He'd shout it at his older cousin Rodric, a glaikit ape who, no doubt, had a big, dumb hand in the abduction.

Thane ran fingers through his tangled hair as he left the better area of Edinburgh. The overripe stench of poverty hit his nose when he reached the broken windows and the sagging two and three-story smoke shops and low rent flats of Bread Street. A man with a patchy beard leaned out from one of the windows above. Paint flaked off the sill and drifted over Thane.

"Lovely coat, richie!" the man said, pointing at Thane's leather jacket. The old man cackled into the midnight street.

Thane threw him a finger and kept on, his mind whirring.

He'd risk a beating if he spoke up about Lewis. Taking a deep breath, he considered it. His mother would want him to be brave for something this important. She'd want him to follow his heart, no matter the trouble it might give.

A sad smile stretched his mouth as he remembered the science fair during his first year in secondary school. When Thane's father had said attending to clan business was more important than going to a silly first prize ribbon ceremony, his mother had threatened to cut her hair off. The clan gathering was set for the next day and Thane's father wouldn't tolerate being embarrassed by his wife in front of so many. After a lorry-load of swearing, his father had finally capitulated and they'd left for the ceremony together. It was the first and last time both of Thane's parents had attended a school function.

A shout broke through the memories, and a cold wind gusted past, tugging at Thane's hair. Two kingsmen—not Campbells, just ordinaries—held someone across the street, in front of an old hardware store. The man pulled out of their grip, ripping his red striped shirt.

"I'm not a sixth-senser," the man said. "I've told you. I'm no Ghost Talker!"

The first kingsman grabbed him again with a meaty paw. "Then who were you talking to just now, your face as pale as my arse?"

The second kingsman snorted a laugh, lifted his stick, and struck the potential sixth-senser in the knee. They threw more questions at the man and shoved him against the mossy brick of the old hardware store. The store's sign—a painted hammer—swung above them in the unnatural breeze.

So that cold wind was a spirit. The man was definitely a Ghost Talker, one of the four types of sixth-sensers currently known. They could speak with the dead and the dead told them secrets of the past supposedly. Thane wasn't sure why the king cared much about that sixth sense. What would the dead have to do with now? Maybe in murder cases or some such. Yeah. That made sense. The other three types of sixth-sensers did seem relevant to gathering valuable intel for certain.

Threaders saw brightly colored strings of light connecting people to people or people to objects when strong emotion was involved. That could really help an enemy of the king find spies like Thane. He swallowed. He hoped he'd never cross a Threader's path. He'd be found out and have to go back to round-up duty and all that blood and beating.

Another type of sixth-senser was a Seer. That type was merely a legend. Supposedly, a very powerful Seer would one day find the Coronation Stone and name an Heir to the Empire's throne. But no one had rounded up a Seer as far as Thane knew. Seers could touch a thing and see a memory. It didn't seem like a sense the king would care about, but Seers remained top of the list for round-ups despite them being as common as a magical unicorn. Maybe the king believed the stupid legend.

The sixth-sensers that made Thane most nervous were the Dreamers. These people dreamed about things that might happen in the future or about what part that person had to play in history as a whole. His own bizarre, recurring dream didn't show him anything as important as all that, but it still didn't seem normal. If anyone ever questioned him about dreams, he knew he'd stumble and say something that could be dangerous. Even though he knew he didn't have a sixth sense.

The second kingsman snorted again and hit the sixth-senser in that same knee. Thane winced and the man fell, yowling.

"The people won't put up with this forever," the sixth-senser said. "We won't! You have no proof against me!"

"Our own word is proof enough for our commander," the big kingsman growled, throwing the sixth-senser into a government car parked at the curb.

Glad that he didn't have round-up duty here in Edinburgh, Thane shoved his hands into his pockets and wound through two narrow, twisting streets before heading toward the back entrance into Bluefoot public house, a Campbell haunt open only to those in the clan. He was known only in here and only by those fairly high up. He'd never worked as a kingsman officially in this area so as to keep his identity a secret. He pushed what looked like a regular wall—a part of a shop that had been closed for years—and it swung open to reveal a dark alcove. It looked like a forgotten spot between two buildings. He kicked the left wall and it popped open, placing him in the back of the Bluefoot. If he'd come in through the front where another hidden entrance sat, he'd have to have spoken to the codekeeper to gain entrance and he didn't want to be seen right now. Or ever really. Only a camera watched this back way in and Bran kept an eye on that screen this time of day. Bran was always on Thane's side.

The sounds of a tambourine and a guitar filled his ears but rage about Lewis filled his chest, stronger and more visceral, taking hold of his mind and heart like a vicious hand as he wove through the back of the club.

In the main room, hammock chairs suspended on plastic links, hung from the ceiling like money bags. Instead of being filled with shining coin, they swayed and dragged toward the cigarette-ridden floor holding men with DRFs, Daily Racing Forms, in their hands. Every man's eyes were on the wall-sized TV screen opposite the copper-topped bar. The screen blinked out another row of numbers and stupid names—horse race stats from Newmarket and nearby Musselburgh—in a chalky white. The lists faded and stomping fillies appeared, ready at the gate on Goodwood's long, green track, far away in England's West Sussex.

The busty Cora greeted him with a sweet smile, a rag in one hand and a glass of whisky in the other. "Good to see you, young man." She probably knew his name, but also knew it was wiser not to mention it.

"Can I get an ale?" He didn't usually drink, but tonight called for it.

Her lips pinched to hide a smile, but she nodded, always obedient to the Campbell name.

The other men eyed him for a moment and went back to their DRFs. Standing beside the hanging seats, the pub's regular clutch of low women laughed and chatted with the patrons. Some women drifted away to perform feats of flexibility on the scarves that dangled from metal bars crisscrossing the ceiling. One girl, upside down, her leg twisted in a scarf, reached for Thane and ruffled his hair like he was a wean—nothing more than a child. Scowling, he slipped around her and found Bran in the workout room.

Beside a well-worn heavy bag, Thane's bushy-haired pal ringed knuckles and palm with a fighter's wrap.

"Just the man I wanted to see," Bran said.

He was about Rodric's age but, alternately, had a functioning gray mass between his ears. Up near Inveraray, where Thane had grown up, local teens spent their free hours at a nature reserve. There, among pines and stolen cigarettes, Thane and Bran had forged a vague friendship, full of secrets but strong enough to get an orphaned Bran to relocate to Edinburgh when Thane had started at university down the way at St. Andrews.

"You look ready for a real fight, my friend," Bran said.

"Aye." A florescent light flickered as Thane paced the small room's red floor, his hands flexing in and out. "They've made a mistake, Bran. A bad one."

The doorway into the main room was empty, but Thane kept an eye on it just in case.

Bran's thick brown eyebrows rose. "You're posing as one *Thane Moray* in the house of that candy chemist?"

"I am. And Rodric and the rest were calling him, asking to get him to...juice up his creations for us."

"Sweets as weapons?"

Thane nodded. "That and more. Ointments, unguents, all sorts of chem work." He hung a hand on the chain linking the bag to the ceiling beams. "The chemist said *no* and they took him. Just like that." He snapped his fingers. "Ruined a good man's life."

"Maybe Nathair will release him."

A laugh jerked from Thane's throat. He took his jacket off and tossed it onto a shabby table near the door. "Right. All sweet and cozy like, I'm sure."

Bran shrugged. "Here's hoping."

Thane leaned his forehead into the heavy bag, inhaling old sweat and listening to his heart drive Campbell blood through his body.

"He has a daughter," Thane said quietly.

The speed bag secured to the wall thumped as Bran—wise Bran—let Thane talk.

"Most of the people I've spied on," Thane said, "they're as looney as Gran on Hogmanay."

Bran snorted a laugh.

"But this girl..." An image of Aini and Lewis working side-by-side in the lab whisked through Thane's mind. "She's so..."

He remembered the fear in her face when she saw the blood.

Heat blazed through his chest and he rammed an elbow into the heavy bag.

"It's terrible what they've done to her and her father." He

gave the bag another hit. "And I don't know what I'm going to—"

Cora appeared at the door, ale in hand. "I didn't mean to interrupt..."

"No bother. Thank you." Thane took the drink and gulped it down. A line of cool liquid ran down his throat.

"And what's this?" a deep, sour voice said from the door. Cora was gone and she'd left Rodric in her place. "Has the wee doggie come out to play then?"

Thane's first memory of his older, second cousin consisted of nothing but Rodric's ducky laugh, the bottom of his boot, and pain. The oaf pulled his flat cap down over his eyes and squared his shoulders. Rodric was big enough he didn't need to act like a tough man. He couldn't help himself. Big, stupid bully.

Rodric sucked the last bit of his cigarette and threw it to the dark corner, where it glowed like a rat's eye.

"Can we not do this?" Thane said. "This whole 'Rodric is tough and older and wiser, and Thane's a wee prick, no matter he stands a foot taller than me now'?"

Rodric answered with a swing aimed at Thane's head. Thane dodged it, ducking and pushing the strike past his ear. His cousin grabbed his shirt and pulled, ripping it along the collar.

"Nathair's wrong, you know," Thane spat. "The candymaker is a good man."

"That lab rat needs to know his place." Rodric faked another shot at Thane, who didn't flinch. "Treasonous rat is what he is."

The ape threw a vicious punch into the heavy bag and Thane stepped back as the target swung wildly.

"He's not a traitor, Rodric. I'm telling you."

Rodric's gaze went up and down Thane, an ugly grin tearing at his mouth. It reminded Thane distinctly of his own father. "What's it to you anyway?"

Bran stepped forward, rubbing an uneven spot out of his wraps. "Thane is only working to keep you from wasting your time, pal."

"You'll mind your own business." Rodric poked Bran in the chest with a sausage-like finger. "Pal."

Thane pushed Rodric back. "Lewis MacGregor is not guilty of treason. He's just a chemist who doesn't want to hurt anyone."

"Oh aye?" Rodric leaned into Thane's face. His breath smelled like cigarettes and hate. "Then why did Seanie find the man on an old Dionadair list just yesterday?"

Thane froze. Why would Lewis's name show up on a search for rebels?

"I see you didn't know about that, huh?" Rodric said.

"It's a mistake."

Rodric shrugged and picked at his teeth with his smallest finger. "Maybe. But what if he only refuses to weaponize his candies for us because he's already doing it for the Dionadair rebels?"

Dionadair meant *Protector* in Gaelic. But from what Thane had seen, the members didn't care about protecting anyone except their precious cause—to liberate Scotland from the English king. Sure, their latest flag stunt hadn't been violent and Thane didn't agree with how his father had handled their punishment, but still, the rebels were low folk and he didn't care for their type any more than he liked Rodric and his.

"You're wrong. I know it." Thane swallowed and set his empty glass on the table.

Rodric spread his arms wide. "Well, make sure you're not leaving any stone unturned, doggie. Sniff him out and prove the chemist's innocence. Maybe then Nathair'll let him be. Not without a bit of obedience training first, of course, but..."

"He can't force innocent subjects to do his bidding," Thane said. "It's wrong."

"Nathair—your own father—is the law. Don't forget it. The rebels are worse than ever and Nathair is sick of playing by rules no one else follows. It's only right we use whatever means we see fit." Rodric popped his knuckles and punched a palm.

Thane's stomach twisted. No. It wasn't right.

He clapped Bran on the shoulder. "I'll see you soon, pal." Picking up his jacket, he shouldered past Rodric and found the back door.

"Remember who you are, doggie," Rodric called out. "Don't forget who your master is. I'll be sure to tell him you've gone soft. He has some new ideas about how to train wee doggies. Best keep up your tinkering and hope you craft something worth a crap to make up for the report I'll be giving to the good chief."

Thane slammed the door. He wasn't giving him anything. Nathair and Rodric could come after him all they wanted. He would not stop defending Lewis, not even if it cost him a beating worse than the ones from training.

He pulled out his phone and rang his mother, but she didn't answer. She could've been sleeping. He pictured her in the big four poster bed, a science journal open beside her outstretched hand and her reading glasses still on her nose. She'd given him her love of science. Through hikes spent identifying trees by leaves and bark. During television episodes on planets and the mysteries of space. She always asked the best questions, ones that had him rifling through her collection of journals in their cavernous library and searching the world information cache online.

It was surprising that a woman so smart could be trapped into a marriage with his father, a man so obviously unfit for a loving relationship. It'd been her passion that trumped her good sense, her sharp mind. She must've fallen for his powerful presence, his standing in their hometown, his way with words.

Thane bowed his head. His own passions pushed him to do things he had better sense than to try. He wondered if his growing concern for Aini and Lewis would be his own undoing.

~

THE TOWNHOUSE DOOR CRACKED OPEN NOISILY, BUT THE front room was empty, the lights out. Thane started toward the bedroom, but moonlight from the window crashed across Lewis's office, tempting him. He took a slow breath, Rodric's words coming back. *Then why did Seanie find the man on an old Dionadair list yesterday?*

The office looked as it always did. Rodric and the rest hadn't searched it. Yet.

After hanging his jacket on the doorknob, Thane sat in Lewis's chair behind the wide, metal desk, smelling only printer ink and bleach, not blood.

Fine. He'd look around. Just to prove there was nothing to find.

He started in the drawers, then moved on to the safe. The combination was his fifth guess—the atomic numbers for the elements in sugar. Hydrogen. Carbon. Oxygen. 1. 6. 8. Inside the metal box, a stack of pounds sat near the deed to the townhouse, permission papers for developing recreational sweets decorated with the royal red wax seal, and a few other legal odds and ends. Nothing interesting.

Closing the safe up tight, Thane began searching more clever spots like behind the loose windowsill and the back of a filing cabinet. Nothing. For good measure, he grabbed a monogrammed snochterdicter—a handkerchief embroidered with Lewis's initials—from the desk drawer and used the fine cloth to wipe the safe's lock clean of his fingerprints.

He was right. Lewis was no Dionadair.

Returning the cloth to its home, he slid the drawer back.

It caught on something.

Thane's pulse knocked on his throat. He crawled under the desk, clicking on the small torch he kept in his pocket. A picture was taped to the underside of the desk, just past the point where the drawer should stop. Some of the tape had come loose and gummed up the drawer's track. Gently peeling the photo from its spot, Thane imagined what it might be. A shot of a lady Lewis shouldn't have been thinking of? A picture of a special creation from the candy lab?

Thane unfolded himself from the small space and turned, leaning against the desk. He pulled his glasses out and slid them on, an ugly feeling uncurling in his wame. The picture showed Lewis MacGregor with a red-bearded man, toasting with what looked like dark whisky.

The two stood directly in front of the Saltire—the banned Scottish flag.

Thane swore and kicked the filing cabinet.

"Thane?"

He crushed the picture in his hand. Aini. Why was she always around? Spinning, he faced her. Suddenly, he forgot to breathe. Her hair fell over her shoulders in a sheet of black satin. The belt of her robe was tied in a neat bow beneath her chest.

"You...you should be in bed, lass."

Though it was nothing but silver and blue in the unlit room, he could still see the color rising in her cheeks. Her hands went to her hips.

"Don't order me around," she snapped. "Why are you in here in the dark anyway?"

Thane slipped the picture into his pocket—and with larger movements to draw Aini's attention—grabbed a pen. "You're right. Sorry. I just saw no reason to wake everyone by turning all the lights on. I thought maybe your father might've left some sort of clue as to where they were taking him, or something."

"Oh. I'm sorry. You're right." Her voice broke.

A fissure started somewhere deep inside Thane. He came around the desk and she let him draw her into his arms. Her hair smelled like sugar and that scent girls always had—like shampoo or lotion.

"I didn't mean to boss you." He pulled away a bit, his hands on her shoulders.

Her dark, wide eyes reflected the window's scant light. "I know. It's just..."

She stared at his necklace, two lines appearing between her slim eyebrows. Good thing he kept the Campbell seal turned toward his throat.

"They'll bring him back, right?" Tears welled in her eyes.

Anger against Lewis simmered under Thane's sternum. Lewis had done this to Aini, put her in this position. Her *and* Thane. The traitor. How could he not have realized the nature of the man? He'd been so wrong, so, so wrong. His teeth ground together.

"I don't know, hen."

He ran a hand over her forearm, and a feeling like electric shock danced up his fingers. Swallowing, he stepped back, giving her what he hoped was a noncommittal, friendly smile. His thoughts and emotions knocked around his body and brain like thrown rocks. He looked out the window. He felt so heavy, so tired of...everything.

The place his mother used to take him washed through his mind.

"You ever been to the Highlands?" he asked her quietly. "Green and gold grasses. Puddles of water so still... Mountains like great castles. A man could hear no sound but his own voice, if he wished it." He was daft. What was he even talking about? His thoughts slipped around like he'd had a boatload of whisky.

"I went there once." Aini's voice was light as star shine. It was surprising she didn't think him completely cracked. "With Father, on holiday."

He turned to see her shudder and wrap her arms around herself.

Thane's watch said it was near midnight. "It's late. Can we talk over everything tomorrow?" What he'd say, he had no clue. Smart as she was, she was blind as hell. Not that he could talk. He didn't have a clear view of anything.

Nodding, she started toward the door, then paused. "What happened to your shirt?" Her gaze slid over his bare shoulder.

"Caught it on the doorframe." His jaw muscles tensed painfully. Lying came far too easy these days.

She looked him over a bit. He tugged his ripped shirt up best he could as heat crept into his cheeks. Running a hand through his hair, he silently berated himself for blushing.

Brushing past her, he snatched his jacket from the doorknob. They traded an awkward, "Good night then," before he sped off to his room.

PACING HIS BEDROOM, THANE STEWED. LEWIS HAD PRETENDED such innocence. Acting as though he cared for the king's law. Saying *that* was the reason he wouldn't do as Thane's clan asked. Stopping at the wall, Thane clenched his fists. Lewis had probably been crafting weaponized sweets for the Dionadair. Thane rammed a fist into the wall, welcoming the pain that matched the hurt inside him. Was there no one he could trust in the world?

Myles's bed creaked. "Hey, Lord of the Tattoos, keep it down, okay? I need beauty sleep if I'm going to battle your handsome tail for the ladies."

"Aye. Sorry." Flexing his now bloodied hand, Thane lowered himself into his own bed.

He was too. Sorry he couldn't leave now and forget about Lewis and Aini and the lab. He had to stay and work on what Lewis refused to. Had to give his clan the terrible things he created. For his mother. And because it was his duty. Campbells who didn't do as ordered didn't enjoy long lives.

Thane fought the droop of his eyelids.

At the edge of his mind, his recurring dream lurked, waiting for him—the one of his fingerprint turning black as a corpse's. It was hours before exhaustion finally washed through Thane's boiling brain and drowned him in a troubled sleep.

## CHAPTER 6
## SECRET

Ani sat on a kitchen chair, fully dressed in tapered trousers and a green silk striped shirt, but she'd no idea how she'd ended up there. Coconut pancakes steamed on a plate in front of her. She folded and creased the napkin someone had thrown beside the fork. Then she aligned the fork with the napkin and plate, making it picture-perfect.

Myles padded barefoot across the room. He smiled kindly, his usual swagger replaced with concern. "You're supposed to eat it, sweetheart. Not organize it."

If anyone else had called her sweetheart, she'd have set them down for a good one, maybe two hour lecture, but Myles actually meant the word as an endearment. There wasn't any condescension in his tone.

"I made these pancakes, didn't I?" she whispered.

He paused, the coffee pot suspended over his blue mug. "You did." Taking a seat, he put his free hand on hers, a brotherly gesture.

She frowned as the black spot in her memory cleared.

Now she remembered wiggling the turner under their crisp edges to flip the pancakes. The cane syrup had come out too quickly when she poured it, and the liquid had pooled against the plate's lip.

"Hey. We're going to figure this out," Myles said. "After all, you're organizing again." Pointing to the folded napkin and aligned fork, he grinned encouragingly. "It's an Aini MacGregor sign of survival and fortitude."

A tentative smile crept over her lips.

Neve scurried into the kitchen, only one of her eyes ringed in brown liner. "I meant to get up before you." She knelt and patted Aini's leg. "Anything I can get you? Seems you already made your own breakfast."

Aini squeezed Neve's hand, closing her eyes and hoping the comfort of her friend's touch would drive out the buzzing under her skin. She took a deep breath, feeling like insects crawled under her flesh. "The Campbells have my father. Right? It couldn't be anyone else, right?" She needed to make a list of possibilities and potential actions to take. "Does anyone know where my phone is?"

Neve and Myles stood, their heads turning and their faces blank. Neve's mouth tucked up at one side. "You're usually the one who tells us where everything is."

Swallowing, Aini pushed away from the table to look in her bedroom as Thane walked in. He held her phone out to her.

Gratitude warmed her. "Thanks." Before she opened a fresh list on the screen, she met Thane's gaze. Red lines crossed the whites of his eyes, and his normally pink, full lips were pale. Swallowing, she put a hand on his sleeve. The rolled edge of the expensive colonial cotton was worn and soft. "Myles made coffee." She didn't know what else to say.

Thane rubbed his face roughly, his tattoos dark against his

fair skin. His hair was a beautiful disaster of gold and honey. She wondered if he'd slept last night.

His eyes flicked open, the irises gray as storms. "You...I... thank you." He pushed past, jerked the coffee pot up, and poured some into a mug, spilling a little over the edge.

Nodding, Aini went to the table and started a list. Her fingers shook and made it tough to type. "First thing." She looked at Myles and Neve. "Who took him and why exactly?"

The two sat side by side, Neve with her fingers laced and a pinched mouth, Myles biting his thumbnail.

"Idea One. The Campbells." With each word typed onto the screen, it became easier to breathe. "They took him because he refused to do what they wanted. He shouted at them over the phone, disregarding their status, and so they acted. Idea Two. A competitor abducted him. They want his recipes. Idea Three—"

"You know it's the Campbells, Aini. It's why the authorities were as useful as teets on a goose." Myles slowly peeled paint off his thumbnail, not meeting her eyes.

With a quick swipe, she deleted ideas two and three. She blinked away tears to see the screen. "Okay. Then what actions to take?"

Neve slid her untouched plate closer, glancing once at Thane, who drank his coffee in silence in the corner of the room. "If they see his behavior as treasonous, they'll question him at the Court of Empire Crimes."

Aini slammed her phone down. "That's ridiculous." Standing, she braced her hands on the table. "He's only obeying the king's laws. He's a loyal subject. More loyal than any other man in Scotland. The Campbells are out of control."

Thane muttered something sharp.

"What?"

"I said," he put his cup down too carefully on the counter and glared. "Maybe your father is not who you think he is."

"Excuse me?"

His eyes narrowed. He took a step. "You ever seen anything to tie him to the Dionadair?"

"The rebels?" Her brash colonial accent was leaking out. "Of course not," she said, careful to soften her consonants.

He looked at her mouth, then shook his head. "You'd never check up on your own father. Would you? It's against your precious *rules*. It wouldn't help you *fit in*."

He turned away, but she grabbed the sleeve of his wrinkled button-down. "Why are you saying this?" she asked.

"People lie, Aini." Bending at the waist, he put his face near hers. "They hide things. Especially from those they love."

Heat flared across her chest. "Don't be an...an ass." Blushing, she leaned closer, her nose almost touching his. "If you've got something to say, say it."

Straightening, he spoke quietly like he struggled to get a hold on himself. "Before this week, did you ever think your father would shout at a kingsman like he did on the phone?"

Aini looked down, her chest hurting.

He pulled something from his back pocket, his face sad and furious at the same time, and thrust it under her nose. "I didn't think he was a rebel either until I found this."

It was a picture. She took it, heart shaking.

It showed Lewis and another man having a drink together. No shock in that. But as her gaze dragged over Father's smile and into the background, she saw it. The banned flag.

Her hand went to her mouth. "The Saltire."

"Aye. It was taken at a club where Dionadair used to meet."

The floor seemed to move under Aini's shoes.

Leaning over her shoulders, Neve and Myles looked at the picture. Neve deflated and dropped into Aini's chair. Myles turned and raked hands through his bright hair.

But it didn't have to mean Father was a rebel. "It's just a picture. An old one. It doesn't mean—"

"Forget it." Thane cut her off and ripped the picture away, his bright gray eyes outlined by black lashes. "If you're determined to live in your pretend world of perfectly organized right and wrong and lists and rules and everyone being exactly who you think they are, nothing I'm going to say will snap you out of it."

Her legs jerked and trembled, threatening to crumble. Like it belonged to another person, her hand drew back, then slapped across Thane's cheek.

Neve gasped.

Thane's nostrils flared. He shut his eyes as his chest heaved. "Aini—"

Twisting, she shoved Myles out of her way and flew up the spiral stairs to the tower lab.

AT THE SHELVING ABOVE THE COUNTERTOP, SHE BEGAN alphabetizing the spices and dried herbs, taking simple pleasure in the clean, white labels and their dark green lettering. Agrimony. Allspice. Angelica. Anise. Arnica. Father didn't like them this way, but he hardly had to measure flavors out anymore so it didn't matter. Bay Leaf. Bergamot. Bilberry. And he wasn't here anyway, so it *really* didn't matter.

A hysterical laugh erupted from her throat, and she paused, a jar of cayenne gripped in her sweating hand.

Thane was right.

People did lie to those they loved. She had.

Her own father didn't know about her sixth sense. She'd been lying for a long time now.

She set the cayenne down and walked across the lab, stopping between Father's neatly arranged work area and Myles's desk, which overflowed with pastel chalk adverts and filthy electronics.

The jars of blue and green sugar sparkled on the far wall. Why were they over there? They really should be stored with the rest of the decorative sugars. She'd take them down. A project would clear her head. On tiptoe, she squinted at the antique bronze hardware that kept the blue sugar jar on the wall. It was a hinge. Hmm. Maybe if she could get to the screw hiding in the hinge's fold, she could undo it. Reaching high, she grabbed the container and pulled it forward. The glittering contents shifted with a hushing sound as the jar tipped toward her.

A jagged rectangle covered in the same uneven stone as the rest of the wall swung open.

A hidden door. Mind spinning, she walked inside.

Secrets and more secrets.

The bare bulb above didn't provide much light, but a layer of dust was visible on the tall filing cabinet and the trunk. The cabinet's tracks squeaked as she slid the first drawer out and peered inside. A brown envelope, worn at the edges and ready to burst, held a huge stack of papers.

She pursed her lips and breathed through her nose. Her world was pulling apart, thread by thread. Slipping a finger under the envelope's flap, she opened it. Drawings. Pictures. Cards. All from her. There was the unicorn she'd made for him in primary school. Her first school picture. Every Christmas card she'd ever bought for him. She hugged the package to her chest and looked up to keep the moisture from leaking out of her eyes. Tucking everything back into place, she returned the envelope and shut the drawer. The middle drawer held all her essay papers from upper school, all the way through last year, when she'd graduated early. In the bottom drawer, large rubber bands held together ticket stubs from her parents' honeymoon trip and anniversary cards from before the divorce.

So far, no terrible surprises.

She eyed the trunk on the dusty floor. Brass grommets stood like sentries along its lid. She pushed on the lobster claw latch. Rust flaked from the metal, but it wouldn't budge. With a fist, she hit the clasp. Pinching the little lever, the latch slid out of the brass loop with a grating sound. She threw the lid open, and the scent of aged paper curled into her nose. The mildewed trunk held an invitation to the king's thirtieth birthday party. Someone —*Father?*—had scrawled the word *Remember* in black over the front. Next to the invitation was a picture of Aini as a child with chubby cheeks and an armful of half-wilted flowers. She remembered picking them out of Grandmother's garden in the colonies. Aini had sorted the bouquet into colors and presented them to Father for Easter. Next, carefully moving a first edition of Father's favorite novel, she uncovered a tuxedo jacket, maybe the one he'd worn at his wedding. She lifted it and something fell from its folds, thudding to the hidden room's oak plank floor.

It was a tiny square of linen sewn like a pocket. Something weighty hid inside. The lightbulb above flickered, highlighting the tiny bumps and ridges in the rough fabric. Stitched words, red as blood, ran across the front.

*For the Seer.*

A chill spilled down Aini's back.

She'd done everything possible to hide her ability for two years. Feigning a stomachache when she touched a coin that someone had kept for a while before dying. Wearing gloves the moment the weather was anything less than hot. Telling Father the secondhand jewelry stores he liked to peruse weren't her sort of thing.

But this trunk had been shut for a long time, judging from the dust layer. And the yellow and brown of age had crept into the fabric. She lifted the small pouch's flap and peered inside. It was a gold brooch, similar to the decorative pin Granny MacGregor had worn on her cardigan. But hers had the MacGregor family crest. This one was different.

She studied this brooch as best she could without touching it, sweat dampening her palms and the back of her neck. Inside the brooch's circle, a golden otter bared jagged teeth. An inscription decorated its edges, but the words were tiny. She squinted.

If she took it out of its wrapping and ran a finger over it, she'd break her number one rule. But her father had some sort of rebellious past, and she had to know if he had any more secrets, and how far this went. She tilted the linen pouch and the brooch slipped into her palm, cool and heavy.

The world dropped away. A vision took hold.

*Face partially covered in shadow, a man shoved the brooch into Father's hands. Fear rose from him, green and black, and he shook his head. Both men turned, something surprising them. The other man ran off. Father still held the brooch. Behind him, a tattered blue flag with a diagonal, white cross hung on the wall. The Saltire.*

The memory disappeared—she'd never see it again—and a new one bled into its place as Aini curled her fingers tightly around the pin, lost in the vision.

*A handsome young man with a wide mouth gripped the brooch. Wearing old-fashioned clothes, he shut his eyes and envisioned a large room with rough brick and stone walls.*

Was this man leaving an emotional imprint on the brooch on purpose? Impossible.

*Water dripped from the ceiling. There was a large knife—a dirk—with a hilt black as coal. He thought of a number. Eighty-five.*

Seer, *his mind said.* Find the knife, first in the *clah-na-cinneamhain* trail.

*An oddly shaped rock came into view. Very large. Sloping upward toward the back, hollowed in the middle like a seat. Circles. Swirls.*

Make certain the time is right, *his thoughts shouted.*

*His dark eyes grew larger and larger, shining, wild, closer, closer.* Seer! See me! Find the knife!

The vision disintegrated, and Aini sucked the air of Father's hidden room as the brick and cement walls bubbled into view. The brooch fell from her fingers and thunked to the floor.

She still wasn't used to her sixth sense, though the process was fairly straightforward. The first time she touched an object with strong sentimental value to someone, a moment of imprinted emotion played out in her head like a movie. At least it only occurred the first time her skin made contact.

She'd seen Mother in a pearly veil when she'd touched Father's watch. That had been a nice one. Unfortunately, they weren't all so pleasant. When she'd touched the chain Myles wore around his wrist, she'd seen a vision of Myles's mother turn her back on him before his trip here to be an apprentice.

And this vision, the first one in the brooch, it showed Father with a stranger, standing in front of the banned flag. She looked at the ceiling, her fingers going cold.

*Father, what did you do?*

She squeezed the brooch and pressed a hand against her forehead. This could ruin everything. It was one thing if the Campbells took him because he'd refused their plan; it was quite another if they found out he was a traitor. She breathed out slowly, trying not to panic.

The second vision in the brooch had been so strange. The man had seemed to speak through the memory. He'd told her to "find the knife."

Crouching, she gathered the brooch. The light glanced off the tiny words around the border. It was a clan motto. Most were in Latin or French. "*De bonnaire...*"

"Graceful," a deep voice said.

Thane walked into the lab, his face pale except for the red mark of Aini's fingers on his cheek. Then he froze. His gaze roamed the hidden room.

She cupped the brooch, then hid it in her pocket. "Is that what the French means? Graceful?"

"Aye." He looked at her, his stare unrelenting.

Standing, she pulled her shirt back into place and wiped the sweat from her forehead. "I didn't know you spoke French."

"You could fill the North Sea with what you don't know about me," he mumbled, running a hand through his hair and looking generally miserable.

Aini wasn't sure how she felt about that. She shut the trunk and dusted her hands together. Thane's gaze burned a hole in her back.

"Aini. Listen. I'm sorry. It's not your fault your—"

She held up a finger, and he paused as she shoved the hidden room's door closed. "You said the picture you found was taken at a club. A rebel club?" She faced him.

His gaze fixed on the jar of blue sugar as it slid back into place with a mechanical clunk. "I did."

"I'm going to that club tonight," Aini said. "What's it called? Where is it? Is it still open?"

"You can't go there. It's not safe."

"I have to know how serious this all is."

"Bad sorts go in there. You can't just walk in there with not a thought to—"

She started down the stairs. The smell of coffee and the cool air of the stairwell cleaned the rest of the vision away. A quick thought of her dark room and bed beckoned, but she couldn't hide away.

"Aini." Thane came up behind her as the stairs opened into the kitchen.

Neve and Myles's heads lifted, their faces drawn.

"Aini. Please. Listen. The Origin is not a Dionadair meeting place anymore."

"The Origin? Perfect. Now I know where to go." Snatching her phone, she searched for the location.

Neve stood and frowned at Thane. "And how do you know so much about the Dionadair?"

"The club is on George IV Bridge," Aini said.

Thane raised an eyebrow at Neve. "*You* know enough to call me on it."

Red splotches rose on Neve's neck. "I hear urban legends and…things…when I lead tours. I have one this weekend…" She chewed her lip and blinked under his stare.

Aini glared at Thane. "Leave her alone."

Neve knew more about Scotland than all of them.

Aini's phone said The Origin opened at ten o'clock. "So who's with me for clubbing tonight?"

Myles snorted and gave a weak version of his normal grin. "I could be persuaded to gyrate under obnoxious lighting while flocked by women. Only if it'll help you out."

Eyes wide, Neve looked from Thane to Myles. "Will someone please tell me what's happening?"

Aini tucked her phone into her waistband and took Neve's

hands, swallowing with the effort not to scream or cry or lose it completely. "That picture Thane found shows Father in a rebel club called The Origin."

Neve started shaking her head slowly back and forth.

Aini squeezed her fingers. "I'm going there to see if I can learn anything."

"This isn't a good idea," Neve said. "I've heard that place is rough."

It was probably true. If it used to be a rebel hang out, chances were the people there liked risking treason to have a little wild fun. Stupid. But Aini couldn't sit around here doing nothing. It was one night. One trip to find out what exactly Father had done in his past and how bad it was. One risk that could give her what she needed.

She met Neve's gaze. "I need answers."

"The Dionadair rebels won't be there with name tags on. You'll never find one, even if they are there and know something of your father's past."

"I have to try."

Plus, Aini had the brooch. A stranger, most likely a rebel, had given to Father. If she wore it in plain sight in the club, maybe the Dionadair would recognize it and tell her more. Information was power, and she needed every bit she could find to untangle this nightmare.

She started out of the kitchen, the brooch warm in her pocket.

She wished she could tell them why a rebel might know to approach her, but she couldn't explain about what she'd seen, about how she knew the brooch had belonged to a rebel. The king and Nathair Campbell called people with talents similar to hers "abominations." And those who covered for sixth-sensers were taken for questioning, and were either sentenced to death for treason or simply never returned to their families, lost in the Campbells' famed prison cells under Edinburgh.

Thane stood in her way. In the dark hallway, his glasses hid his eyes and Aini felt oddly frightened of him. The feeling only lasted a moment, and she felt stupid about it immediately after. She knew him well enough to know he was a little unruly, but nothing to be afraid of.

"This is a waste of time," Thane said quietly. "The kingsmen raided the place countless times. Aside from some rebel wannabes and a few black market operators, the kingsmen have found nothing. Not in years."

"Then it shouldn't be too dangerous to go. Excuse me." She shoved past him to her bedroom door.

When she grabbed the doorknob, he covered her hand with his. His long fingers were smooth. Small calluses on his palm pressed into her knuckles and part of a tattoo—$CaCO_3$—marked his thumb.

"Just because it's not a Dionadair nest doesn't mean it'll be a sweet, little place." His thumb twitched, brushing across the bone in her wrist. They were both breathing like they'd run down the hallway. He pulled his hand away and rubbed his face. "Look, I don't want you to get hurt."

"Just because you're twenty-whatever and I'm seventeen doesn't mean I need you protecting me." She jerked the knob and threw the door open.

A black sweater and a pair of blue leggings lay on Neve's bed. She went to her armoire and surveyed her own wardrobe.

Thane's boots knocked on the floor behind her. "It's not about age."

She picked out a black and blue striped dress she'd never worn and held it up. "This should work, right?"

He put fisted hands against his eyes, shoving his glasses into his messy hair, and leaned his head back. Making that Scottish sound of annoyance in his throat, he stalked out the door.

But it didn't matter what he thought. Aini had to do this.

The dress fit perfectly. She dropped the brooch into her bag, not wanting anyone to ask her about it before they were at the club. The less they knew, the better.

## CHAPTER 7
## THE ORIGIN

Turns out, Aini's dress wasn't going to work. She fought her impatience and tried to be thankful for Myles. He'd picked up some clothes at the thrift shop. Richest guy ever to go into a secondhand store. With his plantation-owning mother, he could've *bought* the thrift shop.

Myles put a hand over his heart, his fresh hair dye bright as spring grass and his sleeveless suit jacket blue as the sky. "One must demonstrate one's lusty beauty before time snatches it away." He kissed his wiry bicep.

Chewing a nail, Aini rolled her eyes. "Maybe in Mylesland." A fleck of gold mascara dropped under her lash.

Myles sighed and fell backward on Aini's bed, arms and legs splayed, knocking bolsters and circular pillows all over. "What a gorgeous idea—Mylesland." Aini hoped he planned on putting those pillows back the right way. "It would be filled with honey and paint and pictures of me."

He and Neve had both been trying to be cheery all afternoon. They'd pushed hope and positive thinking as the group had draped a golden length of taffy over the pulling machine's metal arms. By the end of the six-on-the-dot greens and lean protein dinner Aini served everyone, they'd managed to calm her down, taking her from crushing panic to manageable anxiety.

Now, sitting at the vanity near Aini, Neve made a little groaning sound. Leaving the mess he'd made of Aini's bed, Myles pushed the corners of Neve's mouth up. He stepped back and her feigned smile fell.

"I look a proper idiot," Neve said.

Myles shook his head. "No. You look…delicious."

"He's right," Aini said. "You are beautiful."

Aini had braided Neve's hair into an intricate mess on top of her head. Her outfit consisted of a flowy top with straps and a short skirt. She did not look one bit like a mouse tonight.

"I'm not going to be able to dance in these." Neve pointed to her stacked boots.

Aini smiled down at her own matte gold heels with matching feathers that fluffed out at the ankles. Practical was best, but sometimes lovely things were good too. This dress was another world entirely with its agonizingly short, puffy layers of white colonial cotton and fake gold threading. It was pretty seriously inappropriate.

"Are you sure I can't wear the other dress?" Aini said. "This one is—"

The sight of Thane erased her ability to make words.

His suit jacket had sleeves, but lacked a shirt underneath. His flat stomach was totally on display right there. Right. There. And his dress pants hung way too low on his hipbones. He stood, looking at Aini with those gray eyes framed doubly by black lashes and glasses. His gaze warmed her forehead, nose, the delicate skin over her chest, all the way down to her ridiculously shod feet. His tattooed fingers twitched at his sides.

Aini swallowed, her heart running triple speed. Blinking, she focused instead on Myles and Neve. "I should change," she said. "I'm practically naked."

Turning away, Thane muttered something and shoved his hands in his hair.

Neve bit her lip and gave Aini a trembling smile.

Myles grabbed Neve up and pushed her purse into her arms. "You're fine, Aini. Now it's time to go, people."

Thane made a strangled noise from the door, kicked his heel backward against the frame, then walked into the hallway. Myles trailed him.

Thane spoke to him, voice rolling around the corridor outside the door. "I'm putting a shirt on. This is nonsense."

Aini stopped Neve, laying a hand on her back. "Is this...am I...am I doing the right thing?"

"As if I know. But we're with you. No matter what."

Aini hugged her tight. "Thanks. Thank you so, so much."

She wasn't half the woman Neve was. Working two jobs, Neve supported a sick mother and so many little brothers that Aini could never remember the count.

With a shaky smile, Neve turned and Aini followed her to the front door, worry and guilt hovering like dark ghosts.

The rain pelted them like bullets as they climbed into a taxi Myles had set up.

It was time to find some rebels.

---

Rain clapped against the clear tarp shielding people waiting to get into The Origin. At the front, the bouncer held out a hand for Aini's Subject Identification Card. The pale stone facade of the club towered over them with arching stained glass windows. A body-shaking bass line, cigarette smoke, and the musky scent of incense leaked from its insides.

"Not you. Too young," he said, handing the card back.

Heat rose to Aini's cheeks. She pointed to Myles, who stood beside Neve and Thane at the club's door. "My friend said most places let in fifteen and up. I'm seventeen."

The baldheaded man shook his head and gestured for the next person to come forward. A girl elbowed Aini in the back. Aini turned to say something but ended up staring at the girl's forehead. A tattooed third eye peered back. Aini shook her head.

"Go home, you wee thing," the girl said nastily. "You heard the man."

The boy next in line wore a tight leather shirt that was ripped down one side. "Aye," he said. "Go on." Tiny chains dangled from his lips and ears, and swirls of black paint covered his bare shoulder.

"I am not going home." Aini glared at them. "Nor is this any of your business."

Myles came over and flashed a handful of pounds. He tucked them into the bouncer's shirt pocket. "Let the little lady in, pretty please?"

"Thanks for the tip, pal, but no." The bouncer trained his eyes straight ahead, arms crossed.

Thane said something in Neve's ear as she peered into the club. Red lights colored their faces. Then he waved Myles over and they both looked at Aini. After their tête-à-tête, during which Aini was pushed out of line by the eye tattoo girl, Myles trotted to the middle of the street.

"Check this out!" he called to the bouncer.

Suddenly, he was upside down in a handstand.

Thane walked over as the bouncer looked at Myles and snorted.

Thane took a loud breath, and with one look over the distracted crowd, he snatched something small from his boot and put his arm around the bouncer's big shiny head. He laughed too loudly and swept a finger across the bouncer's upper lip before the man could pull away. The bouncer slumped forward on his stool and Thane eased him to the ground.

"Drank a bit too much, did you?" Thane's voice was too high and his smile didn't reach his eyes. He patted the man's back genially. "I'll get the manager. We're tight." Crossing his fingers and holding them up for the crowd, he leaned toward Aini. "Get inside now." His breath warmed her ear. "I'll meet you."

A broad-faced woman halfway under the tarp shouted, "Don't mind if you get tight with me, blondie!" Several other women howled, and the men laughed.

"What did you do?" Aini demanded. "Did you use something from the lab?"

"Aye. Now go." He jerked his chin toward Neve and Myles, who stared, eyes wide.

"What if the manager comes out? The people saw you and me."

"Aini," Thane hissed through his teeth. "Quit worrying about all the wrong things, will you? Now, go on."

He clapped the bouncer on the back again and scowled at the increasing flow of creatively inappropriate remarks about his backside coming from the line.

Aini rubbed her temples. Thane had used Father's chemicals and herbs on that man. He was trying to help, but that was not okay. Sighing, she stomped across the red and green glass mosaic floor, took Neve's arm, and entered The Origin. Myles hung back, waiting on Thane.

Inside the club, a dance floor, a bar area the size of Aini's bedroom, and two balconies with railings made of what looked like bones greeted them. Red electric lights blended with what had to be a thousand candles, giving the room a sickly pall.

Neve looked over her shoulder. "What's happened to the bouncer? Did Thane hit him?"

Aini's single dress strap dropped off and she tugged it into place. "No. He gave him something. Wiped something under his nose." Her stomach rolled. They were falling further and further from her comfort zone. She had to get some information and get out of here before they all ended up in jail.

Neve bumped into a five foot candle, and Aini caught the thing before it hit the elaborately painted stone floor. "And the stuff knocked the man out?" Neve asked.

Aini nodded.

Artistic vines curled underfoot from the door to the bar. A painted mouth surrounded the dance area like the people were tiny offerings about to be devoured. Over them, an automobile-sized skull with long, stringy hair hung from plastic links.

Shaking her head, Neve followed Aini closer to the dancing crowd. "Did he use stuff from our lab?" she asked. "You'll give him trouble for it, aye?"

"Count on it," Aini said.

A violin and the beat of percussion instruments punched against Aini's eardrums. She inhaled a deep breath of patchouli-scented air. This place was like some outer circle of Hell.

"Okay. The plan is to mingle and keep our eyes open." She lowered her voice. "If you see anything that says *Dionadair* to you, please tell me. I want to talk to anyone who looks like they might be involved."

"I know one thing to look for." Neve wrung her hands. She peered over the mob of sweaty dancers. "I've heard if one rebel meets another, they cross thumbs like this." She held her hands out, low enough so no one would notice, and laid one thumb over the other, creating an X. "It's for St. Andrew's cross. The one on the banned flag."

Coming from behind, Myles raised his arms and jumped into the crowd. "Oooaaaah!"

Some girls, wearing shirts about as appropriate as Aini's excuse for a dress, fell away from him, tripping over one another. Two raised their noses until they noticed his cute face. Then they closed ranks around him.

Neve shook her head. "If you can't beat them..."

Moving onto the dance floor, she wiggled her hips to a rhythm that had nothing in common with the music. But even as Myles shook his shoulders at her, their eyes moved from side to side, scanning the room. They weren't just goofing off. They were looking for signs of rebels. Aini gave them an encouraging smile even though she felt like vomiting or screaming or perhaps some horrid combination of both.

Thane walked up, his false smile from outside gone and only a frown to take its place.

Anger flared through Aini's chest and she crossed her arms. "Want to tell me what you did out there?" Deep scuffs marred the toes of his thrift shop kingsmen boots. "Have you been taking chemicals from the lab?"

He bent to scratch his ankle. The long line of his back and shoulders stretched the jacket's fabric. Small curls gathered at his neck. She wished very, very hard that she didn't like the look of him so much. "It was only an altered cherry drop."

Aini clenched the layers of her dress. "That. Is. Illegal."

Thane threw his head back and sighed. "You're a crabbit, wee thing."

He had no idea why she cared so much about the laws and the rules. If he only knew what she was and what would happen if anyone found out, maybe he'd understand and quit taking unnecessary risks. Not that being here wasn't a risk, but this could be done without drugging people. She almost wished she could tell him about her sixth sense. But no. Everyone viewed sixth-sensers as abominations. Freaks. She'd lose him. And Myles and Neve. Then she'd be alone and Father would be worse off than he already was.

"I'm going to the bar."

"Wait." Thane tried to grab her, but she pushed through the crowd toward the bar.

The banned flag wasn't behind the green and brown liquor bottles anymore, but she could tell it used to be. The countertop was copper like the one in the picture and in the vision imprinted on the brooch. Five hooks marked the mirror above the row of liquor bottles. It was definitely where Father had toasted with that rebel and where he'd received the brooch.

The barkeep, wearing a simple shirt, skirt, and apron, handed the person next to Aini a beer. The froth overflowed onto the keep's finger, and she licked it off.

"What do you want, then?" the woman asked.

A tattoo showed under her short sleeves. It was a woman with a flowing skirt filled with designs. Very specific designs. Aini gasped. It was a cleverly concealed Saltire. Thane elbowed her and she closed her gaping mouth.

"Cranberry juice, please," she said.

The keep nodded and jerked her chin at Thane.

Ignoring a blue-eyed girl to his right who grinned like Thane had invented rainbows, he said, "Ben Nevis Ale."

Drinks in hand, they put their backs against the counter. The juice in Aini's glass quaked in her shaking hand. Thane's sleeve brushed her bare arm with each of his breaths. His eyes trained on the dance floor, he moved a feather's width away. Cold air from the overhead vents rushed down, and she shivered. She was on emotion overload. Worry for Father. Shock at the gall of the keep. Anger and—she hated admitting it to herself—lust toward Thane. She was a total, ridiculous mess.

Muttering something under his breath, Thane faced her. He set his ale on the bar. "I truly am sorry for snapping at you before."

She rolled her dress hem between her fingers. She'd hit him, but that was before she'd seen the vision, before she knew Thane was right about suspecting Father's dark past. But she couldn't tell him about the vision.

"I know you're sorry," she said, not looking up. "It's not okay. The snapping, I mean. But I get it. I do."

A shaky smile pulled at one side of his full lips. A dimple was there and gone in a heartbeat. "I think we should dance," he said.

Her heart snapped like a rubber band, and she slid her juice next to his empty glass before she could spill it. Remembering that Thane was *not a good choice* was going to be that much more difficult in a dancing, bodies-touching-occasionally situation. "Why?"

"You can't hide if you want them to see you," he said.

She narrowed her eyes. He didn't believe there were any of *them* here anymore—any rebels, he meant. He'd said it himself at the townhouse. But whatever his real reason for wanting to dance, it did work toward her goal. She did need to be seen to get this horror show on the road. The sooner she learned something, the sooner they could leave this awful place and return to the order and familiarity of home. She only needed a clue as to what Father was involved in and how to manage rescuing him.

While he paid the keep, Aini pulled the brooch out of her dress pocket—the only practical thing about this get-up. The gold blinked in the sporadic light as she pinned it on and led Thane to the dance floor.

## CHAPTER 8
## DANCE AS IT ALL GOES DOWN

With bodies bumping against her, Aini moved her hips and hands with the beat, not making eye contact with Thane. Heat crept into her face. Her nerves wouldn't stop jumping. She stopped for a second, eyeing the beautiful Edinburgh girls with their stylish, messy up-dos and confident dancing. Closing her eyes, she fell into the music.

From the time she could walk, she'd spent hours and hours next to her mother, dancing to her Balinese music. She smiled. She'd forgotten how much she loved letting go, falling, allowing the sound, the beat, to wrap around her and set her adrift in pure feeling.

Thane's body brushed hers, and she opened her eyes to the black lapel of his jacket, the dark gray of his shirt, and the candle and rain scent of him. The drums pounded around them, seeming to push them together. He stared, and a slow-burning fire spread down Aini's back and legs.

"You look very bonnie." His mouth was very, very close to

her temple. Delightful chills stretched across her scalp and over her neck.

She forced her gaze to the balcony where a few figures stood utterly still in the middle of more dancing. Could they be the owners of the club? Maybe they knew something about the man who'd given Father the brooch.

The music's baseline slowed, and the violin shared time with the sounds of an entire orchestra. Thane looked at her lips. His nostrils flared once, a small movement, and suddenly she was breathing too fast.

Thane lifted her arms. She jumped at the touch, but let him put her hands on his shoulders.

"Just to blend in..." he murmured.

She nodded. His eyes strayed to the balcony. His muscles were tight under his clothes. His light, wool jacket was a strange combination of rough and smooth under her skin. His hipbone glanced against her side.

"Where did you learn to dance?" he asked.

The odd people at the balcony faded into the crowd. A guy in blue face paint fell against Aini, and Thane grabbed his shirt and pushed him away. Thane's arm circled more tightly around her. He was like a big, handsome wall, and considering the raucous group of dancers surrounding them, it wasn't a bad thing to have the shelter his body provided.

"My mother traveled with a Balinese dance troupe. She always had music on, was always practicing."

Two men darkened a side door on the first floor. More bouncers. Were they looking this way?

Thane's hands spanned her lower back, his thumbs pressing lightly into her ribs.

She took one of his hands and turned it over, studying it as they moved slowly with the music. "When did you get your tattoos?"

His chest moved more quickly as she traced a chemical structure that covered the back of his hand and reached along his thumb and first finger. There was a hexagon, a pentagon, and the combinations HO, NH, and $NH_2$.

"Is this what I think it is?" she asked.

Thane's Adam's apple drew up and dropped again. She drew a finger across his palm and he cleared his throat.

"Aye. Probably. The chemical structure of serotonin."

She grinned. "As in, the chemical for happiness?"

Lifting one shoulder, he put his hand on her back. The music's tempo sped up, crushing them with colorful, minor key melodies and a spine-bruising baseline. Incense soaked the air.

She imagined what the gold stubble on his cheek would feel like under her hand. "I like your tattoos. And I think, after this song, we should find a new place to…hang out." Maybe the balcony.

"You do? I would've thought a rule-follower like yourself would hate my unconventional tattoos."

He leaned close and tipped his head closer, though his gaze followed first one stranger and then another.

"There's nothing inherently rebellious about tattoos," she said. "It's merely not a cultural norm as of now."

*Please let someone notice the brooch*, she wished silently.

He laughed, and his eyebrow reached above the line of his glasses. "You do surprise me, Aini MacGregor."

The words felt like praise and she couldn't fight a smile.

His mouth, with its peaked upper lip, was only a breath away. One side drew up into a cocky sort of grin.

Then his eyes locked onto the brooch.

He jerked back a step, and before he could say anything, the chain at his neck brushed her finger. The club and Thane peeled away, and the colors of a vision became pictures.

*A garden. Leafy trees. Blue blossoms like a carpet. A pebble path. A blond-haired boy stood near a tall woman. The woman pulled the boy to her, and he grinned, saying something.* Mother, *his mind echoed. Blue-green happiness and golden contentedness swirled through the boy's mind.*

*A man tore into the garden, breaking a branch from a sapling near the path.*

*He handed a silver necklace to the boy, who took it with wide and innocent eyes. The man tried to put the chain on the boy. The boy shook his head of shaggy hair. His mother held out an arm, stopping the man's hands from circling the boy's neck. The man's mouth opened in a shout. Emotions like a storm of color spun around the boy's head. He looked up through black lashes at the scarred man. The boy's eyes weren't wide and sweet anymore. They were sharp, cold.*

The vision embedded in Thane's necklace shimmered away. The boy—grown now—looked into Aini's face.

"Aini? Are you all right?"

No, no she wasn't. "Yes. Sorry. Yes."

"Let's get you some water." Leading her off the dance floor, he pointed at her shoulder. "Did you know that's a Bethune brooch?"

"Is it?" She hadn't searched for what clan claimed the motto *Graceful.* She should've. Thane shouldn't have been more informed than her. "It was in Father's trunk. In that room."

At the bar, Aini sipped a glass of water, the cool liquid clearing her head.

Thane downed his ale and paid the barkeep. "Do you know about the Bethunes?"

"I just thought if it belonged to Father and certain people recognized it…"

"The last time kingsmen raided this place with any real

success," Thane said quietly, "they found a few of that clan. Seemed to be running the Dionadair here in Edinburgh."

Aini set the glass down and liquid splashed over the side. "What happened to them?"

Thane's eyes went cold as the waters of the Firth of Forth in January. "You really need to ask?"

"Right."

Someone touched her arm. It was a guy with the beginnings of a beard. He would've done better to wait another year before sporting that look. A pudgy man in thick, steel-toed boots stood by him. The liquid in Aini's stomach iced. They were the men from the balcony—the ones who'd been watching. Suddenly she wasn't so confident about her plan.

"Come with me," the first one said, his eyes bright, confident.

Thane made a derisive noise in his throat. "And who exactly are you?"

Neve and Myles appeared, their faces flushed.

Aini put herself between them and the strangers. "First tell me what this is about."

The second man's gaze slipped to the brooch. "You know what."

Aini cleared her throat and tried to stop her heart from beating too quickly. Thane touched her arm, and she gave the men a shaky smile.

"Give us a minute, please," she said.

They stepped back with a nod.

"Please don't do this," Thane said into her ear. "If they're not rebels, they're a waste of your time. If they are...these people don't care about anything but their cause. They're dangerous."

Myles butted in. "I don't know your plan here, but be careful, sweetheart. These people have knives in their fancy boots."

Discreetly, he pointed to the stranger's feet. Something silver showed at the second man's ankle. "If you do go with these losers, I'm going with you. We all are."

Thane nodded.

Myles's mouth fell open. "Wow. You actually agreed with me."

"But you're not going," Thane said to Aini.

"It's Aini's decision," Neve said. "Not yours."

Thane nodded tightly, but Aini could tell it was killing him to let her put herself in danger.

"That one guy looks my age," Aini said. "He can't be that dangerous."

"Shows how little you know," Thane said as he looked over her head at them.

"Number One, you wait here," Aini said. "Two, watch where he takes me. Three, if I don't come back in fifteen minutes—"

"No." Thane said, shaking his head and jabbing a finger. "That's definitely not what we're doing."

Aini may've growled. "This may come as a surprise to you, Thane Moray—I know how geniuses are used to getting their way—but I don't actually need your permission."

"I can't stand here and wonder if you're all right and—"

Aini didn't stick around for the rest of that statement. She started toward the strangers. "Let's go, gentlemen."

Thane slammed a fist on the bar top, rattling bottles and glasses. The keep said something to him that the music covered, and Aini heard Myles and Neve working to calm him down.

The men led Aini to the back of the club and up a wide staircase that led to a large balcony level with its own bar. Black bottles and bone cups made rows against its lighted back wall. Long red booths and sleek tables crowded the area. Past the seating, a hall led to the right, going toward what she could only guess was another interior part of the building. They didn't go far enough for her to find out. Instead, the two strangers stopped at what appeared to be a blank wall. The younger of the two pushed on the chaotically designed green and black wallpaper, and a door swung away from his hand.

"She'll want to see your brooch straightaway," the bearded man said, gesturing toward the hidden room. Then he walked off down the hallway.

"Of course." Aini headed through the doorway. Her pulse raced and she wiped sweating palms on her dress.

Before the man shut the entrance, leaving Aini on her own, she caught a flash of movement. A glimpse of green hair. One wide brown eye. A tattooed hand.

She sniffed to cover a nervous laugh. Myles, Neve, and Thane had hidden behind one of the red booths out on the balcony.

Inside the hidden room, red velvet-like paper covered the walls. Wrapped in a gold and black striped dress and leggings, a dark-haired young woman sat at a round table cluttered with electronics, and oddly, jewelry. A box near her elbow held a nest of shining things—a blue enameled ring, a silver brooch made in the shape of antlers, and several gold brooches. A beefy guy with pock-marked skin stood next to her, chewing on a drink stirrer. He had hair dark as midnight too, but freckles dotted his nose.

They were familiar somehow.

The woman's wide mouth puckered, and she looked Aini up and down. "I'm Vera. This is my brother, Dodie. Now where did you get that brooch?" She scooted forward on her chair, her hands clasped on the table.

Aini coughed, her throat dry. "It was...I found it. In an old trunk."

Vera's eyebrow lifted.

Aini stared the beautiful woman down.

Smiling a smile that would look perfectly at home on a boa about to squeeze someone to death, Vera pushed away from the table, pulled her dress down a little, and sauntered over. Aini silently named her perfume *Too Many Roses*.

Vera bent and squinted at the brooch. "*De bonnaire.*" Her eyes met Aini's.

Aini stepped back.

"A Bethune brooch," Vera said. "I'll give you fifty pounds for it."

"I don't want to sell it. I just wanted to know...have you seen it before?"

Turning away, Vera waved a hand in the air. Her nails were short and chipped. Aini chewed the inside of her cheek. Odd for a woman like her to have messy nails. Aini wondered what she did when she wasn't lounging in a club, buying up black market jewelry.

"There are so many like that," Vera said. "I'm really just paying you for the gold in it."

And yet, here she was, meeting Aini in a private room in a club where rebels used to meet.

"I'll go then." Aini shrugged and made for the door, running her damp palms down her sides again.

Vera's voice went higher, tighter. "Eighty pounds. Last offer."

"I want to know its provenance. Not its worth on the black market."

Vera's eyes widened, but Aini didn't wait for an answer. The walls were closing in, and that big man—Dodie?—had pulled something out of his waistband. A knife? A gun?

"Take it from her," Vera said.

Dodie rushed her. His thick fingers ripped the brooch from her dress, tearing the outer layer of white and gold fabric. Not thinking, just doing, she grabbed for the brooch, but Vera pushed her toward the door.

"Out with you, richie. I've no use for those who live well on English money."

Before they opened the door, Aini jerked hard and shoved Dodie. He fell, and the brooch flew from his hand. She leaped for it. Vera shrieked and came at her, ragged nails like claws. Diving for the brooch, Vera raked Aini's arm. Heat and needles seared Aini's skin. The door swung open behind her and strong hands wrenched her from the room.

"It's us, hen," Thane said into her ear.

Recovered, Dodie charged.

Myles shouted a warning and Neve took Aini's arm. Thane spun and smashed a boot into Dodie's stomach as Vera shot from the room. The two men who'd first led Aini through the club came running from the back hallway. Before Vera could get to them, Myles, Neve, and Aini hurtled down the stairs in a series of teeth-clattering leaps.

"Emergency!" Myles shouted into the crowd.

Aini looked over her shoulder. Still on the balcony, Thane had the bearded man in some sort of headlock. The chubby man waved a knife at Thane. He kicked the man's hand and the knife jumped into the air.

Downstairs, a cluster of girls wearing feathers in their hair separated Vera from Aini, Myles, and Neve. Vera's pretty face contorted as she made eye contact with Aini, but she didn't call out.

"This girl's going to upchuck!" Myles shouted. "Unless you want groceries tossed all over your fab attire, I suggest you move it!"

A girl in a mini skirt and three men with mohawks pushed

people aside as they fought their way through the red lights, candles, sweaty dancers, and skull-numbing music.

"What about Thane?" Neve shouted above the drums and trumpeting horns.

"He's a big boy." Aini helped Myles push the door open. Guilt nudged her, but she figured a man who drugged bouncers could probably take care of himself.

Outside, a mist that was nearly rain filled the air and weighed down Aini's elaborate and quickly dying hair style.

"Let's go, girls!" Myles tried to grab Neve's hand, but she didn't notice.

They tore into the street, dodging a car full of people singing along to the radio. A truck veered around them and blared its horn. The pavement glistened in the damp, slick under Aini's stupid, fancy shoes. At a dip in the road, her ankle rolled, sending a shot of heat up her leg.

"Hold on," she called out.

But Myles and Neve bolted past a pizza place with bright green walls, then a coffee house. They were headed for Candlemaker Row, for home. They couldn't lead these maniacs to the townhouse.

She tugged off her extravagant shoes and held them as she ran. "Stop! Wait!" The weak glow of the street lights teased her, not fully illuminating the wide road of George IV Bridge. It met with Candlemaker and the entrance to the graveyard. "We can't lead them to the townhouse," Aini said, panting.

Myles slicked water from his face. "We'll lose them in Greyfriars Cemetery."

Neve whimpered.

"The spirits can't hurt you." Aini tugged Neve, trailing Myles.

"I'm Scottish. We don't like to tangle with ghosts." Neve pushed the ends of her dripping braids out of her face.

Aini's stomach twisted. She was Scottish too. One half. She loved being Indonesian as well, but the color of her skin tended to make people around here forget her veins could hold blood from any number of countries.

Greyfriars' towering iron gate creaked as they hurried in. The rectangular windows at the top of the guard house doors were dark—it was after midnight—and the only sounds were the drips of rain on the trees that hulked over the old burial ground. At least, Aini hoped that was rain and not footsteps. Thankfully, the surrounding buildings' buttery light illuminated the graveyard well enough to navigate the city of wet tombstones.

"We can cut through the back, right, Neve?"

Aini clutched the brooch like a talisman, the memory of the vision running through her head.

The man handing Father the brooch.

The stranger from the past and the carved stone.

The knife.

The stranger's thoughts, the directions he'd purposely imprinted that almost seemed directed at her, a Seer.

Myles started up the paved walkway past the western façade of the towering church with its arched windows and bone-colored walls.

"If the gate to the Heriot School is open," Neve said, "we can go through their grounds and come around the block the back way."

A chill swept past. A barely audible shushing sound rolled over Aini. Neve snagged her arm, both of them shaking. The walkway was too narrow for all three of them to continue side by side. Aini handed Neve off to Myles and stepped into the grass. Mud squelched between Aini's bare toes. The scent of wet earth and ancient soot, clinging to gravestones like permanent shadows, rose into the air.

Neve began singing nervously. "*Macbeth's Seer rises nigh.*" Her timid voice strained over three minor key notes. "*A stone reflected in his light eye, and he bumped the man upon the chair, ripped him up by the hair.*"

"What are you singing?" Aini asked. "You sound like Myles."

"Say thank you to the lady, Neve," Myles said shakily.

"It's something my mum used to cant in the kitchen."

Aini's foot splashed into a particularly disgusting patch of black mud and Neve's eyes widened.

"Did you know that you're walking on 40,000 bodies?" Neve whispered. "When it rains like this, sometimes bones pierce the ground and come up under you."

Aini shuddered and edged around another cold spot. "Neve. Please. Save it for your tours."

Footfalls sounded behind them. Aini turned as Vera and Dodie rounded the pub at the cemetery's entrance and stopped.

Aini squeezed Neve's arm.

Myles swore.

Vera smiled.

## CHAPTER 9
## AN ANCIENT FEUD

On the club's upper floor, Thane held the bearded man in a makeshift bear hug and kicked the knife out of the other man's hand. The hairy lad wiggled out of the hold and caught Thane with an elbow. Salty blood ran into Thane's mouth as he slipped his head left to dodge another strike. He drove well-worn knuckles into that fool's beard, then spun to face the man's larger associate, who howled and held his kicked, most likely broken, fingers.

"You Dionadair?" Thane knew his smile probably looked a good bit like his father's. His stomach rolled, but he straightened his shoulders. Sometimes cruelty was called for.

The big man spat, the warm blood hitting Thane's jacket and hand.

Keeping the knife within his peripheral vision, Thane glanced at the dark splotch on his jacket. "You'll need better aim than that to down me."

The man launched himself at Thane.

Arms raised, Thane dove and blocked the man's knife arm.

Thane's hand slid to the man's wrist, where he kept the knife low and away from his body as he kneed the idiot in the balls. Clutching his groin, the man fell. Thane kicked him in the stomach and picked up the knife.

Racing down the stairs and licking salty blood from his lip, Thane broke through the club's crowd and rushed into the street. He prayed silently that his naïve lab partners wouldn't head home. Shouting once in frustration, he headed toward the townhouse. He'd tucked his newly attained knife into his boot and the edge bit into his skin a little as he coursed into the mist.

His blood shot through his veins, hot and raging. There *had* been Dionadair at the club still. Four of them, at least. Just the name *Dionadair* molded his hands into fists.

The rebels had long been Campbell enemies. In 1819, Thane's ancestor, wild-eyed antiquarian Donan Campbell, and the man's assistant—Angus Bethune, founder of the Dionadair—uprooted the Coronation Stone somewhere north. The old stories claimed the stone would roar under the hand of Scotland's rightful Heir. What *roar* meant exactly, the stories didn't say.

Thane's ancestor, Donan Campbell, had insisted on bringing the potentially politically damaging stone back to the reigning king of the time. But Angus Bethune hid the artifact. Angus claimed the stone must be used when Scotland was ready for its true Heir.

Whatever that meant.

Donan Campbell had knifed Angus Bethune in the back for his treason. And since that day so long ago, the Campbells had continued the search for treasonous Dionadair.

And two of those vicious rebels were closing in on Aini, Myles, and Neve right now.

Numb with the adrenaline, Thane wished he could run faster.

He was almost to Candlemaker Row when the memory of Aini's mouth, nearly touching his own, burned across his mind.

As they'd danced, everyone else was gray near her bright color. She surprised him at every turn. The violent defense of her father when she'd slapped Thane. Her determination in going to The Origin even after everyone tried to stop her. The courage in her walk as she left her friends and followed strangers in an effort to get answers.

A thrill snaked through him, but he stomped it down, subdued it. If he became involved with Aini, he wouldn't be able to stomach lying about his name, concealing his part in all of this. If he told her the truth...would she understand that he really had no choice, that this was his clan and he couldn't escape? No. She wouldn't listen long enough. And he wouldn't blame her. Not when they'd taken her father. It didn't matter if Lewis was working for the Dionadair, for the rebels. She'd see Thane's involvement as a betrayal, because that's what it was.

Shaking his head to clear it, he rounded the curve in the road. A shout from Greyfriars Cemetery stopped him. He went cold all over. Aini's voice echoed through the fog.

Entering the graveyard, Thane rushed past leaning obelisks and domed, cracked tombstones. A flash of movement shoved his heart against his ribs. He jumped over a mud puddle near the kirk, the grand church's pale walls nearly invisible in the soupy weather.

The two Dionadair operatives loomed over Aini. They weren't waving any weapons around, but they could've tucked them up sleeves or into waistbands. Neve trembled at Aini's side and Myles took a step forward.

If Thane moved in, the Dionadair would attack. Better to wait and see how this played out. He concealed himself behind a massive oak.

Myles's brow knotted. His shoulders were all up around his ears and he bounced on the balls of his feet, ready to spring. "What's so important about a piece of jewelry that you'd waste one of us to get it?"

"My sister wants that brooch, and she'll have it." The huge man's pock-marked face twisted into a grin as he pushed his sleeves up.

Aini's slender fingers clenched the brooch, her knuckles white. Thane put a fist over his heart. She was thinking of her father, and for some reason, she'd latched onto this piece of old jewelry as a key to finding out what was going on with him. Thane shook his head, his chest aching for her. To be so lost, and yet so smart...

Facing the man, she said, "I'll give you the brooch if you tell me why you want it so badly. You wouldn't rough up your own countryman, would you?" She took a shuddering breath. Drops from the trees ran down her face and into her mouth. "You're better than a Campbell, aren't you?"

Thane fell against the tree, the strength gone from his bones. His surprise only proved how she blinded his judgment. Of course she hated Campbells. These days, she'd be crazy not to.

The Dionadair woman's voice cut through the mist. "Shut your gob, girl. You're not even Scottish. You're colonial. And rich as a sheik. Dark as one. You're the furthest thing from Scottish." Her voice grew shrill. "Now hand it over."

Squeezing the oak's trunk until his fingers throbbed with the effort, Thane gritted his teeth. Racist rebel. Ignorant fool. Aini was a Scot through and through. Her pride. Defiance. The courage she'd shown. Her loyalty to her father. Thane fisted a hand and pounded the trunk. The stupid rebel woman's ignorant comment would prick at Aini's soul, he just knew it. The girl did everything she could to fit in here—following every one of the king's directives with regard to the lab work, dressing like the other Edinburgh girls in stripes and leggings, working to shed her colonial accent.

Aini raised her chin, courage shining like stars in her black eyes. "I won't."

A proud grin spread over Thane's mouth and his eyes shuttered briefly.

"Dodie," the woman said, her lips barely moving.

Thane's fingertips tingled. Dodie was going to attack.

Leaving the oak, Thane ran at the man, hoping Myles would go for the woman. But Myles struck out at Dodie, his small fist connecting with the man's stomach. Dodie didn't fall. He just smiled and cracked the back of his hand across Myles's jaw. The colonial dropped like a sack of tatties.

Neve shrieked and called out for help.

Vera leaped at Aini, but Thane was there in a breath, grabbing the woman's hair and pulling her back. He threw the rebel to the wet grass as she shouted.

Aini paled and looked to him. "What can I do?"

He would've laughed at her business-like tone if this weren't the situation it was. "Keep her there," he said.

In one fluid motion, he pulled the knife from his boot, came up behind Dodie, and put the blade to the man's throat. The wet air dragged Thane's hair into his eyes.

Myles lay moaning near a dead man's slab.

Neve ran to Aini and the girls held the rebel woman, each latched tightly to an arm.

Dodie struggled against Thane's hold. The cutting rank of fear and sweat rose from the larger man. Thane couldn't kill him. He'd never killed anyone. Not with his hands. His gut torqued, bringing a sour taste to the back of his throat. He wasn't innocent. He'd doomed plenty with the weapon of information.

Vera yanked her arms free. "Now what, tough man?"

At least she didn't realize Thane was a Campbell. If she said anything and exposed him...

The vial of sleep-inducing gel in Thane's pocket pressed against his side. Aini swallowed and clenched her jaw. Neve's eyes were round as the moon. There wasn't enough left of the gel to knock both these Dionadair rebels out. Could he bring them in? What would Aini and Neve say if he suggested it?

Dodie struggled against Thane's grip, so he tightened his hold. "I'm trying to decide whether to kill you or not. Suggest you behave your sweet, wee self."

The man made a strangled noise as the knife bit a little deeper into his skin. Hot blood trickled over Thane's fingers.

"We'll go our separate ways," Thane said to Vera. "You lost today. We keep the brooch. You keep this man with throat intact."

The woman stared, seething. Studying Thane, she pushed a strand of hair out of her face and pursed her blood-red lips. "Agreed."

Myles lay very still, his chest moving slowly up and down. He'd had a rough knockout, but Thane could tell he was awake.

"Aini, take my place here please." Thane gave Dodie a knee to the kidney for good measure. "I'll help our friend."

Aini moved toward Thane, and he handed the knife off, his fingers brushing hers. Aini's small hands were like ice, but she managed to keep the blade at Dodie's throat as Thane walked over to Vera. The woman stared up at him, anger pouring out of her. This one would have to be dealt with. He grabbed her by the hair. Aini and Neve gasped. Did they think she deserved better treatment? Because Thane didn't. It was really for the woman's own good anyway. If he held her any other way—the wrist, the shoulders—there was a good chance she'd strike out at him and he might have to hit her. He didn't want to do that. Not really.

"Neve, get the vial from my pocket," he said.

Neve twisted her hands together. "The what?" Her voice trembled like a poor recording of herself.

"The vial."

Aini made a noise. Dodie's eyes swung to look at Thane and the lout gritted his teeth.

Thane clicked his tongue. "You'll mind the lady's blade unless you long for a good kick in the teeth."

Neve took three tiny steps and reached a hand in to find the gel. "Got it."

As Vera moved around under the clenched bunch of her hair, Thane pushed her to her knees. "Now open it. Don't touch it, Neve. Drag the opening over Vera's wrists."

"What are you doing?" Vera tried to turn and look up at him.

His fingers curled and she yelped, now staring straight ahead and kneeling as still as a virgin at her prayers. Thane nodded, and Neve moved to follow his directions. People could say what they liked about positive reinforcement—money and lands—but pain did the job in a grimly satisfactory and rather timely manner. Thane took a breath of the wet, night air and wondered what sane people did on their Charlesday evenings.

As Neve stepped away from Vera and capped the vial, Thane locked gazes with Aini. "Now, release him," he said, gesturing at Dodie. "Keep the knife."

Thane freed Vera's hair and she crumpled at his feet. The gel, once again, had done its work.

Dodie stumbled toward her, a hand at his bleeding throat. Red trickled thinly through his fingers. It wasn't a big enough cut to do anything. Just enough to make him think twice about doing any more fighting tonight.

"What did you do to my sister?" Dodie demanded.

Thane hurried the girls out of the cemetery, and left the Dionadair behind like ghosts—one silent, one shouting—among the tombstones.

Myles mumbled something.

Neve put a hand to the colonial's forehead as Thane carried him.

"We need a taxi. Now." Thane waved a car over and they worked Myles inside.

They gave the driver the address for the townhouse, and the curly headed man twisted in his seat. "Don't you think he should be going to the hospital?"

Thane put two fingers under Myles's jaw, feeling for his pulse. "Just do your job, man."

Raising his hands, the driver shook his head. "Fine. It's your friend. Not mine."

"He just had a hit on the head, right?" Aini looked from Myles to Thane to Neve. Her eyes were wet with tears and it made Thane want to punch things.

"Aye." He thumbed a clod of mud from Myles's eyelid. It was just a hit on the head. Not serious. At least, he hoped not.

As they bumped down Candlemaker Row, Aini and Neve's gazes never left Myles's face. Aini kept her hands firmly on his stomach to steady him. Neve cradled his shoes like they were treasures.

Thane looked at the water-stained ceiling of the car. *Your friend,* the driver had said. Aside from Bran, who felt more like family, Thane had never thought of someone like that. He hadn't had the opportunity.

He leaned toward Myles. "You better not go all dafty on us, friend."

## CHAPTER 10
## A QUESTION

"Should I get smelling salts from the first aid kit?" Aini asked, watching Thane carry Myles through the front door of the townhouse. "You should lay him in his bed."

"Where did you think I would lay the man down?" Thane rolled his eyes. He mumbled at a sleeping Myles. "The numpty. Why'd he think he could take on a man that size?"

As they hurried through the entryway, Aini was glad to see Thane moving carefully, his gaze on corners and furniture that might trip him.

Myles had sat up once during the ride home, given everyone an okay sign, and then promptly fell asleep. Aini didn't know much about concussions, but she didn't think sleep was a good thing at the moment.

Holding the boys' bedroom door open, Neve chewed her lip. "And you don't think we should've taken him to a doctor?"

"Nah," Thane said. "It's a knockout. That's all. A rough one.

If we can rouse him again, there's no more to do than let him rest. If we can't wake him..."

Aini rushed into the kitchen. "I'm getting the salts. Just in case."

A yellow nightlight glowed over the stove, illuminating the room. She slipped past the round kitchen table and headed up the dark stairs to the lab, praying silently that the salts were in the first aid kit. The last one to use the kit was Myles. But of course, the first aid kit wasn't where it was supposed to be—by the stove, in the top cabinet.

Aini dashed to Myles's massive desk and began rummaging. She tossed a stapler and two chewed pencils into the first drawer, where a scattering of charcoals hid. She stacked four small blank canvases at the corner of the desk and peered under a tattered portfolio. No first aid kit. Only a calendar of women in bathing suits. After shuffling through some drawings, she turned her attention to the other side. Lifting the edge of a large sheet of green and pink painted butcher paper, she slid the bottom drawer open and finally found the emergency supplies.

"Myles!" Neve's voice came from the kitchen.

Aini looked up, the kit in her hands and her heart pounding.

Myles appeared at the open lab door. He leaned a forearm against the frame and heaved a breath. "Don't wrinkle that butcher paper."

Aini pinched her nose with two fingers. "You come back from unconsciousness to keep me from wrinkling your latest advert idea? When your desk rivals a rat's nest for the Most Horrifying Mess award?"

On the paper, the cotton candy colors and emerald hues blended to form representations of the visions their chewing gum induced.

One of Myles's eyes was nearly swollen shut and the side of

his face was puffy. "The advert is enthralling, right?"

A wry laugh crept out of her. "It is pretty fantastic."

She helped him into a chair as Neve and Thane burst into the room.

"Daft colonial." Thane shook his head of golden hair.

Neve kneeled at Myles's feet. "Why did you go flying out of bed like a dog had bitten you?" She turned to Aini. "He sat up right after we laid him down. We were about to call for you."

Smiling, Aini waved her off.

Myles pointed a finger, then winced and bowed his head. "I knew Aini would be looking for the first aid kit." He cocked his head at Thane and Neve. "And what would our Miss MacGregor do if she had more than a second at my creatively arranged work station?"

Thane and Neve spoke in unison. "Organize it."

Aini raised an eyebrow. "*Someone* should."

Taking a copper pot from the cabinet, she ran a finger over a ding in the side. Her body felt heavy with what had happened. "Those people could've killed us."

She set the pot on the stove and began heating sugar and cornstarch over medium just to keep her hands busy.

Neve hummed two notes, the sounds she made when thinking about new candy flavor combinations. She walked over, eyed the pot, then slid the large cutting board from the lab table's lower shelf.

"Golden taffy, aye?" she said to Aini, her voice as artificially bright as Myles's hair.

Picking up a folded cloth from the counter, Thane cleaned some water from the edge of the sink.

Tears rose, hot and sudden, and Aini dragged a hand over her eyes to smear them away. "I'm sorry I put you all in this position."

Myles coughed. "We knew what we were getting into."

"I didn't," she admitted.

Neve blinked. "Me either."

Thane stared, the cleaning cloth thrown over his shoulder and his eyes weary. Aini wondered if he'd lost his glasses in the graveyard.

"Where did you learn how to fight like that?" she asked him, adding the butter and salt.

"Not everyone had a sweet childhood like your own."

"I just...thank you. For—"

"What did the rebels say to you in that wee room of theirs?" he asked.

Neve gave Aini the container of orange flavoring and the jar of golden dye. "Aye. Tell us. Did you learn anything about Mr. MacGregor's past?"

Aini measured, then remeasured the flavor and stirred it in. After all they'd risked tonight, they deserved to know everything. But if she told them about being a sixth-senser—specifically, a Seer—they'd immediately have knowledge they were required by law to report. If they were caught hiding her, they'd be taken for questioning and possibly be in an even worse situation than Father probably was right now.

The cutting scent of citrus bit into her thoughts.

Neve donned some hefty oven mitts and removed the pot from the heat. She frowned and added the gold.

Myles laid his head on the back of the chair. "Aini, you need to tell us exactly what's going on."

Once she told them, everything would change. It would be a jump off a ledge, the lighting of a match, pushing the first domino. Aini moved her mouth, but the words wouldn't come. Neve asked her something, but all Aini could hear was her own heart knocking. She had to tell them. She couldn't tell them.

## CHAPTER 11
## CONFESSION

"Does it have anything to do with that brooch you're wearing?" Neve poured the taffy onto the cutting board.

Aini swallowed. "I found it in Father's trunk. In the hidden room behind that wall." She pointed to it, certain Thane had told them about it, but Neve and Myles's eyes widened.

"Hidden room?" Neve said. "Does everyone in Edinburgh have a hidden room?"

"Only rebels." Thane's hands fisted at his sides. "Sorry. Ignore me." His fingers went to the chain at his neck, the one that held the vision of him as a child.

Aini suddenly felt crushed under the weight of his judgment against her family.

But he was right.

Father had been involved. Somehow. She didn't know how deeply, but he'd been tied into the underground world of rebels at some point.

Looking at her clothing and touching her updo, Aini gritted

her teeth. She'd tried to fit into Edinburgh society. Talking like the upper class, well-respected Scots and Englishmen. Following every rule that she could. And now Father's past could erase all her efforts to give him the peaceful, successful life he deserved. The life she'd thought he deserved. *No. He still deserves happiness.* Surely his mistakes didn't go so deep.

Her shoulders and back tight, she removed the brooch and passed it around. "The brooch has the Bethune clan motto. Thane tells me some Dionadair rebels are Bethunes."

"Aye." Neve handed the piece of jewelry to Myles. "The ones sentenced to death when we were still in grammar school."

"Yes." Aini pressed the flat spoon into the mixture, inhaling the comforting scent of sugar and oranges. "When I...when I found the brooch and touched it..."

Myles snorted, looking at the pin. "An otter. Real tough." He rolled his eyes and gave the brooch to Thane, who looked at the piece like it would explode in his hands.

"Shut your gob, Myles," Neve chided.

As Aini laid the turner next to the mass of sticky sweetness, Thane slid the brooch down the silver lab table. It scratched across the surface and Aini caught it neatly. The metal was warm from his fingers. She cleared her throat, touching the tiny, rough lines that made up the rebel clan's motto. Her stomach burned under her ribs.

Myles slowly opened his swollen eye, obviously in pain. Neve was pale as milk as she looked at Aini with the kindest eyes. The taffy was going cold, forgotten. A purple and green bruise colored Thane's knuckles.

"I'm a Seer." The words fell from her mouth like they had a life of their own.

Neve's head jerked up. "What?" she whispered like someone might hear.

"I have a sixth sense." Sweat rose along Aini's back, and she grabbed the turner and folded the taffy, once, twice, three times, her arm muscles tensing. "For two years, I've been able to see emotional imprints, memories, on sentimental items when I first touch them."

Neve's mouth dropped open. Myles blinked, frozen, and Thane's face was unreadable.

"I touched your bracelet, Myles," Aini said. "I saw your mother. Curly hair. Not the nicest person."

His lips opened and shut and opened again.

"Thane, I..." She licked her lips quickly. Her mouth was dry as sand. "I accidentally touched your necklace and a vision of you played out in my head. You were little. Your parents were there. I couldn't see them clearly, but..."

"Can you even believe it?" Neve said quietly. Then she clapped her hands once and laughed. "That's amazing!"

"You're...you're not scared? Of me? Of disappearing into prison for knowing me?"

"I'm scared of prison. But not you. Course not you. Aini...it's brilliant."

Aini smiled shyly, but when she looked at Thane, her grin faded. His face was a sketch in harsh lines and tired eyes. She rolled her mother's ring around her finger.

"And I saw a vision when I first touched the brooch too. It was in The Origin. Near where the picture was taken, the picture Thane found in Father's office. A man gave the brooch to him. Father didn't want it."

Thane narrowed his eyes. "How do you know?"

"I can...see some emotions in visions. Father was scared. Unhappy. Worried. Another vision followed. In the second one, a man in strange, old-fashioned clothes said something. It was like he knew he left an emotional imprint and wanted to talk to the Seer who would experience the vision. So weird. It was different from the other visions I've seen." Aini shivered. The man's eyes had been so bright, so passionate. "He said something about a rock or a trail or something." Her mind went foggy with fatigue, and she rubbed her eyes. She needed sleep, but obviously that wasn't happening anytime soon.

Neve's head went slowly back and forth. "I knew there was something special about you."

A strangled laugh bubbled out of Aini. "You don't think I'm an abomination?"

"I know you." Neve played with the braid hanging over her shoulder. "You wouldn't use your...ability to take advantage of people."

It's what many people thought about sixth-sensers—that they'd use their extra sense to one-up everyone else.

"I hope I don't get you all into trouble." Aini blinked back tears.

"Bit late for that," Thane said, softening his words with a shaky smile. "And the king's law is wrong." Venom leaked into his voice. "He should not call your kind what he does. It's not your choice to have this ability." Crossing his corded arms, he popped a knuckle and mumbled something under his breath.

"I've only known one other Seer," Myles said. "An old woman who worked for my mother. You're a truckload better looking than her. Guess you don't have to be a hag or a lying cheat to be," he wiggled his fingers, "in touch."

A sad smile drifted over Aini's mouth. He was a friend. She hadn't had many in her life of traveling with her mother and the dancing troupe. She memorized how he looked right at this moment, with his sly grin and green hair and wide eyes, and tucked the image into her heart.

Neve sighed at him. "Myles. Really." She checked his puffy

jaw and eye with her fingers. Aini guessed growing up with younger brothers almost qualified Neve as a nurse.

"My life's an open book. Read at will, Aini," Myles continued. "I'll warn you, it's not for the faint of heart."

The lab's overhead lights suddenly felt too bright. Aini slid her mother's ring from her first knuckle to the next. Neve helped Myles to the stairs.

"This man needs his bed," Neve said.

Myles put a hand over his heart. "Oh what I could do with that phrase if I wasn't three shades shy of full function."

Neve gave him a look he completely deserved. "Aini, I'll wait up to talk to you. In our room. If you want."

They disappeared into the dark, and Thane turned the oven's temperature up. He scooped the cold taffy lump onto a baking sheet.

"We should get some rest." Aini swallowed. "You don't have to do that."

He pulled his glasses out of his pocket. So he hadn't lost them. He'd prepared to jump into the fray at the cemetery, removing his glasses before fighting.

His eyes were very gray as he looked at her over the black frames. "I know what it's like to need normality. To make taffy when you should probably be thinking over what you've been through."

"You've made taffy when your world was coming apart?" She let out a half sob, half laugh.

"Not taffy, no. But I—I understand."

The oven door closed with its usual squeak. Aini sat on a stool and hugged herself. She felt empty. Confused. Lost.

After eyeing the taffy through the oven's window, Thane leaned back on the table beside her. His left hand was tucked under an arm, his right picked at a thread on his belt loop.

"A Seer, aye?"

"Yep."

"Pretty rare."

"Uh huh."

The corner of his mouth pulled toward a dimple. "So the rule-follower is really one of the King's Most Wanted." He took her hand—his was hot—squeezed it quickly, and then pulled away. "I'm sorry. I shouldn't joke."

"It's okay. It is kind of ironic."

"Kind of?" He nudged Aini with his shoulder. That grin of his would've melted her if she hadn't been so miserable. But his powerful smile faded fast. "Hey, hey, I'm sorry. I'll shut my gob."

And then she was crying and he was holding her against his chest and she didn't even remember putting her arms around his waist. He felt so strong, his muscles taut and coiled with potential.

"I've always held myself back from my ability," she said. "To protect everyone. So I wouldn't see into their personal thoughts, their memories. It's an invasion. I know it is. I never once stayed at a friend's house. Not that I have any to speak of...I was afraid I'd see something I didn't want to. You can't unsee those most important memories. I have to pull back when someone goes to hug me or put an arm around me. Everyone thinks I'm cold, but...I hide what I am so if I'm taken for questioning," her throat clenched painfully, "no one but me will be hurt. But Father, he was always in danger from me. Just for being my father."

Her skin felt too sensitive, raw and hurting. Her chest ached with her father's absence. She wanted more than anything to hear his voice and the people at the club had tried to take her only clue—the brooch—instead of helping to figure all this out and it was too much, too much, too much.

She choked back a rasping sob. "The rebels...they're just so... I don't know how Father could've helped them. They're awful. You saw them! I don't know what to do."

Thane made a soft hushing sound over her head. "Easy now, hen. One thing at a time. You love lists, so let's make one."

Sniffing, she nodded and broke away. They stood side by side, leaning on the lab table and a little on one another. One of her arms was still behind him, her hand on the edge of the cutting board. The scent of sugar and rain filled the air.

"Information Item One," she said, and he laughed sadly, the vibration humming through the place where their bodies touched. "Those were Dionadair rebels. Two. They want the brooch. Three. Father has some connection to the club or what used to be there or both. We know because of the picture and my vision."

As she pulled her hand from behind Thane, her forearm dragged over the waistline of his trousers, rucking up his shirt a little. A sliver of his skin touched the inside of her wrist. He sucked a quick breath and looked down, his eyes serious. She swallowed, feeling very warm. How would it feel to run a whole palm against his bare back? Her mouth went dry. Thane twisted and leaned in, his gaze so heavy on her lips that she could almost feel the pressure and the heat of it. She imagined his breath tickling her chin and—

The oven beeped.

She jumped to get the taffy, hearing his deep inhale behind her. With oven mitts, she removed the candy from its warm hideout and set it on the table. Her heart wouldn't stop drumming. Her lips wouldn't stop feeling that imagined kiss. They both touched the taffy to test its temperature and the mix stung her fingers. The pain faded quickly. She wished these inconvenient feelings would disappear just as easily.

"Perfect temp." She looked to him.

"What?" He glanced at her, and then at the candy. "Oh. Yes. Right."

Together, they lifted the sticky stuff and draped it over the taffy puller machine. Thane switched the puller on. It began humming, drowning the sound of the oven's fan and the small cooler's buzz and clank.

"Thank you." She rubbed her eyes with the back of her hand. "For listening. For helping me tonight."

A length of taffy drooped away from the machine's silvery arms. They reached for it and their hands collided in the warm candy. They lifted the draping, golden strand, then stood there, facing one another. Aini had ended up with two delicate strands of taffy on her fingertips. She ate one and gave him the other.

He grinned and took it between finger and thumb.

The space between them begged to be filled. Aini's fingers twitched and longed to reach out and touch the bruise below his eye, his proud chin. She wanted to feel the strength of this genius who could somehow fight too.

She took a shaky breath. "I'm sorry for all the problems I've caused."

Lines appeared between Thane's eyebrows, partially blocked by his glasses. He bit his lip and shook his head. His mouth opened, shut. Then he said, "Do not say that. Aini, I—"

"I should've listened to you about the club. About the danger. If I had, Myles wouldn't be injured."

She was breathing quickly. Thane too, his tee shifting as his broad chest moved.

"And all you did," she said, "was what you thought was best in a situation I should never have dragged you into. You were amazing. The way you fought. Your quick thinking."

She wanted to kiss him. A terrible idea. But here he was, by her side, with his patience and his eyes going all soft and after what he'd suffered for her tonight and all he'd risked...

It was like a magnet sat in each of them. The pull grew stronger with every breath.

Making a noise in the back of his throat, Thane closed the short distance and cupped her chin in his long, taffy-sticky fingers. Heat bloomed over Aini's cheeks as sparks ignited under her skin and spread down her throat. The scent of summer, embodied in fruit and syrup, soaked the air around them. His body pressed against hers and she was melting like chocolate.

Her heart boomed in her ears. "I should've listened to you."

"No, hen," Thane whispered, eyes half-lidded.

Gently, she pulled his hand away from her chin. "It was wrong. I am sorry."

Thane's eyes matched the sky's light through the window. The sun was rising. "Aini, you're so...good. I've never met someone so true to themselves. And you're insanely brave, you wee fool." A lightness rose inside her at the praise. Then a raw, vulnerable look crossed Thane's features, the same look she'd seen flashes of ever since they'd taken Father. "You make me feel like some daft poet," he said, smiling.

"Robert Burns wasn't daft." She grinned and raised an eyebrow.

"Not like him. A poet without any proper words...only the emotions to make me wish I had them. *Where're you bide in the world so wide, we wish you a nook on the sunny side, With a muckle of love and little of care...*"

It was absolutely lovely, and she felt so much like he was a part of her life here now, that he understood her and what she was going through. She was so lucky to have him here. He was going to help her solve this and save Father. It was all going to be okay.

"What's it from?" she asked.

He looked down, his cheeks going a little pink. "It's a wedding blessing. The only pretty thing I know." His black lashes brushed his glasses. "Aini—"

She couldn't stand it anymore. Rising onto her toes, her lips stopped his words.

He kissed her back—a hard, pushing embrace—and a burn worked its way from his velvet lips, to her mouth, down deep into her heart. Each time he pressed into the kiss, a pulse of heat flared from her chest, all the way to her taffy-covered fingertips. Goosebumps trailed down her legs. Moving backward, she bumped into the table and tasted the taffy again in her mouth and his. She pulled back.

The Cone5, the ingredient that caused the enhanced color vision in the taffy, took effect. A halo of blue-purple shone around the edges of Thane's hair. A teal-pink hue showed in the lines of the tattoos on his hands and in his glasses' frames. Aini put a hand to her head. It felt light as feathers and all her worries dissipated.

Thane's gaze flew over her face and hair and dress. "The colors...it's...I didn't think you could get any more bonnie, but this is—"

He eased against her, his calloused hands on her cheeks, then sticking in her hair. His flat stomach was hot through their clothing and Aini curled her fingers into the soap-scented fabric of his shirt. He tilted his head to the right, and their noses brushed awkwardly before he corrected, grinned against her mouth, and brushed his lips over hers. Aini's pulse beat hard and fast in her throat. She pulled him closer, loving the feel of his breath, his teeth, the quick slip of his warm tongue over her top lip.

Neve hurtled into the lab. She'd changed into pajamas, and

because of the taffy, her purple top glowed in three shades Aini didn't have names for.

"The people from the club," she said, blushing and looking from Aini to Thane and back again. "They're at the door."

Aini jerked away, head spinning. "They're here? The Dionadair? How do they know where I live?"

Neve bunched her pajama top in her small, white hands. "Suppose they asked around about an Indonesian girl. Not a lot of those in Edinburgh. They've brought another man. Never seen him."

The effects of the small amount of taffy began to disappear. Corpse-gray light dragged through the window and gathered in the corners of the lab. Aini shivered.

Thane had gone all still and quiet, his arms hanging loosely at his sides.

Going to the sink, Aini grabbed a towel and ran it under water. "Should we...should we go talk to them?" She cleaned her fingers and handed the towel to him.

A muscle in his jaw moved as he rubbed the taffy off. "I'll go."

Following Neve, Aini started down the stairs. Thane trailed her.

"No," Aini said. "This is my problem. You all stay inside and I'll talk to them on the front stairs."

"We're here in whatever way you want us to be," Neve said, stumbling over her words.

The light of early morning slid into the kitchen and along the hallway where it blended with the shadows. Aini's mind was a buzzing whirlwind. She couldn't contain the dangers she'd brought on herself. Telling Thane, Neve, and Myles about her sixth sense. She'd kissed Thane. He'd kissed back. They'd almost been killed by people who were now at her front door. And she was about to chat with them like it was normal as tea on a Henrysday afternoon.

Staring ahead, Thane set a hand briefly on her back. Neve took Aini's fingers in hers and gave them a squeeze. The boys' bedroom door was closed; Aini guessed Myles was resting. Soft music trickled from within as firm knocks at the front door echoed through the entryway. She nodded at Thane and Neve, and took a breath.

"It's all right," a crisp male voice said through the door. "We come to apologize."

Thane laughed once, low and heavy with sarcasm. "Right."

Unlocking the three bolts, Aini put a hand on the cool, bronze doorknob. Her heart clanked like a kicked tin can.

Thane's phone hummed from his pocket. He took it out and mumbled something fierce.

Aini opened the door to Vera, Dodie, and a man in round glasses and a trim red beard. He wore a pair of striped trousers and a bow tie.

A slick of cold sweat covered Aini's back and upper lip. "What do you want? I'm not giving you anything."

The red-head held out a hand. "I'm Owen."

"You'll not touch her," Thane spat.

"I can speak for myself, thanks," she snapped.

Owen held his hands wide. "No worries." His owl-like stare locked on Aini. "Vera and Dodie are my siblings. They made a mistake. They saw the Bethune brooch and...acted rashly. Our apologies."

Aini kept a few feet of space between them. "We don't want your apologies. I want to know what you know about this brooch and what my father might have to do with its history."

Owen smoothed his beard. "Yes. Of course."

Vera's arrogance had fled her features. She watched Aini with rounded eyes, her hands clenched at her sides. "We think—"

Owen put a hand on her arm. "We believe our father and yours were close friends, associates." Pushing his glasses higher on his small nose, Owen traded a look with Dodie. The big man still looked murderous, but that could've just been the way his face was made. Clearing his throat, Owen said, "We believe you may be...someone important."

Thane snorted. "That's specific."

Neve stood behind Aini, her warmth a comfort against the cool dawn air.

Aini wasn't about to play stupid games with these people. They might've thought of themselves as representatives for the Scottish people, some sort of vigilantes, but she'd felt that woman's nails and heard the crack of that man's hand on her friend's jaw. They would've done worse if Thane hadn't intervened. These rebels were the picture of danger, standing in the flesh on her front steps. They—or those like them—were the reason Father was suffering questioning somewhere. The Dionadair had probably coerced him into doing something long ago. And now, instead of the Campbells simply leaving Father alone when he refused to help them, they had something to use against him.

She crossed her arms. "Explain."

Vera stepped forward, and Owen rubbed his hands together. "If you are who we think you might be, find the knife," Vera said.

"The what?"

"There is a legendary knife. And if you are who we think you are, you'll be led to it."

"Why would I care about some knife?"

Vera sneered. "Because the future of Scotland relies on it. As well as your father's well-being."

"What do you know about my father? Tell me."

Owen rubbed his chin. "When you prove you are the one to find the knife, we will tell you everything." He laid a hand on his stomach and gave a little bow. The three turned as one, walked quickly down the stairs, and disappeared into the lightening day.

Aini stood there, watching them go. "What? No! Tell me now!" She ran at them, but three sets of hands held her back. She turned to see all three apprentices. "What was that? What are they talking about? We have to go after them!"

"You should think first," Neve said, her face drawn with lines of worry and fear. They went back inside and shut the door. Neve locked it. "Have you ever heard your father talk about a knife? Is there one around here?"

Thane's forehead wrinkled and he took his glasses off, shaking his head. "They want a knife now? What in God's name…"

Numb and lost, Aini walked through the entryway, passing Father's glass-walled office. Their reflection looked eerily similar to a vision.

Aini froze.

The doors of her mind flew open.

"I did, Neve," she said. "In the brooch's vision. I saw a knife."

Thane frowned, and Neve cocked her head. "How would they know you saw a vision?" she asked.

"Maybe that's why they want the brooch so badly," Aini said. "They're aware of its embedded vision and want to know if I saw it."

Thane's boots knocked along the floor as he began pacing.

Thinking, Aini chewed the inside of her lip and leaned against the couch that framed the living room.

"Why would this particular knife matter to rebels?" Neve asked, her eyes red with fatigue.

Pausing, Thane shoved his glasses into his messy hair. Five dabs of taffy marked his collar. Aini flushed. Her fingerprints. He glanced from her to the prints. Looking down, he swallowed and continued pacing the wide, wooden floorboards.

She coughed. "I don't know. It doesn't make sense. Even if they somehow knew the brooch held a vision, how would they know what the vision showed? And why would they care?"

"Maybe if we go to sleep, our brains will figure it out for us," Neve said.

She was right. No matter what they decided, their bodies needed sleep before they could do anything.

Neve said good night and went to bed, promising first to check on Myles. Switching all the house lights off, Aini followed in her wake, Thane behind her. Her feet were concrete blocks. She blinked, clearing her fatigue-dry eyes.

At the door to the girls' bedroom, Thane put a hand out to stop her, his glasses on top of his head and tangled in his hair. The stubble on his sharp jaw had grown. In the hallway light, the tiny hairs glowed gold like the taffy they'd sampled. Aini didn't need recreational candy to see the beauty in him. It was all there in his high cheekbones, bow-shaped lips, and those sea-storm eyes that, when they focused on her, smoothed a warmth over her heart, down her stomach, and below her navel.

"Aini, I should not have—"

She put a hand on his chest and his heart beat against her fingertips. Like her dress was made of lead, she felt so heavy, tired. "I know. The timing...but don't think I," she cleared her throat, "that I didn't want..."

His lips quirked to one side and his eyes grew sad. "Go on to bed. I won't bother you anymore tonight." He looked toward the dawn streaming through the front windows. "Oh. Today."

She laughed sadly. "I'll set my alarm and get you up if you want me to."

"Sounds good," he said, but his tone sounded anything but good.

With a quick goodnight, she went into the bedroom.

Sleep didn't want to take her away though. She rolled her mother's wedding ring around her finger. Neve snored lightly across the room, the tiny, square skylight laying sun over her ever-present, painfully messy mound of pillows and blankets.

Aini picked up the brooch and thumbed the Latin words of the motto. How was she going to puzzle all this out? Would her life ever go back to normal? She turned over, carefully folding the end of her sheet over the duvet's edge. *Normal.* What a beautiful word. She longed for her organized days of lists and rules that she could follow.

But she was a living, breathing joke. She'd been breaking the rules all along, being what she was, doing what she did. She was a fake, an illegal sixth-senser posing as a loyal subject who did as the law demanded. Pressing her face into the pillow, every bone in her body ached, longing, moaning for the simple life she'd somehow lost.

# CHAPTER 12
## GUILT AND OATMEAL

The lab air cooled Thane's face. Good thing too because his brain was on fire. Aini was a sixth-senser. A Seer, of all things! And right here, under his nose. Rodric would've had a grand time with that knowledge. Thane pressed his fists against his pounding head. She'd hid her ability so well. This proved what Thane had believed though. That sixth-sensers had no choice at all in being born with their talents, so to speak. Aini didn't deserve punishment. The poor lass had enough of that in her life now.

He took a deep breath, smelling heated metal, oranges, and sugar. The scent produced an image of Aini's face. A pleasant shiver ran from Thane's chest and down.

That kiss.

It shouldn't have happened. His stomach clenched with the thought of her lips under his. He shoved the feelings to a far removed corner of his mind as he gathered ingredients from the mini ice box and turned on the stove. If he didn't turn in a new recipe for weaponized candy to Rodric soon, his cousin would pay him a visit.

The traditional Scottish sweet called tablet normally consisted of nothing more than cane sugar, sweet condensed milk, unsalted butter, and a bit of fresh milk. But Lewis's special formula negated the effects of certain other recreational sweets.

And that gave Thane an idea.

First, he could amp up the color-vision Cone5 taffy recipe—the stuff he and Aini had sampled during the kiss—and make a gas version so it'd be easily dispersible. When released, anyone in the area would see far too much ultraviolet, too much of every color in the spectrum. They'd be temporarily blinded by color. Unless they had also eaten the juiced up negating tablet Thane was about to create. It'd be perfect for undercover Campbell operatives.

Two recipes. Surely it was enough to get him off the black list with Rodric. And it wouldn't be as bad as giving them the paralyzing stuff he'd crafted.

Yes. Two recipes should be fine for now.

*If* Thane turned it in.

As he stirred the pot of ingredients over medium-high heat, steam clouded his glasses. After twenty minutes, the mix's color took on a golden brown hue. Removing the tablet from the heat, he stirred it vigorously, then poured it into a buttered baking tray. Before it could cool, he sprinkled Lewis's canceling powder over the top. It was a combination of powdered sugar, a mild steroid, and a hormone that blocked the vision enhancement chemical in the taffy.

With the tablet complete, he attempted to focus on a formula to turn the taffy's essence into a gas.

He swallowed, his heart as heavy as his eyelids. Aini had

confessed her greatest secret. She was a Seer. And a good one, it seemed. What exactly had she seen on Thane's necklace? His tongue tasted bitter. Served him right if she saw some painful secret, a clue to his true identity, in that vision of his childhood.

Rubbing his face harshly, he scratched out his formula, then started again.

His phone buzzed from the pocket of his pants. It was Rodric. He should report Aini right now. He should report this recipe. He hit the ignore button on the phone. For once, just once, he didn't care about *should*. As if it'd heard his thoughts and had a mind of its own, his long-ago broken rib pinched his side. Rodric had cracked that bone, and here Thane was, basically asking for a repeat performance.

After finishing up in the lab, Thane hurried down the stairs to the kitchen. Weak light drifted from the front of the townhouse and lay in tattered strips along the wooden planks of the floor. Suddenly longing for comfort food, Thane switched the light on over the stove and started a pot of oatmeal cooking. His skin felt too tight. Too warm. Itchy. Like he wanted to crawl out of himself and be someone else.

His phone buzzed again. He tossed it on the countertop and kept stirring.

"If you whisk that oatmeal any harder, you're going to dig a hole to Russia." Myles raised his eyebrows as he ambled in. "Or whatever's on the other side of the planet from here."

The colonial started some coffee, then pulled out a chair and sat backwards in it. His face looked like Thane felt. Bruised. Knocked off kilter. An ill fit for the bones beneath it.

"How d'you feel man?" Thane poured the oatmeal into two bowls and threw some blueberries on top. "Your head aching?"

Myles accepted the bowl and added a boatload of honey. "I'm all right. Not too bad. You know your phone's going off."

Neve and Aini walked in. Neve was all in black, and Aini wore a short, blue dress that hugged her waist. Her eyes were big and haunted, circles ringing them. She'd not slept enough. And no wonder. Aini flipped the kitchen's overhead light on and her gaze went from his face to his bare feet. Her eyelashes were black and thick and pure sexy. His heart clunked hard, just the once, under his breastbone. She blinked, and her apple cheeks darkened a shade.

Myles nudged Thane's wrist with a finger. "Probably shouldn't stare. They don't like that."

Thane swallowed and looked into his oatmeal, his face hot. "Shut your gob, colonial."

Snickering, Myles bid the girls a good morning. Neve poured out some orange juice while Aini eyed the stairs to the lab.

"Neve, I'm going to need your help," she said.

Neve sat beside Myles. "Aye. Course. To find that knife?"

The coffee maker let out a low screech and a puff of steam, its familiar finale. Aini handed a mug to everyone and took the chair between Thane and Myles. She braced her shaking hands on the cup, and Thane's heart cinched in his chest.

"So in the vision on the brooch, I saw a lot of things. One being the knife I believe those Dionadair mentioned."

"Could you tell where the knife was?" Myles slurped his coffee.

"It was in a brick and stone room. And the place was dark." Aini stared into her mug like she could see the vision again. "Water dripped from the ceiling. If the knife is close enough that the rebels think I can just go and get it, it must be here in Edinburgh somewhere. The only place I can think that would look like the location is the underground vaults."

Thane reached a long arm out and grabbed his phone, pocketed it. "A good place to hide something."

Neve hugged herself. "I hate that place. I used to run a tour there. It's full of spirits. And not the nice kind."

Myles laughed. "You Scots are adorable. Believing in ghosts and all that."

Thane and Neve glared at him.

"We'll see how cute you think I am," Thane said, "when I make your right eye match the left."

Myles made an *Oooo* sound and pretended to shake in fear. Thane took a drink, raising his middle finger over the side of the cup so only Myles would notice it.

"The man in the vision mentioned a number." Goosebumps raised the fine hairs on Aini's arms. "Eighty-five."

"Yes," Neve said. "The vaults under Cowgate Road are numbered for sure. I don't know about the others. But those are."

She pushed away from the table, left the kitchen, and returned with the patched satchel she usually brought on her tours.

"Look at this." She took a map from the bag and spread it between the coffee mugs. Steam rose from the drinks as she smoothed out the paper's folds with a palm. "Eighty-five should be about here." Her finger hovered over a spot north of the townhouse. "This is the vault you're looking for. This section was abandoned around 1835. But you can't go in, Aini. They walled plague victims up in certain spots down there. The spirits—"

Aini slammed her fist on the table and everyone froze.

"I'm sorry," she said, her voice shaking. "But I have to go in, Neve. You know I do."

Neve nodded, and Myles patted Aini's back.

Thane stood and took a better look at the map. Running a

hand over the black lines and scrawled names, he remembered red tape and an announcement about the vaults.

"Neve's right that you can't go down in the vaults," Thane said. "But not because of ghosts."

Aini frowned. "Why not?"

"The Dionadair used them to move around the city and orchestrate hanging the banned flag on Holyrood Palace in the spring. The king has closed them up now. You can't get in."

Myles frowned. "How do you know all this?"

Aini's eyes went all fiery and angry. "I have to know what Father did or didn't do. A padlock isn't going to stop me."

"Oh no?" Thane cocked his head. "A past in breaking and entering is it then?"

"No. I...I'm claustrophobic." She swiped her palms on her dress. "Father taught me how to pick locks in case I was stuck somewhere."

She was always surprising Thane and now was no different.

Myles's eyes widened.

"So I'll be fine," Aini said. "I can get in and get out. No problem." She swallowed, not convincing at all in her cavalier attitude.

She was going to get herself killed. Thane stood up, went to the sink, and pressed his hands into the countertop.

Aini gathered Neve's map, smoothing and smashing it until the thing submitted to her demanding folds. "I'm leaving. Thane, will you go with me? Neve can stay here and keep an eye on Myles."

"What about the kingsmen guarding the vaults?" Myles asked. "I'm guessing there'll be at least one of them at the entrance. Probably need to worry more about them than ghosts. Ghosts don't have swords. Oh. Wait." He tapped his head. "I have a great idea."

Thane snorted.

Myles cleared his throat like he was about to sing. "Get a dog," he proclaimed.

"A dog?" Aini put her head in her hands.

"Listen." Myles held up a finger. "Toss a row of sausages at the first kingsman you see. Thane will be wearing one of Neve's dresses and—"

"I prefer blue." Thane shrugged. "Sets off my eyes."

"You're taking this seriously?" Aini asked.

"None of it's happening anyway. You'd never get away with it. No one would," Thane said, his voice rougher than he meant it to be. But he had to stall her. "I may as well have fun with the colonial's imagining."

Myles pumped a fist in the air. "Even our Thane can't deny my fantastic forethought. He can go after the dog while you head for the vaults."

Sighing, Neve grabbed the sugar bowl. "Why does Thane need a blue dress?"

"Don't encourage them," Aini said.

"I told you, Neve," Thane said. "Sets off my eyes." He fluttered his lashes.

"Stop," Aini said. "We need to—"

The colonial clucked his tongue at Neve. "Never underestimate the power of your attire." He shook a finger at her.

Neve dropped a spoonful of sugar into her drink. "I learned all about that when we went to The Origin," she whispered at Myles.

The cocky gomeral's face reddened. "Oh. Yes. You, that outfit..."

Thane smiled, glad he wasn't the only one feeling exposed on matters of the heart.

Aini lifted her shoulder bag off the chair and her ebony hair swung across her back. "I'm going to the vault." Thane's chest tightened as she made for the kitchen doorway. "No matter how many ghosts or kingsmen trouble me," she said, still not facing him. She ducked her head to draw the bag's strap over her shoulder. "Or how much Thane scowls. And yes, Thane, I can feel your dissatisfaction burning into the back of my head."

He couldn't let her do this. She'd be caught. No way she'd hold up under questioning. Brave, she was. Tough? That was yet to be determined. She'd done well enough with Vera and Dodie, but...

He stepped forward. "I'll fetch the knife. You don't need to go."

"Of course I'm going."

"We'd have to go in right off High Street. Right, Neve?" Thane asked. "That's the only door even remotely accessible."

Neve nodded.

"There'll be loads of kingsmen in that area," Thane said to Aini. "And you know it."

"Look. You were right about the club. You're probably right now. But I'm going anyway. I have to. The Dionadair promised information. I'm going."

He shook his head. "Too dangerous."

Myles laughed. "Sorry, my lord Highlander. I don't think this one," he jabbed a thumb at her, "is going to swear fealty to you anytime soon." The colonial grinned and began mumbling something about the merits of female domination and leather.

Thane shot him a look, and Myles clapped a hand over his mouth.

Aini had her planning face on. "We'll find a spot to watch the vault entrance for an hour. See if any kingsmen are specifically assigned there."

"Yeah. Look for patterns of their movement, all spy-like," Myles said.

Thane felt sick. "Patterns? In an hour?"

"We don't have all the time in the world. The Dionadair might change their minds," Aini said. "And Father is suffering. I can't sit and observe them for days like we probably should."

Neve cleared her throat. "Why don't you go around lunch? Maybe they take a break patrolling or might at least be distracted by the crowds heading in and out of the eateries."

Aini nodded. "Good idea. And Myles is right."

"I am?" He made a fist again. "I am."

"We need a distraction," she said. "We could...report something to the kingsmen's office. Over the phone. Maybe they'd send their closest men to investigate, leaving the vault door unguarded."

Neve picked up Aini's phone from the table and handed it to her.

Aini set the device down. "Not from my phone. Not from any of ours. If the Campbells in the office recognize one of our numbers, they'll know I'm not following their directions to keep quiet about Father's abduction. They might...hurt him. Or worse. We have to find another phone to use."

"And what are you going to pretend to know about and report?" Thane asked.

This was getting messy. If Aini created some sort of ruckus, there'd be kingsmen everywhere. Some Campbells would recognize Thane. Some wouldn't. The English kingsmen who worked here in Edinburgh wouldn't. They weren't welcome at the Bluefoot or any other secret Campbell haunts.

"I wouldn't mention rebels," he said. "Keep it something small and simple, so they don't call in more kingsmen. It must be something the men in the area can deal with."

Aini twisted her gold ring around her finger, her gaze distant. "How about a mysterious package at Deacon Brodies Tavern?"

Myles made a face. "Like a bomb threat?"

"Yes. I mean, aye." Aini's cheeks went pink.

Neve smiled. "Just be yourself, Aini. Quit trying to be what you think you should. No need to fash yourself over your language."

"Fash?" Myles asked.

Thane tossed his coffee into the kitchen sink and rinsed the mug. "It means stress, or trouble."

"Thane. I wish you'd get over it and help me," Aini said sharply.

She could've saved her breath. "You know I will," he said.

"Then what? You don't like the plan? If you have any ideas, I'm open to them."

"It's not that." He wanted to tell her everything. But how could he? He was the enemy. It would ruin everything. It would blow his mission. And he had his mother to think about. If Aini could just be stalled until he figured a way out of all of this... "I think we should wait," he said.

"For what?"

"You need to think this through. It's no little thing to call something in, to make a report."

"I know that. I'll keep it anonymous. None of this is little." She tucked the map inside her shoulder bag. Her hands were still shaking and it tore at Thane's heart. "It is terrible and big and horrifying. But oh well." She practically shouted that last bit, then lowered her voice to add, "There's an old phone booth behind the hostel on Cockburn Street. Father used it once. We'll go straight out after I make the report and watch the vault door for kingsmen."

Neve and Myles wished them good luck, and Thane followed

Aini outside, into the summer sun. He took a minute to close his eyes and pray for a better outcome than the one he currently had raging through his brain.

CHAPTER 13
THE VAULTS

Sea birds squawked overhead as Aini and Thane headed toward High Street. Three men in suits—Londoners, according to the accent—strolled into a pub, their ties bright pink, blue, and white. A handful of university students took sadly scant sandwiches from a narrow shop and called out to a friend across the street. Tourists in sunglasses meandered around, snapping pictures and bumping into one another. A few studied the king's latest news release on the public board. If everything went as planned, Aini would have the knife from the vision embedded in the brooch in less than an hour.

She tucked her hand into the crook of Thane's arm, hoping he was okay with that. Honestly, she wanted him here beside her being all stern and big. She knew the dangers they faced. Having a backup that could throw a punch and kept a knife wasn't a bad idea. She had to shake her head at herself. Two days ago she never would've thought something like that.

The rolled edge of Thane's worn button-down was smooth under her fingers, but his muscles beneath tensed. He shut his eyes briefly like her touch caused him pain. She stole a peek at his profile, with its peaked lips and strong chin. He wore a hoodie partly pulled up over his rumpled hair. He glanced back, then away, a reluctant grin tweaking one corner of his mouth. She smiled nervously, her insides fluttering.

The crowd thickened. A group of school-age kids bumped past, their parents mumbling apologies as they wove through, trying to catch them up. Urged into an orderly line by some kingsmen, a bus load of elderly tourists spoke French to one another.

Thane tugged his hood down, and Aini slipped on a funky, black hat she'd borrowed from Myles. If any Campbells had been watching, maybe now they'd lose them.

To the left, a kingsman scrubbed at some silver graffiti. Two thumbs crossed. The Dionadair's sign. Seemed Nathair Campbell, the king's vicious head of security, was having trouble stamping out the growing flame of rebellion.

A memory of the men and women accused of treason and shot down by Campbell's men in the middle of the Grassmarket courtyard splashed across Aini's mind. A sharp chill raked over her. Their wide eyes. The pooling blood. A rush of quiet like a wave washing over the gathered Edinburgh natives. No tourists had been there that day. Had Nathair Campbell made sure of that?

She blinked the memory away as they worked their way through tables of knick-knacks and tourists, and came out on High Street. A street performer in red gloves juggled knives on the pavement. Next to the man, the sun glinted off the shiny brass toe of the Hume statue. Her heart contracted, recalling the superstition Father had taught her about touching the toe for wisdom. An ache filled Aini.

Four kingsmen sauntered down the pavement opposite them,

eyeing the juggler. Street performers were permitted to have weapons for show as long as they weren't sharpened. The shortest kingsman held a hand out toward the performer. The juggler stopped tossing the knives and handed one, hilt first, to the kingsman.

Her hands sweating, she tightened her grip on Thane.

The kingsman said something to the performer and handed the dull weapon back.

"Here's Cockburn Street." Thane touched her hand.

She swallowed and headed toward the red phone booth. *Please let this work.*

Thane stood outside as she slid the door open. Lifting the receiver to her ear, she pressed the gold Crime Report button below the zero. The line rang and suddenly she wasn't so sure she could even talk.

A click. "CR line. What's your situation?" a gruff male voice said.

She tried to talk, but her tongue stuck to the roof of her mouth. *Go away, nerves.* "I...there's..."

"Are you an American colonial?"

"Yes. No. Why?"

Thane peered in, scowling.

"Only English and Scottish subjects may use this line," the voice said and it sounded like he was going to hang up.

"Wait! I'm a Scottish citizen."

"All right then. What is the problem?"

"I saw something strange in a tavern on High Street. A box. It was hidden...under a table in the back. It was black and there were wires going from it into the wall."

"When and what tavern?"

"Five minutes ago. Deacon Brodies."

"We'll check it out. Your Subject Identification Number, please."

"I don't have my card with me."

"You don't...you must! Young lady, I fear—"

Aini hung up. Her heart clawed at her throat.

Thane popped in. "Did you do it?"

"Yeah, but he wanted my SI number."

"You didn't give it to them, did you?"

She shook her head. "I hung up."

Thane shrugged one shoulder. "Guess we'll have to wait and see if it works."

THE DOOR LEADING TO THE VAULTS HAD BEEN PAINTED BLACK and a strip of plastic tape fluttered from the lintel. One kingsman hung around the entrance and a padlock the size of Thane's fist hung from the door handle.

Around the corner, staying somewhat cloaked in a group of university students waiting for food at a place that only served baked potatoes, Aini pulled her pick set from her dress pocket. Her hands were steady, but sweat slicked her palms.

Thane's eyebrows went high. "You weren't bluffing about the lock-picking then, were you?"

The kingsman who paced back and forth in front of the vault door wasn't a Campbell. He wore no tartan, just black military pants. His eyes were half-closed as he watched his own boots. At least he wasn't a horrible Campbell.

"He's never going to leave, is he?" she whispered.

The walkie talkie on the man's belt made a scratching noise. He turned it off.

"Why isn't he answering that thing?" she asked. "I bet they're trying to call him now."

Another kingsman, this one in a blue and green Campbell kilt, stalked down the road and met with the one they watched. She swallowed the growing lump in her throat, wanting more than anything to run at that man and demand to know where Father was and why they insisted on making life in Scotland so much more difficult than it needed to be.

Thane turned away and leaned against the restaurant's brick wall. A sheet including all the king's updated rules fluttered beside him, the words written in a jagged style. "Fantastic," he muttered, scanning the street.

The guard at the door talked as the Campbell threw a hand toward High Street.

"We should go." Thane squinted at the flow of people in the wide avenue.

"Not yet."

"We can't spend all day here, waiting for someone to spot you. Things will only get worse."

"I think they're leaving," Aini said.

Both men faced High now, the one all in black speaking into his walkie.

"They're not," Thane said.

"Five minutes."

"Aini."

"Thane."

The Campbell started back toward them, toward High and the crowd. With one look at the door to the underground vaults, the other kingsman followed him.

"Yes." Aini turned her face to the menu taped to the window and pretended to study the differences between prices for English and Scottish customers. The king was so cruel, so petty.

"They're gone. Let's go," he said.

The buildings shadowed them as they approached the taped-off door. There weren't any crowds here to hide them and they couldn't be sure when the kingsmen would be back.

At the padlock, Aini's tongue moved around in her mouth as she angled the pick up and left. The pick caught the mechanism inside the hunk of metal, but it slipped out of place. She grumbled. It'd been a while. A long while.

Thane leaned against the moss-covered wall near the door and crossed his arms like it was an average Williamsday afternoon, and they weren't trespassing into territory owned by the king. He really was good at pretending a casual attitude. Aini envied his self-control. Her nerves always had her in their grip; he seemed able to rein them in, to subdue them.

The pick finally dislodged the mechanism and the hook popped from its hole.

"Yes!" Aini shouted, then clapped a hand over her own mouth, watching for the kingsmen.

"Come on," Thane grumbled.

They scuttled through the door and shut it quietly and quickly. They had to hurry.

The crumbling steps dove into the darkness, and the air stilled, quiet as the dead.

"We probably have twenty minutes? What do you think?" A chill drew nails down Aini's neck as their steps echoed off the walls.

At the bottom, black tunnels stretched left and right into the bowels of the city. The odor of mildew and muck assaulted her nose. Raising a flashlight, she tried to remember Neve's directions.

"I'd say that's a good guess." Thane's voice seemed to surround her in the dark.

The ground sloped downward and Aini put a hand on the wall. "You know, Father told me about this place." The bricks were moist. Ugh. She pulled her hand back. "He said he got lost down here as a kid when Granny MacGregor brought him to the library." He'd told her about the hatch opening that hid beneath the tiles on the main floor, said all the kids in Edinburgh told stories about it. "He received the whipping of a lifetime when she finally found him." More tunnels loomed around every corner. Aini really hoped Neve's directions were right. "It's like a labyrinth." The walls felt too close and getting closer.

"Will you tell me again what the knife looked like?" Thane's voice rumbled behind her.

She knew what he was doing. He was distracting her from the walls, the stale air, her fear. She forgave him a little for trying to lord over her back at the townhouse.

"The hilt was made of very dark wood," she said as the image flickered through her mind.

"Bog oak."

A drip from the ceiling landed on Aini's cold nose, and she wiped it away. How many layers of ancient stone and dirt and filth were between her and the sky? A tremor bit into her and she gripped the flashlight more tightly. Were bodies really buried behind these walls?

"Bog oak. Yes," she said. "That's what Neve guessed." A rock caught the toe of her flat, and she pitched forward.

Thane caught her under the arm. Although he released her immediately, his fingers left a subtle warmth behind. "Should've worn smarter shoes," he said, not unkindly.

"Black flats work in all situations."

"Did that rock not get the memo about the flats?"

She glared at him over her shoulder and shined the light in his face.

He raised his eyebrows over his glasses. "Sorry. Go on about the knife."

She gave him an eye-narrowing before turning back around. "It was big. Big as your forearm."

"So the man in your...vision said eighty-five, you're certain, aye?"

A rat scurried somewhere not far enough away.

"The man in the vision didn't really *say* it," Aini said. "He thought it. He imprinted the idea, the number, on the brooch. That was the first time I'd ever seen a vision where the person knew they were leaving emotions and thoughts."

She kicked yet another rock across the floor. It clattered until it met with something in the dark and went quiet. Another chill wrapped arms around her.

"Hmm. The man knew he was doing it?" Thane asked.

She nodded. "It scared me."

"So does this wee tunnel, but you're here."

Some of her fear melted at his praise. "Into the dark, to be free of the dark."

"Aye. I'd take physical dark over informational dark any day."

As the tunnel opened up a little, she noticed Thane looking at her, his eyebrows drawn together, knuckle absently rubbing across his bottom lip. Like she was a chemistry formula he couldn't solve.

The flashlight flickered. She smacked the end of it until it brightened.

Before she could focus on anything, the scent of whisky flew into the air. A figure came around the corner and hit her.

*A man. A fist. Pain.*

Circles of red and gray floated in front of her eyes, and her heart beat wildly.

Thane shouted and moved away. Then she realized she was sitting on the floor, holding herself up on her elbows. She hadn't blacked out, but everything had just happened too quickly for her to keep up. She blinked. Blinked again. And there was Thane's face, his hair falling into his eyes. Pain pounded like drums in her skull. The flashlight sat beside her, illuminating Thane in its blue-white light.

"Aini, please. Say something. I'm going to murder that..."

He put his warm hands on either side of her face and Aini's fuzzy brain didn't stop her sigh of pleasure in time. A smile spread across Thane's face. She shut her eyes, cheeks burning.

"Wh...what happened?"

The warmth of his hands disappeared. "A man tried to take your purse."

"He hit me." A knot throbbed on her head, above her ear. She cracked her eyes open and sat up, Thane's hand on her back. "Where is he now?"

Her small bag still hung securely over her shoulder. Thane's gaze flicked to it, then to the nearest corridor that hung open and black like a ghost's groaning mouth. Blood ran down his knuckles.

"Are you hurt?" Her hand flew to the splatter of red coloring his shirt.

"I'm fine. It's him that's hurt." The muscles at the back of his jaw flexed. "He's gone now." He helped her stand. "Do you feel well enough to go on?"

Her knit dress was twisted around her middle, so she tugged it back into place and adjusted her leggings. "I have to." Pain banged against her eyes with each word.

He nodded and handed over the flashlight just as it blinked, faded, and went dark. Immediately his hands were on hers, trailing their way to the light.

"I'll check the batteries," he said as she released the tool to him.

Musty air brushed past. She coughed and squeezed her hands

into fists, longing for the sight of the open sky and the feel of clean air.

A quiet crack sounded above them.

Aini stepped back, catching up on Thane's foot. "Are you hearing this too?" she whispered.

The sound of metal on metal told her he was unscrewing the base of the flashlight. "Aye." He didn't sound scared, only wary. Like he was keeping an eye on a large dog he didn't know.

In front of them, something thudded against the wall.

The hairs on the back of Aini's neck rose. "What was that?" It could've been the mugger returning.

"I'm not sure, but it's not the man who attacked you. I promise you that."

"How do you know?" She couldn't keep the panic out of her voice.

"It's all right, hen," he said softly. "These noises—it's just a wandering spirit. Not an angry one."

The air blew past again, cold and old. "I think Neve was right about the ghosts not wanting us down here."

A click and another metal scrape later, a blue-white glow flooded from the end of the flashlight and spilled light over Thane's sharp nose and deep eyes behind his glasses. He handed her the flashlight and they started down the corridor again, her head aching like something was trying to crawl out of her left temple. She needed to go home and ice her head, but she'd probably never get the chance to find this knife again. Without it, Owen and the others wouldn't tell her what they knew about Father.

To their right, six brick alcoves sat in two levels. Black numbers marked each arch. Seventy-eight, seventy-nine.

"Look." Thane pointed at a spot past her.

She shone the light in that direction. Another arched area was labeled with numbers.

And there was eighty-five.

Excitement zipped through her. She took the light and propped it between two rocks on the floor. The entire room bloomed into view. Pits and cracks in the stone walls had been repaired with rough cement. Other spots were brown and black as if touched by fire. Vault eighty-five consisted of two bricked, arched spaces for storage. The bottom one was big enough to walk into, the top was the size of a small fireplace.

The outer wall of the alcove was rough under her fingers, but there weren't any loose stones. Nothing seemed out of the ordinary, not that she really knew what to look for.

Copying her movements, Thane ran his large hands up and down the bricks on the other side of the vaulted space. Bits of brick and little plumes of dust fell in the wake of his fingers.

A sneeze blew out of Aini. On tiptoe, she reached into the smaller compartment above her head. Dirt, little more than dust, coated her fingertips as she searched the edge of the wall that divided this vault from the next. Half way to the back, the corner of a stone lay a finger's length higher than its neighbors. She inhaled, her heart speeding up. With one hand over the lip to pull herself higher, she tried to slip her fingers over the back corner of the stone. Her arm just wasn't long enough. She dropped back, her toes trembling from the effort of rising up.

"Thane, can you help me?" A muscle in her neck and back twitched. She'd stretched too far. "I found something."

Looking up through his black lashes, he linked his fingers to make a step. "I'll give you a boost."

"You sure?"

"You weigh about as much as a bowl of porridge. Think I can handle it." He frowned and jerked his head at his hands.

Headache worsening, Aini put her shoe in his makeshift step and pushed up. To his credit, Thane didn't grunt as he lifted her high enough to bend over the rough edge of the upper alcove. He put hands around her ankles, holding her steady as she extended an arm. She prayed he wasn't staring at her backside.

She squinted into the near dark. Instead of being surrounded by aged mortar, the stone in question was framed by black space. Leaning all the way on her stomach, with the vault's edge biting into her, she grabbed the stone and wiggled it. With a grating sound, it came free.

"There's a hollow here." Her teeth clacked together. The walls crowded in on her and stole her air.

"All right. Slow that breathing, lass."

She nodded, drawing the chilly air in, and reached into the hollow the brick had concealed and blocked up. The space cooled her fingers immediately. Stone scraped the back of her hand, but there wasn't anything there. Just a hole. And she'd been so sure. Her lungs tight, she put her other hand on the bricks near her head.

"It's not here."

"Come now," Thane said softly. "Why don't you get down? You've—"

As she started to pull her hand out of the hollow, something slightly pointed on the space's wall dragged across her pinkie finger. "Wait!"

She pinched the object and tugged hard. It broke from its hiding place with a scraping sound, and she flew backward, landing in a heap on top of Thane. Their fall knocked the flashlight off its rock supports and illumination swiped across the room like a lighthouse beam, halting at the back corner and leaving them in near darkness.

Her back to Thane's stomach, she sat up holding the item

she'd pulled from the vault, but couldn't get her feet under her. Thane grabbed her arms and tried to help, mumbling something in rough Gaelic. As they untangled, every line and curve of his body pressed into hers.

Finally, she stood, the object in hand.

Thane grabbed the light. "Is that..."

A leather sheath. Black hilt. Despite her aching head and the walls being too close and the air too musty, a light of hope warmed her.

This was the knife from the vision.

Every three inches or so, bronze scalloped fittings wrapped around the knife's case. The bog oak hilt had been carved into the shape of twisting ropes that came together at a bronze tip.

"This is definitely the one I saw, the one that man embedded into the vision."

But she hadn't seen any visions when she touched it. She frowned.

"Maybe you have to touch the blade itself?" Thane suggested. He was so good at reading her body language. He seemed to know her worries and how to potentially solve them before she said a word.

"Good thought. Let's go. I don't want to have a vision here, with that man around and this awful place's walls closing in on me."

A shower of glistening drops fell from the ceiling near the door they'd come through.

"Ugh." She shook it off and Thane smiled a little.


AT THE DOOR, THANE TURNED THE KNOB. A SLICE OF SUN blinded them.

"I'll go first," Aini said.

Thane looked like he wanted to argue, but he stepped aside.

Heart cracking like fireworks, Aini peered out. Crowds filled the main road beyond this one. A kingsman hurried down that main road, but his eyes weren't on the door to the vaults. He was headed away toward the sound of a man screaming. Someone was being arrested. Her stomach turned.

She nudged Thane with an elbow. "I think it's safe for us. Come on."

Outside, Aini ran a hand over the back of her sweat-damp neck and sighed heavily. It was beautiful to be out of that dark, close place. Taking another good look around for kingsmen, she gripped the knife and studied its ornate hilt.

"How are we going to get this thing home?" she whispered. The crowd's rumble reacted to another of the arrested man's shrieks for his family. A sudden thought had her leaning against Thane's solid form. "What if they're taking him for the fake bomb report I made?"

"No. This happens constantly. What are the chances?"

"I don't know. It could've been my fault."

"I doubt it. Now, will you let me take the knife? I can fit it in my waistband easier than you." His eyes were wide and sincere.

If he were caught, he'd be tried, convicted, and imprisoned. Or shot like a traitor.

"Fine."

With a curt nod, he took the knife from her, his eyes scanning the street, and hid the weapon behind him, beneath his untucked button-down. The hilt bulged a little, but she prayed it wouldn't draw any attention.

## CHAPTER 14
## A TANGLE OF LIES

Thane's nerves jumped and buzzed as they continued down the side street, taking a less populated and winding way back to the townhouse.

*That evil creature Rodric.*

He couldn't believe his cousin had attacked Aini in the vaults. There was no way it was on orders—outright attacking the people Thane was meant to spy on? Not very undercover. The ape. Anger lashed through Thane. He must've been following them. Rodric's stupid warning from earlier rang through Thane's memory. *Don't forget who your master is. I'll be sure to tell him you've gone soft.* Thane knew very well who *him* was and that Rodric had overheard the bit about Lewis's daughter, about Aini. Rodric was playing with Thane. His cousin was such a sick waste of space.

Grime lined the doorways and windows of the leaning buildings. One lonely tree drooped in its squared off piece of dirt in the pavement. A tattoo parlor boasted a sign in the shape of a fire breathing dragon with wings and slitted eyes. The road curved past an abandoned hostel.

A kingsman appeared around the corner.

"Just keep on," he whispered.

The man said something into his walkie and tucked it back into his belt, glancing once at them as they passed.

"You there," he said.

Thane and Aini froze.

Thane turned and made easy eye contact with the man. "Aye?"

The man's jacket was jet black against the ash-colored buildings as his beady-eyed gaze flicked over Thane's middle. The man rubbed a hand over the back of his tidy brown head of hair. It seemed like he didn't really want to be where he was. Thane knew the feeling too well.

"What do you have there, Scot? Show me what's under that shirt," the man said. His accent said he was from somewhere in northern England. Lancashire maybe.

If the kingsman did take Thane in, his identity would come out; he'd be released, quietly and for some well-crafted, false reason. He had only to show the man the back of his necklace, which bore the Campbell crest. It'd be difficult, to say the least, explaining his release to Aini without exposing his cover.

"I don't know what you mean." Thane gave a simple smile to the kingsman.

The kingsman frowned. "You have something there. Perhaps a souvenir or..." He gave Thane a mean grin, looking ready for a fight now.

Thane took the knife from his waistband, and Aini stepped forward.

The kingsman's eyes scoured the ancient-looking blade in its black sheath. "So we *do* have something to discuss."

"It belongs to her family," Thane said. "We were only having it appraised." He offered the knife for closer inspection.

Fingers lighting on his gun, the kingsman leaned closer.

Thane eased Aini behind him.

"I'm sorry," the man said to Aini. Now his glaikit smile was real—the complete opposite to the wolf's smirk he'd given Thane. "I'll have to take this." The kingsman nodded at the knife. "I won't report you because I can tell you're not a rebel. Too pretty and smart, eh?" He grinned and gave her a thorough once over.

Thane's stomach clenched. The kingsman could not be allowed to take the knife. Well, it was too bad, but violence couldn't be avoided here.

Thane whistled. "Eh, lover boy." He threw a fist into the idiot's face.

Aini's hands went to her mouth.

With a groan, the kingsman fell to his hands and knees.

"Come on." Thane tucked the knife away and grabbed Aini's slender fingers.

They ran down one street and then another. He was mad for heading this way. He should've fled north. The windows in most of the buildings here sported jagged breaks or nailed down boards. And there, up ahead, was the Bluefoot.

The kingsman would be here in a heartbeat. There was nothing for it. Thane would have to take Aini in through the back door and hope the lot inside would keep to their drinks and not mind him. And pray Aini wouldn't ask too many questions.

"Are we lost?" she asked, grimacing at the filth in the street and the swear words sprayed on the buildings.

He laughed bitterly. "No, hen. I've been to the worst of... never mind." He dragged her into the small space between the buildings, then through the hidden back door of the pub.

"What is this?" Aini's eyes grew as she studied the swinging section of the wall that made up the passage into the Bluefoot.

Smoke and the smell of fried fish choked the air. Two men leaned against the bar top, talking to the keep and drinking pints. Their black kingsman jackets hung over a nearby chair and their Campbell kilts were bright against the dark wood of the bar. Another man laughed with a woman near the stairs.

"I don't like this," Aini hissed. "Those are Campbells!"

God above, this was a mess. Thane pulled her to the back, past the stairs, under the balcony, and into the workout room. The flickering light shuddered off the heavy bag and red flooring.

"Do you come here a lot? Why is the door hidden? You need to stop shoving me around and tell me what is going on."

She was going to get them caught with her blathering. He didn't want anyone seeing her here. Except Bran. "Just come on. It's better if you don't know anything about this place."

"We're well past what's better for me, don't you think? How is hiding in a place where there are Campbells smarter than running?"

"The man will have called reinforcements. We wouldn't have made it another two minutes." He had to lie. There was nothing for it. He had to add another layer of deceit to this or she wasn't going to give in. He knew that determined look on her face. The girl was like a pit bull. "My friend Bran...he...he has connections with the Campbells."

"What? Is he horrible? Why are you friends with him?"

"The Campbells aren't all horrible. They've been helping Scotland...well, until recently."

"Until they decided to start competing with the king for the title of Worst Ever?"

He had to calm her down, steer this conversation. "Bran

wishes he didn't have to...work with them. But he tangled with the Campbells when he was very young—just out of secondary school. You can't just tell the most powerful clan in Scotland to leave off when you choose."

Aini's shoulders dropped and she let out a breath, staring at the heavy bag. "I suppose you're right about that." She bit her lip, her fear probably coming back as her anger receded.

"I can hide the knife under the floorboard in my room. With the brooch," Aini whispered. "If we can just get there. That way, if they come to question us—"

Thane shushed her and suddenly Cora was there, frowning. She gave Aini a tentative smile. "May I help you somehow?" Cora asked.

"Aye. There's a..." He peered toward the stairs where the man and woman joked. If they heard him worry about a kingsman, their ears would surely perk up and he'd be in an even more awkward situation. He lowered his voice. "There's a kingsman after us." Pinching his lips, he looked from Cora to Aini, willing Cora to understand what was going on.

Cora's mouth opened, but she shut it again, her brow tangling.

Thane glared at her.

Her face smoothed slightly and she said, "Well, all right then." She pushed them toward the stairs. "Up here."

Aini stared at the scarves flowing from the ceiling. "Thane—"

He put a hand over her mouth. "Stay quiet. Please." He had to keep this as simple as possible.

She nodded, trust and mistrust warring in those big, cat-like eyes of hers.

Cora led them up the creaking stairs to the row of closed

doors that faced the open area of the balcony. The rest of the pub spread out below them like a circus after hours.

The couple at the bottom of the stairs went quiet, and Thane looked over his shoulder to give them a glare. The man mumbled something, and the woman laughed.

Thane had never been upstairs. He knew full well what sometimes went on here.

Cora stopped them at the last door. "Go inside. You'll want to see Bran as usual, I'm guessing. And we'll keep the man away from here if that's what you need."

"Thank you, Cora."

"No bother," she said quickly, not meeting his eyes.

Thane opened the door for Aini. "I'm sorry to take you to a place like this." Heat flooded his face. "I just know Bran can help."

Arms crossed over her chest, Aini took three steps to the bed at the back wall. It was covered in a dingy, calico print duvet.

A knock made them both jump. "Have fun in there!" a man's unfamiliar voice said.

Aini's cheeks matched the red in the calico print. Thane was fairly certain his own did too.

He swallowed and rapped a fist against the door. "Be gone with you."

A laugh echoed from outside, then faded along with the sound of footsteps.

Thane rubbed his face.

Another knock drummed against the door. *What now?* Thane cracked it open to see Bran's warm eyes and bushy eyebrows.

"Do you need me, friend?" Bran's gaze stayed on Thane's face. Most men, knowing what these rooms were for, would've peeked right over Thane's shoulder. But Bran was not most men.

Thane nodded. "I have a...friend here."

He stepped aside and opened the door fully. Aini gave Bran a wave. Bran smiled at her.

"We have a weapon," Thane said. "And a kingsman followed us. He's seen the thing and won't leave us alone now that he has."

"There's news," Bran whispered. "Nathair has ordered every kingsman in Scotland to pledge allegiance solely to the Campbells. It's being done quietly. On paper though. And I strongly doubt the king knows of this."

Thane gripped the side of the door. Edging out of the room, he kept an eye on the pub's first floor, watching the front entrance. "It's madness."

"Aye. It is that," Bran said.

As Bran opened his mouth to say something more, the front door of the pub banged open, knocking the codekeeper off his stool. The kingsman raged in, blood dripping from his nose.

"Anyone seen a big, fair fellow about twenty or so?" he shouted across the pub. "I don't care that this is an illegal gambling den. I need to find the man."

Thane made a fist and pressed it against his mouth. "What can I do, Bran?" He flicked a glance at Aini.

Bran's gaze followed the line of Thane's eyes and clicked his tongue. "Hmm. Wait for a count of ten, then go out the window."

"The window?" Aini leaned to look out the glass.

"The roof's not a far jump," Bran said. "You'll be fine. The building next door has a fire ladder down the back side."

Before Thane could argue, Bran pushed him back and shut the door in his face, his deep voice booming over the pub's TV.

"Saw the very man," Bran shouted. "Ran right past to the next bus stop. Just down to the corner."

Heart thudding, Thane jerked the tight window open. "...eight, nine...go, Aini."

She rolled her eyes and huffed, but climbed out. Thane followed, and they stood on a slim ledge outside the window, staring at the neighboring low roof.

Aini dusted old paint off her hands. "Well," she said shakily. "No use waiting around. The roof isn't coming any closer."

Thane reached an arm out as she leaped over the four foot space, her hair flying behind her like a cloak. His heart jumped too. Right into his brain. His hands went to his knees as she landed safely in a crouch.

She scowled at him over her shoulder, then stood.

First bending his knees, Thane exploded off the ledge and ended up a good foot beyond where she'd landed. The roof's black top pulled heat from the sun and shimmered in the air around them.

Aini put a hand up to block the light. Her features worked into a frown. "Did you do a lot of roof-jumping in your childhood too? Along with the punching and kicking? And befriending Campbell lackeys?"

She was too smart for her own good.

"Aye."

He didn't wait for her to ask more, but hurried to the rusty handles of a ladder. He went first, averting his eyes as she, still in that short dress with leggings that clung to every curve, made her way down after him. The knife's sheathed tip dug into his right buttock as he climbed. He paused to adjust it.

At the bottom, they took off for the townhouse, him leading the way and hoping against all that the kingsman would be put off their trail and that none in the pub would remember Aini's face. As if they wouldn't. Half Indonesian and more bonnie than any girl he'd seen, they'd remember. But there was nothing to be done for it.

As they ran, the sun burning their heads, Thane wondered

where this all would lead, what the endgame would be. Once they gave the Dionadair the knife, then what? Would the rebels tell Aini what they knew of Lewis? What was their motivation behind the telling?

He didn't like it. Not a bit. This was a dangerous game Aini was playing and Thane wished she'd just go back to the lab and stay there. If Rodric heard about the knife, if he found out Thane had it within his reach and didn't turn it in to the clan, he'd be insane about it. Nathair would want to at least *see* this artifact the rebels were going on about. Even if it wasn't really what they thought it was.

As if she knew his thoughts, Aini glanced at him. "Thanks for all the help," she said, her words breathy from running. They made it to the townhouse and she unlocked the door and went inside. "I am sorry—"

"New rule," he said. She gave him a scathing look. She liked to be the one doing the bossing. "No more apologizing," he said.

Taking a deep breath, she nodded. "Agreed. May I have the knife, please?"

He pulled the weapon from his back and held it out to her, a knight to his queen.

"Are you going to tell me more about Bran and that pub?" she asked archly.

Thane looked at the floor.

"They knew you there."

Aini raised an eyebrow.

"Bran deals cards there sometimes. For extra money. I gamble with him. He's a good man and I don't want to end our friendship just because he has a less than perfect...situation."

"I like him."

"He's a good guy."

She held the knife closer. "And so are you."

They stood quiet, the compliment burning down Thane's walls.

"I'm going to examine the knife. See if there's a vision in it."

"Of course. Yes. I'll be…around if you need anything."

With a serious look on her face, she disappeared into her room.

He'd told her more than he should've, but she needed something to chew on or she wouldn't have let it drop.

Heading for the kitchen, where it sounded like Myles and Neve were arguing jokingly, Thane raked fingers through his hair. His eyes filled with heat, moisture. He'd not cried in an age, but now, he wanted to. Seeing Aini in the Campbell pub. Her innocence, her goodness, against that place filled with people who were daily being drawn further away from doing right… His clan seemed driven now by a madman, by Nathair. A prickling ran over Thane like one thousand knives scratching his flesh. Willing the wetness in his eyes back to where it'd come from, Thane put his mask-like, blank expression on and went to the kitchen to wait on Aini.

## CHAPTER 15
## A CASTLE ON THE SEA

Sitting on the bed, Aini set the knife on her lap and took a deep breath. Her head still ached and her jaw was sore, but she couldn't think about resting. Not even if she'd wanted to.

Thane spent time at a secret Campbell gambling den. He had a friend tied up with the Campbells. She rubbed her temples. Things were going from bad to worse.

The ancient weapon gave off an odd smell. Metal, certainly, but also mildew and some kind of herb. Sage, maybe. Cloves? It was so strange, a scent that stirred an irresistible need to inhale it again, to try and pin it down. A deep, quiet fear laced the curiosity, like the knife had been touched by something not normal, something not of this world.

Lifting the age-old weapon, she wrapped one hand firmly around the cool, black hilt and slid the steel from its ornate bronze and leather sheath. She lay the casing beside her and held the vicious-looking thing vertically. The light coming from her lamp flashed off its slanting angles. It weighed her arm down, heavier than it'd seemed earlier. Shadows danced in the corner of her room, echoing the movement of the light on the steel. The ceiling fan whisked air over her head.

The other apprentices knocked around down the hall. Myles's colonial banjo music carried through the house like sprites bouncing off the stone walls and wooden floors.

Thane's voice punched through the noise. "Turn that down!" His *ow* came out as *oo*.

Aini pressed her fingers against the flat side of the knife.

With a shiver, the vision dropped over her.

Seer! *The wide-mouthed man in the old style clothes, the same from the first vision, spoke.* Waymark Wall! *His face dissolved.*

*Sandstone walls rose from a green lawn. Castle ruins. The structure was weather worn, the edges soft. Holes marred the once solid construction. A marking was set in one wall. A spiral. The curling line spun until it morphed into a sea bird, then a flock. The birds squawked. Waves rushed and roared, gray and sea-green, in the background. A piece of land hunched like an animal's back in the field of ocean. Then that odd, black stone appeared again—the one from the brooch's vision—its surface carved with swirls too. It stood chest-high, hollowed like a seat.*

The images flickered, and the real world washed them away.

Aini's wood-paneled room appeared again. The rose carvings on her bed posts. The light on the metal. The ceiling fan pushed a piece of tickling hair over her face as she sheathed the blade. Her legs shook as she crossed the room to the vanity and jotted down what she'd seen on a slip of white paper.

*Castle ruins.*

*A spiral carved into a wall.*

*The ocean.*

*The black stone marked like the wall, with spirals.*

Pulling the stool out from the vanity, she sat, her head splintering.

The information from the vision explained nothing. Nothing.

A picture of Father sat on her vanity. She traced his face with a trembling finger. Her mother had taken the photo the day she'd presented her *wayang* show, a Balinese shadow puppet performance. Seated on a stool with one leg crossed over the other, Father looked on as she held her cutout puppet in front of a white sheet. A traditional coconut husk lamp lit the cloth from behind. Mother had helped her make it. Father's eyes were cinched up, partnering with his smile, as he focused on Aini, a nine-year-old at the time.

Keeping hold of the knife, Aini lifted the picture and carried it to bed. She curled into a ball around the wooden picture frame, and with one hand gripping the antique knife, let exhaustion take her under.

∽

"Wake up, sweetheart." Myles's voice floated above her head.

His face and Neve's slowly came into focus. Myles's eyes were bright and Neve's were pinched with worry.

"I'm glad you had some rest," Neve said.

Thane snored lightly in the rocking chair by Aini's bed. His glasses were askew and one of his long legs stretched over her duvet, his dirty boot marking the fabric. She frowned, but a glow filled her chest. His mouth turned down, and a flicker of sadness, or maybe frustration, wrinkled his brow as he dreamed. Soft light draped over his exposed throat and the proud lines of his collarbone. The scent of candles and chemicals wafted from his clothing.

"How long has he been there?" she asked Neve and Myles.

"A while," Myles said. "I know you don't feel well, but...did you see anything with the knife?"

An island. The sea. A castle.

The vision flooded back and she sat up. "Should I wait for him to wake up?"

Myles's trainers squeaked on the floor wax as he walked to where Thane slept. He shook Thane's arm roughly. "It's almost midnight, man. We need your brains and bulk on this mission."

Thane blinked, pushing his glasses into place. His eyes found Aini and he heaved a sigh. He pulled his leg off the bed and stood to check his phone. He groaned.

"Bad news?" She pointed to the phone.

"No. I just didn't sleep so well."

"A bad dream?"

"Not so much bad as it is confusing," he said. "Same one I always have."

He didn't seem to want to share. Letting it drop, she placed the picture of her father back on the vanity.

"The knife did hold a vision." Her note crinkled in her hand. The whole day and night felt like one big dream. "I saw castle ruins, birds, and that strange stone again. The ruins sat on the coast somewhere. A spiral marked one of the walls. Does any of that sound familiar, Neve? You know Scotland's landmarks."

Neve crossed her legs, making the bed squeak. "There are a few ruins that sit at the sea. I'll have to think. Something about that marking is tickling the back of my head."

"A spiral?" Thane asked.

Aini nodded. "Ring any bells for you?"

He looked away. "For a second, it reminded me of something. But...no."

She found a dark ruby ribbon Father bought for her years ago, maybe at Christmas, and tied it into her hair.

"Are we going to The Origin to show the rebels the knife?" Neve asked.

"I guess," Aini said. "But should I bring the knife *and* the brooch?"

With paint-stained fingers, Myles drummed a beat on his thighs. "I say hide the goods. That way, you'll have something to bargain with."

"I have to show them the knife. If I'm going to get any information out of them, I have to do that at least. But I can hide the brooch."

Thane pocketed his phone. "You're sure I can't talk you out of this?" His voice was cold as the dull morning after a great party.

"You know I have to do this," she said, quiet and sure.

"Aye."

It almost sounded like he'd given up. She tried very hard not to let his lack of faith crush her determination to find a way out of this mess, a path back to a life with her father.

Myles marched into the hallway, Neve following him. Thane stayed behind, an unreadable look on his face and his hands in his hair. He'd put on a thin and wide-necked, ivory sweater, and for once, his trousers weren't well on their way to totally unusable.

Remembering how she'd tripped in the vaults, Aini tied on a pair of flat boots. "Myles," she called out to him, "being knocked unconscious is not something to ignore. I wish you'd stay home."

"No chance. Besides, I heard you were hit too. A mugger, right?"

"Yes."

"You need all of us," Myles said. "End of discussion."

"You sound like me," Aini mumbled.

"I know. So bossy and sensible. Neve," he said, his voice

echoing down the hallway outside her door. "Say something I can turn into a dirty joke. I'm not feeling like myself."

Shaking her head, Aini dislodged the loose floorboard near the foot of her bed. Thane's gaze burned the back of her head, but he stayed quiet. Aini's childhood diary sat inside the hidden spot beneath the floor, dusty and full of forgotten, naive poetry. She took the brooch from the vanity and nestled it beside her diary. The board back in place, she stood and dusted her hands.

Fighting panic, she took a slouchy sweater from the armoire and slipped it on. Thane lifted the bog oak knife from the bed, sheathed it neatly, and handed it to Aini. Like Thane had done before, she tucked the weapon into the waistband of her leggings. Her dress slid easily over it, and the sweater covered its odd shape pretty well. Her mind wrapped around a new list of things to do. None of them were simple.

Number One: manage not to panic and get to the club without anyone seeing the weapon.

Number Two: show the rebels the artifact.

Number Three: keep eyes on the exit and listen to what they had to say.

Number Four: use the information to develop a plan to help Father. Even if he had done something unthinkable, he was still her father.

"Are you coming, Thane?" she asked, walking into the hallway and working the words so they didn't show how much she wanted him to say *yes*.

Without a word, he came up behind her, his warmth a solid comfort at her back. He held up a finger for her to wait, then ran through the kitchen. His boots pounded up the lab stairs. A minute later, he returned with a flat bag sort of thing with a strap and buckle. He lifted his shirt and secured the bag to his side, buckling the strap over the distractingly nice lines of his bare stomach.

"What's that?" Aini asked as they trailed Neve and Myles outside.

Talking in whispers, Myles and Neve passed under the skinny maple at the base of the townhouse's front stairs.

Thane smoothed his hair—a valiant, yet fruitless move—and regarded the rising moon before opening his mouth.

Aini raised an eyebrow like a weapon. "Save it. I know what you're going to say. The less I know the better. You know I'm not okay with that answer."

Thane shook his head and chuckled.

But she actually trusted him. The fact didn't sit easy on her shoulders. He was a rule-breaker, her opposite in so many ways, but his crooked path put him by her side. He cared for her, for her father, for Myles and Neve. He'd proved it. When he broke rules, it was for a good reason.

Thane clenched and unclenched his fists. His boots splashed through a shallow puddle left by the street cleaning machines. Aini sidestepped the murky water. The moon's blue light oozed off everything—the flat pavement, a tall street lamp missing its bulb, the massive wall that surrounded Greyfriars Cemetery. The quiet between them grew, the weight of it pressing on Aini's chest. It was so obvious he wanted to say something, but was afraid to do it.

"Thane, just tell me."

His eyes widened. "I said, the less you know—"

"I'm not talking about whatever you have in your little bag there. I'm talking about the other thing you need to spill."

He swallowed and stared at the pavement. "There's nothing."

"Whatever it is, I'll understand. You've been amazing about all my secrets."

"It's not that easy. I...I want..." He shoved his hands in his pockets.

"When you're ready, I'm here," she said. "And I'm not telling anyone. Not about the gambling or the Campbells or Bran. Don't worry."

Speeding up, he mumbled something like "...probably shouldn't be..."

Aini pulled on his sleeve. "Come on. It can't be that big of a deal. Not after all this."

Wincing, he said, "Ha. Right. Well, when we finish this mad quest you're on. Maybe...maybe I can tell you."

He probably had a gambling debt. Or public fighting on his record. Both. She didn't like it, but it didn't mean she couldn't trust him in important ways, ways that mattered.

They caught up to Myles and Neve. Myles had linked arms with Neve, but she detached from him and slowed to walk beside Aini.

"What will we do if you have trouble getting into the club again?" Neve asked. "Will they be looking for you?"

Aini shrugged. "They told me to bring the knife. I bet they'll find me."

Darkness swamped the street. The stillness crept along Aini's scalp. The nearby grocery's windows were black, the fruit and cereal left alone in the night. A car drove by, its engine whining about the hour.

"It's not open," Thane said as they neared the club.

No music drummed from the interior of the former cathedral and no light spilled from the stained glass window above their heads.

"It's WAN." She'd forgotten this was Weekly Address Night, when everyone gathered around the TV to listen to the latest mandates from the king. There was a new one, something about marriage between English and Scottish citizens. Ridiculous.

She led the group to the door.

Thane touched the place where his hidden bag hung around his body, and curiosity nudged Aini. She tied her questions up inside her and ignored their struggle for freedom.

Myles noticed Thane adjusting the bag though. "What do you have there, big man?"

Eyeing the club's gothic, arched door, Thane said, "Our escape plan."

"Um..." Myles ran a hand over the geometric designs on his bright blue shirt. "Care to explain?"

"Later, pal. Let's get this over with."

Myles began singing another Mint song. *"Be brave, bind boring burdens blue..."*

"That one truly makes no sense," Thane said. "Blue? Really?"

Myles crossed his arms. "You know nothing about poetry."

Aini put a hand on the door knob. "Should I knock or..."

Rolling his eyes, Myles kicked the door open and Neve squeaked in surprise.

"Subtle," Aini said.

Myles grinned with all his teeth.

Thane pursed his lips and nodded. "Well done, colonial."

The inside of the club smelled like old cigarettes and sour beer. It wasn't nearly as sexy without all the fancy lights and wild music.

"Hello?" Aini called out into the darkness, walking quickly toward the stairs that led to the room where she'd met Vera and Dodie.

A man burst from the corner and threw a sack over Thane's head.

## CHAPTER 16
## ATTACK

Aini's heart jolted. She started toward Thane. Myles and Neve shouted, and rough hands grabbed Aini from behind. Thane called her name and almost managed to toss his attacker over his shoulder, even with the sack over his head. People came out of every shadow, every corner. They snatched Neve and Myles, covering their heads with burlap like they had Thane. Aini caught one frightening flash of her friends, faceless, before she too was blinded. Myles's muffled and creative swearing echoed in the empty club as they dragged them back toward the door.

The night air hit Aini's forearms and an engine rumbled nearby, its smell of petrol and oil strong. Hands pushed Aini into a vehicle of some sort and onto a cold seat. The antique knife poked her back and began to slide out of her waistband.

Someone who smelled strangely like horse and sea air began to tie her hands with scratchy twine. Her pulse rammed against her wrists, neck, and temples like her blood wanted out, and the knife, pressing painfully into her spine, didn't make things any better.

"Sorry for the treatment." The man's voice was gravelly and calm. "But we know you and yours are fighters. We need you to come along nicely, then we'll have a good talk at the end of this."

He pushed her farther down the seat.

"Easy," she snapped, kicking out in his general direction. Something hard blocked her foot, most likely a gear shift or console.

"Aini?" Neve was suddenly beside her.

"I'm here," Aini answered, hating the fear in her own voice.

The vehicle's door slammed. Another opened. There was grunting, and the car or truck or whatever they were in moved around with all the activity. The radio blared guitars, a measured drumbeat, and a woman's soaring voice. She guessed their abductor was coming around to the driver's side.

"This is one heck of a welcoming party," Myles said from behind, making Aini jump.

"You're here too?" she asked, her hands like ice.

"Myles." Thane's voice, coming from beside Myles, eased her heart a little. "Stay quiet. Don't give them anything to use against you."

"What are you, some hostage situation expert?" Myles said. "You'd think being every girl's wish on a four leaf clover would be enough."

"Shut it, colonial. Save your nonsense for later. He'll be back in here in a breath."

The door of the vehicle they'd been tossed into creaked open. The seat eased toward the driver's side, and the same man said, "Comfortable? Good. Now keep still and everything'll be all right. Just taking a wee trip."

Aini's eyes strained to see in the dark of the black-dyed

burlap bag. "Are you Dionadair?" The blood rushed away from her face. A memory of gunshots exploded through her mind.

Neve made a little noise and bumped her shoulder.

The man laughed. "You're a brave one, aren't you? That's good."

"Why?" Aini wiggled her hands to loosen the ties' hold on her wrists.

"Keep quiet." Thane's voice was low and strained like he was in pain. "Please."

"You might want to listen to your friend," the man said.

The vehicle lurched and turned. Aini leaned into Neve. Sweat covered Aini's palms and back. She bounced an impatient foot on the floor as the axles croaked. The sounds of traffic faded, giving way to the hush of speed on an open motorway. She curved her thumbs toward her pinkies to make her hands as skinny as possible and tried to ease them out of the twine.

"Behave," the driver said quietly as the truck sloped downward like they were taking a roadway junction off the motorway.

Aini froze, the memory of gunfire popping through her mind.

WHAT FELT LIKE YEARS LATER, THE VEHICLE RUMBLED TO a stop.

"All right, beauties," the man said, clicking the locks.

His movement shifted Aini on the seat. His accent was light like Neve's, and his voice was annoyingly cheerful considering he'd just kidnapped them. The twine bit into Aini's wrists as the man cut her free.

"You may take your hoods off now," he said.

Aini's vision took a second to clear as she removed the bag

and adjusted the knife so it wasn't jabbing her as badly. They'd parked in a grassy area, spotted with boulders and surrounded by fields. A road ran between the nearest field and the next. Their kidnapper, a short man with a large forehead, cut Neve's ties and climbed out of the truck.

As he took the sacks off Thane and Myles, he leaned across the back seat and said, "Don't get any ideas about fighting or running." His pocketknife made quick work of their ties. "There are a good number of people in that barn who do both those things better than any of you."

Thane's face was full of murder as he slid out of the truck, Myles next to him. Thane's eyes narrowed at the fields, the fences, and the sloping ground surrounding a huge barn.

Aini scooted across the seat and out of the truck behind Neve.

Under the dusky light of the half moon, a three-story, stone barn huddled like a grave marker against a rolling hill. Windows glinted every few feet along the walls and a set of double doors sat at the base. The roof, made of wood shingles, slanted up into the star-sprinkled sky.

"Oh, nearly forgot. I need your mobile phones," the man said.

Thane pulled his out of a back pocket, pushed a side button Aini was fairly sure didn't exist on her phone, and threw the device against a rock at his feet.

Her mouth dropped open. "What did you do that for?"

The driver raised his eyebrows and mumbled something.

"We're not going for a picnic with these people, Aini," Thane hissed.

She handed her phone over, still intact. "I realize that, but what if we get away? Don't we need to be able to contact people?"

"The risks outweigh the benefits." Thane watched the kidnapper pick up the broken phone.

The man marched toward the massive barn, his arms pumping at his sides.

Behind Myles and Neve, Aini walked close to Thane. "Do you have any idea where we are?" The darkness in the barn's windows made her walk even closer.

"We traveled mostly east. A bit north." Thane looked right and left over moonlit fields of waving winter barley almost ripe and ready to harvest for whisky. "We're nowhere near a town of any size, I'd say. Farms for miles."

He glanced at the man leading them, then jerked her to a stop. "I have to talk to you."

"What?" she asked. "Now? I thought you wanted to wait to talk after we'd met with...them."

"Aye. But that was before they brought us way out here. I don't know, I'm not sure..." His eyebrows furrowed, and his knuckle rubbed over his lip.

"What's wrong?" Her heart tapped an impatient rhythm on her ribcage. "Other than the obvious."

The driver waved. "You two." He and the others had reached the double doors and a woman in a short dress and tall combat boots held the entrance open wide.

Thane growled in frustration.

"Now." Their kidnapper pulled a gun from his belt. "I'd like to keep this pleasant, as I've been ordered, but I'll do what I must."

He corralled them into the barn.

In air scented with musty straw, mud, and machinery oil, electric lanterns shone from the hand-hewn beams crossing the impossibly high ceiling. Thick climbing ropes, knotted in places, reached down to the wide planks of the barn's wooden floor. At the far left side, four circular, black and green targets hung on the wall, flanked by row upon row of guns and knives in every shape and size. Guns had been illegal, for anyone besides kingsmen, since the last uprising over twenty years ago. Of course, some rural people still used them for hunting, hiding them away when anyone came around. Father had told her all about it. Maybe these were for hunting? She squinted, eyeing their black shapes.

They were for hunting all right. But not for deer or birds.

On the right of the barn, colored hand and foot holds dotted the wall. Near the door, a black cage of barbed wire surrounded a raised, rubber mat floor. Three jumbled pairs of boxing gloves lay scattered within the cage, dried blood marring the surfaces.

Neve rubbed a hand over her arm like she was cold. "What is this place?"

"Dangerous," Myles said. He chewed the inside of his cheek.

A set of metal stairs led up the side of the barn to a landing where a table with tubing, jars, and scales sat. A lab.

Below and beyond the small landing, a crowd of men and women sat on benches and stools and chairs around long wooden tables. There had to be over three hundred people dressed in everything from ragged trousers and T-shirts to suits and ties. Every face turned. Young. Old. In between. Aini recognized three people immediately.

Red hair, round glasses—Owen, who'd come to the townhouse with an apology. Barrel chest, bulging eyes—Dodie. Black hair piled high, combat boots, dress, and a curvy figure—Vera. All three had the same wide mouth. The room tilted. They reminded Aini of the man in the visions from the brooch and the knife.

Snarling, Myles jolted toward Dodie.

Thane's hand landed on the back of Myles's shirt, stopping him. "Whoa, colonial."

Myles whirled his arms around but didn't break Thane's hold. Thane said something in his ear, and Myles stilled, grimacing. Thane released him, and Myles straightened his shirt, his eyes throwing knives.

Dodie stood, his mouth parting to speak, but Owen rose and pushed him back into his seat.

"We're very sorry, friend," Owen said to Myles, no trace of sarcasm in his voice.

Aini's heart pounded in her ears. Every pair of eyes searched her face. She lifted the bog oak knife and held it out. "Is this the weapon you wanted to see?"

The room held its breath. Owen stepped forward and touched the hilt. His brown-orange irises developed a feverish sheen.

"Why is this so important?" she asked. *Somebody say something.* "Whose knife is it?"

"Your father knows," he whispered.

"What do you mean?" Her voice started tight and small but grew to a shout. "What can you tell me about my father?" She hadn't meant to walk away from Neve, Myles, and Thane, but suddenly she wasn't ten feet from Owen, Vera, and Dodie.

The crowd stayed utterly still, hands on knees, eyes blinking quietly, arms crossed, fingers linked.

A grin flashed over Owen's mouth. "He is a good man, your father." He spoke loud enough that all could hear.

The knife's cool sheath pressed into Aini's hands. "How do you know him? Even if he knew one of you once, he's not a...traitor like you."

"Aini," Neve hissed from behind.

The gathering murmured. Vera put a hand on her generous hip and snorted.

"Vera had to remind me who he was," Owen said. "She's our historian here. Lewis MacGregor used to work for the cause, for the Dionadair."

It was as if someone had poured a bucket of ice water down Aini's back. Her body quaked in the aftermath. This was exactly what she'd been afraid of. That Father truly did have a dangerous past. That this whole thing wasn't simply a mistake and easily solvable. Her own dear, sweet, genius father was a traitor to the crown. And being that, he was also an enemy to the most powerful clan in Scotland, the increasingly vicious Campbells.

"Your father and mine were good friends," Owen said.

Neve was whispering feverishly to Myles, who looked like he'd downed a sour cup of milk.

Aini swallowed, her throat on fire. "Who is your father?"

Owen, Vera, and Dodie traded a look, all downcast eyes and burdened shoulders. The people on the benches and sitting in the chairs around the tables set their mouths and straightened their own shoulders, protecting their leaders like a seawall shields a bay.

Owen quickly licked his lips. "Our father was a Bethune, as are we."

"The line of the first Dionadair!" a man called out. Another beside him patted his back and smiled grimly.

Owen gave his supporter a nod. "Yes, thank you." He looked at Aini. "And together, your father and mine had developed an invisible tracking powder."

Aini's hands shook as she gathered the knife closer, holding it, squeezing it, wishing it had some inherent power to help her out of this situation. She breathed once, slow and determined, through her nose. The air here smelled foreign. More metallic. Electric. And also like deeply churned earth.

"The powder worked well," Owen said. "But one of the ingredients had a traceable source in Isle of Man. The Campbells knew my father had contacts there. They came for him soon thereafter."

Vera trembled like a ghost had walked through her. "They sentenced our father to death."

"No." Aini's lips were cold and she touched them briefly, her fingers shaking. "My father is a sweets scientist. Not some wild insurgent. He can barely handle the tax men. He doesn't have it in him to rebel."

Owen raised his eyebrows. "From the stories, Lewis was a different man before he lost his closest friend, my father. The last of his rebellious streak was subdued when your mother left him."

She couldn't breathe. Her mother. That's why she'd divorced him. Because she found out he was a traitor. Her collar choked her. She tugged at it with icy fingers. "So, the Campbells do have my father."

"Yes. We're not certain what Nathair has planned for Lewis, what with the statements the man has made of late. It was easier when we had one enemy, the king, and knew what his motivations were. Now...Nathair may have more than a criminal trial in mind for your father."

"They tried to persuade him to craft weaponized candies."

Owen nodded. "But for who." It wasn't a question. He'd said it like he wanted Aini to think it out.

"To hurt you," she said, "the Dionadair?"

The red-bearded man slowly shook his head. "By now, they've guessed about his past work with my father. The Campbells know we're aware of the possibility of weaponized candy. They know we'd be wary. Of course that doesn't mean they wouldn't try it. But..."

Thane stepped closer, his arm brushing Aini's.

Owen's gaze went to him, then returned to her. "We believe the Campbells want to use weaponized candies on the Scottish people."

"What?" Thane and Aini spoke together.

"After we realized who you are, Aini, and who your father is, we put out some...feelers. The Campbells are interested in a fear campaign."

"But why?"

"To persuade the people to rise against the king and back Nathair as an independent leader in Scotland." Owen pushed his wireframe glasses higher on his nose.

Thane made a grumbling noise. "What a load of cack. No matter what...interesting tactics he's using, Nathair can't possibly believe he can win against the king."

Vera laughed, and Aini fought the urge to cover her ears. "Is that not what *we're* doing here, Handsome?" Vera said. "The king *can* be beat and he will!"

The crowd shouted. It sounded like a blend of *Ha!* and *Muah!* Probably Gaelic, Aini thought.

Thane stepped back. "Yeah, well," he whispered to Aini, "Nathair is not as daft as this bunch. Mad, yes. Daft, no."

Owen's head jerked up and his hands fell to his sides. He'd heard Thane.

"My father won't help the Campbells use weaponized sweets against innocent people. He wouldn't even do it against not-so-innocent people. Like you."

Owen nodded. "Aye. Vera found one of our own father's diary entries that said as much about your father. Very against the whole idea, Lewis MacGregor was."

"Is," Aini corrected.

Vera glanced at her with pity pouring out of mascara-heavy eyes.

A fusion of frustration and anger buzzed through Aini. "He is alive. I'd know it if they'd killed him."

Owen stepped in and took her arm. Thane's nostrils flared and he looked at Aini like *Is this okay?* She shrugged and let Owen hold her elbow lightly, like an old man would.

"We do believe he is still alive," Owen said. "We have a plan. But first, we need information to shape that plan." He leaned closer, his voice a stage whisper, loud and soft at the same time. "Tell me, what did you see when you touched the Bethune brooch?"

Aini's heart solidified.

She should've been prepared for this moment. After all, she'd found the knife the brooch's vision showed. But still. Admitting her ability aloud, discussing it in front of three hundred or so strangers who may or may not—probably not—have her best interests at heart? One could even be a Campbell spy. A breath shuddered out of her. She could never really prepare for something as big as this.

"I don't know what you're talking about." Her words trickled out of her mouth when they should've marched, strong and defensive.

Vera's purple dress stood out in the crowd of brown, blue, and white. "Oh yes, you do. You know very well what we're speaking about. You wouldn't have the brooch if you were not meant to."

"Meant to?" Aini asked.

"It's the prophecy," Vera said.

Dodie came forward and grabbed Vera's arm in his meaty hand. "She might've just found the thing." His curly, black hair fell over his heavy eyebrows. "She might not be the one."

Owen detached Dodie's grip on their sister. "She is. Enough of this, Dodie."

"What prophecy?" Aini leaned forward.

Neve and Myles gathered around Thane and Aini.

"Macbeth's Seer." Vera pointed at the knife, and cold perspiration slicked over Aini's face. "That's the old king's knife. Macbeth's knife. And I'd bet you saw the stone in your vision from the antiquarian's brooch."

Thane's eyes went wide and he staggered back a step. "My God. She's right."

"What's right?" Aini looked to Neve and Myles, who seemed as lost as she.

A ripple of whispers rolled through the crowd.

Owen held his hands wide, inviting the whole room to listen. "In the eleventh century, Macbeth, *MacBheatha mac Fhionnlaigh*—the real man, not the Scottish play—ruled Scotland. When threatened by a Scots leader who worked for the English—much like the Campbells do today—Macbeth hid a very special stone. Concealed it in the earth, deep, where no one would find it. That stone was the royal seat for the ancient Dal Riata Gaels. Every ruler from *Loarn mac Eirc* to Macbeth had been crowned upon it. It was called the Coronation Stone."

Neve gasped.

Aini wrapped her arms around herself. "A one-thousand-year-old legend doesn't have anything to do with me."

Owen stepped forward, his gait slow and regal, his hair copper in the overhead lanterns' light. "In 1819, my ancestor Angus Bethune and his spineless, betraying bossman, Donan Campbell," he paused to spit on the ground, "found the stone. They were antiquarians, relic-hunters. Angus Bethune hid it before that sleekit Campbell could give it to the English king and ruin Scotland's chance to free herself from tyranny.

"Donan Campbell killed Angus Bethune—knifed him in the back—when he found out, but not before Angus planted a trail, aided by Macbeth's ghost. Yes, he was a Ghost Talker and a Dreamer, seems like. In a dream, the ancient King Macbeth told Angus a Seer would rise. He said Angus must set a trail of visions embedded in artifacts, beginning with the brooch, that would lead the Seer to the resting place of the Coronation Stone, the rock that, when the true Heir to Scotland's throne touches it, will cry out and both its promise and its curse will free us from the English king and all in league with him."

As one, the Dionadair stood. They reached high and crossed their thumbs over their heads, faces solemn as gravestones. Every eye turned to Aini. These people, their hope, it burned with ferocity, a surety she'd never seen. Goosebumps rippled down her arms.

Neve made a sound like she'd breathed her last breath. Myles shook his head, and Thane paled, his glasses very black against his honey hair and fair cheeks.

The room spun. "Wait." Aini held up her shaking hands. "It can't be true."

She heard the unbelieving tone in her own voice. Felt it. On the surface, anyway. But the wild story rang through her bones like music she'd never heard before but somehow loved.

"Just give me a minute." She pinched the bridge of her nose, her heartbeat in her ears.

"Of course," Owen said quietly.

"Aini..." Neve edged closer, but Aini stepped away for space to think.

The whole thing came together in events, feelings, and visions, with the Dionadair as the good side in all of it. But they were rebels. Outlaws. People who threw rules back in the king's face. They were as dangerous as people could be.

But the king was worse.

He treated Scots like lesser beings than the English, prohibiting marriages without permission and laying out prejudiced taxes. The king had long ago abolished Parliament and taken away any chance they once had for a say in government. He was a tyrant. If he had his way, everyone like Aini, every sixth-senser, would be dead.

"It's because of this prophecy, isn't it?" she whispered. "This is why the king sees us—sixth-sensers—as abominations. He is afraid of me, of the stone, of the true Heir, the person who is meant to rule Scotland, the one the people would rise up and support."

Owen smiled sadly. "Of course it is, Seer. You understand it now, don't you?"

She put a hand to her churning stomach. Their theory, the story they'd told, drummed persistent and unrelenting through her flesh and bone. If she accepted this idea as truth, she'd forever be known as a sixth-senser, an abomination to the king, a person destined to die sooner rather than later.

Vera began to chant.

*'Macbeth's Seer rises nigh, a stone reflected in his light eye, and he bumped the man upon the chair, ripped him up by the hair.'*

Stepping back and holding his hands wide, Owen nodded. "Aini MacGregor, you are fated to free not just your father, but all of Scotland. You are fated to find our true Heir. You are the Seer."

Her blood halted in her veins, then sang and burned and made her want to scream. The Seer. It was crazy.

*It is true,* her blood whispered.

She sucked a breath as the crowd surged and cheered, a

moving tangle of smiles and bodies and hands lifted over heads. Thane stayed back from the rest, his fist on his mouth, thinking, overwhelmed, and she didn't blame him. She felt the same. The celebrating crowd crushed Neve and Myles into Aini's sides, their faces shocked, but joyful.

Neve squeezed Aini's hands tightly. Now Aini was not only a sixth-senser. She was not only an unintentional rebel. She had become the figurehead, the guide of the Dionadair.

The Campbells' greatest enemy.

## CHAPTER 17
## SEER

The excited voices, the chanting of the old song—all the sounds echoed off the barn walls and reverberated inside Thane's skull like alarm bells.

Aini was the Seer. Not just a Seer. *The* Seer.

She was the one the old stories said would find the Coronation Stone. Why had he never truly believed the legend? Rodric did. Nathair certainly did. He'd railed on about it at a clan gathering last autumn, his scarred face red in the bonfire's scattered light.

It really *was* more than a dream formed of whisky and Nathair's growing lust for power.

Head ringing, Thane's mind wheeled around and around. If there was one thing he could report to forgive all his recent shortcomings with his clan, this was it. If he was the Campbell to locate the Seer and destroy the fabled stone, he'd rule the clan. They'd flock to him like disciples. He shivered. What a thought. Rodric looking to Thane with respect? He shook his head. If Rodric respected an act, that act could simply, easily, quickly be categorized as pure evil.

As Thane shook his head to clear it, the Dionadair started ringing contacts on beat-up phones, heading through back doors with paperwork in hands, talking in groups. Two big men doffed boxing gloves in the cage to train. They were preparing for war.

Reporting this nest wouldn't be evil, would it? Even if it did please people like Nathair and Rodric. It was Thane's duty to his clan. To the good people in Clan Campbell.

But reporting Aini?

There she stood, so slight in her dress and open-front sweater. The woven piece of clothing swallowed her arms and hung below her knees. With that red ribbon in her ebony hair, she looked younger than she was. The skin on the back of her neck was smooth and he knew exactly how sweet that spot would be to kiss. To think of her taken by his clan...

Something stuck in his throat and he coughed. He rubbed his lip, the small scar on his thumb rough and familiar. He remembered getting that scar. He'd beat the sense out of a man who'd spoken against the king. It'd been up at his family's home. In Argyll. He'd been ten years old. In Thane's memory, his father was quiet, slick, and sure. Everything ten-year-old him was not, in his too-long arms and legs and squeaking voice.

"Hit him again, young Thane," his father had said then. "He's a traitor and you're doing the king's work."

After Thane had hit the man twice—the second sloppy punch hit the man's mouth and the traitor's tooth had cut Thane's thumb—Rodric and the others had hauled the man off to prison.

Eels swam in Thane's belly at the memory.

He blinked, pushed his glasses into his hair, and rubbed his face to clear the image away.

Now only Owen, Vera, Neve, and Myles made a loose sort of circle around Aini.

"I did not see that coming." Myles looked like he'd been hit in the back of the head, stunned and wondering how much pain was headed his way once his body caught up with the blow. "Of course, I'm not a Seer so…"

"Oh, Aini!" Neve grabbed Aini by the arms. "I can hardly believe it. It's amazing."

Aini stood motionless, until she turned and looked at Thane with coffee-black eyes. She needed support now, going through this madness. But all she had was him, the enemy, the wolf hiding in the trees. Thane grabbed his sweater at the chest and gripped it tightly, the loose weave distorting the curves of his fingerprints.

Vera snorted and swaggered up to Aini. "Think you can handle it, Seer?"

Aini's mouth worked, but nothing came of it.

Owen pulled Vera and Dodie aside. They spoke, heads together. Vera and Dodie joined a group at one of the many rickety wooden tables across the barn. The climbing wall stood behind them, covered in ropes like vines.

Owen waved Thane, Aini, Neve, and Myles toward the back of the barn. The wall there didn't sit quite flush with the rest of the wood. It was an exit. Or an entrance to another area. Thane didn't know where it led, but it was no place he wished to go. Not being a Campbell.

"What did you see when you touched the brooch?" Owen asked Aini. "Don't be afraid. We have several sixth-sensers here. Threaders. Ghost Talkers. No dreamers, yet… Sixth-senser skills are valuable to the cause. Yours, of course, especially so."

Raising her chin, Aini looked at Owen. "I touched the brooch and saw a stone. It looked like…like a seat. Someone had carved swirling shapes and circles in it. It's the Coronation Stone? The one that will announce the Heir when that person touches it?"

"Aye. It is." Owen rubbed his hands together. "It's mind-blowing. You've seen the stone in your visions." Throwing his head back, he laughed. "My siblings treated you terribly at the club."

Myles raised a finger. "Yeah, I expect a seriously beautiful *I'm sorry for punching your face* card from that thug you call a brother."

Owen pressed a hand to his chest. "Apologies, Myles."

Myles's head jerked back and he looked from Owen to Neve and back again. "How do you know my name?"

Owen raised his eyebrows. "As I mentioned earlier, when I guessed who this young lady might be, I released a few operatives into your part of Edinburgh. They told me you were Myles Smith, son of a successful plantation owner in the southern American colonies."

Myles's scowl could've melted the altered tablet candy hiding in Thane's secret bag. "Let's get back to this vision," he said quietly.

"I think I saw Angus, your ancestor, in the vision," Aini said, changing the subject. "He looked like you, Vera, and Dodie."

Nodding excitedly, Owen pulled on a thick rope, and with a snick of a mechanism, the uneven back walls slid to the side, revealing a rock passageway leading into the side of the hill. "He was the first of the Dionadair."

"What does that word mean anyway?" Aini asked.

Owen led the lot of them through the door and into a dimly lit, but large tunnel. Aini's gaze traveled over the dug-out passageway. She shouldn't have been too claustrophobic in this place, Thane thought. An elephant could walk through that passage. But what did he know of the phobia? He couldn't judge.

He squeezed his eyes shut. Where was his head? Here he was worrying over small things when they were about to stroll into a secret passageway with the head of the Dionadair. He'd gone mad, that's what this was. Thane had gone completely off his head.

"*Dionadair* means *protector*," Owen said. "We're protectors of Scotland and the stone." Owen blinked like an owl behind his glasses.

Cursing himself silently, Thane trailed right along behind Owen, Aini, and the rest. Every five feet or so down the passage, lights glowed—orange and inconsistent—from the rock walls. Scuffed beams lined the roof and made crude archways. Thane touched the chain at his throat. Quite the nest these Dionadair had here.

Aini looked over her shoulder at Thane, and he sped up to walk just behind her. If Owen tried anything, he'd be ready.

"There was a vision on the knife, too," Aini said. "It showed a wall marked with a spiral. The shape was reminiscent of the one on the Coronation Stone."

"The Waymark Wall," Owen said reverently. "When you find the wall and touch it, it'll give you the final vision and lead you to the stone. Where did you see it?"

Aini sure was giving away a great deal of information. Thane's mind whirred around the threats, risks, and the possibilities of this new world they'd been dumped into. The girl would be wise to keep some information back. He put a gentle hand on her shoulder and she glanced at him, a wrinkle appearing between the delicate slant of her black eyebrows. Turning slightly away from Owen, he put a finger to his lips. Her gaze going over his face, she began to scowl. He knew she didn't like being bossed about, but maybe she'd take his nonverbal advice anyway.

A droopy-faced woman in a dark shirt and corduroys came out of the back of the tunnel. "If you give us five minutes, we'll have the rooms ready."

Owen gave the woman a nod and she scampered off.

Chewing the inside of her lip, Aini kept quiet on Owen's last question about the location of the Waymark Wall. The way she was working that lip, she had to be making mental lists of what to do now. At least she'd taken his advice to keep quiet.

That Owen was wise. He kept his tongue as well, not pushing Aini to answer. He'd earn her trust backing away like that. Rodric could've taken a lesson from the man.

Aini sighed and nodded, as she'd come to some conclusion with herself. "I don't know where the Waymark Wall was in the vision. Near the ocean, I think."

Thane ground his teeth. She was going all in then.

Her eyes went bright like the time she'd thought of a new way to organize the lab stock. "What is our plan? So, what if I find the Coronation Stone, and somehow, the Heir? What then? It's not like the Campbells are going to simply hand my father over and make for the border with their tails between their legs."

She was right about that.

A daft smile slicked over one side of Owen's mouth. Thane was truly starting to hate that man. "They'll have to," Owen said. "They'll have no choice. Once we reveal the stone and the Heir, and Nathair Campbell's plan to poison his countrymen and blame it on the king, Scotland will rise behind us. We will force the Campbells out."

Thane pressed a fist against his mouth. They were getting a bit ahead of themselves. But his heart clanged inside his chest painfully. If the Dionadair were ready to go this far, and with Aini, Neve, and Myles in the midst of it, things were about to become very, very ugly. Thane paced a small circle as they waited on the corduroy woman, his feet hot in his boots and his palms sweating. If they knew Myles's name, they might know more. They might know something about Thane. The tunnel's ceiling was more than high enough for him to walk comfortably, even stretch, but Thane began to feel as Aini did in closed-in spaces. Like he was being buried alive.

He returned to her and touched her arm. "You all right in here? It's not that tight, is it?"

Her eyes shuttered closed and she swallowed roughly. Looking at the walls like they might bite, she whispered, "I'm okay."

She turned to Owen, who was watching Thane and her in a way that made Thane want to kick something. Someone.

"Where does rescuing my father come into all of this?" she asked smartly.

Thane crossed his arms and stood a bit closer to Owen, smiling at the head of height he had on the man.

"If we get their feathers up about a possible sighting of the true Coronation Stone," Owen turned a black and gold ring on his pinky finger, "it'll be easy enough to infiltrate their ranks and steal him back. They won't see this coming. It's their pride that'll make it doable."

Thane snorted and took up pacing again. It'd take more than Campbell ego to trip Campbells up. Maybe if the Dionadair had the weaponized sweets and could get the stone to roar in public —not that the thing most likely truly roared. Probably only a metaphor for something, but if the Dionadair could present it properly, they might have a chance at defeating Nathair. They'd still have a lot to deal with.

He stopped. His fingers unclenched, and a breath like a sigh or a cynical laugh floated from his mouth. He'd just been planning a revolution. A revolt against his own clan. Of course, if

Nathair truly did plan on trying to push the king from Scotland...

"What's your story, Moray?" Myles whispered. "You think these people are out of their gourds too? They do have a pretty boss hideout though." He elbowed Neve. "If you join the crazies, I'm in."

Neve whimpered and put hands on her head. "This is too much."

Myles rubbed her back.

Aini pressed her palms into her eyelids. "I don't know about all this."

"You'll have to trust me, Seer," Owen said quietly. "There's no other way out of this with your father alive and Scotland free."

"But...but why me?" Aini listed to the left.

Thane rushed to grab her by the arms.

"You need to sit down?" There wasn't a bench or anything in this stupid tunnel. Thane turned to Owen. "When are your blessed rooms going to be ready?"

Owen's mouth twisted into an ugly frown, but Vera was suddenly there, shiny as a beetle and blethering on with her brother about something. She held a walkie-talkie in one manicured hand and kept glancing at Thane.

Aini's lashes fluttered a little as a sad smile poured over her full lips. "Thank you," she whispered to Thane. "I just forgot to breathe for a minute."

"Let's not do that, all right?"

She laughed a little, and he forgot he was under a hill swarming with people who would happily murder him if they knew his real name.

"Agreed." She gave his forearms a little squeeze.

She had her weight under her again, so he released his hold, his stomach swimming. She was so brave and strong, but even the brave and strong needed backup.

Vera's gaze tore down Thane's body, and he tensed. "What is your story? You don't have the innocent look of the rest of these." She pointed to Aini, Myles, and Neve.

Myles mumbled an *oh please*, but Vera ignored him and ran a finger across Thane's chest. His lip curled. He lifted her hand off his ribs and dropped it, glaring.

A sideways grin pulled at Vera's lips. "We found out plenty of information about that one." She pointed to Neve. "With her many little brothers, alcoholic mother, and admirable work ethic."

Neve's eyes narrowed.

Vera licked her lips. "And we know all about Myles Smith. His plantation-owning mother in the Carolinas is a real horror story in the making."

Myles's eyes burned. He looked like a different person. "Shut up."

Vera laughed. "Don't get your knickers in a twist, colonial. It's not your fault mummy doesn't love you the way she should."

"Vera." Owen tilted his head, his voice warning his sister.

She crossed her arms. "It's only the truth."

"You soulless dog," Neve hissed.

Everyone froze.

Vera was the first to move again. "Ooo. The mousie has a mean bite, eh? Good. You'll need it."

Owen looked at the ceiling. "Forgive my sister. We've had our share of tragedy and it's sharpened our edges."

Myles whipped away from the group and strode farther down the tunnel. He couldn't know where he was going. Thane supposed the colonial didn't care. Just wanted to get out of here. Poor lad.

Myles tore back toward them. "You don't know anything about me."

Vera's face went from taunting with an eyebrow cocked, to sad, her eyes tipped down at the sides. "I'll not say another thing about it." She was a slippery one. Then she blinked at Thane. "But you. You've been naughty in your past. Shows in the eyes."

Thane's pulse slowed and his training kicked in. "I'm Thane Moray. I'm nobody."

Sneering, Vera said, "I doubt that. You can't go around looking like that and stay a nobody for very long."

She gave everyone except Aini a haughty look. With Aini, she seemed cautious, jealous maybe. Her eyes held questions.

"St. Andrews uni student," Vera said. "A friend named Bran, is it? And you're an orphan with an auntie near Glasgow? You don't dress like a Glaswegian."

Owen shook his head. "Vera, really. Stop."

Following Vera's touch, Aini's gaze was hard to define. Sucking a breath, Thane grabbed the woman's wrist and threw her hand away.

Aini stepped between them. "Enough about my friend."

"I agree," Owen said, eyeing Thane. "Aini wants to know *why* her. Let's focus, sister. Don't you have a little theory on that?"

"I do. I believe you're Macbeth's descendant."

Thane shook his head slowly.

"I'm a Threader," Vera said to Aini.

Thane's hands fisted. What would she see connected to him?

"Don't look so shocked." Vera raised an eyebrow at him, then at Aini. "Why do you think I've been the one to search for the brooch, to believe it was real? I see...connections from people to people, or people to objects. I saw the link, a slim silver line between you and the brooch, and assumed it was only a sentimental attachment like most have with a family heirloom. But no. You are Macbeth's Seer."

"This is all insane," Aini stammered. "Even if we find the stone, we don't know where the true Heir is that can supposedly 'bump' the king from his 'chair' as the song says. How are we going to, as you put it, *get the Campbells on the run*? Where does rescuing my father come in?"

"Exactly," Thane said before he could stop his mouth doing so. "You can't expect Aini to trust a band of cutthroat rebels, can you?"

Owen stared at the onyx ring on his own right hand. "Cutthroat."

"Aye. Tell me you wouldn't use weaponized candy yourself to take down the Campbells. You act like they're the only ones interested in new ways to control a group of people. What about that wall of guns you've got there in the barn? Unless I'm mistaken, those steely decorations do a bit more than make loud noises."

He knew he should shut his mouth, but the way that Owen wouldn't meet his eyes, the way they made themselves out to be saints all set to save Scotland—it was a load of bull.

Owen raised his head. "You wouldn't do what must be done to defend yourself? You'd let the kingsmen shoot you down, imprison your family and friends?" He nodded at Aini. "You'd stand by while they sentence the Seer to death?"

"I'd do no such thing, Dionadair," Thane spat. "I'm only saying you should avoid vague notions and be clear about your intentions and not pretend your plan does not involve violence. Because it does. It always has."

Aini put her graceful hands, one each, on Owen's and Thane's chests. Her hands were stronger somehow for their delicate beauty in this difficult place, but she could've saved herself the trouble. The fight had dissolved from Thane's fists and heart.

He was a Campbell.

He *would* have to stand by while someone sentenced Aini if it came to that.

The back of Thane's tongue tasted sour. His glare, aimed at Owen, faltered.

Owen cocked his head and a question crossed the man's eyes.

A line of sweat rolled down Thane's back.

"I won't help until you promise you won't try to…murder people," Aini said.

"The Campbells won't release your father," Owen said. "You'll have to take him back, and you'll only be able to do that if you help us take down the lot of them and reclaim Scotland."

"He's right, Aini," Neve said, her voice timid but steady.

Myles nodded.

"No," Aini snapped. "All we need to do is find the Waymark Wall, then the stone. Then we can leak the find to the Campbells to spook them and divert their attention from my father."

Owen turned and ran two fingers over his beard. "Yes."

Vera put a hand on his shoulder, but he gave her a look and she backed off.

"Yes," he said, louder this time. "It might work. After that, you can do as you wish, keep your father safe, and we'll find the Heir on our own and leave you to participate as you see fit."

Thane crossed his arms, his sweater pulling tightly against his skin. He might not have known exactly where he stood in this, but he knew very well where Owen was. At the center of a rebellion—not getting Aini's back.

"As she sees fit, aye?" Thane said, his tone woven to help Aini see the man's false front.

"Of course." Owen was a good liar.

Aini took a breath. "It's settled then."

Thane sucked a breath. Why did she believe Owen? She was smarter than that.

Vera's walkie talkie scratched and a voice carried through the tunnel. "Rooms prepared."

Thane wondered what the Dionadair had hidden while Aini and the others had waited with Owen in the tunnel. Maps of underground access tunnels the kingsmen hadn't yet found? Loot stolen from Campbell headquarters? Falsified papers and manufactured royal seals?

Owen and Vera led them to a large, dirt-walled room. Clusters of hammocks hung from the roughhewn ceiling beams. Several men and women polished guns and read books in the harsh white of overhead lights. A bank of filing cabinets stood on the back wall. Tiny, bronze keyholes stood out against the drawers' blue paint. On either end of the space, laundry lines suspended drop cloths that had been pulled back to reveal neat stacks of pants, shirts, and pullovers. Reed baskets overflowed with buckled boots, red-laced trainers, and steel-toed construction footwear.

The people in the room inclined their heads politely to Aini, their eyes bright with excitement. Wiping a rifle with a cloth, one man with a shockingly white mohawk smiled widely and said something to the people nearby. They nodded and went back to cleaning their portion of the Dionadair black-market arsenal.

Thane took a deep breath. They were obviously giving their Seer some space, but wished more than anything to ask her questions. Their gazes stayed on her as Owen led Thane and the others around the room.

"Sleep for a bit." Owen ran a hand over his beard. "There's food down the way in the kitchens."

"I can smell the bread," Neve said, raising her nose into the air.

Only the grease on the weapons reached Thane's nose. He felt simultaneously at home and nervous as he picked at a hangnail and kept to Aini's heels. This was her show right now. All he could do was hold on for the ride and hope they made it out of here alive.

Aini stopped abruptly in the center of the room. The big, overhead lamp shone down on her in strong beams, making a cage of light around her.

"I'm not resting," she said, her voice growing stronger. "My father is out there. With the Campbells."

Thane flinched, the truth nipping at his heels. He wasn't going to escape this thing intact. No matter how this played out, Aini would hate him and it would rip the best part of him in two.

She pulled a slip of paper from her sweater pocket. "I've thought about it. And I have a good guess on the Waymark Wall's location."

Owen clapped his hands together. "I'm as anxious as you, but it's obvious you need rest or you'll collapse before we've gone a mile. Sleep, and I'll have someone rouse you after just a few hours."

Thane wished he could sleep until this whole nightmare was over.

CHAPTER 18

WORRIES UNDER THE
NIGHTTIME SUN

In the Dionadair's sleeping room, Aini sat on the very edge of a dilapidated sofa with Neve, who couldn't stop trembling. Owen's associates had just now roused them. Owen had let them sleep the rest of the night, and the entire following day. It was night again. She gripped the hem of her sweater and squeezed. They'd lost so much time.

Leaning his head against the wall, Thane slung one leg over the arm of the couch to sit. It seemed like a practiced sort of nonchalance. His foot wiggled, and he kept fooling with his thumbnail and touching that small scar.

Myles, who'd gone to the kitchen for them, walked through the entrance, water bottles under his arms and holding a loaf of fresh bread. He held a piece out to Aini. She surveyed her hands. Pretty disgusting. But there was no sink nearby. She wiped her hands on her leggings and reached for the snack.

"I know you're not checking the cleanliness of your hands while we wonder whether we're going to live or die in a rebel's secret hangout." Myles smirked.

"No reason to die from contagion in the meantime."

Myles smeared a hand over his face, and Thane chuckled, though sadness darkened his smile.

At the back of the room, two men in overalls played cards on a wooden crate.

"I can't believe we slept so long," Aini said.

"We needed it." Neve nibbled her piece of bread. "You may be part of a legend, but you're still human." She smiled weakly, and Aini tried to return one but failed.

Glad that she didn't feel trapped in the room, Aini breathed in and out slowly. The ceiling was high, and the wide entrance to the tunnel leading to the barn gave the illusion of an easy departure if necessary. But she did feel trapped in the situation.

Her best guess on the Waymark Wall's location was the ruins of St. Andrews. It was on the coast. She'd been there with Father once and remembered a green lawn similar to the one in the knife's vision. It was near Edinburgh, where the first Dionadair had hidden the knife. It made sense. If they made it to St. Andrews, she'd have to feel around the structure's walls, searching for a vision in front of everyone. She'd be all but admitting to the Dionadair that she really was this legendary Seer they were so excited about. There'd be no turning back after that. She'd be the Seer. Forever. Never again simply Lewis MacGregor's daughter. Not the upstanding manager of the most successful boutique candy lab in Europe. She could never go back to her old life.

Thane put a hand over hers to still it. She'd completely unraveled her dress's hem. His beautiful mouth parted and his eyebrows furrowed together, but he didn't add words to his gesture. Maybe there weren't words for this kind of thing.

Thane's watch was close to touching her, and she pulled back out of habit. She sighed internally. She'd already touched the watch and seen nothing. It didn't hold any memories. Even if it did, wasn't it about time she gave up avoiding who she really was?

She relaxed under his hand and took simple pleasure in the way his bare arm brushed hers, the way the gold hairs on his skin disappeared under his sweater's rolled sleeves, the movement of his iron muscles and sharp tendons, the fact that this strong arm was here to help her.

After handing out the supplies, Myles stared at the floor, his eyes unfocused.

"I'm sorry Vera said what she did." Aini hoped she wasn't pressing a bruise by bringing up his mother.

He shrugged. "I can't really get ticked off when it's the truth. My mother is not a nice person."

Neve reached a hand out and touched his knee briefly. "Even when you were little?"

"Nah." He shoved his hands into the pockets of his extremely wrinkled pants. "She shoved me off on nannies and servants. Said she never planned on having children."

Thane looked Myles up and down, a serious look on his face.

Myles moved his weight from foot to foot. "The nannies were fine."

Aini paused, not knowing what to say or if there's anything anyone could say to address that sort of twisted pain.

"May I ask about your father? Did she lose him and that's why..." She probably should've kept her mouth shut.

Myles rubbed the back of his neck. "He left right after I was born. Mom claims it's because of what I did to her waistline." He looked at Aini with a smile that wasn't happy but was better than the vacant look he'd worn a second before. "But my math tutor—God bless the patience of that guy—said it had more to do with a new blonde in town."

Neve made a Scottish kind of *hmm* noise. Thane nodded.

One of the men playing cards slapped the table and laughed as Vera and Owen entered the sleeping quarters. Vera wore a ridiculously tight dress in the same brown as her heavily lined eyes and more lipstick than anyone should ever even think about.

Walking over to Aini and the others, Owen slid on another out-of-style tweed jacket and clasped his hands together. "Dodie has the truck running. Are you ready, Seer?"

The reverence in his tone made Aini's stomach hurt, but she stood. "Yes, but I don't think we should travel with a huge group."

Owen frowned. "But if the Campbells trail you and realize what you're doing—"

"All the more reason to keep our party small. Just send..." Aini took a second to think: who was the least flamboyant of the group? Definitely not Vera. "Maybe Dodie. He's quiet, but big, in case it comes to a fight."

Thane agreed.

Owen glanced at Vera, who frowned but nodded. "Aye, then," Owen said.

Vera looked at Aini's shaking hands. "Sure you aren't scared, Seer?"

Aini pushed past Vera. "Not any more than I should be, Threader."

The woman laughed. "Maybe so. Maybe so."

∽

Thane leaned his head against the truck window. The glass cooled his temple but not his mood swings. He'd gone from shocked, to enraged, been mired down into guilt, and rushed head long into hope, only to burn up in cynical self-doubt again. In the seat in front of him, Dodie—silent and thick-skulled—turned the truck's steering wheel as they entered the town of St. Andrews. Thane knew these streets well, the slope and rise of them under the inky blue sky and between the whitewashed buildings. When it wasn't summer holiday, he took classes at the university as part of his feigned life as Thane Moray.

Beside Dodie, Aini cracked her window. The sound of sea birds and mildly frustrated traffic poured in through the space, and wind threw strands of hair like black ink across her soft, round cheek. Could he somehow escape his clan and be with her? If he were any other Campbell, maybe.

Myles leaned over. "Staring at her like she's an experiment gone wrong ain't going to win you any points."

Thane jerked. Then he closed his eyes. Forget points. When it came to any possibility of a relationship with Aini, he needed a whole new game.

"I can give you some tips, you know," Myles said. "There's this one move called the rub-behind-the-head that gets them every time."

Thane opened one eye to see Myles raising an arm so that his excuse for a bicep stuck out like a kid's bicycle tire.

"Best if you stop that," Thane said. "I don't want to jump you in front of the girls."

On the other side of Myles, Neve snorted. "Thane."

Thane straightened, going hot around the collar. "Sorry, Neve. I didn't know you were listening."

He'd thought she'd been asleep. Not that it was late. Just that they were all still exhausted. It was after eight, though the sun hadn't set yet, this being a Scottish summer.

Ahead, the crumbling ruins of the former cathedral and castle reached toward the heavy-bellied clouds. Windows—

empty of glass, but full of the darkening sky—decorated what used to be the cathedral's nave. Part wrought iron, part stone, a wall surrounded the worn architecture and the scattering of tombstones. Like a king's mantle thrown on an old man, a groomed lawn draped the decrepit grounds. The ruins grew even more hunched as they approached the flinty North Sea until they were indistinguishable from the rocky cliffs above the black sand.

Dodie parked along the street near an overgrown garden crowded with tree boughs cloaked in thick leaves. They all climbed out, except for Dodie, who stayed behind to keep watch.

"I'll join you if need be," he said.

Aini regarded Dodie with an appraising eye. She was probably wondering the same thing Thane was. What exactly would he do if there was anything to worry about? If anyone headed toward the group at the ruins, he wasn't the type to handle it with clever distraction. He'd most likely bash heads.

The briny air stuck to Thane's skin as they made their way down the curving street to the ruins. A ticket office sat in front, looking closed.

A small car zipped past while another vehicle parked up the street, across from a pub and not in Dodie's line of sight. The parked car spit out two kingsmen in black jackets and Campbell kilts. Thane whispered a curse.

## CHAPTER 19
## ST. ANDREWS

The kingsmen dropped out of sight, hidden because of the street's curve.

"I don't think we're going to get in the way you'd like, Aini." Thane cleaned the wet and salty condensation off his glasses with the edge of his sweater.

She raised a pretty eyebrow, her plummy lips pinched. "None of this is how I'd like it to be," she said, but she kept heading toward the dark ticket window like her body acted from rule-following muscle memory.

He leapt the ruins's fence and held a hand to her over the metal bars. "Just come this way."

Aini evaluated the top railing, the bottom, then examined his hand. She waved it off politely and climbed the fence, landing pertly at his side.

He couldn't fight a grin. "Don't look so cocky. You're not proving anything I didn't already know about you."

"You knew I could climb fences?"

"I've learned you're quite good at breaking rules when the situation demands it."

She made a noise.

Myles pointed and laughed. "You made that Scottish noise."

Neve put a boot on the lowest railing, it slipped, and she caught herself on the fence.

"Allow me, milady," Myles said. He got down on all fours. "Mount up."

"Really?" She took a pure beamer, her cheeks going bright red.

"Go on," Myles urged.

With a laugh, Neve stood on his back. Her foot pulled at his shirt and she almost fell, kicking the lad smartly in the ribs. Finally, she made it over with a hand from Thane and Aini. Still laughing, she apologized to Myles.

"No need to be sorry," Myles said. "Sometimes you have to show your mount who's boss."

He backed into the street and took off at a run. With a whoop, he jumped and did an awkward, painful looking shoulder roll to land at Thane's feet.

Thane pulled at his own collar, covering his face a little just in case. But it seemed the kingsmen had vanished. He grabbed Myles by the back of the shirt and hauled him to his feet. "Hurry, pal."

"You sure are more concerned about getting in trouble today."

"It's about time," Aini said, Neve at her side.

Thane strode toward the stone arch that led to the inner courtyard.

Myles began singing. "*Tails tied to trees too tall, goals gone, gore growing go...*" That stupid band he loved gave Thane the worst headaches.

"Shut it, Myles." Neve hurried past him.

"Just come on," Thane snapped, gently shoving Myles, the last of them, behind the arch and out of view. His nerves were raw as the sea's biting wind. "Tell us what we can do to help, Aini."

She was already crouched at the base of the stones, running a hand over the weather-beaten, vanilla-and-smoke colored rocks.

"Look for a spiral carved into the stone," she said. "It may be very faint." Mumbling to herself, she stood and dragged her palms over the wall and up over her head as far as she could reach.

"Should I lift you?" he asked, part of him forgetting all about kingsmen and prophecies and thinking only of her little waist and nice—

She turned, her cheeks red from either wind or shyness, he wasn't sure. "I'll finish looking where I'm able, then maybe...yes."

"All right."

Myles and Neve moved on to what remained of the cathedral wall near the cemetery. She said something to him and he hunkered down like an old man, making her laugh.

Thane wasn't seeing anything like a marking. Just stones and old walkways and empty windows. "Want me to lift you now?" he asked Aini.

"I suppose. Although wouldn't Angus Bethune stick with somewhat easily accessible spots?"

"You think getting into and out of Edinburgh's locked-up vaults was easy, do you?" The minute he brought it up, he regretted it, thinking of Rodric's attack. He clenched his fists so hard that his nails burned into his palms like brands.

"I'm sorry," Aini apologized. "It wasn't easy. And it's not your fault that person attacked me. You saved me from being hurt worse."

He sighed forcefully, so weary of all of this, strung so tightly he felt he might explode. "Let me lift you just a bit. To my height, at least. Then you can move on to where you see fit."

With her nod, he bent, one hand to the fine, soft grass. She climbed onto his shoulders, one leanly muscled leg on either side of his head. Her little boots were muddier than anything she'd ever worn.

As she sat on his shoulders, her legs warmed his neck and chest. She reached and touched the wall, her stomach tensed against the crown of his head. If Thane hadn't been concerned about the kingsmen, and wondering if he should come clean with Aini, this would've been a fine day.

"Am I hurting you?" she asked.

"No."

A minute later, she tapped his shoulder. "I'll get down now."

As he lowered her to the ground and they untangled themselves, she looked at her hands.

"What if this is all a big mistake?" she asked quietly. The wind blew over her head and lifted strands of her hair.

He took her fingers in his. "All we can do is our best. Look for the Waymark Wall here. If we don't find it, look at another spot. When you feel you've searched all you can, then decide what to do next."

A sudden smile rose on her face like a sunrise. "Why, Thane. I think you just made a to-do list."

He laughed. "Aye. I think I did. You see the effect you have on me, hen?"

Aini leaned close, her shampoo and candy scent tempting. Her gaze brushed over his lips and he felt it like a touch. Her breath dusted his chin. Her small white teeth drew him nearer. What would her mouth taste like right now?

"Thane," she whispered with that mouth. "I—"

"Hey you all!" Myles called out.

Thane gritted his teeth. Aini broke away to see what the colonial was pointing to.

"Look at this!" Myles waved a hand.

Across the lawn, a metal railing and stairs led to a narrow opening in the ground. The stairs were slick and rounded from use over centuries. It looked like the entrance to a tomb.

Aini crossed her arms over her stomach. She seemed nervous. "What is it?"

Neve craned her neck to look into the tunnel. "It's a countermine." Her loose shirt whipped around her. "Protestants holed up here and defended themselves from Catholics in the sixteenth century. They dug these tunnels to intercept and demolish their enemies' mines—the ones dug to get into the place."

The railing cooled Thane's fingers as he entered the tunnel's damp mouth. After two steps, his boot slipped. He grabbed hold of the metal with both hands.

Aini shook her head. "I don't really want to go down there."

Neve sucked a breath. "I'm not claustrophobic and I still don't want to go down there. But they did open these up around 1800, so that's perfect timing for Angus Bethune to make his mark."

"Good thing you know so much, Neve," Thane said, looking back into the courtyard.

A flash of black and blue and green showed past the largest remaining section of the ruins. His heart leapt and practically hit his chin. Was it the kingsmen?

"You can do this, Aini," he said quickly. They needed to get out of sight. "We'll be right beside you. Just for a quick peek, aye?"

She inhaled and nodded, going in.

Continuing deeper into the dark tunnel, the rock remained like ice. Myles made a comment about snogging in slippery places.

"Do you know what people say of men who brag about their prowess?" Thane asked as Aini ran her fingers along the wall.

Myles took on an innocent look. "That those men are named Myles Smith and the bragging is as just as the day is long?"

Neve frowned over her shoulder. "That's a Mylesland answer."

"You know you want to visit, Neve."

"For what purpose?" Neve gripped the railing and looked up at the weak light on the ceiling of the tunnel.

The sea threw a gust of salty breath down the place as Thane tried to see the entrance.

"Mylesland has a fantastic library. Full of historical volumes."

Neve laughed. "Then I might consider the invitation."

"Of course the history is slightly skewed toward promoting licentious behavior. Only true libertines win in Mylesland."

"Libertines aren't necessarily licentious," Aini said. "They're simply fond of freedoms we can only dream about."

"Can you imagine having the freedoms the Dionadair want?" Thane asked, talking more to himself than anyone else.

"I thought you hated them," Myles said, nudging his way between Thane and Aini.

Thane swallowed. "I...I'm not sure how I feel actually." The lines between his real feelings and those he was using to maintain his role as spy were growing too wrinkled to smooth out.

Myles clapped hands over his mouth. "Seriously? Thane has no grouchy, superior answer?"

A growl rumbled in Thane's throat.

Neve eyed him. "You are a rebel of sorts like they are, Thane.

In the market, you stole those drinks because that man cheated Aini the week before."

Thane lifted one shoulder. "That doesn't mean anything."

"It does," Aini said, pausing to look at a rough spot in the wall below the railing. "You break the law, but only when you think it leads to justice. Or to help friends." She was thinking of Bran. If she only knew...

"But you hate the Dionadair." Myles clucked his tongue and ran two hands over the opposite wall, searching for carvings. "If they aim for justice for Scots—freedom to marry who they wish without permission, freedom to wear clan tartans even if they aren't Campbells, freedom to vote on taxation—why don't you love them as much as I'm beginning to?"

"I love them." Neve raised her chin.

Aini raised her eyebrows. "Neve, the rebel. I never thought I'd see the day."

Neve shook her head. "Sadly, I've no more drive to fight than a wee chicken."

They'd made it all the way to a black iron gate that blocked the tunnel's exit out of the ruins. Aini put a hand against the wall.

Her eyes went blank.

Thane began to take her arm, but held himself back. She was having a vision and he wasn't sure touching her was a good plan or not. What did it feel like to see things like that? Her lips moved once, twice. It was strange how Thane had once thought of sixth-sensers as people he would never understand. He didn't really understand Aini now, but he had realized such people were so much more than only their extended abilities. Aini was who she was, and then she was a sixth-senser. It didn't define her; the sense added another facet.

She gasped. Her knees gave out.

Thane caught her as she looked at him, her eyes alert again.

Neve and Myles hovered.

"Was it Angus Bethune again?" Neve bit her lip and pushed a fallen lock of Aini's hair behind her friend's ear.

Aini stood and brushed herself off. "It was a man in armor. He was choking on smoke...fighting someone he knew." She pressed her hands against her cheeks and inhaled deeply. "I need to get out of here."

Neve pointed to a spot on the wall. "There's a bit of metal embedded here. Must've belonged to some long ago Protestant or Catholic fighter." She shook her head as they hurried from the tunnel. "You are a wonder, Aini."

Cold air blasted through the passage.

Words slipped, barely audible, over Thane's ears.

"Ghost," he whispered, very glad he wasn't a Ghost Talker.

Myles whistled and looked around, wide-eyed. He looked a bit green around the gills. "I'm beginning to be a believer."

Neve smacked his arm. "Hush. Don't speak of it."

"Ghost or no ghost," Aini said, "let's go."

Neve crossed herself and hurried after her.

Then a real voice, not a ghost's, trailed through the tunnel.

Thane's heart tripped and he snagged Myles's arm. "Grab a girl. Let's see that snogging you've been going on about." He pulled Aini to him and gave Neve a gentle shove toward Myles. "Apologies, girls. But we're about to be caught."

Myles stuttered but eventually got out, "Ah. Gotcha." He laid a kiss on Neve.

Aini's eyes widened as Thane drew her face close to his. He dragged his mouth along her soft neck and was pleased to see chill bumps bloom along her skin.

"What are you doing?" she asked breathlessly, making Thane

feel like he was floating and he never, ever wanted to come back down to earth.

The stranger's voice said, "That's exactly what I wondered, lass."

It was a woman.

Squinting, Thane could only see her tall outline with the last of the late summer sunset behind in shades of blood and rust. Pulling away from Aini, he kept to a bend in the tunnel that the overhead lights didn't quite reach.

Aini spun, her cheeks going a bonnie shade of deep red. She looked to Thane, then to Myles and Neve, who weren't snogging, but stood very close together.

"Oh," Aini said, recovering. "We were...it was..."

Myles smoothed his shirt with big movements. "Just having some fun, miss. We'll move on."

"Come with me, please." Waving a hand, the woman started toward the entrance. She wore a black government uniform with red stripes down the sleeves.

They emerged into the dusk. Purple and blue battled for chunks of sky above the tombstones and the bones of the old cathedral and castle.

The gaunt-faced woman took out a walkie talkie and turned a knob. She was maybe fifty, fifty-five. "I'll have to report you. I am sorry."

Her nails were long and very red and gave Thane an idea.

∼

Giving Aini a loaded look, Thane let go of her arm and approached the ruins guard. Aini immediately missed the warmth of his touch. This evening had been pointless. Frustrating. Longing for a shower, for a solution to all of this, for something other than wandering around and failing her father, she wiped her filthy hands on her leggings. She put a hand to her throat, wanting to feel the spot where Thane's mouth had been.

"Ah, now lass," Thane said to the guard in a sugary, deep voice.

Aini's insides melted.

Neve's mouth fell open.

"You don't have to tell anyone we were here, do you?" Thane strengthened his West Scots accent, and the guard smiled, which completely changed her face into something far more manageable. "We weren't doing any harm." He looked up at her through his black lashes. Two gorgeous dimples appeared in his cheeks as he smiled and angled his body toward her.

Aini pushed her sleeves up, suddenly very warm. That voice he was using...it was like a sixth-sense ability of its own.

"I bet," Thane went on, "that not so long ago, you yourself enjoyed similar activities."

Smiling, the guard pulled at the collar of her unattractive uniform. "Well, that's none of your business." A laugh pealed out of her throat.

Thane put a hand on his well-built chest and dipped his head, hanging a thumb on his trousers and looking like the most gorgeous thing in the universe. Those tattoos. Those glasses. Aini blew out a breath. Those arms. She knew she was being pathetic, but still. Still.

"Aye. Course not," he said. "But if you let us go, just this once, maybe we'll see you at the pub up the way later on tonight."

The guard's face lightened. "Oh?" She shook herself slightly and cleared her throat. "That's not, that's nothing I can…" She waved a hand. "Just go." An easy smile poured over her mouth then. "Go on, the lot of you. I was young once too."

Thane took her hand and kissed it slowly, his head bent like a knight.

Aini's heart clattered around like a broken mixer. It wasn't the most fun thing knowing she could've been conned by Thane too. Beauty was a powerful possession. Neve said Aini had it. Even if Aini could be convinced of that, she had no idea how to wield it like a weapon as Thane did. Thane, the Heart Bender, Drool Maker, Thought Swayer. She rolled her eyes at herself and almost laughed. What a sixth sense that would be.

"Thank you," Thane said, straightening.

He gave the rest of them a quick nod, and they were off, trotting back toward the truck before the guard could change her mind.

"Thane," Myles said as they climbed the fence. "You are my hero. In fact," he dug in his pocket, "I have twenty quid. Do you want it? I'll give you anything. I fully support the usage of male sexiness in times of need. And you, my friend, are a master of the art."

Thane glared at him and hopped off the pavement. "Shut your gob." He kept glancing down the road and at the painfully untended garden beside the truck.

"What are you looking for?" Aini asked, but he didn't answer as they made it to the truck and waved to Dodie.

Dodie pointed at a pub across the street. "Why don't we go in there and eat before heading home?"

The door opened, and happy music danced out along with the smell of something smoky and pleasant. Aini's stomach growled.

Thane opened the truck door. "We should go."

Dodie was already getting out, and Neve and Myles crossed the road.

Aini had failed and they had to eat. "Just for a quick meal. I have a headache and I want to get back to safety too, but…" She held out a hand toward the intoxicating drumming of a bodhran and a set of pipes' lilting tune.

Thane shut the truck door but didn't smile as he followed them to the pub.

Aini hoped the music would help her think.

## CHAPTER 20
## A REEL AND A STRAMASH

In the pub, three stag heads large enough to impress Thane, who'd grown up surrounded by wildlife, decorated a wood-paneled wall. With their proud racks, the dead creatures presided over a group of musicians taking a drinking break. Tables of locals and tourists crowded around a dance floor. A man—with a nose that looked like it'd been broken several times—poured drinks for the patrons. The place smelled like everything had been doused in old ale and frying oil. Nabbing a seat facing the door, Thane sat at the closest table.

Myles dragged a chair out, making a racket. "I need a drink."

"You never drink." Aini peered around the room.

"Well, I need to start sometime, don't I? It fits my whole licentious behavior thing."

Neve sat beside him and put her purse on the table. "Don't let your idea of yourself rule you."

Myles blinked. "That was very wise, Neve. I...think I'll take your advice. I tried beer once and it really is pretty disgusting."

"I used to smoke," Thane admitted. "It was a stupid habit."

Dodie took a chair between Myles and Thane.

Smiling, Neve pulled a stick of something from her purse and slicked it over her mouth. Her lips looked no different. "But don't stop me when I order a whisky."

"A whisky?" Myles asked.

"I'm Scottish. It's like apple juice to us."

Thane nodded approval, and Dodie said, "Aye."

Thane snorted. That'd be the only thing a Campbell and a Dionadair rebel could easily agree on.

"Don't drink too much." Aini sat beside Neve. "We need to stay alert. Owen warned that we are being watched."

Cringing a little, Thane waved the server over. If he had to be miserable, he could at least do it on a full stomach.

Aini's phone rang. "...right. No, we didn't. Okay." Pocketing the phone, she scanned the pub with wary eyes. "Owen says we should go back to the townhouse for the rest of the night," she whispered across the table. "He says it will keep...certain people from wondering what we're up to."

The man with the bent nose appeared with a notepad to take their order.

"What's that smoked haddock soup you're always wishing you had?" Myles asked Thane.

Thane pushed his glasses up. "Cullen Skink."

"That is not a good name for something you want to put in your mouth."

"Suppose not. But I'd have thought green was not a good color for your melon either." Thane pointed at Myles's hair.

"Shows what you know."

"You're the envy of mold spores everywhere, colonial."

Myles started to frown, but then laughed loudly, startling a bonnie, older woman at the next table.

Everyone ordered, and Thane sat back and kept an eye on the door.

The musicians began puttering around. A bald man drummed a round, skin bodhran with a small stick. A woman wearing a yellow snochterdicter as a headband perched a fiddle on her shoulder, made the instrument whine twice, and turned the small knobs at the end of the fingerboard to tune it. Another member of the group, a man with ears far larger than God should've given him, strummed a guitar. Then they started a reel.

"The Riverside Rant," Neve said.

"My sister likes this one," Dodie said.

Everyone looked at him.

"Hey," the man said. "If we're going to be around each other, might as well be civil."

"It's not that," Aini said. "I just didn't realize you cared much for conversation."

Myles glared at him. "I'd like it better if you kept quiet."

"Get over it, pal. This is a war we're in. When you don't seem to be on my side, I'm going to plow you down. When you're with me, I'll do all to keep you standing."

Myles threw Dodie one last mean look, then turned his attention to the music, pretending Dodie wasn't there.

Following the rhythm, Myles banged his knuckles lightly on the table. Neve smiled and watched the fiddler like she'd never seen one before. Aini's delicate fingers moved and curled an inch above the table in some imagined pattern.

"Did you ever think of being a dancer like your mother?" Thane asked.

The server handed him a hot crockery bowl. Aini took her own bowl of the same soup he'd ordered.

"No. I love being at home. The candy making business suits me." She smiled like a memory had touched her.

"I didn't mean to make you sad," he said quietly.

Myles made up lyrics to go with the band's music. Neve laughed and spilled a little of her whisky.

Aini looked at Thane, the corner of her mouth tucked up. "You didn't. I just remembered having competitions with Mother to see who could spin the fastest without growing dizzy." She frowned. "I've always been angry with her. For the divorce, for leaving Father. Even when we were having fun and getting along, there was a part of me that stayed angry. She'd see it sometimes when I snapped at her or chose Father over her, but she never said anything. She could've told me. I might've been on her side. I wouldn't have blamed her when I missed Father. I might've understood when she was demanding with him about petty things. She was hurt by all this too."

"Are you angry with your father?"

She swallowed. "I should be, I guess. But no. I know who he is, in spite of the secret part of his past. My life is so different from what I thought it was. I was blind. Even though he's still an amazing person, Father isn't the innocent I thought he was. And Mother wasn't the cold, bitter person I'd believed her to be."

The whisky fuzzed Thane's thoughts, and a memory of his recurring dream blinked through his mind. His fingerprint, and the feeling of falling and rushing forward. How his skin turned black. He wished he could call his mother, check on her. Beg her to go to Great Uncle Rabbie's for some invented reason until he figured everything out. He knew something bad was headed his way if he continued on like this, riding the line between his clan's demands and this girl's needs—his heart's needs.

The music had pulled in couples from around the tavern. The people lined up, crossed their arms, and walked circles around those next to them.

"Even I know this one. Strip the Willow," Myles said. He

lifted his soup bowl with both hands, downed what remained, and pushed away from the table. He held a hand out to Neve. "Care to take me for a spin?"

Neve shot the rest of her drink. "I believe I do. Or the whisky does. But I'm not of a mind to argue it just now."

They walked to the start of the lineup. Myles linked his arm in Neve's and tugged her around, stopping at the second couple and dropping his hold on her. She took up the next man's arm. Myles wiggled his eyebrows at a portly woman and shimmied. Thane sighed, jealous of his easy nature and more jealous of his ability to shrug off his troubled childhood. Why couldn't Thane throw off what he'd been born to? Why did it feel like his childhood, his family, grew over him like unbreakable vines, tight and tightening still?

Aini dabbed her mouth with her napkin. "We should dance, too. I feel terrible. I can't think. A good reel will help."

Thane didn't feel like dancing. Not even a little. But that smile she was giving him...

"All right," he said, standing. He nodded at Dodie, who kept his seat and chewed a toothpick.

Snagging Aini's hand, Thane pulled her into the reel. They both knew the steps, their feet and hands turning and moving in time.

A look of surprise showed on Aini's glowing face. "You're a great dancer. I mean, club dancing is one thing, but this?"

"I've all sorts of yet undiscovered talents," he said.

She missed a beat, then continued.

He tore his gaze from her curving neck and soft-looking face. "I'm sorry. That sounded..." he stuttered.

Spinning once under his arm, she came up against him. Her chin tilted. Her mouth was so close. "It's the whisky, isn't it?"

"It washes a person's manners clean away." A strangled laugh came out of him.

She grinned like a devil, and they joined everyone in making a circle, surrounding one dancer. The man in the center did an impressive jig, then returned to the edges of the crowd.

Thane gave Aini a little shove to the middle. She eyed him, grinned again, and began to dance. Taking the hem of her dress, she moved slowly, toe, toe, heel, heel, following the slow driving beat. The musicians, by now on their feet with the rest, built their tempo, challenging her. She moved her feet behind and in front of one another, moving faster and faster, spinning every fourth time, and giving a great leap at every one of the violin's high notes. Eyes closed, she became a piece of the music.

Thane couldn't take his eyes off her.

Her arms were lines of low and high, her fingers moving beautifully, and her feet punching staccato drum beats on the wooden planks of the floor. She began to spin, round and round, like a top.

The song came to an end and the room erupted into applause. She opened her coffee eyes, a lock of sweat-wet hair over her face and a real smile stretching her lips.

Aini MacGregor was definitely going to be the death of him.

Here he was gawking at her when they had a true storm coming down on them any minute. Rebels. Kingsmen who he had to avoid to protect his cover. Lewis in Nathair's hands.

The dancing broke into a mess of blethering and couples goofing around. Thane and the others headed to the bar to get water. Thane wiped his face with his sleeve, then peeled his lightweight sweater off. He'd left the bag of chemicals and candy under a cot at the Dionadair barn, so wearing only a T-shirt wouldn't be a problem. There was nothing that needed hidden.

As he leaned on a wood post waiting for Aini to order, a

couple of guys started mouthing off at the barkeep. They downed another shot of whisky and said something pure awful about the keep's mother.

Though the keep went about his job, this show of patience wouldn't last. The lads should've kept their tongues, considering the size of the keep and the look on the man's face. He didn't look like one to take it in stride, not with that cricket bat he had stored near the cash register. The only sport that bat had seen was the kind that ended in blood and bruised ribs.

The pub door opened.

The kingsmen walked in.

Thane swore under his breath.

One man with a shock of black hair was familiar. He'd been to the Bluefoot. Through the smoke and crowd, he squinted right at Thane. Preparing for the possibility that the kingsman—who'd obviously recognized him—would fail to retain his cover, Thane shook his hair down over his eyes.

"Forget the order," he said into Aini's ear. "Grab Myles. I'll get Neve. We're leaving."

Aini turned and saw the kingsmen too. "Okay. What about Dodie?"

"He'll get out. He knows what to do."

As the first kingsman dragged the other to the bar, Thane and the others made their way behind the crowd, nearer the door.

The barkeep and the guys were still arguing.

Back at the table, Thane waited until the keep had his back turned. Then he picked up his whisky glass and hurled it over one punk's shoulder. The glass hit the keep in the back of the head and crashed to the floor. A man and two women shouted as the keep whirled around, the bat already in his hands.

"Whoa!" Myles raised both arms and laughed.

The keep swung it at the guys. "Get out!"

They tried to argue it, pointing back in Thane's general direction. "We didn't—"

The keep swung again and this time, the punks had to duck. The bar erupted into a full-fledged fight.

Thane gathered everyone up and slipped out the door, the black-haired kingsman trying to get to them but blocked by the stramash.

In the street, they ran to the truck. Dodie drove them quickly out of town.

Dodie squinted, eyeing the motorway. "We'll have to get rid of this vehicle."

Neve was breathing too fast and Myles looked ready to faint.

"Aye," Thane said. "Dump it soon as we're within Edinburgh proper and we'll cab it the rest of the way. Neve. Myles. You're fine now. It's all right. How's the head, Myles?"

"I can't believe you just started a bar fight." Aini's eyes narrowed at Thane.

Out the window, night blurred by. "It was going to happen anyway."

Dodie shifted gears and the truck groaned.

Aini hugged herself, fingers pinching into her skin. "I have to think of another place to look for the Waymark Wall."

"We'll figure it out," Neve stammered.

Aini nodded, but Thane could tell her heart wasn't in it. Thane squeezed his eyes shut and laid his head against the window. After all they'd been through, could she be convinced that he'd see her through this somehow? Could he even make such a promise?

He lightly knocked his head against the glass. He wanted to make that promise, wanted it to be true. But the whole thing was so tangled and dangerous. Maybe if he could talk some of the other Campbells into backing him up instead of Nathair. Putting his elbows on his knees, knowing full well he was crazy for even thinking it. The minute they were at the townhouse, he had to send a message to Rodric. Further silence would be seen as disobedience. He'd mention the blinding powder that could be teased into gas form—the stuff he'd developed—and the negating tablet. Maybe if he could manage it, he could get Aini and the others to make a batch of the gravity-reducing hard candies and he could alter the mix to make the effects more extreme. He could report that too. That would keep his clan off his back until he figured out what to do. It was a mess that was certain.

The quiet of the rest of the drive was punctuated only by Myles's occasional bursts of song.

*"For fire fight for friends, run ragged rings round reason, 'tis too tame to talk, touch, win wildly, wearing wounds wound with worship..."*

*Wearing wounds wound with worship.* That line pretty much described Nathair Campbell. The chief of Clan Campbell, Earl of Argyll, wore the scar on his neck like a badge of honor. Anytime someone spoke up against him, he pointed to the thing like it was a holy relic and asked them what they had given of themselves for king and country.

A shudder wrapped around Thane. Outmaneuvering his clan was not going to be easy.

## CHAPTER 21

### FULLY LOADED

"No." Aini slammed a hand on the lab table the next day. The cool metal sent a chill over her. "I won't let you do this."

Thane paced the floor. He looked like he was going to be sick, but she wasn't going to ease off. Dawn's orange fire glowed through the high, leaded glass window, shining over him like a broken, unmoving lighthouse beam.

She'd discovered that, while the rest of them had slept, Thane had reworked the formula for Father's gravity-reducing hard candy, but it wasn't only to accomplish a punchier grape-lavender flavor. He wanted it strong enough to lift a person clean off the ground and keep them floating freely like a bird for a half hour.

"That is a weapon," she said.

The scent of burnt sweetness fit Aini's mood rather well.

"It wouldn't hurt anyone," Thane said.

Aini pointed a finger and stubbornly ignored his looks. It didn't matter that he was like something she'd dreamt up as he grabbed one of the low, black wood beams that crossed the ceiling. His slightly wrinkled, gray T-shirt shifted. The movement revealed the fine slope of his strong arm and a peek of his hipbone above his low-slung cotton pants. She looked away, staring instead at the colored sugar on the far wall.

Neve walked in, still braiding her hair. She paused and took in their scowls. "Surely Aini, at this point in our lives—with rebels and corruption and visions—you're not as worked up about paperwork, are you?" She must've heard part of their arguing. "So, what is it?"

Myles, nibbling an orange, came up behind her and frowned at Aini. "I wonder. Is there specific paperwork for a sixth-senser working in a candy lab?"

"Shut up, Myles," Thane and Aini said in unison.

Aini spun her mother's ring around and around her finger, its edges cutting.

"Don't you understand this at all?" She quieted her voice to keep it steady. "Father was taken because he refused to do exactly what Thane wants to do. Weaponize candy. Push its limits. Use it to alter people in ways that could truly affect lives." Spinning, she faced them and crossed her arms. "I will not go against my father's idea of right and wrong with regard to crafting sweets. This is HIS business. Not mine. Not yours. HIS. He spoke against the Campbells, risking everything, to fight the idea of stretching the effects of his sweets. I will not betray him now. Especially since I'm the worst possible kind of child he could have."

A sob tried to choke her words, but she forced it down and set her jaw.

"No, you're not," Neve said, her own chin trembling.

Thane's mouth turned down and he cocked his head at Aini. "Don't say that, hen."

"You are definitely not the worst," Myles said. "Not great, but not the worst. *I'm* the worst child someone could have. You should've seen my graduation. They're probably still cleaning the paint out of the dean's hair."

They all argued quietly against the fact, but it remained a fact. For a candymaker—a job you had to specifically apply for— to have a sixth-senser in the family? A mistrusted abomination? It didn't matter that Father had stopped helping the Dionadair. He was doomed because of Aini and some prophecy. She shook her head. A sick twist of fate.

Neve stepped around the table and stood beside Aini, her face pale. "Your father was against this. But that was before they ignored his right to a trial, to justice. He was against it before they hurt him. Before they kidnapped him."

"So, now you want me to make crazy concoctions so we can fight against them?" Aini said.

Shoving his glasses into his hair, Thane leaned on the table. He pressed his hands against his face. He really did look ill.

Neve raised her chin. "I do."

Aini's mouth fell open. She turned to Myles. "And you?"

He laughed and spit an orange seed into a napkin. "You know I do. If we're going to go up against those Campbell kingsmen, I want to go in fully loaded." Pretending he had some kind of enormous gun, he blasted the list of the king's rules hanging on the wall.

Fury rising, Aini jerked the stove's knob and turned the heat off. "No. We're not making anything. This lab is closed." She marched to the light switch and threw the room into darkness. "If I do this, Father will never be able to craft sweets again." She waved a shaking hand at the mixer, the rainbow of ingredients along the wall, the taffy puller, and Father's desk. "Our whole way of life will be over."

Thane stood tall, his face all lines and sharp angles. "It already is, Aini."

Her stomach lurched. "No," she whispered. "If we can spook the Campbells with a picture of the stone," she said, louder now, "and distract them and help Father escape, they might give up their plans for him. They might let us—"

Neve and Myles stared, their eyes sad and deadly calm.

They didn't believe it could happen. Everyone thought her life, their way of life, was actually over. It was all over.

Head spinning, Aini ran to her room. She refused to cry or rage in front of anyone anymore. Sitting on the bed, hands clenching the duvet and heart hammering, she suddenly wanted everything of Father's around her. She wanted to see him in everything. To somehow keep him close. Her heart clenched. She wanted to see him in a vision.

Rushing from room to room, she gathered his things. Dodie woke from his temporary bed on the couch and asked questions she ignored. She collected Father's favorite dark blue coffee cup, a keychain he'd bought in the Dominion of New England—where he'd visited her and her mother—and a tumble of chemistry and math volumes. Back in her room, she poured them onto the bed. Over and over again, she brushed fingers along each item of rough crockery, silver-plated metal, worn cloth, and leather.

None held a vision.

She started to drop onto the bed to forget this stupid idea—she needed to think of where else the Waymark Wall could be—but then she remembered she'd hidden the brooch under her floorboard. Maybe there was a place she hadn't touched yet, a sliver of memory left, one little vision.

The slat came up easily and there was her diary.

Her stomach dropped. The brooch was gone.

"Thane!" She didn't know why her mouth called for him when they'd just argued.

He banged into the room, his face worried, his glasses hanging from one hand. "What is it?" His tattoo of the chemical formula for salt had been splashed with purple food coloring.

"The brooch. Someone stole it."

Thane swore in Gaelic. Aini echoed the sentiment.

Myles stuck his head in, eyed her stash, and whistled like a bird. "What's going on in here?"

"The brooch is gone," Thane said. "I'm going to question Dodie."

The very man came to the door. "I heard you. And I don't have the Bethune brooch."

"Did the Campbells come here again and take it?" she asked. "But they didn't touch anything else."

Thane swallowed. "Guess it's all they needed."

Myles whistled low again, and Aini suddenly remembered the birds in the knife's vision, the ones on the island.

What if the island wasn't just another separate thought like the sight of the stone was? What if there was an island near the castle ruins, near the Waymark Wall?

She knew of one island in the area, one that fit the bill. It was covered in birds, which would explain the strange white color in the vision. She'd been a fool. This made sense. This had to be important.

"For now, forget the brooch. The candy. I have another idea about the Waymark Wall."

## CHAPTER 22

## A DOISTER

They left Edinburgh in a rush, met with the Dionadair on the motorway, and headed to Tantallon Castle, another jumble of ruins on the North Sea. Aini's palms tingled as if they somehow knew the Waymark Wall was there, waiting for her. Or maybe the stress had finally broken her and this was simply the beginning of her end.

Dodie agreed that the Campbells probably took the brooch. Somehow they'd learned she had it. What else they knew was still a mystery and that was no good. If they made it to the stone first, that would be the end of the road.

Dodie's lumpy form sat behind the steering wheel, Vera beside him, and Aini was squeezed between Thane and Myles in the back seat. Neve was on Myles's right, all of it making for a really tight fit. It didn't help the discomfort of the situation that Vera kept bumping her knife hilt on the roof, and Neve's nervousness was spilling out of her in the form of random historical tidbits.

Wind kicked last year's leaves into the cloudy sky as they

sped down the curving, narrow country road. Another truck drove in front of them, puffing foul exhaust through the open windows.

"Tantallon," Neve said, blinking too quickly between words, "is a castle of *enciente*, meaning it has a curtain wall. Forty-nine feet high and twelve feet thick, if you can believe it. Walter Scott wrote extensively about the castle in one of his poems. It's the one that everyone quotes. *Oh what a tangled web we weave, When first we practice to deceive!*"

Vera turned suddenly. Aini thought for a second she might cut out Neve's tongue, but she held up her phone, a serious look on her beautiful face. "Owen sent a message. A scout in Edinburgh says some of the Campbells are meeting to discuss something. Said even Nathair will be there. They know, Aini. We need to get to the wall and to the stone before they do or the game is up."

Icy fingers curled around Aini's throat.

His foot bouncing on the floor, Thane rubbed his knees. His tattoos blurred in the darkening truck cabin.

Vera made a call. "Gavin, take the tail." She was talking to the truck in front. "Call Tom Hunt. Tell him we'll be in his territory in twenty minutes."

Thane bumped into Aini as the truck moved down a hill. His hand pushed against her thigh. "Sorry," he said, his gaze shifting across her face.

She couldn't tell what he thought now. Fear? Anger? Regret that her mess of a life had snared him? It was impossible to tell. He'd retreated into himself since they realized the Campbells had the brooch. Or maybe because of their argument about the candy.

Leaning over Myles, Neve smiled. "You'll find it. You're fated for this."

"I wish I had your faith."

Vera sighed. "I wish our Seer wasn't such a wee feartie."

Thane raised his head. "She's not a coward. It's only that she cares about the people around her."

Vera stared Thane down. "Oh, and I don't care? Why do you think we're out to throw the Campbells and the king down? For the money?" Vera laughed loud and batted her thick black lashes. She slammed a fist against her chest. "My parents were shot to death." Tears shone in her eyes. "And I'm risking my life for my countrymen. I do it every day."

"And you put your cause before those you love," Thane said. "It's pointless to fight against the Campbells. You're leading us all to the slaughter."

Heart drowning, Aini shuddered. Didn't he have any hope in her at all?

Myles shoved a tiny apple into Aini's hand. "Ignore them and eat, sweetheart." He produced another like a magician and gave it to Neve. "You too, love."

Aini held the apple, turning it in her hands. They had to quit bickering. They needed to be a team if this was going to work. She had to be strong enough to bind them together in this madness. But they kept on arguing and shooting glares at one another.

She put a hand on Thane's back and eyed Vera. "Please, stop. We're in this together, for the moment anyway. There's no purpose in fighting right now."

Thane twisted. His nostrils flared out and in. "Are you ready to do as the Dionadair do and risk all? Because these people, they're not putting your father first. I can tell you that."

Vera snorted. "You think the Campbells are just going to hand him back? He's good as dead if we don't take all of them down."

The truck bounced, sending Aini's apple to the floor. Myles retrieved it and traded fruit with her.

"Please," she said. "I need to think. To remember the vision so I can find the wall."

"Aye. Of course," Thane and Vera said in unison.

Sighing, Aini put her head in her hands.

Neve whispered, her tone joking but her words shaky. "For a lady so lovely, Vera sure can give a mean growler. What a scowl."

Peering at the expression Vera directed at Thane in the rearview mirror, Aini laughed shakily, agreeing, then closed her eyes to try and bring every detail of the vision to mind.

Thane's mouth was suddenly at Aini's ear, his soft lips moving and making her breathe unevenly. "Take this," he said and handed her something small.

It was a square of tablet, the sugar and butter candy Father altered to negate the effects of the golden taffy. "Why?"

Keeping an eye on Vera, Thane handed a piece of the tablet to Myles and Neve too. "Just keep it. Eat if I ask you to."

Neve stared at it.

"What are you up to?" Aini asked.

Thane shuffled on the seat and adjusted the hidden bag under his sweater as Vera swore at Dodie. Myles shrugged and slipped the candy into his shirt pocket.

"I'm just making sure we have an escape plan if we need it," Thane said.

"Escape from who exactly?" Myles asked.

Aini studied Thane's serious face. "He's worried about the Campbells. But how will this help—"

Vera had stopped fighting with her brother. She turned. "What's this you're blethering on about?"

"Nothing," Neve and Aini said.

Thane rolled his eyes.

Vera sniffed. "Right," she said, but she did drop it, thankfully.

Aini pretended to cough and stored the tablet in her bra, wondering what Thane had in mind. Especially considering he hadn't shared the plan with the Dionadair. She didn't like this. Not one bit. Too many variables clashed around, too many things not planned out or reasoned properly. What she wouldn't give to spend a week figuring this all out and writing a proper list, a plan of attack.

DODIE DROVE THEM INTO A PARKING LOT FRAMED BY TALL grass. Thane, Myles, Neve, and Aini piled out of the truck. The moonlit ruins of Tantallon Castle loomed past a tourist shop and a mown field.

"Go on ahead, Seer." Vera locked the vehicle's loading doors and nodded to Dodie. "My brother and I'll keep watch. Our other truck will be here soon."

Tantallon was a child's sand creation made real in the starlight. Below lacy clouds, a curtain wall of red sandstone reached across the headland, a gatehouse at its front. Aini shivered. It was just like the vision. The North Sea hissed at the cliffs beside and behind the old castle.

"That's the Douglas Tower," Neve whispered as they walked through the clipped lawn. Grass snicked at their shoes. She pointed up to the left. "Seven stories. Circular, originally. There's a pit prison down below."

Myles looked at his feet and smiled. "I'll stay near you, Neve. Don't be so nervous. There aren't any Campbells out here as of yet. Plus, we've got two truckloads of black market, gun-wielding rebels on our side even if they do show."

Neve sighed heavily and put her hand in the crook of his arm. "You do know how to sweet-talk a lady." She rolled her eyes.

Taking a breath of the briny air, Aini studied the uneven line of the ruins. A far-off noise hovered in the air like someone plucking poorly tuned guitar strings. Sea birds. Beyond the castle, an island sat in the waves. The moon lit its sloped face as well as the water that rolled around the island's base.

Aini pressed her fingers into her eyelids, picturing Father the last time she'd seen him. His bushy gray eyebrows. His salt and pepper beard. His sparkling, smart eyes surrounded by new wrinkles that made her want to take his hand and ask him about his day. In her mind, he called her *squirrel* again, the childhood nickname she'd earned by climbing the maple in front of the townhouse. Her throat convulsed, but she pulled air in through her nose.

They passed through the time-chewed gatehouse.

"Look for a spiral in the stone," Aini said. The wind was chilly and salty. She pulled her sweater more tightly around her. "I think it was at the base of a wall inside a room. I'm going up."

"I'm coming with you." Thane's voice was low and strained.

A retort rose inside her mouth. She wanted to tell him she was fine on her own, that she'd be all right, but he looked like he needed the company and his worry had just washed his tone in acid.

Myles and Neve walked through the open grass of the courtyard toward the shell of rooms near the sea cliff.

With Thane, grouchy but quiet at her back, Aini found a stone, spiral staircase, much like the one leading to the tower lab. They wound up and up and up. These ruins were huge. Desperation weighed down her shoulders and eyelids.

They reached the summit of the castle. The parapet stretched along the top, a slim road of stone and low wall, overlooking the courtyard. Myles and Neve's silhouettes moved far below Aini, and farther still, the North Sea's waves shifted. The wind tugged Aini's hair, and water crashed beyond and below, its surface as silver as the dress she'd worn to King John's birthday masquerade last year in London. The king had accidentally brushed her arm during one of the dances that night, and his smile had given her chills. Pushing the memory away, she ran a hand along the base of the wall. Thane knelt beside her and did the same.

"When did you start seeing visions?" he asked, his words nearly lost in the wind and his hair flying around his head. He took his glasses from his pocket and slid them on.

"My visions...um...around my sixteenth birthday."

"Does your father know you're a sixth-senser? Tell me the truth. Please." Thane moved into a crouch to examine the middle row of stone.

Touching the gritty top of the wall, Aini stood, stepped closer. Dust and grime from centuries ago fell away where she rubbed the stone.

"I couldn't tell him. I was afraid it would somehow get him in trouble. And I was afraid of what he would think of me."

"So, you lied to keep him safe and to maintain his high regard for you." There was no questioning tone in his voice. "Because you...you love him."

Aini glanced at him out of the corner of her eye. The wind threw his hair sideways. The moon danced over his shoulders, across his glasses, and the line of his crouched shape. What was he getting at?

"I hated hiding my ability from Father," she said. "He would've loved me anyway—I know that now—but he was terrible about keeping quiet when it came to any kind of surprise. At Christmas or with things in the lab. I was afraid kingsmen would question him and he wouldn't be able to keep my secret." She laughed, but it wasn't funny at all. "Guess he kept the secrets he really needed to."

Thane gaze went to hers. "We all have secrets."

Her breath caught in her throat. "I'm not mad at him for hiding his past. Not anymore. He's a good man. He took care of me. Spent so much time and money to travel overseas to visit me every month. He never said a mean word to Mother, even during the divorce. He did what he thought was best for us."

Thane reached out a hand and touched her cheek, and she shivered under the wonderful heat of his skin.

"To have you think like that of me..." he whispered.

The wind gusted, and rain drifted down in a cold, misty sheet, covering the castle grounds.

One hand running along the pitted wall, Aini pulled him to the staircase. Halfway down, they ducked into a small, circular chamber. A glassless window opened to the fields out front and the grassy lawn beyond the gatehouse. With bobbing flashlights, the Dionadair waited in clusters. Her neck and shoulders tensed.

Myles and Neve ran into the room, their hair hanging wet over their foreheads.

"Find anything?" Myles slicked his green spikes back.

Talking over the search so far, the four of them scoured the walls as the rain lashed in through the window. The wind howled once, loud and long, around the ruins.

Vera appeared in the doorway. "We need to go. The wind's rising. There's a doister coming."

"We can't go yet."

"What's a doister?" Myles asked.

"A big storm. A nasty one," Neve said.

Aini's head began to pound. If she didn't find the wall tonight, the Campbells would track her down. The Dionadair would be destroyed, along with her only chance at getting her father back.

"I'll just go look at a few more places." Aini tore past the rest of them and ran down the stairs.

The only room they hadn't collectively checked at all was the rectangular space that used to serve as the great hall, where people had once feasted and drank by the massive hearth.

The roof was long gone. The hall stood open to the churning clouds overhead. Rounded supports protruded from the walls where thick beams once ran side to side. The place looked like the rest of Tantallon, the skeleton of something that had once been powerful, protective, a shield against the storm of armies and intrigue.

With the rain increasing, Aini worked her way to the base of the closest wall. The salty water lashed out, fogged the stones in front of her, and flavored the moisture that ran into her mouth.

Thane ran up, rain streaming down his face and sticking his sweater to his strong chest, revealing the edges of the bag he'd hidden beneath.

"We need to go. The storm is—"

A gust ran fingers through her hair and yanked out her scarlet ribbon. The slip of fabric flew through the storm, catching the diffused moonlight, until it snagged the nearby corner where the back wall and the outer met in a triangle of darkness. She couldn't stand the thought of leaving it out here in the cold rain near the crashing ocean. A hard shiver rocked her and she fought a sob, Father's face in her mind, bleeding and dirty.

She raced to retrieve the ribbon, and crouching, curled her hand around the soft fabric. Her fingers brushed a curving indentation in the sandstone. She pressed a hand fully against the wall.

It was a spiral.

The wind kicked up, and the stone bones of Tantallon's ancient great hall cooled her flesh. Everyone else ran into the great hall and crowded around her. Excitement buzzed through her veins.

A looping shape had been carved into the base of the open room's back wall. She traced the curve and remembered her vision of the Coronation Stone, the one imprinted on the brooch. As her finger dragged into the heart of the spiral, Thane's furrowed brow, the rain falling sideways around him, Myles, Neve, Vera, and the ruined castle walls—it all shimmered and disappeared, leaving the world gray around the edges.

A man's face appeared.

Angus Bethune, the first of the Dionadair.

*Angus raised his chin. His palm lay against the spiral in the wall. Closing his eyes, he pictured the black stone with its metallic flecks. The Coronation Stone. A hollow sat in the stone's center, more circles and spiraling shapes decorating its exterior. Over the stone, a shape came into focus, a black and white space surrounded by churning movement.*

*The island.*

*A bird darted to the crashing sea. The air was thick with briny moisture. A stone building sat against the island's rough terrain. Inside, there was a small, underground room lit by candles. A chapel?* There. Seer. Seer! *Angus called out.*

*The earthen floor of the small room grew hazy, but there, somewhere, was the stone. Sitting, waiting like a beast in hibernation. Power hummed around the ancient throne like the black rock was alive, breathing, ready to strike.* Tear our land from the wrongful king! You are the Seer. You have the gift! *Angus shouted. His words became unintelligible, his brain flying through pictures. Emotions like colors streaked the scene.*

*Murky yellow fear, blue truth, green trust.*

*Faster. Faster.*

A shout tore out of Aini. Thoughts brushed along her mind too quickly like she was running through a forest and any minute she'd slam into a tree. She shook her head, and at last, the vision faded.

As she tilted to the side, nausea squirmed in her middle, but a sense of joy soaked through her, waiting for the sick feeling to pass.

Her hope roared to life.

The man from the vision—Angus Bethune—had been so sure, so very sure, about her role to play as Macbeth's descendant, the Seer. His faith lifted her to her feet. The strength she'd felt in the Coronation Stone poured steel into her limbs and steadied her.

Maybe the Dionadair, with her help, really *could* succeed in their quest to free Scotland. She could find the stone, find the Heir, and take down the Campbells and the king. But before the rebellion, and so much sooner, maybe Father would be in her arms again.

"Aini."

She whirled around and Thane stood there, waiting. The wind whipped his hair, and his eyes matched the tumultuous sea beyond. The darkness that had always hounded his features cleared. He smiled, and her heart surged. It was a real smile, like he somehow realized what this vision had meant to her.

"You truly think this can be done," he said over the weather. "You can change everything."

Myles and Neve stared, wide-eyed. Vera, Dodie, and several other Dionadair surrounded them, awe coloring their faces.

"I...I do," Aini said, shocking herself. For a breath, she imagined a Scotland with a good ruler and a Parliament, a place where people had a voice.

Vera took a step forward and held out a hand. "Let's get you out of this weather, Seer."

The rain unleashed its wrath then and came down in lashing whips. They splashed into the muddy courtyard. The storm nearly obscured the island from the vision—Neve had called it Bass Rock. Aini kept glancing at it as they hurried through the towering gatehouse and sped toward the trucks' yellow headlamps.

The rain tasted bright and salty on her tongue and the world was suddenly sharper. Like everything they'd been through shone in stronger contrast.

CHAPTER 23

REVELATIONS

Back at the Dionadair's barn and underground facility, Aini squeezed rain from her hair. The wind howled through the double doors until Dodie latched them tight.

"Did you see it?" Neve asked. Her clothes hung on her like a wet rag.

"I did," Aini said, turning to Owen, who'd come from the entrance to the tunnels. "It's on Bass Rock, the island off the coast near Tantallon. It's in a chapel. Some sort of buried chapel."

"I know about that place!" Neve said. She began telling Myles about some saint and the history of the island.

Thane came up and took Aini's hands, warming them. Wonder had replaced the darkness in his eyes.

"It's amazing," Aini said. Everyone had gone quiet and turned an ear toward her. "The Coronation Stone has this...power to it." Goosebumps ran over her skin.

A tentative grin spread over Thane's mouth. "I cannot

believe I'm saying this, but if we can get it and find the Heir... things might truly change."

Thane cupped her chin, his eyes light gray and brimming with concern. The circles under his eyes said he needed rest, though he was nearly buzzing with energy. Or was that her?

He leaned in and spoke near her mouth, throwing shivers down her neck and chest and shoulders. "I'm proud of you. None of what I've been worried about will really matter if—"

Owen clapped his hands together once, shattering the moment between Thane and her. "If you'll follow Vera to the sleeping quarters," he said, checking his phone, "she'll find you some dry clothing." He addressed the teeming mass of Dionadair. "Once the storm has passed, we head to Bass Rock!"

As they made their way through the tunnel attached to the barn, Myles whistled a southern colonial tune, punctuated with lines that rhymed with Neve's last name Moore.

"I only wished my sweet faced Neve would give me more, my heart is sore, my Neve thinks I'm a bore, to love me be a chore!"

Thane muttered something about strangling, then looked over his shoulder at the circle of light coming from the main tunnel they'd just left.

"Hey, if this doesn't go the way we want it to or if the Campbells find this place," Thane whispered, his lips grazing Aini's cheek and making her mouth go dry, "eat that tablet I gave you and get Myles and Neve to the truck. Dodie leaves the key in his. Go toward a port city. Get out of Scotland."

Any warmth she'd found faded fast. Her teeth chattered from both fear and her wet clothes. "How can I do that? It'd be—"

"Mr. Moray," Vera said, her voice singsong and falsely sweet.

Aini spent half her time hating that woman and the other half deciding whether she should be her next hero. "It's not polite to share secrets in front of others."

"You need to teach your wandering hands about manners before you can do any preaching on the matter," he spat back.

Myles and Aini laughed as they came to the sleeping quarters.

Vera snorted. "You are a spicy one, Thane Moray." She pointed to a rack of hanging shirts, coats, pants, and dresses at the back wall. "Grab something to wear. All of you."

Securing some dry clothing, Aini and Neve went behind the hanging drop cloth on one side of the room. The guys found their own screened area on the other. Aini pulled a sea-colored long shirt over some dark blue leggings, and after grabbing a pair of unmatching but clean socks, put her damp boots back on since there weren't any shoes available in her size.

Neve threw on a green v-neck T-shirt and some trousers that were several sizes too big. She latched a belt on and found a pair of men's black boots. As she tugged the laces, her copper brown hair fell over her eyes. Aini thought about how much Neve had been through for her and Father.

"Think your brothers are doing all right without you to check up on them?" Aini straightened her heavy hair over her shoulders.

"Suppose they're getting into all sorts of trouble." Neve grinned, but there was a gravity to the look. "Clive's old enough now that he can make sure everyone has food on their plates."

Neve was risking so much. "Thank you for being a great friend. It sounds stupid, but thank you for staying by my side. I couldn't do this without you. Or what you know about Scotland."

Neve raised her head and smiled, her front teeth too large,

but somehow pretty anyway. "Scared as I am, I wouldn't miss this for anything, Aini. Don't doubt that for a second. I have a question though." Aini nodded, and Neve's eyes took on a faraway look as she sat up. "Did you see the Heir in your visions?"

It was a good question. "No."

"Could it be you?" Neve bit her lip.

"I'd know it, wouldn't I?"

Neve shrugged. "It's not like there's anything to go by."

An alarm blared through the room, a shrieking, piercing wail. A cold sweat spread over Aini. She and Neve traded a panicked look and hurried out from behind the screen.

The Dionadair shouted at one another and ran into the tunnel, cocking shotguns and shouting directions.

Hair still dark and lank with rain, Thane and Myles emerged from their own screened spot. Thane wore a slightly baggy pair of brown pants and an ivory shirt that was only buttoned halfway up. Aini noticed he'd removed his silver chain. Maybe he'd lost it. The edge of his secret bag showed.

Dressed in mostly black, Myles hopped on one foot, tying on his second boot.

"Someone has breached their perimeter," Thane said.

The breath went out of Aini.

*The Campbells.*

Thane waved for them to follow him into the tunnel. The lights along the bare rock walls flickered. The alarm screamed, searing Aini's ears.

"Do you think it's the Campbells?" she asked, panting as they ran.

"Well, it isn't Owen's granny coming to call." The orange lighting made him look sick. "Just when I'd thought maybe life could be different," he hissed under his breath.

The entrance to the barn was closed. Owen came flying up from behind, a rifle in his arms. A scream and several loud bangs sounded behind the door. The whites around Owen's eyes were bright in the low light.

"Stay here," he said, jerking the entrance open.

The barn was in chaos.

Faces twisted in anger, kingsmen in Campbell kilts poured in through the double doors. Swords and clubs swung in quick arcs from their hands. Guns fired. The Dionadair swelled and met them with fists and knives flashing. Shots blasted off the barn's towering wood slat walls and rock foundation.

A rush of people flowed out of the tunnel, pushing past and shoving into Myles and Thane. Owen grabbed a man with a dragon tattoo peering out from the neck of his shirt.

"Get the rest of the guns down. Find Dodie," Owen ordered the man. "I'm here!" he shouted at Vera, who'd hitched up the mini skirt she now wore and was scaling the shelves of weapons, reaching for a bronze-handled rifle.

"Then get to it!" she screamed back, her face wild.

Thane spun toward Aini, Myles, and Neve. His voice was loud and steady despite the horror behind him. "Eat the tablet I gave you. Here's more." He fished some from his bag and handed it to Myles. "I'm going to blind everyone else. Though it'll be uncomfortable, you and only you all will be able to see. Keep to the walls and edge your way out the doors. Remember what I told you, Aini."

Her lungs seized up. Noise and fear battled for space in her brain.

Myles's and Neve's gazes followed the action left and right.

People were everywhere.

Thane pulled a flat, glass container and a fold of paper from his hidden bag. He crouched in the corner where the earth met the wall of the barn and tugged the cork of the container out with his teeth.

"This is a spin on Lewis's golden taffy made into a gas. It'll give you time to escape this mess."

Aini looked over his shoulder, her curiosity overpowering her anger that he'd once again gone against her in this. "But it's powder."

"It is until I mix this in." He held up the fold of brown paper. "Then it'll become a gas. It's some of the Cone5 and a five to six ratio of—"

"What about you? You act like you're not running away with us."

"I'll make sure you get out alive."

She grabbed his shirt.

Ignoring her, Thane shook the package into the container and immediately a cloud of yellow snaked from the glassware. He coughed. "I'll find you. Don't worry."

"No way, man," Myles said, bouncing on his toes. "We're not leaving you."

Neve agreed.

Thane met Aini's eyes and something dark crossed the gray of his irises.

"I will worry," she said. "No matter what you have up that sleeve of yours. Why don't you just come with us?" Her heart was breaking. This was supposed to be the beginning of a new life for everyone, not a horrible ending.

Across the barn, near the double doors, a tall man in a muddied kingsman jacket and a Campbell kilt raised a huge handgun.

"Traitors!" the man shouted. A scar puckered his neck like a gruesome smile, but otherwise he was a fairly handsome man with wavy red-blond hair and broad shoulders.

Aini's stomach turned. It was Nathair Campbell, the king's head of security.

"Death to the traitors!" he shouted.

A strangled noise came from Thane's throat. As he stared at Nathair, he fell back and gripped the wall. "It's him."

The vial crashed on the stone, and the yellow haze curled quickly into the air, spreading into the barn. Aini helped Thane away from the smoke he'd created.

Neve gripped Aini's arm hard. "That's him. Chief of the Campbells. Earl of Argyll. The King's Deathbringer."

Myles pulled at them. "Let's go." He looked at Thane. "You're sure about this?"

Thane nodded tersely. "Get Aini out of here. She can't be in the same room as that man."

Aini didn't even get a last look at Thane as Myles dragged them into the barn. There were too many people moving, fighting, shouting, pushing. Thane's chemicals whirled around the room like sickly ghosts. Every man and woman shrieked as it touched their faces. Dionadair and kingsmen alike put hands to their eyes, blinded and running into one another. They struck out with weapons and pulled triggers, some killing and maiming. Swords and axes hit tables, walls, and people before clattering to the floor.

Shaking, Aini took the lead and shepherded Myles and Neve along the left side of the barn toward the fighting training cage near the exit.

At the cage, a kingsman, his eyes rolling as he tried to see past what had to be a blinding, glaring rainbow of colors, swung a club at a Dionadair, way too close to Aini's head. She dodged the thing, the fighting cage's barbed metal biting into her back and her heart pounding.

Through the press of bodies, they eked their way to the double doors and into the predawn light.

Outside, three kingsmen knelt by strange boxes. Their kilts partially blocked Aini's view.

"They say a chemical's been released," the first one said into a walkie talkie, not noticing them. His associates swore and spoke into their phones and to one another. "No one can see," the first one said to them. "That yellow fog—it's screwing with their vision. Call for the false retreat. Then raze the front section." The second man held a black box with a red handle. "Explosion on my count. Are you clear?"

Aini's knees shook. Explosion. They were going to blow something up.

The men shifted as more kingsmen with streaming eyes rushed from the barn, some Dionadair trailing them. Thane's concoction blossomed into the air and dissipated.

"Retreat!" the man shouted as they rushed toward Dodie's empty truck. "Soon as you see the chief clear the entrance, raze the barn."

*Thane is in there.*

Aini ran free of Myles and Neve, with nothing in her mind but buzzing and white and panic, she dove at the man with the black box. She hit him hard, her cheek bruising against his shoulder as more yelling rose around her. Then all the noise and movement was swallowed by a flood of golden light. As she fell to the earth with the kingsman under her, the ground beneath the three-story barn erupted into the air. Splinters big as a man. Foundation stones. Sprays of dirt. Bodies. Everything in sight shot into the dawn.

She landed, ears throbbing, and jumped off the kingsman. Myles was near, on his knees, Neve at his side and lying on her stomach. Her hands shielded her ears.

Surprisingly, most of the barn's other side still stood, but the front area near the doors was nothing more than a pile of rubble overrun with kingsmen and Dionadair, scrambling up to continue their fight or holding bleeding comrades. Moans and screaming came from the rubble as the yellow haze dissipated.

*Thane.*

Aini tore toward the damaged barn.

At the first cluster of wooden debris, a man shouted, "Aini MacGregor!"

She froze.

The man was partially covered in broken wood planks and dirt, his body trapped beneath one of the barn's doors. Reaching from the rubble, his hand snagged her ankle and she screamed, pulling with everything she had. His fingers dug painfully into her boot and the skin underneath. He held on, the scar at his throat vivid despite the mud and dust.

Nathair Campbell.

The man who had led the public execution of rebels last month. The Campbell who seemed to be going mad. The one who gripped his own countrymen by their throats and squeezed money from them and their businesses, who had ordered so many innocents shot to death or imprisoned for life in the famed cells under Edinburgh. The memory of the boy crying on market day blazed through her mind. He'd lost his parents to a ridiculous law about Subject Identification Cards all because of the king and his beast, this man, Nathair.

*And Nathair controls the men who have Father.*

Keeping his hold on Aini and blinking repeatedly, Nathair used his other hand to dig beneath the stone, into his pocket. He tossed something at her. A roll of rag cloth. It fell to the ground at her feet. With Myles and Neve shouting to come on to the truck, she unwrapped the cloth. But she couldn't understand what she was looking at. Flesh. Pale and blue and streaked with blackened blood.

A finger wearing a ring. The MacGregor ring.

Gasping, she dropped it, and the ring fell away from the flesh. A rushing sound filled her ears, bile rising in her throat. She braced herself on a boulder and bent to vomit. It was Father's finger. His. Finger.

The ground dropped away, and she took hold of the boulder with both hands.

"Is he still alive? Is my father still alive?"

"Aye," Nathair hissed, working his way out of the debris to stand.

The earth stopped rushing away and she managed a breath.

"You should look to what side you choose, girl. I don't think you'll enjoy losing." His words rose and fell unevenly, his body swaying and his head cloaked in blood.

"Father," a low voice said.

Nathair and Aini both whipped around.

Thane stumbled out of the boiling mess of fighting and bleeding men and women.

A cool rush of relief ran over Aini. Blood masked the left side of Thane's face. Like a wraith, his cheekbones were sharp in the sunrise, and his eyes were deep and dark, but he was alive.

Nathair held his arms open wide, a twisted look on his face. "Son."

The word cut Aini at the knees.

Shaking, weak, choking, she met Thane's gaze.

Regret blackened the light in his eyes. A shiver rolled through him, and he clenched his hands and threw his head back as a vicious shout of frustration and rage erupted from his throat.

He launched himself at Nathair, fisting his hands in the man's shirt and jerking him roughly. Nathair shoved Thane back, but Thane drove at him again. Shouting unintelligible words, he rained down wild strikes. Tears mixed with the blood streaming over the line of Thane's jaw. His shirt absorbed the wet and clung to his chest.

Aini was frozen. Neve and Myles were suddenly beside her, but she felt no relief. It couldn't be true. She shook, worked air into her lungs. The trees, grass, the mess of the explosion, the people—hurting and shouting—spun once, fast, around her, before she could focus on Thane and Nathair again.

Though he was unsteady on his feet, Nathair dodged most of Thane's blows. Staggering, he ripped a silver chain from his neck. "You left this at the MacGregor house." It was Thane's necklace. "You should not forget who you are, son."

Tearing it from Nathair's large hand, Thane threw the chain to the earth. The silver dropped to the ground like a piece of the morning moon had fallen from the sky.

Aini choked out one word. "Why?"

Nathair smiled. "Because I told him to."

Chest heaving, Thane's rage took him again. He was a lion, his strikes quick, strong, vicious. A hit to his father's stomach. A knee to the groin. Two elbows aimed at Nathair's temples. Nathair's eyes dazed, and he fell at Thane's feet.

Myles and Neve seized Thane by the shoulders and dragged him back a step. His shirt ripped down the back as they pulled him away.

Aini's stomach reeled. Her fingers were numb.

A terrible smile tore across Thane's face. "I'm as terrible as him. As the lot of them."

Jerking away from Myles and Neve, he laughed like a madman, wiping tears and blood from his face. His torn shirt hung loose and showed his shoulder, the tendons and muscles moving beneath his skin as he looked at Father's ring in the mud. He closed his eyes, his black lashes making lines above his cheekbones.

"To think I believed all this could change...I've always been a Campbell." He punched a fist against his chest. "That's all I'll ever be. *Ne Obliviscaris*. Forget Not. That's our dear clan motto. Forget not how we beat you down until you're bleeding and begging to serve us."

He performed an exaggerated bow, almost seeming drunk, stumbling but catching himself on another pile of rock.

"I tried to tell you, Aini. But I should've known. How could you care for a man who has a part in this? I'm a fool. A spy. I'm the worst thing that's ever happened to you."

"No," she whispered. "Bran is working for them, but you, you're my father's favorite, like a son..."

Aini's world fractured into a million pieces. Was anything she believed actually true?

Scooping up his Campbell necklace, Thane rushed toward the damaged fencing surrounding the property. A black horse trapped in the space between a fallen section and a tree shied from him, but he caught the animal and threw a leg over its back.

Myles ran after him. "Thane!"

Thane pushed his heels into the horse. "Yah!" His voice cracked, and he rode toward the dawn's light, the sun making his bare shoulder and tangled hair glow. The horse's hooves kicked up chunks of earth as they disappeared down the road.

The fight went on around Aini. A shot rang out and something stung her ear, but she didn't flinch. Father's finger lay in the grass beside the MacGregor ring.

Myles and Neve put hands under her arms.

Myles pulled Aini toward Dodie's truck. "We have to get out of here."

Neve shuddered. "I never would've guessed Nathair's own son...right in front of our faces. There was something odd about him, yes, but this? I never thought the genius lab rat could be *that* Thane!"

"Wait!" Aini pushed away from them, running to Father's ring. She cupped it in her palm, then returning, clambered into the truck.

Though she'd already played out the vision embedded on the ring, memory brought it back, clear and beautiful and sharp as glass. The vision—a memory so important to Father that it had sunk into his signet ring—had shown the day she was born. Her mother, sweating and smiling, held a red, newborn Aini. She screamed like babies do, her face scrunched in a fierce scowl. Father took her into his arms, his face glowing, and Aini's crying stopped.

Aini suddenly felt far away from where she was. Her mind took her...somewhere else, a place foggy.

White.

Numb.

Then the truck bumped harshly to the right, and the daze slipped away. Myles was behind the wheel, silent and eyes narrowed. Dirt covered Neve's knuckles as she stared out at the road. There was nothing in front of the three of them but ruined plans and the coming crash of grief.

## CHAPTER 24
## CREATURE

Thane slid from his horse under the broad branches and clustered leaves of an English oak, maybe five, six miles from...everything. He was in a bracken and weed-strewn fallow field beside long, flat runs of barley and something green and short. Blood slugged through him as he moved his fingers slowly in and out, fisting and unfisting. Dried red flaked from his knuckles. His father's blood.

Thane's eyelids shuttered closed against the struggling dawn. He pictured a finger in the grass and mud. Stomach roiling, he dragged a hand over his sore face and swollen eyes.

What was wrong with Father? What had they all become? But it was a question he already knew the answer to. They had become people Aini could never forgive. Shouldn't forgive.

Exhaustion lay over him like a lead blanket. His last thought he had before sleep pulled him under was of his mother. Her eyes, pewter like his, always smiled even when her mouth did not. His mother was scarred, her spirit lashed and beaten into submission by a love she shouldn't feel.

Almost every Monday morning of Thane's childhood, his father went to London and his mother took him from their Georgian mansion, Inveraray Castle, and out to the wishing well, hidden among the clean-scented pines and dense oaks outside of town. He remembered reaching a hand toward the arch of carved stone that stood over the sacred spot. The air smelled like it did here in this farmer's field, green and good. She'd picked him up, her hands gentle on his sides. When she nodded toward the spring bubbling from under the earth, he'd made a silent wish that every day would be Monday. Now the king had taken the very day's name away.

His dream came to him then.

It showed his hand, five fingers, then the palm, then closer and closer, until the dips and swirls of his ring finger's print were walls, valleys, canyons. The flesh darkened, blackened, grew sharp and strong, and Thane was lifted by a thundering storm and driven through the curves, flying, rushing, the sound like one thousand drums.

EVENTUALLY, THE SUN'S WHITE LIGHT CHASED THE CONFUSING dreams and tender memories from Thane's mind, and he lifted his aching head, his hand going to his ribs. The dull pain didn't crack him apart like a true break. It only made him slow in rising to his feet. A cut pinched at the side of his head, but it wasn't serious. He pulled a twig from his hair and rolled his tongue around in his mouth. Thirst almost seared away the pain in his body and his heart. Almost.

Past the oak's wide-reaching and dappled shadow, the horse he'd ridden snapped up grass with velvet lips. Bracing himself against the tree, Thane stood. The summer breeze blew across the bare skin of his shoulder. When had he torn his shirt? Everything was a blur of violence. Fists, fury, and shouting.

But it had also somehow freed him.

All his life, a creature with burning eyes and grabbing claws had lived inside him. He'd thought the creature to be a sense of justice. But now, no. He knew better. It was his father's growing need for power, his madness. Nathair had nurtured the creature with nights by the hearth spent repeating why Campbells were special and owed fealty. The creature knew the names of generations of Campbells, MacArthurs, MacIvers, Burnes, and MacConochies, and Orrs. It was well versed in the wrongs done them by the Dionadair. And what Campbells did about it when they found the rebels.

Thane put a hand over his chest. His heart beat slow and sure.

The creature was gone. The crippling fear and anger absent.

He only hoped Mother would understand.

Taking the horse's loose reins, he searched the saddle bag for water, ale, anything to wet the desert of his mouth. A hawk's sickle shape soared high, swooped low to the golden grasses, and rose again to search for prey, ready to strike. Thane's fingers tightened on the reins. The ragged leather twisted in his grip. Even with the creature exorcised, his father would always be there, watching, waiting, wanting.

Mounting the horse, running a hand down the animal's warm, ebony side, he made a promise to himself. A secret promise.

Swallowing disgust with what he had to do, he took off at a gallop toward the road to find a town, a train, any path back to Edinburgh.

CHAPTER 25

MY ENEMY'S NIGHTMARE

Aini sat at a wide table in a stranger's kitchen, looking out the window at a dead tree. Owen had caught up with them on the motorway and detailed the loss of lives, injuries, and how the Campbells had reportedly left the area to regroup, their bruised leader shouting orders to go after his son. A widow—mother to one of the rebels—had offered her house to the Dionadair, so they'd holed up here in borrowed blankets, cots, and hammocks, not far from the site of the violence. They wouldn't be staying for long, Owen had said.

He and Vera were talking to Aini about Thane, his loyalties, and their fears. Really, they were talking *at* her. Toying with the bandage on her ear—it turns out, a bullet had just missed her—she was still processing, picking apart every moment she'd had with Thane.

"But he never told you a thing," Vera said.

Neve was quiet beside Aini, her hand gently perched on Aini's knee. An anchor Aini needed to keep from drifting into swells of hopelessness.

Owen's voice was careful. "And he was responsible for that blinding gas, aye?"

Aini stared out the warped window panes, the dead tree's branches black and twisting toward the sky.

What was real?

Thane had handed her Macbeth's knife with his head bowed in the exact same manner he'd used when conning the female guard at St. Andrews. So that one, that moment she'd thought they'd had, was false. A lie. A stage direction in his play.

But their kiss. That had been real. The blood had risen to his cheeks. And the way he'd looked at her... Not even Nathair Campbell's own master spy and son could fake that. Could he?

The memory of Father's ring and severed finger washed the tree and the window from sight. She put her head in her hands.

Father.

She wanted to drive a knife through Nathair's chest. She wanted to scream, hit, to destroy. Gripping her hair, she stared at the table's deep grain, seeing veins and blood. Anger was more than a feeling. It was a person she'd become.

How could Thane have been part of kidnapping him? The way they'd been in the lab together, trading ideas... Father had loved him like a son.

But he didn't really know anything about Thane.

She'd shared so much about her childhood. Her unjustified anger with her mother. The divorce. How she'd been angry with Father, but how she finally understood his choices. Her parents had been doing what they felt was best for the people they cared about.

Father had lived to make up for what he'd felt was a wrong choice. He'd gone out of his way to visit Aini and her mother in the colonies, month after month, year after year. Every time her mother demanded he reschedule a trip for some invented reason, he went along with it.

Her mother had been trying to protect her. She'd left her new home of Edinburgh to live in the colonies to keep Aini away from rebels and what she viewed as stains in her father's past. She'd endured what Aini had: the pain of not fitting in anywhere.

Aini had tried to keep her sixth sense a secret to protect her father, Myles, Neve, and Thane, worrying they would go to prison just for knowing her. She'd struggled every day not to touch rings, watches, bracelets, treasured books, sentimental gifts at Christmas and birthdays. She'd been called *cold* more than once as she clung to rules and structure to protect herself and everyone around her, to keep from invading their privacy, to shelter them from suspicion if she were ever taken for questioning. She'd held herself back from hugs and close friendships, from spontaneity, to live a safe life.

But while she'd shared her pains and confusion, Thane hadn't told her a thing. She knew about Bran. That awful pub. But that could've been a lie. She didn't even know where Thane was from or who his mother was. And his father...she supposed Thane was from Argyll. If he was the Earl of Argyll's son, he'd grown up at Inveraray Castle, a sprawling estate where he'd have been treated like some sort of Campbell prince. But had he? Pain had always shown in his eyes, a shadow that had haunted him until he'd started to believe Aini really could find the stone and the Heir.

And when Father had spoken kindly to Thane, listening to his hypotheses and working with him, Thane had seemed so unaccustomed to the behavior, so maybe he hadn't been treated like a prince. Maybe Thane had been mistreated growing up. It was a guess she'd made long ago, why she'd never been jealous of their close relationship. Nathair had no doubt expected a lot from his son, educated him, taught him to fight, paid for amazing schooling and fine clothing, but he maybe hadn't loved him in a healthy way. Did that excuse Thane's betrayal?

No. No, it didn't.

Aini pressed her fingers into her eyelids, angry tears burning out as Owen and Vera murmured a blend of kindnesses and opinions. Neve's stillness and quiet comforted far more than anything they could say or do.

Thane had never reported discovering the Dionadair. If he had, his father's presence wouldn't have sparked such surprised rage in him. Thane had fallen against the tunnel's wall, stunned, when they'd first glimpsed Nathair in the barn. The angry side of Aini demanded, *It doesn't matter.* He'd lied, hidden who he was. He'd had so many chances to tell her.

This was how her mother must've felt when she found out Father was working with the rebels. Aini wondered if he'd told her, or if she'd discovered it on her own.

Aini pressed a fist against her chest. It just hurt so much. *I'm sorry, Mother.* She squeezed her eyes shut. If only Aini could've known, realized why her mother had never answered Father's questions with more than a few words, why she handed the phone to Aini immediately when he called. The pain on their faces when they were together—it all made sense.

Now, the kind widow who'd invited the Dionadair in pulled a pot of oniony stew from the stove as a Dionadair with shaggy brown hair ran up to the table.

"Someone's left a package," he said to Owen. "Found it at the end of the road. Near the turn off."

After glancing at the door, Owen looked to Aini, and a frisson of fear jarred her spine. He was thinking the package contained explosives.

During the Campbells' attack, they'd lost five people and

more than twenty were seriously wounded and being treated at an underground hospital near Stirling.

Thane could've reported the Dionadair right after they'd run into them at the club. But he hadn't. The attack on the barn had nothing to do with him, aside from the probability that another Campbell had been watching him, an operative that *did* report everything to Nathair.

Vera threw her legs over the table's rough bench and started toward the door, the kitchen light shining off her midnight hair.

"Wait," Owen said, hurrying to follow.

Aini watched, buttoning and unbuttoning the mandarin collar of her blood-stained, sea-colored shirt. Standing, she tied her hair into a loose bun and put Owen's pencil through it. She ran a hand over her forehead and swallowed, her throat raw from crying on and off. Her phone sat in the waistband of her leggings, still quiet, still with no word from Thane. She wasn't sure whether she wanted a call or not.

Gritting her teeth, she closed her eyes and tumbled questions around her mind. Over and over and over as she trailed Neve to the front room.

One second, her anger with Thane blistered her skin, not caring for any cool reason. The next, she was sad, anxious, longing to have Thane here so they could spill out all their fears and worries and see what withstood the flood.

Two things bore down on her shoulders, heavy and unrelenting. One: Thane was still missing. She had no idea whether he'd go to Nathair, or if he was off on his own, hating himself, or maybe even dead by his own clan's hand for attacking their chief.

The second item that weighted her was that Thane wasn't just the son of a Campbell, which would've been bad enough. Thane was the son of their chief. No wonder he'd never come clean. If Aini hadn't seen his fury after the explosion at the barn, the idea of him going against his own father, a man everyone in Scotland feared now more than ever, would've been very, very difficult to swallow. But the way Thane's eyes had burned with the knowledge that he couldn't change his blood, and had been trapped with his father's mad schemes, had shown her what she needed to know: though he'd started his assigned task—it had to be spying on lab work and developing weaponized candy—as a firm Campbell follower, he'd changed.

*No. Yes. Maybe. No. He was who he was. He lied again and again.*

Owen and Vera had the mysterious package open and inside the door. It was a wooden crate loaded with crumpled newspaper and bags of round beads.

Aini blinked, rolling Father's signet ring around her finger. It clicked against her mother's wedding band. "Those are my father's cherry drops."

Crouching beside the crate, Owen adjusted his round wireframes. "And why are they on our doorstep?"

Vera opened one of the plastic bags and lifted a drop. "What do they do?" She began to pop it in her lipsticked mouth, but Aini knocked it from her fingers.

"Normally, they're aphrodisiacs."

Vera wiggled her sculpted eyebrows and went for another.

Aini put a hand on hers. "Normally. Nothing about right now is normal."

Nodding, she pulled her hand back.

Bending, Aini looked through the crate. Under the five one-gallon bags, a square of lined paper showed scrawled writing. Slanted. Slightly looped. Thane's hand.

She snatched it up and held it under a green glass lamp on a side table, tracing each letter with a fingertip. She could see him in her mind, holding the pen too tightly like he always did, his knuckles white. His tongue touched the inside of his bottom lip as he concentrated. His hair curled slightly around the frame of his glasses.

Neve looked over her shoulder and read the note. She let out a breath. "Aini, you know what this shows."

"What does it say?" Vera said.

Aini had to laugh at herself, her throat tight, because she hadn't even read it yet. She'd only pored over his handwriting, the little bit of him she had there in her hand.

"It says, *If we don't become his worst nightmare, none of us will dream again.*" She shivered. "It's from Thane." She folded the paper into a neat square and cupped it in her palm.

Owen was beside her in a blink, his hand out like she might share the note.

Her mind brought up the memory of Thane's face as he fought his father. Tears dragging through blood. The necklace, thrown to the mud and grass. A wrenching suck of breath as he saw Father's ring on the ground.

"Thane wants us to somehow use these," Neve pointed at the crate, "against the Campbells."

"We can't trust that git," Vera snapped.

Neve glared even though Aini thought Vera was so, so right. "You're not the only one with an opinion," Neve snapped. "You don't even know him. Nathair Campbell is his father! Can you imagine the childhood Thane probably had?"

Owen rubbed his nose, then put his hands behind him. He walked toward the kitchen and back again, giving Neve a look. "Pull the claws back in, Neve. Vera is right and you know it. He's Nathair's own son, for God's sake. We won't trust him. Not ever."

"If Thane had a chance to alter these cherry drops, we should use them." Neve's voice didn't sound like her own, the words cracking like dry branches and whipping around the room. "No matter what you think of him." She glanced at Aini. Neve's eyes flashed with a quiet strength and a silent question. *Do you agree with me?*

Out of the corner of her eye, Aini saw Dodie bend to pick up the drop she'd smacked out of Vera's hand. "Dodie, don't!"

He pushed it into his mouth and chewed. "What's that?" he asked before falling promptly to the pine floor.

They rushed to him.

Vera put his head in her lap and lifted Dodie's eyelid. "Brother!"

Owen tried digging the drop out of Dodie's mouth, but Aini pulled his hand away. "I wouldn't touch the inside of his mouth right now. Not if he bit the candy and released its gooey center," she said, sitting back on her heels.

"They're not aphrodisiacs anymore, and that's for certain," Vera said snidely. "Wouldn't want a man in my bed snoring like this lout is." She pressed a gentle hand on Dodie's cheek and smiled. "But you think he'll be all right, then?"

"I do." Aini hoped. "Thane put a man at the Origin to sleep with something that acted that quickly. Maybe it was the same sort of formula, a sleep agent or some sort of paralyzing concoction."

Owen called three men over, who took Dodie away. "Watch over him," he called out as Dodie's caretakers disappeared down the dark hallway. "Ring me if he seems troubled at all."

They resumed their spots at the kitchen table. The room smelled like stew and the hot lemon water the old woman had used to clean the wooden surfaces.

Leaning forward, Owen folded his hands. A new scab covered three of his freckled knuckles, but the lean muscle and taut tendons seemed to be working fine.

"Why do you believe Nathair's son—"

"Thane."

Owen pressed his lips together. "Why would *Thane* send us a crate of weaponized candies?"

"Because he's on our side," Vera said, oddly quiet.

Owen probably looked as surprised as Aini.

"Exactly." Neve crossed her arms.

Vera shrugged and picked at a nail. "Neve is right. The thing didn't explode on us, and he left that note. The only thing that makes sense is that the lad is as Neve claims. A good man. A man for Scotland. A man for the Dionadair." She paused, pondering something. "I saw a golden thread between our Seer and him at the Waymark Wall. Sparkled like pure gold. I'd thought it was only because of who you are to Scotland," she said, looking at Aini, "who you are to him, to everyone, but now I think…I think it's because he loves you."

*He loves you.* Aini's hand went to her chest.

Here was truth: it didn't matter what Thane had or hadn't done. She cared for him. Her heart couldn't be bothered about evidence. It raged, beating for him and nothing else mattered.

She was an idiot. She could never forgive him. She was doomed.

"I don't trust him," Owen said.

Aini fisted her hands on the table. "Me either."

Neve inhaled and exhaled slowly. "He gave us this gift, this weapon to use for our side."

Owen looked over his glasses at Aini. "I thought you wanted nothing to do with such a thing. You were completely against using your father's creations to fight."

Aini swallowed, her mind and heart warring. "I don't. But at least they don't kill anyone. They're not so bad, I suppose. Unless this is a trap Thane has set."

Vera snorted. "Oh, so it's all well and good for the Campbells to off our lot, but killing them would be bad?"

A bitter taste covered Aini's tongue. Her head pounded. She wanted Thane here, to ask him questions. No, she wanted him gone so he could never lie to her again. Her thoughts whipped through her head, beating her with stinging truths and unbearable feelings. "I'm going to bed."

Vera opened her mouth, but Owen gripped her wrist and shook his head. She settled down as Aini and Neve stood.

"I suppose you need some rest, Seer," Vera said without any vinegar.

"We can talk when you're ready," Owen said as Aini and Neve walked toward the hallway.

"Fine." Aini's legs were jelly. She felt like she had sand in her eyes and down her esophagus. "Give me four hours. Then I'll be up and ready."

"Five."

"Okay."

"Okay," Vera said back in a faked northern colonial accent like Aini's.

∽

After washing her face in a big, white porcelain bowl and doing her very best not to disturb all the other sleepers in the front room, Aini sat on her assigned cot. Neve snored lightly two beds down, blanket tangled in her legs already. Aini's pillowcase had a foul, brown stain so she flipped it.

A square of paper the size of her thumbnail flittered to the floor.

Across the room, Myles snorted in his sleep and she jumped. Heart racing, she picked the paper up. This wasn't Thane's writing. It was blocky and full of sharp edges. She squinted to read the tiny print.

*We'll trade your father for the stone's location. All offenses wiped from the records. Meet at the bend in the road. One hour. It can be over tonight. Done.*

Her heartbeat was loud enough to wake everyone. She pictured Father reading Robert Burns by the fire, his salt and pepper beard illuminated by the flames. She imagined him being hit across the face and dragged like a criminal from the MacGregor townhouse steps.

Sliding the note into her bra, she lay down, eyes wide open.

A Campbell operative had sneaked into the widow's house, past the guards, through the hammocks and cots, and somehow found her pillow.

They'd known exactly where she was going to sleep.

The note's words ate at her. *It can be over tonight.* She took a slow breath. Another. She could have Father safe in her arms, could see if he was recovering from his awful wound, could go with him back to Edinburgh and lock the door on all of this.

On all these people.

But five people had given their lives for her, for this mad quest. More would probably die from their injuries. Nathair might agree to protect her and her father, but what about Myles? Neve? Owen and Vera and Dodie? If he knew she was here, he knew they were as well and was most likely assembling another attack right this second.

She rolled onto her side and pressed a fist against her mouth. Another slow breath.

In. Out. In.

Then she climbed out of her cot and headed for the door.

Her fingers rubbed together, remembering the feel of Father's wool suit jacket as he walked with her to the train station. She inhaled, thinking of his soap and shoe polish scent. She bumped a cot as she grabbed the side door's handle. The tenant shuffled in her sleep and drew her knees up under a thin blanket. Aini opened the door and walked into the pale light of a Scottish summer night.

A guard with wide-set eyes adjusted the black gun at his belt. "Do you need something, Seer?"

"Just...need some air. I'll be right back."

She was only going to talk to the Campbell messenger. If they had Father, if she could just see him for a minute... Her boot hit a dark spot in the dirt drive, and she stopped.

Blood.

It was from earlier when they'd moved a man still bleeding, a man who'd missed the truck to the safe hospital. She remembered him from the sleeping quarters in the hillside. His white mohawk hair style had contrasted with his quiet, polite smile.

What was she doing? If they had Father there, they'd only use him against her. To murder her friends and the rest of the Dionadair, the people who risked everything to fight against Nathair's mad quest for control.

Even if the Campbells did release her father, were he and Aini supposed to go back to their lives with the knowledge that the kingsmen could scoop them up at any minute and put them to death for treason or whatever infraction Nathair cared to invent?

Aini looked up. The stars shimmered, fighting to shine in the fading blue sky. Before Thane, before the slaughter, before meeting the Dionadair and seeing their passion, she could've made peace with a life lived in determined ignorance. Safety for safety's sake. A quick memory of the vision she'd seen in Thane's necklace poured over her thoughts. The cold edge to his father's movements, the pain in his mother's face, the twisted loyalty Thane felt as a child.

Aini couldn't allow Nathair to win. Not this time. No matter what.

Father wouldn't want her to fight. He'd left this life to keep her in his life, to try and make amends with her mother.

Dizzy from lack of sleep, and the pull and stretch of fear, she tugged her hair free and let it drop over her shoulders. Taking a shuddering breath, she raised her hands to the sky and crossed her thumbs. Maybe the Campbell messenger would see her and know her decision.

She wanted the Scottish people to be free from Nathair. She wanted her father to be free from Nathair. She wanted Thane to be free from Nathair.

Back at the farmhouse, she nodded once to the guard and went inside.

Owen was waiting beside her cot. "So, you're finally ready."

"I am," she said, her blood hot in her veins.

## CHAPTER 26
## IF ONLY FOR A FEW MORE MINUTES

Under a flint gray sky, five Dionadair trucks shed their hiding places on the old woman's farm.

"If it doesn't confuse them—though I think it will—it'll surely keep them busy," Owen said, helping Aini brush straw from a truck's hood.

Aini bent her head and climbed inside. Myles and Neve went around and scooted across the seat. Vera and Dodie sat up front with Owen.

The first truck to leave, recently tarped and covered in branches behind the barn, headed to the townhouse to see if any Campbells were stationed there. Another Dionadair vehicle, that had shared the barn with a dozen operatives and five cows, drove south as a mere distraction. Maneuvering out of a struggling orchard, a third truck carried the Dionadair's finest fighters toward the Campbells' holding cells beneath the Signet Library in Edinburgh's Old Town, just down from the townhouse. They were going after Father.

Aini put a hand over her aching heart and said a silent prayer.

*Let him be okay. Let this all work out. Please. Let me have my only family back again.*

That wasn't quite right though. She had more than her father. Her friends had become family too. Myles and Neve sat beside her in the cabin's back seat, their faces pinched with worry. Aini laid her cheek on Myles's shoulder, breathing in his paint and cotton smell. He patted her hand and Neve leaned over. She gave Aini an encouraging smile, her front teeth over her lip.

Their truck, and the one going with them, bumped out of the farmhouse's dirt drive and aimed at North Berwick.

They were headed for the stone.

"When do you think we'll hear from the Signet cells team?" Aini took a small bite of another of Myles's quietly procured apples. A real breakfast wasn't really happening on a day like this.

Vera sipped an aromatic dark roast from her travel coffee mug and answered for her brother. "We'll hear from them when there's any development."

Myles picked at some paint under his thumbnail. "As in, when they find Lewis?"

"The poor man." Neve looked out the window.

Aini flicked a glance at Myles and forced another bite of the tart apple down. "Yes, when they find him. If they fail, the Campbells aren't going to let them give us a ring to chat."

Neve made a little noise and Myles shut his eyes.

Wishing for a message from Thane, Aini took her phone from the wide, military belt she'd borrowed from Vera. It had a good sized pocket and a place for the Macbeth knife. She felt better with the weapon at her side even though Owen had only given her two, one-hour lessons on the ways to use it yesterday. She'd probably hurt herself more than any attacker.

But at least she wasn't going down without shedding some enemy blood.

Rolling hills, clusters of painted buildings, and roads smaller than the one they were on made up a patchwork of faded green, white, and black beyond the truck's windows. The landscape had probably changed little since Angus Bethune set this trail of artifacts, guided by Macbeth's ghost. The roads, of course, were different. The billboards too. But the growing things were most likely much the same and the lay of the land.

"We have a tail," Vera said, leaning over Owen and looking at the side mirror.

Owen slowed and moved into the next lane on the wide motorway. Myles, Neve, and Aini moved to see. In Owen's mirror, a black sedan nosed out of the mild traffic and took a place three cars behind the truck of Dionadair traveling with them.

"They've been with us since we entered the motorway." Vera bent and came up with a pistol. She cocked it, and Aini's heart clicked like it was preparing itself too.

Her hands began to sweat. She hoped it wouldn't come to a battle. She didn't want to see more blood. Bile rose in her throat. The metallic smell of broken people still haunted her. Surely they could do this without anyone else getting hurt. Maybe Nathair Campbell would realize what he was doing wasn't going to win him more power, that the Dionadair would always find a way to protect their loved ones from his ruthless plans.

Passing through the small, cobbled town of North Berwick, they approached the docks. Boats, red and white, bobbed in the choppy water along the rugged coastline.

Myles, Neve, Dodie, and Aini followed Owen, Vera, and ten other Dionadair heavies down the long, wooden dock to a middle-sized fishing boat. A gust of wind blew across the Firth of Forth, a slice of the North Sea, and sprayed Aini lightly with salt water. Eyeing their boat's tall mast and the netting strung along the side, Myles leaped onto the craft and helped Neve board. Aini grabbed the side of the boat as it dipped in the water. She jumped onto the deck with fairly steady legs, but her mind was still with Thane and wondering whether they'd been followed.

Dodie started the boat's engine as Vera and Owen untied their lines from the dock. They started into the leaden slab of ocean, Neve's hair and Aini's tangling together in the wind. Aini pulled her borrowed, light wool sweater higher at the back of her neck. The red fabric was soft under her fingers and she wondered who had originally owned it. Were they dead now? And how did they die? Or was this simply a loan from Vera or another Dionadair, maybe one of the operatives who'd volunteered to drive the distraction truck in the opposite direction?

Myles rubbed a hand over Neve's back and Aini's. Aini smiled, and he gave her a wink. Half of her wished they weren't there, but the other half was so glad they were. She'd told them about the Campbells' offer and filled them in on Thane's message too. They had a plan for those cherry drops that had put Dodie down for four hours. She didn't like it, but it was better than having a bloody shoot-out, because every single Campbell could have a gun. The Dionadair only had as many as they could scrounge from the black market. The king was a much better provider.

Promising rain, a blue fog curled around the rocky cliffs of Bass Rock Island as they approached its southern side. White plumed gannets soared above, every so often tucking their ebony-tipped wings and diving from impossible heights into the water like spears thrown from heaven.

As the boat sidled into a small, walled-off harbor, a mother seal hissed like a banshee. Dodie stood with one foot on the prow, ready to throw a rope around a weather-beaten post.

Looking through the salt-crusted windows of the cabin, Owen lifted the lid of a storage trunk and removed three hunting rifles, one hulking shotgun, and a few shovels. He handed them out to Vera and the other Dionadair before they tied up and climbed out of the craft.

A modern staircase made a jagged line up the face of Bass Rock Island. A lighthouse rose like a white mushroom from the blackened decay of a former fort, and a rectangular stone building perched to the left, about halfway up. Plants reached over its moss covered walls and through its missing roof. The empty, round window on the end reminded Aini of the Waymark Wall's vision.

"That ruined stone building is the chapel." Neve pointed, then grabbed a tire secured to the side of the boat to steady herself as she disembarked after Myles. "St. Baldred's. It was built on top of his monastic cell in 1542, if I remember right."

Anxiety tremored through Aini's limbs as she gripped the worn edge of the boat and made her way onto the dock. The stone could be right there.

"So," she said and coughed as they started up the rough stairs, "you agree that this is the place to look."

Neve nodded. "What you described, the hollowed-out chapel and the earthen walls...it says monk's cell to me. I've studied a great deal of history."

"As if we could ever be ignorant on that fact," Myles said, giving her a gentle elbow.

She smiled and pulled her sleeves over her hands.

"I just wish I had your faith," Aini said, hurrying to catch up with the Dionadair, who'd almost made it to the rectangular chapel ruins.

Dodie held a shotgun over one shoulder and a shovel over the other. Vera sauntered up the stairs with a rifle tucked behind her arm. Holding his own firearm, Owen kept checking on Myles, Neve, and Aini, his glasses reflecting the scant light.

Gannets, yellow-tinged heads tucked against the weather, nested close enough that Aini could've touched a chick's fuzzy white crown if she'd wanted to.

Myles clicked his tongue. "What'll these crazy Dionadair folks do if the stone roars for one of us?" He ran fingers upward through his hair, making it stand up like grass. His gaze landed on the back of Vera's head, his eyes worried.

"There's only one written record mentioning the roaring and the curse," Aini said. Neve had told her about it.

"What curse?" Myles asked.

"It's pretty vague." Her legs ached from the steep stairs. "Neve, didn't you say the record mentioned that anyone who went up against the true Heir to Scotland's throne—meaning the one who makes it shout or roar—would have some sort of punishment?"

"The history books make no mention of the curse." Neve kneeled to retie her boot. "But the texts on legends and myth give an archaic, brief description. It's the power of the old to protect their own, or something of the sort." She straightened and they continued on.

A cold breeze floated through Aini, raising bumps along her forearms.

Neve crossed herself and said something in Gaelic.

A whisper tickled Aini's ear, and she heard something that sounded like her name. Her palms tingled. "Did you hear that?"

"No, but I doubt the message was for me, Seer." Neve

frowned at the air around them. "And I think you can add Ghost Talker to your sixth sense resume."

Myles looked from Aini to Neve, to the Dionadair, then shivered violently.

*Yes*, Aini's mind said. Neve was right. She'd heard words in Greyfriars kirkyard. Whispers had followed her when she toured the old battlefield of Culloden with Father as a child.

"But everyone hears ghosts a little bit."

"Aye, but only Ghost Talkers can hear all of it and understand the meaning." Neve swallowed and kept her eyes on her feet.

Neve had been fine, excited even, about Aini's Seer ability, but this... "Why do the spirits make you so uneasy?" she asked Neve.

"It's like having a multitude of stalkers, isn't it?" Neve slowed her pace. "You'll hear them whether you want to or not. They can follow you anywhere."

Myles grimaced. "They can? Like even into the toilet?"

Neve scowled at him. "You are a piece of work, you know that?"

"A fine piece." He winked and she rolled her eyes.

Aini's thoughts swamped their conversation, muffling everything else. She hadn't had any trouble with ghosts trailing her so far. Would she now that she'd begun to really use her sixth sense? Would it all grow stronger? Become even more problematic?

The path went left and led to a view over the wide waters of the Firth of Forth, back toward Tantallon. Red against the plumes of cloud and mist, the castle ruins where Aini had found the Waymark Wall seemed to hang on the edge of mainland Scotland. Under the Douglas tower, grass lay in patches on the northern side of its rocky seat over the shoreline.

They neared the chapel ruins, and a gannet flew from the

space where the roof used to be. Aini leaned back to watch it disappear into the cloudy sky, almost wishing she could escape along with her.

Owen and his band stopped. Some brows were furrowed with curiosity. Vera wore a challenging look, like she wanted Aini to prove her status as the Seer. Dodie twisted his hands around his shovel's wooden shaft. The scent of green things and the tang of a coming storm cleared Aini's head.

Lightning blinked, far off, and she headed into the former chapel. Thick grass caught her boot as she moved toward the center of the hollowed out structure. Untangling herself, she said, "We need to get into St. Baldred's cell." She pointed down. "It's here. I...think."

Everyone with a shovel took up digging into the weeds and earth. Myles shed his shirt on a nearby sapling growing in what used to be the aboveground chapel's floor. Aini couldn't seem to stop praying silently.

∽

After an hour of taking turns with the shovels, they found a slab of rock.

"I've found it!" Dodie jabbed his shovel underneath the hard surface.

With help, he wedged the slab up. Squirming creatures and musky-scented ground fell away from the edges. Dodie and Owen pulled the slab to the side, and it thudded to the grass near their dirt-caked boots. Owen rolled his sleeves higher, the storm lifting a few of the red curls on his head, and wiped his face on an arm. A square of black yawned where the covering had rested. Aini hugged herself as Dodie directed his flashlight into the hole to show a set of earthen stairs leading into darkness.

"I'll go first," she said, nodding thanks as Dodie handed her his flashlight.

The gathering steel clouds argued and sent a blast of thunder over them. A movement at the chapel's door made Aini pause. Owen said something sharp. All the Dionadair, except Dodie, Vera, and him, disappeared over the walls and into the tangled brush and waving trees surrounding the chapel.

Aini's skin went cold. "What is it?" She looked from Owen to the others. Dread climbed onto her back, a heavy, clinging thing.

In the gloom and kicking gusts of wind, Campbells poured through the opening wearing their kingsmen jackets, muddied boots, and bright blue, green, and black Campbell kilts. Next to a beast of a man wearing a flat cap, Bran and Thane appeared.

Aini's heart hung useless in her chest.

Thane wore the same kilt as the other Campbells. His face was unreadable. Bran's eyes were slightly closed and the corners of his mouth turned down. Wearing plain trousers, he didn't seem to belong. What were they doing here? Was there a plan they had in mind or had they simply returned to following Clan Campbell orders?

Lightning washed the clouds and the coming storm boomed, almost covering the sound of guns being cocked and shouts of warning from both sides.

Neve spoke in Aini's ear. "He's not with them. Remember that. He has some reason for being here, dressed like that."

Myles took a step closer. The saint's cell at Aini's back breathed ancient air.

"This is not your business, Campbells," Owen said to Thane and the big man.

The man laughed. "Now that our good earl is at home

mending," his eyes cut to Thane, "everything in Scotland is my business, Dionadair. My name is Rodric Campbell and I'm leading the clan. I speak for Nathair."

Rodric looked at Aini like she was something dangerous. Probably the same way she'd been looking at him. Like if he stared long enough, he'd glimpse claws at the ends of her fingers or horns coming out of her head. He crossed himself. She glared at his hands. They'd killed people, she was sure of it.

"Seer." He spat and adjusted his flat cap. "The stone rests somewhere down in that hole, aye?"

"I'm not telling you anything, kidnapper, murderer."

She felt Thane's gaze on her. She glanced at him, but his blank face told her nothing. He wore what the rest of them did, a black kingsman jacket and the Campbell kilt, his muscled legs showing above his boots.

Rodric's lip curled. "You are as naive as they come, Seer." He turned to Thane. "Bring the chemist."

Myles caught Aini's arm as her knees gave out.

Thane nodded obediently and left through the arch.

Owen looked to Aini, and she pulled her arm gently from Myles and stood on her own. Owen gave her an almost imperceptible nod and trained his gaze on Rodric again.

"I suggest you lower your weapons before anyone gets themselves hurt," Rodric said.

None of the Dionadair lowered anything.

Thane returned, gripping a hooded man's sleeve.

Father.

Aini realized she'd yelled his name. She closed her mouth, feeling all the blood drain from her cheeks. His head was covered in a burlap bag, his hands were bound with twine, and a dirty bandage covered the hand now missing one finger. Rodric took a silver pistol from another man and pressed it against Father's leg. Aini's stomach rolled.

"Aini," Father said. His voice was Christmas morning, oatmeal with honey, warmth and safety and promise. Tears leaked from her eyes, not caring at all that she wanted to appear as a leader and failed.

"If I shoot him here," Rodric said, his knuckles white as the blink of lightning overhead. "He'll die slowly."

Dots floated in front of Aini's eyes. She jumped in front of Owen and the others, and pushed their rifle barrels down.

"Here," Rodric aimed at Father's gut. "Well, let's just say he won't like how that one goes. And neither will you, Seer, considering the shade your face has taken on. I did give you a chance to do this a nicer way."

Vera and her brothers flicked a glance at Aini. She hadn't told them about the message under her pillow. Only Myles and Neve.

Aini cleared her throat and traded a look with Thane, whose hair curled into the wind and whose eyes matched the rising storm.

Did he have a plan? How many different ways could this go?

He pursed his full lips and tilted his head a little, just a small movement that seemed to say *It's your decision.*

She'd known this outcome was a possibility. That if the Edinburgh team couldn't secure Father, and the Campbells found them here, her father and the rest of them would be at the Campbells' mercy—a thing no one seemed to think existed. But she couldn't just give the word to fight and throw Father's life away. She couldn't do it. Not like this. Not unless there was no other way to go.

"I don't even know if the stone is in there." She pointed to the rectangular square of black in the ground.

Rodric's eyes narrowed. "Then take a peek, aye?"

His hand shook. He was scared of the stone, wanted nothing to do with it. How could they use that fear?

"Fine. But my father stays whole and alive."

"Or what?" Rodric laughed again.

She gritted her teeth and Thane closed his eyes, one hand still holding Father's arm. The big, horrible bully was right. She had nothing to hold over him if the stone was here. He could take it and, as Owen explained, destroy it and ruin Scotland's chance to find the one meant to rule, the one the curse would protect, the one person who could fight the Campbells and the king and their cruelties.

Strangely, Aini wished she could hear a spirit's voice, something to encourage her to move forward, a word saying everything would somehow work out. But the only cool wind to blow across her face came from the storm that quickly approached over the hills and sea water.

To keep Father alive, if only for another few minutes, she turned, walked over to the earthen stairs, and descended into the ground.

## CHAPTER 27
## AND THE EARTH TREMBLED

Aini's heart slammed against her chest as she made her way down the stairs. Clicking on the flashlight Owen had given her, she breathed in the smell of wet dirt. The side of the chamber was smooth stone and dirt. Someone, presumably Baldred, had rubbed the earth's body to a level, sloping shape, creating a domed cavern. In the damp air, the light painted the long room the pale shade of bones and the dusky blue of bruises. Shapes and shadows moved in the corners. The stone? Other things Baldred kept here? Ghosts?

"Wait," a deep voice said from the top of the stairs behind her.

Her pulse surged in her throat. She spun and shone the light upward. Thane stood there, a tattooed hand on the wall as he climbed down, his kilt swinging as his knees moved. A prickling sensation spread across her back, a mix of fear and desire, her blood glowing in her veins.

She took a tentative step. No one stood directly at the entrance behind him.

Thane ran a hand through his hair as he studied her face. "Rodric sent me down here. Doesn't seem to care much if either one of us dies from whatever horrible thing he thinks will happen. But...he can't hear us now."

Aini's lungs wouldn't expand. Her throat wanted to scream at Thane. Her arms longed to pull him to her.

He took a step. "Aini, I don't know how to tell you, how I...I know you hate me and you've every right to feel it, I—"

"Don't explain. Just apologize." Anger and the pain of betrayal heated her skin and thinned her voice.

"I'm sorry." His eyelashes shaped black rings around his stormy eyes. Mist dotted the edges of his glasses. A jagged crack marred one lens.

Without realizing what she was doing, Aini touched his face. It was slightly stubbled and warm. His lips parted. "I don't hate you," she said, swallowing confusion and wonder and fear. "I should. But I can't seem to do it. You had better be done with lying." Tears heated the corners of her eyes.

Sighing, he covered her hand with his much larger one. "I should've just told you. I should've never obeyed my father as long as I did." Dropping his hand, he turned toward the stairs and his fingers curled into fists. "I have no excuses."

"You aren't back on their side. You're here..."

"So I could follow them to you. To unhinge their plans. To work from the inside one last time."

"Why did they take you back? You fought your father, their leader. How did you make them trust you again?"

Thane stared at the wall, beyond Aini's head. His lips were pale and bloodless. "I did something—" He squeezed his eyes shut. "They had to see me do...I did a horrible thing."

Aini didn't want to know. She'd had enough of this. If Neve trusted him, if her own heart trusted him now, maybe that was enough. She laid a hand on the drape of soft wool tartan over his jacket, waist to his shoulder, and kept one eye on the cell's opening. Why did she want so badly to forgive him?

His father was a monster, a murderer, and a liar. He was obsessed with power, mad, a man who didn't care about the people who he was meant to lead and protect. Thane couldn't possibly respect the man's decisions, his clan's decisions. He had to see how wrong Nathair had been for so long. Especially after he'd executed those rebels and sixth-sensers without even the ruse of a trial citizens were supposed to get. It was plain; there was nothing anyone could say to defend his horrifying abuse of power. Why had it taken Thane so long to see it and act against it?

But Nathair was also Thane's father, the most important man in his life so far, the one who'd been there since he was born, at every milestone, there for every decision. Nathair, head of Clan Campbell, had been there when Thane had learned to walk, talk, to ride a bicycle, maybe, and a horse. Maybe the man had taught him to drive. It was a lifetime of habit and a twisted normalcy.

She assumed Thane had fought hard against the normal drive to stay devoted to one's father. In some ways, he had gone against Nathair.

It couldn't have been easy to go against your own father. It would be heart-breaking, frightening, overwhelming.

"Get on with it!" one of the Campbells shouted down, fear of the stone soaking the voice.

Aini's father had sided with the Dionadair and she'd still followed his trail. Granted, she now believed the rebels were the answer for Scotland's problems. Or, at least, the start of a powerful conversation between the people and those who ruled them. If Father had been on the wrong side of things, how far would Aini have gone along with him? If he thought what he was doing was right, it would still be near to impossible to cut him out of her life. If he was mad like Thane's father surely was, it would feel even worse. The urge to talk him out of his madness, his wrongdoing, would be hard to turn away from. The desire to do as best she could to smooth the situation would be a powerful thing.

She'd never truly understand what Thane was dealing with, how it felt, but one thing was certain—it had to be truly terrible.

His light eyebrows drew together. The crack in his glasses blinked in the uneven light.

"I forgive you," she whispered. Her chest ached with the truth and pain of it. "I know you're with us now."

He swept her wind-tangled hair from her cheeks and cupped her jaw in his warm, calloused hands. "I am with you. I don't know what we're to do now, but I'm with you and Lewis and the foolish Dionadair all the way now."

Her chest pressed against his as they breathed the same air, warm and getting warmer. They'd been through so much that no matter what was going on, she wanted so much to disappear into the brush of his thumb over her lip, the touch of his mouth, the hard lines and muscle of his body leaning into hers.

"Aini, I've been so..." He dipped his head and lightning flashed close, thunder ramming through the space and making them pull apart.

But she had to touch him, to know he was all right. She had to feel those lips on hers.

Lifting onto tiptoe, she tugged him to her, and kissed him hard. He started to draw her into his arms, began to say something, but a strange hum from the back of the cell had her dragging him farther in. The flashlight ghosted over the walls and the shapes toward the back.

"Do you feel that?" Thane asked, rubbing a hand over his arm.

A buzz ran over her skin like electricity. Everything else was forgotten. "Yes."

A wide, wooden chair squatted along the wall. The seat section, mostly disintegrated, had fallen to the earth below support frame. A table with roughly shaped, square legs sat beside it.

The hairs on the back of Aini's neck stood on end. "Either we're about to be hit with lightning or that's…"

And there, in the very back of the saint's cell, black and covered in carved spirals, was the Coronation Stone.

For a breath, Aini's heart stopped.

The ancient royal seat was really here. She'd found it. Her pulse stamped against her wrists as her heart started up again, loud in the dirt-walled chamber.

The white-blue of the flashlight illuminated the carved swirls and circles in the stone's surface. Made of rock dark as the night sky, the stone stood hip-high and looked like a shapeless hand, curved and hollowed to serve as a seat.

"The carvings," Thane whispered, "the swirls, they remind me of my dream."

She glanced at him.

"Ever since I was a wean," he said. "I've dreamed of my fingerprint. The pattern grows dark like…like rock. It's…it's the stone I've been dreaming of."

Shock held her as she took a step toward the ancient artifact. "Then you're a Dreamer, Thane." She felt like she was in a dream now. "You have a sixth sense. All this time, you've had one too."

The stone heated the air. Waves of its buzzing energy filled the cell. The power hummed in Aini's fingertips and through the blood pulsing in her veins.

They stood beside the Coronation Stone, close enough to touch. Shivers flew up her back.

As a Seer, she wanted nothing to do with touching the thing. She could get lost in the centuries of emotions embedded on the stone. Her hand was wet with the air's moisture and her own perspiration, and the flashlight tried to slip from her fingers. She gripped it tightly.

A wash of close lightning brightened the entrance to the chamber.

Thane's whole body leaned forward, toward the stone, his eyes wide. "My God," he said reverently.

Before he could touch it, he pulled his hands back and exhaled slowly. He studied the bare skin below his rolled up and muddy sleeves. Goosebumps raised the blond hairs on his forearms.

"He—Rodric—he," Thane said, his voice flat, "he wants you to touch the stone. He wants to know what you see."

Aini's shivers rose again and spread so that her skin matched his. "What about the curse? What if it's more dangerous than we think?"

His eyebrows lifted, but his mouth still turned down at the corners. "It won't hurt you. The curse will only hurt those who go against the Heir. I'll do it first. Or together. We'll do it together."

Thunder growled outside, and rain lashed through the opening.

Someone outside shouted, and Rodric's order to one of his men echoed into the chamber. Then Rodric himself pounded down the stairs. He pulled his flat cap lower to hide his eyes, then motioned to the stone with a handgun.

"Get on with it." He stepped toward Aini.

"You're afraid of the stone, aren't you?" Aini said quietly, watching his shaking hand and the gun gripped in his meaty fingers.

Thane glared. "Rodric, I—"

"I knew you hadn't gone back into the fold," Rodric spat. "You worthless traitor. Rabbie believed you. But me?"

Thane got between Aini and Rodric. "I'll die before I let you touch her again."

"Still angry about the fun in the vaults, aye?" He snorted. "Save your hero crap for a girl who's not good as dead." He raised the gun.

Realization lit Aini's memories of the Edinburgh vaults. Rodric had hit her in the vaults. It hadn't been a mugger. It'd been this older Campbell, who obviously had some further conflict with Thane.

Thane cut him with a string of Gaelic words.

Out of the corner of her eye, she saw Thane reach across the stone. She twined her fingers in his. Lightning poured white and blue into the room.

"For Lewis," Thane whispered. "He'll kill him if we don't do this. We'll do this, then figure out what to do."

Aini nodded. "For Father."

She slammed their linked hands onto the humming stone.

Wind blasted around them. It kicked dirt into the air, knocked the flashlight to the ground, pressed Thane's kilt against his legs, and turned his jacket collar up. The earth rumbled, shook, and the supernatural storm tossed Aini's hair around her head.

A sound like a lion's roar vibrated from the stone and smashed against her eardrums.

The stone chilled Aini's palms, and a vision wiped the cell's close quarters from sight.

*A whirlwind of colors—orange and green and blue and gold and iron and bronze—spun through the air around the stone, slowing to become pictures. Men in all kinds of patterned clothing—white tunics, plain shirts and dark cloaks—touched the stone, then sat and raised their eyes to their people.*

Voices echoed in her mind, a tangle of sounds she didn't understand. Then, slowly, the words crawled out of the noise, clear as a bell.

*The spirits' mouths moved, calling out their names. Kenneth Mac Alpin. Donald I. Constantine. Malcolm. Dubh and Culen. Macbeth. They were bearded and old, wide eyed and young, muscled, thin. Every one sat tall, straight, and possessed the fire of purpose in their eyes.*

They were ghosts. And they were kings.

Aini yanked her and Thane's hands from the stone. As quickly as the tempest had begun, the chamber quieted. Her hair fell back onto her shoulders, and Thane's collar settled against his neck. From outside, lightning flashed.

Both of them were in a terrible situation. But one, *one* of them was directly, inseparably lashed to a political storm to rival any in their country's history. A tempest of powerful men and women, desperate to curl hands around money, people, farmland, cities, towns, and businesses.

She spoke first, her chin shaking. "You're the Heir. The wind and that noise, it all started when your hand touched the stone." She didn't want it to be true for him, but it had to be true, because she knew it wasn't her.

"Your hand was on it too," he said.

Rodric had fallen. He swore, found his feet, and ran up the stairs, shouting orders Aini didn't hear.

"You're *the Seer*," Thane said. "It only makes sense. You're the Heir, Aini."

She shook her head so hard it was in danger of falling off. "I'm less than half Scottish."

"You think any one of the line is fully Scottish by blood? Course not. They're all married into English, German, French families. What matters is...the stone has called us."

It did feel that way. Like the kings had set a quest at their feet. Because of Thane's bloodline—Campbells did hold a tenuous line to the old rulers, as did many clans—but also because of who they were. Seer and Dreamer. Merlin and Arthur. Hearts ready for sacrifice.

Thane pressed a fist against his mouth and studied the stone. The fallen flashlight and the storm's intermittent waves of white and silver cast a haunting light over both man and throne. It had to be him with his broad shoulders, quick mind, and high cheekbones. His tartan completed the picture. Thane had been through so much. A military upbringing under a madman's hand. Life-threatening situations when he had to make split second decisions. A moment when he'd had to go against everything he knew—father and clan—to become the man he wanted to be. And he'd grown a good heart and a brave soul throughout his struggles.

*The Coronation Stone has chosen well,* Aini thought.

Outside the entrance, gunshots blasted through the rush of rain.

Leaving the stone, they ran from the cell to see a fight already in motion. The bulk of the Dionadair—who'd concealed themselves at Rodric's arrival—worked in pairs, grabbing Campbells from behind and bringing them to their knees. One of the two would hold a gun to the Campbell's head and the other would grab him by the hair and force a cherry drop down his throat. The Campbells fell one by one, paralyzed with Thane's concoction.

Myles and Neve were back-to-back, brandishing a gun and a knife, their faces ghostly as they held off two Campbells with wild movements. The Campbells circled Myles and Neve like wolves do their prey.

Bran traded punches with a Campbell who kept shouting, "Traitor!" Blood ran in two thick rivulets down Bran's chin, but he smiled anyway and threw another fist.

Thane put a gun in Aini's hand and cocked one of his own. "Stay beside me," he said. "Please."

Rodric had Father and was dragging him away from the fight, toward the arched door. He fired off two rounds into the fray. Owen jerked, hit.

"Brother!" Vera shrieked and fell with him to the mud.

At her scream, the other Dionadair lost focus and ran to their leader. Some shouted for Aini; others were captured immediately by Campbells who hadn't been dosed with the sleeping agent. At the shoulder, Owen's shirt was black with blood and his cheeks had gone white.

Aini scraped at her throat, feeling like she was suffocating.

"It's over!" Rodric shoved Father to the ground, and Thane and Aini took off at a run toward him. "Rabbie," Rodric growled at a lanky man with deep-set eyes, "destroy the stone."

Bran stepped over the Campbell he'd knocked out and started toward Rabbie, but Rodric pointed the gun at him.

"No, Bran. You've shown your colors. Get over there with the rebels where you belong."

Bran held up his hands and joined Vera and Dodie. He bent and felt Owen's pulse as he whispered something to her. Vera shot curses at Rodric. She took a wad of cloth from another Dionadair and pushed it into Owen's wound.

Rabbie hefted a massive canvas roll from his back. He pulled out five sledgehammers and handed them out. The men pushed past Vera and Dodie and Owen, who moaned and tried to lift an arm. They stormed into St. Baldred's cell.

"That abomination must be eliminated," Rodric said, sounding so much like Nathair had during his announcement on the square. Then, Aini hadn't understood why the king called sixth-sensers abominations, why he drove his head of security to destroy them. But now she knew. He was afraid—terrified of the possibility of a Seer finding the true Heir and the people who would support that Heir.

Myles waved his knife to drive back the Campbells surrounding him and Neve. The Campbells dodged Myles's knife and the taller of the two kicked at the gun in Neve's shaky hand. Hair tangled around her face and nose running, brave Neve managed to keep hold of it.

The weighty ping and smash of sledgehammers battled the increasing wind's howl and the cracking thunder.

"You're going to smash the Coronation Stone?" Aini shouted up at Rodric. "Aren't you afraid of the curse?"

"My dear uncle Nathair is the curse you should fear. His will crushes through my hand. That is the real threat." A feral smile creeped over his mouth. He held a hand out toward Owen, whose lips were blue, glasses fallen to the ground beside him and his siblings. "Isn't that right, Dionadair?" He spat the word into the rain, full of arrogance, but his eyes gave him away as he glanced toward the saint's cell. Fear flickered in his gaze. Perhaps that's why he wanted to destroy it. He thought that would end its power.

Hands trembling, Aini worked the burlap bag off Father's head. He looked up at her, one of his eyes swollen shut and bruised to a purple she could see even though the storm had blackened the sky. She cradled his head and wept over him, her stomach sucking and pulling as she cried, in relief, in rage, in absolute terror. A line of dried blood divided his gray and white beard. Dirt stuck in the lines of his forehead and the crow's feet at his temples.

"Aini." He coughed.

Thane went to one knee and, pushing wet hair out of his face, pulled a knife from his kilt belt, then cut Father's hands free.

"I didn't want you here," Father said to Aini, his voice a croak. "This is my fault." He was shaking his head as the rain poured down, sticking their clothes to their skin.

"It's my doing, Mr. MacGregor," Thane said, his face dark as the sky.

Father put a hand on Thane's knee. "No, son."

The Campbell nearest Neve launched forward and ripped the gun from her. The second slapped Myles's knife away.

"No!" Aini shouted, fear scratching through her bones. Why wasn't the curse doing anything about this?

"Hold them. Hold them all," Rodric ordered as one of his men cocked Neve's gun and pointed it at the Dionadair. "They'll meet our firing squad for this. It'll make for a braw show."

Myles, veins sticking out on his forehead, struggled against the Campbell who had an arm wrapped around his neck. Neve whimpered and stomped her captor's foot. Holding her by the arm, the Campbell smacked her across the face and split her lip open wide. Aini's stomach rolled.

Rodric tapped his gun against his own head. "Nathair has a fine plan for a show in Edinburgh. Remind the people who is in charge in Scotland and who they should pay fealty to."

Fury raged inside Aini, a storm of her own, made of blood and heart and refusal to bow to the Campbells, to the clan who'd maimed her father and ruined her life.

"It's not your fault," she said to Father. She stood, water

shucking off her leggings and dripping from the loose ends of her hair.

Thane leaned toward her. "Aini...what are you doing?"

"I'm not going to let this happen." *For Father. For my country.* "I will not let him win."

Tucking his gun in his belt, Rodric crossed his arms like there wasn't a man bleeding, maybe dying, not ten feet away. "And just what are you going to do about it, Seer?" He spoke casually, but terror flickered in his black eyes.

Her heart lodged between her ribs like a knife. "I am exactly as dangerous as the king thinks I am." She flew toward the cell.

"Aini!" Thane's and Father's voices followed her down the stairs.

Vera called out, "Seer, wait!"

Their work lit by a battery floodlight, the men inside lifted their hammers and drove them into the throne, breaking Aini's heart in a million ways for a million reasons. There were pieces of the ancient throne everywhere. Then as the men hit the center, a large crack etched down the black, glittering stone. A corner of the stone fell away and tumbled toward Aini. The men didn't turn, didn't seem to hear her above the noise, as she lifted the rock. One spiral marked the piece, its edges like a giant's fingerprint.

She tore out of the cell and into the storm.

Lightning poured over Rodric, his boot now on Father's chest, and two of his men pointing guns directly at Thane.

Campbells restrained Dodie, Bran, and Vera.

Owen lay on the ground, partially covered in Dodie's coat and shivering.

The wind rippled kilts and the ends of jackets, grabbed at hair, and threw sounds of hammering and crying and thunder around like leaves. The air smelled like steel and blood.

"I'll not settle for a cousin who knows nothing of loyalty," Rodric said, his voice broad and curling with his West Scots accent. "I'm the son Nathair should've had and it's time I rid him of you for good."

"Thane!" Aini shouted and her voice cracked, her throat on fire. She threw the heavy piece of the Coronation Stone.

Squinting, Thane spun, his kilt twisting above his boots. He caught the piece.

Everything happened at once, but slowly, like in a dream.

The dirt under Aini's boots began to quake. Growing in strength, the Coronation Stone's tremor knocked her to the sharp bracken and sucking mud. A frigid wind whipped through the chapel's skeleton walls, stinging her cheeks. Crackling like a fire, a blue-white haze oozed from the stone, and Thane's face went slack as he held the stone tight, arms shaking. The pale fog formed the appearance of men with stoic faces, beards and crowns, long shirts and draping robes that snapped in the wind.

They were the ghosts of the kings of Scotland—ancient Celts, the Gaels, the men of Alba.

With gray hands like claws and eyes empty but burning with purpose, the ghost kings rose. Aini smelled woodsmoke, pine, and a deep, complicated scent like sage or cloves. Their voices filled her ears. Pleading, asking, retelling old tales.

She stood tall, wind tearing around her. The urge to speak to the ghost kings pressed against her mouth, but what could she say? Only the truth and a request.

"They want to kill Thane Campbell," she said to them, her throat aching and her heart in pieces. "He is the stone's chosen ruler. Protect the Heir!"

The blue-white light sighed and brightened. Gunpowder flashed, orange and blinding, from the Campbells' guns.

Surrounded by the kings' twisting light, Thane didn't fall.

The spirits grew, unfolding from the stone, their draping tunics and tartans fluttered over their seemingly solid bodies. Scrolled metal decorated the nearest king's belt. The blue glint of an ethereal light flashed from another's simple crown. Which one was Macbeth?

The ghosts opened their mouths as one, releasing a sound like a broom dragged across a dry floor. They rushed forward and swamped Rodric, Rabbie, and the rest of the Campbells, engulfing them in milky blue, their odd, magic scent increasing, overpowering the salty sea and the metallic flavor of the rain. The men's guns splashed as they hit pewter puddles on the ground. Shouting, Rodric and all the Campbells in the chapel, except Thane, grabbed their chests and pulled at their shirts and jackets.

They collapsed, white-faced and still.

The ghost kings faded into shining dust and disappeared into the biting air.

The curse of the Coronation Stone had worked its magic. Rodric and the rest had tried to kill Thane, the Heir, and they'd paid the price. *The power of the old to protect their own.*

Blinking and ears ringing, Aini scrambled to Father. Thane lay the piece of the stone down and they helped him to stand.

Black lines of makeup marred Vera's face. "Thane Campbell." Her voice shook. "You are the Heir and we, the Dionadair, promise to serve you."

Vera, Dodie, and the rest of the Dionadair crossed their thumbs over their heads as the storm pulled its ashen cloak from the island.

Bran took a knee as the sun battled its way out of the clouds. "I swear fealty to you, Thane Campbell."

Thane's throat moved in a swallow. "I may be the Heir, but I'm not the chief of Clan Campbell."

Bran smiled sadly. "I think you'll need to claim that too if this is to work."

Thane's eyes shuttered, then he looked to Aini, his face grave. Tentative joy and relief flew through her like birds and she drank in the sight of him, strong and able, and of Father standing tall too. Whatever must come next, it was over for now.

It. Was. Over.

CHAPTER 28

SWEET AND SOUR

"Don't think you're getting my side of the room just because of all this," Myles shouted over at Thane. Aini slapped him because Neve wasn't there to do it. Neve was checking on her family. "What?" Myles frowned and stacked some card stock at his desk. "He can't have everything."

Aini shook her head and joined Thane at the taffy puller. He gave her a sideways grin that turned her bones into butterflies. Last time they'd made taffy... Aini's gaze went to his parted lips.

"Don't lose focus over there, squirrel," Father said. "It's a lot more expensive now that it's loaded with more Cone5."

Cheeks going hot, Aini forced her eyes away from Thane's broadening smile. "Of course not, Father."

The taffy was finished aerating. As it dropped from the puller's silver arms and onto the tray, Thane and Aini used plastic scrapers to remove every last bit from the machine. Who knew when they would have access to the candy lab again? Probably never. Tears burned Aini's eyes, but she willed them away. They'd won the first battle. Now they had to prepare for the next. That involved moving whatever they could into the Dionadair safe house on the outskirts of Edinburgh, where Owen was healing with the rest of the rebels. There was no time for sentimental tears.

"The hard candies are ready," Father said, closing the small, purple treats up in a tin. "These will make some brave soul float like a leaf in the wind."

They hadn't decided how exactly to use these intensified sweets. But using candy to improve abilities seemed the best way to help the Dionadair and fight Nathair. Poisoning people could be done in more efficient ways. The rebels had a full armory. Aini hated that she had to consider such things now. But this was war, not a party.

Aini had suggested eating intensified altered candies to form a sort of improved team of operatives. She hadn't realized the idea would result in her being in charge of said team. "I hope that's not the one I end up using," she admitted quietly to Thane.

He chuckled. Sadness still pulled at him, darkening his eyes, but he smiled easier now. "It would be good to see an area from above in a pinch."

"Then you do it."

"Maybe I will."

"I think I'm going to be the one eating the taffy." She'd had another idea late last night when they'd returned from Bass Rock. "Maybe the Cones will allow me to see more spirits, to communicate with more of them."

"Ah. Good thinking."

"We'll test it when we get to the safe house. Vera said there's a cemetery nearby."

"We could test it when the rest take the first load. The house will be ours."

His voice sent good shivers down her back. She tried to breathe evenly so he wouldn't know how much he affected her. It was embarrassing how he could melt her with a word.

"Maybe," she said.

His eyebrow twitched near the frame of his glasses and that grin appeared again.

"All right," Father said. "Myles. Help me take these tins downstairs. Bring your supplies. The lorry should be out front. You two, finish wrapping that taffy, please, and meet us there." He threw a stern look at Aini, then said something under his breath. Even patient Father had his limits.

The second Myles and Father were gone, Thane threw the taffy and scraper down onto the tray, took Aini's face in his sticky hands, and covered her mouth with his. Aini fell into the warmth of his lips, the strength in his chest and stomach against hers. She ran her hands into his hair, not caring one bit that it would make the ends stand up and everyone would know exactly what they'd been doing. He said something into her neck, a piece of that old poem, and she couldn't stop smiling, her lips stretching and her hands smoothing the back of his skull. His scent had changed. Still the clean cotton of his clothing was there, but something like sage, like magic, cloaked him. She pulled back to look at his eyes, the steely gray of the cold North Sea, swirling with power and pull.

She raised an eyebrow. "I told you that you were the Heir."

A little laugh escaped him. "Aye. And I see that, though you're fine with breaking rules now, you've not lost your love of being right."

Lifting her chin, she smiled. "No. I have not." She chewed the inside of her cheek, not wanting to ruin the moment, but needing to talk about what was to come. "You have to go to Inveraray and claim your place as Chief of Clan Campbell.

And Nathair will have something to say about that when he is well."

He swallowed and looked away. "I suppose I must try. We need the clan behind us against him and against the king, if it comes to that. It will be a fight. A terrible fight. I'll need you with me. As Seer. The clan will want to hear about the kings you spoke to and how they followed your commands."

"They weren't following my commands. They were fulfilling the curse."

"I disagree, hen. Regardless, do you think they'll rise up to help us again? Or is the curse a one-time thing?"

So, he didn't see it. In addition to the magic scenting the air around him, a very subtle aura of blue light shone around him since that night on Bass Rock. "Look." She turned him toward the mirror beside the lab sink.

"I don't see anything but how you messed my hair to prove you've had your way with me." The corner of his mouth lifted.

"The blue light around you? You can't see that?"

He shook his head. "No."

"I thought everyone could." That was going to make convincing Clan Campbell he was the Heir and deserved total respect much more difficult. "Maybe you'll see the aura if you eat some taffy? The clan could see it then, if they ate some?"

"Another good idea. But," he smiled down at her, "I think we've time for a wee kiss first. Don't you? What's saving my life if I don't do my best to enjoy it?" His sad smile widened into something brighter as the late night sunset turned the lab's high windows purple.

"I'm not judging, but how can you smile like that when you know war is coming and we're going to be in the thick of it using experimental candies and ghosts to stay alive?"

"I've had a rough go of it so far. I'm not complaining. I just...

now that I have someone who understands me, who likes me despite who I am and what I've done."

She turned his chin so he faced her. "And I do. I forgave you. For all of it. And I hope you can forgive me."

"What for? You did nothing wrong."

"I lied to everyone for a very long time."

He nodded and ran a palm over her shoulder. "I can't let the bad things that will happen ruin what time I have with you. Nothing in life is safe, permanent. I know that much at least."

Aini's heart squeezed once, twice, then she pressed her mouth to his. The tip of his tongue swept gently across hers and a fever rode down her back and into her thighs, making her knees weak. This humble, brave man was hers. For now, anyway. She was determined to soak in every ounce of sweetness while they had this time together. Thane ran a palm up the back of her head and tangled his sticky fingers in her hair.

"Got you back," he whispered, chuckling.

She grinned and caught a glimpse of his tattooed hand as he traced a thumb, just barely touching, over her cheek. Soft, gentle. He dipped his other hand to her lower back and eased her body against the strong lines of his.

"I'm glad you've decided to go claim your place with your clan," she whispered, amused that her voice sounded so husky.

"Aye? It'll be dangerous."

"Yes," she said, "but I'll get to see you in a kilt again."

Taking his top lip between her teeth gently, she kissed him thoroughly, inhaling his new scent. A rushing, lovely heat twisted through her veins and filled her with happiness, and legends, ghosts, and revolutions took second place in her heart.

USA Today Bestselling Author
# ALISHA KLAPHEKE

# the Edinburgh Heir

EDINBURGH SEER BOOK TWO

This is a work of fiction. All events, dialogue, and characters are products of the author's imagination. In all respects, any resemblance to persons living or dead is entirely coincidental.

Text copyright © 2018 by Alisha Klapheke
Cover art copyright © 2018 by Damonza

All rights reserved.
Visit Alisha on the web! http://www.alishaklapheke.com

Library of Congress Cataloging-in-Publication Data
Klapheke, Alisha
The Edinburgh Heir/Alisha Klapheke. —First Edition.
Summary: Fate chose Aini MacGregor and Thane Campbell to change the face of Scotland forever and lead an unconventional rebellion using supernatural elements.

[1. Fantasy. 2. Magic—Fiction.] I. Title.

Printed in the United States of America
10 9 8 7 6 5 4 3 2 1
First Edition

✻ Created with Vellum

## CHAPTER 1
## SUGAR-COATED PLOTS

Aini popped the hard candy into her mouth and waited for her feet to leave the ground.

"How does it taste?" Thane was heating another batch on the stove, but his gaze kept straying from Aini to the window.

The lane curved away from the lonely rebel safe house that was serving as their temporary living quarters. The small town of Greenock, just northwest of Glasgow, exuded the sleepy feel of a good long, nap, but Aini knew better than to be lulled into a lack of vigilance by its quaint charm. At any moment, Campbell kingsmen would spring out with guns blazing.

"It tastes fine. Maybe a little less sweet than normal. So you're sure Nathair didn't tell anyone other than that group?"

The temporary lab's overhead light blinked across his glasses as his chest moved in and out. "That's what I overheard when Rodric spoke to him over the phone. Just before Bass Rock. Said he wanted to keep this all quiet until the right time."

Aini's head began to feel a bit funny. She went to the window and the late summer chill seeped through the glass and into her fingers. Despite it being only the very beginning of September, the trip from Edinburgh to Greenock had been flecked with what felt like winter rain. She drew the curtains and took a breath, watching Thane and Myles work.

"What is that face you're making?" Thane pushed his blond hair away from his black-framed glasses and eased the thermometer into the bubbling sugar.

"I was just wishing I didn't like the new lab so much."

At the townhouse in Edinburgh, the lab had been tidy—she'd obsessively wiped the long, metal table and the marble countertops—but the building had been ancient. The whitewashed walls still showed pitted rock and they harbored dirt she could never quite clean.

This lab was tucked into the guest house kitchen of a twenty-year-old home. Smooth walls. Electricity a person could rely on. Stools, windowpanes, and drawers made in this century. It was heaven.

"I feel guilty that I love it so much," she muttered.

The old lab had been home and here she was mixing candy, doing experiments, and whistling merrily as home sat far away in Edinburgh, alone and dark. Well, maybe she wasn't exactly whistling merrily, but the rest of it was true.

Gold stubble shone on Thane's sharp chin and along the curve of his jaw. He rubbed at it with his tattooed fingers as he studied the temperature of the hard candy mix. It was odd to see him with a little scruff. But it made sense that he'd forgotten to shave or hadn't felt like bothering with the routine. Nothing was routine anymore. Aini simply chalked it up to yet another difference in this man standing in front of her. He was no longer a spy. He'd gone against his own kin to save those he believed needed his protection. This was the new Thane. And she was the new Aini. Both of them in hiding, and on the surface as well as beneath the skin, they were rougher, brighter—more.

"Guilt will get you nowhere, Aini," Myles said, responding belatedly to her confession and looking around the lab she was trying not to enjoy.

She gave him a smile. "You're right, but I can't stop feeling it, or worrying about when they'll find us here."

Her fingers were drawn to the Adam's apple moving in Thane's strong throat. She curled them there for a second, enjoying the warmth of his skin and the beat of his pulse. A small smile pulled at his mouth as her feet left the floor.

Her stomach dropped as she focused on rising, floating—any thought that would lead to breaking gravity's hold. A little lightheaded, she rose and rose and rose.

"Um..." The floor was suddenly very far away.

Thane reached up a hand and grabbed her shoe. The black flat slipped off and he held it gently. "You all right?"

"I guess." The ceiling's ivory paint was smooth under her fingers.

Myles clapped once. "Well! That is a record height, isn't it?"

"It is." Aini put a hand to her head. A mix of fear and pleasure ran through her body. It was great they'd made such a successful altered sweet, but she wasn't so sure she could control this. How would it help them in a fight if she just floated away like a balloon?

"Is it making you sick?" Thane's eyes pinched with worry.

"Not really. I just feel...odd."

"Can you move around?"

Imagining the air was water, she moved her arms and feet and aimed for the arch of the guest house door.

"I don't think that's working so hot," Myles said.

He was right. She needed to pinpoint the way she usually

controlled her movement while under the candy's influence. Her tongue clicked against her teeth as she thought. She normally just looked at the place she wanted to go and her body obeyed, floating lightly over the floor. Maybe she simply had to focus a bit more now that the candy's effect was stronger.

The spot between Aini's eyes almost seemed to hum. Zeroing in on the sensation, embracing the feeling, she mentally "pushed" out from that point, toward the door. She sped over like she was on a zipline from the buzzing spot on her head to the door's archway.

"You figured it out," Thane said. "This will be great for visuals on a larger field of battle."

"Field of battle." Myles rolled his eyes, but it looked forced. Was he afraid? If so, she didn't blame him.

"It will," Thane said. "You'll be able to see who needs help and you'll be able to get away from enemies."

"Not if they have flyers." Myles clamped his lips shut.

Thane glared.

Myles held up his hands. "I'm sorry, but seriously. She'll have to be really careful about that."

Now Aini did feel sick. They were so not ready for this. She focused on the ceiling's peak and drifted like a leaf in the wind, her short dress shifting against her ribbed leggings. With a spin, she reached her arms wide and surveyed the makeshift lab in its entirety.

Thane's mouth had fallen open. Myles elbowed him, and his lips snapped closed.

"You do look really amazing up there," Myles said. "Like some kind of avenging angel."

Aini couldn't help but grin. "I like that."

Myles shoved Thane so he was directly below her. "And here is your deadly devil on the ground."

Thane pushed Myles off him. "Is it wearing off at all? That lightheadedness?"

Aini nodded and sure enough the hum between her eyes faded and she began a slow descent to the floor. "Your timing was spot on. So if I need to stay afloat longer, should I take two at a time?"

"We can try that out if you're up for it."

"Of course I am," she said. "I am definitely up for it," she added in a louder voice to cover the tremble in her words.

Thane pulled her into his arms. His back muscles moved under her hands and she breathed him in, loving his familiar cotton scent and the newer sage that permeated his skin beneath the slight aura of blue.

"I wish we could stay here," she said.

She hated how wistful she sounded, but the idea of being here with Thane in the lab, Father, unhurt and well fed, downstairs helping the Dionadair, and Myles, Neve, and Bran to keep them company, it was just so wonderfully...safe. Neve's mother and brothers had been moved to another Dionadair house with the code name Potato Casserole. No one here knew the location so if they were caught, they couldn't expose her family's whereabouts. It was all so much better than what Aini had imagined their situation would be at this point. She'd thought they'd all be dead in the street by now or crowding one of the king's prisons. Everyone was safely tucked away and very much alive.

But none of this was even close to being permanent.

They'd defeated Nathair's meathead thug—Thane's cousin Rodric—but there would be retribution once Nathair realized no one from the operation on Bass Rock was answering his calls because they were either dead or had gone to the rebels' side—though Thane and Bran were the only two who'd done that. This small pocket of time when Nathair didn't know what had actually happened on the island wouldn't last. Owen and his Dionadair rebels had to figure out what to do and act quickly. Everyone felt the pressure. Everyone had a guess on how Nathair would strike back and when. None of it was pleasant.

"We really need to get moving, though. I don't understand why it's taking Owen so long to come up with a plan."

"He did almost die." Myles pursed his lips. "That gives him at least two days to sit around and do jack, doesn't it?"

"We don't have two days. It's been one and a half already. The Dionadair need a plan. I mean, what are we even doing right now?" She looked at the window again.

"One day at a time, hen," Thane said. "You can't plan this. Not fully anyway."

She frowned up at him.

Myles laughed and greased a baking sheet with an oiled brush. "That is not Aini's M.O. and you know it, man. Players are going to play. Planners are going to plan. No matter how much they stress themselves in the process."

Thane held up the thermometer. "It's go time. For the candy."

"I'm not planning this part of our adventure," Aini said to Myles as she squeezed the dye bottle. Two drops fell into the sugary bubbles and spread like octopus tentacles. "Owen is going to get better and he'll have a plan that will work. The two Dionadair that went to Edinburgh and the other one that went south will be back within hours. They'll have information about Nathair and where kingsmen have been stationed and what the word is around. Owen is going to lead this. Not me."

"We'll all need to give our suggestions on how to proceed," Thane said. "That's the only way we'll find a way out of this alive.

God knows just because I'm the Heir doesn't mean I know what to do."

"You've helped the Campbells plan for years. You do know military strategy," Aini argued. "Plus you're a Dreamer. I don't think it's farfetched to think you'll Dream up something we need to know along the way."

"I don't know. Last night I did Dream about an ice storm. It gave me a headache like the recurring stone Dream I had until we went to Bass Rock. But how does a Dream about a storm help? I don't even know where the rough weather will take place."

"It could be important though. We should tell Owen."

He shrugged. "As for the work I've done over the years…a full-scale rebellion isn't anything like rounding up pockets of criminals or spying on traitors." His gaze lingered on the pale scar marring the back of his hand. "We need allies."

Myles tossed the pizza cutter and scissors they'd used to cut the candy onto the countertop. Uncapping a marker, he began drawing swirling lines on his trousers. "Vera said she had ideas to talk about."

"That woman is crazy," Aini said.

Thane chuckled. "You're not wrong." He added a single teaspoon of the lavender-grape flavoring and two full tablespoons of the boosted anti-gravity concoction he and Father had come up with. "I don't think this will kill anyone," he said, eyeing the candy, "but whoever eats these will not feel normal for a good hour or more after the effects wear off. Not to mention how bizarre they'll feel during the experience." A loose curl of dark blond hair fell over one eye as he muttered something about hormones and adrenaline, then rattled off a formula interspersed with strings of Scots Gaelic.

Rain began to fall against the roof and its metallic scent

permeated the room. The smell reminded Aini of blood, of the night on Bass Rock Island where she'd thought she was going to lose everyone. An unseen pull tugged her fingers away from the pot's covered handle and onto Thane's forearm. She brushed her thumb over his skin and soaked in his warmth, the solidity of his presence. He was the true Heir to the Scottish throne, the one meant to free their homeland from the hands of the tyrant English king, but he was also the one who made her heart whole. He belonged to everyone. But he was also *just hers*.

His big hand covered her fingers and he smiled, though his eyes darkened. "Do you think they'll follow me?"

He was talking about the clan chieftains. At some point very soon, Aini, Myles, Neve, Vera, and several other Dionadair rebels would have to travel to Thane's massive estate in Inveraray to meet with the men and women who influenced the bulk of Scotland's people and, most importantly, its weapons. It'd be a huge meeting of all the clans loyal to the Campbells and the vast majority of Campbells themselves. Thane and Aini would have to convince them that Thane should lead the clans instead of Nathair. Then there was the little bit about a full-on rebellion against the king.

Aini poured the hot, colored sugar mix onto the baking sheet. "I'm not saying it'll be easy to persuade the clans, but surely when they've heard what really happened to Rodric..." She fought a shiver remembering how the ghost kings engulfed him and the others. "And how the stone roared for you, they'll come around."

To say the least. No one would want that curse on their head. Vague folklore said the Coronation Stone's curse promised *the power of the old to protect their own.* On Bass Rock, the power had shown up in the form of the dead rulers of Scotland supernaturally killing Thane's horrible cousin Rodric and the other Campbells there. Aini wasn't sure how the curse would work if another enemy threatened Thane. Even Neve with her substantial knowledge of legend and history didn't know the true nature of the stone's curse.

"After all, you're a Campbell too," Aini said. "And a more powerful one. Or, you will be. I mean. Come on. Nathair doesn't have the spirits of old kings on his side."

"He has a huge army. And the very-much-alive king's army too. And these clansmen, they've been trained to follow Nathair. To fall in line. To support his agenda and my grandfather's for generations. When someone has been brainwashed, it's nearly impossible to persuade them of anything that contradicts what they've been taught. Look at what I've done in my life. But I'm no fool. And I do have a soul. A heart. Despite that, I did as I was told almost every time Nathair asked me to do unspeakable things. Years spent by the fire and at clan gatherings, reciting Campbell oaths and lies…breaking through that conditioning… it's an impossible task we have, my Seer."

He said that last word a little wryly. The Dionadair had fallen into the habit of calling Aini "their Seer" lately and it felt uncomfortable at best. Wrong on some days. She did See memories implanted on items that were important sentimentally to others. She also had the sixth sense they called Ghost Talking. She'd commanded the ghost kings to protect Thane on Bass Rock. But she had no idea how to call up ghosts when they might need them, if Nathair attacked suddenly.

"The clans that support Clan Campbell, and Clan Campbell itself, they must realize they're being misled," Aini said. "Mistreated. The king has shown more and more that he hates and fears the Scots. With the marriage laws. The taxes. The firing squad deaths after only the pretense of a trial. He's taking our people and executing them as he sees fit. And Nathair is at the head of it. I'm sure some of them have lost loved ones to the prisons or the firing squads. There have to be sixth-sensers within their ranks. We can convince them. Surely, just the fact that they aren't permitted to wear tartan unless they're in Clan Campbell should show clearly enough that Nathair doesn't respect the other clans."

"Most will be Campbells." Sadness drew Thane's voice down a few notes.

Aini touched his shoulder, feeling the muscle and bone beneath his shirt. "We just need a real plan. Owen has to come around. His color looked better today. He'll be fine soon, right?"

He had to be. Vera could not run this operation, and despite what the others claimed, Aini couldn't either. She was completely unqualified. The rest of the rebels were so used to Owen running things that none had come forward to suggest a plan either.

Aini's father jogged up the stairs, a wrinkled paper in his hands. His clothes were ironed to perfection despite the multiple threats going on in the world around them. He'd shaved too. The line around his tidy beard was sharp as the edge of a candy cutter. Aini approved.

He held up the paper and eyed everyone. "I have a very wild idea, my dears."

Myles's eyebrows lifted. "Okay..."

Aini peered over his shoulder to read the words inked onto the paper. "What is it?"

"Well, it appears to be a grocery list," he said. "But I don't think it is."

Thane looked up from the candy, his eyes narrowed with intense focus.

"Do share," Myles said, standing next to Aini. "Wild ideas are probably good for a rebellion."

"Agreed," Aini said.

Her father shook the paper out and studied it. "You see the odd use of a single letter for people's names?"

"They've just abbreviated family members though, aye?" Thane had made his way over.

"I don't think so. It fits too well. Think about the leaders of the French forces in the Channel."

"Um, I honestly can't say that I've been paying enough attention. Been busy, you know." Aini raised an eyebrow.

He replicated the gesture. "Of course. But I heard the Weekly Address while in captivity."

Just the mention of Father's time spent in the hands of the Campbells made the room sway in front of Aini's eyes. It had been the worst time in her life. And when she'd seen his finger on the ground after that fight at the barn...

"You all right?" Thane had come around and was now circling her waist with an arm to steady her.

She welcomed the support. "Yes. I'm fine. Sorry, Father. Go on."

He nodded smartly though she could tell he was worried about her. "Seven names came up frequently in the reports about the last clash with the French off the coast. I rejoiced in every mention of them because they're truly giving King John some real trouble. He deserves some trouble, wouldn't you agree?"

"That's one way of putting it," Aini said.

The murdering king deserved more than trouble. He deserved death for all the sixth-sensers he'd ordered killed, those he'd starved through higher taxes, the couples he'd torn apart simply because one was Scottish and didn't have his approval, and most of all, for the children orphaned and left in the streets when their parents never returned from what he and Nathair called *questioning*. Once those poor souls were in the famed cells under Edinburgh, waiting to be questioned, they were lost to their families. Aini had only been without Father for a short time. She couldn't imagine worrying and waiting for years upon years. It was the worst kind of torture and no one should have to suffer it, let alone sweet little children.

Father ran his finger down the list. "Well, of those military leaders named, one begins with a B, one with a C, and another with an A. All those letters are shown here."

Aini read the list to herself.

*B's milk*

*C's big box of oaties*

*two dozen eggs for C too*

*A's bag of apples even if they're a bit overripe*

"Or it could just be a list of groceries, Mr. MacGregor," Myles said, shrugging.

"You may be right, Myles. But I think it is at least worth looking into because of its source."

"Did you find it?" Thane asked.

"No. Rob did. One of the Dionadair. The one with the cap?"

"I like him." Myles smiled. "He made me a great cheese sandwich this morning and told me two dirty jokes I'd never heard."

Aini smacked Myles. "Focus."

A grin flickered over Thane's full lips.

Father cleared his throat. "Rob found it in the house of a prominent banker who the Dionadair suspect is the contact for an English operative in France."

"You should've led with that." Myles elbowed Father gently.

He laughed. "It's not like I'm Dionadair. I don't know how these things work."

"So what does this mean in your humble opinion?" Aini asked.

"I think it's a report on the number of ships outside Calais, near the disputed territory. I believe these are the ships England's forces will come up against during their next attack. B is Beauchamp, that artillery expert they dug up from Provence. He was in the Weekly Address, remember? C is General Caron. He has a flyer carrier out there and his entire fleet of fighters."

"And A must be that Captain Abbe," Aini said. "Even I've heard of him."

"Oh!" Myles slapped his leg. "That's the old man with the fleet of sailors from the last colonial war. We colonials love that guy."

"He saved your arses when the king decided he wanted half the cut on exports, right?" Thane handed the list back to Father. "Made reducing that tax a part of the peace treaty."

"Yep. The leader of Mint has a tattoo of him."

Mint was Myles's favorite band. Aini thought perhaps they overused the banjo a little. "What an honor." She handed the list back to Father. "Did you tell Owen yet?"

"Owen's not in his right mind, squirrel." Father's eyes were kind, but Aini didn't want to hear that news.

"Are you coming with us when we go to Inveraray? You can change your mind. You don't have to stay here."

"If you truly need me there, I will go. You know I will. But I don't think having an old man with you is a good idea. You need fighters. I'd only be in your way."

Aini pulled him into a hug. "You are never in my way."

"And you're not old," Thane added.

Father smoothed the hair at the back of Aini's head and she breathed in the wool scent of his sweater. "I'm off to talk to Rob," he said. "He and Samantha will have thoughts on what to do with this information. I'm also hoping I can make contact with Darnwell. The king is keeping a very close eye on him and his wife, I'm sure. But maybe they can help us somehow."

Lord Darnwell was an eccentric noble—his mustache was phenomenal—who just happened to be married to the French queen's half-sister. He and Father had bonded over how to operate Enliven. Darnwell had his own boutique business. He painted miniature portraits. Most of the nobility looked down on his quirky art, but Father had, rightly so, appreciated the man's unique talent. Aini herself had danced with the lord at several elite parties over the years. Contacting him, well, who knew what kind of situation he was in with the war in France? To think that he might be able to somehow help them, that was surely a long shot.

"You're sure making contact won't put him and us in danger?" Aini asked.

"I will get the Dionadair to help me use a code. I'll only go forward with it if Owen agrees to it." And with a sad smile, Father left the makeshift lab.

Aini's heart warred with itself. She wanted Father with her through this nightmare, but she also needed him to be safe. He'd been through so much. Having him out of the direct line of fire was also a necessity to her mental health.

Myles switched on the television. A man in a sharp, blue suit stood in front of two cages that each held a sixth-senser. Aini shivered. Their hair was matted and bruises colored their cheekbones and arms. The kingsmen had gagged the sixth-sensers. The king was still so afraid of what they'd say. They'd been *questioned*, the reporter said. Aini shook her head. Not questioned. They'd been tortured. She couldn't wait until the slimy king found out he wasn't going to be able to hold Scotland in his vicious hands for much longer.

Myles cut the finished hard candies while Aini worked on

another batch. Thane set a plastic tray of finished taffy on the end of the counter. Inside, golden strips of sugar and Cone5, wrapped in pale wax paper, sat ready for the experiments they'd planned.

If things went well with Thane's mother and the clans in Inveraray, the team would run the tests at the estate.

If things at Inveraray went badly, and the clan decided not to believe Aini and Thane's story and came to the conclusion more sixth-senser blood should be spilled right then and there, well, there wouldn't be any call for altered sweets or battle plans. The rebellion would be over before it started.

So many lives hung in the balance.

As Aini stirred the second batch of hard candy, the pink-lavender hue in the pot darkened into a deep purple, like circles under tired eyes. "I added too much dye. These look awful."

Myles peered over her shoulder, smelling faintly like the white pepper and nutmeg chewing gum he'd munched on this morning during his quest to fool his eyes into seeing some version of the Loch Ness monster. He wouldn't listen when Neve told him this wasn't even close to the right area for that story.

"The color is fine," Myles said. "A little depressing maybe, but maybe since it's darker, we'll remember how much more powerful it is."

Breathing out through her nose, Aini took the candy from the heat and poured it out on the baking sheet. She locked eyes with Thane who was cleaning the taffy puller with a wet rag. "Will you two finish up here? I'm going to see Owen."

Thane met her at the door. His shirt collar was nearly worn through. It hung loosely to one side, showing off his collarbone and the spot where not so long ago his Campbell necklace hung.

"Do you want me to come with you?" he asked.

He cleaned taffy from his fingers and Aini couldn't help but remember the time they'd kissed in the middle of making the candy. Sugar, sparkling colors, the heat of his body against hers...

"Aini?"

"What? Oh no, that's okay. If it's important, I'll grab you and the others."

"All right then."

He went back to his work, stoic as ever. She smiled at his broad back, then trotted down the stairs. She wished they had time to have fun together. But every minute the Dionadair waited to act was another minute Nathair might find out what happened and move to get the king to help him crush the burgeoning rebellion. There wasn't any time to lose.

Through damp, browning grass dotted with purple mushrooms, Aini hurried to the main house. She would tidy up this situation and get things moving. She didn't want to plan their next move, but she was more than fine with putting a fire under those who did know how to take down a monster.

CHAPTER 2
EXPERIMENTS AND FEAR

Thane grabbed the box of caramels he'd made before everyone woke up this morning, said bye to Myles, and slipped out the safe house's back door. Wind bumped against his cheeks and pressed into his glasses. It was colder than it should've been for this early in the autumn. Behind the house where they'd been since their quick escape from Edinburgh, steep hills sloped into a narrow stretch of tall, yellow grass and moss-covered rock.

The box lid slid off easily and the smell of caramel wafted into the crisp air. The others might think of him as the Heir or some great genius, but Thane knew well he'd made plenty of mistakes. This candy might end up being one of his most embarrassing ones. Better to test it outside, away from everyone. Safer too. That first batch had developed a nasty slime and he hadn't wanted anyone to touch it let alone test the stuff. This batch looked fine, but he really didn't know. Who knew what this blend of blood and muscle altering chemicals would do? He didn't want to accidentally explode all over everyone in the guest house.

With a deep breath, he bit off a corner of one caramel. It was delicious. At least that part was right. Despite what was coming, what he had to do very soon, he really hoped this altered sweet didn't drop him dead where he stood.

A slow heat rose from his heart and into his throat. He touched his cheeks as they flushed hot. His quadriceps spasmed. It wasn't painful, but it felt very odd. He swallowed. He really, really didn't want to die. He wanted to enjoy at least one more day with Aini.

Muscle spasms squeezed their way down his body. Trapezius. Rhomboids. Obliques. The tendons around his groin even tightened.

"Whoa. Take it easy," he mumbled to himself, extremely glad he'd made the decision to do this away from prying eyes.

Then his body seemed to settle into a low hum of tension and heat. Like he was a car idling, ready to take off fast from the line and leave the rest of the traffic behind.

"That's much better."

With a grin, he started to run.

Wind sheared over his face as the surrounding hills blurred to each side. He hurtled easily over a boulder coated in orange moss and veered left to avoid a patch of black mud.

It felt amazing.

Struggling to keep up with his muscles, his lungs burned hot as his blood. He was almost flying, his long stride eating up the distance between the house and the end of the valley. Peeking over his shoulder, he saw the roof and the sturdy walls—now just a spot on the horizon.

He threw his head back and laughed out loud. "This is madness!"

Turning quickly, he ran back toward the house, his legs moving too quickly for him to see properly. His lungs shook inside his chest, and he slowed, legs humming still. Back where he'd started, he put his hands on his knees and gulped the cold air.

When he straightened, five faces appeared in the back windows. Dionadair. Their mouths hung open. They looked at him like he was a god.

He snatched up the box of caramels and held it high. "It was just the candy. Anyone could do it."

But they either couldn't understand what his actions meant or they refused to believe he was any less than what they wanted him to be because they kept staring and raised crossed thumbs high as a sign of respect.

Thane shook his head and tucked the caramels under his arm. He almost wished he thought of himself as highly as they did. Maybe then he'd be as confident about claiming the roles of Clan Campbell chief and King of Scotland as they were about the whole mad thing.

He thought of the storm Dream he'd had last night, the feel of the ice on his skin, the sound of the wind against a car window...

Yes, he knew being a Dreamer and the Heir was in his blood. Yes, he knew the prophecy and the ghost kings all proved he and Aini were meant to do all of this. But a big, fat chunk of him still couldn't accept it. He knew his own limitations. He was only twenty-years-old, for God's sake. He didn't have the life experience of someone like Lewis MacGregor or half the Dionadair.

Thane knew Aini could play her role. She'd been bossing people about for years. She had the very soul of a leader, the practicality of a general, and the ability to learn very quickly what she needed to know to lead the Dionadair.

But Thane, he'd never wanted to lead. He'd longed to leave Clan Campbell, not rule it. He did love Scotland though. To his core. It was his breath and his heart. He only prayed he wouldn't destroy it trying to live up to the prophecy that tied him to this green and lovely land.

He decided to try one more run to see how long the caramels lasted. Taking off toward the valley again, he recited the Periodic Table to calm his nerves. ...N, Nitrogen...

A sudden memory of his father's face blinked through his brain.

Nathair was smiling and it was terrible like it had always been.

"No!" Thane sped up though the caramel's effect was wearing off. "I am no longer a Campbell like you. I will fight you. I will fight your influence."

His legs stretched to jump over a shining puddle of rainwater. The silver surface flashed the reflection of an angry man who looked far too much like Nathair Campbell, despite the different coloring. Thane dragged himself to an abrupt halt. He fisted his hands and let the bones of his knuckles painfully strain against his skin. The world tilted a bit. Taking a breath, Thane threw his head back and shouted into the wilderness. Another breath and he'd purged some of his fear and rage.

He brought the memory of Nathair's smile to mind. "I will not be like you. I will never hurt those who love me. I am not your son. I am not your son. I am not your son."

If he said it enough, he hoped he'd begin to believe it.

Thane could only allow himself to rule the country he loved if he completely and totally broke away from his father and turned the meaning of the name Campbell into something else entirely. Children could not go around afraid of the name. Women could not worry about their intuition, praying it was not some latent sixth sense surfacing. Men could not lie awake at night and wonder if a Campbell would be coming for them in the morning.

Campbell had to become a name the people loved.

"I am Thane Campbell. First of the new line of kings. Thane Campbell, named by the Coronation Stone, paired with Macbeth's Seer, and fated to help Scotland break free and rise up."

Suddenly bashful, he spun to make sure no one had followed him. Only a small bird hopped from a wide fern to a mossy rock. It chirped lightly at him.

"I am Thane Campbell and I'm a fool." He rubbed his face harshly, shoving his glasses into his wind-tangled hair.

When he turned toward the house, he saw Myles coming out and heading toward the caramels.

"You shouldn't eat those!" Thane gestured toward the box. "You just had the gum this morning!" It might be too much for his system or even for his brain.

Myles obviously didn't hear because he lifted the box lid and popped one into his mouth. Waving a hand, Myles chewed while Thane began the run back. When Thane was still a stone's throw from the house, Myles leaned forward to boak his treat all over the unsuspecting grass. The Dionadair who'd cheered Thane on were still at the window. One pointed and another laughed.

Myles, always a good sport, wiped his mouth with his sleeve then bowed to his audience.

"I tried to stop you." Thane put a hand on Myles's shoulder. "Why don't you have a seat? I'll fetch some water. You shouldn't mix altered sweets."

"I hadn't had anything for over two hours."

"This is all experimental. I really don't think it's a good idea to eat more than one type of candy in forty-eight hours. You must metabolize through one—"

Myles held up a hand. "Got it. Got it. Only one type of yummy at a time or you spill your breakfast all over granny's petunias."

"Oh I don't think it would merely be vomiting if you'd eaten them closer together."

Myles's frown deepened. "So like…" He held his hands near his temples. "Kaboom?"

"Aye. Maybe. Probably less dramatic but just as deadly. Seizures. Cardiac arrest. Something of that sort as a first step toward the grave."

"You are kind of a poet."

Thane glared.

"No, really. That was like a song lyric. First step toward the grave…" He began humming.

Thane assumed he wouldn't boak again, so he started to leave, but Myles grabbed his sleeve.

"Hey, I need some advice, man," Myles said. "I love my mother like a snowman loves summer, but I'm thinking she should at least know some of what's going on over here with me."

Myles's mother ran a cotton plantation in the southern colonies. From what Thane had heard, she was a horrible woman who paid her workers very little. She acted like some sort of queen in her remote corner of the world. Had loads of money, for certain.

"You'd have to be very careful."

"No kidding."

"I just mean…she may want to get involved."

"To save me? Yeah, no. She won't. That won't be a problem."

Thane put a hand on Myles's shoulder. "Sorry she's like that, pal."

"I'm used to it," Myles said, but the pain in his eyes told another tale. "I just don't want her trying to contact me at the townhouse and screwing something up."

"Aye. Well, get with Lewis and the others. See if you can come up with a coded message to send to her via a safe phone. Just to tell her there has been trouble, but you're fine."

"For now. Should I mention I might be dead soon?"

Thane laughed without humor. "Might want to leave that bit off."

Myles saluted him. "Thanks for listening, Master of the Universe."

Thane rolled his eyes. "No problem." He clapped him on the back and went inside to find Aini. He needed someone sane to talk to, and that someone was neither himself nor Myles.

## CHAPTER 3
## TO LIGHT THE FUSE

Bran spread the materials for a low explosive and a high explosive on the table by the safe house's garden shed. He ran a careful hand over the complicated high-end detonators he'd nicked from the Campbell stores before Bass Rock. They'd been hidden in the lining of his coat and he wasn't sorry at all for taking them. They were tricky buggers to make and having a good example to study would help Bran's assistants craft more just like them to use against their enemies. A sealed, small barrel of gunpowder sat at the end of the table. He hoped they wouldn't have to travel with it, but he had a sneaking suspicion they would.

The sound of boots on fallen leaves crunched behind him and he turned to see the three Dionadair that had agreed to work with him on the explosives side of this rebellion. All three were skinny malinky longlegs, to be sure. Their limbs were like saplings gnawed bare by overzealous wildlife, all pale and straight beneath their shirtsleeves. Despite their less than hearty bodies, the lads' eyes held fire, and that was the most important thing.

To deal with this kind of thing, they had to have a pretty serious helping of courage inside them.

"All right then, my men. Study what I've gathered here. This is what a deconstructed low explosive looks like. This kind are set up to burn. They won't blast unless tightly cooped up in a proper container. This here is an example of a high explosive. These must have a detonator and will explode like the world is coming apart. This is very similar to what the Campbells used at your rebel barn the night they nearly offed their own leader, the idiots." He pointed to the detonator. "I need help constructing a few more of these. I'd like to have four fully functional high explosives on hand when we head out of here to God knows where. Then, depending on what plan our leaders decide on, you three can make more and send them to where the fighting takes place. That's not for us to worry about now, though. Our part of this is simply to get the explosives prepped. Do you understand? Any questions?"

"Aye. My brothers and I have all made explosives. We know what you're wanting." The tallest of them touched the detonator with finger and thumb. "What we'd like to know is why you're in charge of this team and not the other way around?"

Bran wasn't sure if he meant brothers as in blood kin or brothers as in brothers in arms. Regardless, they seemed to be of one mind as they stared him down. But Bran knew exactly how to deal with passionate folk dedicated to a cause. He'd had enough dealings with that to last a lifetime.

"I'm leading this group because your Seer and your Heir told me to do so, may they rise together." He held up his hands and crossed his thumbs over his head.

The lads nodded and copied his gesture. The distrust in their faces faded. "Let's get to work then," the tallest said.

Side by side, they twisted metal, tucked components into

their proper spots, and used pliers to make adjustments. The men did well, Bran thought. They were moving carefully, slowly, methodically, and keeping a good eye on that gunpowder, showing it the respect it deserved.

When they had the four completed explosives ready, Bran shifted them into a straw-lined wooden crate. One of the lads fit the top onto the crate and together they pushed it tightly closed. Bran dusted his hands and surveyed his team.

"If we get the call to head out into this madness as a group, good. If we don't, and the opportunity to join me later arises, please speak up to your elders and do come find me. I trust you now and I hope you trust me too. I'd rather not work with this stuff around strangers. Do you agree?"

They nodded and Bran worried for a moment whether their skinny necks were up to the job of holding their heads on.

"It wouldn't hurt for you to eat more and...do some pushups, for God's sake. You're too thin, all of you."

Bran took the long way around to enter the safe house through the kitchen door, his mind throwing out scenarios as he walked over gravel and grass.

Where exactly was Nathair now and what was the man up to? Nathair had lost his core unit, the men he trusted to do the jobs he considered highest priority. If he knew what had happened on Bass Rock, if he knew they were dead and gone, he'd build a new group, wouldn't he?

The man had a knack for finding those who would follow him into the fire. The poor, the desperate, but the rich too. He had a way of persuading everyone within earshot that he had the truth of things and knew the way the world should be.

Thane had always fought it. Bran had seen the fight in Thane's eyes a thousand times, that look he had when Nathair raged on about how the Campbells were God's gift to the world.

Bran seemed to have an antidote to Nathair's rhetoric flowing in his veins. He was the only one Thane used to confide in and he alone spoke up in agreement with Thane's tentative, early arguments with Nathair. It's why Bran had stayed by Thane's side. He wanted to be there for him always. The battle Thane fought, mentally and quite often physically, against his father was one no man should have to fight alone.

Bran pushed the safe house's kitchen door open with more force than he'd intended and the white wood banged against the frame, startling a Dionadair in an apron.

"Sorry," he mumbled, slipping out of the haze of cooking smoke and the scent of butter, into the low light of the main house.

If Nathair did have a new core unit of operatives, they would be fearsome to be sure. Nathair wouldn't play around with the possibility that more kin would go to Thane's side of things. Nathair's new men would be even more ruthless, if that was possible. They'd be cold and professional.

A shiver ran over Bran as he closed himself into his small bedroom to think. The bed creaked under his weight and he put his head in his hands, remembering Bass Rock island—the ghosts and the wind, the roar and the truth.

"I hope it's enough," he said to the empty room. "Or we're all good as dead where we stand."

## CHAPTER 4
## SLEEPING LEADER

The stairs leading to the room where Owen slept zigzagged like a mountain trail. With every step, Aini practiced what she would say to rouse the head of the Dionadair rebels. Surely she could help him shake off the lingering stupor from the blood loss he suffered and put his mind to the task of the rebellion. This was Owen Bethune after all—owlish, practical, a cutthroat in herringbone—and this was the moment he'd been waiting for, working toward his entire life. He would know what to do next. The job of organizing rebels and supplies and attacks didn't have to fall onto Aini's and Thane's shoulders.

She would ask him how he was feeling. Tell him about the candy they'd crafted. Inform him that she and Thane were ready to follow his orders and work as a team to defeat Nathair and, eventually, the king. His people needed him and his experience, his passion. Now was the time. He'd rise up out of bed, face flushed with resolve, and lead them to the future they were all hoping for. A future with the true Heir on the throne,

Scotland as its own master, and freedom for all, including every single sixth-senser that chose to make this green land their home.

Dodie, Vera's ox-like brother, stood guard outside Owen's room. He gave Aini a respectful nod and mumbled, "Morning, Seer," as she passed.

Pale yellow light soaked through Owen's closed curtains and into the rumpled duvet. The sun illuminated the blue half-moons under the rebel leader's eyes and the new wrinkles spanning his temples. Aini smoothed the blankets and pulled a straight-backed wooden chair beside the bed. She folded her hands in her lap and cleared her throat.

Owen's eyes opened. "Seer."

"How are you feeling?"

He ran a knuckle over the red stubble on his chin and reached for a glass of water on the nightstand.

Aini grabbed it and helped him take a drink. "Your informants should return soon. We need to know what your plans are."

His eyes shuttered closed. "Ask Vera," he mumbled.

Setting the glass back very carefully, Aini took a breath. "Vera isn't you. We need you to lay out a plan."

"I can't."

"You can."

"My mind...I'm still...foggy."

Behind a tower of clean, folded cloth, a man bustled in. "Our leader needs his rest, Seer. Please." He began unwrapping Owen's wound with sharp movements.

"Fine. You can rest, Owen. But first, just tell me how we can approach the clans and get their support. Do you have any thoughts on that? And what should we have them do if we manage to talk them into joining us?"

Owen's eyelids fluttered shut and he turned toward the nurse.

"With all respect, Seer, you must leave now," the nurse said.

"This is the revolution you and your family have struggled toward." Aini gripped Owen's sleeve. "Now is your moment. Just tell me what to do and I'll do it. Please."

The nurse stood. "Seer. You'll never get anything from the man if he has no time to recover."

Aini sighed, deflating.

The nurse shooed her out of the room with a nod and expectant eyes.

Shaking her head, she left as ordered. She didn't want to hurt Owen, to keep him from healing properly, but surely he could still think up some strategy that would get Thane and her to Inveraray without trouble. Or tell them to do something she hadn't even thought of, like go to another town and use part of the rebel network to contact some of the chieftains. There were countless ideas he might give them if he only had the will.

"Now Seer, it's not polite to snarl at sick men." Vera sashayed around the corner and put a hand on her hip. "I hear you don't trust my guidance."

Aini blew out a breath. "It's not that I don't trust you. It's just that Owen is your leader. Our leader."

"No. You're right. He does have a better head for strategy. But I have a plan and you'll listen to it, won't you? Besides, Owen will be up and well soon and then you can side with him against me again." A sad grin passed over her mouth. "Ready to hear my thoughts?"

"Of course." Aini was pretty certain this plan would involve maiming multiple people for no apparent reason and driving like madmen into a line of Campbells armed with nothing more than a bludgeon and some attitude.

"We head out at night once we hear Nathair is gone from the area along with his best men. Travel quick—"

Aini crossed her arms. "And arrive at the gates of Inveraray like bandits begging to be shot on site?"

"We'd stop first and clean up. We'd make a fine entrance." Vera raised her chin.

"In the middle of the night."

Vera spread her arms wide. "Then we send word first."

"To whom?"

"Thane's mother."

That wasn't a bad idea. "I'll talk to Thane about discussing this with his mother and what he thinks the risks may be to her and us. You go talk to your brother. You know as well as I do that we need his brain."

"Aye. I can't argue that." Vera gave Aini a respectful nod before heading into Owen's room.

The door swung shut, and Aini stared at the clear plastic knob. She didn't want to wrap Thane's mother into this before they had a solid idea of what they were going to do and when. The heating vents switched on and blew Aini's hair across her face as she walked downstairs. Gritting her teeth, she tucked the wayward strands of her unruly mane behind her ears. Her mind was full to bursting. Owen simply had to snap out of this.

In the small guest room she shared with Neve, Aini slid the top drawer of the sleek, modern dresser open. Two rows of tiny glass jars clinked together lightly, their green lids labeled in clear white letters. She grabbed up the rosemary, basil, juniper berry, peppermint, and clary sage. With the lids unscrewed, she took a small spoonful of each and shifted the ingredients into her mortar's smooth, marble interior. She twisted and pressed down with the pestle and the sharp scents of the concoction filled the room.

"If this doesn't wake Owen up," she mumbled to herself, "and get him planning for us, nothing will."

"What are you up to?" Neve appeared at the door with a wooden spoon coated in melted chocolate. She licked the back and cocked her head at Aini.

"We're headed into war, real war, and you're eating chocolate?"

"I'd say that's the best time to eat chocolate. A person needs comfort now more than ever."

A smile broke over Aini's mouth despite her worries' attempt to drag the corners of her lips into a frown. "I love you, Neve."

"Back at you, darling." Neve offered the coated spoon.

Aini waved it off. "I'm making a little something to rouse our Owen."

Neve sniffed at the mortar, then jumped back. "That would rouse my dead great aunt."

Aini set the mortar down and dusted the dried rosemary off her hands. "Then it must be ready."

Concoction in hand, Aini headed back toward Owen's room. Dodie was gone and a new guard had replaced him. He didn't say a word to Aini or Neve when they opened the door. Thankfully, the nurse wasn't there, but Vera was drawing a fresh sheet up to Owen's chin. Aini settled herself on the bed's opposite side, beside the nightstand.

"What a smell!" Vera's nose wrinkled at Aini's concoction.

Aini scooped a portion and began to shift it into Owen's untouched soup.

Vera reached across her brother and pushed the mortar away from the bowl. Herbs scattered over the small table. "You're not feeding my brother that stinking mess."

The guard at the door sucked a breath and leaned in to see what would make someone talk to the Seer that way.

"I mean," Vera said, schooling her tone, "I don't think it'll help, Seer." She fluttered her lashes, obviously trying to look young and penitent and failing miserably.

Aini rolled her eyes. "It might. And it won't hurt him regardless."

She dabbed a bit of the mix into a spoonful of yellow soup and nodded to Neve who put an arm behind Owen to help him sit up. His eyes remained closed.

"Owen. We have something that'll make you feel better." She set the spoon against his lips.

He took a sip, then spat it back out, eyes flashing open. Groaning, he pushed the spoon away and spilled the rest of the portion on the blankets and Aini's arm. "I don't want to feel better."

Aini froze, her gaze on Vera. Vera touched her lips, her face pale.

"What do you mean, brother? We're on the verge of what we've been fighting for our whole lives." She sat, making the bed dip a little as she reached over him and ran a hand over his cheek. "This is the rebellion. It's actually happening. Of course you want to mend so you can help in the fight. Our Seer is here. She is ready to lead."

Aini put a hand to her suddenly throbbing head. This was not going the way she'd planned. They could not run this revolution without its leader.

Owen rolled onto his stomach and pressed his face into his pillow. "My mind...I can't..."

Vera stood.

The nurse pushed into the room. "Seer, with all due respect, this man suffered extreme blood loss and is fighting temporary memory loss and what I'm sure is a crippling mental fog." He sniffed the air. "While I appreciate your knowledge of natural remedies and do support their use, know that our leader will continue to heal in his own time and we must make adjustments as needed. Now, please consider my advice and let him rest."

He didn't have to yell. Something squirmed in Aini's chest. "I'm sorry. You're right."

A strangled sound crawled out of Owen's mouth. Aini spun to see him thrashing on the bed.

Vera pinned his arms down.

"No!" The nurse put a hand on Vera's arm. "Back away. Give him space. He will get through this, but he needs space."

Owen kept seizing. Aini went cold all over.

"What is wrong with him?" Vera's hands went to her mouth.

"It's a seizure. He had one two hours ago. It is normal with as much blood loss as he experienced," the nurse said.

Owen finally settled and Vera's hands went to her sides.

The nurse held a hand toward the door. "Now, please leave him alone for a while. I'll be here the entire time. I promise."

The hallway outside Owen's room was too quiet. Neve, Aini, and Vera just stood and stared at one another.

A girl who looked a little younger than Aini pounded up the stairs, cheeks bright red. "The informants returned, Seer. None of them managed to get a 100 percent solid take on Nathair Campbell's current location or where he may be heading. Nothing conclusive."

Vera whispered a curse.

The girl continued. "One scout did overhear a report on a kingsman radio frequency that stated the earl was seen at an Edinburgh judge's house, but that information is sketchy at best seeing as the reporter didn't specifically mention Nathair's name."

Aini rolled her mother's ring around her finger. Hmm. They really needed to know if Nathair was nearby. Everything hinged on that information.

Neve bit her lower lip. "We can't wait around forever though, right? He'll be coming after us sooner rather than later."

"Tell us what you want us to do, Seer." Vera clasped her hands and swallowed. "Some of the elder members will want to meet, to hear what you have to say." She glanced at the door to Owen's room. "You and Thane."

Aini spun and rubbed her temples. This was all moving too quickly. She didn't know what to do. "Why do you want me to lead you? Let the elder members lead."

Vera grabbed Aini's arm in a viselike grip. "Why do we want you to lead?! Because you're the Seer, woman! The prophecy called you. You are the entire reason for the existence of the Dionadair. You are Macbeth's Seer and I knew you would come to us and take us into a world where Scotland is free. You are born to this. Don't doubt it." Her eyes were wild and a strand of her dark hair had fallen over one cheek. "They will only follow you. I love my brother and I hope he comes around to help, but you are who we need. Who we must have. It is destined. This is fate."

"Should we talk?" Thane said from the bottom of the staircase, his face full of concern. Sun streamed through the front windows and shone across his light hair and the corners of his glasses. Pink spots colored his cheeks like he'd been outside in the cold.

The twisting feeling in Aini's chest tightened in time with Vera's hold on her arm. Whatever she told the Dionadair to do, whatever she and Thane decided, the outcome would sit squarely on their shoulders, hers and Thane's. She didn't want the responsibility. Not like this. Not without Owen and his guidance. No matter how much this was supposed to be her fate.

She took a breath and detached Vera's claws, finger by finger. "Yes, please, Thane. That would be wonderful. Let's go ahead and get together with the Dionadair elders."

Vera jerked her chin in a quick nod and marched down the stairs. "Rob! Samantha. The rest of you lot. We're having a meeting!" She disappeared around the corner along with the girl, leaving Thane and Aini to themselves.

CHAPTER 5

FEEDING THE FIRE

At the base of the stairs, Thane cleaned his glasses with the edge of his shirt. "What did the scouts say about Nathair's whereabouts?"

"They couldn't find out anything for sure," Aini said. "They think he might be in Edinburgh."

"Should we move forward or stay until the informants gather more concrete evidence on where he is? I tried to call my mother, but she isn't answering."

"I don't know. We can ask the others and see what they think. By the way, where is Bran?"

"He'll be in soon. Right now, he is meeting with an explosives team," Thane said. Aini's fear must've shown all over her face because he quickly added, "For later. For the true battle that'll come later."

She took a shuddering breath and nodded. The war. Yes. It was going to happen whether they wanted it to or not now. "I don't want to be in charge of this," she whispered.

"Neither do I. I'm guessing not many would want this job of ours." A wry grin washed the frown from his face but didn't clear the fear from behind his eyes.

She wanted to take his hand and feel that warmth that only he had, the heat that tingled against her skin and made her feel both challenged and protected at the same time. It was a strange, perfect combination that she was quickly becoming addicted to.

With everything that was going on, they hadn't had any time alone in what felt like forever. Did he even want to hold her hand? To feel her skin on his? Maybe his head was too full of their fate and what they were trying to do. She wouldn't blame him. But it would hurt. It would hurt a lot. The twisting inside her flared into her throat and made it difficult to swallow. She moved her fingers toward his, but he was looking at the gathered Dionadair in the room down the hall and didn't notice.

Once the group—including Neve and Myles—was assembled on couches and around the floor in the living room, Aini followed Thane.

The sun bled through the red curtains, giving Neve's and Myles's faces a strange hue as they talked, heads close together. Black shadows clung to the corner beside a tall grandfather clock that ticked away the seconds they had until Nathair realized what had happened and came after them in force.

All eyes went to Aini. It didn't seem like she had much of a choice about leading. These people believed in the prophecy and the Seer and she had to fill the role or risk the rebellion falling apart and everyone dying in vain. It had to be her.

"Okay fine," she said, ignoring her jangling nerves. "We don't yet know where Nathair is, so we're going to send someone into the local kingsman's office tonight to break in and nose about.

We have to know where he is. Once we know for certain he isn't breathing down our necks, we'll move forward and a team will depart from this safe house."

"Bran can handle the kingsman's office," Thane said. "He knows how to keep from being caught, and if he is, his looks are so average that it most likely won't be an issue if Nathair has put out descriptions of us. Bran can talk his way out of a lot of things."

"He's better looking than average," Aini said. Neve and Vera nodded knowingly and Thane cocked his head. Aini shrugged. "Well, he is. But I see what you mean. Brown hair. Brown eyes. Average height. Yes. Good plan. As long as he fully agrees and is okay with the risk."

"I'll talk to him after this," Thane said.

"Once we learn where the King's Deathbringer is lurking," Vera said, "we'll leave here at night, right?" She was nodding like they'd already agreed and a few of the elder members of the Dionadair with her.

"I don't think it's smart to sneak around like we're guilty. Then if we're caught, they'll know we're up to something. If we travel by day, on the main roads, unafraid of being stopped at any checkpoints Nathair has set up, then a handful of fake Subject IDs will do the work for us. We'll hide the stone, wrapped up tight, in the back of the truck, and have a full load of...what do they sell off up here?"

Rob pulled his flat cap off and raised a hand. "Colonial cotton. In from the ports just south."

"Okay. So..." Aini chewed the inside of her cheek. "I'm guessing we don't have access to a bunch of raw cotton, but we could simply bring clothes in for resale at the market, right?"

"I suppose," Rob said.

Thane paced a line behind Aini, his boots knocking along the wood floor. "Who all should go? Because I think we should travel in two groups with the first communicating with the second on what lies ahead."

"The first vehicle will serve as a scout?" Vera asked.

"Yes. Agreed," Aini said. "Who wants to go? I think we should have a decent-sized group to make a strong showing at Inveraray."

Thane clicked his tongue. "I see what you're saying, but remember the Campbells and the clans who support them hate the Dionadair. We don't want it to look like we're staging a coup."

"But we are."

"Aye, but let's say it's more of a changing of the guard with a Campbell still in place as chieftain."

"Yes. That makes sense. So Thane, Bran most likely, Neve, Myles, Dodie, Vera—"

"You couldn't stop me if you wanted to," Vera said.

"And that's why I added you to the list," Aini said. "We need someone who knows the area. Maybe a former kingsman or two to sway the unwilling?"

Vera pointed out two Dionadair. A woman with a long, skinny neck and thin lips and Rob. He kept looking from Vera to Thane to Aini with worried eyes.

The woman bobbed her head to Aini. "I'm Samantha."

Rob shook Aini's hand. His palm was sweating.

"You sure you're up to this, Rob?" she asked him.

"I am. But we are going to take proper weapons, right? Because you know they'll be ready to off us the second we don't seem like we are who we say we are," he said.

Thane clapped a hand on each of the rebels' shoulders. "We'll have weapons. Hidden, but ready."

"I really don't think they'll expect us to come right down the main road in bright sunlight. I think this will work," Aini said.

*Please let me be right.*

"Well we won't know until we try it," Dodie said gruffly.

"What are we doing about the arrival? Do we just walk up to the door and knock?" Vera asked.

"I have the password for the gate codekeeper. But I'll also speak to my mother," Thane said. "She might have an idea who would support us. I have one idea... I tried her once already. I'll do it again now." He walked under the door's white arch, phone on his ear.

"I think we should leave tomorrow afternoon," Aini said.

"That soon?" Neve said, eyes wide.

"We have to. Nathair is gone. Who knows when he'll turn around and come back. We should go now while he is out of the way."

Thane stepped back into the room. "Her phone's been disconnected."

Aini's heart gave a jolt. "Has this ever happened before?"

"No."

"Maybe it's just the service," Neve said. "Sometimes when I tour up here the towers don't have enough—"

"It's not the service." Thane pressed the phone against his forehead. "Something has happened. I have a bad feeling about this."

Aini rubbed a hand over her stomach. She had a bad feeling too, but she wasn't about to tell him and make his worry worse. "Let's get the IDs made and dress to leave. There's no reason we can't leave when you want to."

"There is one clan leader who will fight this no matter who shows up at Inveraray. My old second cousin, Sorley Menzies."

"Now *that* is a name," Myles said.

"What is it that makes him a problem specifically?" Aini asked.

"He hates everyone."

"Everyone? Come off it." Vera crossed her arms.

"He has never liked my father. Loathes me. Never approves of what anyone does really," Thane said. "He wants to be the cock that rules the roost. He caused a big fight back when I was fourteen or fifteen. Something like that. Nathair hired a group of covert experts from Cornwall and Menzies didn't like it."

"You don't know why?" Aini asked. "If we could untangle his motivations, we might figure out a way to get him on our side. Is he simply after power for power's sake? Or does he want money? Does he have a family?"

"She's kind of scaring me and I like it," Myles said.

"I suppose he wants power for power's sake," Thane said. "He has a family, although I've not seen them for ages. Not since I was a wee mite. He has two boys near my age and a wife who cares more for her own side of the family than his."

"It'd be very good if we had someone to help us go up against him," Rob said.

"Honestly, I think an ally is key. We should make some inquiries. Discreetly, of course. Bran could help with that," Thane said. "Maybe even head into Perth to see my family there."

Aini bit the inside of her cheek. "But we don't have time."

"We must make time. We need a strong ally. Especially if they've decided my mother isn't to be trusted. She'll be no help to us and we'll be no help to her without more internal support."

"We should go to Inveraray first. See what is going on and who has sworn sole fealty to Nathair, outside of the king's knowledge, and all that. Pretend to be all in. Your mother will help us sell that. We can make a plan there. Then maybe search for more support if she says it'd be a good idea."

"We can't rely on everyone else, Aini. You and me, we have to make the decisions here. Everyone is looking to us."

"And we will. But we need to scope out the situation there. They don't even know you are on the rebels' side yet. You can use that. Until Nathair knows the truth of what happened on Bass Rock, you're still a loyal Campbell and welcome at your father's estate, right?"

"I believe so. When I went back to gain their trust before Bass Rock, I went off with Rodric and only Rabbie and Seanie were there. Rodric reported back to Nathair about my...return. No one else knows what went on outside of their group, the group who went to Bass Rock."

"We only have a tiny sliver of time to use the rest of the Campbells' ignorance. I say we go for it."

"By ourselves."

"With the Dionadair that don't look like Dionadair."

Thane spun and growled quietly, rubbing his hands through his hair. "This is a mess."

Tentatively Aini smoothed her palms down the warm muscles coiled around his shoulder blades and lower back. The shape of him comforted her and made her feel like they could do anything. She only hoped he wanted the touch as much as she did. It seemed like maybe he was all right with forgetting about love when they had a war to conduct. She felt like an idiot wanting it herself. But she did. She needed the comfort, the camaraderie.

He turned, then looked at her through his fingers. Streaks of pure white shot through the gray in his eyes like there was a lightning storm inside him just waiting to be released. "I have an idea. But I don't know if it's a good one. It's risky." The room's red light painted his tattooed fingers and made them look muddy.

"Tell us," Aini said, loud enough for the rest to hear.

"I spent a lot of time at Uncle Callum's estate, learning to shoot and doing some ground fighting training. He isn't like…Nathair."

Aini could tell he'd almost said father.

"He used to talk Nathair out of his rages. I'm thinking he might be persuaded to join us. If he doesn't agree, then he'll definitely report us."

Vera shot out of her seat in a cloud of perfume. "How many men does he have?"

"I'm not sure. But more than most of the other clan leaders loyal to the Campbells. I think he's second only to my clan."

My clan. He'd claimed his clan. This was progress. Aini imagined him in Campbell tartan and tried to feel good about it. This was what they had to do. Make it so that everyone in Scotland who saw Campbell tartan began smiling instead of running off in a panic.

"Where is this benevolent uncle with the army and a good head on his shoulders?" Myles leaned forward, arms on his paint-stained trousers.

Bran walked in and took a seat beside Thane.

"In Perth," Thane said. "He lives in the old castle there. It'll take…about two hours, maybe less, to drive there. Then a couple hours travel to Inveraray."

"Ah, so we're going to visit your Uncle Callum?" Bran nodded, thinking. "That's a good idea. He'll take some persuading though."

"Aye. And I'll need to talk to you about a job after this if you're all right with that," Thane said.

Bran nodded. "Course."

The sun rose higher in the sky, and the room's light shifted from red to orange, dispelling the shadows by the clock as well as some of the bad feelings in Aini's chest and stomach.

"We can do this," she said. "Let's get started."

## CHAPTER 6
## HAIR DYE AND SECRETS

In the basement of the safe house, Thane followed Aini, Vera, and the rest of the group that would head toward Uncle Callum's estate. Two other Dionadair trickled in holding scissors and bottles and strips of silver foil. Aini tapped a finger nervously against her peachy, light brown cheek, and all Thane wanted in the world was to scoop her into his arms and take her away from all of this. Preferably to a room where they could be alone for a few minutes and talk. He'd love to listen as she discussed a list of tasks that had to be accomplished, fingers ticking off each item and eyes narrowing as her mind whirred. It'd be heaven to touch the velvet skin just under her chin, then to reassure her that he was behind her every step of the way on this wild journey.

So much was happening so quickly.

Aini smoothed her borrowed shirt with quick hands, then leaned toward Neve, saying something that made Neve take her arm and give it a comforting squeeze. Myles crossed his arms as he looked at Dodie; he'd never forgiven him fully for the fight in

Greyfriars kirkyard. Long-necked Samantha and that level-headed man with the cap, Rob, talked quietly, their gazes flitting from Aini to Vera before landing on Thane. Their faces were unreadable under the strange basement lighting. They gave him a respectful nod. He smiled back, hoping it didn't look too strained.

The recessed lights' pearly haze made the whole room and everyone in it look like a dream—faces blurred a bit, Thane's heart beat too quickly, and he felt as if the odd lighting would grow paler and paler until he was overcome and stopped breathing entirely. That last feeling, the sensation of being overwhelmed, reminded him of his Dreams. The prophetic ones. It was wrong to wish it, but he definitely wished he never had those Dreams. They would most likely help the rebels succeed and detach the English king's hold on his homeland, but who knew for sure? And in the meantime, they were very, very unsettling. Trying to grab hold of their meaning, to be certain it was a *Dream* and not just a *dream*, was like reaching out for a minnow in a storm-flooded river.

After a Dream, Thane experienced pain in his head as well as a feeling of being overwhelmed, taken under. The ache, now that he recognized it, told him whether his sleeping visions were prophecy or simply his brain processing stimuli from the day gone by. But what if the headache faded before he really woke up and he missed it? It wasn't easy. Not even a little. He suddenly craved the surety of a formula written in pencil on a piece of paper and the bubble of carefully measured chemicals in a test tube. Why couldn't life be more like science?

Vera raked through her large, silk bag, then held up a stack of paper—tiny slips that she handed out. There was a sketch of a person on each one, done in some kind of colored pencil. "Here are the ideas we have for how to change your looks."

In Thane's, he had jet black hair that had been shaved on the sides and was longer on top. And his alter ego was wearing eyeliner.

"Why must I always wear eyeliner when we go undercover?" He breathed out through his nose.

Aini peeked at his, her own held against her chest. Her mouth popped open, but she quickly closed it.

"Seems I'm due for a haircut." He tugged on his floppy, blond locks. "And to become some sort of rock star."

"But your hair..."

Thane came close, breathing in the scent of Aini's shampoo and forcing himself not to kiss her right then and there. "Aw, hen," he said, leaning in, "don't look like that." He brushed his lips over the soft curve of her ear. Goosebumps traveled the length of her neck, which of course made him feel very hot and bothered. He couldn't resist making her just as warm under the collar. "If you need something to hold on to during our private time, I'll still have these lugs." He tapped his ears.

Her cheeks darkened. At least she wasn't biting her cheek nervously any more.

Myles shoved his sketch at them. "I've got to take it all off."

Neve squinted at Myles's likeness. "You're bald!"

Sure enough, Myles's fake persona had an extremely short buzz cut that followed the lines of the skull.

Myles rubbed both hands over his mint green hair. "Well, if anyone can pull it off..."

Neve smacked his bum lightly. "Cheeky." She frowned at her own drawn image. "I'm going blond and it seems I'll have blue eyes. How are we going to manage that?"

"We have contact lenses ready for you," Vera said.

Aini flipped her sketch so everyone could see. It was her face but with heavy eyeliner and cropped, colored hair. "Purple?"

"Sure." Vera winked.

"What happened to the whole 'Our Seer' respect..." Aini mumbled, tucking the ID into her waistband and starting toward the long, trough sink where the two other Dionadair that had followed the group set up bottles of what had to be hair dye.

Aini sighed. "I'm going to look like an eggplant."

Thane wanted to chuckle with her, but his heart started hammering again and he suddenly wanted out of this room.

Vera snickered as she headed for dye. "You'll look great. The lot of you. In a few hours, someone will come to take our photos, then our ID man will have everything ready in minutes."

Sweat dampened Thane's back and palms. They were doing this. Changing their looks to head into the fray. There was no escape after they did. And he would have to lead them after all was said and done. If they made it through. He couldn't picture himself as a ruler. Not even a little bit. Especially with a stick of eyeliner in his hand.

"Are you okay?" Aini's big brown eyes stared up at Thane.

"Not really, but I have to be anyway, don't I?" He swallowed and tried for a smile.

"You can take a break upstairs. They can't complete all the cutting and dyeing at once."

A weight pressed against his lungs. "No. I'm not leaving. The heir can't be off for a kip while the rest go on to fight for glory."

Aini's mouth stretched into a grin. "I'm glad you're staying."

Thane forced himself to breathe slowly in and out. He wondered if this was how Aini felt when she was in tight places. What was his problem though? Just the stress of this?

Shoving his glasses into his hair, he walked over to where Myles sat in a chair. Under the snip of a young Dionadair's scissors, his hair came off in thick, green chunks. Thane allowed a slim girl to swathe him in a barber's gown and settle him into a chair. Aini stared at him from across the room where Vera shook one of the dye bottles. He realized then he'd walked away from her without saying anything. He hadn't meant to.

The girl snapped the barber's gown tight around Thane's neck. It itched. "So you'll be Chief of Clan Campbell in a matter of days and leader of all Scotland in as many weeks if we don't all die in the effort." She whistled. "That's a lot to take in, aye?"

The air suddenly left the room and Thane's eardrums pounded.

"I suppose. But one thing at a time, as our good Seer likes to say."

First, travel to Uncle Callum's in Perth without getting caught.

The wooden chair squeaked under Thane and bits of his hair slipped by his face to fall into his lap.

Thane looked at Myles from the corner of his eye. "I had no idea a rebellion would be so..."

"Hairy?" Myles supplied.

"Exactly."

Aini let Vera lean her head into the sink. Water hissed from the tap. "Thane," Aini said, "did you finish that batch of Bismian?"

Bismian was a powerful blend of bismuth and various other chemicals. He hadn't tested it properly yet, but Thane's hypothesis was if as much as a teaspoon came in contact with a victim's skin, the result would be a headache that would keep them from putting up a fight. The stuff would also erase the day's events from their memory. Bismian would be a good weapon to have on hand.

"I did. Have two vials of it in my bag and ready to go," he said.

Thane suddenly missed Bran. He was the only one who truly

understood what all this meant to Thane. He knew what Thane had gone through, had listened to all of Thane's stories about his rough childhood and how Nathair brainwashed him from the moment he came from the womb. Soon as this hair and clothing stuff was finished, he'd go find Bran and make certain he still wanted to go with them to Inveraray.

Neve came out from behind a white screen. A billowy top and pencil skirt made her look more like her fake persona. That skirt would make fighting difficult. Thane wondered if he should suggest a change.

Samantha adjusted the collar of Neve's shirt. "It fits well. Now take it back off so we can get your hair done."

Neve headed back behind the screen. "What else do we have in our unusual arsenal?"

Aini winced as Vera splattered purple dye over the top of her head. "We have the Cone5 taffy. It might help me see more spirits." She frowned. "That sounds so strange," she said to herself quietly.

Myles shivered dramatically.

"We also have a batch of gravity-reducing hard candies," Aini added, "the vision-inducing gum, aphrodisiac cherry drops—the regular formula—and we also have the strength chocolate Thane's been playing with—"

"The what now?" Myles blinked and sat up. His hair person shoved him back into the chair and lifted the razor to finish the job.

Thane cleared his throat as his own barber switched on an electric razor. "The strength chocolate drops should increase blood flow to the muscles." The razor buzzed over the back of his head and near his temples. It tickled like fiery fingers. "It should allow for a ten to twenty percent increase in—"

Neve squeaked as shards of pottery fell from her hand and clattered to the floor. "I just broke my coffee."

"Weren't you eating chocolate earlier?" Aini asked.

"Yes."

"I have a feeling that little treat wasn't just a little treat."

"Oh." Neve went pale. "I picked them up off the kitchen counter. I...I didn't think they were altered."

Thane smiled. "At least we know they work. Be careful with any small animals you may pick up."

Myles winked at Neve. "And be careful with me later tonight." He ran a palm over his almost bald pate. He looked like a brawler. It wasn't a bad look for him.

"I tested the acceleration caramels. Or whatever we're going to call them," Thane said. "They definitely work."

"I heard about your impressive sprint outside from some of the others," Samantha said. "And about Myles being sick."

"I ate them about two hours after having the gum. Thane thinks that's why I puked."

Thane nodded. "We should remember that, everyone."

Aini's nose wrinkled. "I'm sure you're right. There could be counter effects between the ingredients."

"Aye. And unexpected outcomes," Thane said as he was moved to the dyeing sinks.

"I'm not taking any of that stuff, man," Myles said. "Not unless you make me."

Neve took a pen from her hair. It cracked as she folded it like a napkin. She grinned and Aini laughed.

"That was so hot," Myles said as Neve threw the ruined pen in the bin and rubbed her hands together.

By late afternoon, they were different people.

"We look bizarre," Aini said.

"No. We just look different," Neve said.

Thane had shorter hair now, a little longer on top than it was on the sides. With a glance in the mirror, he thought maybe he looked older. It was the dark color of his hair. Contacts in place, his gray eyes were now green as Myles's hair had once been.

The Dionadair had dyed Neve's hair a honey blond and her eyes were now a dark blue, or so Vera said. Thane couldn't tell in this light.

Aini touched her own purple hair, shrugged, and turned to pick up her bag. "I hope this works."

She did not look like an eggplant. Her elegant neck peeked beneath the back of the shorter cut and Thane's fingers longed to explore the ups and downs of the tendons beneath the skin, to kiss the spot where her neck and shoulder met.

"Wake up, sweetie." Myles bumped the back of Thane's knee with a foot and jostled him pretty good. "Time to rock and roll."

There was no more time for thinking and debating and wondering if he could handle this. When they left this safe house tomorrow and headed for Uncle Callum's, the rebellion would be beginning in earnest.

He glanced at Aini. She studied her small hands, fisted them, then took a deep breath. Were they ready? No. Did it matter? No. It was time whether they wanted it to be or not. Only the strongest of them would survive. Aini was strong enough. Thane prayed he had the same strength to find himself standing at her side when it was all over.

# CHAPTER 7
## A LITTLE BREAKING AND ENTERING

"If you ask me again if I'm sure I can do this, I'm going to call you *Granny* for the rest of the week," Bran said, pulling a black, woolen cap over his thick hair.

Thane frowned and Bran saw Nathair in the look, not that he'd ever say that to Thane. "I'll make you some cookies to go along with all my granny-style worrying if it means keeping you from being the next one shot in Greenock Square," Thane said.

For all that Thane's mannerisms sometimes reminded Bran of the earl, Thane had a heart of gold. Bran would gladly risk anything and everything for his closest friend.

Myles came around the corner of the safe house. "And you don't want me along?" He shivered and rubbed his recently shaved head. "Because I will totally ride along if you need me. I've learned a thing or two from this guy and that Seer of ours." Myles poked Thane in the shoulder.

Bran smiled. "No. It's best if it's just me. I can move in and out quickly. I know the layout of a standard kingsman office. I'll be back before midnight. If I'm not, maybe send Dodie and Rob out to see if I've been taken. All right?"

Thane handed Bran a small pouch. "Aini said to give you this."

Bran upended the bag to find a half-diamond pick, a small torsion wrench, a bump key, and rake snake. An impressive little set. "Our Seer knows the business of breaking and entering."

"Aye. Her father showed her how to crack locks because she has a touch of claustrophobia."

"A good man, Lewis is."

"Definitely," Thane and Myles said in unison.

"Good luck, Bran," Myles said as Bran tucked the pick set into his jacket. "I'll set some whisky out for you."

"You're moving up on my list of favorite people, colonial," Bran said.

Myles saluted him and left for the house.

"I'll share that dram with you when you return, pal." Thane tucked his hands into his pockets as the wind kicked up.

Somewhere someone was burning a fire. The smoke carried through the night and reminded Bran of playing chess with Thane, by the wood stove in a flat Bran had years back.

With a nod to Thane, Bran faded into the crisp night, hoping he'd indeed be drinking whisky when this was over and not eyeing the end of a kingsman's bullet.

A BLOOD-RED DOOR MARKED THE FRONT ENTRANCE TO THE local kingsmen's office on Union Street. Rob had dropped Bran down the way a bit. It hadn't been much a jog to get there, but Bran was already sweating. Maybe because everything was more dangerous now than it had been. At least, it felt that way.

The office was only manned by one kingsman on a weekday

night like this one. He'd most likely be at an interior desk on the first floor, watching the television. Not too much went on in this wonderfully quiet little town. Samantha had talked to Bran before he left, telling him the radios he needed to access were on the second floor. She'd worked in this very office before going over to the Dionadair side of things.

An oscillating camera mounted above the office door turned south, away from Bran's shadowy spot beside a closed down pie shop. Bran rounded the corner of the three-story building, passing a hand over a cold pillar and sliding into the black space between the office and the neighboring post office. An industrial-sized bin sat against the wall. A second-floor window leaked weak emergency light onto the rubbish stuck under its lid. He might not need Aini's lock-picking tools after all.

Pulling himself onto the manky bin, Bran eyed the corner. Every noise he made sounded like a cannon's boom. Greenock was a little too quiet for this kind of work. The window glass was thick and old. The wood frame could be opened by a brass lever —there for firefighters—but a horribly rusted lock kept the thing from turning. If he smashed the glass, it would surely alert the kingsman on the first floor. The television wasn't that loud. Bran put an ear to the window, listening. All he could hear was outside noises—the rush of the wind and a faraway lorry several streets over. He pulled out Aini's set and went to work.

The half-diamond pick worked like a charm. The lock opened with surprising ease and the window slid smoothly out of the way. This was going too well. He stepped one foot through the opening, straddling the frame and ducking his head inside.

"Eh! What's that you're doing?" a voice called from the alley.

Bran's heart scrambled up into his throat. He leaned his head back out and eyed the swaying man shouting at him. The man belched. He was drunk, big, and twice Bran's age. Bran quickly slipped back onto the bin's lid, leaving the open window behind him. He hopped onto the street.

"I was about to steal some things. So if you don't mind, I'll be back to my business."

The man's jaw dropped.

"Oh." Bran held up a finger. "It would be very helpful if you didn't shout loud enough to raise the dead again. Thanks, pal." He pulled a flask from his jacket and tossed it to the man, hoping against all odds the idiot would catch it and not create more noise by letting it crash to the ground.

Lurching forward to grab the flask, the man belched again and nearly fell.

Bran caught him and winked. "Best get home before I decide I don't want a witness to my horrible crimes, aye?"

"Aye. Course." The drunk blinked and grinned like Bran was a fairy here to grant his wish.

Before the man had even left the alley, Bran was back through the window. A chair—or something—rubbed loudly against the floor downstairs. The kingsman was moving about.

The room across the hallway housed a wall of radios, some of which were from the last century. These small towns didn't get much in the way of financial support. It was better though really because they were simple machines and easy for Bran to work, going on Samantha's instructions. He flipped the silver switch on the one labeled Southern Route and crackles exploded from the speaker. Bran turned the thing off, his pulse flying. Controlling his breath, he listened for the kingsman. Footsteps knocked along the ground floor. A stair creaked and Bran put a hand on the cool metal of the gun in his pocket.

The kingsman coughed from what sounded like the bottom of the stairs. "Haunted. I've told them already..." he mumbled.

"...won't listen to me. Sarah's right. I shouldn't take these night jobs..."

Bran had to smile. He was happy to play the ghost. With the radio's volume dial twisted down, he switched the thing back on. Pressing the button, he spoke quietly into the speaker.

"Please report on latest location of Nathair Campbell. King's update."

Samantha had said they did a regular update on important persons from time to time. Midnight would be an irregular moment for such an update unless there was an emergency, but it couldn't be helped.

The crackling turned into a high-pitched voice. "Kingsman Broch here. Respond."

The kingsman on the radio wanted Bran's name to check against his roster. Thinking of Samantha's list of who used to work in this office, he picked one name at random. Hopefully, the person still worked there. Conversation wouldn't be an issue. Kingsmen weren't permitted casual responses.

"Kingsman Alan. Respond."

The speaker whirred and snapped. Bran turned the volume up a little to make sure he wasn't missing Broch's answer. Should he repeat himself? Or wait another minute? He strained to hear the television downstairs or the shuffling of feet.

"Earl Campbell," the radio kingsman said, "was last seen two hours ago on the M6 nearing Preston and heading south.

Bran let out a huge breath. The farther Nathair was from them, the better, and it seemed he was on his way to London. But what was he going to do there? Was he on his way to meet the king to discuss what happened on the island? Would he plan a huge attack? The king was busy with the French war, but he had plenty of advisors.

"And just who are you?" a voice said suddenly from the door.

The light from the hallway illuminated the outline of the kingsman from the first floor. He had a hand on his shiny new gun and was squinting into the dark radio room.

Bran popped up, heart pounding, and kicked the chair out behind him. He lunged, then cracked the kingsman across the chin with a right cross. The man fell to the floor.

Standing over the unconscious man, several things went through Bran's brain. He had to make this look like a petty crime, committed by bored youth, instead of a break-in carried out to gain high-level intel on the king's head of security.

Bran hurried down the stairs and into the spot where most kingsmen's offices kept the petty cash. He grabbed a night stick and smashed the cash box lock. Tucking bills into his pockets, he found a permanent marker in a pen cup by a desk. On the wall in the petty cash room, he wrote an obscene phrase about someone's mother and a hippo, then topped it off with the drawing of a raised middle finger.

"That should do," he mumbled, tossing the marker to the ground.

He went back out the upstairs window, making sure to bash the glass right before making his escape off the bin. Young, bored criminals didn't pick locks. This had to look sloppy and pointless.

A dog began barking at the sound of the glass breaking and Bran wasted no time running back into the shadows that would lead him to Rob's pick up point and the safe house.

## CHAPTER 8
## A DREAM COME TRUE

Aini read over the coded message her father and the Dionadair had come up with to send to Lord Darnwell. "I think this word should be capitalized, if I understand the code correctly."

Father nodded, murmured something to Rob, then made the correction.

Sent directly from Father, this message asked Darnwell and his wife, Elodie, whether or not they approved of Father's efforts to begin talks with the rebels about joining the French in their fight against King John. It was very risky. If they were loyal to the king, they would report Father.

"You're sure this is worth the possible trouble? If they show this to King John, the kingsmen will be after you until you're dead." She hated saying it like that, but this was no time to dance around the truth.

"As soon as Nathair learns what happened on Bass Rock, he'll most likely tell the king. I'm already up to my neck in this, and you know it, squirrel. No use pretending otherwise. In for a penny..."

She smiled sadly at the old phrase. "True. Now, hug me because I don't know when I'll see you next."

He held her tightly and kissed her forehead. "I will always be with you in spirit, squirrel."

Tears ringed Aini's eyes. She fought to keep them from falling down her wind-chilled face. Her mouth wouldn't work, so she simply squeezed him once more, then turned toward the road where Dionadair scurried around, readying the two vehicles they'd use for the trip.

Without looking back at Father, she climbed into the truck's front cab. It was time to go. Bran had discovered that Nathair was far away, in Birmingham at least and most likely nearing London. Now was the time to go. Tilting the rear view mirror, she watched the tear-blurred shapes of Dionadair loading the back with sacks of folded shirts and trousers. The sedan in front of them held four other Dionadair, who would serve as scouts on the road, going a little ahead of the truck.

This was it. The start of the true rebellion. One truck and one car of people who believed wholly in a prophecy made way before they were born. Aini swallowed a sour taste in her mouth. She was leading a group of rebels to tear down a local tyrant and a king. A king!

But she had no choice. Nathair had left. They had to strike now and get this moving or they'd be dead where they stood in a day.

The side mirror briefly showed Bran before he disappeared behind the truck to join the bags of clothing. Thane and Vera found spots to the left and right of Aini, Thane at the wheel with white knuckles. Myles, Neve, and Dodie sat in the back. Along with Bran, Samantha and Rob rode in the truck's cargo area to keep eyes on the Coronation Stone—in its unassuming burlap sack—and the weapons and Bran's explosives, which were hidden under a false bottom near the cab.

If someone had asked Aini a year ago how rebellions were born, her answer would've included detailed strategies and seasoned soldiers. She traded a tight look with Thane, then glanced at Vera, who nodded like she somehow knew what Aini was thinking. This was what rebellions truly were. A ragtag bunch who shared a belief in something greater than them. A collection of deviants determined to shape their homeland into what it needed to be.

As the small entourage left the tidy town of Greenock, and the group's last chance at remaining hidden to their enemies, Aini realized rebellions were born of passion and desperation. An amalgam that would either get them killed or create the life of their dreams.

Driving along the River Clyde, the land grew less and less populated. Sheep dotted flat fields, and distant hills gathered up dark, sapphire clouds. Myles began to sing. Thane swore.

"*She sipped sweetly soft singing, shouts stirring...*"

"...not a bit of sense," Thane mumbled, "...such a glaikit, bald..."

Aini shushed him. "At least he's making us think about something other than what we're driving into. What are the odds on your uncle supporting you?"

"*Burn bright blue blaze befit born bawling...*"

Thane swallowed and glanced in the rear view mirror to glare at Myles with his whole heart. "I'd say less than a twenty percent chance of him agreeing with us."

Aini's shoulders weighed one hundred ton. "Okay."

Myles kept on and someone began drumming a beat through the wall of the cab.

Thane's frown faded and a grin like a memory of a smile flashed over his eyes and mouth, making Aini's stomach do a little flip. "That'll be Bran drumming," he said. Thane's contacts made his eyes green, but the gray was still there, darkening the hue.

The drumming grew more complicated, and Myles, pretty much shouting at this point, matched the song to the rhythm. Aini tapped her disgusting boots against the floorboard and tried to think positive. After a bit, Bran stopped thumping from the cargo area. Myles laughed and gave him a quick rhythm which Aini supposed was a thanks for joining in.

"That's the River Teith." Neve pointed at the waterway they were approaching. "And there?" She nodded to the right. "Castle Doune rules the bend of the river. If you visit the courtyard, you can clearly see the rich tastes of the man who had it constructed."

Aini couldn't help but grin. Neve hadn't run a tour with Caledonia—the company she worked with—since all this madness began, so the urge to detail history to an audience was probably nigh to unbearable.

Under the castle's shadow, water undulated like a blue and silver snake. White teeth of light pierced the shimmering surface like a beast fought desperately to break through. The wind kicked up, and the truck swayed along with the tops of the dark pines reaching over the road.

"Fine Scottish weather, huh?" Myles grimaced as he looked out the back passenger window.

The scout car sped up and was soon out of sight.

Thane turned the steering wheel and leaned forward to look up at the pewter sky, his Adam's apple moving above the dip in his throat. "Aye. We might get a bit of snow before the day's out."

"It's so early in the year." Neve buttoned the top of her sweater with awkward fingers, her tongue sticking out of one side of her mouth.

"Trying not to rip anything?" Aini figured it must feel odd to be suddenly stronger than you'd ever been.

"That's right. I don't think Blaine McGruffin has any holes in her sweater." Neve tossed her newly blond hair over her shoulder and pursed her lips.

"Oh Tav Laney does." Aini rolled her eyes at her own fake ID name. She lifted one of the scuffed up boots she'd been given to wear. "Good old Tav could've at least replaced the ridiculously short shoelace, don't you think?" She wiggled the frayed end of the string on her right boot at Thane.

Neve peeked over the seat at Aini's less than fabulous footwear. "Blaine is probably going to take her shopping later for better shoes."

"I should hope so. It isn't even safe walking around with one boot half unlaced."

"Not safe at all."

The window beside Vera didn't quite wind up the whole way. Air zipped through the opening and bit Aini's ears and nose. She moved closer to Thane, enjoying the heat of his body through the canvas trousers and lumpy, knit sweater he'd been assigned to wear. His false identity was heavier than him and the Dionadair had done their best to make Thane look thick around the middle. Aini knew better. She could picture the flat stomach hiding under there and she had a pretty good idea of how warm and strong it would feel under her hands. Despite the fact that she had to keep checking the mirrors to be sure death wasn't coming at them in the form of Nathair or the king, her heart tripped around in her chest at the thought of having him to herself again sometime soon.

Tiny spheres of ice began to crack against the windscreen.

"Sleet." Thane made a Scottish sound in the back of his throat.

The clouds closed in around the sloping hills and the long, winding stretch of road as the wind whipped against the truck. Soon, the green and copper growth along the roadside disappeared behind plumes of mist and the lines of ice shooting from the heavens.

Vera's phone—rigged to block any hacks—buzzed. "Aye. What? You..." Then she held the phone out and stared at it. "We lost contact. I think they ran into some trouble."

"What kind? What did they say?" Aini's stomach knotted.

"Something about the road conditions, then the call broke off."

"Will we find them if we stay on this road?" Neve's large front teeth worried her bottom lip.

"Aye." Vera tapped the phone against her palm.

The wind blew hard, ice flying across the windscreen, and their truck surged left. A wheel caught the edge of the paving and Thane swore. He jerked the wheel and righted them. "We've got to stop somewhere. I can't see a thing."

"This is what your dream showed, isn't it?" Aini remembered what he'd said in the lab about seeing ice and the headache he had after he woke up.

"Most likely." His frown said the storm was only going to get worse.

Vera put her ear to the phone again. "Are you making a pot of stew, Shelby?" she said tersely. Then she clicked the phone off. "There's another safe house coming up. About fifteen minutes off. Just past a hard left turn. Beyond the river's bend. We can stay there until this passes."

Thunder rumbled, and Aini tucked her freezing fingers under her legs. "And there'll be stew?"

Vera snorted. "That would be nice. But the question was a code."

"Right. Of course." Seemed like half of their conversations lately were code. "Why do all of your code words have to do with food?"

"Easy to visualize and remember."

Aini raised her eyebrows. "Solid point."

Thane squinted to see through the storm. "There. They're in the ditch."

The lead car sat, bum up, in the long grass beside a low, stone wall, hazards flashing and a hand waving out the passenger window.

With Bran keeping a watch on the road, everyone gathered around the wreck. The windscreen was cracked in three places. It looked like a limb from the maple above them had fallen against the hood. The driver door was smashed in badly. The Dionadair behind the wheel moaned and held his arm against his side.

Sleet bit into Aini's cheeks. "We'll get you out of there."

The others in the scout car blinked. They probably all had concussions. The man in the front passenger seat was bleeding pretty badly. Blood covered his right eye and ran over his cheek. He wiped it with the back of his hand.

Vera threw up her hands. "Well this is fine. They'll all have to stay at the safe house. We can't have scouts with brain injuries. And the car...it's done in."

Thane wrenched the passenger side door open and soon they had everyone out. Everyone's noses were red with cold and the weather only seemed to be growing worse. Aini put an arm around the man with the broken arm and helped him into the back of the truck. She and Bran propped him up with bags of cotton clothing. When the rest were tucked away, Thane started their journey again.

Vera leaned over the seat and pointed. "The safe house is just there."

Thane growled. "This hard left might put us in the loch."

The wipers squeaked and lashed along the glass, but they did little to clear the view. He swore again and made the turn. A small house with limed, white walls and a thatched roof peeked out of the sleet in a field beyond the road. It looked like it hadn't been updated since the 17th century. The icy rain paused for a minute and a barn materialized behind the house, a low, gray rock wall surrounding it.

The rain, starting up again in earnest, cut Aini's cheeks as she led the group to the door, Vera at her side. Vera knocked on the chipped paint, and a woman with very short, light hair answered holding a cup of something steaming. That little cup looked like the cure for every ailment in the universe.

"Please tell me that's tea." Aini wiped her boots thoroughly on the beaten down doormat.

"Come in then. Come in," the woman said. A silver chain ending in a copper star hung from one ear. "I'm Shelby. I don't have much, but the Dionadair are welcome to it all." She began to fuss over the injured, pulling bandages and alcohol swabs from cabinets and drawers.

Bran shut the door as everyone twisted and huddled, trying to find somewhere to stand or lie down between the round kitchen table and two sad lumps that had probably been chairs once upon a time. A fire snapped from the hearth and brightened the room.

Thane put his backside to the fire, eyes closed. "Ah. I can feel my arse again. You all right, man?" he asked the one who probably had a broken arm.

"Of course he's not okay," Aini snapped.

Shelby looked up from her work. She was wrapping a length of flat wood against the arm. "He'll be fine. It's a clean break."

"How do you know?" Neve asked gently.

"I used to be a nurse. Worked with the coast reserves until that sleekit king of ours cut my wage, raised my tax, and gave my poor sister a heart attack." She glanced at a picture hanging above the fireplace. Two blondes stood side by side, smiling and holding fishing rods heavy with a salmon each. Shelby muttered something in Scots Gaelic.

Bran found a spot next to Thane and slicked ice from his thick, brown hair. Some hit the fire and it sizzled.

Shelby seemed to know not to ask questions, but Vera gave her a minimal explanation that would keep the woman enough in the dark as not to be in danger if someone came asking questions. Shelby nodded as she brewed up two full pots of tea.

Neve took a steaming cup from Shelby and handed it to Bran. He smiled and handed it on to Vera who downed it in one go. Shelby and Neve doled out more tea around the room. The scene reminded Aini of the family gathered after a funeral. She coiled her fingers around the tea Shelby gave her and inhaled the bittersweet scent. The hot drink eased down her throat and dispelled her shivers.

As if angry they'd escaped, the storm beat against the three square windows, sleet clicking like claws against the panes. It looked like night, although it wasn't past four in the afternoon.

"I'll send up some transport for you lot," Vera said to the injured scout car group. She looked to Aini, then Thane. "We'll have to go on without them, I think, and take our chances."

Shelby sipped her tea. "You probably shouldn't have taken

this main road. There are kingsman at every crossroad. They're tailing some escaped sixth-senser, as I heard it." She jerked her chin toward a radio above her sink.

"May we turn that on?" Aini asked, heading toward the old device.

"Of course."

The knob creaked, and a voice echoed through the scratchy speaker.

*"...and the forces assembled along that coastline had to fall back. The French have stated they will only hold the port until King John agrees to the first step in the peace treaty process. For now, London suffers shortages that we are certain King John will address in the near future..."*

Neve snorted. "Right."

*"...and the recently exposed plot to abduct the French ambassador..."*

"May I suggest some rest? You lot look like you could use it." Shelby gestured to an open loft level above the kitchen where a single bed had been pushed against the wall. A woolen quilt hung from pegs and a space heater sat at the top of the narrow ladder. "It'll be tight." She eyed the group. "But it'll be cozy." She winked at Thane, who looked down fighting a grin.

They didn't have time to rest though. Nathair could find out that Thane and Bran had betrayed the group at Bass Rock at any moment. He could be sending men to find them now. Or alerting those at Inveraray, which would ruin the plan.

"We really need to stay awake," Aini said. "We'll have to get going as soon as possible."

Shelby maneuvered around Dodie to get to the kitchen sink. She filled the larger of the two tea pots again. A teal cat with a hopeful grin covered the side. Its tail ran along the handle. "I can tell you, I've lived here all my life and you'll not be leaving here until the morning."

The radio kept on.

*"...weather keeping kingsmen on alert as they search for the woman accused of being a Ghost Talker. She was located originally in Skye where she told locals the spirit of a Viking raider warned of a coming political upheaval. Ridiculous and traitorous, both..."*

Aini rolled her mother's ring around her knuckle, then slipped it to the next finger. Everyone stared at the radio.

*"...and it spurred a group of insurgents to raid local law enforcement. Nine of the rebels were killed in front of the kingsmen's office. A man speaking for the Campbells stated that the king should see this as a sign that Scotland needs help."*

"Speaking for the Campbells...I wonder who it is," Thane said quietly. "He is certainly brave, calling King John out like that."

"You all look half dead," Shelby said. "Go on and rest. You can plot to your hearts' content after you've dozed a bit."

Thane looked at Aini, a question in his eyes.

Aini sighed. "I guess we'll sleep for a little while then. If you're sure this weather isn't going to improve."

"Och, I'm sure. I'll keep an eye on the road," Shelby said.

Myles was snoring before Aini had even finished rolling out her blanket beside Thane. He covered his mouth and laughed. "Feels like home."

She snuggled up beside him, breathing in the scent of him, soaking in the warmth of his long, lean body. "Is this okay?"

His chuckle rumbled in his chest and against Aini's cheek. "Course it's okay. Why would you even ask?"

"You seemed...distant earlier today. In the basement at the other safe house." She didn't want to accuse him of keeping something from her, but that's really what she feared.

"Och. It's just a big heap of madness, this whole venture."

She leaned back. He'd removed his contacts and stored them in his bag. The nightlight Shelby had plugged into the wall near the top of the ladder and the grassy color of Thane's sweater turned his eyes the color of a summer ocean.

"So you still..."

His gaze touched her forehead, nose, and chin. She knew her skin was oily after being in such tight quarters. She should've washed it properly when she had her allotted time in the one tiny bathroom.

"Yes, Aini MacGregor. I still." His breath warmed her skin.

She was suddenly very aware of how their stomachs pressed together. His hand lay on his thigh, but his fingers twitched like they wanted to move toward her. His chest rose and fell and she was definitely breathing too quickly.

"Do you think everyone is asleep?" Aini whispered.

The nightlight flickered and someone beyond Bran, who slept beside Thane, shifted and made the loft's floor creak.

"I think so." It was odd to hear a nervous note in Thane's voice. He reached out a hand and ran a thumb along Aini's jaw.

She really and truly hoped everyone was sound asleep. Because she wasn't sure she'd be able to slow down once they started this. Thane's waistband had slipped down and his boxers showed just a little. Aini brushed a finger along the cotton edge. Thane exhaled and swallowed loudly enough for her to hear. She fanned fingers over his bare stomach. Her heartbeat drummed in places she'd never known it could. Thane covered her mouth with his and he pulled her even closer.

"Sorry," he whispered.

"Don't be." She was breathing like she'd run all the way from Greenock.

Her hand had a mind of its own. It slid down his side, feeling his goosebumps, then rose and fell over his hipbone before stopping under the edge of his boxers. The skin was so warm there. And if she went further...

Her face was on fire right along with the rest of her.

He kissed her earlobe and caught it gently between his teeth. "Aini," he breathed.

With her other hand, she pressed his lower back and urged him closer, closer, closer. She could tell he was as happy to be here as she was. He rolled, and she was under him, the longer hair on top of his head hanging down and tickling her face. Adjusting his elbow, he arched his back a fraction and his body pushed against hers. Fingers of heat rose under Aini's skin, before traveling down her torso, arms, and legs. Aini thought maybe the world had ended and she was in heaven. This was their own beautiful space filled with hope and heat, trust and wanting. The muscles of his arm tensed as she clasped his neck to draw him in for another slow, soft kiss. He broke away, his lips floating above hers.

"We should stop." His gaze went to the others. "I need to stop now."

"Please don't. I might die."

He laughed quietly and put his forehead to hers.

"You're not as crafty as you think you are," Vera said, her back turned away.

Aini's heart stopped.

"Get to sleep, you two," Vera said. "You'll have plenty of time for that when we're at your fancy uncle's place."

Thane glared Vera's way and growled something in Gaelic before rolling off Aini.

Aini had no idea what to say, so she simply curled against him, one arm across his chest, and tried to stop thinking about what could've happened. As she pushed the wanting out of her mind, her earlier worry surfaced. Thane was definitely keeping something from her. Not a terrible secret like he had before with his father and who he really was, but another type. How worried was he about claiming the role of chieftain and Heir? Would he follow through or disappear when push came to shove? He wasn't a coward. Definitely not. But that look in his eyes when he said he was fine...

He wasn't. Somehow she had to get him to open up. If he didn't, he might not be ready when they needed him most. Worse, he might destroy himself from the inside out.

"So the storm Dream. It did come true."

"Aye."

"Have you had any other Dreams?"

"I don't know."

"How could you not know?"

Turning onto his side, he slid out from under her arm and faced her. "It isn't easy to know."

"But why? You said they gave you headaches."

"I'm asleep when I'm having the Dreams obviously. I could be sleeping through some of the headaches. They're dreams. It's not like I can study them properly and come up with some way to deduce what means what and which are important."

She put a hand on his cheek. "Calm down. I'm trying to help."

Gently, he pulled her fingers away from his face and his eyes hardened. "I'll deal with it," he said. "I'll figure it out. It's my calling, right?"

He rolled to his other side. His sweater stretched against his shoulders and along the lines of his back.

Aini tugged her blanket higher. "If you need to talk about it. About anything..."

"You're here. I know. And I thank you very much for it." His head turned like he was trying to look at her without rolling back over. "I really do, Aini. But let me be on this, all right?"

Her blanket was too thin for this kind of weather. A chill spread through the thin fabric and made her shiver. Pleas and questions flew through her mind, but all she said was, "Okay," and watched the green and black spots behind her eyelids until she fell asleep.

## CHAPTER 9
## BLOOD AND MAYBES

*A dark, deep red blanketed Thane's view of the well outside his childhood home in Inveraray. Mother faded away slowly. First her arm, then the side of her face, her white hair. Then it was all gone in the red-black blur. The sound of the birds in the pines faded to a buzzing silence. A sour odor—sweat—blocked out the scent of the resin on the tree bark and the minerals of the well water.*

When Thane woke he remembered nothing of any dreams, but there was a pulsing in his right temple.

Probably just from sleeping on the wood planks of the loft.

Aini was already up, but he could still smell her on his clothing. He prayed she wasn't too angry with him. He'd snapped at her a bit last night and only because she'd been trying to help him. It was just frustrating that he didn't know exactly how to use his sixth sense.

Standing in the kitchen on the lower floor, Aini bent over a map that had been stretched across Shelby's round table. Aini's arm moved quickly as she scratched a pencil on a piece of paper. Vera, Rob, and Bran looked over her shoulder. Bran's hair was a creature born from his odd way of sleeping in one position all night.

After what almost happened with Aini, he was horribly glad his friend slept like a day old corpse. Bran would never have let him live that one down.

Aini pointed to what she'd written and took a cup of tea from Shelby. "From this map, it looks like we'll be at Huntingtower Castle by nine fifteen, depending on traffic."

"Huntingtower?" Shelby lowered her tea cup, and her fingers covered the little yellow cats decorating the side.

Vera poked Aini in the ribs. "You weren't supposed to say that part out loud."

Aini made a guilty face as the ladder creaked and Thane joined them on the lower floor.

"Well," Shelby said, "maybe the ghost of Lady Greensleeves will tell you if your next move is doomed or not."

"Super comforting." Myles smiled with all his teeth.

"Don't let Callum hear you talk about any ghosts," Thane said. "He doesn't like anything not of this world."

"I bet he isn't a big fan of sixth-sensers then, hm?" Aini finished her tea and rinsed the cup over Shelby's demands that guests should not lift a finger.

Thane recalled the first time Uncle Callum had spoken of a sixth-senser. Some men's silence is honestly more frightening than others' shouting.

"No," he said. "He is not. I don't know why. I think it has something to do with his grandsire. The one who won their family lands back by pleasing the king."

"It would be good to know what exactly happened." Aini clicked her tongue.

Her mind was probably racing as fast as the winner of the Ayr Gold Cup. He shouldn't have compared her to a horse, he supposed, although she was lean and mean like those beauties. Good thing he hadn't said anything out loud.

OUTSIDE, THE ICY GROUND CRUNCHED UNDER THANE'S BOOTS and the wind nipped his cheeks and tossed his newly black hair around.

Bran punched Thane softly in the liver. "Think old Uncle Callum will be pleased to see you? How long has it been?"

"Too long. He won't recognize me. Even if I didn't have this," he motioned to his face and hair, "happening. I can tell him about our talk at the clan gathering when I was thirteen though. Then he'll know it's me for sure."

"Was that the year Nathair had you jump the biggest fire and take the blood oath?"

"Aye. And Callum took me aside and told me no matter what oath I took, I had to follow my heart."

"What did you say to that piece of very non-Campbell advice?"

"I didn't say a thing. I thought he was daft."

Bran smiled sadly. "I wonder what you would've been like if Callum had raised you."

Thane touched his chest, rubbed his breastbone. "I'm not that bad, am I? Not now?" he whispered it, wishing he could take the questions back as soon as he'd voiced them.

Bran squeezed his shoulder. "Ah, lad. I'm sorry. I didn't mean it like that. You're the only one I'd follow into death. And I'm not being a prat. I'm serious. I only meant I wonder how much happier you would've been if you'd had Callum as a father instead of Nathair."

"Callum is a good father figure for the people of Perth and Kinross," Thane said. "Mother told me he built a fine orphanage for the children who'd lost parents in the factory explosion two years ago."

Bran nodded. "So he doesn't just spend money on parties and killing people like our lovely king."

"No. Callum is a good man. I truly hope we can lure him to our side."

"It's a grand idea, Thane. I think it'll work."

"It better. We won't succeed without him."

"No chance?" Thane was surprised Bran was being negative. The man was usually fairly positive in his thinking.

"I wish I felt differently." Bran frowned up at Thane's face. "I can't believe they dyed your eyebrows too. You look ridiculous."

"And I'm not even wearing the rockstar eyeliner they gave me. They can kiss my arse on that one."

"Why didn't I get a new look?" Bran plucked at his shaggy, brown mane.

"You got a fake ID, right?"

"Aye. I'm Craig Dunkirk. Aged 23." Bran wiggled his thick eyebrows and flashed his ID.

"Och, you're getting younger."

"I think Vera made this one for me. She's trying to get on my good side." He frowned.

"You're too smart to tangle with that one, Bran."

"Aye. I can't stand the woman. But someone needs to tell that to the rest of my body. In Branland, there are two warring sides."

"Time to go!" Aini waved an arm at them before disappearing into the cab.

Thane neared the truck door. "Branland. You're beginning to sound like Myles."

"You're welcome!" Myles called from the cab.

Bran barked a laugh as he started toward the back with Rob and Samantha.

The weather steadily improved as Thane drove the group along the main road toward Uncle Callum. Blue sky pushed out the steely clouds.

Sunlight made Aini's purple hair glow like amethyst. Her smile was radiant. "This is all going to work. I feel really good about it. You?" She touched the sleeve of his bulky sweater.

"Hey, I'm sorry about last night."

Vera rolled her eyes, then looked out the window. "Sorry it ended, you mean," she mumbled, chuckling to herself.

"Shut it, Vera," Thane and Aini said in unison.

"I meant I'm sorry I barked at you a bit. About the Dreams."

"It's okay. I imagine it's tough to get your head around being a Dreamer and the Heir."

"Ah no. It's easy. Predict the future. Rule a country. All with zero experience. Kid stuff, really." He'd tried to joke, but his tone had been tight in all the wrong places and he saw it in Aini's softened gaze.

She ran a finger over the curve of his ear, sending shivers down his back.

"You're not alone."

Her lips lifted into a half smile and he wanted more than anything to press his mouth to hers and taste her lip gloss and feel the tip of her tongue on his.

"Road, Campbell. Eyes on the road, if you please," Myles said from the back seat. "I want to die in a blaze of glory. Not the blaze of a car crash, thank you very much."

"No one is dying." In the rear view mirror, Thane watched Neve cross her arms. Then she seemed to think better of it. She grabbed Myles tight and nuzzled into his neck.

"I'll talk about dying every other minute if this is the response I get," Myles said.

"Shh," Neve said. "Don't ruin this lovely moment with your mouth."

"I hate that we have no scout," Vera said.

The road twisted and showed a truck parked and blocking three cars.

The side of the truck boasted the lions of England. Hanging from a huge hook on the back of the truck, a metal cage bore the sign *Sixth-Senser*. It was an exact copy of the cages the king always had at his parties.

Thane's stomach turned to ice.

"No." Aini's voice was a whisper.

Thane wanted so much to hide her inside his stupid, giant sweater. No side roads branched from this one. There was no escape. They would be seen. They might be questioned.

Myles's hands appeared on the seat, his knuckles white. "Turn around. Just turn around and get the heck out of here."

Thane shook his head. "It'd be too obvious."

Six kingsmen—one in Campbell tartan and the others in government black—poured out of the truck and toward the nearest car. They shouted something unintelligible at the driver.

"Who cares about obvious if we can get away? I don't want to be killed before we even have a chance to do anything." Myles's voice was raw like he'd been screaming. Purple circles hung under his eyes.

The driver of a red car lowered the window to talk to the kingsmen.

Aini clasped Thane's arm, her fingernails biting his skin. "What are they doing? I can't see." She craned her neck to look out the windscreen and see beyond the cars behind the red one.

"Well, I think we all know they aren't doing anything

awesome," Myles said. "Get us out of here, man." He pulled at Thane's sweater.

Aini gripped Myles's wrist. "Calm down. Everyone calm down. They might just ask her a few questions, maybe rough her up a little, then let her go. It's best we stay here and stay quiet. If we make a fuss, they'll take us all in, including that poor woman."

Thane was very glad to hear her managerial voice. That's what this group needed. A level head. But despite her sure tone of voice, sweat beaded on her forehead and upper lip.

The kingsmen ripped the red car's door open and pulled a woman from the driver's seat.

A man crawled from the car, reaching for the woman. "Leave her alone. She isn't a sixth-senser. I told them that already. She was already questioned. We are loyal to the king!"

The woman spat at the two kingsmen who held her. The tallest of the two cracked her across the mouth. The man with her flew at the kingsmen who easily shoved him to the road. With a shout, the woman drove a knee into the closest kingsman's groin. His associate threw her to the ground and raised his stick.

Thane saw Aini there on the road instead of the stranger.

Her terrified eyes.

Her hands raised to defend herself.

Blood streaming from her mouth.

Thane was out of the truck and running before anyone could stop him.

"Stop!" Aini was behind him, but Thane couldn't hold back now. They were beating that woman and man and it could've been Aini. His mind didn't see the error—the fact that he'd now dragged Aini right into the fray. His heart pounded and he had to DO SOMETHING.

"Hey!" Thane waved a hand. "I doubt you've put her through a proper trial, hm?"

Rage stretched his voice and sharpened his senses. The road smelled like oil. The sky was too blue, too dark, too much. The blood on the woman's face was the brightest red he'd ever seen. Aini's and Vera's boots, only a step behind his, popped along the ground like gunshot.

As a group, the kingsmen straightened. "And that's none of your business," one with a wide face said.

"It's everyone's business!" Vera stuck out her chin and looked ready to fight.

So was Thane.

Thane hit the kingsman hard in the throat. Another set of hands was on him, tugging and hitting, then Thane was punching another kingsman.

A woman screamed. Not the sixth-senser. Samantha landed in the tall grass on the side of the road, her face contorted in pain.

Rob's cap flew off as he lunged at a kingsman Myles was kicking between the legs. The kingsman shoved the kick aside expertly and spun to throw an elbow at Rob.

A fist rocked Thane's head back and light flashed behind his eyes. He stepped back dazed, then was shoved to the ground.

Beside him, the kingsman downed Myles. The colonial struggled against the man as he tried to tie him up. Myles threw out insults about the kingsman's mother that would've been funny on another day.

Vera elbowed another kingsman in the face, but he took the blow like a real fighter. The man grabbed her arm, pulled her close, and hissed something probably really vile into her ear. He tossed her against the kingsman truck and held her in place with his wooden baton.

Aini lay near Myles's feet, her eyes on fire. A Campbell kingsman started rummaging through her pockets. The Campbell colors on the man's kilt were another punch to Thane's spirit.

"Get your hands off her!" Thane rose up and was knocked across the head.

"Search them for their IDs," the kingsman above Thane said.

Where was Bran? Rob, Myles, Aini, and Neve were all captured. Samantha lay bleeding and still, near the roadside. Her trousers were bunched up and she'd lost a shoe.

The kingsman jerked Thane's back pocket open and ripped out his wallet.

"You should have to take me to dinner before you enjoy yourself like that," Thane said.

"Nice eyeliner." The kingsman snapped the fake ID against Thane's nose.

Thane threw the man a finger. It was better the kingsman think he was merely a minor thug rather than a true criminal.

The kingsman's boot pressed into Thane's lower back. "That's enough now, lad. Settle yourself."

Aini's captor eyed her ID. "This says you're from Glasgow."

Racist prat. He thought because she had light brown skin she couldn't be from here. Ignorant ape.

"Just moved there," Aini said.

Smart girl. That would cover her very non-Glaswegian accent.

"Eh, Hal!" the Campbell kingsman shouted. "Didn't we get a new list of rebels to keep an eye out for this morning?"

The boot in Thane's back pushed into his spine and sent sparks of electric pain down his legs. "Aye. Haven't read it yet." Thane twisted to see Hal turn on his phone.

The sixth-senser—the one the kingsmen had beaten—moaned. Someone was sniffing like they'd been crying.

Hal held up his phone. "Your girl there looks like number 23. Minus the purple hair."

The Campbell nudged Aini with a toe, and she thrashed, ready to snap the man's foot clean off. "You a rebel, darling?"

Anger roared inside Thane, fear cowering just behind it.

"Hmmm, she does," Hal said. "Get her up."

Thane put his hands under his shoulders and shoved his way to his knees. Hal kneed him in the side. Thane's breath went out of him in a blast, and he dropped to the road again.

"This one's very concerned about her safety." Hal put his face in Thane's. "There is something familiar about your features, pal."

People didn't usually see the resemblance between him and Nathair. But maybe this one did. Or he'd seen him at a gathering. Doubtful. It was only the top ranking clan representatives and members of the closer sect of the family that came to those. If this man did recognize Thane, could Thane use that fact? Maybe craft some story about traveling under cover? Only if Nathair didn't know yet what had happened on Bass Rock and therefore hadn't reported Thane as a traitor. If he knew and these men knew...

Hal lifted his phone and held it beside Thane's cheek, bumping his face roughly. "I think that you might just be—"

A great shout came from the greenery at the side of the road and Bran blasted into the Campbell kingsman, knocking the lout to the ground.

Vera did something too quick for Thane to catch, then somehow she had the baton. "The stone!" She locked eyes with Aini.

Freed, Aini scrambled to her feet and leaped onto another

kingsman's back. As Thane rammed his forehead into Hal's nose, he noticed Aini slide an arm around the other kingman's neck, choking him and bringing him to his knees.

Thane was so relieved he'd taught her a couple moves.

A kingsman near the downed sixth-senser from the red car pulled something from his belt. He raised it up.

"Tav! Down!" Thane shouted, using Aini's false name.

She hit the ground as the kingsman's gun fired one ear-splitting shot, then she scrambled toward the back of the truck.

Thane and Neve rushed the gunman like fools, but what other choice was there?

Thane took out the man's legs and Neve tore at his arms, but he got off one more shot.

Where was Aini? There was no sign of her behind the truck. Was she taking cover? Thane hoped she was, but it wasn't like her to hide when her friends were in trouble. No. She was up to something. He'd bet it all on that.

Grabbing the blazing hot gun barrel, Thane pushed the weapon in the kingsman's hand up, then jerked it free, popping the kingsman's finger loudly. Thane cracked the man's temple and watched him fall to Neve's feet. She dusted her hands and tried to look tough, but her whole body shook.

Bran dispatched the last of the kingsmen, Myles and Rob at his side.

All the kingsmen were down, on the ground, injured and vicious as hungry dogs.

The sixth-senser and her husband lay close and quiet on the road near two of the wooden batons that had bloodied them both. They weren't groaning or asking for help so hopefully they were fine.

Aini flew out from behind the truck with the Coronation Stone in her small hands and its burlap bag under one arm.

The kingsman eyed the stone. Only one seemed to react. His eyes widened with curiosity as he lay inert, injured enough not to move, beside the sixth-senser's tire. He didn't seem to know what the stone really was, but he knew enough to wonder. He'd talk. He'd tell the others. That couldn't be allowed to happen. If the kingsmen spread the word about seeing them and also a stone, Nathair would know what was going on and winning the rest of the clans over would become an impossible feat if it wasn't already. Nathair would prep a story, a great speech, and Thane and Aini and the rebels would lose this war before it even really started.

"Here!" Aini held out the stone and hurried toward him.

Then she noticed one of the kingsman who'd been knocked out. Drool pooled from the man's mouth and onto the roadway. She stopped, and her gaze dragged to the kingsman at Neve's feet. His broken finger stuck out at a nasty angle as he moaned and tried to get up. A nice goose egg was already rising from his head where Thane had clocked him. When Aini saw Samantha, bleeding and still beside the road, her shoulders slumped. She wrapped the stone up and went back to the truck.

Thane reached out a hand to call her back and tell her it had been a good idea to get the stone, even though she'd left it a bit late. But he let his hand fall. Would the stone have helped here? Why didn't it?

Rob kneeled by Samantha.

"How is she?" Neve asked, keeping one eye on Myles who'd put a foot on a kingsman's back to keep him down.

A smear of red colored the wrinkles between Rob's eyes. "She is alive. But I think her leg is broken and her nose too. She has a cut along her ribs. Pretty deep. We have to find someone to stitch her up."

Neve pulled a small bag from her pocket. "I'm no Shelby, but

I can do that." Before Thane could wonder at how amazingly courageous these people who hadn't grown up with violence were in this moment, Neve was threading a needle and whispering comfort into Samantha's ear.

"Eh, man," Thane said to Myles, not wanting to use his real name. The colonial met his eyes. "We can't leave these men here." They knew too much.

Aini appeared again, rubbing her eyes. Blood caked the skin around her wrist and a red slash glared above her eyebrow. "We can tie them up. Leave them behind the hedges there."

"But the truck. More kingsmen will see that truck and find the men and our story will be told."

"We have to..." Aini's tone flattened. "We have to kill them."

"You were hoping the stone would, so what's the difference?" Myles scratched his almost hairless skull. Bones gleamed under his skin. "Why didn't the curse work for this? Where were the kings this time?"

Neve looked up from her stitches. "I'm thinking our friend here must be in contact with the stone for the curse to function," she whispered, obviously meaning Thane.

Aini swallowed and held her stomach with splayed fingers. The blood on her hands was still vibrant and horrible.

"Aye," Vera said. "I think she may be right on that one. The connection between him and the stone blazed when Tav brought it out, like it wanted him to come closer."

"We won anyway," Rob said quietly, gaze on Samantha.

The weapons they'd knocked from the kingsmen's hands were black marks on the pale road.

"They are arming regular kingsmen with guns now." Thane shouldn't have been surprised. "Everything will be more dangerous now."

They were very lucky the Campbell kingsman hadn't pulled

the gun he surely had too. Must've thought he and his could handle this group. Pride in Aini and the rest swelled inside Thane, but the knowledge of what killing these now-unarmed and injured kingsmen would do to Aini crushed it flat.

"So we must kill them," Aini whispered. She tugged the gun from the Campbell kingsman's belt and held it like a venomous snake.

Thane hated himself. Despite the fact that he was rebelling, that he was the Heir, this was still his fault. It was his blood causing her this pain, his own father, his own clan.

"I'll do it." Thane took the gun, checked it for bullets, and aimed.

Bran let out a curse. "They're dead." He covered his mouth and looked down on the sixth-senser woman and her man. "Beaten to death. Gone."

Neve's head dropped and her stitching hands hovered over Samantha's bright, bloody wound.

Suddenly Thane just could not do it. He couldn't spill this blood. Not today. At least not today.

"No. We're not killing these injured in cold blood," he said. "I won't have us be like them. Help me tie them up."

Aini was nodding.

"We'll chuck them behind the shrubs and shove their truck into the loch so they won't be found as quickly."

"What loch?" Aini squinted into the distance.

"There's one not a mile from here," Neve said, staring at Samantha. "I know close to nothing about these kinds of injuries, but my guess is that she needs a doctor. Now."

Rob lifted the bleeding woman like she was nothing more than a rag doll. "I'll take her back to Shelby's. Our special friends have docs that can come there to help her," he said, meaning the

Dionadair. Thane was glad none of them knew Shelby's real name. That good woman didn't deserve trouble.

"If she worsens..." Neve bit her lip.

Bran put a hand on Neve's arm.

"She knew what she was diving into." Rob pressed his lips together as he looked at Samantha. "This is her cause and she'd be happy to suffer for it."

Rob settled her into the back seat of the sixth-senser's red car and he was gone before Thane could muster up a word.

The group gathered around the dead sixth senser and her man.

"What do we do?" Neve whispered.

They couldn't very well cart two deceased with them on this mission. But Thane couldn't leave them here on the road like this. "Help me out?" He lifted the man onto his shoulder.

Bran, Myles, and Aini worked together to gently lift the woman. They set the couple in the grass beside the road.

"We'll cover them as properly as we can." Thane began stacking stones on the bodies. The group joined in until the dead rested, protected and together.

Aini whispered a prayer and retrieved her gun from where she'd set it on the ground at her feet.

"Now!" a stranger's voice crowed.

The Campbell kingsman shoved himself up, the rest of his men with him. He grabbed for the gun in Aini's hand, but she sprinted toward the Dionadair truck. The engine groaned to life as Thane dodged a blow from Hal, then took a blow to the stomach.

Kingsmen were coming at all of them, bleeding, angry, and dangerously efficient.

Thane raised his gun and fired it into the air. Hal leaped back.

The man fighting Myles jerked, surprised at the gunshot. Myles rammed his shin into the man's groin.

Vera shrieked like a banshee, grabbed up a baton, and whipped it into another kingsman's knee.

"To the truck!" Thane snapped a palm into Hal's already broken nose, then grabbed the back of Vera's dress and pulled her toward the vehicle.

Aini drove into the fray. Everyone took hold of the open passenger door or the side mirrors, grabbing whatever they could. Neve hung off, feet swinging.

Hal held his face. "Stop them!"

A kingsman snared Neve's leg and swiped a knife at her. Blood spilled down her ankle as she broke free and clambered into the cab, past Thane and Vera.

Bran stuck his head into the window on Aini's side as Aini sped up. "We're done now, you know. They have our new descriptions. They have a good guess at least on who we are." He was looking right at Thane, his dark eyes hard.

"Nothing more we can do about it."

Aini took a curve and they fell into the cab, piling on top of one another, feet on top of feet and shoulders and hips painfully shoved together.

Gunshot smacked the back of the truck.

"We just need to drive and drive fast," Thane said. "They'll be following us until they have us or we're safe hiding with Callum. If he doesn't decide to hand us over which he probably will."

"It'll be tough for those numpties to trail us without these." Vera dug a set of keys from her bra and dangled them from a finger.

"Nice!" Aini grinned viciously, hands white-knuckled on the wheel.

But the victorious feeling died as they drove on toward Huntingtower Castle. Samantha might've died already. Rob was with her and so they were short another operative. A solid group of very angry kingsmen had seen Thane and Aini and would most likely figure out who they were and make a full report. Said report would land in Nathair's inbox along with a mention of a certain stone.

The window of Nathair being in the dark was closing fast if it wasn't already shut.

They may have escaped with their lives but that battle had been a big, bad loss, and Thane didn't see how they would wiggle their way to freedom now. Not with Nathair prepared for battle, prepared to argue against Thane's claim to chief.

He was a master brainwasher. A mighty voice one could hardly argue with. He had no sixth-sense but his ability to manipulate could definitely vie for the label. When and if they ever made it to Inveraray to talk to the clans, Nathair would have already swayed the leaders, the representatives, the cousins and kin.

Thane would end up Heir to nothing but a cruel and bloody end. Not even Aini's ghosts could protect him from a battle tipped in Nathair's favor.

## CHAPTER 10
## A HIDDEN ENEMY

Silver lochs and sage green fields slid past the windows as Aini followed Thane's directions toward Huntingtower Castle. Rain that was partly ice leaked from the sky and wept onto the windscreen where it froze before the wipers could do their work.

"Why didn't I listen?" Aini tapped her fingers on the steering wheel, ticking off each thing she'd done wrong in the last twenty-four hours.

Thane covered her hand with his very large, warm one. "To what? This wasn't your fault, if that's what you're thinking."

"It is though. Partially at least."

"What?" Neve scooted forward to lean over the seat that divided the front of the cab from the back. "How in the world would anything about this be your fault? This is Nathair's fault. The king's. Not yours. Not mine. Not any of ours."

"You fought well. Especially considering you have no real training. You were amazing," Thane said quietly.

"I persuaded you all to travel during the day on main roads. I put the Coronation Stone in the back in a bag instead of in your hands where it might've done some good."

Vera shook her head and studied her broken nails. "No, no, no. We decided together, Seer. And none of us thought to have that wild candy you all make in our pockets just in case we were stopped."

Thane nodded, put a hand on Aini's leg, and rubbed circles on her thigh with his thumb. "She's right."

His newly black hair hung over one light eye. She resisted the urge to tuck it behind his ear or shift it out of his face. This road was far from straight and she needed both hands on the wheel. Especially with Thane touching her leg like that.

"You are all very nice to try to make me feel better, but this is reality. I'm not afraid to admit I made mistakes." She pressed on the gas to speed up a little as they drove past a black car that looked like it could've been an undercover kingsman. "We should've traveled less known back roads. Samantha and Rob would still be with us if it weren't for my suggestion to stay on the main routes. I should've agreed to the others' suggestion that we keep our heads down instead of throwing us into the open."

An image of Samantha lying in the dirt and grass, bleeding and broken, blinked behind Aini's eyes and speared her through the middle, making it difficult to breathe.

"Aini. Hen." Thane scooted closer and put a hand on her back. "It's all right. It's not your fault."

Stupid tears burned Aini's eyes. "Let's just get to your uncle's. We have to keep moving forward."

Vera tuned the radio to a station playing a sad song about a strange tide going out and taking a lover away. The gray tide would never bring him home again...

Swallowing, Aini focused on the winding road and began a list in her head.

*We need to have altered sweets and the Bismian on hand at all times.*

*Unless we believe we will be searched in the near future.*

*We need a plan on what to do with the stone and how to protect it and use it at the same time.*

*The kingsman will all have guns soon.*

*We need more training on disarming and handling such weapons ourselves if we are to win this.*

"What is our plan when we get there?" she asked Thane. "Are you just going to walk up and tell them who you are and hope things go well from there? I think maybe you should..." But her idea died before she could say it aloud. So far all her ideas had done is get Samantha seriously injured. She'd almost been at fault for getting them all killed.

"Tell us," Thane said.

"No."

He shook his head. "Fine, but you'd better snap out of this, hen. We need your brains. We should stop a few miles from the castle and arm ourselves with the altered sweets."

"And guns," Vera said.

"No, no guns. They'll see those and then it'll be over before it starts."

A crumbling car park appeared around the bend, beside a closed down convenient store.

"How about there?" Aini asked. "It's out in the open but..."

"Yes. That'll work."

Aini pulled them into the lot, and they set to work on dividing up the gravity-reducing hard candies, aphrodisiac cherry drops, vials of Bismian, speed caramels, strength chocolate drops, vision-inducing chewing gum, and golden taffy.

Bran crossed his arms. "This is too much for each of us to carry. We'll be stuffed like Christmas geese."

"I'm not having any trouble." Vera was cramming wrapped candies into her cleavage.

Neve shook her head, grinning.

"How about we each choose two to have on us?" Aini took a handful of the lavender hard candies since she'd used them several times in the past. "How high up will I go with these new ones? We haven't tested them yet, right? Neve? Did you test them at the safe house?"

"No, I didn't have time."

Aini really hoped she didn't end up on the moon. "I'll take the taffy, too. I want to give it a swing on this ghost that supposedly haunts Earl Callum's old castle. Maybe I'll see her and figure out how to better make use of the ghost kings that Thane can summon with the stone."

"That is the most kick butt statement I've ever heard in my life," Myles said.

"Just be sure you don't take the taffy and the gravity-reducing hard candies at the same time," Thane said. "Both access areas in the back of the brain—parietal and occipital, specifically—and we haven't tested the combined effects on brainwaves and heart rate and—"

Myles shushed him. "Okay, science man. She's heard enough and so have I. She won't take them at the same time, right Aini?"

"No. Definitely not." She was pretty glad Myles had cut off the warnings.

"We have enough risks going on now," Myles said as Thane nodded and walked over to inspect the candies for damage. "No need to test out the idea that science lectures can kill." Myles raised his eyebrows and let out a little whistle.

Thane whipped around, the shining aura around him glowing. "What was that last bit?"

Myles held up his hands. "Nothing, Lord Highlander. All is good. You are fabulous and science rocks."

Thane scowled, then turned back to the candy. He scooped up a vial of Bismian and some of the speed caramels. "I'm going with knocking folks out and being really fast."

"I like it." Myles grabbed the strength chocolate and some vision gum. "Can we be twinsies?" he said to Neve.

Her one crooked tooth showed in a wide smile as she snatched up some chocolate and gum too. "Definitely."

Vera had a bit of everything down her dress and Aini wasn't about to question it. She was just glad Vera was on their side.

Bran fisted some hard candies and cherry drops. "I'm good at explosions and maybe there will be a moment when we need one up high?"

Vera eyed him, almost shyly. Aini was shocked to see her look anything but brazen. "You don't need those cherry drops, love."

Bran's mouth fell open, then he broke into a laugh. "You're gorgeous, but I know better than to open myself up to one like you."

Vera huffed and stomped away.

Thane pressed his finger along the bridge of his nose, moving glasses that weren't there right now. He ran a hand over the shaved sides of his head, then through his dyed hair above. "The rest we'll store in the secret compartment in the truck along with the stone. We can't let Uncle Callum see that we have the stone until we're sure he's on our side." The glow around his hands showed up brighter against the section of hair he still had.

"Good thinking," Aini said. "We don't want to have some very visible, very wild battle that won't get us closer to beating Nathair and the king."

"I'm still impressed you can just say that sort of thing out loud without a tremble in your voice at all. I love it!" Neve patted her back. "Should we show off the stone if we win Callum over?"

"Thane, what do you think?" Aini asked.

"We'll see what the old man has to say. Play it by ear, so to speak. All right?"

"Agreed," Aini and Neve said together.

The rest gathered up their goodies and talked strategy. Myles found a boulder to sit on while he loaded candy into the secret pocket inside his thick shirt. Vera wiggled her dress higher and a candy fell onto the grass. Neve headed toward the truck.

Aini caught up with her. "Can you drive? You know this area well and I think I should sit in the back with Thane and have a talk about what he's going to say to his uncle."

"Aye. No bother." She took the keys from Aini with a sad smile. "It's not going to be an easy confrontation. No matter how it goes. This is the first time Thane will be open with who he is. With being the Heir and all. He'll really have to own it."

"Yes."

"And so will you, Seer," Vera said from behind. She pinched Aini's elbow lightly and shouted at Bran. "Will you sit with me in the back of the cab?"

"Only if you promise to keep your hands to yourself," Bran said.

Thane said something that made Bran chuckle and go a little red in the ears. "No, I won't be driving down that road, I can promise you," Bran said.

Aini eyed Thane. "Can we sit in the cargo hold and talk?"

"Sounds like you're in trouble, lad," Bran called over his shoulder.

Myles jumped off the boulder and nudged Neve, fluttering his eyelashes. "I want to be in trouble."

"This is too much," Aini said. "All these couples. I think those cherry drops leaked into the air somehow."

Thane gave Aini an appraising look. "I think we all just almost died and this is how humans respond. It's purely chemical."

"That is such a Thane thing to say."

"Is that such a bad thing?" he asked, following her into the darkness of the cargo hold.

When they'd settled onto some sacks of cotton shirts in the corner, knees nearly touching and backs pressed against the cold, metal walls, Aini plunged right into the topic at hand. There was no time for mincing words or being careful with feelings.

"What are you going to say to your uncle to persuade him? How do you know he won't have us shot on sight?"

"I'll tell him I want to discuss Clan Campbell and Nathair. He's brought up complaints from his townsfolk many times. It's no secret he has problems with the way Nathair helps King John oppress our own people. Rabbie told me he argued his way into a near fist fight with Rodric about the tartan law last time he was at Inveraray with the clan representatives. Said he should be able to wear any tartan he feels tied to and so should the rest of Scotland."

"So he's a passionate man?"

Thane gave her a wry grin. "When you said you'd like to spend time with me in the back of a truck, I didn't think you'd be asking me about my uncle's passion."

"Thane." She gave him a look. "I mean, passionate people make the best rebels. Look at Vera. She's a maniac."

"True."

The truck bumped them both off balance and they each put a hand to the wall.

"So we use his passionate nature to work him up," Aini said, "and persuade him to support us in convincing the rest of Scotland to do it too."

"You're a little bit scary, you know."

"I'm practical."

"Exactly."

Aini brushed her purple hair out with her nimble fingers. "How is Callum related to you?"

"Oh, his deceased wife was my mother's sister. She died a long while back."

"Why hasn't he tried to help your mother escape Nathair?"

The question scratched at an old wound inside Thane. "Because she refuses to ask for it. She is a stubborn woman, let me tell you."

Aini smiled, her teeth very white in the dim. "I'm going to like her."

"Yes, yes you are."

THE ROAD GAVE WAY TO A GRAVEL DRIVE UP TO A HULKING castle of stone. The brakes squeaked as Aini parked the truck by the gate.

Rain seeped from the grass and soaked the toes of Aini's ratty boots. Crows called from a tree desperately holding onto the last of its leaves. Trailing Thane to the pathway into the modern gatehouse—which appeared to have been added well after the construction of this old place—Aini fought a chill and shook each boot to dry it.

"Why aren't there any guards?" Myles asked, stepping out from behind Neve.

"Oh there are guards." Thane's sharp chin brushed his collar as he turned to check on Aini.

Sure enough, a man like a dragon slid out of a side door, his face ruddy and scarred. He spread his arms and smiled a smile that could definitely set someone on fire. And not in a sexy way.

"Good day, all. You do know this castle is not open for touring, aye?"

Thane's shoulders straightened. "We need to see Earl Callum."

"Do you have an appointment?"

"No. Tell him the last person to jump the fire is here."

"If I'm wasting my lord's time with a joke…"

"You're not. I swear on my mother's life."

The nasty smile faded from the man's mouth. He gave a curt bow and faced the door he'd come from. "Out here, lad," he said to someone they couldn't see. "Keep a good eye on these new arrivals."

A sallow-faced man about Thane's age walked out and glared. He had a walkie talkie clipped to his belt.

"Any news lately?" Myles asked.

Vera and Bran elbowed him hard from both sides. Aini agreed with the sentiment.

The man's eyes widened. "News?"

Myles shoved Vera away. "Has the king issued any new decrees? Are the kingsmen searching for anything in this area? What's the weather look like for tomorrow?"

Vera kicked him in the back of the leg. "Real subtle."

Sweat beaded across Aini's upper lip. "Ignore him. He's not

quite right." She gave Myles a sad smile and he sighed dramatically, throwing up his hands and heading outside. Neve stayed with him.

Thane leaned over to whisper in Aini's ear. "If they'd heard a report, we'd already be in chains."

"But they could hear about it any minute."

"Yes."

The dragon man returned and waved a hand. "Come with me."

"Myles. Neve." Aini motioned for them to catch up.

EARL CALLUM STOOD IN FRONT OF A FIREPLACE AINI COULD'VE used as a parking space. His gold-red hair shone in the flickering light, and as he turned to greet his nephew, Callum's bulbous eyes squinted. "Although I'm puzzled why you're here, lad, it is good to see you." He clapped a ham-sized hand on Thane's shoulder, jostling Thane a little which really was no small feat. "I've not seen you since you were, what, twelve? Thirteen? Christ above, you're tall."

"I've missed you too, Uncle." Thane smiled.

"What's this you've done to your hair?" He ruffled a hand over Thane's head.

"I'll explain everything. I just need you to promise you'll listen until I'm finished."

Callum's eyebrows lifted, and he motioned to a circle of leather chairs. Once everyone was settled, he leaned forward, elbows on his knees, and steepled his fingers.

"Does this have to do with Senga? You know she won't listen to me. I tried again to talk her out of that house just a year back and she hung up on me. I swear it."

"No. It's not that. But it does involve my family."

"Well, I'm ready, lad. Let's hear it. I'm not getting any younger."

Aini was relieved he hadn't shaken their hands in greeting. A family ring sparked from his left hand and having a vision right now would ruin everything.

Thane stood up even though he'd just sat down. Aini began to stand with him, but changed her mind. This was his show, and it was probably better if she stayed on the sidelines here.

Hands linked behind his back, Thane paced. "You've never liked the way Nathair runs things."

"Now, I never said those words and you know it," Callum said.

Thane held up a hand and cocked his head. Callum waved him to go on.

"It's growing worse," Thane said over the flames popping in the fireplace. "He murdered those people in Edinburgh without a trial."

"They were questioned. Some were sixth-sensers. All were rebels. They attacked Holyrood Palace, did they not?"

"There was no attack. They only hung a saltire flag on the outside. A fight started when the kingsmen showed up of course. Several were injured. None died. Their actions, while illegal, did not call for the firing squad opening up on them in a planned killing in the square."

"Why tell me? Why not talk to your father about it?"

"Come on, Uncle. You know very well how that would go."

"Do I?" His tone said he disagreed wholeheartedly with Thane, but his body language showed his true thoughts. He'd stood and gone back to the fire, his face revealing the frustration that could only come from his knowing Thane was right on all counts. Their leader was unmovable. Mad. Never swayed by the thought that what he wanted to do might not be right.

"Are you still listening?" Thane asked.

"Go on. Go on." Callum rubbed his belly like he might be sick.

"He supports the latest moves King John has made against us, against Scots, his own people. The new marriage rules? The taxes that will cripple our businesses further? You can't say you agree with his stance."

Aini wondered if he'd heard of Nathair talking to some Campbells about swearing fealty to him above the king.

"Of course not," Callum said, "but we can't fight the king."

"Especially not with Clan Campbell and its chief against us too." Thane was setting up the conversation so it'd come around to making Thane chief.

Callum spun around. "What are you saying, lad?"

"I'm saying that I found out something that changes everything within Clan Campbell and gives those like you and me—Scots who know what is right but have until now lacked the ability to speak up—the power to rise."

Callum called for his man at the door. "Take them to the guest wing. Give them each a set of clothes and take their soiled ones to the laundry. Fetch them some food. They're all exhausted from their travel and are talking nonsense." He locked eyes with Thane. "I won't hear any of that here, lad. And that's that."

Thane was losing him. The frustration and confusion that had been in his eyes, all over his face, was gone, replaced by a wall of cold eyes and thinned lips.

He had to be convinced.

Aini gripped the arms of her chair. "Aren't you even a little curious about what we found out?"

"It's a game changer, Earl," Bran whispered. His brown eyes glittered in the near dark.

Callum crossed his arms. "If Scotland were wrenched from Earl Nathair's hands, what then? You can't just go around shucking leaders off. The king would only send in another, maybe worse, replacement. An Englishman. Someone who doesn't care at all about us." He eyed Aini, then watched Thane. "This may seem honorable and worthy to you now, impressive to your lassie here, but you can't go around thinking with what's under your kilt."

Aini's fingers pinched the chair's leather arms. "How exactly could another ruler be worse?" she asked, ignoring the jab. This was bigger than her own pride. "The very man in charge of security is murdering our people with no trial. He takes innocents into his cells under Edinburgh and tortures them until they tell him what he wants to hear. How could anyone do worse?"

"Maybe let's not tempt fate with questions like that, sweetheart," Myles said, grimacing.

"Scots that don't have a job catering to the wealthiest in Scotland and England are in the worst spot imaginable. Because of the new taxes on factory workers, soon mothers and fathers won't have the money to buy food for their children. They'll starve in the street. They'll freeze to death in the winter when they lose their housing. I know Edinburgh—it is my home—and I can already see the sickness of poverty creeping up on the people there. The desperation in the kids who sell apples on the corner and the way people shrink from a kingsman who is simply walking his beat. It is the calm before the storm, Earl Callum."

The lab genius morphed into the Heir—eyes flashing, jaw clenching, and nostrils flaring. "And we intend to hold off that storm with everything we have, Uncle. Even if it means death."

Callum threw his hands up. "You're too young to know when to shut your gob, lad. I love you, but you've gone mad. To bed.

The lot of you. I'll breakfast with you and you'll be gone tomorrow just after. This conversation never happened." He gave a nod, turned on his heel, and left the room.

All the air went out of Aini.

"That went well," Myles said.

Neve smacked his knee. "Shut it."

Vera swept from her chair, dress rustling. "Sleep will help our side too. He'll be in a better mood to listen and he'll have time to think on the truth you've set at his feet."

"I disagree." Bran crossed the room and faced Thane. A lock of his brown hair fell over his cheek, but he didn't bother pushing it away. "Go after him, Thane. Make him listen. He may very well report us the minute fear sneaks into him. I'll go with you, if you like, but you must go. Now."

Thane rubbed his face and growled in frustration.

Vera glared at Bran. "What do you know about it, card dealer?" Bran dropped back a step, face going slack as Vera continued. "I can tell the connection between Earl Callum and Thane is strong."

She was talking about her Threader ability. Here, her eyes alone glimpsed the colored light connection between Callum and Thane that showed their relationship. But the guard at the door couldn't find out about any of their sixth sense abilities.

"Give your uncle some space. Time to allow the shock of this to sink in. I mean, you show up on his doorstep looking like a totally different person and you're with a load of strangers...it's no surprise he'll take a bit of working to move him to our side."

For once, Vera was making good sense.

Thane blew out a breath. "All right. Fine. Sleeping will be so simple to do now that I've cracked the world open and my psycho father could be on his way here right now."

Aini touched his sleeve. He looked down, and the pain in his eyes speared her. "He won't call it in," she said.

Vera eyed the guard. "Your...relationship with your uncle is strong. Bright and true. He loves you. He won't report you. Not yet anyway."

Aini smiled. "Listen to her, Thane. We'll talk again in the morning. We still have a chance."

"Fine. Fine." Thane let her lead him by the hand behind the rest of the group and the guard. Aini hoped the man couldn't tell they'd been talking about Vera's sixth sense. That was all they needed, some vigilante ready to be the hero.

She looked to Vera, then glanced at the guard. Vera nodded and elbowed the guard.

"Where does your family hail from, pal?" Vera asked.

"What? Umm. From Inverness actually. I came here when I was ten to start schooling with the earl's fighters."

"And your family name?"

"McConoughy. We have a place up near Travars Pub."

Vera smiled like the cat who'd swallowed the bird. "And that's all we need to keep you quiet, you glaikit thing, you."

Confusion twisted the guard's features. He gave an awkward shrug and gestured forward.

The dark stairwell led to a long hallway.

"Watch your step," the guard mumbled, obviously put off by Vera. "This covered walkway's flooring is very uneven."

Warped wooden boards pressed into Aini's boots as they knocked along and came into a more open space showing more stairs and two levels of rooms.

"What happens if we see Lady Greensleeves tonight?" Vera asked the guard.

The man sniffed. "You won't. No such thing."

Vera looked at him like he was about as smart as a slug,

linked an arm each with Aini and Neve, and pulled them into the nearest guest bedroom. "Sometimes I believe we'd be so much better off without the men in the world. Too bad they're the only ones who can flip my switch."

Aini threw Thane a sympathetic half-smile which he returned before the door closed. She wished she could have time alone with him, to feel the warmth of his arms and tell him it was all going to work itself out. That this was their fate and they couldn't fail. Too bad she didn't really feel that way. She was just as worried as he was.

## CHAPTER 11
## LADY GREENSLEEVES

With a wink, Vera sauntered away from Aini and toward the first bed in the low-ceilinged room. She flung herself down, not bothering to even take off her boots before sleep grabbed her eyelids and tugged them shut.

"Guess we should do the same." Neve took her shoes off and set them by the second bed, a narrow cot covered in a thick duvet. "You take the good one, Seer," she whispered, smiling.

Aini didn't have the focus to argue. The four poster bed squeaked a little under her weight and she tugged her clothes and shoes off, planning to sleep in her bra and underwear. The sheets smelled nice, like soap and lavender, and she hauled the heavy duvet up to her chin. Vera was already snoring. Neve waved and turned over, but Aini could tell she'd have the same trouble sleeping as Aini.

As Neve plucked at her duvet and scowled at the yellow color of her hair dye, Aini's mind churned like the taffy puller, stretching out tonight's conversation and combining it with the one she had with Thane in the back of the truck. Why would Callum be any different in the morning? He'd just say no to helping them again. He wouldn't listen. How could they stir his passion?

Eight large paintings covered the guest room's whitewashed stone walls. One was of a double bridge keeping company with a plethora of ferns, sunlit saplings, and thick moss. Another showed an old manor house with too many chimneys and lighter stone marking the edges of each corner. Several boasted a crowd of smiling people, all lined up for the photo. Children grinned and showed missing teeth. Women in fine, striped silk dresses or plain work trousers turned to look thinner or hugged friends to pose. Men sucked in stomachs and smiled over bow ties or work shirts.

This was what Callum loved. His town. His people. Somehow Thane had to relate this problem directly to them. It already was, really, but how could they argue the cause to tie it more immediately to Callum's beloved home?

Somewhere a clock chimed out the time. She'd been in bed for over an hour. Sleep wasn't happening. She swung out of bed and grabbed a guest robe hanging from a wooden post in the wall. There weren't any slippers and she had zero desire to put those ratty boots back on anytime soon, so she slipped out of the room on chilly, bare feet.

"Tav?" Vera hissed Aini's fake ID name from her bed, but Aini just closed the door, pretending she hadn't heard. She needed to walk alone to think.

Moonlight flowed over the outer room and along the stairs leading up to Thane, Bran, and Myles's room. Surprisingly, Myles snores were absent. Normally, his snoring would be shaking the floor.

"Hey," a quiet voice said, making Aini jump. Myles sat cross-legged at the far end of the covered walkway that spanned the space between the two parts of Huntingtower Castle. He waved, something small and light-colored in his hand. "Sorry. Didn't mean to scare you."

She wasn't going to get any thinking done with him around, but she didn't want to be rude so she crossed the cold floor. The wooden boards moaned and sent a shiver up her back.

Myles held his sketchbook. A chalked cow with dragon wings was paused in mid-flight on the page. "What do you think?" He held it up proudly.

"Is it a metaphor explaining the way I felt trying to talk Earl Callum into going up against Nathair?"

Myles chuckled. "Yeah no, but I like it. Really, you did well. I don't think he's coming around anytime soon though. Seems pretty ticked off about the whole thing."

"We are asking him to commit treason. That's not something you agree to right away."

The moon illuminated Myles's skin. He still looked tanned from his life in the southern colonies, but maybe his skin was just that shade.

"Did you send a message to your mother? Thane mentioned it."

"Yeah. Some of the old guys at the safe house helped me with a code based on their occasional communication with the rebels over there."

Aini wasn't about to ask if he hoped his mother would write back. She already knew he'd deny that hope even though it would be obvious in his eyes. "Do you think you'll ever go back?"

He blinked, chalk frozen above his paper.

"I'm sorry," she said hurriedly. "Forget I asked."

Wishing she was more sensitive, she pinched the bridge of

her nose and contemplated how many mistakes she'd made just today.

"I'll go back. Someday. I miss the people. They're a lot like the Scots, but more...changeable. Individually. Don't you think?"

"I've changed a lot, that's for sure. I never would've rebelled five years ago. Rules were my lighthouse beam."

"Oh, you still love the heck out of some rules, lady."

"But I break the ones I don't like."

Myles opened his mouth to reply, but a scratching sound came from the roof. It sounded like the slate tiles were moving around.

"A raccoon?"

"I doubt it."

"Because there aren't raccoons in Scotland or because you think it's something else."

"Both."

Myles scrambled to his feet and dropped his chalk. "Let's get out of here."

A light voice sang a line. The words were tangled, unintelligible. Goosebumps rose along Aini's arms.

Myles swore. "Yeah, raccoons don't sing," he whispered. His chalk sat beside his foot, forgotten.

The strange noise moved to the spot right above Aini's head and the moonlight from the window lit the painted vines and circles on the ceiling.

"I am thine, my love, and I will come to you," a deep, sweet voice said.

Myles swore some more. Loudly.

Vera popped out of the door, and Aini about leaped out of her skin. "What's that racket?" Vera demanded.

Aini shushed Vera and pointed up. "Lady Greensleeves?"

"It's not." Earl Callum emerged from the shadow behind

Myles. "There is no ghost here. And you should all get back to bed."

"I have zero problems with that directive. As you say, sir." Myles saluted and ran off past Vera and toward his room.

Aini picked up his piece of chalk and faced Callum. "And who do you suppose is singing on your roof? One of your guards?"

"He has a right lovely voice." Vera smirked.

"I didn't hear anything. Now go on. The both of you."

The scent of sage filled the air and the wall beside Aini shimmered like disturbed water.

"I don't think..." Vera started, hand going to her lips.

A woman's head, cloaked in white-blue light, moved through the walkway's wooden wall.

Aini was face-to-face with what had to be Lady Greensleeves.

Her body followed her head and Aini stepped back to give the ghost room. An emerald veil covered most of her hair and a darker green dress wrapped her small body tightly. The world shivered around her, white and blue. Her skin was a pearly gray. Her eyes were like banked coals in a hearth, burning, ashy, black, and red. The scent of sage and smoke was nearly overpowering.

"You will not stop me," the ghost said quite clearly and Aini wondered if she'd ever get used to being a Ghost Talker.

"What's she saying?" Vera asked.

Callum stood frozen, his face contorted in a mix of shock and outrage. Why was he so angry?

Aini told them the ghost's words.

Lady Greensleeves lifted an arm slowly, her dress and veil billowing around her like she was underwater. "He is to blame for my unhappiness. Before there were others, but now, now it is him." She extended one finger and aimed it at Callum.

The air was so, so cold.

"Why is she blaming you for her unhappiness?" Aini asked Callum.

Callum kept staring at the lady. "She lies. I've never seen her before tonight and I have no idea who she is, outside of the old stories. Those things happened well before my time or even my great, great grandsire's."

"Oh no. That's a lie." Vera came closer, keeping an eye on the ghost, but angling her body toward Callum. "I'm a Threader, dear Earl, and I can very clearly see a bright green and purple line reaching between you and this lady. You know her and you know her well. What did you do to her?"

"Nothing! And you—you're both sixth-sensers! You shouldn't be here. You..." Callum swallowed and schooled his tone. "I've done nothing wrong. No matter what you abominations claim this spirit says about me."

Aini clenched a fist, ready to show this earl what she thought of his opinions.

"It was my resting place," Lady Greensleeves cooed. "It was where I waited for my lover."

Aini fought the instinctual urge to run. Facing an angry ghost was less than comfortable. "Did you disturb her grave?"

Callum scowled, and his hands shook at his sides. "No."

"Come on, Earl Callum. Whatever you did, just come clean and we'll figure it out. You are a good man. Thane told us about how much you care for this area, for your home. He said you recently added a new wing to the orphanage you started when you were first given your title. I'm sure you didn't mean to hurt this lady. Be honest and we'll figure it out."

"The orphanage..." The lady began singing quietly, almost too low to hear.

"What is it that bothers you about it?" Aini asked her.

Vera and Callum stared.

The ghost covered her face in her nearly transparent hands. Bones moved under the opal skin. "He killed her right on my grave. He desecrated my resting place. He ruined it. The blood, it pains me. Pains me!"

Aini knew neither Vera nor Callum could understand what the ghost said. Only her mind could unravel the language and the spirit's noises and somehow turn them into words that made sense.

"Earl Callum," Aini said, "was there an accident near the orphanage, near the kirkyard there?"

"How do you know there is a kirkyard just there?"

"Answer my question."

"I don't know what she is telling you, but I—"

"Enough of this." Vera pulled out a knife. Where had she found that? "Tell us what you did, you evil man, you traitor to your people, tell us or I'll finish you right here."

"Try to gut me, girl, and see what happens," Callum snapped.

Aini had no doubt Callum would win this fight. She could see it in his confidence. There was nothing faked about that.

"Maybe don't wave knives at people we're trying to persuade to support us, okay?" Aini held out a hand and lowered Vera's weapon.

Vera's lip curled, but she let Aini take the knife.

Lady Greensleeves' hands fell away from her face. She glared at Callum. "She would not have spoken against you, coward. You should have given her aid."

The area around Callum's mouth had gone white and he looked ready to fall over. "What is she saying?"

"That you killed a girl on the lady's grave and you didn't need to. That the girl you killed wouldn't have gone up against you about whatever you did."

Callum fisted his hands and pressed them to his forehead,

blowing out a loud breath. "There was a car accident. I ran off the road after going to the pub. I hit a girl in one of those tiny cars, and when I checked on her, it was...it was clear she'd broken both legs to the point...to the point that she'd not walk again. She was our pastor's daughter. I'd paralyzed our greatest holy man's only child. I would've been hated. I hated myself. Still do."

Vera crossed her arms. "So you offed her so she couldn't talk."

Callum's head fell forward. "No. She isn't dead. She lost a load of blood and doesn't remember seeing me. I drove off, and no one ever found out I was the one who'd driven her into the ditch beside Lady Greensleeves' grave. No one knows. They think it was a stranger. A tourist, maybe. That it couldn't possibly have been one of us."

"She could've died on the side of the road because of your fear," Aini said, shock pealing through her.

"That's why you built an orphanage." Vera rolled her eyes. "Guilt."

"Aye." Callum wiped his face with his hands. He knelt. "Lady Greensleeves, I am sorry for what I did and how it hurt you. I will do whatever you wish to put you at rest again."

Lady Greensleeves turned to Aini. "Speak to him about honor. Clean the stain. Help me rest."

"I'd say a huge house for children who need it was a good start," Aini said. "What else would you like him to do?"

"He should conceive a plan and I will be satisfied."

"He needs to come up with it himself?"

But the lady didn't answer. Her form dissolved into nothing more than a sparkling kind of floating dust as she eased backward, into the wall. With one more line of singing about her lost lover, all noise and the sage scent faded.

Callum looked up at Aini. It seemed like he wasn't the same man they'd met earlier, the one with a straight back and the walk of a soldier. This one was humbled with red-rimmed eyes and a cross to bear.

Words crawled out of his throat, raspy and thick. "What can I do?"

"She said you had to think of some way to show her honor and clean the stain from her burial place. I have no idea what that could be." A cold lump formed in Aini's stomach. Somehow she knew she was supposed to use her other sixth sense, her Seer ability. The surety of it pressed against her heart. "Give me your hand, please. The one with the ring."

His eyes widened, but he slowly extended his left fingers. Before she could let that old fear rise up and overtake this intuition to use her gift, she gripped his ring finger.

The walkway's damp wood scent, the shadows around Callum's kneeling form, and the warped floor fell away.

A vision rushed over her head.

*A rust-haired boy ran down a path guarded by twisted pines and ferns.* To the boat, *he called out, coming into a clearing. A group of boys and girls with dirt smeared on their cheeks and sticks in their hands turned. A crumpled form lay on the ground. The rust-haired boy drew up, panting. Purplish blue and sick yellow swirled around his head, fear and the sense of betrayal mixing equally.* "What have you done to Lolla?"

"She can't say the oath right. The oath to the Campbells. She's a disgrace."

"But she's a Gowrie." *She was his sister.*

*He pushed through the bigger children and threw himself on top of her.* "Don't you ever strike Lolla again, you beasties. I don't care what she can or can't say!"

*The children lifted their sticks and each took a whack at young*

*Callum before heading back into the big, gray house in the distance. Tears blurred the sight of the house's sun-hued flowers.*

The inside of Huntingtower Castle and the face of its repentant master blinked back into being.

"What did you witness, Seer?" Vera said, her voice awed.

Callum's mouth opened and shut.

Aini helped him to his feet. "I saw you sacrifice yourself for Lolla, for your sister, when the children were beating her."

Jaw clenched, Callum breathed loudly through his nose. "So you have two sixth senses?" He shook his head. "Lolla died the next day. Accident, they claimed. But it wasn't. They pushed my good sister out of the tree she liked to climb and she broke her neck. I never told anyone what I suspected though. I kept it from my father and mother. They thought she was mad." He whispered a prayer and kissed his ring. "But what does that have to do with the lady?"

"Maybe you need to sacrifice more than money and time to clean the stain of what you've done. You need to tell the truth about Lolla and also about the car accident."

"My people here will hate me for my part in the accident. As for Lolla, there's not many left who even knew her."

"You'll never know if it matters until you do it," Aini said.

Without a word, Callum left them.

Aini had no idea whether she'd helped or hurt their situation.

## CHAPTER 12
## IN THE KINGDOM OF ALBA

Thane and Bran slipped out a side entrance to the upstairs guest room right after Myles pulled his own escape. Thane had to leave the stuffy, old place, breathe some fresh air, and try to muster up some hope for tomorrow's discussion with Uncle Callum.

"Where are we going exactly?" Bran jumped down into the trimmed grass of the castle garden from the new wall, trailing Thane like a shadow in the moonlight.

"I thought we'd go to Scone."

"Want to check out your predecessors' old stomping grounds?"

"Something like that."

Thane opened the driver's side of a sad little auto and set to work hot-wiring it.

"Ah." Bran stretched back in the seat and pretended to be relaxed when he was really keeping an eye on the road. Careful Bran. Good man. "This is just like our days before you went to uni."

"Never thought I'd miss the days of petty crime."

"Stealing cars isn't actually that petty."

"Compared to rebelling against one's father who works for one's king?"

"Point taken."

The engine rumbled to life. The road curved between a sloping hill and the rough growth no one wanted to mow.

Last time Thane had been to visit Uncle Callum, his mother had been with him. It'd been Christmas and snow had blanketed the ground. Now, the town was slicked with dark ice instead of nice, clean powder. He'd been thirteen when he was here with his mother and all he'd wanted to do was tie Callum's old hound up to a sled he found in an outbuilding and go for a ride. Mother had rescued the dog from what would've probably amounted to accidental torture and given Thane a job to do.

A science-enthusiast and baker herself, his mother had asked him to learn the secret ingredient in Uncle Callum's famous venison stew.

He remembered the moment like it was yesterday. After two solid years of doing terrible duties for Nathair, the idea of simply finding out an ingredient had been amazing. This wasn't knocking a nobleman's son into the drink to distract him while Nathair's men searched his car. No one had to be beaten down or scared to their bones with a dead rabbit in their post box. This was a clean job, a mission he could feel good about and not have to vomit over when he was through.

He'd hurried to the kitchen faster than Callum's hound could track a deer and set to bugging the cooks about cinnamon and types of Mediterranean salt.

Maybe that was why Lewis's lab had felt so right. It had been a good job. A nice thing to do. Well, aside from the spying.

Thane sighed and drove under a crumbling stone arch. Scone

Palace rose up, pointed and arrogant and lovely, lit by tacky floodlights that weren't good enough for it. Pulling into the car park, Thane couldn't help but hear Neve's voice in his ear, telling him about Robert the Bruce being crowned here. She'd know the exact year and how the clothes would've looked on that day.

Thane and Bran climbed the gentle slope to the moot hill where it was said the long-ago crownings had taken place. All Thane knew was that the wind through the towering pines and the cool air on his face was like a welcome. He felt as if he'd come home.

Bran, however, watched the wood like something was about to pop out and grab him. "I don't have a weapon. Just so you know."

"No need for one tonight."

"That is the best news I've heard in weeks."

Thane smiled at his friend and tried to hide the stirring in his wame. He wanted to appear composed and casual to Bran, not like some fainting idiot all pleased with himself, so he pushed the conversation far, far away from here. "So you really do hate Vera? She likes you, you know. And she's not hard on the eyes."

"She has a beautiful backside and a laugh I could fall into, but the woman is a snake and I won't invite a snake into my bed, I can tell you that."

"She is on our side."

"She is on the side of the rebellion. Vera would slit our throats in a heartbeat if she thought it would speed the revolution."

"I thought I was the only one who saw that. I've been trying to persuade myself to trust these Dionadair. It's no easy task." Thane took a circuitous route to the red stone chapel that backed up to the wood. The chapel wasn't what called to him, but he wasn't ready to stand where his predecessors had taken on the mantle of kings.

Bran peered into one of the chapel's windows. "You're right to watch them. Although I do think it would set their plans back a good step if they offed their Heir."

"Aye, I suppose I'm safe as long as they still think I fill that role."

Bran poked Thane's arm. "You don't think you are? After all that's happened?"

Thane shrugged. "The stone roared. The kings defended me. But am I truly meant to rule? I don't know a thing about politics."

"Och. There are plenty around you who can handle that bit for you. You're meant to inspire the people and carry out the plans you think are best for them. You can do that. I know you can. You're a good one, young Thane."

"I wish you would stop with the *young*," Thane smiled to take the bite out of his tone.

"Can't let you grow too big-headed." Bran punched him lightly in the pressure point on the outside of the thigh.

Thane stumbled a little, swiping back at Bran's mop of hair.

Snow drifted from the black sky like the stars had come down to light the hill. The air nipped at Thane's cheeks like small, rough kisses. With every step through the low grass, he wondered if *Cineád mac Ailpin*—the supposed first king of the Scots, Kenneth MacAlpin—had pressed down this same piece of earth. What had gone through that great man's head when they decided to crown him? He'd had advisors certainly. He'd been raised to rule. Thane had not. Well, Thane had been groomed at first to take the role of chieftain. But that had changed when Thane showed signs of weakness, as Nathair called it.

Thane had shown mercy to wrongdoers and to those not in

thick with the clan. Nathair had quickly decided Thane would not lead Clan Campbell, though Nathair never had settled on who actually would take over for him. Thane hadn't thought much about it. His mind had tried hard to think on it, to wonder what might happen if his father couldn't lead anymore. But he'd always pushed those wonderings away. Hopelessness had a way of making him pack his feelings and questions into certain boxes, some of which he never opened.

The wind blew again, pine-scented and soft. Thane stepped onto the flat red stones that surrounded the fake Coronation Stone.

Without any preamble, his veins lit up like he had gunpowder for blood.

He exhaled in a gust of white plumes.

Bran's eyes were wide. "My God, lad. That's..." Bran was looking Thane up and down. "I can see this *light* around you."

"Aini said she can see that light all the time since the stone roared for me."

Bran rubbed his forehead and whispered under his breath. "Amazing."

Thane closed his eyes and let the wind wrap him up, allowed the feel of the place—a heavy, sweet embrace—soak into his shoulders and along his limbs. There was a rhythm hiding in the wind's noise through the trees. Aini would've understood it, he was sure. A coolness filled his left hand, a roughness along his fingers.

"Open your eyes, lad."

Thane did as Bran said and looked down to see a pale, flickering broad sword in his hand. He flipped it upside down and set the tip on the flat stones, taking the hilt in both hands. Closing his eyes again, he whispered to the spirits of the rulers of ancient Alba, of his home, his people.

"Please help me be the leader they need. Help me find my way. Give me the formula for bringing their enemies low and healing their hearts."

When Thane opened his eyes, Bran was grinning. "Only you would ask the spirits for a formula."

Joy suffused Thane's chest and came out in a loud laugh. "I can only be who I am, pal. No more. No less."

The sword dissolved in a shower of illuminated particles and Thane was comforted with the knowledge that somehow he'd done the right thing in coming here and paying tribute, in asking for aid. Now if he could just translate this experience into practical capabilities as the Heir.

"Let's go on back, aye?" He stepped away from the crowning spot and clapped Bran on the shoulder. "I need some sleep before I battle with Uncle Callum."

The stars shimmered in the black sky. Bran stared up at them. "This is some wild adventure you've dragged me into. I never could've guessed this forgotten boy would live to serve a true born king."

He may never have known his family, but he was definitely not forgotten. Not to Thane. "I'm just glad you know how to serve a good whisky," Thane said.

With a wry grin, Bran tripped Thane, and they traded a few easy punches before heading back to the castle for some hard-earned rest.

SLEEP DID NOTHING TO CLEAR OUT THANE'S MIND AND GIVE him a rest. Sleep brought a new Dream and there was no doubt this time that it was a dark tale of a very possible future.

In the Dream, Thane stood on a mountain top that was really nothing but an impossibly huge pile of round rocks. His foot slipped. The drop to the valley below yawned wide open like a great beast ready to swallow him up. Heart in his ears, Thane steadied himself and grabbed the exposed root of a gnarled pine. He turned to see Aini. A blood-red dress whipped around her as she stood like a statue, not breathing, not blinking.

"Choose," she said.

Her dress, face, arms—all melted down and reformed into Nathair scowling, scar puckering the skin at his neck. He held up Thane's Campbell necklace and shouted.

"Choose!"

Then Nathair melted away too, leaving nothing but a stain of red-black blood on the mountain top's stones. Thane fell backward. The wind rushing past his ears as he plummeted sounded like a man's voice, Kenneth MacAlpin's voice.

"Tagh. Chì sinn dè an seòrsa rìgh a bhios thu." *Choose. We will see what kind of king you'll be.*

Before Thane hit the earth, he raised his hands and saw he held the ghostly sword from the moot hill. It was covered in blood.

CHAPTER 13
DECISIONS AND FIREWORKS

Uncle Callum's chair was empty when Thane and the rest followed a guard into a large feast hall. A mound of bright, scrambled eggs and bowls of steaming porridge crowded the table. The guard, who obviously wasn't just a guard but a butler of sorts, too, gestured to the high-backed chairs. When Thane visited as a child, he used to pretend the chairs were ships, the spindly backs like masts.

Thane sat beside Aini and to the right of Uncle Callum's place. "When will my uncle be down?" Thane asked the butler-guard.

"I don't know, my lord. I think he had a difficult time sleeping last night. May I suggest you eat? The earl won't mind at all."

Myles looked a little green around the mouth. "I wish I had an appetite."

Neve frowned. "I feel like there's something everyone knows but me." She spooned some porridge into her mouth.

Aini elbowed Thane. "I need to talk to you."

"And I you, hen, but maybe it can wait until we've talked to Uncle Callum."

"You need to know what happened last night," she said.

"I went to Scone." He wouldn't tell her about the Dream just yet. He'd wrestle with that one on his own. But he could tell her about his experience on the moot hill.

"You what?" Neve's spoon hung still in front of her chin.

"Bran and I," he said, "we drove to the moot hill where the Coronation Stone used to rest. Where the old kings were crowned."

Aini gave him the MacGregor eyebrow lift. "I want to hear all about that, but that's not what I'm talking about. Last night, Myles and Vera and I—"

"How come no one thought to invite me on one of these little nighttime outings?" Neve said. "You know what? Scratch that. I'm glad I, for one, had a good sleep." She shrugged and finished her porridge, moving on to the eggs.

Myles gave her a weak grin. "You're the smart one, Neve. You are lucky you didn't have a run-in like we did. Now, can you see any blueberries or strawberries around for the porridge?"

"You should eat it with salt and butter only at Uncle Callum's table," Thane said.

The man himself walked in. "He is right. That's the only proper way to eat porridge." The memory of a smile graced his weathered face. "I think we all have some stories to tell, aye? I'll start."

Then Uncle Callum's voice took on that rise and fall cadence he used during clan gatherings by the bonfires. He told them about Lady Greensleeves and a terrible accident. He'd called the city council that morning and told them he was responsible for the car wreck and that'd he gone to the lady's grave at sunrise to leave a blood sacrifice.

"What did you leave?" Neve asked.

"The spirit smelled of sage so I tied up some dried lengths of the herb from my kitchens and dragged my cut palm over them to bless them."

"Perfect." Aini smiled and folded her napkin on her lap.

"So...you're no longer against all sixth-sensers?" Thane asked. Uncle Callum had always railed against them, although he'd protected Perth from the worst waves of questioning Nathair set into motion.

"No, lad. I'm not. It was my own fear that drove that anger. I'm ashamed of it. Truly."

"It takes a real man to admit when he's being an arse," Bran said, giving Uncle Callum a nod.

Thane took a sip of black coffee and cleared his throat. He had to tell him. "You know the old stories about the Coronation Stone?"

"Aye," Callum said, "of course." He steepled his fingers and watched Thane carefully. The white bandage around his hand was like a flag of truce he'd raised to sixth-sensers and Thane had to make the most of his uncle's open state of mind.

"Aini here, Aini MacGregor, daughter of a chemist who once worked for the Dionadair, is the Seer. The Seer. She found the Bethune brooch and followed the trail that led to the Coronation Stone's resting place on Bass Rock Island."

Callum's face was unreadable.

"And when we touched the stone, it...well..."

"It growled like a beast and took down all those idiots working for Earl Nathair!" Myles, halfway out of his seat, raised a fist.

Callum stood and walked to the door.

"I know it's difficult to believe," Thane said.

Taking a deep breath, Callum returned to his seat. "You're saying that the Coronation Stone protected you, young Thane."

"Aye."

"And so you claim you are the Heir to Scotland's throne."

Aini raised her chin. "He is the one that will knock the king from his seat."

"You're his Seer. He is your Heir."

Neve clasped her hands and grinned. "Merlin and Arthur is my favorite way to think on it."

Callum swallowed and grabbed his glass of water, drank it down. He wiped his mouth, gaze roving the faces gathered around the table. Thane couldn't stop clearing his throat and the room felt too small even though it was honestly too big. His fingertips tingled like he was about to be attacked.

Beside Callum's hand, a phone reflected the morning sun and sent a ray of painful light into Thane's eyes. With one call, it would all be over. They'd be taken into custody and thrown in prison if they were lucky. If not, they'd be shot the moment Nathair's crew showed up in answer to Callum's report.

Thane's hand searched for Aini's under the table. She found his and gripped him tightly in her soft but strong fingers.

Callum pushed away from the table again and turned his back on them, arms crossed. "What do you suppose I do about this?"

"Support Thane, of course," Aini snapped.

Callum whirled around, and Thane wished a little that Aini hadn't jumped to that so quickly.

"In what way?" Callum demanded. "With guns? Fighters? How do you plan to overtake the entirety of Clan Campbell's forces *and* the king's, which will back them? What do you know about fighting against the king's Head of Security?"

Thane wondered...should they tell him? In for a penny...

"Uncle Callum, meet Vera Bethune, daughter of the most influential leader of the Dionadair rebels."

Vera stood up and curtseyed. "Good to meet you, Earl Callum."

Callum's mouth dropped open. "God above. You've already gone in with the rebels, then?" He glared at Thane. "And brought them to my house. Without any thought to my safety."

"Aye, but I did worry about your safety and ours and that's why I have black hair and contacts and we all have fake Subject Identification Cards. We're committed to this, Uncle. We can't back out now. Will you support us or throw us to the wolves?"

"If I do throw you to these metaphorical wolves, will a non-metaphorical, actual curse take my life?"

Thane didn't want to say. He wasn't sure how the stone's curse really worked and he wanted his uncle to do this because he believed in it, not out of fear.

"Probably!" Myles grinned and scooped another heap of eggs onto his plate.

"I need time to think," Callum said.

"Aye. Of course. But will you give me your phone as a sign that you're actually just thinking?"

"You know I have access to any number of communication paths."

"I do. It's merely a symbol of your action. A promise, of sorts."

Uncle Callum slid his phone to Thane, who pocketed it before the man changed his mind. "Thank you, Uncle. I hope you'll come to me with any questions you might have."

With yet another heavy breath, he nodded and left the room. Poor old man. They'd probably end up giving him a heart attack.

"How long do we give him?" Aini arranged her used fork and spoon on her plate, then finished the last of her coffee.

"I'll find him in an hour. If he doesn't know by then, we need to find a way out of here."

Vera brushed a little egg off her dress. "Agreed. In the meantime, we should practice with those candies of yours." She wiggled her eyebrows at Aini.

Aini grinned. "It's time for dessert, friends."

Thane looked out a window to see Callum walking the garden, hands in pockets and shoulders hunched. He didn't envy his uncle's decision. No matter what he decided, his life was never going to be the same. It wasn't so long ago that Thane had gone through that same decision.

Aini came up beside Thane and steered him out of the dining area and into the hallway. "You never told us what you and Bran did last night."

Thane broke into his tale about Scone and the sword. "I'm not sure what good it did, but..."

"I can see what good it did," Aini said. "Your aura is brighter than ever. Do you truly feel like the Heir now?"

"I don't think I'll ever be comfortable with the position."

"Me either. With being the Seer, that is. Leading the rebels. I've done everything wrong so far."

"You have not."

She waved his arguing off. "I want to talk about you."

"Well, I do feel different today. After going to Scone. Is it mad to say I can feel the blood of those kings inside my own veins?"

"Of course not. You do have their blood in you."

"But I *feel* it. It's as if I've fireworks setting off under my skin sometimes."

Aini reached up and put her arms around his neck. She smelled lovely and her skin was so warm and smooth. Her lips parted to say something, but she stopped. The corners of her mouth tipped down.

"What is it?" Thane made circles on her cheek with his thumb.

"I want to enjoy you, enjoy us. To say that I'd like to give you some more fireworks, if you don't mind. But..."

He pulled her close and ran his nose along her forehead. "I'd like that very much."

"But I feel awful. I should've had us arm ourselves with the altered candy and taken the back roads at night. I should've been more careful. I messed up during our talk with Callum, too. I always blurt things out and I wish I was more like you, so measured and smart."

"Hah. Right. I'm so even keeled. Sure."

"You do have a temper, but yes, you seem to know what to do all the time."

"I don't. Hardly ever. I'm making this up as I go along, just like you, just like all of us. And I certainly think we should firework one another while we can."

She smiled sadly, tears shining in her big eyes. "The others will be busy with the candy for at least a few minutes. I saw a quiet spot on our way in yesterday. Is there a library here?"

"Aye. Just here." He pointed to a wooden door covered in carved thistles. A likeness of Scone Palace sat below the plants' tangled roots.

Aini tugged him into the dark library. He shut the door with a foot.

His hands had a mind of their own. His palm smoothed the fabric covering Aini's hips, all the way to the stripes over her flat stomach. His thumbs stopped just below the curve of her breasts. Body thrumming with want, he closed his mouth over her lower lip and she let out a small noise that undid him. She kissed him back, her teeth nipping lightly, before her mouth moved to the spot behind his ear. A kiss there, and heat raged down him, through him, making coherent thought near impossible. His hands were in her hair then and she pulled back, her lipstick everywhere.

"Do you miss my long hair?"

"No, hen," he said, laughing, "I'd be mad for you even if you were bald as Myles."

"Please don't bring up Myles right now."

"Don't have to tell me twice." He touched his mouth to the smooth lines of her collarbone and slid his hands down her back. The feel of her body against his was too much. She was so soft and so strong. He wanted more than kisses in a library corner. "Aini. What if we—"

A knock on the door cut him off. "Sorry to interrupt, but," Neve said through the thick oak, "we're supposed to be practicing with the altered sweets, right?"

Thane squeezed his eyes shut and tried very hard not to be rude. Neve was fantastic and she didn't deserve the rough end of the chemicals currently raging through his body. "Of course, Neve. Be right there."

Aini laughed against Thane's chest. "The rest of our fireworks show will have to wait."

Thane adjusted his clothing and things. "Ugh." It wasn't as easy to switch gears with this amazing girl of his. Finally, he took Aini's hand and they left the library.

## CHAPTER 14
## COLORFUL TRAINING

Candies—red, purple, pink, brown, and gold—covered Aini's neatly made bed.

"Be sure about which one you want to try." She chose the golden taffy.

"Yes," Thane said, "because I truly don't think you should intake more than one type. I worry about brain damage."

Myles patted his own head. "I really don't want to risk the little I've got up there."

"No one is going pressure you, Myles. You do what you feel is best."

He smiled genuinely. "Aww, I need to do it. I don't want lovely Neve to think I'm a coward."

"Giving in to peer pressure makes you more of a feartie, darling," Neve said, picking up a chocolate drop.

"You people kill me." Vera pulled a cherry drop out of her pocket, walked up to Bran, and shoved it into his mouth.

"Vera!" Thane ran over to him and patted him on the back as he sputtered and spit the thing onto the floor.

Bran straightened and rubbed a sleeve over his mouth. "I'm fine." He nodded to Thane, then turned to Vera. "You need to stay away from me."

"What are you doing?" Aini grabbed Vera's arm and spun her around. "It is NOT OKAY to shove altered sweets down throats."

She laughed loud. "Calm down. I was just having a bit of fun with tall, dark, and handsome."

"You two have zero in common," Aini hissed in her ear. "I don't know why you think you can seduce him."

"Seer, let me have my fun."

"That is not fun," Neve said. "That is assault."

"You wouldn't know fun if it hit you in the face," Vera said to Neve.

Neve socked Vera right in the nose.

Both girls bent, howling. Neve held her hand and Vera, her nose.

Blood seeped between Vera's fingers. "You glaikit girl. So you want both boys, do you? Myles, you can have. Bran, now he will be mine before this thing is through."

"Don't I get a say in it?" Bran asked, looking pretty thunderous.

Thane examined Neve's hand. "Good thing you used your palm and not your fist. You would've broken it if you'd tried that."

"Vera!" Bran started toward her.

But Vera didn't answer. She sauntered from the room, dripping blood. She was terrible, but she was tough. They would definitely have to rein her in. Unfortunately, Aini thought that was probably her own job.

"I really, really want to call her very bad names." Neve glared at the door.

Aini couldn't agree more.

"Go right ahead, love," Myles said. "Let it flow. We support you. Better in than out. Or something."

Thane's mouth lifted as he put the remaining candies back into the containers Aini had organized. Bran said something to him that made him laugh darkly.

"All right, everyone," Aini said. "I'm going to head toward town and to find a kirkyard. I want to see if this improved Cone5 taffy helps me see spirits more readily. Anyone want to come?"

"As enticing as that is," Myles said, "I think I'd rather have a fight training sesh with Thane and Bran here. Blood before boogie men, I always say."

"Boogie men?" Thane cocked his head.

"He means ghosts." Aini headed toward the door. "All right then, have fun with some fighting. Neve, want to come along?"

"Yeah. I don't want to, but I will. For you, Seer." Wincing, Neve shook her hand. Her palm was splotchy.

"Please just call me Aini. You're my friend, not my disciple."

Neve hugged her and just about broke a rib.

"Take it easy." Aini stepped back. "Your chocolate power is dangerous."

"Och. I'm sorry." Neve covered her mouth with her hands. "I didn't mean to hurt you."

Myles sighed dramatically. "I know I'm about to hear that same phrase from Thane one thousand times."

Thane grinned like a maniac and cracked his knuckles. "It was your idea, colonial."

Aini paused by the door. "How about we watch a bout or two first?"

Neve bit her lip. "All right."

Myles shrieked and ran at Thane, one hand raised like he could hammer Thane into the floor somehow. Thane caught

Myles's forearm, stuck out a foot, and Myles landed in a heap at the foot of Aini's bed. Bran put a shin across Myles's stomach, his other leg extended for balance.

"Don't show me what you're trying, colonial," Thane said.

"Don't break my back in the learning process, Lord Heir."

Bran helped Myles up. "Keep your hands up, near your face, to protect yourself. Don't look where you're about to strike. Don't hesitate."

"And less screaming would be good," Aini added.

"Aye," Neve said, "but did you know when ancient Highlanders went into battle, they often shrieked wildly to throw their enemy off?" She raised both eyebrows like this was the most exciting thing ever.

Bran tilted his head toward Neve. "She's right."

"That is interesting," Aini said, giving Neve an indulgent smile.

Myles threw a punch, and Thane pushed it off to the side, past his ear. "That's called a parry. Doesn't need to be much, just a wee shove."

Thane began throwing slow punches at Myles's chin. Myles used the parry to keep from getting hit.

"Good job!" Neve clapped once, grimaced at her palm, then rested her hands gingerly on her hips.

A sheen of sweat made Thane's cheeks and forehead shine. His undershirt stuck to the planes of his chest and the curve of his upper arms and shoulders. "Now we'll go the ground and I'll teach you how to sweep a man off you."

"Or a woman," Aini said. Then she blushed realizing how this sounded.

"I need to practice that one," Bran said, an eye on the door, watching for Vera's return. "Or maybe I don't since Neve Breaker-of-Bones Moore is around."

Myles covered his heart with his hands. "Breaker-of-hearts."

Bran and Myles traded a look that said they might have a bit too much in common in the way of Neve.

Myles's mouth switched from grin to glare. "I had her first, you handsome Scottish devil. And I make her laugh."

"I won't take her from you, lad," Bran said gently.

Aini was so glad Thane had Bran in his life. With all the horror he'd endured, Thane needed a good friend like Bran. Myles did too.

The boys began to tussle again, sweating and laughing as they threw punches and tossed one another onto the floor.

"Let's let them have their fun," Aini said, checking to be sure she had the golden taffy wrapped well. "They should enjoy some laughs while they can."

A FAIRLY NICE DAY TURNED INTO AN ICY, FOGGY ONE AS AINI and Neve passed the first of the gravestones.

"Why did I agree to this?" Neve tugged her sweater so it came right up under her chin.

"Because you're the best friend I've ever had."

Neve squeezed Aini's arm gently, using just her fingertips.

"Appreciated," Aini said.

With the effects of the taffy fully in play, the fog's white plumes took on more color. A pale, iridescent green shifted through the air and wove into a deep wine color that moved more slowly. Aini waved a hand through the myriad of colors.

"I wonder what all this really is."

"What is?"

"The colors I'm seeing. There is this green and a burgundy... is it gases in the air or what?"

"I have no idea. That's a question for Thane."

Then they had no more time for speculating because a human shape was forming not ten feet from where they stood. Over a head-high grave marker of an angel, a ghost shimmered into view. The blue-white light that had been around the ghost kings and Lady Greensleeves was nowhere to be seen. Instead, the air around the vague shape shimmered a color Aini had no name for.

"Can you see that?" Aini pointed.

Neve shivered. "No. Is it a spirit?"

"I think so. But it doesn't have that same color."

"The kind of light the kings had?"

"Right."

The unnameable hue faded and the bluish white light replaced it. Neve gasped.

"Ah. There's that color they usually have," Aini said.

The ghost drifted closer, the colored fog stirring around his bulky frame. "Do not come here." His eyes darkened.

"We need to get out of here." Aini snagged Neve's hand and they ran to the far side of the kirkyard.

Another ghost materialized near a snowdrift by the kirkyard's stone wall. With the Cone5 working, Aini saw it first and pulled Neve to a halt before they could sprint straight through him. This former person wore clothing from at least two hundred years ago. A patch covered his right eye.

"It's another one," Aini said as the blue-white light that would allow Neve to see bloomed into being.

Neve gave a single nod and seemed to gather herself up. "You should ask him about the earl and see if he has any suggestions on how to sway him."

The spirit spoke before Aini could say a word. "Command me, Seer."

A shudder danced through Aini's ribcage. "Who are you?"

"A salmon trader's son." His words wavered, fading in and out, making it nearly impossible to understand. "...your strength...could call one such as me without the Coronation Stone."

Aini's heart lurched. "What did you say? What do you mean?"

He inclined his head. The scent of the river—wet banks and minerals in the water—rose off his glimmering form. "I am no king. I come because you are the Seer."

"What is he saying?"

Neve leaned closer as if proximity were the reason she couldn't understand the spirit's words. Of course that wasn't true, but this ghost did seem more human than any of the others they'd run into so it made sense Neve's first reaction was to come close to hear him like she would a person who was speaking softly.

"I can command you even though the Heir isn't here with the stone?"

The ghost nodded. "I am no king."

Aini turned to Neve. "I think this boy is willing to do what I ask because he somehow knows I am the Seer."

"Could he fight for us?"

The spirit lifted, then fell, his shoes dipping into the earth. Aini felt desperate to squeeze information from him before he faded away. "Can you fight?"

Confusion twisted his face. "Touch? No. I am no king."

"I don't think he can physically affect the living world," Aini said to Neve.

"What about a message?" Neve jerked her chin back toward the castle. "Maybe he could persuade the earl to make a decision we like."

"Would you do that?" Aini asked the spirit. "Can you tell Earl

Callum to support the rebellion against Earl Nathair, Chief of Clan Campbell and the king's Head of Security?" She felt the odd need to be formal with this boy.

"As you will it, Seer." The ghost's form exploded into a shower of glittering dust and the kirkyard fell silent. The click of the icy rain on the tombstones was the only sound.

"He is going to talk to Callum," Aini said. That was unexpected.

"What if he threatens the earl?" Neve walked at Aini's elbow. The heavy fog still shrouded the kirkyard's entrance.

"I hope it doesn't come to that, but if it does, well…it'll be for a good cause."

AINI FOUND THANE IN THE DINING ROOM WHERE HE WAS scribbling on a piece of paper. Numbers and letters filled every inch of the sheet except for one spot where he'd sketched a brain coded with patterns that showed which altered sweets affected which region.

He mumbled under his breath and pushed up glasses that weren't there. "Scandium, Titanium, Vanadium, Chromium, Manganese…" A smile lifted Aini's cheeks. He was rattling off the periodic table of elements.

She put a hand on his shoulder, feeling the muscles under his shirt, warm and strong. He hadn't donned that terrible sweater yet because Callum's staff had taken most of their clothes to be laundered and given each a spare set of something simple to wear. "It's going to be okay. I found another ally for us in the kirkyard."

Turning, he looked up at her with wide eyes.

She told him about the salmon fisherman's son and the effects of the Cone5.

"I wonder if it'll work."

Callum strode into the room, boots covered in grass clippings and his face pale. "I'll help you, lad. Lassie. It'll be an awful mess, but I'm in it with you. To the end."

Aini longed to ask if the ghost's message was what had moved him to this decision, but she didn't want to push it. Too often lately, she'd blurted things out and acted rashly. Bravery was one thing, but she'd gone past that a time or ten and sailed right into foolishness. She had to regain her strong practical instincts and be smart about what she suggested, said, and did.

"Are you truly ready to rebel against your father and your king, young Thane? How about you, Seer? Are you prepared to go to your deaths if the chaos calls for it?" As Callum spoke, Myles, Vera, Neve, and Bran walked into the room.

Thane stood. "I thank you for siding with us, Uncle Callum. And yes, I am ready. As ready as I'll ever be."

"It's not as if we have much of a choice," Aini said. "We're called to do this and fate won't let us ignore the situation at hand."

"Yeah the baddies are going after you all regardless, so you might as well give them some good trouble," Myles said.

Thane cracked a smile, but Callum's face remained serious.

"What do you suggest we do first?" Callum asked. The butler/guard/server came in with a tea tray and Callum waved the man out of the room.

"Will you call a clan gathering at Inveraray for me, Uncle?" Thane's jaw cast a shadow over the tendons in his neck and the worn edge of his white undershirt.

"You're certain that's the right choice."

"I must detail Nathair's and the king's wrongdoings. Then we'll expose who we are and what we plan to do." He nodded toward Aini. "I have to make my plea, answer their questions, and win them to our side."

Callum smiled sadly. "Aye. To do this and come out alive, you will need to do a great deal of very fine talking."

"As long as I don't have to jump any more of your bonfires, I'll be fine."

Callum barked a laugh. "I can't promise you that won't happen after a few drams of whisky."

Relief loosened Aini's tensed muscles and relaxed her fists. The revolution was about to begin in earnest, but at least they had this powerful earl to back them.

## CHAPTER 15
## A CALLING OF THE CLANS

Thane had only seen it done three times. Never from here. Uncle Callum put five of his loyal men and women onto horses. The saddles bore skirts showing his coat of arms, and as the riders burst from the front gates of Huntingtower, the colored fabric fluttered in the vortex of the horses' speed and the opposing wind. Hooves threw chunks of grass and soil behind the mounts and Callum blew a horn taken from a Highland cow. The sound reverberated in Thane's chest and reminded him of the kings' blood inside his veins.

Thane stood close to his uncle, near enough to smell his shaving cream and the wet wool of his coat. No one in his family, extended or immediate, had ever risked this much for him.

"I thank you, Uncle," he said softly, feeling very young. "If there's anything I can do..."

"You can win, that's what you can do. Win, then let me come back here, to my home and my people."

The beat of hooves faded as Aini drew up beside Thane. "Why horses and not cars?"

"It's tradition," Thane said. "No other news is delivered this way. Only the call for a gathering. The moment the horses are spotted in each county, word is spread and the traveling begins. It won't take nearly as long as you might guess." He faced her and set his hands on her shoulders. "Are you ready to stop doubting yourself and act as the Seer that you are?"

Smirking, she covered his hands with hers. "Say that into a mirror, love."

He pursed his lips and nodded. "Are *we* ready?"

She studied the space around him, most likely watching his aura glow. "I know one thing for sure."

"What's that?"

"I am more than ready to stop sneaking around in dirty boots, pretending to be someone else."

"Is it the pretending or the unclean footwear that has you most bothered?"

"Shut your gob, laddie." Aini pinched his stomach and marched back inside.

Thane said a little prayer that she would make it through this. It would kill him if she…no, he wouldn't say it. Not even in his mind.

THE LATE AFTERNOON SUN WARMED THE STEERING WHEEL AND Thane's knuckles. The road was empty. Too empty. He didn't want to mention it and worry the group more as they approached Inveraray. The quiet back roads gave way to salt-white shops, black roofs, and…gray pavement devoid of any tourists or locals? A dark feeling crawled down Thane's back.

"Do you have your taffy on you?" he asked Aini.

She'd told him the young ghost claimed she could command

him and other lesser ghosts. Hopefully, they'd scare the stuff out of their enemies.

"Yes. Do you have your caramel?"

"Aye. But no gun."

"Well, we agreed on no obvious weapons, right?"

"Right," Bran said from the backseat.

Myles snorted. "Besides the caravan of Callum and company behind us who are surely toting buckets of guns."

"Yes, besides that, we come in peace." Aini's lips bunched to one side like she was thinking.

Thane's palms began to sweat. "I never took the stone from its hidey hole in the back of the truck." He lowered the visor to block the harsh, lowering sun. "How am I supposed to do anything with that big boy anyway?"

"I really want to make a joke right now," Myles said.

Neve tsked at him. "Restrain yourself."

"It's a valid question," Bran said.

"You commanded that ghost to talk Callum into his decision," Neve said. "So why do we need the stone now? Aside from making it roar in front of the people to show them you're the Heir."

Aini shook her head. "The ghost I used to send the message to Callum said he couldn't do anything physical to this world. It's my guess that only the ghost kings can carry out any true defense of the Heir. We need the stone in Thane's hands to call them up."

"Which leads back to my question: how do I use the stone properly? It's no small rock."

Aini snapped her fingers and some of Thane's worry faded at the sight of her mind at work. "We can break off another piece of the stone. A small piece. You could wear it on a chain around your neck."

"Och, that's a braw plan," Bran said. "Does anyone have a drill in their back pocket?"

"Are you being sarcastic with our Seer?" Vera hadn't spoken since the nose-breaking. Thane had hoped she was working toward being amenable. But maybe she was merely angry as a wet cat. "You can slight me all you like, you and your bizarre threesome you have going on back there." She looked at Myles and Neve in turn. "But the Dionadair won't put up with you disrespecting our Seer."

"I meant no disrespect at all."

Bran's voice was dangerous. He may have been the kindest man Thane knew, besides Lewis MacGregor, but he had beaten deadlier people than Vera down, and Thane had no doubt he'd take the whole rebel crew on if he thought it was the right thing to do.

Thane blinked at the sun and took a right turn. "We'll stop at the car park just there, near the apothecary, and see if Callum's group has a way to make this chip of the stone."

A HALF HOUR LATER THANE WORE A LEATHER STRING AROUND his neck. A chunk of the Coronation Stone, roughly the size of a pound sterling, hung heavily from a metal ring. Bran had drilled the tiny, careful hole, using his explosives skills. Thane kept the stone between his undershirt and his sweater, not wanting the magical object to touch his skin.

"Does it feel strange?" Aini asked as they started toward home.

"It does." The fire in his blood burned hotter with the stone so close to his flesh. It was a scary sensation. Like he might come undone if he kept it so close for too long.

"Your aura is brighter. What are you worrying about?" She

squeezed against him to look in the mirror at the trail of trucks and cars behind them, probably double-checking Callum was keeping his word.

"Not about my uncle, if that's your fear. I've never seen him break his word. I don't like the look of the streets, if I'm honest."

"There's not a person out today," Neve said, "and with this better weather, you'd think they'd be at the shops." She spoke the truth. After all that rain and ice, folk should've been on the streets, buying and talking and drinking.

Everyone in the truck went quiet as they drove past a sign for the castle.

"I've never seen Inveraray Castle." Aini leaned over Thane's arm to peer out the window as he turned the truck toward the new gatehouse at the base of the drive.

A woman and a man in Campbell tartan and kingsmen jackets stood at the barred entrance. Codekeepers. Thane's pulse ticked faster. Faster. This was the moment. They'd be shot on sight if Nathair had found out about Bass Rock and the death of Rodric.

Thane lowered the window. "Gallowglass," he said.

Aini shared a puzzled look with Myles. Thankfully, both kept quiet.

The woman pressed a button and the black, iron gates swung open.

The pebbled drive curved between hedges that threw dark green shadows. The flickering shapes of birds shook the tiny leaves, making the plants themselves seem nervous.

Vera cleared her throat noisily. "I just hope you have the stones to lead, Heir."

Maybe it was just the stress of everything, but Thane was

fairly certain Vera was growing meaner by the day. Thane threw the door open and Aini climbed out behind him.

"Stones the lad has," Bran said. "It's his sense of self-preservation I'm not so very certain about."

The group cleared the truck to catch the first view of Thane's childhood home.

Aini sucked in a breath.

Thane tried to see it as Aini would. Larger than Huntingtower. Less ancient, more majestic. The structure blocked the orange-pink glow of the setting sun. Its smooth, stone exterior had a corpse's pallor. A series of conical towers, graced with medieval style turrets, stood guard at the ends. Gothic, arched windows looked down on the group. The newer stone surrounded what looked like an older, more square version of what castles started out as—fortifications. Part of this house was very old. Part of it was much less ancient.

"Can you see the old keep within the structure?" Neve said.

"I noticed that." Aini just kept staring.

Whistling low, Myles took Neve's arm and followed Thane. "Let's hope we live long enough to show this place our backsides as we leave."

"From your lips to God's ears," Neve said.

Thane's took a breath and tried to calm down as he surveyed his childhood home. He could not drown in that overwhelmed feeling right now. "Welcome to Inveraray Castle, everyone," he said darkly.

Vera fluffed her short dress and fell into line behind Aini.

Bran looked like he was about to vomit. Made sense. He'd seen more of what Clan Campbell could do than the rest of them combined, save Thane.

## CHAPTER 16
### DEMONS TO WRESTLE

No kingsmen guards in Campbell colors flanked the door. Aini wasn't sure that was good. A woman with white hair piled high on her head and a long woolen skirt emerged from the front door. Something about the set of her shoulders and the shape of her head reminded Aini of Thane.

Thane's face softened as the woman smiled at him. "What happened to your phone? And where is Jimmy?"

The woman squeezed her eyes shut and pressed her fingers tightly against the back of his neck. Her skin was smooth for someone with white hair, her face nearly free of lines. Why would a woman of her age—perhaps a little younger than Aini's father—have lost all the color in her hair?

"Oh I'll tell you everything, but first let me meet your friends." A shadow crossed her face. It could've been fear or worry, or maybe she had a secret.

Thane hugged her again, then presented his mother to Aini and the others. "This is my dear mother, Senga Campbell."

"I knew it," Vera whispered. "Maternal threads are a very peculiar shade. I'm getting better at this every day."

Aini put her hands over her heart. Her own mother would never meet him. Her eyes burned. At least her mother wasn't suffering through this.

"Welcome." Senga's voice was a little shaky, like she was nervous. She touched her silver ball earrings nervously and opened the door. "Please come inside."

The group gathered awkwardly under the chandelier of the entry hall as Thane took his mother aside.

"Have you heard any talk about me?" he asked her.

"You know no one tells me much of anything."

"I also know you have your way of finding out what you need to know."

"Not any more. Your father lies and lies and all anyone around here does is parrot him."

She led everyone into a mint-colored parlor covered from ceiling to floor in tapestries.

"Two days ago, one of the guards took my phone. No one will admit it, but I had it next to me while I was reading the paper. A woman came in to retrieve something from Nathair's desk, then the phone was gone. It was her. I know it. But why, I have no idea. And Jimmy. He disappeared."

"When did you see him last? Was there an argument?"

"Who is Jimmy, if I may ask?" If he was Thane's brother, surely Aini would've heard about him before now.

Thane swallowed. "Jimmy is our butler. He has run the household for more than three years now. He's a good sort."

Senga agreed. "I've told the kingsmen here to look for him, to ask after his family in Inverness, but we haven't heard anything."

"Probably wise of him to fly the coop before the foxes get hungry."

"What do you mean, son? Are you in some trouble?"

"The streets are empty, Mother. Have you been out today? No one is around."

Aini hated the stress in his voice. She wished she could take him away from all this or annihilate those who caused him pain. But that person was his own father. Her stomach rolled. To have that kind of man as a father. She thanked God his mother seemed like a good person.

Thane went on. "Has there been some sort of announcement or a curfew or something?"

"Not that I know of," Senga said.

"I have a great deal to tell you." Thane touched the spot where the piece of the stone rested under his sweater. "First, you should know that Uncle Callum's entire retinue is here, just outside the main gates."

Senga lowered her gaze on Thane. "Start at the beginning of your story."

And so he did, with some moments filled in by Aini and the rest.

THE LONGEST HALF HOUR IN THE HISTORY OF THE WORLD passed finally. How could Senga possibly believe all of this madness?

Senga looked at Vera. "You are Dionadair?"

A grin tugged at Aini's mouth. Senga trusted them.

"Aye," Vera said. "And I hope you'll join us and become a rebel too."

Senga rubbed a spot between her eyebrows and went to the window. Then, as if what they'd told her had finally sunk in, she hurried over to Thane and grabbed him, pulling him into her arms. She said something to him and he patted her back.

"It'll be all right," he said quietly.

He gave her a smile, and Aini could see the little boy he used to be, all blue eyes and bright hope. Hope Nathair had all but ruined. Anger at the Earl of Argyll burned inside her, and it was all she could do not to rage around the room, destroying everything the man had touched.

"Are you all right, Aini?" Neve touched her knee.

"Yes. Sorry. Yes."

"Of course I'll do whatever I can to aid you." Unshed tears glistened in Senga's wise eyes. "It's long past time I stood up for myself and for you." She pressed two fingers against her forehead. "I've been a terrible mother." With a deep breath, she regained her composure and waved off Thane's and Bran's attempts to comfort her. "I'm fine. It does no good to wallow in self-pity. We have work to do. First, we must bring Callum in, have a meeting, then we'll set you up in your Campbell tartan and have you fully look the part of the true chief of Clan Campbell. I must say I am very glad to have Callum here and on our side of things. My sister would've been proud. She always hated Nathair. I should've listened to her when she warned me of his angry streak on our wedding day."

Aini couldn't stop herself from getting up and throwing her arms around Senga. "I hope this is okay."

Senga's shining eyes were the same color as Thane's. "Where did he find you?"

"In a lab."

Senga laughed. "Of course he did. Thane, do you know how lucky you are?"

Thane did a double-take. "How did you even know we're together?"

Vera and Neve said in unison, "Please." Then they glared at one another.

"It's obvious, my dear," Senga said to Thane, who'd adorably gone a little red around the ears.

AINI LAY IN A CURTAINED BED IN THE CASTLE OF THE MOST powerful family in Scotland. She was dating the son of said family. He was about to overthrow the entire clan.

How in the world had she come into this situation?

Sweat pricked at her forehead as she got up to dress. The world was spinning too fast. She hadn't slept a wink last night. It wasn't the different smells of Inveraray—those were nice. Roses, wood polish, evergreens. The lack of noise didn't hurt her state of mind either although it was odd to not hear Neve lightly snoring or the lorries squeaking by like they did at all hours back in Edinburgh. No, she hadn't slept because two hundred and sixty, give or take, clan representatives and every adult member of Clan Campbell were currently driving sports cars, utility vehicles, and probably, horses directly to this very spot. *Insane.* Aini put a hand on the cold sink in the room's private bath. These men and women, of the Highlands mostly, would either raise Aini and Thane up to lead, or rip them down and feed them to Nathair.

Aini brushed her teeth and flossed twice because it made life feel better somehow.

At least the meeting with Callum had gone smoothly. That was a good start, a good omen perhaps. He'd even apologized to Aini, Thane, and Vera for his comments against sixth-sensers.

When Senga brought up her deceased sister, Callum had given out another apology—this one to Senga for not looking into her well-being here at Inveraray more recently. He knew exactly how

Nathair was and he claimed he should've done more to help her escape. He admitted to fear for himself and his county. After promising every weapon, resource, and able-bodied and willing man and woman of Perthshire to this new cause, he'd bent the knee to Thane and sworn fealty. Thane had jerked the man back up though, telling him it wasn't official, so Callum shouldn't swear yet. Thane had to first receive approval from the leading members of Clan Campbell, then they could move on to gaining fealty from other clans such as Callum's. So far, this venture was looking up.

But Aini's nerves couldn't feel the optimism that her practical mind wanted them to. They just kept vibrating and itching and pulling her thoughts apart so she had trouble remembering whether she'd told everyone she needed to tell something to.

Wearing the blue and brown short dress Senga magically drummed up for her, she found everyone else downstairs where breakfast had obviously started long ago. Usually, Aini was the one making breakfast, or at least the one of the first in the group to get out of bed. Not today. Today, she'd hidden behind those bed curtains and ignored the sunrise, her mind dizzy.

Neve handed her a blueberry scone wrapped in a linen napkin. "I actually thought you'd died."

"I bet the sun tried to go back down this morning because it thought something was wrong with Aini not buzzing around." Myles poured her a cup of coffee.

Thane took the coffee and handed it to Aini.

Sun poured through the windows and turned Thane's hair to gold.

"Your hair isn't black," she stammered. It wasn't what they needed to discuss on this most important day, but the words just poured right out of her mouth.

Thane grinned with one side of his mouth and her stomach flipped pleasantly. "No, hen. I had it dyed back last night. I need to look like who I am now. Well, except for the glasses. Those are far away and will have to wait. Thankfully, my prescription isn't so bad."

Aini wiggled her feet which were now, thank the stars above, wearing clean black flats. "I didn't get rid of the purple," she pointed to her hair, "but at least my feet feel like my feet again. Those old boots…" She shuddered. It was one thing to deal with dirt you'd earned on your own adventures, but someone else's dirt? Too much.

"I'm sticking with the blond for now," Neve said, tossing her hair over her shoulder awkwardly and making Myles snicker. "It's completely me."

"I can grab our stylist to fix that if you'd like," Thane said.

"Our stylist." Myles slapped a knee. "You are too much."

"Oh as if you lived in squalor back in the colonies on your multi-millions worth plantation," Thane said.

"We did not have a stylist."

"The Campbells have one because Nathair has to make public appearances. It's part of his job."

Myles's eyes went wide. "Did you just defend Nathair Campbell?"

"I defended the Campbells."

"I guess that's something we're going to start doing," Aini said.

Bran took a loud sip of coffee, then refilled the cup before the attendant could get to it. "Thane will lead the clan, and we'll be sided up with them."

Vera's hand went to her stomach. "I'm going to boak."

"I'm used to backing them as needed," Bran said.

"Why did you always stick with me, Bran?" Thane sat back while the household staff cleared his plate and Bran's beside him.

"Because you stuck with me. I love you, lad."

Thane winked. "And I you, friend."

"No really. You're my only friend and you saved me from my own natural inclination toward self-pity."

"This is just beautiful." Myles leaned back in his chair and propped a knee against the table's edge.

"I didn't know you were having problems when I met you, Bran." Thane touched the rim of his coffee cup and stared into the black drink. "You seemed to have it all together. You made a killing tending bar up here. You had a smile for everyone."

"And I wanted to off myself every single night. Until I met you and you needed me."

"I needed you?"

"You did. You still do. You always will. I see your dark spots, have lived with you through the dark places, and will launch into more darkness until one of us stops breathing. You were a boy with a golden heart. Now, you're a man I can follow instead of lead. It's a relief, really. I've done well."

"You sound like his daddy." Myles raised his eyebrows. "Doesn't he?" He nudged Aini.

"Yes. I do think Bran served Thane in ways Nathair never could."

"And at times when I couldn't," Senga said as she walked in, a small, white dog at her heels. "I couldn't trail you like Bran. I also had my own demons to wrestle."

"You are the best mother a man could have." Thane stood and pulled a chair out for her.

Aini melted. "When you're finished here, Thane, would you meet me in the gardens out back? If you think we have time before the representatives get here that is."

"You have time." Senga said something to an attendant who set a plate in front of her. "Go on, Aini. Just allow me a moment with my son first."

"Of course." Aini gave Neve a brief hug and found the door to the outside.

## CHAPTER 17
## AMONG THE TWISTED VINES

Under rolling clouds, Thane strode around the side of the castle and searched for Aini. Myles had tipped him off that she'd gone in search of a quiet place to take a breath but hadn't taken a car into town or anything. She just wanted some time away from the arguments and discussions about what might happen when the clan representatives arrived. Thane couldn't blame her. It'd been a wild few hours, and she had to be thinking of her father back at the safe house and wondering if he was truly safe.

He wasn't. None of them were.

He found Aini leaning against the pointed arches of the southwest bridge, her form tiny under the frame of solid stone. A lock of her hair had escaped and blew the way she was looking, toward the snow-touched vines of the sleepy garden and the low hills beyond.

She has so much more than shallow beauty. A sharp mind within and a brave heart beating in her chest.

With a silent prayer that she would still want him after all of this, despite what he'd done during his time with Nathair, Thane approached her. At least she didn't know every crime. If she learned what he'd done to persuade Rodric to include him in the operation on Bass Rock, she'd never speak to him again. Even if it was truly the one way he could've been there, in that position, to help Aini and the Dionadair survive that night.

As always, Thane wrestled the horrible memory down, then buried the blood and guilt in the farthest reaches of his mind, and tried to remember who he wanted to be, not who he'd had to be all these years. He started toward Aini again, his heart drumming an uneven tattoo on his ribcage.

She didn't look up as he walked up and touched her on the back. Her skin was warm under her dark blue short dress. The brown stripes in the fabric matched her eyes.

Maybe she'd come to her senses and decided not to be with him. He wouldn't blame her a bit. "Do you wish I'd leave you alone?"

A smile pulled at those full, plum lips of hers. "No," she said, staring at frozen spots in the evergreens spilling over the earthen walls. Her flats crunched the gravel as she adjusted her weight away from the arch. "Is this going to work? Will Callum's support be enough?"

Thane swallowed. "There's no way to know. I think maybe that's not what you really want to say."

She spun to face him. "Should we get your mother away from here? Just in case this all goes badly? If she has to lose you, right in front of her..."

"So you think I'll be shot down the moment everyone arrives, aye?"

"That's not what I meant. I just don't want her to suffer. She has been through so much."

"And we should tuck her away safely, hm?"

"She would hate that. She wouldn't go."

"No, she wouldn't. You're a bit like her, you know."

Aini smiled. "I should be so lucky."

"Thank you for coming here. For risking everything."

"I'm still amazed you put me up as leader of the rebellion." Her eyes were so dark they were nearly black. Like the peat water in the lochs. "There aren't too many people who would give up the chance to rule it all."

He frowned at her. Her eyes were open and true. What did she mean? He'd done it because they were a team and he wanted to do everything with her at his side if she willed it.

"You could've claimed all that power for yourself," she said. "You know you're the Heir, but you don't care about that part of it, do you?"

Not after the life he'd had and what he'd seen of power in one man's hands. He shook his head. "I only want us all to be free of my father."

"What made you decide this is what you wanted to do, to claim your right and fight Nathair?"

The fire in her eyes, the strength he'd seen that had made him want to destroy his father and all the man had created, was still there in the brown-black depths. It was quiet now, smoldering, but still there.

"You."

He brought her fingers to his lips. Her lids, slightly purple at their edges, pressed together and a single tear escaped each one. If only he could take her away from all this and escape to the quiet of the Highlands. They could find peace in a wee house with nothing to do but mind the sheep and make love. Not necessarily in that order.

"It'll be over soon. For good or bad. It'll be over." He kissed her fingers. They were soft and light and smelled like the herbs and grasses she touched in passing.

Through her thick lashes, she looked up at him. It was like his body had a burning thirst and only her touch could quench it. He clapped a hand around her waist and crushed her sweet mouth with his. She made a little noise, and his chest heaved with wanting her as he eased into the kiss. Her arms circled his neck, and he ran his lips along her warm throat. As they fell against the arch, his entire body—from the tip of his head to the toes in his boots—sparked and burned.

"They'll be here soon," he said. "I should stop."

She grabbed his coat and whirled them both around to bump against the arch. "Oh no you shouldn't." She kissed him firmly. A punch of desire hit him. "If we have to deal with the pain of this world," she said against his lips, "we get to enjoy the perks of it too. I'm pretty sure you said that first."

He grinned. "How can I argue with you, my Merlin?"

"You can't. Now shut up and kiss me," she said, and he did.

When he knew they had to stop or risk moving into something she might not be ready for, he found a bench for them. While Vera, Bran, Callum, and the rest worked on forming the best arguments to win over Clan Campbell and those clans loyal to Campbell, Thane and Aini told jokes Myles had taught them and made up stories about each of the sheep on the hill.

## CHAPTER 18
## WITH A SHOUT AND A TURN

A riot of rumbling engines, loud voices, and an explosion of ravens soaring into the snow-gray sky tore Thane's attention from Aini's troubled face.

A gun fired.

They traded a confused look, then ran toward the shouting.

In the drive in front of Thane's insanely large childhood home, two armies had assembled.

Callum bellowed over his group of currently unarmed men and women from Perthshire toward a group of newcomers. "Calm yourselves. I called a gathering to talk and that talk includes why there is a disguised Dionadair truck alongside my vehicles. I wouldn't call you if there wasn't a very good reason. We need to listen to Thane and his group here. They have information vital to Scotland's well-being. To its future."

"How did they know the truck belonged to Owen and the rest?" Aini craned her neck to look at the truck they'd come in.

The rebels had painted it just before the group had left the safe house. It bore no telltale gunshot wounds or the bright blue color the rebels sometimes painted on bridges and roads.

Thane shrugged, eyes narrowing behind his glasses. "I'm sure they'd have changed the plates." He should've made certain.

Menzies—the very cousin he'd warned everyone about—raised his crooked nose and waved a gun at Thane. "Here is the man of the day. I know full well you're the one who put Callum up to this gathering. You think you can show up here with people we've never seen before," he gestured toward Vera and Aini, "and suddenly we're at your feet? Earl Nathair may've gone off the map, but we're not desperate enough to need you and your wild ideas, whelp."

"We're not desperate at all," a man in Campbell tartan said.

"Earl Nathair hasn't disappeared," a red-cheeked woman said. "He is just on the job, man. Watch yourself. Don't go calling our chief's son a whelp, Menzies."

"Aye," another agreed. "Go easy. That's the earl's son, remember."

More voices joined in to defend Thane, but it wasn't exactly what he needed them to feel. "Thane is the heir to Clan Campbell and fights as well as his grandsire once did."

"Menzies," Callum said darkly. "You know me. Do you think I'd call a gathering just for the giggles?"

"And I thought you had brains enough not to pull something like this. Ah. I'm seeing it now." Menzies rubbed his chin. "You want to move the lad around like your puppet. You want control. You know you should be content enough that the king forgave the Gowries for their bitter past and enjoy the lands you have."

Mother walked down the front steps and it was all Thane could do not to run to her and push her back inside the house. "That's some fealty you're showing there, Menzies," she said.

Menzies glared her way. "Stay out of this, Senga, and there

won't be a need for too much violence. I'm just trying to teach your son here the lessons you failed to."

Anger seared its way down Thane's fingers and his hands became fists.

Senga crossed her arms, her voice carrying. "Did you or did you not bend the knee to Clan Campbell, offer the hilt of your family sword, and swear to be loyal to our cause?"

Thane remembered this was how she used to look all the time—confident, tall, sharp.

"You think this falls in line with that oath?" Menzies snapped, looking flushed despite his barking tone. "You're attempting to yank your father's role as chief from under his boots."

"I want to put it to a vote," Thane said. "The representatives, yourself included, will decide that. I will accept the outcome, whatever that may be."

"Well, I won't." He pointed the gun at Aini and Thane's heart stopped. "Have you told these disciples of yours what you did to gain back Rodric's trust, Thane?"

Thane shut his eyes. He couldn't tell them. Aini would never forgive him. It had been necessary. But it was a horror—committed after he knew better than to ignore his conscience and do as Nathair and Rodric demanded—and Aini could not find out.

"Och, I can tell you have not." Menzies laughed, an ugly sound that pebbled Thane's flesh. "Let me take you down that road, will you? I'll enjoy that. What do you think? Are you his whore, you pretty little thing? Did you realize you were bedding a man who cares so little for human life? For the pain he inflicts on others?"

Aini stepped forward, eyes on fire. "I'm no whore. And I know exactly who and what Thane is."

Thane's stomach lurched. He remembered bone and blood. Lies and pain. It had nearly been the end of him.

Menzies watched Aini like the threat she was. His thumb rose over the gun's hammer and he clicked it into place, leveling the barrel for a clean shot.

Thane's whole body buzzed. "Wait. Just listen." He forced himself not to run, not to panic, not to rush Menzies' finger into pulling the trigger.

"Seer!" Vera, paled and panicking, hopped onto the bumper of the Dionadair truck, ignoring the weapons aimed at her head and staring at Aini. She ripped her sleeve. A phone was strapped to her arm. Pressing a button, she shouted, "Aini MacGregor, MacBeth's Seer, needs our help to defeat a man named Menzies!" Thane couldn't breathe as she turned to glare at Menzies. "Now the entire Dionadair are headed here with your name on their blades."

Menzies swore. "Seer, aye. I know exactly what that title entails. Allow me to put you out of your misery, traitorous abomination."

Thane pushed away from Bran, who held his sleeve, and two women he didn't know. He had to get between them. His heart and lungs shook inside his chest, threatening to pierce right through him.

He reached under his sweater and clasped the Coronation Stone.

The world shivered. The fire in Thane's blood raged hot. A blue-white light appeared around him, a circle of what he knew would form into mantles, swords, helms, and bearded kings of old. There were gasps. Shouts. The rattle of a gun hitting the drive.

Menzies eyes were big as moons. "What am I seeing?"

Thane released his hold on the stone. The light faded.

Callum picked up Menzies' gun. "I told you I wouldn't call a gathering unless I had good reason, man."

Thane put his hands on his knees and tried to breathe, watching Aini talk to Neve, unhurt, alive. The house behind her tilted. He took another breath. That gun. That was too close. He was going to kill Menzies. Someday. Somehow. Or at least keep the man from ever holding a weapon again.

The memory of what Thane had done to gain Rodric's and Nathair's trust flashed through his mind. Aini would ask about what Thane had done, what Menzies was talking about. And there the thing growing between them would die.

The clan representatives along with what appeared to be most of Clan Campbell worked their way into the house under Mother's direction. She ordered all guns and ceremonial swords onto three tables the kitchen staff had produced at the base of the front steps. Two cooks in aprons watched over the dangerous collection.

"Just in case a foul plan sneaks into your heads," Mother said, as the crowd nodded respectfully to her and streamed under the arched lintel.

Aini found Thane's side. Her mouth leaked a little blood. She must've bitten the inside of her cheek too hard. "I need to know." She crossed her arms and locked him down with her MacGregor eyebrow.

Thane was definitely going to be sick. "Please don't ask me to tell you."

"I thought we were building a relationship on trust. After the whole spying-on-me-and-my-father thing, I'd have thought you'd be keen on honesty between us."

"I am. I know. But this..."

Vera, Myles, Bran, and Neve closed a circle around them.

"You all right, pal?" Bran cocked his head.

"Aye. No. Well..." Thane rubbed his face harshly. "You don't understand, Aini."

"Make her understand," Neve said.

Myles shook his head like a fly was in his ear. "Why do we need to know really? Hasn't there been enough of this? Nathair is an arse and he messed with Thane. We know that. Why are you torturing him and making him drag out the past?"

"This isn't the past. This happened less than a week ago. After Thane had come to his senses about what his father was and what was wrong and what was right. Whatever he did, it wasn't under the influence of brainwashing."

Vera shoved into the center of the ring. "Oh, you think it's like that, aye? Know so much about it, do you, Seer?"

Thane hated Vera's tone. "Vera. Don't."

"No, I suppose I'm not aware of everything to do with brainwashing," Aini said, face open. "But I need to understand this if I'm going to risk my life, yours, my father's, as well as Scotland's future, on his ethics."

Vera laughed and held her stomach. "Forgive me, Seer, but don't think for a second that those with what you think are *proper ethics* are the ones who can run a country."

Bran coughed. "I hate to say it, but she has a good point."

Vera gave him a nod. "To beat the baddies, you must sometimes become one."

"Then just tell me, Thane. Tell us what you did so we can understand."

Aini's brown eyes swallowed him up. God, he loved her so much. The way she opened herself to criticism. How she accepted new realities with such courage. The sharp mind she paired with a good, strong heart. He owed her this truth. Even if it tore them, and the rebellion apart.

He pictured that night. The fog and the sea. Rodric's mocking looks as Thane approached, hands open, weaponless.

"I'm surprised they didn't fire away the moment I walked up," he said. "Rodric was primed for hurting. I'd always been his favorite target. Now that I'd shamed myself in the eyes of Clan Campbell in full, I was more open to injury than ever before."

Thane leaned against the banister, trying to ignore the ongoing arguments about him going on in the next room. He heard Callum's voice, then others. Some positive, others aggressively inquisitive.

"At that moment," he said, continuing, "I had none of my father's rancid protection. I'd gone to the other side. I was the enemy. And Rodric was more than ready to end me slowly and painfully."

Thane blinked. The group watched him with careful eyes and fisted hands. Like they had been there with him. His heart thudded once for each of them. Despite their flaws. Despite his own blazing flaws.

"I had to completely flip what he thought I'd become."

Aini shuddered and hugged herself, but she didn't take back her demand for an answer. Thane steeled himself to continue, running a hand through his hair, then over the bump of the stone under his sweater.

"Rodric and Rabbie had a man there. A man who distributed traitorous flyers at concerts and clubs. He wasn't a true Dionadair, I don't think, but he was a rebel in his own right."

"Was he from Inverness?" Vera asked.

"Aye. They called him the Third Fiddler of Inverness."

Neve brightened. "After the old tale about the two fiddlers who spent one hundred years trapped with Thomas the Rhymer in the fairy hill?"

Thane nodded. "Most likely. This man hid flyers in a false

back of a fiddle that he played for coins. When no one was watching, he tucked statistics on the king's ordered killings in Scotland, as well as the instances of disappearances, under car windscreen wipers and into purses and through mail slots. He always disappeared before the kingsmen could get their hands on him."

Vera rubbed her hands together, obviously forgetting this tale didn't end well. "What did he look like?"

"Just an old man. Thin. Wild-eyed. He'd been handsome when he was young, probably. Had a strength to him. He fought back—"

Thane's stomach heaved and he had to stop and breathe for a moment. Aini and Bran both reached a hand out to steady him. Aini pulled her fingers back first and traded a heavy look with Myles. Thane recalled the trip home after Dodie knocked Myles out. Myles was Thane's friend now. Would he still be in five minutes? Aini wouldn't. There was no way she'd accept this. Not after how his clan had treated her father. He knew full well she could still picture Lewis's family ring on the ground and...

He had to finish the telling before he lost his nerve. He refused to lie anymore. "Rodric demanded I extract information from the fiddler. They wanted to know where the man found his information and where he hid when he wasn't on the streets. Whether the man knew more about the Dionadair than suspected. Of course, the fiddler was no coward. He clamped his mouth shut for the ones who'd taken him in and took several hard hits to the stomach and groin for his efforts."

"So they left him with you?" Vera buttoned her coat up to her chin as snow began to fall.

The icy designs drifted into Aini's hair, one thousand geometric patterns forming a crown of white.

"Aye," Thane said. "He would not break." The mask Thane

had worn his whole life, the armor of unfeeling fortitude, it slammed over Thane. It didn't fit like it used to. His heart thrummed under its weight, his new brand of thinking shining between the cracks. "I took three fingers from the man. Two from his right hand. Then one from his left before he crumbled into something far less than what he'd been."

No one said a word. The only sound was the distant rumbling of the groups inside the house and the shift of wind in the pines outside the open front door.

"Was it your tool that took the man's fingers?" Bran's voice was steady, calm.

"Ah, no. I used garden shears. Rabbie's, I suppose." Thane squeezed his fists so tightly that blood refused to flow to his knuckles and gathered painfully in his fingertips.

Bran's hand on his shoulder made him jump. "It was not your weapon. It was not your order."

"It was my choice. I could've done it another way."

"Truly?" Vera's arms fell to her sides. "Would they have taken you to Bass Rock if you'd shown anything less than total, brutal commitment to the Campbell cause?"

"No, but—"

Neve stepped closer. "You had no time. No time to make some grand plan that would save us and keep your new way of living whole. You sacrificed yourself."

"Don't call what I did heroic. I won't stand for it."

Thane's anger surged and rolled over him. It shoved him and pushed him and forced him away from the group and into the cold garden. He let the chill seep into his bones, punishing himself for the deed by imagining the fiddler's shrieks over and over and over.

## CHAPTER 19
## THE WEIGHT OF LOVE

Aini watched Thane walk away. Her feet wouldn't move. His hands had held her, touched her cheek, brushed her lips. And just days before, those same hands had maimed a brave, good man.

"Forgive me, Seer, but don't go thinking you're too good for him." Vera dipped her head to show some respect but her actions didn't match her tone.

"It's not that. It's just..."

Myles and Neve stood near the door, heads together, talking. He pulled her into a hug and she stayed there as he sang a silly song above her head, quiet and ridiculous and perfectly Myles.

Why couldn't her relationship be so simple?

Bran frowned at Vera. "Those sweet ones there don't carry the weight you and Thane must. You can't go around comparing yourself to them."

"I thought you didn't have a sixth sense," Aini said. "I'm pretty sure you just read my mind."

A sad smile flickered over Bran's face. "It doesn't take being a

Threader," he glanced at Vera, who was talking into her formerly hidden phone, "or a Seer to make good guesses. May I share a story with you, lass?" Bran's honest face showed the beginnings of wear, of lines around the eyes and mouth.

"Of course. And don't think I think I'm better than Thane. I just can't imagine him being the same person I spent time with right after that..."

"It's confusing. You saw Senga take a bit of control today, aye?" Aini nodded and Bran went on. "She used to do that all the time. But Nathair beat it out of her. Beat the courage out of her, both literally and figuratively. She can't handle doing the bad things it takes to fight him properly."

"She doesn't need to. We can help her."

"Exactly. Because we are now the kind that *can* do the terrible tasks a rebellion calls for." Bran leaned back a bit and studied Aini. "You'd do anything to keep your father from the king's firing squad. Wouldn't you? I can see it in you now. That ferocity. The fire and the ice. You have both. Like Thane."

"I...I don't know."

"You do. Only you aren't sitting well with it yet. Thane's had a longer journey to this spot. He knows well what it will take to defeat his father and his king. And he knows he'll get his hands dirty. He'll bend his ethics to win."

"But doesn't that make us as bad as they are? Shouldn't we stick to what we believe is right?"

Vera clenched her jaw as she studied her phone. She must've received a message from the other Dionadair. "No," she said quietly. "The win is all that matters."

Bran held up a hand. "I disagree. If we win but along the way become monsters ourselves then it's not a win, is it?"

"It's not. Not at all," Aini said. She tried to see Thane in the garden, but he'd gone past the corner and was hidden in the stone and evergreen growth. "That's what I worry about. Will this rebellion throw Thane right back into the life he fought to leave? He doesn't want to be like his father. I will not let him be like him. If that costs us the rebellion, then so be it. I will not let him become a person like Nathair Campbell or King John. There has to be another way."

"You know there isn't another way, Seer." Vera touched Aini's wrist gently. "Fate has called you both."

Aini refused to give in. Bran kept watching Aini like her face might tell him some big secret.

"What do you suggest we do when we are put in a place where winning and being a good person can't both be accomplished?" she asked.

"You must decide moment by moment," Bran said. "There is no rule or plan you can follow with this." How well this friend of Thane's already knew her. "Sometimes you'll be wrong. You'll take a false step and hurt yourself and others. But the fact that you stop and consider each move for its place on the spectrum of good and bad—that is what makes you who you are."

Myles had snuck up beside them. "You're like the old wiseman in every movie, Bran."

Bran threw a light, quick punch into Myles's stomach.

Aini's heart lifted. "You say there's no rule or plan," she said to Bran, "but that really sounded like one to me."

"If it makes you smile like that, lassie, take it for whatever you like." He hugged her, then yanked Myles and Vera into the embrace. "I love you, people. Despite your edges."

"Because of them!" Vera mumbled a shout into Aini's sleeve.

Neve jumped on top of them and let out a *Whoop!* Her mouth ended up near Aini's ear. "It's going to be all right, my friend. We're in this together. Until the end." She turned and smacked Myles's hand. "Keep your hands off until we're in private, you lout."

"I was appreciating your edges, sweetheart. My apologies." He winked at Aini, but did indeed keep his hands to himself. He was flirty, but he never seemed to press Neve into anything without her approval.

The group hug fell apart.

Vera held up her phone. "I have news. Dawn—an operative at the Glasgow main safe house—found a message from one of Nathair's code names to a kingsman that details a plan to use chemicals on the people of Edinburgh. Just as we suspected, he will blame it on the king to rouse support for himself."

"We can use this when we talk to the gathering here. I need to talk to Thane now. How long do I have?" Aini eyed the house.

"I'd say you have an hour while everyone catches up, spreads gossip, and finds something to eat," Bran said. "Then you'll both be needed inside to address the gathering formally in proper attire. There will be the fealty ceremony. After that, of course, is the dancing. Unless this goes badly."

Buzzing with fear and anticipation, Aini walked toward the garden to find Thane. She'd never thought about how fighting to be a good person made you a good person. For what felt like the thousandth time, she thanked God he'd sent Bran to Thane.

THANE TENSED WHEN SHE TOUCHED HIS ARM.

She didn't say a word. The wind blew, cold and quick, across Thane's pinked cheeks as she looked up at him. The pain on his face, in his gray eyes, tore her heart—bright, burning strips of pain across her chest. She was part of the reason he felt this way. Why had she questioned him again? Faith had to come into play here. Without it, and a heaping measure of trust, they'd never make it through the uprising.

Taking handfuls of his sweater, she pulled him close and set her forehead against his. The muscles in his arms relaxed as they slipped around her middle. His breath was soft and his skin smelled like sage and cotton. They stayed that way, a warm cocoon in the light snow shower, until a smile washed Thane's features and Aini's heart felt whole again.

Then she told Thane about Vera's news.

Thane's face was grim. "This is good. It's a stroke of good luck at last." He touched her chin. "We are going to win this thing, Aini MacGregor."

"Did you Dream it?"

"I don't need to. Reality has provided all the necessary ingredients."

"A perfect mixture for a rebellion."

"Exactly so."

IN INVERARAY CASTLE'S HIGH-CEILINGED ARMORY, AINI SAT in a red velvet chair at Thane's right hand. Vera, Myles, Neve, Bran, and Senga filled the other chairs at the head of the room. The large table had been cleared away to allow a crowd. A circle of Brown Bess rifles—all burnished steel and polished wood— made a sort of wreath over the hearth. Lochaber axes, muskets, and Scottish broadswords hung on the gold-painted walls. The tattered British flag hanging on the far wall, evidence of the Campbells long-running support of the monarchy, was disturbing to say the least. Long-handled, axe-like halberds fanned out from the rifle collection.

Aini squinted. Blood stained one of the weapons. Though

the room was cool, tension had her feeling like she was in the Grassmarket under the July sun.

Vera licked her lips in excitement. Win or lose, she was having a fine time. Aini wished she could get excited about the idea of a fight. She was ready for it, but joy was definitely not part of that.

Every time Aini glanced at Thane, he took her breath away. He'd swept his golden hair back from his face, and his gray eyes snapped clear and ready above his high cheekbones. Wearing his clan's sage green, black, and blue tartan in the old-style—hanging as a long kilt and draped over his jacket—he looked the part of a powerful chieftain.

One of Senga's men strode into the room wearing a simple black suit with a gold and black brooch in the shape of a boar's head. "The representatives are prepared to meet, Master Thane." The man bent slightly at the waist.

"Jimmy!" Thane left the table to embrace the man.

Senga smiled. "He came back as soon as he heard what was happening."

Jimmy studied Thane's face. "This is all we could ever hope for."

"Thank you for being here," Thane said. He slapped Jimmy on the back, then returned to his spot beside Aini to straighten his tartan.

This was all so formal. Aini felt completely out of place. She could almost feel every wrinkle in her new dress. Kind Senga had bought it over the phone and a girl had delivered it just fifteen minutes ago. There hadn't been time to iron the black-striped, colonial cotton skirt properly. The top was green velvet so at least no wrinkles marred that bit.

Thane stood, squaring his shoulders, and a rush of pride

soared through Aini's chest. He held a hand to her. She gripped his fingers briefly and squeezed them.

Her pulse drummed in her ears. What exactly was she going to tell these men to push them from Nathair to the Dionadair, to support Thane? Would they listen, or would they just start ripping the ancient weapons from the walls?

The thud and slap of boots carried from the dining hall and kitchens until a crowd of kilted men and finely dressed women—every age and size—had filed into the armory. Some took seats, others stood against the walls, their arms crossed over their chests.

Thane spread his arms wide. "*Fáilte*, cousins, neighbors, countrymen."

A hunched man cleared his throat loudly. He hadn't been here earlier, or at least, Aini hadn't noticed him. He squinted at Thane. "What are you planning, my lord's son?"

Another stranger, ruddy-cheeked and new to the group, pointed at Vera, Myles, and Neve. "Who are they? If you don't mind me asking."

"If you'll give me a moment, MacCoran." A muscle twitched in Thane's jaw.

Aini pulled at the high neckline of her dress. Myles winked. She gave him a weak smile. Vera bristled at the end of the row of chairs like she was ready to tackle every Campbell in the room.

Thane held up his hands. "My father, Nathair Campbell, has gone mad."

Menzies stood at the back of the room, face unreadable. Callum sat beside Senga. He rubbed his mouth with a knuckle, a mannerism Aini had noticed in Thane from time to time.

"He ravages his own countrymen—from Glasgow to Inverness to Edinburgh—for his own gain and that of the

English king." Thane pounded a fist on the table and the pillar candles flamed higher. "He no longer acts like a Scotsman."

"This is foul talk, young Thane," a woman in Campbell tartan whispered. "Are you sure we just heard you right? And I want to know about what happened outside."

Callum's sharp eyes found the woman's face in the crowd. He stared. Aini wasn't sure whether he planned to shout back at her or have her shot.

But it was Menzies who spoke first. "Just listen to the man, Hawes. He...there is more happening here than you think. Believe me."

Hawes blinked, obviously surprised a man like Menzies would say something that sounded so reasonable.

Aini touched Thane's hand. *Go on. Do it.*

Senga put a hand on Thane's shoulder, tears shining in her eyes. "It's true," she said to the room. "My husband has become Scotland's worst enemy. A snake in our own grass. He is as much a monster as the false king, John III."

A man near the door threw up his hands. "Now that *is* treason!"

Others joined in, calling for Thane's arrest and spewing obscenities about the Dionadair.

But no one denied the fact that Nathair had become Scotland's worst enemy. That was something, at least. Aini's palms left marks on the table. Her heart knocked around inside her ribs.

"No." Thane's voice was thunder. "It's treason against Scotland to deny the truth. The Dionadair are our enemies no longer. To rescue our people from the machinations of my father and the false king, they follow the lead of this woman, Aini MacGregor, MacBeth's Seer."

She knew it was coming, but it didn't stop her stomach from flipping.

The room erupted into shouts and jeers.

"Criminal!"

"Take her!"

Senga, Myles, Vera, Bran, and Neve gathered around Aini and Thane. Men and women bumped against them, raising their fists. Some angled themselves toward the crowd, backing Thane and Aini.

Sweat drew down Aini's back and she reached for Thane's hand. He wrapped his long fingers around hers and held tight. She memorized the feel of the callouses and lines, and the bones of his hand and wrist.

Thane's voice stormed over the crowd. "Quiet."

"Don't you see what Nathair has become?" Aini raised her voice, making eye contact with everyone she could. "He has asked many of you to swear fealty to him alone, outside of the king and his mandates, hasn't he? Admit it."

Many looked from side to side, obviously not wanting to admit what they'd done.

"I did," one man said, raising a hand briefly. "He demanded it."

"And you think he'll do something to help us Scots? Do you truly believe he is in this to improve your life and increase your freedoms?"

"Listen to her. Do you think my father will do anything that doesn't simply feed his own power?"

"The power of the Campbells is our power too, if we support him," the man said.

Aini shook her head. "We have proof that Nathair plans to poison the people of Edinburgh."

The talking died to a murmur of questions and whispers.

"He'll put the blame on King John to gain power."

"What does he want all this power for?" a deep voice said from the back. "What claim does he have to the throne? He's not of the royal line and we'd only get more trouble from France if he wrested control away from the one who does. Am I wrong?"

There were those who spoke up in agreement and some that just put their mouths into tight lines and crossed their arms.

"Even if it did help Scotland—which most of us realize it definitely will not—is that something you can live with? Men, women, children—innocents—dead in the streets? It's horrible enough that he rips sixth-sensers and those merely accused of it from their homes."

"Where is your proof?" another voice asked. "How do we know Nathair really is ordering the city of Edinburgh poisoned?"

Callum took a slip of paper from Vera's outstretched hand and held it high. "This is the message. I believe it's valid. And I've known Nathair my whole life. You can poke holes in this all you want. But I think you know what the man is capable of."

The tension in the room weighed on Aini's shoulders. All around her, hands remained on belts where knives surely hid, sharpened and ready. One wrong move and this became a massacre with losses on all sides.

Aini cleared her throat. "When I touched the Bethune brooch, I saw the Coronation Stone." She closed her eyes and remembered she was meant to do this. "It was shaped like a seat, an ancient throne." A shiver ran up her arms. "I found MacBeth's dirk and the legendary Waymark Wall. Thane and I finally found the Coronation Stone on Bass Rock in Saint Baldred's underground cell."

Vera hefted the stone in its bag onto the table with a thud.

The gathering craned their necks to look as she pulled the burlap away to show the shining black rock.

"That's not the Coronation Stone," Hawes said. "It's too small."

But her voice trembled. They all had to feel it. The stone hummed like a beast about to spring. The gathering simply needed to see the magic for themselves.

"Thane? Shall we?" She held a hand out to him.

His smile was a sharpened blade. "Yes."

They slammed their palms onto the stone.

A roar crashed through the room, jangling the rifles against the walls and blowing the candles out. People covered their ears and cowered as the wind rushed over them, whipping around Thane and Aini, lifting their hair like flames around their heads.

Thane took their joined hands away from the ancient stone.

MacCoran grabbed his own shirt front like he was having heart trouble. Several men crossed themselves and others muttered prayers.

Thane looked ten feet tall, and Aini was pretty sure she looked just as mighty.

"Swear yourselves to your new earl," she said, "and the Heir of Scotland."

Thane's eyes found hers as he spoke to the hushed group. "We will go to Edinburgh and save the people. We will crush my father's mad quest for power. We will free Scotland from the tyranny of the English king!"

With a great shout, the representatives of the clans—kilts and skirts of peat brown, heather, blood-red, rose, midnight, and sea green—threw their fists in the air. "Aini MacGregor, our Seer, and Thane Campbell, true Heir of Scotland!"

Callum and Senga cleared everyone away.

"Back, back," Senga called out. "Time to make your allegiance official."

Jimmy and several others handed out the ceremonial swords the gathering had left on the tables. Once they had their swords on their belts, they made their mark beside their vote for Thane as chief of Clan Campbell, replacing the unfit Nathair.

MacCoran slipped out a side door. *Not today, Master MacCoran.* Aini worked through the thick of bodies and steel, following him to the corridor beyond the armory.

"Where are you going?"

The old man stopped and turned his head to glare with dark eyes. "I won't break the oath I already made to Earl Nathair. Besides, Thane cannot claim to be earl without approval from the king."

"He doesn't need the pretender's approval. He is the Heir." Vera, Neve, and Myles joined Aini. "The stone's demand overrides all," she said. "There is no shame in correcting your mistake in swearing allegiance to the wrong man."

"With all respect, I disagree." MacCoran eyed the group.

"That's fine. Vera, Neve, Myles. Would you mind helping me?"

"As you wish, Seer," Vera said before putting a gun to MacCoran's back.

"You're just going to kill me, eh? For being honorable. So glad we're gaining a new leadership. It'll be such a change."

Myles snickered. "I like him."

"We're not going to murder you, MacCoran," Aini said. "But we can't let you leave and warn our enemies of what we're up to. Vera, do you have a place you could keep him?"

"I'll think of something. Neve, give me a hand, please."

Neve jumped to open the back door and they disappeared with the man.

"That was neatly done," Myles said. "Now, I think it's time for a bunch of Scots to promise their souls to you and Thane or something."

"I don't think souls will be mentioned. Just defense."

"Tomato, tomatooooeeee." Myles held out a hand toward the armory and nodded for her to go in first.

"Thanks." She grinned.

"Of course, my liege."

"Please stop."

"I don't think so. This is the fun part."

Incorrigible.

## CHAPTER 20
## BE IT KENNED TO ALL

※

One by one, each clan representative and their associates lined up in front of Thane and Aini.

Callum was the first.

His wiry, gold-red hair swept away from his wide face, he went down on one knee and set his sword on the ground. Holding his palms up, he spoke low, but loud enough that most could hear.

"Be it kenned to all, I bind and oblige my heirs and myself by the faith and truth in my body to maintain, assist, defend, and concur with Thane Campbell, Earl of Argyll and Chief of Clan Campbell and his heirs and sundries their quarrels, actions, debates, and causes from this date."

Thane took Callum's hand in both of his. He nodded his head, then looked to Aini. Callum inclined his head to her. He put a hand over his heart.

"I give my respect to you, Seer. I'm amazed this old man has the chance to see this prophecy come to fruition."

Aini copied the gesture and rested her fingers over the soft, velvet neckline of her dress. Her heart beat, sure and steady, under her palm. "I promise to do my best to fulfill the role Fate has given to me."

One by one, the rest came forward and bent the knee to them.

Thane wasn't wearing a crown, but he sure did look like a king with the sun streaming through the windows and touching his head, and the crowd in quiet reverence as they listened to his responses. Aini never would've said it aloud—too crass, and it wasn't important right now—but that look of power and capability was very, very attractive.

When the ceremony finished, Myles and Neve found Aini and handed her a glass of wonderfully cold ice water. She drank it down and felt more hopeful than she had in days.

"The real question of the day is, what the heck does *kenned* mean?" Myles took the glass and ate one of Aini's ice pieces.

"Known," Neve said. "Let it be known."

Myles gave her a nod. "All right. I'm satisfied. Now, when does this dancing they've been bragging about start up? Let it be kenned I'm ready to set the floor on fire." He shimmied against Neve's hip and she bumped him, grinning.

The twang and pluck of musicians readying their instruments trickled from the saloon.

"I'm guessing now?" Aini led them to the saloon's door. "I'm going to freshen up a little. I'll meet you in a minute or two."

They took off to mingle with those already gathered on the pale wood floors as Aini escaped to the restroom to have some much needed quiet.

A HALF HOUR LATER, VIOLINS AND DRUMS FOUGHT FOR attention in the long, wide expanse of the saloon. Everyone was dancing the same reel, but it looked like poorly managed chaos to Aini.

"Good evening, lovely," Thane said from behind her making her jump. His warm hands circled her waist and the length of him pressed against her gently. "Are we going to dance or stand here plotting?"

"There is a lot of planning to do." Weapons. Locations. Information. Father had sent coded intel from Edinburgh an hour ago regarding Lord Darnwell—the French queen's brother-in-law—as well as kingsmen movements near Edinburgh. The rebels had a true army to assemble. And Nathair was still "off the map" as Menzies had put it. Disconcerting, to say the least.

"I know planning *is* your favorite past time, but could you spare a few minutes for me?" Thane's breath on her neck turned her insides to molten silver.

"I think I can do that."

She led him into the reel, her body finding the music and settling into its rhythm. His grin lit her up as she spun, then returned to his hands.

"Are you wearing the stone?" she asked. The leather strap wasn't showing on his neck.

He tapped the tooled, black leather bag attached to one of two belts on his kilt. "It's safe in my sporran." With a wink, he started dancing again.

The room was hot, but it wasn't unpleasant. A ton of candles scented the air with beeswax and brightened the wood-framed portraits of Thane's fancy ancestors. Vera and Bran argued beside the perspiring musicians.

Thane nodded toward them as he took Aini's hand and moved right two steps. "Should we intervene?"

"They're just two very different people," Aini said.

"Hopefully their shared interest in this rebellion will bridge the distance."

"Like the recent study that showed how agrin and acetylcholine surprisingly work together to develop our synaptic connections..." Thane trailed off as Aini gave him a look. "You know," he said, sounding casual which only made Aini want to laugh and punch him a little, "like our muscle cells and motor neurons and all that."

"All that. Yeah."

"I'm not the only nerd here, Organization Queen."

She patted his back. "Truth." They moved away from the dancing and toward the armory.

Menzies stood talking to Senga. All the faces that had stood out in the fighting and arguing were here except maybe Callum. He was probably off doing some of that organization she should've been overseeing.

Aini drank in the sight of Thane walking in front of her. The flash of his leg and boot below the edge of his kilt. The broad lines of his back. The quick, mischievous smile he threw her over his muscled shoulder.

Yeah. She could wait on the organization for an hour or three.

Candles in the room where they'd shown off the larger chunk of the Coronation Stone flickered in sconces beside the arrays of swords and axes.

"Will you come up to my rooms with me?" Thane asked, his voice a little rough.

A thrill went through Aini. "Yes."

A stairwell hid behind the armory. Aini let Thane lead her further from the noise of the celebrating. The stairs brought them to a small room papered in silken black and green stripes.

A massive four poster bed boasted a Campbell tartan canopy and a twisted, dark wood frame.

"Is this really your room?" Sometimes Aini forgot how Thane had grown up. Then she saw things like this. "This bed could eat mine."

A spark lit his eyes. "It's nice to have plenty of room."

Aini's mouth dropped open and her knees were suddenly about as sturdy as a bowl of pudding.

He held out a hand. "Did I say the wrong thing?" He looked genuinely worried.

"No. No." She cleared her throat and put a hand on one of her burning cheeks. "I just wasn't expecting that." She laughed, enjoying the fact that everyone else was very, very far away.

As he stood there, looking delicious, Aini gave up any thought of clever talk.

She pretty much attacked him.

They fell onto the bed and Aini froze for a second, her chest on his. She reached out and brushed a fingertip over his eyebrow, then down his temple where his pulse tapped quickly. Something was pressing into her.

"Ah," he whispered, wiggling hands beneath her and making her gasp. "It's my sporran." He pulled off the small bag and threw it to the floor.

"Might want to be a little more careful with that, seeing as your most powerful weapon is sitting inside."

His gaze flamed hot across her body. "I have other weapons, hen."

Aini swallowed. His hair was wild. She realized she was straddling him with very little clothing separating them. She met his eyes and saw what she needed to see—permission to keep up her attack.

Her mouth found his jawline. The soft stubble on his skin

pricked her lips lightly. His large hands smoothed their way down her back, then drifted over her hips before latching on with a strong grip that made her head swim wonderfully. She started unbuttoning his shirt, taking moments here and there to run fingers over his warm skin. He made a growling sort of noise, and before she knew it, she was on her back, his hips pinning her down delightfully. He raised himself up and looked down. One of her legs was between his, the kilt swinging and tickling her leg through her stockings.

She reached forward and set a hand on his thigh, daring herself to go further. His chest rose and fell like he'd sprinted miles after eating altered caramels. He seemed barely able to hold himself still. His fingers shook, and she couldn't help but love that she had that effect on him. The candles along the wall flickered and snapped, sending shadows across the striped silk walls.

Thane put his hand over hers and scooted her fingers a little higher. Raising an eyebrow, he grinned wickedly. "Go on then, aye. If you want…"

Then a knife appeared at Thane's throat.

## CHAPTER 21

## BOOM

The staccato of gunfire broke across the house, shattering a window not far from the saloon. Bran slowly set his whisky glass on the table as men and women shouted and went for weapons hidden inside their fine clothes. Senga hurried in from the hallway beyond. A piece of her silver hair had broken free and curved under her chin.

"It's Nathair's men," she said to him. "I know it."

"How?" Bran joined her at the saloon's door as another volley of shots pounded the stone walls outside. "Why aren't they coming in? What do they want?"

"It's him. And a small group he recently brought together for the jobs that matter most, he says. A new group of sycophants he picked up in the roughest parts of Glasgow and Birmingham. They're petty gang thugs who think they'll get the best spots when he pushes the king from Scotland. They aren't loyal to any clan. Only to him. They're outside our politics, really, and I have no idea what he's ordered them to accomplish here now."

"He could've been in here with all of us dead by now

considering he wiggled past the guard already without us knowing." It didn't make any sense.

"Aye." Senga's gaze tore across the room. "Where is my son?"

"With Aini. Upstairs." Bran gave Senga a knowing look and she almost smiled, but she knew as well as Bran that they were in serious danger.

Vera, a few of her rebels, and two of Callum's men spoke together in a corner. Vera was pointing toward the back of the house.

"I'll see what I can do to find Thane and Aini. To secure them," Bran said to Senga.

"I'll arm everyone here." Senga slipped back out of the room with her trusted butler in tow.

"Vera," Bran called. She looked up at him, eyes wild. Neve and Myles gathered beside them. "We need to find Thane and Aini."

"Mac," she called to a man turning tables over to block the entrance. The man hurried over and she spoke quickly in his ear. With a nod, he ran off.

Bran wanted more than anything to go warn his best mate himself, but he had other duties at the moment. At least Thane and Aini were in an interior room. "I have three explosive devices armed and ready in the back of the truck out there," Bran said. "Right beside their gunners."

"What are they doing? It's Nathair, isn't it?" Neve turned toward the door.

"Senga thinks so," Bran said, stomach clenching with dread. "Whoever it is, they deserve some boom, I'd say."

"Agreed." Myles nodded and squeezed his hands into fists at his sides.

Senga returned and began handing out revolvers and rifles and night sticks.

"When do you think I should put them off—" Bran's question was cut by a loud crash coming from the front steps and a rain of bullets into what sounded like the upper story windows.

"Now is good, right? How about now?" Myles grimaced.

Bran pulled three tiny switch boxes from his interior jacket pocket. "Sounds good to me." They'd have to time this right though. They couldn't hit their own people and they had to take down as many of Nathair's group as possible. "I'm going to need some eyes on the scene out there."

They followed him through the house and into the dining room beside the front entrance hall.

"Don't turn the lights on," Bran said to Myles who had a hand on the dial.

Myles slowly removed his fingers from the light switch.

Shapes moved in the moonlight outside a broken window. A man shouted at the house, but his words were drowned by his own handgun firing, bright white in the near darkness.

"They're not close enough to the truck," Bran said.

"But you have three high explosives?" Vera pulled the curtain aside a fraction and peered south. "How strong?"

"They'll blow the back of the truck apart and take anyone within, say, ten feet."

"I have this," Neve said, holding up one of those caramels Thane had made. "I...I can eat one. Maybe run out there and draw them toward the truck?"

"Nope." Myles crossed his arms and shook his head.

"I appreciate your courage, Neve," Vera said, "but we don't need a suicide mission on this. Ideas, Bran?"

Bran pursed his lips, thinking. "Maybe if they believe we need something in there, they'll investigate it. Do you have a walkie?"

Vera handed him one of the small ones the Dionadair always used. If he spoke into it in a place Nathair's men would overhear him, if he handled it right, he might push them into checking the truck out, then *kaboom*, and hopefully Thane would escape what Bran feared would be his end.

In the room opposite this one, wind blew the fine, black curtains, fluttering them like giant corbie wings. "Has your Mac sent word back about Thane and Aini?" Bran asked.

"No." She followed him to the room across the hall, Myles and Neve on her heels.

Bran held the walkie to his mouth to begin his acting. It took nothing to make his voice sound strained. "It's in the truck. We have to get in there before they do. We can't move forward without it."

There was no guarantee the men outside the broken window would hear him and take the bait. He could hear feet on the drive and the occasional shout of orders to move. Another walkie talkie was loud with white noise, but Bran couldn't catch any snippets of conversation. There was too much other racket.

"Yes," Bran said into the walkie, louder now. "We need inside the Dionadair truck. Now."

Vera gasped. She knew as well as he did that mentioning the presence of the rebels would end any chance they might still have had for surprise.

He gripped Vera's arm.

Myles and Neve cocked guns and held them ready for anyone who might come through the door.

"I think they're here for Thane and Aini," Bran said, realizing this was the truth and that he'd really known it from the first moment.

Vera pulled away and flew out of the room, obviously heading for Thane and Aini and those she'd sent after them. "Mac! Greta!"

Outside, three men crept toward the truck. It wasn't all of them, but it was better than none.

Bran flipped all three switches. Three red lights bloomed in his hands. "Myles. Neve." He gave each of them a detonator, keeping an eye on Nathair's men. One man threw the back of the truck open. "Hit the button exactly when I hit mine. All right?" They nodded. "Now."

All three pressed their detonators, and with a blast to make ears ring, the night was day for a few seconds of horror. The truck belched flame and smoke as it leaped from the drive. The explosion sent all three of Nathair's men into the grass where they lay knocked clean out. They were lucky they weren't dead. An engine revved in the muffled aftershock of noise in Bran's ears.

Someone was leaving.

He tore out of the room, beelining for Thane's bedroom. Why hadn't he gone himself when he'd first heard the shots?

If Nathair had done what Bran feared, Bran would never, ever forgive himself for this mistake. Palms soaked, heart driving into his mouth, praying, praying, praying, he raced past the Dionadair, Campbells, and Gowries and into the darkness of Inveraray's secret passages.

## CHAPTER 22
## DEADLY DREAMS

From Heaven to Hell. In a blink.

Cold metal bit into Thane's throat and he heard his father's rasping voice at his ear. "Stop rutting and listen to me, just for a moment?"

Thane silently berated himself. Why had he thrown his sporran to the floor? "How did you find me, Nathair?"

"This is my house, boy."

Aini's face paled. She tugged her skirt down. Thane stepped off the bed and marched backward, the edge of the knife pushing him. He was dizzy and couldn't seem to get his feet under him properly.

"We have an army here," Aini snapped, hair over one side of her face and cheeks bright pink. "Even if you kill both of us, you'll never get out of here alive." She eyed the door, probably wondering what was happening in the saloon right now.

Nathair stopped. "That army down there is mine, you traitorous witch."

Thane turned and took the sting of the knife.

"Aye," Nathair hissed. "I do know what she is. And you too. Dreamer. Seer." He snorted and let the knife release a stream of hot blood down Thane's neck.

Thane felt no pain. Only panic. His heart was in his mouth because Aini was here and so was this beast of a man who'd killed so many like her so many times in so many ways.

"It is a bit of a mess though. I'll give you that, my son." He said the last word like it put the taste of poison on his tongue.

Then Thane's most recent Dream flooded his mind. The mountain of loose rock and how his foot slipped, the faraway ground looming, shimmering, dizzying. He saw again Aini's blood red dress and heard the old king Kenneth MacAlpin's words.

*Choose. We will see what kind of king you'll be.*

This was the choice.

Would he fall like he had in the Dream? His throat tightened and bobbed against the sharp metal edge of his father's weapon.

"If you let her go, if you leave those downstairs alone, I'll go with you willingly."

He could almost see Aini's face dissolving as he fell away, off the mountain in his Dream.

Her eyes blazed. "You're not doing this, Thane."

"What makes you think I'd do that?" Nathair asked.

"Because," Thane said, "Rodric told me you wanted a show. And you could put on such a great one with me as Heir and Dreamer and asking for mercy at your feet."

This was the only way Aini and the others might just have a chance to escape with their lives.

Aini's fists loosened and she held out a hand, tears shining on her cheeks. "I won't just go. Not without you."

"You will."

"You'll do exactly as I say, lass." Nathair put the knife against

Thane's ear and drew a line of lancing pain from lobe to temple. "If you want this fool to live."

"You're the fool," she said to Nathair.

"Aini, please." Thane would beg. He would do anything to get her out of this room. "Just go. Stay quiet. It'll be all right. I love you, hen. I do. And this is the only way I save you. It's too late for me. I should've known. I am a Campbell and I'll always be trapped by my family name." Tears burned the edges of his eyes. He'd never see her again after this. Or if he did, he'd be under Nathair's control and he'd be her enemy. "Please just flee Scotland. Go back to the colonies. Anywhere. This rebellion was doomed from the start." He had actually believed they'd be successful. Why did he keep tricking himself? His father was right. He was a fool.

She snorted and crossed her shaking arms. "I'm not going along with this, Nathair. Absolutely not. You'll kill us regardless so I might as well make life difficult for you." She locked eyes with Thane. What was she doing?

She opened her mouth and screamed.

The door swung open. Callum walked in and Aini's mouth clamped shut. Thane sighed. They were saved.

Callum lowered a hunting rifle at Aini.

Thane frowned. What was the man doing?

The initials CG were etched into Callum's gun barrel, elegant and proud. "Shut it, lassie," Callum said, "before things grow far worse than you ever could've imagined."

But Callum was on their side. "Uncle? What is this?"

Aini's face showed a war between confusion and rage as she took a step back.

Callum kept his gaze on her, but spoke to Thane. "I wanted to support you, young Thane. I wasn't lying to you."

No. NO. This could not be happening.

"But your father has a way of persuading people to do what he needs them to do."

Thane's anger was a fist around his chest, keeping him from taking a breath. "Father. What did you do?"

"Callum is a good man," Nathair said. "He is most concerned about the well-being of the people of Perthshire. I simply let him know that it wouldn't go well with them if he made a wrong choice in this little...disturbance."

"This is a rebellion." Aini was the embodiment of righteous anger.

Thane regarded Callum like he was some strange creature he'd never seen. "So you told him where I would be. You set up the empty hallway. Did you kill the guards we had set on the stairs?"

A flicker of unease crossed Callum's face. "No. I gave them a chore and it was all very peaceful. I'm not the enemy here."

Aini stepped closer to the gun and made Thane's legs go limp. Nathair caught him under the arm roughly.

"You're the worst kind of enemy," she said. "You betrayed us!"

"My people are my only family now." Grief gave Callum's words weight. Thane was forced to believe his uncle truly hadn't wanted to do this, to report Thane's whereabouts to Nathair and make this turn possible. The fact just made Thane's hatred of his father grow deeper, darker.

"I don't think she's going to let you make this choice, son," Nathair said.

She had to. "Aini, please." He poured all his love into his pleading. "Go. I can't stand the thought that the world wouldn't have you anymore. I can't..." Tears broke free of his eyes and joined the warm blood on his throat. He didn't care that his nightmare of a father was listening and sneering. This was about Aini's life. The life of the woman who shoved the heavy cloak of evil away to see the good hiding deep inside Thane's shattered soul. "If you live on, the best part of me will too."

A sob choked Aini. She drew a hand across her cheek.

Callum kept the gun on her, but his face had gone white.

"Enough." Nathair dragged Thane out the door. "You make sure she stays quiet until we're gone and I'll keep to my end of the bargain, Callum."

Callum nodded once, then lifted a boot to shut the door between them.

The last thing Thane saw was Aini's face glistening with tears, and panic in her eyes. Then Nathair struck him hard on the temple and he knew no more.

Thane woke up in the back of truck, his hands and feet bound with twine and attached to the wall via a zip tie. Looking through the window between the cargo hold and the cab, he could see Nathair's sharp profile in the driver's seat. The events in his room at Inveraray hadn't been a mere nightmare. All of it had actually happened.

The stone.

Thane scanned the floor, longing to see the sporran that held the stone necklace but also praying it was far, far away from Nathair. There. In the back corner—barely visible because of both the lack of light and the absence of Thane's glasses—sat his sporran and the larger chunk of the Coronation Stone in its burlap bag. Nathair had secured both. All Thane needed to fight off Nathair was right there. So close, but completely out of reach. Thane knew his father well enough to realize Nathair had arranged this situation to further deflate any hope Thane might have. Thane shut his eyes and leaned his head against the vibrating truck bed.

He would never see Aini again.

His cruel mind brought forward an image of her laugh, the dimple in her cheek, the sound of his name on her tongue. Then he saw Callum's gun and imagined a gun shot and could almost see her falling, bloodstained and broken, to the floor at his traitor uncle's boots.

Thane was turned inside out, emptied.

The truck bumped down some unknown road, and his head rapped sharply on the metal grating, reminding him that his father had nearly cut his ear off. But Thane didn't move to relieve the pain. He pressed into it, relishing the way it burned the imaginations away.

What would happen to the rebellion now that they had no Heir? He prayed with all his might that they would go on without him and defeat the king and bring someone else to power. At the same time, he begged God to get Aini out of the country before any more harm came to her. Maybe wise Bran could talk her into leaving.

Bran. Thane wouldn't see him again either, he supposed. Bran had been the brother Thane always wanted. What would Bran do now? He was caught between two worlds—the Dionadair and the Campbells. No matter what Bran did, someone would want him dead.

Thane couldn't stand the fact that he wouldn't be able to communicate with any of them, to see what was going on and if they'd escaped Nathair this time. They could all be dead right now. Aini, Myles, Neve, Bran, Vera. Senga.

Mother.

Thane swallowed bile. "Did you see mum?" he shouted toward the glass dividing him from Nathair.

# THE EDINBURGH HEIR

"What's that?" Nathair barked back as he buzzed the window down.

"I said, did you see my mother?"

"She surprised me. I had no idea she could stir up so much trouble. She's been dealt with. Now it's best if you remain ignorant on the details. Be a good lad and keep your end of the bargain or I'll find that girl of yours and she won't like what happens then." He raised the window back up and the truck lunged, increasing in speed.

Thane fought the urge to vomit. He was lying. Mother was fine. She had to be fine. If she wasn't...

He could almost smell her perfume and hear her singing at the well where she used to take him on Sundays.

## CHAPTER 23
## IN THE DARKNESS

---

The door swung shut. Aini's arms wouldn't move to tear Callum's rifle from his hands. Her feet were stuck to the dark carpeting of Thane's bedroom and a pathetic fluttering between her ribs said there used to be a functioning heart somewhere inside her. She couldn't let this happen.

*Move*, she demanded her body. *Do something.*

With Callum's side to her, his gaze not directly aimed her way, she jammed her shoe into the back of his knee. He exhaled in a great huff and nearly toppled over.

"Stop that." The gun barrel lifted, level to her nose. "I don't want to hurt you, so stay still, lass. Just for a few more minutes. Then it'll all be over."

"It won't be over. You gave Thane to Nathair and I will never, ever stop fighting to free him."

Callum studied the ceiling and sighed heavily. "Then you'll die and your friends with you."

"We are prepared for that."

"Are you? Do you even know what it feels like to lose someone you love, you, just a slip of a girl?"

A memory of her mother's hands flashed through her mind. Delicate. Strong. Music made flesh. "I know exactly how that feels." But she wasn't about to share the loss of her mother with this betraying arse. "Didn't you learn anything from Lady Greensleeves?"

Callum's face went red with rage. "I did. I made my apologies. This is nothing like that. I'm actually saving your life. If you rebel now, I will simply act as ordered by the one I swore fealty to. The first one. My men know nothing of this yet, but I will explain it all and they will understand. Everyone downstairs will. Maybe even you. I'm only protecting us from Nathair's rage. He is the man we must follow or we'll all suffer. I'm protecting you, my people, and those loyal to Clan Campbell. There's no shame in that."

"Isn't there?"

"I'm protecting my people. And following the king's law."

"King John isn't supposed to be king. Don't you get it? The prophecy and the stone named Thane as the Heir. John is a pretender, a monster, a fraud we must rise up against. You don't think someday Nathair and John will come for you again? You don't think they'll ask something horrible from you and your people? You truly believe they'll leave your little bubble in Perth happy and free? And even if Nathair does for some wild reason keep his word and protect your people, he is rising against the king himself. The king will come for you. Do you truly believe you'll make it out of this mess without a scratch just by playing the role of submissive subject?" She let out a Vera-like laugh. "You're an idiot. Thane gave you far, far too much credit."

The sound of his name made her stomach tighten. Had they already left the grounds and escaped? Were Nathair's men murdering and maiming everyone downstairs? She tried to look out the window, but Callum knocked the gun into her shoulder. He started to say something, but she cut him off.

"He loved you." She stared into his bulbous eyes, forcing him to see the truth. "And you betrayed him. Do you know how many people Thane trusts? How many he loves like family?"

Callum blinked. "His mother stands with him and I'll see she is cared for."

"She doesn't want to be cared for. She wants to be able to trust a man who called himself her brother-in-law and in heart to keep his promises. Senga is a rebel who refuses to live in a bubble and ignore the rest of the country's needs!"

There was a shout outside the door, then the ground shook. The glass in the window buzzed. Callum let the gun fall, and Aini launched herself into him, knocking him to the ground. Untangling herself, she kicked him in the nose and jerked the door open.

Bran was on the stairs, fear written all over his face. "Where is Thane?"

Aini tried to say the words *He is gone*, but they wouldn't come. Her throat was thick and her tongue stuck to the roof of her mouth.

Bran took a labored breath. "That's what I was afraid of. It was Nathair himself, wasn't it?"

Aini nodded, then started quickly down the steps, going past him. "Callum is back there with a broken nose to match his broken promise."

"Really?" Bran's footsteps were close behind. "He ratted Thane out?"

"I don't think he planned on doing it, but yes. Nathair threatened Perth as a whole and Callum folded under the weight of immediate danger rather than using his good head to realize we're all trapped and starving with the government the way it is right now."

"You sound like a real Dionadair," Vera said as she appeared from the armory to meet them. "Bran. Nice explosion."

"Thane is gone," Bran said, sparing Aini from having to say the words aloud. "Nathair has him."

"Did Nathair sic his men on you?" Aini's stomach clenched and rolled over. She gripped Vera and Bran. "I need...I need a second." She bent and let her head hang between her knees until the nausea faded. "Okay. I'm all right. Tell me. What's going on?"

Bran held up a hand. "Mac is injured, right?" he asked Vera.

"Aye, but I can send someone else to deal with Callum."

"We need to keep Callum here. And quiet," Aini said. "His men don't know—and they can't be allowed to find out—that he betrayed us. It'll only weaken us. Do you think you can change his mind about us, Bran? Get him to support Thane and me?"

"Maybe. Doubt it. But I know a secret passageway from Thane's room. Vera, can you get two of yours to take him under the house? If you get Senga's butler to help them, he can show you where to hide Callum until we know what to do with him. They can take Nathair's men injured from the blast too."

As Vera spoke into a phone, she led them through the armory. After giving her orders, she turned to Aini. "Nathair only brought a small contingent of armed men. They were obviously here as a distraction, so Bran gave them something to deal with. We figured you and Thane had some trouble coming at you."

"You were right." The blades on the walls seemed to stare down at them, silver, steely eyes. "We should use these weapons. They're antiques, right? If Senga thinks it's a good idea, we should carry them and tell everyone we have them and use them to show the clan representatives that we can return to the glory days when Scotland was a power on its own and France was its ally against England."

Bran was nodding. "Aye. Not many here have family fighting the French. Not yet anyway. If we can angle things so that they see France as a potential ally against King John—"

"You mean the false king John," Vera said.

"Exactly that," Bran said. "Then they may see this rebellion as having a better chance of ending in success and peace."

"Even with the Heir in Nathair's hands?" Vera stopped, and Aini nearly ran her over. "Wait. Did he take the stone necklace, Aini?"

"He did. But we have the larger piece still, don't we?"

"No. Nathair's men mowed our four guards down and nabbed it from Senga's room."

"She is okay though?" Aini asked.

"She is, but when she learns her greatest fear has come true..." Bran traded a look with Aini.

"I'll go to her." She didn't want to be the one to give Senga the news, but it felt right somehow. Thane would want Aini to tell her. "Where is she?"

"In the library, looking for a coded letter Nathair wrote to the French years ago. She thinks it might help drive a wedge between him and the false king," Vera said.

"I'll go there now. I'll meet you both in the armory with anyone who wants to discuss strategy in one hour."

Because of what she'd gone through with her father, Aini knew fear for Thane would come again and freeze her where she stood. She had to get as much accomplished as possible before she was locked in the ice, worrying about a loved one trapped in the hands of an enemy.

SENGA'S HANDS MOVED QUICKLY THROUGH A STACK OF PAPER on a huge, mahogany desk in the corner of the library. Books lined the walls and soaked in the sound of Aini's footsteps.

Senga must've heard her anyway. Her head lifted and she set those gray eyes, so much like Thane's, on Aini. Her fingers released the papers and fanned over the stack. "Where is Thane?"

Aini cleared her throat and pushed the words out of her reluctant mouth. "Nathair took him at knifepoint. He wants to use him in a display of sorts to quell this rebellion."

Senga's hand went to a knife tucked into her belt. "We will find him and free him."

"Nathair doesn't have a chance."

Senga smiled as tears welled around her pale eyelashes. She held out her hands and Aini squeezed them. The fear Aini had been holding back stole over her with a corpse-like chill. Her teeth chattered.

"Here," Senga said. "Sit." She motioned toward the desk chair.

Aini had tried to act like they would be able to rescue Thane and tried to believe it herself. But it was impossible. Nathair would never leave his side again. He'd have a true army surrounding him. Even if they could charge at Nathair, Aini had no doubt Nathair would shoot Thane down before he let him escape. Thane was as good as dead.

"It'll be all right," Senga whispered, turning to pick up a fuzzy, tartan blanket. Tucking it around Aini and settling her into the chair, she knelt. "We will make a plan. That'll make you feel better."

Aini should've been doing this for her, not the other way around. "I'm sorry. I'm fine. You're right." She reached for a tissue on the desk and wiped her nose. Her hands shook so hard she dropped the tissue, and Senga retrieved it.

"I'll get you some tea." Senga stood and hurried out of the room, head held high.

Would she give in to her fear in the kitchens, away from Aini?

Aini hated herself. She had to be strong, but all she could see behind her closed eyes was blood running down Thane's throat and the terror in his eyes. The finality in that look he gave her—that was the thing that stopped the blood in her veins and dissolved her hope that he'd fight his way out of Nathair's hands or someone was coming to help. That look had said goodbye as loudly as the slam of the door.

Tugging the blanket more tightly around her, Aini covered her face and recalled every moment with Thane. She had to burn the images into her head so she wouldn't lose them. It was all she had left now. It would have to be enough to get her through this rebellion.

Should they even go on with the rebellion? What was the point now? There was no Heir. No ghost kings to fight John. Callum had left their side. The Dionadair would lose. They would all rot in prison or fall to the firing squad's bullets.

"Thane," Aini whispered into the blanket. "I hope you know I loved you."

She imagined his tortured look, the goodness all tied up in the pain. She could almost feel his hands cupping her face and the brush of his mouth on hers. He'd battled such terrible darkness to become a man she could be with. Gone against his own father. Fought for hers. He'd tortured that poor rebel for her father and for her. He'd given up his very soul to protect Aini, her father, Myles, Neve, and Senga. He'd done horrible things to keep them alive.

"I will never forget what you did for us."

The bruised light streaming through the curtains slid over her hands, shadowing them and making her bones stand out like she was a corpse herself. A part of her had certainly died and there was no way to bring it back to life. The words came at last and brought with them a finality nothing else could. Her skeleton trembled under her skin as she spoke quietly to the dust motes floating around her face.

"Thane. Is. Gone."

---

THE LIBRARY DOOR OPENED AND SENGA CAME IN WITH A TEA tray. Myles and Neve trailed her. Myles was straight-faced. Neve's eyes were too wide and she clenched and unclenched fists at her sides.

Senga set the tea on the table and began pouring out the amber liquid. Steam rose to join the dust in the purple light. Aini wanted to throw off her blanket, serve the tea herself, and demand Senga take some time to mourn the day's events, but grief held her in unmovable claws.

Myles sat on the desk in front of Aini, then decided to lie down, asking Senga permission with a look. Neve sat on the arm of the chair and set her chin on Aini's head. They didn't say anything, but their simple presence stopped Aini's shivering.

She shut her eyes and leaned into Neve, letting the world crash around her.

## CHAPTER 24
## A BROTHER LOST

**B**ran fell against the garden wall, his back hitting the hard surface and knocking what little breath he had out of him.

He hadn't wanted to break open in front of Aini or Senga. Lord knew they didn't need further evidence that Thane in Nathair's hands was the worst of nightmares. A chill rushed over Bran's flesh and he closed his eyes.

Nathair would know exactly how to hurt Thane. He'd have someone beat him, of course, as punishment for being a traitor, but that wouldn't be the worst of it. The mind games would be darkest part of Thane's time with him. He'd twist every deed Thane had done and peel it apart to somehow make it seem like Thane was the reason for every problem in the world.

And that promise the foolish lad had believed about Nathair leaving Aini alone? It was only a matter of time before Nathair launched some plan to get her as well. Bran wasn't sure why he hadn't already taken her. It wasn't easy untangling a man's mind. Not an evil genius's mind like Nathair's. Bran would bet all that it was meant to create the utmost torture for Thane and the best angle for Nathair's play for power in Scotland.

Maybe he'd use Thane against the king. Or hand Thane to the king to soften the king toward Nathair. There were a million possibilities and every one of them ended with Bran's best mate, his chosen brother, in terrible pain, and after that, most likely dead.

Bran kicked the wall with a heel and let out a curse, sending a flock of black birds into the lead sky. Without the Heir, without the stone, where did they all stand? Was there any chance here to turn this around?

He thought of Aini's fierce eyes, her tears only making her passion all the more genuine. Aini. The Seer. She was what they had, and she might be enough. She had to be enough.

Bran pushed off the wall and stared toward Edinburgh. He would stand with his best mate's girl and together with the rebels; they would at the very least give that evil genius some real trouble. He headed toward the Dionadair crowding the drive.

"Who has Macbeth's knife?" he demanded, hope surging inside his aching chest.

A woman raised a hand. "I do. Been keeping it safe on Vera's orders."

"Then come with me, please." He started toward the door. "Our Seer needs us now more than ever."

The vibes of the group behind him gave him the strength to open the door and begin the next grueling step in this revolution.

## CHAPTER 25
## THE STEEL TO RISE

※

Minutes, hours, days, an eternity later, the door opened and one of the older men from the safe house back in Greenock strode up to the desk.

"Vera just spoke to a Ms. Smith, of the Magnolia Plantation in the southern colonies. She claims to have wired a very large sum of money to a coded account for Myles and what she called his *difficulties*."

Myles popped up. "Since when does she care?"

The messenger nodded. "Ms. Smith declared that no one is permitted to treat her son poorly. That she will not allow it."

Myles threw up his hands. "Yeah. Only she can treat me like crap. Tell her she can shove her money. I refuse to take it."

"But Mr. Smith…"

"It would be useful, Myles," Neve said.

"I can't." Myles sat back down. "I just can't let her be a part of my life. Not anymore."

Aini touched his shoulder and nodded.

The messenger looked to each of them, then seemed

resigned to Myles's decision. "Fine then. I will inform those involved. The money will be not be used."

"I wonder what she'll make of that," Myles said. "I've never turned money down."

Neve kissed his temple.

Bran walked in. What appeared to be the entirety of the gathering of clans and Dionadair behind him. They filed in and stood silent.

Aini studied the gathering and swallowed.

"We come to honor you, support you, and arm you, Seer," Bran said, rather formally.

A woman stepped forward and placed a familiar knife in Aini's hands. Bog oak hilt. The scent of history and power clouding around its ancient fittings and blade.

Her hand clasped it with a mind of its own and strength flowed through her like a shot of adrenaline. She tucked it firmly into her waistband and raised her eyes to the group, her pulse steady and loud in her ears.

"I won't go over what we already know. What you may not know is that I am never going to give up on Thane or this rebellion. Not until my hearts stops beating. And if you're with me, I say we put our heads together and make a plan to liberate our Heir!"

Vera crossed her thumbs and shouted, the room joining in. Myles, Neve, Bran, and Senga stood by Aini's sides, determination sharpening their features.

She turned away from the group to stare into the starlit sky. Her heart thudded in her throat, pushing her blood through her body so quickly she felt like she was falling. Her mind showed her images of every vision she'd ever had.

Mother in a wedding gown.

Father holding her as a baby.

Thane in the garden with Senga and Nathair.

Myles's mother.

Ghosts and memories, emotions like a whirlwind of color nearly overwhelmed her. She put a hand to the cold, cold window and spoke like Thane still stood next to her, powerful and prepared.

"We will rise, Thane. We are coming for you. Never forget who you are."

USA Today Bestselling Author
# ALISHA KLAPHEKE

# the Edinburgh Fate

EDINBURGH SEER BOOK THREE

This is a work of fiction. All events, dialogue, and characters are products of the author's imagination. In all respects, any resemblance to persons living or dead is entirely coincidental.

Text copyright © 2018 by Alisha Klapheke
Cover art copyright © 2018 by Damonza

All rights reserved.
Visit Alisha on the web! http://www.alishaklapheke.com

Library of Congress Cataloging-in-Publication Data
Klapheke, Alisha
The Edinburgh Fate/Alisha Klapheke. —First Edition.
Summary: Chosen by fate, a Seer and a spy must lead a revolution to save their loved ones and the country of their hearts.

[1. Fantasy. 2. Magic—Fiction.] I. Title.

Printed in the United States of America
10 9 8 7 6 5 4 3 2 1
First Edition

❋ Created with Vellum

CHAPTER 1

STRANGERS AND CONCOCTIONS

Aini crossed the wide stones of Senga Campbell's basement kitchen and soaked in the familiar scents of mint, rosemary, white pepper, and cinnamon. The delicious smells of candymaking helped her rein in the vicious anger and crushing frustration she'd felt since Callum betrayed them and Nathair stole Thane away. The scents kept the flashbacks at bay and helped her act somewhat normally.

Neve stood by an ancient oven. A black pot hung from an arm over open coals and Neve stirred the contents with a wooden spoon. "The caramel is ready for the speed chemicals."

Pretending she wasn't about to fall apart, Aini nodded shakily and examined her ingredient list. Thane had created the new caramels, but thankfully, he'd told her what he'd included. She unscrewed the glass vial one of the Campbell family doctors had provided and carefully removed one dropper-full of the adrenaline-hormone mix. They were very lucky the doctor understood Thane's amounts and ingredients.

Aini approached Neve with measured steps. Then, eyeing

the candy thermometer, Aini waited until the red marker rose to the right spot and in the chemicals went. Both of them exhaled with relief.

Neve wiped her forehead with her sleeve. "I hope they work."

"They will."

Aini set the vial beside the sink where some of Senga's cooks were helping to clean up. The men and women wore bright green gloves up to their elbows according to Aini's directions. Thane's mother didn't want anyone who wasn't familiar with this kind of work to accidentally come in contact with something that might hurt them or throw them for a mental loop.

Aini watched as Myles cut pieces of vision-inducing chewing gum. The long, wooden table sat against the far wall under a third set of copper pans. "We still need a way to incapacitate the enemy without killing them."

Myles whirled, his butcher knife paused over the pink slices of gum.

"Careful," Aini said, watching the knife.

Myles ignored her. "We could weaken the Bismian formula," he said. "Then we could wear gloves and—"

"I just don't think that's going to work. We really need Thane's formula for those altered cherry drops. The ones we used at Bass Rock."

Standing under the archway leading out of the kitchen, Senga spoke to someone on the phone. "Already? She'll be so pleased, I'm sure. Good bye."

Aini frowned. "Who was that, if I may ask?"

"You may ask anything you like, my Seer." Senga's sad smile was genuine. Despite everything going south, she still respected Aini's role and was behind the revolution all the way.

"Aini." Myles pointed his knife out the window. "Seer.

Whatever I'm supposed to call you. Come here—a certain man who may or may not be obsessed with perfectly ironed clothing is walking up the drive like he owns the place."

Aini's mouth fell open and she glanced at Senga. "Is that who you were talking to?"

Senga gave her a half-grin and shooed her toward the window.

Aini ran to join Myles and Neve.

Lewis MacGregor, Aini's illustrious chemist father, hurried past the ice-slicked greenery, eyes squinting against the fall sun. And the earth righted itself a fraction.

It wouldn't sit evenly though until Thane was in Aini's arms, but with the lab and her friends and Father here, Aini could walk the ground instead of scrambling along in the dirt, desperate and terrified beneath her strong shell of duty.

Lewis met them in the lab. His mouth tipped down at the edges, and Aini battled tears. She hugged him tightly.

"We will take him back, squirrel," her father said. "He is strong. It will be all right."

They both knew his words were a naïve comfort. Aini, herself, held prisoners in a hidden dungeon under their feet. The worst of men—King John and Earl Nathair—were both after her blood. Thane was in the hands of his most feared enemy, his own father. Nothing was going to be *all right*. But she let the promise cloak the chill in her heart despite its holes.

"You didn't have any trouble on the way, Mr. MacGregor?" Neve cleaned her sugared fingers on her apron.

"I did. Just a bit. But there is time enough to tell that story. I'm here and that's what matters."

"You still going to help out with the intel branch?" Myles shook his hand.

"Aye. I can do that just as easily from here. If the elders approve it."

"Of course they will," Aini said. "Now, we have a problem."

Father rubbed his hands together. "Let's get to it."

"We need a way to incapacitate Nathair's men but in a way that is safe for our operatives, and if possible, can be administered from a distance." Aini helped Myles wrap pieces of gum while Father studied the list of chemical additives in the caramel.

"You need darts. Poison darts. Like they use in big animal veterinarian services."

Aini smiled. "Yes. Exactly. But the only thing we currently have on hand that puts people out is the Bismian."

"What about those cherry drops you used on Bass Rock?"

"We only have a few left, and I don't know what would happen if we melted them down to coat dart tips."

Father traded a look with her. Aini knew very well what he was thinking. She needed Thane. In so many ways. "If I'm careful, I can come up with something that might work. Do we have someone who can procure an actual dart gun and darts?"

Senga lifted a hand. "I will see to that." She left the room, already talking to someone on her phone.

"We need a tiny copper pot." Father pointed to one high on a hook.

"I'll monkey up there and get it." Myles grabbed a three-legged stool and climbed on top.

Father rubbed his tidy beard. "And three full vials of the cherry drop hormone."

"On it." Crates sat on the big table in the middle of the room. The glass containers with the hormones were nestled in straw that poked Aini's fingers as she retrieved three of them.

"I'm trying to think like our boy," Father said, speaking of

Thane. "He would've distilled our basic recipe, but he had to have added something to hit the nervous system. Some anticholinergic ingredients." His gaze went to the window. "Is there a medicinal garden on the grounds? Do we have access to dried herbs like nightshade? Or maybe henbane?"

One of the kitchen workers raised her green-gloved hand. "We do, aye. I can get them for you. If you like." The woman couldn't seem to look at him.

"That would be wonderful. Thank you."

The worker motioned to the other kitchen folk, then they all hurried out of the room as a group.

"They're off to tattle on you, Mr. MacGregor." Myles tapped a rhythm on the little copper pot he'd retrieved, then hopped down from the stool. "*The handsome chemist wants some deadly herbs, my lady.*" He'd adopted a ridiculous accent that no one here actually had. "*I want to refuse him for fear of what he'll do, but he's so dreamy.*" Myles fluttered his lashes and held his hands against his cheek.

"Nonsense." Cheeks going red, Father pivoted away to answer his ringing phone. The voice on the line sounded curt and military, but Aini couldn't catch what they were saying. "Yes, I think so," Father said quietly. "It was sent just this morning." He mumbled something about a code and French troops.

Neve grabbed the copper pot and knocked it against Myles's stomach. "You're embarrassing Mr. MacGregor. Shut your gob."

"Yeah, colonial. Shut it." Aini grinned, her eyes burning with unshed tears as she mimicked Thane's voice. He should've been in the lab with them, laughing and working.

"Ah, Aini." Neve came to her and crushed her in a hug. "We'll get him back. We will."

Vera exploded into the room. "I heard Aini's da is here and is ready to craft some sleep darts for us?"

She looked left and right, then saw Father on his phone in the far corner. He ended his call and turned as Vera grabbed his face and planted a kiss right on his mouth.

Aini's own mouth fell open.

"You're a grand addition here, Mr. MacGregor. Thank you for joining us again!" Vera spun and was gone from the kitchen before anyone had time to react.

Father wiped red lipstick from his face. "Well that was...nice."

"Why is everyone suddenly in love with my father?" Aini asked, frowning.

He smiled. "I don't think everyone is in love with me. There's most likely some fascination with me being the Seer's father. You have a magic in you, squirrel, and many will think it runs in my blood too. Now, enough of this silliness, we have work to do."

Aini relaxed into the rhythm of lab work. Measuring chemicals and hormones. Stirring. Counting down time on the clock as something warmed to a bubbling boil. She tucked her fears for Thane away for the time being, knowing well they would hit at night when the work wasn't there to distract her.

THE GRANDFATHER CLOCK CHIMED MIDNIGHT WELL BEFORE Aini climbed into Thane's bed. Her mind was bursting with gun counts, kingsmen reports, darts and levels of toxicity. They'd discussed Gilmerton Cove—the labyrinth of underground passageways and rooms the rebels would use as a new headquarters. It sat under a sympathetic noble's estate outside Edinburgh proper. The noble had been paid well to keep his and his family's mouths shut on the deal, but Aini had her doubts. She'd seen that very nobleman share a drink with Earl Nathair

Campbell, the King's Deathbringer and Thane's own father, once at one of the king's parties. Nathair had allies crawling everywhere.

Needless to say, sleep wasn't coming to visit Aini anytime soon.

She rolled to her side and ran a hand down the emerald velvet duvet, remembering her last moments with Thane. The feel of his calloused fingers under her jaw and the warmth behind his knee and on the inside of his thigh. She could summon the scent of him, the timbre of his voice in her ear, the electric feel of his presence in the room.

"Aini."

She sat up. That had been his voice. Right then. In her ear.

Her rational mind gave her a terrible possibility.

*He is dead. You are a Ghost Talker and you are speaking to the dead.*

But she threw that out immediately, crushing it with gritted teeth and an anger that surprised her. It was her imagination. Her fatigue. She needed sleep. Shock had taken its toll. That made sense.

Forcing herself to settle down, she pulled the duvet to her chin and shut her eyes. Aini refused to be dragged into foolishness and useless worry simply because her body was breaking down. That would not be allowed. Pure determination finally brought her a sleep with no dreams.

THE NEXT MORNING, AINI LACED UP A NEW PAIR OF BOOTS and began tightening the wide belt Vera bought her in town last night. Wedged between the belt's two layers, Macbeth's knife pressed comfortably against Aini's hip. She'd sewn a pouch to the belt too and it held altered sweets, specifically the Cone taffy that helped her see spirits, and several hard candies in case she needed a better view.

There was knock on the door. Aini touched her once-again black hair—some of Senga's stylists had helped her return it to normal—and tugged the sleeves of her fitted sweater into place. She adjusted the thick leggings under her short, split skirt, and turned the brass knob to find Neve.

"They're ready for you." Neve was talking about the entire rebel group. They'd gathered for a final send off. "Are you ready for them?" Neve somehow looked leaner, meaner, and Aini was glad to see it. She would need that hunger to survive this.

"I am, but first I'm going to the...holding cells." It was a dungeon, but saying that word was truly frightening. How could she have people in a dungeon? This was all madness. "I wanted to be there when Bran questions Callum, and Nathair's captured men too. Do you have what you need?"

Neve nodded and patted the pocket of her heavy, nicely tailored wool jacket. Aini knew very well the tailoring wasn't to show off Neve's waistline. It was made so the shoulders and sleeves wouldn't hinder movement in a fight. The pocket was also filled with strength chocolate and ammo for the gun tucked into the waistband of her wide-legged trousers.

On the stairs, Myles waited. He'd shaved his head again and his coat collar stood up to block the cold from his neck. His blue eyes studied something small and shiny in his palm. "Aini. Rob found this and said maybe you should have it." He held up the Bethune brooch and Aini's feet froze in place.

This was the object that had started everything.

Knowing she wouldn't see the vision again—she never saw imprinted visions more than once—she slowly extended her hand.

"They said as the Seer, you should wear it along with MacBeth's knife," Myles whispered.

The metal cooled Aini's fingertips. She ran a thumb over the clan motto. *Graceful*, the scrolling words said in French. Thane had translated it for her in the lab in Edinburgh. It seemed as though years had passed between that day and this one, but it had only turned from summer to autumn. If she and Thane had been honest with one another from the first, would they still be trapped by Nathair and the king or would they have won already? She closed her hand around the old piece of jewelry. There was no use in *What If*s. Nathair had Thane, and the rebellion had spun out of control. But Aini wouldn't stop fighting for Thane and Scotland until she was dead on the ground.

Neve took the brooch with a sad smile and slid its pin through the thinner edge of Aini's belt. She looked up, then her lips parted. "Aini."

Myles whistled. "Did you just see that, Nevie?"

"Nevie? See what?" Had they lost their heads?

Myles blinked.

"Aye. I did see that." Neve touched Aini's arm like it might burn her. "You had this light around you." She squinted. "Maybe it was my imagination. I could've sworn though..."

Aini frowned. "Like an aura? Thane has one. I can see it all the time now."

"The...aura is gone, but yes, maybe?" Neve shook her head and rubbed her red eyes.

"We are close, you and me," Myles said to Neve, "but we don't share an imagination. That just happened, lady. That. Just. Happened." He wiggled his fingers around Aini's shoulders and head. "But you look normal now."

Aini adjusted the brooch and the knife. "Gee. Thanks."

Neve raised Aini's chin with a finger. "You look exactly as you should."

Myles knocked a fist against his pocket. There was something solid sounding hiding inside. "I have my chocolate. And a pair of lovely brass knuckles Bran gave me."

"Ah." Aini was glad those two were getting along.

"Won't your candies melt in there?" Neve asked.

Myles shrugged. "I think they'll work more quickly when they're halfway to melted."

Aini led them through the disturbingly quiet house. "Could be."

The morning sun speared the lush carpets and dark wood furnishings of the house with a blade of bright white. The light hurt her eyes and she squinted, her head aching. Dread was a constant companion now. She remembered this room filled with Dionadair rebels, and Campbells and their kin too. They had sworn allegiance to Thane as the new chieftain of Clan Campbell and rightful heir to the forgotten Scottish throne. The men and women had shown they believed in Aini—Seer for the Heir, Macbeth's chosen, the one who would command the ghost kings as they upheld the curse and protected Thane, the Heir. A sense of joy and triumphed had suffused this room then. But that was before Nathair, Thane's father, had crept in and stolen Thane away. Now, there was no joy. Only fear. And that terrible dread. Every second since Nathair had taken Thane, Aini worried the phone would ring and it would be news of Thane's death. That she would lose him forever.

"I have a good feeling about it," Myles said, though his face showed that his words were a lie. Pale and jittery, he seemed as scared as Aini. "And y'all, I am so ready to smash some baddies' heads." He grinned like a maniac and cracked his knuckles.

Neve nodded. "Me too."

Aini's mind spun, bits of their plan rising to the top of the whirlpool. "All right. I'm headed to the holding area. I'll meet you out front when we're finished."

"You're sure you don't want us to come along?" Neve asked.

"No, but thank you. I need *you* to make sure the vehicles are prepared and that the talk out there is...what we need it to be."

The mix of Campbells, Dionadair, and people from all over Scotland was spicy to say the least. Little arguments kept breaking out over which routes to take to Edinburgh, how loyal they were to the Heir and the Seer and Scotland itself.

"They just like to hear themselves talk." Myles looked toward the front door. "Once we get moving, it'll be fine."

"I hope you're right."

"He is." Neve hugged Aini. "Don't let those traitors in those cells down there make you feel bad, Aini. They deserve death and you're kind enough to give them a chance to live."

"Yeah, don't let them B.S. you, love," Myles said.

"I'm well past being snowed. Don't worry," Aini said, feeling the truth of it. She was a leaner, meaner version of herself too. She wasn't going to take any mind trips with the men who wanted Thane and everyone she loved under Nathair's and the king's nasty thumbs. Not a chance.

Myles saluted her and Neve handed over a small flashlight —a torch.

Before they could say another word, Aini was tugging back the tapestry in the house's green room to reveal a secondary entrance to the secret room of cages under Inveraray Castle. Another passageway went from there to Thane's bedroom, but she and Bran had blocked that with a heavy trunk before she'd gone to sleep last night. Not that she'd slept at all.

The passageway wasn't lit, so Aini flipped the switch on Neve's torch. Warped wooden stairs wound through the darkness. They flattened out, then dropped again, now even steeper. Muffled voices rose from the distance—Bran's low rumble, Callum's raspy answer, then a shout.

The passageway opened into a stone-walled room. Three sconces flickered, orange and white. Under each sconce, a cage stood, a cage just like the ones the king used for sixth-sensers. Aini gripped the doorframe, head spinning. Nathair's men scowled, two in one cage together, the other on his own beside Callum.

"They won't talk. Not a surprise." Bran was decked out in black kingsman boots and a sling of grenades. He stood beside two converted Campbells Aini had seen talking with Senga yesterday. "Would you like to have a go at it?"

Aini steeled herself. "I would."

She walked slowly toward Nathair's men, studying them. One wore a flat cap, a nasty smirk, and a freshly black eye—most likely courtesy of Bran's fist. The other two men were short and brawny. She wouldn't have been surprised if they were brothers.

"So Nathair gathered you up from where exactly?"

The first man's smirk broadened into a full smile. "Buckingham Palace, my lady Seer." He curtseyed and his cohorts chuckled.

"I thought so," she said. "You have the look of royalty. Just like me." She raised an eyebrow.

Surprised, the men barked a laugh. The Smirker came closer to the bars of his cage. "Yeah I don't think they'll like you running the show up here in Scotland, even if you do win this thing. Which you won't."

"They?"

"The Scottish nobility."

Aini looked down her nose at him. "I've had plenty of clients in those circles. They are just like you and me. Some good. Others, not so much."

He brushed his lapels off dramatically like some nobleman's son. "Oh sure. They'll definitely support the *candymaker's daughter* in her quest to rule the country."

One of the brawny ones snorted.

"I'm not going to rule anything. Thane is the Heir. Not me. And he'll give power to the people. He doesn't want it for himself like Nathair does."

"Good thing he's nice," the Smirker said, "nice folk always come out on top."

Anger crawled up Aini's chest. "Bran, do you have any more of those brass knuckles like you gave Myles?"

"Sorry, but I could get you some."

"No. I have something I can use."

The Smirker rolled his eyes like her threat was empty.

It wasn't.

Aini unsheathed Macbeth's knife. "Bran, would you mind opening that man's cage? I think we need to give him some motivation towards being cooperative."

Bran made a grand show of pulling a piece of molded brass from his pocket and fitting it onto his right hand before opening the cage's lock. He gripped the Smirker's sleeve and pulled him out. Shoving the man quickly against the cage, he pressed the brass into his throat. "Watch yourself, man."

Aini still felt lightheaded. This all seemed like a terrible dream. But this had to be done. A little blood was fine if it helped her find and free Thane.

She set the tip of the knife under the Smirker's eye and let the steel nip the skin. A tiny drop of blood rose to the surface. Aini fought her nausea down and set her jaw. Once she had herself in check, she looked into his face, using all the rage inside her to make her determination clear.

"I don't like doing this and I'm sure, as a man of violence, you are aware. You see my reluctance as a weakness, perhaps. I know it to be a strength. A horrible strength like a wild stallion, reckless and untamable. I don't want to hurt you, or anyone. But I will, and I doubt I'll have the measured control over my actions like a seasoned monster such as yourself. Once I begin hurting you, I will be overwhelmed and I might not know when to stop. I plan to start with your eye in exactly ten seconds unless you tell me where Nathair took Thane. And don't tell me *Edinburgh* because I already know that. I want the building, the room, the set up. Ten, nine, eight, seven…"

Aini's heart knocked loudly against her eardrums. Sweat broke over her palms and back. She was going to have to cut this man's eye out. What was she thinking? She couldn't do that. Could she?

She glanced at Bran. He was staring at her with a strange look on his face, a blend of sadness and respect.

"Zero."

Aini tilted the knife's edge and drew a shallow circle around the Smirker's eye. He jerked and gritted his teeth, spittle showing at the sides of his mouth.

"Go on," he said. "Do it. Nathair will do worse if I talk."

Nausea flooded Aini's senses as the blood seeped down his face. She stepped back, panting. It wasn't deep, but it was still ugly. "Lock him back up, please, Bran. He is no help to us." She sheathed Macbeth's blade and walked on shaking legs to Callum's cage.

Callum wouldn't meet her eyes.

"Feeling a wee bit guilty?" Aini pinned him down with a stare.

He did look at her then. Anger flashed through his pupils. "I am not. I just...I don't enjoy making such choices. I do love him, you know."

"You love Thane? The man you threw to the wolves? I find that very difficult to believe." Callum started to say something else, but Aini ignored him. "Do you have any paper down here, Bran?" she asked.

He lifted up a stack of paper and a pen. "I have some here to write directions for these men." He indicated the two Campbells beside him.

Aini faced Callum. "Earl, I need you to write a missive to your men. Tell them to continue the fight and back us as we move to rescue the Heir."

"You know I can't do that. Nathair will destroy Perthshire if he finds out."

"I'll order it destroyed right now if you don't."

"You wouldn't."

She held a hand out, jerking her chin at Bran's walkie talkie. He gave it to her and she clicked the side button. "Vera."

"Here, my Seer."

"Please send twenty men with the green box of extra explosives to Perthshire to wreak some havoc. I want water lines, electricity, and main roads torn to shreds. Please tell them to wait until after midnight to minimize injuries and death."

"Affirmative."

Callum gripped the metal bars of his cage. "You won't do it."

"I just did. This is war, and though I'm not the unfeeling beast Nathair is, and I refuse to hurt when I don't have to, I will rain down vengeance on those who don't support us." Aini handed the talkie back to Bran. "I think it's time to leave."

"Fine. Fine!" Callum reached a hand through the bars. "I'll write the missive."

Bran handed the man pen and paper.

"Be sure to say you'll join us as soon as you finish the task you're working on now. And instruct your men here not to ask about this covert operation. It's too bad, Callum. Instead of rotting in a cage, you could've been doing some good yourself."

"I hope you're as right as you think you are, lass." Callum's voice dipped as he shook his head slowly and handed the completed letter over to Bran.

Bran pocketed the missive, then handed another piece of paper to the two Campbells guarding the cages. "These are the contact numbers you'll need, lads. Keep to the directions concerning our prisoners, please."

The two nodded, then Bran joined Aini in the passageway.

"They'll have Thane in the upper rooms, just down from Nathair's office." Bran switched on his own torch and the golden light spread over the ancient, stone walls. "I'll show you on a map."

Nodding, Aini flipped Neve's flashlight on—*torch*, she reminded herself, knowing she still sounded colonial when she wasn't paying attention—and led him away from the secret room as quickly as her feet could carry her. Callum's words bit into her confidence, gnawing the corners off. She needed to see everyone gathered out front and primed to go into Edinburgh as a unified force.

AT THE FRONT OF THE CROWD OF VEHICLES, VERA WORE TWO guns next to her pouch of cherry drops and Bismian, one pocket pistol and a larger piece for longer distances. Aini wasn't the best with shooting—practice last night at the Inveraray range had proved the fact once again—so she'd stick with commanding ghosts as the situation demanded.

"Seer!" Vera raised her arms and crossed her thumbs, the group echoing the motion. Even the Campbells and their kin—Thane's mother Senga, the perpetually antagonistic Sorley Menzies, questioning yet loyal Hawes, all of them—joined in.

Callum's needling words faded from Aini's mind and she gave the rebels a fierce smile.

"We don't know our Heir's exact location, but Bran has given us a good guess. You have your orders. We will see this through. Our Heir will be free to fight by sunrise tomorrow!"

The gathering shouted, cheering her on, as she climbed into a lorry with Bran, Myles, Vera, and Neve. Each of her friends nodded, determination shining in their eyes. With Bran already unfolding a map of the Signet Library and the surrounding government buildings that had belonged to the now defunct Parliament, Aini started the engine and began the journey to take back Thane.

## CHAPTER 2
## A NEW KIND OF DEVIL

Thane raised his chin and tried not to show the defeat he felt in his heart.

Nathair laughed, pushed past the guard at the door, and dragged Thane into his office inside the Signet Library in Edinburgh. The guard followed them, one hand on his gun.

"So your darling fool is on her way here." Nathair chuckled. "Did you know she would follow us?"

It was like a punch to the stomach. Thane bent at the waist and glared. He was afraid she would, but prayed she wouldn't. "Your source could be misleading you. With Callum defecting to your side, the group will be cracked into at least three different pieces. There's no way they'll pull together again." Unless Aini decided on going forward. That woman could organize the world into submission. His heart contracted, and he grabbed his shirt, the pain of losing her very, very real.

The feeling grew electric—piercing and distinct—and became less about pain and more about longing. The sensation buzzed through his chest and somehow he knew Aini was thinking about him. He touched the back of his knee where he somehow felt the brush of her silky fingertips. The scent of her filled his nose.

"Aini," he whispered.

Shivers ran down the length of his body.

Nathair, not noticing Thane's odd behavior, poured some whisky into a crystal glass and downed it. He didn't used to drink like that, Thane thought.

"I am surprised they're so quick to move," Nathair said. "You're the Heir, after all." His voice held an odd tone.

Thane shook off the sensation of Aini's presence, straightened, and poured himself a glass, deciding to drive right into this mess just to see if he could shake Nathair up at all.

"It doesn't matter if I'm gone. Aini is their leader. If she decides to do it, she will rule this thing whether I'm around or not. You took the wrong one, Nathair. She is the power in the rebellion." He forced himself to laugh, loud and strong. "What I can't understand is your reaction to what happened on Bass Rock. I made the stone roar. Your own son. You must have heard about it from someone. Somehow. You always believed the old stories. Why can't you accept that fate chose me? I am your blood." The whisky burned its way down his throat just as his words did.

Nathair looked out the window, strangely still. "I do believe. I do accept it. You are the Heir. You are going to rule Scotland. If we can beat the king. If you can make the right choices."

"Ah." Thane finished his drink and set his glass down, banging the desk and nearly shattering the thing. "There's the rub, aye? The right choices will be your choices, won't they? And how will you get me to behave and be your puppet? I won't do it to please you. I certainly won't do it to save my own skin." Anger surged through him. He longed to jump onto Nathair's back and break the man's neck with one strong snap.

An ugly grin pulled at Nathair's mouth. "Don't worry, son. I have a plan to rectify that situation. And our Seer is playing along nicely."

Nathair had sworn to leave her alone. Why had Thane believed him? Why did he always believe him, over and over and over and over and over?

He shoved his palm against the back of Nathair's head and he slipped to the carpet. The guard jumped on Thane and pressed the metal of gun barrel against his temple.

Thane grabbed the barrel and pulled it against his forehead. "Just shoot. Do it."

Fire lashed across Thane's shoulder. Nathair had cut him and was drawing his knife back again for another strike. Blood poured from a gaping wound on Thane's right arm. He blinked as the room tilted.

"Get him sewn up and put him in his room," Nathair said to the guard.

Stars flickered over Thane's vision and he allowed the guard to steer him away. His brain didn't want to work. He was bleeding so much. Too much.

His worries flipped over one another like devils playing in the flames of his pain. Aini. Coming here. Nathair's plan. What was it? How was he going to get Thane to do as he wished? Thane knew exactly how. He was going to hurt Aini every time Thane did something Nathair didn't like. Somehow, he had to get word to Aini that this was all a grand trap and they could not come to Edinburgh, no matter what.

Before he could think of any possible way to accomplish that

# THE EDINBURGH FATE

feat, the guard was shoving him into a plastic chair and another man was injecting his arm with numbing solution.

Ten neat stitches later, Thane lay in a fine room down the way from Nathair's office with a tube of fluids feeding him. He jerked the tube out of his arm and pressed the spot to stop the bleeding.

A message. How could he get a message to Aini and the rest? His arm throbbed dully, and he looked out the window into a closed courtyard.

Men and women in suits bustled through the square of dead grass, cobblestones, and past the dry fountain. He could kick the glass and escape through the window. But then what? He'd be caught in a minute. There were guards everywhere and cameras too. But maybe he could be free long enough to get a note to someone who might do as he asked. He crammed his hands into his pockets, looking for money. If he offered a bit of money for the deed, the messenger may just take him up on the offer. If he offered too much, they'd be wary. But he had no money on him at all. What else? A desk sat beside the bed. The drawer slid out easily, showing a pad and pen. That was something.

Thane leaned on the desk to write, racking his brain to remember the codes he could use in case the message was found. It had to be a really strong code. Not that ridiculous food code they'd used on the way. He'd write the message in the number code. Yes. That one hadn't been put to work in a while. Hopefully, it was still safe. The code used the letters' number in the alphabet, then subtracted two. Operatives were also required to insert a nonsense number every third time. It wasn't that tough to figure out. But it was enough, hopefully, to protect this information from prying eyes or Nathair's men if they intercepted the message.

He worked quickly, his brain fuzzy but functioning. That should've been his motto.

The message hopefully stated:

*Do not come after the Heir. It is a trap.*

*Fight Nathair as if the Heir is with you, because he is in spirit.*

*Infiltrate the city quietly and take St. Giles first. Nathair is using it as an armory.*

*He will tempt you into going after the Heir in the library. Do not attempt rescue.*

By the time Thane finished the message and tucked it into his boot, the sun was long gone and so were the people in the courtyard. He kicked the window out, using his heel to clear the smaller bits of glass from the frame so he could maneuver his way onto the ledge. One finger-sized length of glass winked. He pocketed the piece, knowing it could serve as both weapon and tool in the future if needed.

Outside, it was dark, but there was plenty of light for anyone to glimpse him. Former Parliament buildings came together to create the courtyard, their windows illuminated squares on the stones below. A tension buzzed through the air, like someone was about to scream. An errant, late worker walked quickly, gaze darting here and there. What did he know that Thane didn't?

Thane lowered himself into a squat, his stitched arm proclaiming its unhappiness with his activity. Then he made a go for the drain spout. With one hand, he cupped the ledge, lay on his stomach, and gripped the spout with his boots as best he could.

What was it Lewis always said? In for a penny, in for a pound.

He slid over the edge, keeping a hold on the spout as best he could. His boots squealed against the metal as he slipped down, down, down. Each new section of pipe jarred his hand and cut his palm, but he couldn't let go or he'd drop to the most likely very unforgiving pavement.

One more floor to go and he'd be there.

"What's that?" a voice called out below him.

"Go!" Another voice rose above that one.

Thane's thumb caught the last section of drain spout and ripped his hand away. He grasped for the pipe, but couldn't regain his grip, and fell hard on his back. The wind knocked clean out of him, he sucked a breath, glad at least that he'd had the sense to tuck his chin to protect his head. Those new men Nathair had taken on, all in flat caps and wearing the look of the devil himself, poured out of the courtyard door toward Thane.

He jumped to his feet, head spinning from the earlier blood loss, and took off toward the exit and freedom. He only needed a moment to pass the message on.

Free of the courtyard, he found a side street and a plain-faced vendor selling scarves and mittens. Thane paused to take the message from his boot, then shot toward the vendor.

"Please take this to Gilmerton Cove. South of here. Ask for Vera."

"I don't know what that is." The woman eyed the street and put a hand to her chest. "What do you mean, man?"

"Just ask around. For Gilmerton Cove. Please. You'll be rewarded. They will give you what you ask as long as it's—"

Someone jerked Thane backward. He fell against three of Nathair's men. Thane stretched to see the vendor. She was slipping her hand inside her pocket. Maybe she had kept the message. Maybe she would deliver it. Or maybe she thought he was a madman and had thrown the message to the ground already.

He pushed a man off him and tried to see the street near the vendor's boots. "Get off me, ape!"

He didn't want to hope if there was no hope. Above all, he didn't want to be blind in this situation. But there wasn't any paper on the roadway. The vendor had kept the coded message, for whatever reason.

Thrusting upward, Thane rammed the back of his head into one of the men's noses. The man howled in pain, cursing Thane in a creative way Myles would've appreciated.

"There's more where that came from if you want it," Thane said.

Fingers gripped Thane's hair. A thumb and a finger pressed acutely into his jaw, sending sparks of fire down his neck. A voice he'd never heard before echoed in his ringing ears.

"I don't think that's how you should behave, future king," the voice whispered in his ear.

The words tilted up and down with a thick Birmingham accent and Thane was struck again with how his father could bend so many people to his will—even those whose backgrounds had nothing to do with the Campbells.

"What did he give you to become his dog?" Thane shook his head and pulled away, heading back through the exit he'd escaped from. There was little use in running right now. He wouldn't get far. Thane turned to see the man who'd held him with expert, exact force.

The first thought Thane had was: here stood a man about to defy a rebel army and a king, smiling coolly, gallus as anything. He wasn't taller than the men around him, though it seemed he had a good foot on the rest. His suit was far too fine for this kind of bloody work. Thane had no doubt if he took a keek at the man's right hand, he'd find blood there under the fingernails. The man's smile and chilling eyes told Thane he wasn't even going to respond to the dog insult.

"My name is Jack Shaw." He made a little bow, flipping his

long coat aside to show a red, silk lining. "Your father invited us into his confidence and I, for one, consider it a fine gift."

Thane felt like he was drowning. Jack was too refined. Too professional. Not the kind of enemy Thane knew how to handle in situations that called for violence. "Shows how little you know of what my father's gifts look like in the light of truth."

Jack swept past him, his men surrounding Thane, guns and knives barely hidden. "He does sound like a prophecy come to life, doesn't he?" Jack whispered, his men laughing.

"That's right, Jackie," another man said.

The others joined in the laugh as they corralled Thane to his room. A guard stood outside the door and inside too, by the broken, boarded-up window. They'd worked fast to undo what Thane had done. The men shoved him toward the bed, then left him with Jack.

"You best get some rest." Jack sniffed and ran a finger over the unbroken side of the window. "Your friends will be here soon. We'll have an exciting evening, for certain. Then, when we've dealt with them, it'll be time to prep for your appearance on the television. You see, Thane Campbell, we are all on the same side."

Pretending to nurse his stitched-up shoulder, Thane leaned over far enough to slide the glass from his pocket under the mattress. Then he stretched out on the bed. His shoulder wound pounded in time with his pulse.

"Things may not go exactly as you'd like," Jack said, "but they will proceed in the same direction. We will usurp the king on your behalf. We will take back your country for you. You will be king of Scotland. You see? We are but your servants in this endeavor."

Two of Jackie's men returned, one with a pint of beer and the other a plate of bangers and mash. They set the stuff on Thane's night table.

Thane wasn't about to ask Jackie any questions. Anything they told him would be tainted with misinformation and could lead to a misstep. No, better that Thane talk to Nathair again. At least now he knew if Nathair was lying. He could see it all over Nathair's face and he wondered how he'd never before noticed the shift of features.

"You will be king of this fine land. And I will return home to Birmingham, some of these lads to Glasgow, and we'll all be happier for it. Embrace our assistance and this will all go rather smoothly, I like to think."

"The chemist isn't listening to you, Jackie," a man from Glasgow said, his accent familiar to Thane. So the two groups Nathair had taken on were blending. Bad news for the good side. Rough men from two of the roughest cities would make for a very difficult gang to beat in a fight. Especially with this sharp leader orchestrating things with that blood-stained hand.

"He thinks we're not being truthful with him." Jackie lit a cigarette right over Thane's head and sucked it. The tobacco crackled lightly. There it was—the dark brown lodged under Jackie's fingernails, just as Thane had guessed. "He'll just wait and talk to daddy about all this and see what the old man gives him."

Thane's stomach flipped. Jackie had just about read his mind.

Jackie leaned closer and pressed a thumb into Thane's bandage. Heat leaked from the wound and down Thane's arm, dragging a bitter pain alongside.

"Maybe you'll have a nice Dream about what's to happen tonight, hm?" Jackie raised both eyebrows. "That would be a good thing for you, because I don't think you've guessed what your father has up his sleeve." He grinned and turned on his heel to go, his gang trailing after him like long, dirty coattails.

The guard at the window cocked his revolver and set it on his forearm.

Message received. There would be no easy escapes from now on. Thane shut his eyes and prayed that vendor had delivered the message. Aini could not come here. These people would rip them limb from limb and Jackie would add her blood to the dregs under his manicured nails.

## CHAPTER 3
## A BLESSING

The plan was complicated, to say the least, and Bran was about sixty percent sure it would go wrong. The problem with it was that the rebels—Campbells, Campbell kin, Dionadair, Aini, Neve, and Myles—believed Nathair wouldn't see it coming. He definitely would. Rodric and Seanie would've agreed with Bran. Thane would have. But Bran had been outvoted on spending time coming up with a new plan. So here they were, trucking it to Edinburgh, straight toward Nathair who was always five moves ahead of the rest of the world.

"Can you tell me one more time?" Myles scratched his head, then pulled his black beanie over his scalp again. "I just want to be sure I know exactly where I'm supposed to be and what I can maybe do if I don't end up in the right spot."

"Of course." The steering wheel squeaked a little as Aini pulled the lorry into a car park near the Edinburgh train station.

Street lamps glowed under a cloudy, starless night. The radio played a quiet song about an owl who had morphed into a girl at midsummer. Could've been a lovely night if they weren't about to make it explode. Bran silently chastised himself for being so bitter. Even if they were about to ruin everything, it didn't have to spoil the fine moment. What was life other than fine moments mixed into the bad?

"First, we'll set up three diversions within Edinburgh. One here at the train station. A second near Edinburgh Castle. And a third on Forth Bridge. You are part of the castle team."

Two more rebel vehicles pulled in behind Aini's parking spot —a blue car and a plain white lorry similar to the one they were in.

"With Vera, Hawes, Bran and his explosives team, you'll walk to the castle and set up your explosive device beside the ticket booth. The inner booth, beyond the open entrance."

"Got it."

Myles tapped his head while Bran opened his bag and rummaged around for something to eat. Bran was trying very hard not to think of it as a last meal.

Aini opened the lorry's door and climbed out. The chilly wind picked up her hair and tossed it over her shoulder. Her face was straight lines and sheer will. The lass was ready for war, that was obvious. "While the bulk of our forces infiltrate the cathedral that is serving as Nathair's secret armory and the Signet Library, all explosives teams will put off their detonations at the same time. We hope Nathair won't have the time to realize—and pass on the fact—that this is organized and is only a ploy to spread out his forces here. I will be with the group here. We will set off the explosions, then all head to our posts around the Signet Library and the old Parliament buildings where we know, from Bran here, Nathair holds his prisoners, both those he treats well and those he does not."

"And we're just hoping Nathair thinks we're a bunch of

quitters who won't go after their Heir?" Myles gave Neve a quick kiss and a firm hug.

"Yes," Aini said. "He believes I promised Thane to stay out of it for my own health. I do know that I endanger Thane's life in coming for him. But I don't see any other way to free him. We have to do the job. There's no one else who will do it for us. I'm certainly not sacrificing Thane to save my own skin."

"Agreed," Neve said, handing Aini a walkie talkie.

Blood going cold, Bran slid out behind Myles and adjusted the sling of grenades under his coat. He wasn't sure which way Nathair would treat Thane. Would Thane be in a cell under the building? Or in a nicely appointed room upstairs, guarded and tied to his fate? Bran watched Aini give some orders over her talkie.

"Has there been any word on whether or not the king knows about Nathair asking Campbells to swear to him? I'm only assuming what we've done thus far hasn't been pitched around yet."

Aini strapped the device onto her belt. "Our intel says there isn't any chatter about our infiltration of Inveraray or the gathering. There was one mention of the king planning a visit to the North though. We don't know if he wants to check on Nathair's doings or what."

"There's so little we know going into this." Bran moved his fingers in and out, trying to get the feeling back into them.

Aini was suddenly right in front of him, fierce eyes blazing. The wind whistled past as she lifted his chin gently, her other hand propping her jacket to the side. Macbeth's dirk poised, dark and ancient, from her waist and the Bethune brooch glittered beside it, promising Aini's role here, Seer, Ghost Talker, Protector of the Heir.

Aini smiled, and Bran saw a beautiful, female incarnation of

Merlin, magic swirling around her in blue flames and reflecting off her shining hair. He shook his head, not sure if he'd actually seen that or imagined it. "You are my soldier," she said, "and I *will* succeed in this. Don't let fear break your quick mind, Bran. We need you. I need you."

The urge to bow broke over Bran, but he felt silly, so he settled on lowering his gaze respectfully. "Thank you, Aini. I will do my very best for you and for Thane."

She set a hand on his shoulder. "I know you will. I would never doubt you. This won't go like we plan, I'm sure. I'm not an idiot. But we must push on and think on our feet. There will never be a day when we are fully prepared for this."

"True."

She spun and took her magic with her, leaving Bran feeling oddly baptized. A sensation like power lingered over the spot she'd touched.

"That was mint." Myles blinked. Awe had pulled his eyes wider.

"Come on, then," Bran said to his team as the other groups disappeared into the night, heading toward the Forth Bridge and the train station.

"I'm ready." Vera slicked on some bright red lipstick and joined him, not a trace of her earlier antagonism in sight. She only wore that I-love-to-flirt-with-Death look she'd most likely been born with.

Hawes strode over, hands gripping the straps of her satchel. Her dark eyes watched the night. She'd seen some rough times during a fight between the clans during her childhood. Bran remembered the story Thane had told him about her and two much larger girls. Hawes was a born fighter, Thane had said. She used her surroundings to give her an edge.

Bran started toward the wooded area beyond the street, his

lads at his heels. They could move along quickly there without being seen quite as easily. "You're pretty comfortable toting a sack of things that explode," he said to Hawes.

Hawes jerked to a stop, face going pale. "I thought they weren't live."

Okay. She was tough, but not a macho idiot. Good. "They aren't. But they're also not made of candy, you know."

Vera snorted. "Candy isn't the safest thing in this group."

Myles nodded along with the rest of the lads.

Bran laughed quietly. "Just please be sure to keep your footing, aye?"

"Course." Hawes swallowed and watched her feet as they crossed the road, nearing a turn off.

HEADING DOWN A SIDE ROAD TOWARD EDINBURGH CASTLE, the team saw several kingsmen. One in a Campbell kilt, the rest in black. All stood straight and armed with guns on their belts. None so far had noticed them creeping along the streets. The nighttime crowd, though sparse at this hour, poured laughs and music from pub doors and into the streets. The noise did a fine job covering their own footsteps through the shadowed spots on their route.

Vera led the team up a set of narrow, stone steps. Cold water dropped from the rooftops, some falling onto Bran's neck and slithering down his back. He kept close to Vera and Myles. Hawes stayed right behind him.

"Keep an eye on our tail, lads." Bran came up beside Vera to look down the street.

A kingsman stood guard in front of a tall, wooden newspaper stand that was closed up for the night.

"He just glanced over here," Vera said.

"Now he's looking toward the castle though."

"Aye. There's no way past him."

Myles popped a chocolate into his mouth. "I'm ready to take him down. Just give me a minute." He cracked his neck.

Bran shrugged. "I guess it's worth a shot. We'll be here if your distraction goes south."

Myles walked out of the dark, putting a lorry-load of swagger into his walk. "Hello, kingsman. How is the evening treating you?" He laid the southern colonial accent on thick as clotted cream. Or, Bran supposed, thick as sausage gravy?

The kingsman jumped and pulled his gun free. "Fine and thank you. Move on, now. Get back to your whisky."

Myles ventured closer. Closer.

The kingsman pulled his gun's hammer back and raised the weapon. "I said, move on."

"Awfully angry lately, aren't you all? What is going on in this country these days? Everyone is acting like there's going to be some kind of ruckus. Should I be worried?"

The kingsman lowered his gun. "No. We will take care of any...issues that arise. Everything is under control." He looked down to slide his gun back into place.

Myles kicked him in the stomach. The man flew back against the newspaper stand. Wood splintered around him, but Myles didn't wait for the man to find his feet in the aftermath. The colonial, chocolates giving him ridiculous strength, lifted the kingsman up by the coat. He released the coat with one hand, then threw a nasty hook into the man's jaw.

The kingsman fell to the ground, unconscious, as Myles dusted his hands off. "That was fun."

Fun. Bran pressed his palms into his eyelids, a hysterical laugh climbing up his throat. He shook off the mania and jogged to catch up with Myles. If anyone noticed that unconscious kingsman, they were in for trouble.

Edinburgh Castle's bridge stretched out in front of them and Bran led the team past the statues of Robert the Bruce and William Wallace, two of Scotland's greatest heroes.

He drew up short.

Thane was following in their metaphorical footsteps. If the rebels won, Thane would be a grand leader of Scotland. He would be king.

"Bran. You all right?" Vera elbowed him. She looked from him to William Wallace. "Interesting, are they? Get it together, tall, dark, and handsome. We have a job to do."

Scowling at Vera's swaying hips as she walked away, Bran hurried through the gate and up the incline.

"Take the contraption out carefully and set it there," he said to Hawes, pointing to the ticket booth. His explosion team watched him with wide eyes. "Yes, lads. This is your moment."

The ticket booth was nothing more than thin metal and wooden slats. It would go up easily and make a good sound doing it. No one was inside this time of night, so they wouldn't have to harm anyone unnecessarily.

Hawes did as ordered, then the lads arranged the plastic contraption and its fuse. Vera and Myles kept watch on either side.

Bran stood and wiped his palms on his trousers. The air smelled like metal, like rain was about to fall from the billowing clouds overhead. "It's ready."

The group moved to a spot near the downed kingsman. The man groaned as Hawes gagged him and tied his wrists together. The clock on the building across the street chimed lightly, old brass bells doing the same job they had for at least one hundred years. It was almost time.

Bran breathed the cold air in through his nose. "Three, two, one." With a swell of healthy fear, he pressed the chilly metal lever down. Light bloomed in front of the castle, noise following in its wake.

Myles had hit the ground. His hands covered the back of his head. He started to say something but two other, far off explosions boomed across the city. "That means we go now, right?"

"Aye, and this looks a fine way to do it." Vera hopped on a motorbike parked in front of a hotel. She gestured to three more behind hers. She revved the engine. "What's wrong? Haven't you been on a motorbike?"

Tucking his explosive materials neatly away, Bran climbed onto the next bike. "I have." He cleared a green button of mud and pressed it. The engine rumbled to life. "But..." He looked at the rest of the group, then wondered how long they had until the kingsmen arrived to see what had blown to Heaven near Edinburgh Castle.

Myles raised a hand, then claimed the next motorbike. "This is what I drove when I first came over from the colonies for the apprenticeship with Lewis MacGregor." He talked too loudly, like the blast had messed with his hearing.

Hawes motioned to the rider seat behind Myles, and Myles nodded. The explosion lads looked more nervous about the bikes than they did the explosives.

"Just run, then, lads," Bran said, taking off into the night. "It's not far."

Vera shouted over her shoulder. "Anyone else worried about how there aren't enough kingsmen around?"

Bran studied the dark spaces between the buildings—alleys were the perfect place to hide a small unit set for an ambush.

The bikes buzzed down the street and they took a corner. Myles pulled up next to Bran, Hawes with him.

The wind threw Hawes's hair into her face. She held onto Myles with one hand and tangled her locks into a knot with the other. "But our explosions drew the kingsmen away. Should we be worried?" She glanced at Vera, who ran her bike much too close to a tree.

"Definitely," Vera said loudly. "This stinks of Nathair. Even with some of the kingsmen heading off to investigate the explosions, there should've been more around."

Myles's bike wobbled a bit and he leaned forward, his elbows sticking out awkwardly. "Why would Nathair want us to infiltrate Edinburgh?"

"To trap us here?" Bran followed Vera over a rough spot of pavement and the bike jarred his teeth together. "To wipe us off God's good earth once and for all?"

Myles caught up.

Hawes shouted to be heard over the engines. "If he downed us all, he'd have a lot less ammo to use against the king when he comes. It takes a good amount of work to dig bullets from corpses."

Myles glanced over his shoulder, then trained his sights on the road ahead. "I do not want to know how you know that. You can keep that little tale to yourself, please and thank you."

Bran's stomach churned. He recalled a night spent digging very suspicious holes in a forest with Thane and Seanie.

Now, the flashing lights of kingsmen cars lit up the sky, near the explosion sites. So there were some kingsmen out. Just not as many as there should've been. He swallowed as they zipped down Johnston Terrace, coming to a stop just past The Little Inn.

Bran parked the bike in the shadows beside the inn. Vera and Myles followed suit. A few people peeked out the front door.

"What's the story?" a man with an Irish accent said.

A hand pulled him back inside and a woman's voice scolded him. "Get in here. They said not to go out this night." The front door was promptly slammed.

"You'll have no story if you don't break the rules sometimes, lovelies!" Vera knocked once on the door, then began a quick jog toward the Lawnmarket.

The cathedral stretched a long gray neck into the cloud-strewn stars as Bran, Myles, and Vera slipped beyond St. Giles and behind a shuttered ghost tour ticket office at the mouth of Mercat Cross.

A solid group of twenty kingsmen—most in Campbell tartan —stood at the Signet Library's front door with a secondary group beside the fiercely ugly statue of King John. The Parliament of Scotland used to meet in one of those buildings beyond John's bronze profile. Now it was home only to Nathair and his machinations.

The rebels were doing as they'd been ordered by Vera. Creating chaos. Some darted from one building's moonshadow to another. Three women shrieked, "Freedom!" before high-tailing it across the cobblestones and back to relative safety down the street. A kingsman shot his gun into the air. Another aimed at more rebels running from the shadows, but it was an off shot. Nathair's men weren't trying to kill. A baby cried somewhere far off, and the sounds of hand-to-hand fighting echoed from the darkness. There were shouts and orders given through walkie talkies.

Vera took a wrapped candy from her cleavage. "I'll take one of the caramels and drag their attention toward me as you slip around the side, to that door there. Our team from the road behind should be inside now and ready to help you in."

Bran's explosion team ran up behind them, panting like dogs. "There are some rebels downed by gunshot in the inner courtyard," the skinniest of the lot said. Bran hated himself for forgetting the man's name. It was something basic like John or James. "We overheard it on a kingsman's talkie as he ran past. They ordered all of their own to stop firing though. This is wild, aye? Anarchy in the city."

Vera was already on her phone. "Yes. Send in another unit to retrieve the wounded…no…but…she wasn't supposed to be there. She should be over by the—hello?" Vera banged her phone with the heel of her hand, then tucked it away, swearing. "We need to move now."

Bran grabbed her arm to keep her from taking the caramel. "No, we need you when we get inside. As a Threader. I need to see the connection if there is one to see. If the men have a stronger connection, or markedly lesser, to someone inside one of the holding cells or upstairs in the rooms, we need to know about that. If any of us show a strong tie to anyone there—it'll help us find Thane."

Vera clicked her tongue as gunshots sounded far off. "Fine. Who goes then?"

"We'll give a go." The explosives team looked at the gathered kingsmen, then held out hands for speed caramels. It was like they shared a brain.

Shaking his head, Bran handed each lad one of the candies. "Scatter once you're clear of this corner."

They did.

With shouts and warnings and gasps of shock at the men's speed echoing around them, Bran and the rest slipped through the shadow of the king's assembly chambers next to the library, where Nathair ran his business beside a slew of other government workers.

Bran had briefly considered having them all take the caramels, but Myles couldn't since he'd used the strength chocolate so recently. Thane had been very clear about the possible damage to the brain and nervous system. And the rest of them might need to use another type of altered sweet to finish this job.

At a side door, Bran pulled the group up short and said a silent prayer for the lads who'd drawn off the remaining kingsmen. He tried the doorknob, found it locked, and peered through the old, wavy glass. An emergency light glowed over a hallway and a set of stairs carpeted in green and gold. An elaborate *J* had been carved into the baluster. King John sure was a humble man, Bran thought wryly as he smashed a fist through the window and twisted the lock.

Bran moved into the carpeted area, his boots crunching on the broken glass. He switched on a torch. Myles, Hawes, and Vera did the same behind him.

"Where should we go first?" Hawes had obviously decided they had enough light because she put her torch back in her satchel and pulled out a gun instead.

Bran patted his shot pouch. The tranquilizing darts hid inside, tucked side-by-side in a sardine tin. "It's a good guess that he's in one of two rooms upstairs. Near Nathair's office,"

They started up the steps.

"Guard," Myles hissed.

He pushed the lot of them against the wall with a long arm as a man in a kingsman jacket left the hallway and walked right past.

Bran held his breath. Vera put a hand on her gun, but Bran covered her fingers with his to stop her. The kingsman lifted a foot to show the glint of broken glass in the carpet. He clicked the button on his walkie talkie and began to turn around. He was going to spot them. Even though it was dark and they'd covered their torches with palms. Bran's heart beat hard against his chest. If they waited to play their cards, one of them would most likely fold. If they attacked and didn't need to, they might alert a score of waiting kingsmen and lose the hand completely.

Vera leaped off the fifth step and landed on the kingsman's back. Bran couldn't breathe. She roped the man's neck with an arm and he thrashed against her, hitting her tucked head and arms but not getting much of anywhere with it. The man fell to his knees, gurgling, then Vera set him down gently like she was a kind nanny seeing to her ward. She ruined that quite well with a kick to the unconscious man's stomach.

Dusting her hands, she began climbing the stairs. "Come on. No time to waste!" Two steps at a time, she led them, Bran shaking his head.

At the second level, Bran shut his torch off and waved at the rest to do the same.

A quiet creak sounded behind them, down the stairs. Every nerve buzzing, Bran turned to see some of their own approaching. It was one of Callum's men and another man in Campbell tartan. Hawes nodded at the second man as if she knew him.

"Can we help?" Callum's man whispered.

Bran motioned for the idiot to shut his mouth. The man nodded, then Vera gestured for Bran to join her as she moved forward. Myles and Hawes and the other two pulled out their darts and guns, holding them ready. Together, they peered around the corner. Four men guarded two doors in a long corridor. Vera frowned, most likely trying to distinguish between the strings of light she saw as a Threader.

"One room is a decoy," Bran said into her ear. "It's one of Nathair's favorite tricks."

She yanked him down and whispered, barely audible. "God above there are threads like mad here. It's tangled. Bright. I can't...The guards have a bright connection with the person in the first room there. It's a violent connection. I'm guessing they hate the person. They would hate him. He is their enemy. That is most likely the jagged violence I see in the thread. Has to be Thane."

Bran nodded. Vera's sixth sense had been improving of late. She'd told them plenty about it at breakfast. He didn't mind the bragging. It was better than the vitriol she'd been tossing about before Thane's abduction.

Vera tapped her red, red lips.

"Any threads connecting them to the person in the second room?" Bran whispered. Myles peered around the corner. Bran scowled at him and he jumped quickly out of view. "Or is it just empty?"

"There is a fine silvery thread there..." A wrinkle appeared between Vera's eyebrows. "They have someone important in there. Could be a trap. I, I'm just not sure."

Bran lowered his tranquilizer gun and slid darts into each one of the five slots in the cylinder. It was quieter than a gun. And these men would be left alive to fight against the king if they managed some kind of truce. This was a complicated war to be sure.

He pulled the trigger, and in quick succession, he landed darts in one, two, three, four guards. The men slumped to the floor in varying degrees of uncomfortable-looking positions. "Myles, Vera. You watch there. Hawes, take the far end of the corridor."

They raced down the hallway and Bran stopped at the first

door. He tried the knob, not surprised when he found it locked. It'd been reinforced and was more of a prison lock than a guest room type of handle. Good thing he'd brought Aini's lock picking set.

He pulled the tiny set out of his shot pouch and went to work, fingers shaking and heart in his mouth. If they heard him, if they opened this door, if anyone came up the stairs...

The lock gave way. Tasting metal, Bran kicked the door open and fired at the first person who wasn't Thane. Bran missed. His target—a grimace tugging at the man's thin lips—slipped right, and came up beside Bran. A fist clocked Bran hard on the ear, making the room ring. Bran put his hands up and looked around.

Where was Thane?

"Not here," said the man who had hit him. He was pale, looked underfed, and spoke with a strong Glaswegian accent. One of Nathair's new gang—the Glasgow branch anyway.

A gunshot sounded somewhere outside.

"He's not here!" Bran hoped the team could hear him. He prayed they were inspecting the next room.

The man put a gun to Bran's temple and forced him to the window. An inner courtyard splayed below. Men and women from the rebel groups threw punches at Nathair's kingsmen and new gang members, who were all wearing charcoal gray. It was an ugly fight with most of the rebels retreating, outnumbered.

Aini ran across the night-shrouded cobblestones. She paused to look over her shoulder, then shouted something.

Why was she sprinting toward the side of the courtyard that Nathair's men still held strong? Maybe it wasn't as it seemed. Maybe Bran was mistaken.

"Aini!" Bran pulled away from his captor, toward the glass, as if she could somehow hear his warning.

Beyond her, where she was headed, a light flashed. The crack of a gun popped Bran's ears.

Aini jerked back, then fell.

Bran couldn't understand what he was seeing.

The distance masked most of the details, but a darkening stain showed on Aini's shoulder. Her open mouth moved and her eyes were wide, shocked. The strength went out of Bran's legs and he caught himself on the windowsill.

The man dragged Bran backward, out of the room, then threw him to the carpeted floor.

Bran's mind spun. "You shot her," he stammered.

The man pulled the curtain further back and peered down. "If that is indeed the Seer, we will care for her. We are on the same side, even if you don't believe it."

The Seer. Their leader. Thane gone and now her. He was shaking hard enough to rattle his teeth. "But that shot..."

"Aye." The Glaswegian looked again. "I do think she's left us. Dead before her time. A sadness. Shouldn't have rushed our man like she did." Nodding, the Glaswegian removed his cap, then held it to his chest as if he was already at a funeral for Aini. "We will make sure her body is properly cared for. Now, off with you before I do the same with you."

Bran found his feet and rushed toward the next room. "Thane. Thane!"

But the next room was locked and his team was nowhere to be seen. Vera hadn't managed to get in. Where was the team now? The corridor was empty. He kicked the locked door hard, panic rising in his chest.

Aini was dead. Aini couldn't be dead.

He had to see Thane, to tell him, to get him out of this hell.

"Ah, ah. Don't do that. Go on, now." The thin-lipped man

had followed Bran down the corridor. "You don't want to meet the man on the other side of that door."

But Bran could hardly hear him over his own heartbeat. The carpet at his feet exploded. Over the ringing in his ears, he heard the man saying, "Move on, now." Smoke leaked from his gun and a sulfuric scent rose into the air.

The Glaswegian had shot the floor right in front of Bran's boot.

Bran couldn't draw his own gun in time to do anything. His grenades were useless too. He'd only end up blowing himself up and possibly Thane too if he was on the other side of that door. Holding his hands up in defeat, Bran backed away, down the other side of the hallway, but before he left, he said, "We will get you back, Thane. Have faith, man."

He hurried down the stairs and out a side door, finding the chaos of the rebels' retreat.

Aini was dead. The Seer was dead.

Finding Vera, he began to run with her, but a tingling sensation spread over his back. He turned to see a man in a gray coat and white shirt, standing at a window. The room couldn't have been far from the one Bran had broken into. The man smiled coldly and tipped his flat cap at Bran. They wanted the rebels to get away without much trouble.

Why? What was Nathair planning?

Bran blindly followed Vera—a shrieking leader speeding down the road, totally ignorant of the fact that not only had they not rescued the Heir but now their Seer was lost to them, to everyone, forever.

"Vera, we don't have him. He wasn't in there," he said, his words flimsy against the hard sounds of the night—sirens and shouting, engines and gunshot.

"Don't be fooled, my fellow Scots!" Vera raised a fist as she crashed through the streets, heading for the train station with Bran and the rest in her wake. "Nathair Campbell wants to poison you and blame the king! Don't be fooled!"

Windows opened, and men with unshaved chins and women in nightgowns watched the rebels rage onward. Two girls in braids shouted down, excited but too young to know the horror and blood a rebellion delivered at innocent people's doorsteps. Their parents tugged them out of the window and slammed the shutters closed.

"The Dionadair will rise again!" Vera's hair came loose. It flew behind her, tangled and wild. She looked every inch a madwoman. "The true and loyal Campbells—the ones who love our country—will be with us too. Take up arms. Be ready. The Coronation Stone has spoken and we will listen and take down Nathair and the false king John!"

Bran's feet were leaden as he did his best to rush through Edinburgh, toward the lorries and cars they'd parked at the train station. Questions swamped his mind as he ran. What had he just seen? Why had they shot Aini and let him go? Who was that man at the window, a man who obviously worked for Nathair but who had simply tipped his hat to Bran and watched him escape? Bran forced himself onward, throat thick with grief and chest tight with fear. What had Aini been thinking? What had she seen as she ran into the lion's den?

# CHAPTER 4
## ALL THE ROSES FALLING

Aini counted in whispers, watching the train station's massive clock. "Three, two, one."

Neve and the other operatives flinched along with Aini as the explosion punched the quiet evening. Aini's heart pounded too quickly. She touched the knife at her belt to remind herself of who she was. The explosion didn't hurt anyone and it was entirely necessary to draw as many kingsmen as possible away from where they held Thane.

Not waiting to survey the damage, Aini led her team away from the station and down the sloping road. With every step, she saw images of Thane. His smile when they finally had a successful taffy back in the lab. The determined look in his eyes when he'd addressed the Campbells and Dionadair at Inveraray. The mischievous grin he'd worn when she pulled his hips against her. Other images swamped her mind—worries about what was happening to Thane now. Blood running over a lip. A hand held against a bruised rib. The sadness in his eyes when he looked at his father.

"We're coming for you, love," she whispered as they veered around a corner. Her heart responded to her words, backing up her vow with a powerful drumming.

NEVE'S THICK, BROWN BRAID FLEW BEHIND HER AS AINI AND the team zigzagged down side streets in the dark. Lamps bled weak, yellow light onto the pavement and tiny pockets of ice made the cobblestones slippery. Aini had already eaten some Cone5 taffy. Along with the lingering taste of sugar on her tongue, she ran with the sight of ghosts all around. An elderly couple with a dog beside a store under construction. A girl her own age floating in the wispy memory of a sixth-senser cage, trapped by her own memories of fear and horror.

"Can you help us?" Aini asked over her shoulder as they sprinted by.

The sixth-senser ghost's cage wavered until it was almost invisible. She streamed along with Aini in swirls of blue, green, and silver as the team found the street that would lead them into the action. Gunshots and yelling already crowded the nighttime air.

"How?" The ghost wore a dress from the time of the king's great-grandfather, when it was rare for a sixth-senser to be found and caged. These days it was the new normal. The spirit's hair was tied into complicated braids that had mostly fallen out. A dark bruise marred her cheek.

"I'm not sure yet. Are you able to come with me? To stay by my side?"

"Who are you talking to—oh..." Neve's eyes widened at the air around Aini. She had guessed what was going on. Smart girl.

The spirit glanced at Macbeth's knife hanging on Aini's belt and swallowed. "I will try, Seer."

"Thank you." Aini was out of breath.

The street around the back of the government buildings was dark and damp. The steeple of St. Giles peered over the Signet Library and the old Parliament buildings. Neve pointed at an entrance to a sort of inner courtyard, through an arched, open door not twenty yards away.

Aini pulled everyone to halt beside a cluster of maples that reminded her of the tree in front of her home, the maple she used to climb. Moonlight leeched the color out of the leaves and highlighted Neve's forehead and chin.

"The extraction team is in there." She nodded toward the building on the right, beyond the inner courtyard.

Neve's walkie talkie buzzed and a voice came through. She spun the knob so the words were barely audible. "...ordered the kingsmen not to shoot us, so do as you like, rebels!" Neve's sideways grin lifted her cheek as she tucked the talkie away.

"Okay." Aini eyed each member of her team to be sure they were listening. "A whistle will blow five strong times when they have Thane in hand. If you hear it, get back to the train station as quickly as possible. No further mischief. Do you understand?"

"So we're headed in there to create more chaos while the extraction team works, aye?" The Campbell speaking had a slight lisp. He was a lean man with scarred knuckles and a mean look to him.

Aini was glad he was on their side and not the other way around. "Yep. Let's go."

They raced inside to find the fight.

Several groups were fighting hand-to-hand. One kingsman had a nightstick out and was using it to knock a rebel off his arm. A gun went off, but the kingsman holding the weapon had shot into the sky, only scaring off the rebel who'd come up to choke him from behind. A rubbish bin by a side door erupted into flames and two rebels cackled and ran through the arch and back into the street.

In an alcove leading into the building proper, a tall man stood. He looked very familiar.

Aini's heart thumped like the time she'd fallen from that maple in front of her house.

"Thane," she whispered, the sound was a prayer that it was him in the shadows.

The ghost girl hissed in her ear, but Aini ignored it. The man in the alcove definitely had the build of Thane. She could see one side of him in the dim light from a window. She couldn't tell if Thane held a gun or was waving to her. Squinting, she waited for a moment when all of Nathair's men were occupied with fights and hurrying after rebels, then she ran.

"Thane!"

She shouldn't have yelled, but his name was on her tongue before she knew what was happening. The warmth of his skin would wash the cold from her fingertips. The heat of his eyes would make everything all right again. He was the Heir. She was the Seer. This was how it was meant to be.

He lifted something. A gun. Aini twisted to see if an enemy was at her back, but there was no one, only chaos here and there, not immediately around her.

The man stepped forward and the moon caught the edge of his face. Not Thane's proud nose. Not Thane's strong jaw. The gun flashed. Not Thane at all.

The cloudy, night sky filled Aini's eyes as she flew backward.

The sixth-senser ghost touched Aini's shoulder. A strange mix of cold and hot seared her through. The aroma of magic stirred the air—sage and something similar to a match's burning scent.

"What are you doing?" The cold overtook the hot. Aini shivered hard. "What's happening?"

With translucent, shimmering eyes, the ghost watched the courtyard around them, hands on Aini's chest and shoulder.

A song drifted through the air—or was it only in Aini's head?

*...when ye come and all the roses falling*
*And I am dead as dead I well may be*
*Go out and find the place where I am lying*
*And kneel...*

With an ache that felt like a horse's kick to the heart, the cold finally won, and the world went black.

# CHAPTER 5
## A TORTURED SHOUT

Thane's guard had left him for reasons unknown and he was going to use every second he had alone to try to get out of this hole. The piece of broken glass was where he'd left it, under the mattress. Careful not to slice himself up like a Christmas goose, he used it to cut a strip of sheet away from the fancy linens. Wrapping one end of the glass, he fashioned a sort of knife, then stood beside the door so he'd be hidden when the guard returned.

The sound of a single pair of boots knocked down the hallway outside, then the doorknob rotated. The door eased open a fraction, and a smooth and lilting voice crept into the room.

"Let's see you cut me. With that glass you hid in the bedding? Yes, that would be a grand fight, I think. I'm up for it." It was Jackie.

Thane looked to the ceiling and cursed the day he was born. With a mumbled Gaelic swear, he launched himself from his hiding place. Jackie went low and Thane went high. Thane threw his right hand toward the back of Jackie's head as a distraction and simultaneously jabbed the point of his makeshift knife at the Brummie's side, aiming up and under the ribs.

He felt the glass hit but they were tangle of limbs. Jackie's knee rammed into Thane's thigh, though the man had been aiming for the groin. Thane's boot then connected with a knee. Jackie caught him with an elbow to the nose and Thane dropped the glass. Jackie had a gun out and cocked between Thane's eyes faster than he could blink.

"Now settle down." Jack bent to pick up the glass shard. He slipped it into his pocket, showing a small spot of blood on his vest, near his ribs. Nothing serious, unfortunately. "I've told you. Your father wants you alive and still handsome enough for the crowds to come. I don't care to disobey him on this point, but if it comes to you or me, I know which side my gun lands on."

Thane held up his hands. "Fine. I'm good." He got to his feet because by God he wasn't going to sit there on the floor with a gun to his forehead while Aini was on her way here. "I need to talk to my father." He swallowed bile at the term. Nathair didn't deserve it and never would.

Thane's heart squeezed as he realized Lewis was the father he'd always needed. Lewis would be worried to madness when he heard what was going on. Bran too. Och. Bran. Poor man. He'd kill himself trying to free Thane. That was fact.

Jackie's cool eyes studied the emotions that were most likely pouring over Thane's face. But maybe it'd lend truth to his lie. "All right. We'll visit your dad then. Though I may have to explain that bleeding nose of yours."

Thane pushed past Jackie's lowered gun and out the door. "He needs to schedule my makeover for my moment in the lights," he joked through gritted teeth.

Jackie chuckled behind him and poked Thane's back with his gun.

At the stairs, the sounds of guns and men and running echoed through the building.

"Back to your room, Heir." Jackie rushed Thane down the corridor, then locked the door, putting himself by the window.

Someone knocked. "They're here, Jackie. I'll take this door if you want to leave."

"No." Jackie looked out the window and didn't stop Thane when he moved to do the same. "It's fine, Michael. You keep to that door and I'll be fine here."

Everything inside the building grew quiet.

There was a noise from the man, Michael, at the door. Then the unmistakable sound of him falling limp to the ground.

Thane stepped forward.

"Just stay out of it, Campbell," Jackie warned.

Thane eyed the door, then the clear side of the window and the courtyard below. Shapes were moving in the dark. The street lamps' light eased over the walls, casting a sallow gaze onto the scene of small groups darting this way and that.

An explosion blasted just one room away.

The muffled sounds of a fight mixed with two angry voices worked their way to Thane's ears. Thane lurched toward the door, then felt Jackie's cold hands grab his.

"I think you need some help keeping your control." Jackie zip-tied Thane's hands behind his back and thrust a snochterdichter into his mouth as a gag, the colonial cotton choking Thane. Jackie kicked the back of Thane's knees and dropped him to the carpet.

Thane craned his neck to see out the window. Gunshots punctuated the night. A woman was hurrying across the courtyard, her hair like ink spilling out behind her. She chanced a look back as she sped up.

Thane knew that run. He knew that hair.

The woman rushed toward a dark alcove into nothing Thane could see. "Thane!"

"Aini!" The gag tortured Thane's shout.

A gun sounded.

Aini fell.

Nausea washed over Thane as he watched blood pour from her shoulder, her mouth gasping like a fish out of water. She turned her head. What was she seeing? *God, no, don't let her die.*

"Aini!" Thane threw himself against the wall, under the window, his whole body shaking and sweat rolling down his temples. "Aini."

Something slammed into the door. Jackie looked from the window, to the door, to Thane before knocking Thane's pounding head with the butt of his gun.

The world slipped through Thane's fingers and he was glad to see it go.

## CHAPTER 6
## TORN

Aini opened her eyes to see blue light and a man in a long, gray coat. Two figures. One in this world. The other in a world between this and the next.

The light filtered away. *A ghost,* her mind told her. It was as if her mind and her body were two different things. Separate. One functioning. The other, not so much.

Thane had shot her.

No.

A man who'd looked like Thane had shot her.

"What kind of sick game are you playing?" She glared at the cocky man standing over her.

Surrounded by more men—mostly young and wearing more gray—the man smiled, showing a beauty that cut like the sharpest knife, a numb cut undiscovered until it begins bleeding. The man's head brushed the green silk canopy above the bed she lay on, his hair dark and trimmed into perfect lines. Muscles bunched under his fine clothing and a ruby ring weighed down his finger as he flicked ash from his disgusting cigarette into a tiny dish on the side table. His eyes were so cold and his smile so warm. It made Aini's head spin like she was seeing things that weren't there. Maybe none of this was real. She'd felt frozen on the cobblestones outside. After the gunshot. She'd known she was going to die.

"Why am I not dead?"

"Full of questions, this one." The man's half-lidded eyes moved like a bird's as he took her in. "I'm Jack Shaw. I work for your man, Thane, and his father, the earl."

"You don't work for Thane. I wouldn't be tied to this bed if you worked for Thane."

"Then why don't you answer your own questions if you don't like my responses?"

"I will. You set up someone who looked like Thane to lure me close. You had me shot. I don't know why I'm not dead..." Well, she did have a good guess, but she wasn't telling this monster. "The rebels must have failed to take Thane back or you wouldn't be grinning like a smug piece of shite."

Jack put the cigarette between his horrible, sultry lips and clapped slowly. "You about have it. Things are about to get a little ugly though. Once we're very sure you're not going to pass on to the other side to see your mother."

"What do you know about my mother?" Just hearing him say that word was enough to make her shiver.

Jack didn't answer, he just spun on his heel, waved a hand at his men to come along, and left her alone with the ghost in the corner. Aini couldn't see her now, but there was a strangeness to the light there.

"Did you heal me?" Aini asked the spirit quietly.

The sixth-senser ghost brightened and became visible for a moment. She nodded.

"You kept me from dying. Thank you."

## THE EDINBURGH FATE

The ghost smiled although her eyes still looked desperate and sad like they most likely had when she left this life. "Do you need more?" The spirit's voice was like a wind chime or maybe a wind through bare branches as she faded again.

Aini swallowed, the pain and chill in her shoulder threatening to tip into something she couldn't control. The ghost didn't wait for an answer. She floated to the bed—a whisper of shimmering light—and set a translucent hand on the gunshot wound. Despite the cold the spirit put out simply by being there, the ghost's fingers released a stream of warmth that flooded Aini's damaged shoulder. Aini let out a sigh. The sound of horses' hooves, clinking glasses, and voices drifted through her ears.

"What am I hearing?"

"My memories, I think." The ghost smiled sadly and the scent of magic rose again.

Once the shock and pain were under control, Aini's mind began clicking things into place.

She was in some holding area that Nathair controlled. Everyone thought she was dead.

"Can you send a message to someone in this building? He should be nearby. His name is Thane Campbell and he is—"

"He is the Heir."

"Yes. Please tell him I'm alive. Can you tell me where he is and tell him where I am and...I don't know..."

What should their plan be? They were surrounded. The rebels most likely thought she was gone. What was the best move? Well, first everyone needed to be informed. That at least was one thing she could accomplish here. Plans could wait until her mind was working better. Or until the rebels somehow messaged her to tell her where they had fallen back to.

Oh! There was that cave they were going to use as a

headquarters for the full attack. Gilmerton Cove. Yes. And then Neve would make sure Father knew she was alive. He wouldn't have to mourn.

"Number One. Please find the Heir. Tell him which room I'm in if you are able."

"I was a Threader. I can see the connection between you two."

"Number Two. If you can, if you are willing, please go to Gilmerton Cove and tell the rebels I am alive."

The ghost flickered and nearly disappeared. Aini couldn't hear her voice. She needed more taffy, but her belt, weapons, and all her materials, including Macbeth's knife, were nowhere to be seen.

The ghost vanished completely.

Aini closed her eyes and focused on the tingling heat moving in and around her gunshot wound. What was it that the spirit had bled into her? Energy, maybe. Could she ask the ghost to do that for anyone? Or was that a Seer perk? Thane was most likely injured himself. Aini hoped the ghost would heal him too. A sad smile spread over Aini's dry lips and a tear ran out of one eye as she tested the plastic ties holding her wrists to the bed posts. She was alive, Thane was alive, and that was a start. She knew very well it could be so much worse.

AINI WOKE TO A WHISPER FROM AN INVISIBLE SOURCE. EARLY dawn light oozed through the window and glided over the sixth-senser ghost's barely visible cheek, nose, and arm.

"The Heir knows you are alive."

Relief sang through Aini. At least she'd accomplished that. At least he wouldn't mourn her anymore.

"I will try to make it to Gilmerton." The spirit shimmered, faded. "They are coming and mean you harm. Be strong!"

The voice trickled away, and Aini fought the fear scratching up her throat. "Who is coming? Jack? Nathair?"

The door opened and Jack walked in. A very thin man came in behind him carrying a video camera that looked like something from a television studio.

Aini's whole body tensed.

He began plugging things in and lining up the camera to face a chair in the corner. Aini wanted to close her eyes again and pretend she didn't have a very good guess as to what was coming, but she forced herself to look straight at Jack Shaw.

"So you're going to do something to me and record it. May I ask the purpose?"

Jack sniffed lightly, checked his phone, then eyed her. "The Heir needs some additional motivation to embrace his fate."

Aini swallowed. Motivation. Yes. She knew exactly what this meant for her. "May I have a drink of water and would you please untie me? I'm not going to fight or run. I can't possibly beat you two up nor can I escape with you two right here. I simply would like to feel my fingers again before I quite possibly lose them."

Jack closed his eyes. "I won't take your fingers." He glanced at the thin man, who then cut Aini's wrist ties with a switchblade.

She sat up and rubbed the skin the ties had bruised. "So you have your limits when it comes to torture, do you? How nice."

"I do."

"Your employer has no such qualms."

"No, I'd say you're right on that. Earl Nathair is an… impassioned man."

"He is a monster, and you're helping him devour our cause."

"It takes a beast to defeat a beast. King John will not have limits and so our leader must sometimes go beyond the pale, so to speak."

Aini clamped her lips shut. She was finished talking. She'd already had a much wiser, kinder, and higher-level version of this conversation with Bran. Jack and Nathair's vision of war was nothing she'd ever accept.

She drank all the water in the glass on the side table. It tasted like the smoke curling away from Jack's snuffed-out cigarette in the dish. "Let's get on with it then so I can weigh my challenge here."

"Brave as a lion," Jack murmured. "Fine then. Go sit in that chair and take this." He handed her a card. "Hold it up and look at the camera when the light turns green."

The thin man maneuvered behind the big, black thing and flipped a switch.

Aini sat and read the card.

*I suffer when the cause suffers. Be the Heir. Do your duty.*

"So the camera has no sound." Her voice sounded like someone else's.

Jack lashed her ankles to the chair legs, his fingers warm and quick, his face devoid of any emotion. "Correct. Hold up the card now."

The light glowed and flickered. Aini stared into the camera's wide lens. She held up the card. Jack looped a rope around her neck and tied it to the chair's back slats. The rope was loose enough that she could breathe just fine. It sat against her esophagus, the pressure like a snake ready to constrict at exactly the right moment. Her fingers were numb and her heart ticked like a broken clock. The material at the back of her shirt and jacket clung to her skin. She licked a drop of sweat from the side of her lips.

The camera stared. The men stared. Thane was on the other end of this video feed. He was reading the card right now.

Aini pinched the top of the card, middle finger and thumb, middle finger and thumb.

Staring right into the lens, she ripped Nathair's message in half.

# CHAPTER 7
## SEARED BONES

Jack's men escorted Thane to the toilet. He'd been sick twice in the last hour since Aini had been shot. He wanted to see her body. But he didn't want to see her body. His stomach kept wanting to turn itself inside out, but he really didn't feel anything. He was numb and cold, unable to blink. The faucet water ran over his hands and washed the soap bubbles down the drain. Like some kind of automaton, he dried his hands on the gold-lettered paper towels. There was a shining letter for each of the king's names on the towels, glittering and ornate.

Back in his room, his prison, he stood at the window and watched a watery ray of sun break through the dark gray clouds to illuminate the stain of Aini's blood on the courtyard stones. He made his lungs move in and out. They had no desire to do it, but he forced them into it.

*Why did you run right at them, hen? Why?*

There had to be a good reason. She was smart. Careful. She wouldn't have simply rushed at an enemy like that.

Grief seized Thane's throat. A cold that seared bones—like the winter night he'd spent in John O'Groats with Bran and Rodric years back on orders to watch a suspected traitor's hideaway—wrapped around Thane and pulled the grief right out of him.

A voice like tiny bells whispered in his ear. "She is here. She is alive. Your Seer sends you word…"

Thane looked left, but there was nothing there. He gripped the windowsill and strained to hear more. "Say it again, please? I'm listening." His heart galloped through his chest, bumping into ribs and flesh and driving him mad.

The Glaswegian and Birmingham guards surrounded him, and he obediently held out his hands to be tied again, this time in front of him. "What's that he's saying?" one guard asked the other.

"He's gone off," the second man said. "Ignore it."

Breathing slow to keep his head, Thane closed his eyes and tried to believe he'd heard what he'd thought he'd heard. That Aini wasn't dead. She was alive. Was it madness to believe it? Maybe. Maybe not. She'd used a ghost to communicate with Callum. She could've done it again. But he'd seen her bleeding. She'd gasped for air like a person does before they die of blood loss, the brain lacking oxygen the blood provided and the mouth working as if it could do the job instead. He knew how death looked and he'd seen her go through it. Hadn't he?

The men finished tying him. He would fight them again. He would get out of here, dead or alive. But not right now. Right now, he was a husk of a man. Getting his lungs to draw in air was a feat in itself.

Nathair strolled into the room wearing the whole cat with the canary look. God, how Thane hated him. "Have a seat, Heir," Nathair said.

Thane took note that he didn't use the word *son*. That was just fine by him. One of Nathair's new men set up a small television on the dresser. He switched it on, and all Thane saw before the man blocked the view to adjust the knobs was a black and white image. A room like his maybe. Two people?

The bed gave under Thane's weight. Hands tied behind him, he sat up straight, but ducked his chin a little like he was about to go into a fight and wanted to protect himself from a knockout.

Nathair put his hands on his hips and looked down at Thane. "You and yours did a fine job finding allies."

"We did, aye? I suppose that's why I'm tied up and my better half is dead." He forced his lungs to work through the pain of being the one left alive. But was he? Had he really just heard that voice? It could've been ghost. But he was no Ghost Talker. Confusion pounded against his temples.

"No, you did," Nathair said, oblivious to Thane's state.

Thane was more scared of hoping the message was real and true than anything. If it wasn't and he was crushed again…

Nathair bent to stare into Thane's face, his breath smelling like the cigarettes he only smoked when he was feeling down. Broken blood vessels made his cheeks looked flushed. Thane's Coronation Stone necklace slid out of Nathair's collar and rested against his throat's massive scar.

A pressure built in Thane's ears and he leaned close. Closer.

If he could touch it, even with his forehead, he might be able to enact the curse and take all of them down.

Nathair frowned and tucked the necklace back into his shirt, turning away. "An anonymous donor left a barge of anti-aircraft weapons and some serious guns at our dock last night. They look French."

So Lord Darnwell had received Lewis and Aini's message for his French wife, Eloise, kin to the French queen.

"Why your dock?" Thane asked.

"We intercepted your coded message and added a line or two." Nathair's predatory eyes glittered. His claws weren't out yet, but it was only a matter of time. "And we have reason to believe the French will protect our coastline from John's future advances too. He won't be able to sneak up on us there. We have France's support even though it is being kept quiet."

This was huge. With France's support at sea and with guns, they truly had a solid chance against King John. If Aini was alive. If Thane could get that necklace. If. If. If.

Nathair opened the armoire that stood against the wall. The shelving inside held sweaters and Campbell tartan. He ran a hand over the Campbell colors, then closed the armoire door gently.

"So you see, Heir, our teams are working well together. It will all end in you being on the throne for our Scotland and King John leaving us to it, taxes and all. We'll be rich, you and I. But neither of us care for that, I know."

He paced the floor, passing back and forth in front of the Glaswegian who stood in front of the television.

"We will change Scotland for the better. Now that I know all about sixth-sensers, they'll be permitted to live as anyone else. And we'll make taxes more beneficial to the Clan Campbell. No English will be allowed to cross our borders. We're done with that. And all business licenses will run through Campbell hands or my loyal men I've hired here. We will get a cut of everything and make sure to protect the people from anyone who dares to infringe on their freedoms as Scots."

Thane's jaw tightened. "You don't see yourself as the one infringing on freedoms currently?"

Nathair's hand cracked across Thane's already sore face.

But Thane smiled. "You'll come to realize I won't go along with your madness. I don't want to be king. I will never be king of anything now. You've ruined it by shooting down the only one who could lift me into such a complicated, challenging position. You killed Aini."

A vein pulsed on Nathair's forehead. "Did I now?" He held a hand toward the television and the man moved to show the screen.

Aini sat in a chair. Jack Shaw stood beside her. She held up a card.

Heart shunting away in his chest, Thane stared and stared. The ghost had spoken to him. He had heard the truth. It was too much for him to grasp. His head spun. There she was, right there on the television screen. "It's not real. This is a fabrication. You've used—"

"It's no camera trick, Heir. That's Aini. The one who should've been the Seer and a strong member of the upcoming monarchy, but now she is simply your motivation."

She was alive. Aini was there, heart beating, eyes flashing, soul filling his own with light.

His eyes burned with unshed tears. He blinked, trying to read the card she held up.

*I suffer when the cause suffers. Be the Heir. Do your duty.*

Her mouth titled up at one side and she tore the thing in two.

On the television, Jack moved quickly toward Aini and another set of hands came toward the camera and the screen went black.

Stomach heaving, Thane ran to the television. "Stop! Stop now. What happened? What is he doing to her?" It was too much. He was going to smash the television and rage through the door on sheer will to get to her.

"He is a bad man. I won't lie. But he listens to me because I pay for his vices. Horse racing. Women. Expensive whisky."

Thane's anger festered like a bad wound.

Nathair paused. "Don't growl at me, Heir. It's your doing that led to this. If you would've simply done as I'd asked, we wouldn't be where we are. You chose this."

Thane felt as though a sword had pierced him through and all his life was draining to the floor. He had to find more strength to fight through this, to win, to get Aini safe. He took a breath, nostrils flaring, and braced himself.

"And as for Aini," Nathair said, "all I need to do right now is call Jack and tell him to keep her safe and sound."

"Do it then. Do it or you'll not get a thing from me for the rest of my life. I'll fight you at every turn if you hurt her."

"Exactly. You have the logic now. Tomorrow, we'll put on a lovely show for Edinburgh and you'll claim your role as the true Heir to Scotland's throne. We'll declare our break from King John. You'll raise me up as your Prime Minister and I'll create a new kind of Parliament here to assist you. The king will come soon after. I'm sure. But by then the people of Scotland will have seen our combined might of Campbells and Dionadair, France's support of our cause, and of course there will be no more tolerating the king after the horrible event following our show."

"What horrible event?"

"King John's spies will poison one branch of Edinburgh's, Glasgow's, and Inverness' water supplies with some of the Bismian solution you developed and Lewis MacGregor so kindly explained during his time with me."

"Lewis would never tell you that formula."

"He didn't handle sleep deprivation very well. I'd guess the man doesn't even remember telling me all the ingredients and the proper process for its creation."

"Turn the camera on again. I need to see her."

"You don't get to make demands, traitor turned king. Life as a royal will be tough. There will be sacrifices. You'll get used to it. It is your fate, after all. Oh, Lord and Lady Darnwell offered their condolences via coded message just now. On the death of your Seer."

How did they already know? They were in close contact if a message came and went that quickly. Or Nathair was simply lying. "I'm supposed to go along with the lie that she is dead? For how long? You can't keep that going—"

"We'll see how it works out. If the lie becomes too much trouble, Jack will simply turn it into truth. Quickly or slowly, depending on your behavior as ruler of our country. Now, I'll be back soon to be sure you're ready to speak to the crowds. Now, rest that nasty cut. Maybe read one of the books there." He nodded toward the shelves lining the wall and tied a strip of cloth across Thane's mouth.

Nathair and his man locked the door behind them.

Thane lifted his tied-up hands and tugged the gag away from his lips.

"I am here, Aini!" His throat burned with the shout, his head pounding with blood and rage. "I will never stop fighting for you!"

Turning his back to the solid oak door, he launched himself at the surface and the zip-tie snapped. He pressed his head and hands against the door, breathing through his nose and trying to rein in his anger. Possibilities, variables, the damage he could do if he got his hands on such simple things as cleaning supplies from the toilets—all of it spun through his mind in letters, numbers, formulas, lines, and charts. He would not follow

Nathair's plan out of fear. He would change this. Fix this. Or burn the whole thing down trying.

He rammed his good shoulder into the door. Again. Again.

An unfamiliar voice with a Birmingham accent similar to Jack's spoke outside. "Settle. I have permission to break your arm if need be."

Thane took three steps back, then surged into the door. The hinges popped. One screw came loose and hung limply.

The lock clicked, the knob twisted, and there was the guard.

Thane threw a punch right into his chin and he dropped like a stone.

With one glance down the empty corridor, Thane headed further into the building and to a set of back stairs. The metal steps—made for the help to use when delivering papers or tea, and for cleaning crews—clanged lightly as Thane swept up to the next floor.

She had to be right above him. He'd recognized the room on the screen where she'd sat on the chair. It was one of Nathair's guest rooms, all carpets and velvet and brass. The other wings were more modern and sleek. Nathair liked decor that reminded him of his golden youth when Grandfather, in all but name, ruled Scotland and no one was strong enough to question the Campbells. Back then, the Dionadair had been quiet and in its infancy.

Peering through the window of the stairs' door, he saw a long hallway with red carpet and two guards standing outside the third door down. Aini was in there. He knew it. His heart could feel her there, being proud, strong, fierce. His body thrummed, wanting her, longing for the sound of her voice, the feel of her warm skin and soft mouth.

Thane went back down the stairs and slipped into the tiny wash room that the help used. He hated that term. The help. It was just like Nathair to use a term that gave none of their employees individual recognition for their labor. The cabinets under the wash room's sink held an aluminum tray with a bottle of toilet bowl cleaner, some scrub brushes, bleach, rubber gloves, and toilet paper. Heading into the first stall, Thane found a pack of cigarettes and a lighter. Nathair had fought the bad habit since Thane was a child. Nathair didn't like the addiction he had to the nicotine. He always said it was no good to have a substance making his decisions for him. But Nathair had been sneaking smokes in wash rooms as long as Thane could remember.

He snatched the lighter, smiled, and began rolling up a piece of the aluminum foil. Combined with some of the other items under the sink, he could easily create a nasty something to toss at the guards, giving him time to rush them.

When he finished his contraption, he rubbed his hand knowing well it would be burned during this move. But a burn was nothing to what Aini was suffering at the hands of that Jack Shaw.

Running quietly up the stairs and praying no one knew he'd escaped his room, he shoved the stair door open with a hip. He lit the glove portion of the explosive contraption, and threw it at the first guard who noticed him.

The glove exploded with a bang that made Thane nearly deaf. He grabbed the guard who wasn't holding his ears, flipped him toward Aini's door, and slammed the guard's head into the wood. The man fell to Thane's feet as Thane twisted to dodge a punch from the other guard. He let the man throw another strike, but this time when the man's fist came at him, Thane pushed the punch to the side, then bumped the man's elbow and wrapped the guard in his own arm, choking him.

"You're going to give me that gun," Thane said, his mouth

right near the guard's, "and unlock that door, or you're going to say *Fare thee well* to your stones, pal." Thane kneed the man in the groin to push the point.

"Mr. Shaw is in there."

"Open the door."

The man fumbled with his belt with his free hand. Shouts came from the stairwell, beyond the closed door. More of Nathair's men were coming. Thane shoved the guard to the ground with all the force he had in him, then jumped on him for the gun. The newly arrived men pulled Thane off the guard.

"Aini. I'm here. Be strong." Could she hear him?

The men dragged him down the way he'd come.

"Thane." It was her.

"I hear you!"

"I won't give up. Don't give in!"

The pain behind her words broke his heart into pieces. The strength in her voice welded them back together.

They dragged Thane back to his room for what felt like the thousandth time. They threw him onto the floor.

"And now we'll have to do some damage," one of the men said. "It's a shame."

A fist came down on Thane's side before he could shake himself out of the moment when Aini was shouting, and this moment in the here and now. He felt a rib bend nearly to the point of breaking. He shifted to protect it and tried to get his feet under him. A foot landed in his gut and he blew out a gust of breath, spittle, and curses. Pressing against the bed, he worked his way to his knees. And took a mouthful of knuckles. Blood warmed his tongue and slowly pain rose to his lips.

He jerked himself up and his feet found the floor properly. With a quick thrust, he kneed the man in front of him. Three more sets of fists came at him and he fell again, curling himself up to keep the damage to his head at a minimum.

They hauled him onto the bed like a sack of very sad tatties. Pain sat on him like a heavy blanket, covering every bit of flesh. Nothing was broken. These men knew how to beat without breaking. Nathair had instructed them well. Jack had trained them.

The biggest of the group jabbed a needle into Thane's arm, and sleep took him down like a prize boxer.

## CHAPTER 8
## THE CRUMBLING LABYRINTH

Bran would've loved this cave if it wasn't today, the worst day, a day he had to tell everyone an amazing person, a leader, their leader, was dead. His whole body felt raw.

They'd spent the last hours fleeing Edinburgh's city limits and gathering everyone they could to Gilmerton Cove. The place had an entrance below a pub in the small town of Gilmerton, but also another secret entrance on a nobleman's property. With eight rooms carved out of sandstone and its off-the-beaten path location, it was a quiet hideaway, perfect for planning a revolution.

Watches had been set up and weapons relocated. Bran had filled the elders in on how the plan went awry in the upper floors of the old Parliament building, but he still hadn't told anyone the worst of what he'd seen.

Aini, bleeding and pale, on the ground at Nathair's headquarters.

No one else had seen it. There had been too much going on and most had already fled or were inside or outside that area during the operation. She'd just been another fallen soldier. As soon as Myles and Neve and Vera had finished their immediate tasks of patching those who were fighting death themselves, they'd be on him and asking. *Where was their Seer?*

Neve had a handful of fresh bandages. She was headed toward the makeshift infirmary in a room to the left, but stopped to talk, her voice strung tight with fear. "Did you know a blacksmith built this place? There are stories that, later on, the Covenanters used it to hold meetings and maybe even the Hellfire Club met here. You know that sick group with the rituals and all that? Some say there is a now-crumbled passageway all the way to the Templers' 15th century Rosslyn Chapel from this very room. Eh, have you seen Aini yet? I'd feel a load better if I could clap eyes on her."

Feeling the strain of the terrible news, Bran put a hand against the table the long-ago blacksmith had carved into being. Patient as ever, Neve shifted her load of white linen and pushed her braid over her shoulder. The torches set in the hideaway's walls as well as the dirt on the lassie's face made Bran feel as if they were cave people from long, long ago, just starting the arduous journey toward civilization.

Bran removed his sling and the two unspent grenades. Rough benches lined the rock walls and he sat on one, breathing in the dark scents of the earth around them. "I saw her in the back courtyard of Nathair's building. Neve..." He lowered his voice. "It's not good."

Neve set the bandages down beside him and touched his arm.

Myles bounded up, fists bunched and dried blood on his forehead. "What's up?"

It was time to tell them all. "Vera!" Bran raised a hand to get her attention. She helped an injured man onto a cot carried by Dodie and another big lad, then hurried over.

"I need to tell you something." Bran's voice sounded far away. "Something big. You should sit down."

He stood and offered all of them the bench. How was he going to do this? Not only had they lost their Heir, they'd lost the Seer too. Invisible talons of grief clawed across Bran's chest and he sucked a breath.

"First, I want you to think about how we were able to leave the building. That man I fought with, he shooed me off like a fly. They wanted us gone and didn't try to hurt us. It's worth considering. What is Nathair's aim? Will you talk to the elders about it, Vera?"

She swallowed, nodded, and eyed him expectantly. The woman knew he had more to tell.

Bran's shoulders fell and he closed his eyes briefly. "In the courtyard, I saw Aini fall."

Neve shot up. "What do you mean?"

Vera had Myles's arm in her grip, eyes wild.

Bran fought the burn in his heart and told him what he'd seen—the way she'd run at whoever stood in the alcove, how she'd looked over her shoulder, how she'd said something before he was driven off by gunfire.

"They shot her. She is...she is dead. I saw her bleeding out myself."

Closing his eyes, he let the chaos rise over his head.

Vera shrieked and ran off to find someone whose name was lost in Myles's swearing and Neve's questions.

"But you don't actually know for sure." Neve took Bran by the hands. Hers were ice cold. "Maybe it was someone else. It was dark. Why would she rush Nathair's men?"

Myles pressed the heels of his hands against his eyelids. Tears leaked from the corners. "Because she thought she could save Thane. She couldn't accept that our plan failed."

Neve's hands fell to her sides and she stared at the cave's uneven rock floor. Her head moved side to side as if she was silently saying *No* over and over again. Myles took her in his arms like a good man and held her tightly.

The question now was *Did Thane know about Aini's death and if so did that change anything for him?* He was still the Heir. The lad loved Scotland. He'd rise up from the ashes of this grief, wouldn't he?

Vera climbed onto a table at the back of the cave's main room. "Gather around, rebels!"

Bran put a hand on Myles and Neve and steered them that way, whispering nonsense at them, hoping it would somehow help.

When Bran lost the girl he'd thought of as his sister—a wild red head a bit older who lived at the orphanage with him—nonsensical but kind words from the nuns had actually smoothed the horror of her death. It'd been like having a soft cocoon in which to mourn. It didn't take the pain away, but it was good to know the easy boundary was there when he or if he needed it.

"Rebels." Vera's voice echoed off the walls and all was silent except for the occasional drip of water from the ceiling. "We failed today. Not forever. Just today. But we lost in a way I…I never thought we'd lose." She took a shuddering breath. "There is no time for reflection and proper mourning. We must act now and keep on until we break the shackles of Nathair and John's reign. I won't hide the truth from you. You'll know soon enough anyway."

A man in a torn, blue jacket traded confused looks with a woman holding what Bran guessed was her teenage son firmly to her side. The boy was a good head taller than her but had the slimness of a thirteen or fourteen-year-old lad. He glanced over his shoulder at Bran with inquisitive gray eyes.

Something inside Bran shattered.

Pain swelled over his ribcage and up his throat until he wasn't sure he was still standing. The boy's eyes reminded him so much of Thane. Thane had lost his love. He'd lost her while in his evil father's grips. He'd lost her in the middle of a war started by terrible people, a war he would have to fight with a broken heart. Bran put his head in his hands and wept for his friend, not even caring that everyone around surely heard him.

"Och, pal. I do pray for you, lad," Bran whispered to a distant Thane, a best friend he would do his best to deserve. "Please know somehow we're thinking of you and we're going to get you out of there. Away from him. Away from that bastard father of yours."

In his mind's eye, Bran saw Aini's smile when she looked at Thane, back at Callum's. Bran relived Aini's fear, anger, and sadness when she'd learned what Thane had done to the fiddler. Memory pushed the image of her standing proud in the library to the front of his thoughts, then dashed the colors into fragments. They collected again and created the replica of her blood pooling around her small frame on the blackened cobblestones.

Shaking the thoughts away, he focused on what Vera was saying.

"Our Seer gave her life for this rebellion and we will do the same. We will give our lives!"

Not a dry eye in the place, the crowd raised their crossed thumbs above their heads—even the Campbells and their kin— and shouted assent.

"We strike again at dusk. Prepare yourselves to bleed for your country!"

Dusk? So soon. Bran blew his nose on a snochterdichter and straightened his shirt. He had work to do. He would not fail Thane this time.

The room buzzed with a dark energy, a vicious zing ready to strike at the heart of the enemy. Bran found Myles and Neve and squeezed them once.

"Vera will want to meet with us." He noticed the elders, Menzies, Hawes, and two bearded Highlanders grouping around the table where she'd made the announcement. "Come on."

"Last night sucked hard." Myles sniffed. "Today is going to suck some more."

"You've got that right." Neve took her hair out of her braid and tore her fingers through the thick locks. Her eyes were puffy and still wet. "I can't believe it. I would've thought I'd feel it if a friend died."

Bran knew what she meant. It should feel like you've lost a limb, but it doesn't, and somehow that's worse.

Myles took Neve's hand in his as they moved through the crowd. "Same here. But I guess not. I'm going to miss that bossy little sweetheart." His last word crumbled on its way out of his mouth and he staggered a little.

Neve propelled him forward. "We will mourn her. I demand it. Even if we have to go to war tonight, we will have a funeral for my friend. Nothing will keep that from happening. I'll have my own wee rebellion if the elders or Vera or those Campbells—"

"What are you angry about, aside from the obvious?" Hawes loaded a gun and tucked it back into its holster.

"Before we head out again," Neve said, her voice a little shrill like she was very near to breaking like Bran had, "we must have a funeral for Aini. Here. Now."

Menzies set his hands on the table, open and stained by gunpowder. "We don't have a body."

Myles flinched. "It doesn't matter. She deserves a moment of remembrance."

"Even if that moment loses us the rebellion?" Vera put her hands on her hips. "I'm devastated, but you know they are already assembling their answer to our attack and—"

"Ignoring our passion for the ones whose fate led us here will lose us the rebellion," Bran said.

Vera dropped her chin to her chest. "I agree." She eyed Menzies, then the rest. "What are your thoughts?"

The men and women nodded and traded grim glances.

It was decided. The rebels would host a funeral for their Seer in a cave. Bran prayed this damp place wouldn't prove to be a tomb for the rest of them.

THE REBELS' NUMBERS GREW AND THE CAVE FILLED. EVERYONE had found candles somehow and the walls were alive with shadows and watery, yellow light. Never in a million years would Bran have guessed he'd find himself in a Dionadair cave, mourning the fabled Seer. And in the role of best friend to the Heir. He shook his head and rested his hands on the back of his sticky neck. What an absolute mess this all was. King John was going to rout the lot of them, Nathair too, and paint the country with rebel blood. It wasn't a possibility. It was a surety. With Thane under Nathair's thumb and the forces divided into so many factions, King John would be shooting fish in a barrel. The French wouldn't know who to help or why. Even if they did show. The people of Scotland would be confused, unsure. That was no potion for rebellion. The rebels needed decisive moves and clear objectives. Confidence and fervor.

Neve and Myles had talked to Lewis, Aini's father. He was on his way here. They'd begged him to stay where he was, to keep up his intel work. He was safer far, far from here. But the good man would hear none of it and he was most likely not an hour away if he wasn't already in the hands of Nathair's corbies.

Vera and the rest had set up a chair and piled it high with rowan branches. The berries, just beginning to turn, were bright as blood. She placed a large, flat rock in front of the chair, then sliced her hand open with a knife. Using her blood, she wrote Aini's name and title on the stone. Dramatic Dionadair.

No one was going to speak. Bran supposed it was meant to be a silent ritual of remembrance.

One by one, Dionadair, converted Campbells and their kin, and those recently inducted into the rebels' forces streamed by the makeshift altar. Each touched the black-red letters of Aini's name. Their lips moved in prayer and blessing.

Bran trailed Neve and Myles to the spot.

Neve rested her palm on Aini's name. "You showed me who I am, Aini. You tugged me out of my vanilla life and led me into one with all the flavors of life. I will never regret our choices. I will always remember you. I will see you again someday, friend." Neve's tears latched onto Bran's heart and jerked at it painfully.

Neve glanced at Myles, who stepped forward. He put a fist on Aini's name. "No one can boss like you, sweetheart. I really hope you are able to haunt the hell out of Nathair right now. Scare the piss out of him for me."

"Myles." Neve almost smiled, then wiped her face with her sleeve.

It was Bran's turn. He swallowed, looked at the man waiting behind him in line. "Aini. I will do all I can to help our Thane. You know I will. Bless you, love. I hope you find peace." He pressed a thumb against the flaking letters, then kissed it.

Voices near the mouth of the tunnel that led out of the cave rose, and someone shouted.

"A Ghost Talker received a message!" A boy came running, cheeks flushed and eyes shining.

A woman followed the boy. She slid her light hair over her shoulders with slim hands. Her eyes shifted from left to right, like a camera lens slowly collecting images, as everyone gathered around to stare. Vera pounded over and the two looked like creatures from different dimensions. One ethereal and graceful, the other brazen and bright.

"What did you hear then?" Vera put her hands on the woman's shoulders, bracing her, maybe to give her courage to speak. But Bran would've bet a handful of good money the Ghost Talker didn't need outside support. Her movements had a confidence to them that reminded Bran of Aini, though she looked nothing like her.

"A girl spoke to me. A spirit. She had a message from our Seer."

Bran fell back a step and the rebels quieted. No one said a word. The larger candles popped and hissed along the walls. The smaller ones, held in hands, lit shocked faces and wary eyes. Was it true?

Vera dropped her grip from the Ghost Talker's shoulders. "But she is gone. Maybe this was before she died?"

The Ghost Talker shook her head. "No. The ghost said our Seer is not dead. That the spirit somehow healed her. With..." The woman cocked her head and pursed her lips, thinking, "Energy. Psychic energy is what I believe she meant."

Neve's mouth popped open and she grasped Myles up in a hug. He still looked doubtful as did most of the crowd.

Hawes stepped forward and handed her candle to a short

man. "So she didn't meet the Seer in the afterlife or something? Aini truly is alive?"

"That's what the spirit told me."

"Any other information?" Vera asked before whispering something in Rob's ear. The man nodded, then ran off towards the back of the cave. He disappeared down one of the many tunnels.

"She said there is to be a presentation," the Ghost Talker said. "The earl will show the Heir to the crowds. Mid-morning today."

Everyone began talking at once. Vera clapped three times and the place quieted.

"The spirit was a strong one," the Ghost Talker said. "Not many could hold a message and come this far, I don't think. There was the shadow of a sixth-senser's cage around her. She told me she'd been a Threader in her day and was executed beneath Parliament in one of the Head of Security's secret cells. I don't know how long ago that was. She didn't share anything further before fading from my...senses."

"She was visible?" a voice asked from the back.

"Aye. Strong, as I said."

Bran found himself beside the woman. It was as if she'd pulled him there with a fishing line. "What is your name, if I may ask?"

Her luminous eyes dialed in on his face. She didn't smile, but she didn't frown either, so Bran figured she was all right having a blether with him. "Viola Campbell."

That name. He knew it somehow...

The woman tilted her head. "Yes. I am the Heir's illegitimate sister. Now, stop making that face. You look like your head is about to explode."

Bran found himself and cleared his throat. Thane's sister.

Born of a woman Nathair had fooled into bed on the Isle of Skye. Senga had spoken of the girl at dinner one night when Bran was headed out for a shoot with Thane on Inveraray grounds.

"I won't pretend I don't know about her, Nathair," Senga had said that day, years ago. "Bring her here. I won't hold what you did against the child."

But Nathair had denied the affair every day since the rumor arose and Thane had never met this half-sister as far as Bran knew.

Now, Bran locked his gaze on Viola. "Your father's wife, Senga, wanted to welcome you into her home. When you were a bairn. I overheard her say it myself."

Viola's eyes widened. For the first time, she seemed less than the very definition of confidence. "Senga. How kind of her." From most people, that phrase would've sounded too sweet, and would've reeked of sarcasm, but from Viola's lips it rang true. She met Bran's gaze and he felt suddenly very warm. "Thank you, Bran." She took his fingers in hers. Her skin was silk. "I've heard you're kind, too." Leaning forward, she kissed his cheek like he was some kind of knight headed to battle. "I find that an amazing thing. Kindness. You get little thanks for it most of the time and it is far more unwieldy than many believe." She left before he could say a word.

"This changes everything." Myles ambled up and crossed his arms, watching Viola go.

"It really does," Bran said. "I'm afraid to hope. What if she's wrong? What if that ghost was sent here by a Ghost Talker working for Nathair or the king?"

"Can they do that?"

"Get a ghost to lie? Why not?"

Vera was waving her arms to get everyone's attention in the

back of the cave where Rob had been. "Viola's news about the presentation has been confirmed. The Heir is set to speak to all of Edinburgh, televised to all of Scotland, in one hour. Aside from a lorry with hidden guns and grenades, we will send three groups to the city, all armed with altered sweets because that's about the only thing they might get through with the kingsmen on high alert. It's still a mighty risk, but one we think we should take because we need to weigh the scales a bit more in our favor."

"A bit more. Understatement like wow." Myles whistled low. "They have the queen, the king, and all those important chess pieces I can't remember, as far as I can see. We are bound to lose this game. You know they'll be using Aini to get Thane to do what they want, right?"

"Aye. And Vera and the elders know this."

"One unit will infiltrate the crowd near the stage they're building in Mercat Cross," Vera said. "A second to surround the area for intel. A third will drive a lorry as close as they can to the center of the action. The back will be filled. Pray on everything you hold dear that the weapons team makes it close enough for us to grab and go. They have our Heir. They have our Seer. We will go in quietly, see what is happening, and decide what to do from there. If you see a blue flag raised, hung, held up anywhere —head for High Street where we'll either have the lorry or we'll have some sign as to where to go for your weapons. If you see nothing there, find the nearest rubbish bin. We'll do our best to slip some guns here and there when we can. Risk it all, rebels. This is it. This is what we've been waiting for. But be mindful of the signal flag. If our Heir and Seer are in immediate danger, we must move carefully, strategically. We will communicate via our cloaked phones and talkies. Keep them on silent, but watch them. We must be a cool-headed singular unit in this, rebels."

"Never in my life..." Neve joined them. "Vera preaching about keeping calm." Her eyes glittered with the hope Bran feared to feel. "Our girl is alive. I can't stop smiling." She held her cheeks. "We'll have to be careful. They'll probably have her on stage too, won't they?"

Vera jogged over, checked her phone, then looked up. "Our one inside man says he hasn't seen Aini anywhere. But that tailors have been to Thane's room. And one held a crown."

Bran shivered, remembering that night on Moot Hill when the ghostly sword appeared in Thane's hand. "He is going along with it for now, aye?" He lightly punched his own palm, thinking. "If we come to Nathair and say we know about Aini's death— wait, hear me out—pretend we think she's dead, we can act as though Nathair's plan against King John is our only hope."

"If Aini is too injured to command the ghost kings, Nathair *is* our only hope." Myles set his chin on Neve's head.

Vera chewed a nail, then huffed. "Aye. You're right. Stay with me. All of you. We'll go with the group closest to the stage. It's cold as a witch's left breast out there, so we can bundle up to hide our faces well enough. I hate the risk, but we have to do it."

"You've changed a bit, Vera," Neve said. "I thought you were risk forged to create a woman."

"I've come to love you idiots. The cause is only good if the best of us survive the war. You know?"

Bran was the first to recover as Vera trotted away on business again. "Well, life will never stop surprising me."

"What's next?" Myles tried for a smile, but they were all still shaken. "Me beating you in a fight?"

"Don't get carried away, colonial."

# CHAPTER 9
## A CROWN OF BEATEN GOLD

The small fireplace in Thane's fine prison flickered with warmth and light—two things he definitely wasn't feeling right now. In a high-backed, green velvet chair, he leaned forward and rested his forearms on his thighs. His hands had been freed at dawn, but his thoughts were tied into strategic knots.

If he made another escape, they would punish Aini. If he managed to get her out, great, but that left the problem with the French queen's kin, Lady Darnwell, and her confusion concerning who she was supporting. If they yanked her around too much, she might very well report those guns and supplies as stolen and garner some reward from King John. That would benefit her husband, an English nobleman who struggled to make ends meet in a court he didn't really fit into.

Maybe if Thane went along with Nathair until he had control of the country and had driven King John out of Scotland for good, Thane could then have Nathair, Jack, and the rest of them thrown into very dark, very permanent prison cells.

That way, he'd keep Aini safe and retain the support of the French.

But would the rebel forces come around? If only he could speak to the Dionadair and the converted Campbells about the complicated situation. He could explain that Aini was alive, but he would pretend she wasn't to achieve their ultimate goal—John and Nathair ousted from Scotland's government and Aini safe and secure in her role as Seer and Thane's right hand. But how would he ever get the chance to lay all of that out for Vera, Bran, Myles, Neve, and the rest? If they came up against Nathair in the middle of a battle with John, it would ruin any chance of Thane's strategy working to the right end. Aini would be killed along with countless rebels and they'd lose Lady Darnwell's support.

The fire snapped. Thane sat back in his chair. Fight this or embrace it? He had to make the right move or Aini was dead, he was dead, the rebellion was dead.

The other thing banging around in his head was last night's Dream. He rubbed his temples, trying to chase the lingering headache away. The images were so bizarre. He couldn't really make any sense of them.

He'd seen Myles with his bald head leaning close to Neve, Vera, and Bran. In the Dream, water streamed around their ankles. Green and stinking water with a filmy, oily surface. The liquid gathered into the shape of a hand three different times during the Dream, grabbing for Vera but never quite reaching her. The Dream spun out of focus, then cleared. As one unit, the group—Bran, Vera, and Neve—spun outward. A mass of strangers had their backs to the group and the people were walking away, slowly sinking into the manky water as they left. The green water rose and rose. Then Myles shouted something Thane couldn't hear and Vera, Neve, and Bran threw a bunch of pink squares at the sinking men and woman and children.

And there had been another half to the headache-inducing Dream. This one even worse. Aini had stood across from him, holding a black shape that changed in size and form every few seconds. Even the memory of the absolute darkness of that... thing turned Thane's stomach. *Undo*, Aini had said, in the Dream. *Or repeat*, she'd said, then pointed to a line of consecutive hills. On each hill, a man, a woman, and a child pushed a jagged rock up toward a raised Saltire flag. The flag of the rebels. Their hands were red with blood and sweat poured down their faces and soaked their clothing.

Thane squeezed his eyes, trying to figure it out. If he'd been forced to guess about the first half of the Dream, he'd say the pink squares were vision-inducing gum. But why in the world would that save people from drowning? It made no sense at all.

The second part of the Dream seemed clear enough. Aini's darkness was death. If they didn't use death in the fight to come, all of Scotland was doomed to live through this revolution again and again. There could be no mercy when all was said and done.

Staring into the fire, Thane tried to forget the nauseating Dream for now. He had bigger things to worry about.

A man in a chef's apron walked in with a tray and set it on the table beside Thane's chair. "Breakfast for you, Heir. Just ring the bell if you need anything further." His knuckles were scarred and a gun hung beside his apron's ties. Here was one heck of a chef. Thane gritted his teeth.

The door closed and Thane stared at the meal. Steaming tatties and a herbed breast of chicken. A glass of whisky. A bronze bell. He picked it up and rang it.

The chef returned. "Yes? How may I be of assistance?"

"If I'm going to go along with this, I need to see that Aini is fed and cared for and I need promise of her release once we are finished with our war."

"That isn't my business, Heir, but I can say they said you are not to make demands beyond your own meals and messages sent to Earl Nathair."

Thane stood. "Then tell Nathair what I said."

"You already tried that demand, with all due respect, Heir. It was denied and will be again and again. You are not to make demands. You must simply embrace your fate and follow the plan your father has set. I can tell you that your Seer is alive. She is injured, but will improve as your behavior allows." The chef who wasn't really a chef dipped his head and left, locking the door.

The next people to enter this cushioned hell were tailors. A woman and a man with arms full of clothing and a large sewing basket adorned with the symbol of a tailor—three needles crossed.

"If you've finished breakfast, Heir, please stand here and spread your arms out. We have your basic measurements, but we want to be sure you have the best fit we can manage."

Thane stood and did as he was told, his brain running over what he could do.

How to save Aini.

What steps to take to save this rebellion.

How to get a message to the rebels.

The woman ran a tape measure along his shoulders being careful with his bandaged cut. She made an appreciative noise, then lifted up a deep green frock coat with antique bronze buttons. The man took note of the width of Thane's waist, then organized a plain shirt, an old-style Campbell kilt, sturdy woolen socks, and a new pair of dark brown, bucket-top boots on and beside the bed.

And on the side table, a crown of beaten gold shone dully. Thane swallowed.

The woman clasped her hands. "Please dress behind that screen, then we'll check you for fit."

"Oh." The man raised a finger. "We were supposed to tell you some news too. What was it?"

"About the street vendor."

"Aye. A vendor tried to send information about you to a band of brigands, but thankfully, she was stopped at the city limits by Campbell kingsmen."

A weight descended onto Thane's shoulders. He already knew the rebels hadn't received his message, but it was salt in the wound that these two here thought they were doing him a favor sharing this information with him.

"I do hope you'll improve the Campbell kingsmen's behavior," the male tailor whispered. "Though I am of the upper middle class and have no problems with the laws, I do think they are getting a bit full of themselves."

"They took my auntie with no proof at all." The female tailor covered her mouth with shaking fingers. "I don't know why I said that out loud. Please forgive me. Please don't tell Earl Nathair. I'm sure they'll do justice for her. Forget I said anything."

"Don't be afraid." Thane eyed the clothing. "You can say anything you like to me. Just so long as you don't share my response with any of the earl's men. Especially his new ones."

The tailors traded confused looks. "But you are the Heir. They are your men now, are they not?"

They most definitely were not. Not when they had Aini. He was at every one of those men's mercy.

"Aye. Of course." But an idea sparked inside him. "During this...presentation and speech I'm meant to do today, could you do me a favor?"

"Maybe..." The woman chewed her lip.

The rebels needed a message from him. They had to know Aini was alive and that Nathair held her. He had to warn them about the Dream even if he wasn't sure what it meant. They would surely come to the presentation. They'd come in all quiet. Some of them at least. He couldn't know who they would send for sure, but somehow he knew Myles and Bran would come. His best mates would come to see him. And Myles would be the easiest to spot for these two tailors.

"I won't say a thing about your breach in lawful behavior just now if you'll find a man in the crowd for me during the speech."

"I don't know if we can do that, Heir." The man tilted his head, still listening.

"There will be a man with very, very short hair. Almost bald. He has a colonial accent."

"Why in God's name is he bald? That is very out of fashion." The man tsked.

"Find him please. Quietly. This must be kept secret. It's for a back-up plan. Just in case Earl Nathair's plan doesn't work. In case the people of Edinburgh don't respond the way he needs them to. Find the colonial." Thane went to the table and picked up a pen and paper. He'd use the number code again. He tapped the pen against his bottom lip. "You have to be sure you can deliver this without being caught. This must remain secret. Do this for me and I'll look into freeing your auntie." He began writing numbers on the paper with the tailors looking over his shoulder.

"Oooo. It's a code, then?" The tailor grinned, the fear in her features dissolving like sugar in boiling water.

"Aye."

He had to warn the rebels about Nathair's insane plan to poison the water in Edinburgh, Glasgow, and Inverness. Surely Nathair wouldn't really go through with it. That could go so wrong, hurting his own men and backfiring on his own reputation. But it was best to warn the rebels anyway. Oh. Wait. He wouldn't risk injuring his men or any of the Scottish nobles. He'd taint the poorest area of the cities, thinking them worthless. Thane eyes shuttered closed. He'd never understand the man that was his father.

Rubbing a hand through his hair, he turned phrases for the secret message over and over in his brain. He didn't even know what to tell their units to look for. Thane paced, his mind knocking around. He chanted the Periodic Table out of habit. Finally, he settled on a set of phrases, used the letter four spots down the way in the alphabet from the proper one, then switched them all to their numbered slots. When he wanted to spell a word that began with C, he used G but wrote 7 because that was G's position in the alphabet. He held the message firmly in his head as he worked.

*They hurt the Seer when I don't obey.*

*Hand out vision-inducing gum when I raise both arms.*

*Water poisoning in city's poorest area. Send word to Inverness and Glasgow too.*

*Play along with this ruse.*

*Soon, we will turn.*

That last line threw goosebumps down his arms. What would that turning look like? It wouldn't be pretty. It would end in death, that much was certain.

Finished with the message, the string of numbers looked like nonsense. Hopefully, this wouldn't endanger these two much. Thane swallowed, praying his Dream wasn't turning him into a fool. He still had no idea how that would help the water situation.

"What is your auntie's name?" Thane held the message out.

The woman leaned forward to take it, but the man's hand

shot out and held her back. "No. This is not what we're here to do."

The woman shoved the man's hand off her shoulder, then grabbed the paper and folded it. "Then you go on out," she said to her associate, "and I'll take care of this. You don't have to be a part of it. I want to help my innocent mother's sister if I can."

The man looked from the clothing to Thane to the woman, then hurried out the door in a huff.

"Her name is Meggie." The woman tucked the coded message down the front of her ample bosom. "Meggie Staunch. They took her just outside Glasgow." She kissed Thane's knuckles. "Thank you, Heir. Now, here is your speech. I'll go ahead and leave and if you need clothing adjustments just ask the guards for me."

She ducked out the door and left him to it.

The sound of hammering trickled through the building. Nathair's crews were raising the stage where Thane would wear his Campbell kilt and crown, where he would say what Nathair ordered.

Thane straightened the speech the tailor had given him and began to read. There were notes explaining what would be happening around Thane as he spoke.

*King John is a fine king for England. A great king, even. But for Scotland, King John is thief, liar, rapist, and con man in one. He thrashes our factories to produce more only to reap the profits himself, leaving only scraps to our people. With ringed fingers, he rakes through our politics and twists good men like Earl Nathair so they end up hurting those they love.*

*(release the formula)*

Thane crumpled the speech and threw it into the fire. The formula was Bismian. And in high enough amounts, it could kill a child. He glared at the fireplace, the light flickering over his face. He couldn't go along with this. Not even with the message he'd sent. No way. It was terrible. Families would be dead and he'd be a party to it. Aini too. She wouldn't want him to do this. No matter what she or he suffered. His hands shook. One move, and innocent children, men, and women died. Another move, and the love of his life died in a long, painful way at the hands of that terrible Jack Shaw.

The door opened. Nathair strode in. "Why aren't you dressed? Are you prepared to rescue your countrymen from King John's greedy, fearful hands? To save the common man, the sixth-sensers, and your Seer too?"

Thane whirled to face Nathair. "I'm not doing it."

Nathair's face morphed into the very image of hate. He grabbed Thane, gripping flesh through his sleeve, and Thane let himself be dragged out of the room, down the corridor, all the way to a set of windows that looked out on the blackened cobblestones of Mercat Cross.

Looking outside, Thane glared at the gaudy statue of King John atop the old stone structure that marked the place where Edinburgh's market traditionally took place. He'd changed the thing into a fountain and it was all ridiculous. Like he was some kind of god. Emerging from flowing and gilded robes, the king's bronze hand reached out like he was chucking wisdom around kindly-old-man-style. Thane shook his head. He knew goats with more wisdom than that curly-headed man.

Nathair released Thane, then switched his phone on. "You'll need to move into a stronger position," he said to someone who muttered something back that Thane couldn't hear.

Nathair tapped the phone against the window ledge. "Why are you always fighting the windfalls that come your way, lad? Listen. I know I've made mistakes. I know I'm not a good man. You are the good man. Let me raise you up." Nathair pressed his fists against his own chest, that vein in his forehead throbbing. "I can make you the best ruler this country has ever known. But you need the evil in me to carry out the good in you. Don't you understand?"

Thane remained silent, simmering and afraid of what that phone call meant. Every inch of him felt exposed, vulnerable to attack. There were no easy choices here and his strategies had struggled under Nathair's warped logic since day one. He would have to stay sharp. Look for outs. Be vigilante.

"Just stop, Thane Campbell," he whispered, his voice going quiet and deadly. "Stop that mind spinning and fall into your fate."

Thane squeezed his eyes shut as if he could shut out Nathair's slick words.

## CHAPTER 10
## GALLOWS HUMOR

The door flew open and a man and woman Aini didn't recognize poured in. They wore all gray wool and slim, flat caps like Jack Shaw. The mess of these new hires of Nathair's were beginning to remind her of some sort of bird. Ravens seen through a Scottish fog. Something poetic that they certainly didn't deserve. Big, fat rats is what she should've imagined when she saw them. But no matter how hard she tried, they were sleek, quick-witted ravens and not rats at all. Rats would've been easier to deal with somehow.

They untied her and jerked her up. Her bullet wound pulsed and she bit back a hiss of pain. The ghost had healed it, but not completely.

"Where are you taking me?"

Electric sconces lit the corridor's striped wallpaper and the carpet under Aini's boots was soft as swollen flesh. The two dragged her through a door, then down a set of wooden stairs that smelled like lemons, but not in a good way. Going through a labyrinth of passageways, they ended up on concrete steps stained with something that could very well have been blood. No one cared to clean this area. Not a great sign, she had to admit. She looked over her shoulder, wishing she could catch a glimpse of the ghost she'd asked to send the message to the rebels. But without the Cone5 taffy, they were as invisible to her as they were to everyone else unless they chose to show themselves and had the strength to do so. She could hear them if they chose to speak, if they had the motivation to say something. Now would be a nice time to hear a word of encouragement.

As Nathair's ravens—no, rats, she corrected herself—escorted her through a brick wall that wasn't a brick wall but really a terrible, horrible door, she focused on the idea that maybe even if she couldn't see the ghosts, she may be able to sense them. Had she felt anything when talking to that sixth-senser ghost? A coldness, yes. What else?

"It's very difficult to think when you're pushing me around like this."

One rat sniffed, a version of a laugh, before throwing her into a cell.

More hidden prisons. Nathair definitely had a solid aesthetic he was building. Rusting cells under beautiful, historic buildings. Well-dressed thugs. A firm grip on his role as Only One Who Knows Best and To Heck With Ethics.

The two began fussing with some ropes on the wall.

"What's keeping me from just sprinting out of here?"

"There's another of us on the door we just came through. Plus, Earl Nathair is on his way here and it's likely you'd run straight into the man himself if you did. Go on, though. It'd be entertaining and I, for one, am bored with Edinburgh already." He said something decidedly rude about tourists.

"I figured as much. What is the story with the ropes?"

Maybe it was fatigue. Maybe it was desperation. Aini could

not muster the right kind of fear right now. She was in a hyped-up sort of panic that produced a humor in her that she wasn't sure was entirely healthy. They were going to string her up and Nathair would be here in less time than it took to scream, not that anyone would hear her in this concrete tomb.

"Does she ever shut up?" One rat asked the other. This one sounded Glaswegian. The other, Brummie.

Had she said something? She didn't remember more than that last question she'd asked about the ropes.

"I've heard she does when she sleeps and when she is doing her little meditation thing."

"Meditation thing?" What were they talking about?

"You commune with the ghosts, aye?"

There was really no point in hiding it now. "I do."

"You've been using them to heal you."

Aini touched her wound. "Yes, I suppose I have."

"We're going to put that to use, I think."

A tiny spot of proper fear began to grow inside Aini's bizarre and desperate courage. She could almost see it inside her. It was a black mold, a disease set on killing good cells and breeding bad.

"So you know the plan here. Care to share?" Her voice was shaky. She set her jaw to hide its trembling.

But it seemed the rats were finished with their chat.

One pulled an ancient stool close to the five ropes attached to the wall via embedded, metal hooks. "Climb up."

Seeing no good reason to refuse, she did so.

"Put out one foot." They secured her right ankle in one of the lower ropes. "Now your hand. No, that one."

She raised her left fingers, and they looped one of the upper ropes around it. By the time they were finished, both ankles, both wrists, and her neck were encircled by ropes. Most of her weight hung on her ankles, but the pressure on her wrists and the strain of her stomach muscles made the whole thing really very awful. She shifted slightly this way, then that, trying to find a position that didn't make her feel like she was about to choke to death or come apart at the seams. Her eyes filled with tears, but she would absolutely not, not ever, let them fall.

"You look like rats. Not ravens. Just so you know," she choked out.

The two looked at her like she was a madwoman. Madness was better than misery, right?

The secret door groaned and slid open, raising dust she hadn't noticed on her way in.

Nathair had that stupid smirk on his face. She'd never hated a facial expression more in all of her life. His clothes were ironed and smart, Campbell tartan everywhere. And he—

Thane walked in behind him.

Aini's heart stuttered, and she clamped down on showing any kind of discomfort. Nathair was using her to control him. She wouldn't make it more difficult on Thane if she could help it. What was the solution here though? Keep on being tough and getting hurt and Thane does what Nathair orders? She had to get out of here. To remove herself as the tool of control. But how. How. How. How.

They were talking but it was white noise in her ears. Shock, she guessed. Or severe stress. Then a voice spoke into her ear, clear and sure.

"I'm here, Seer. I will ease your strain." It was the sixth-senser ghost that had healed her.

Hope burned the disease of fear out of Aini's middle. "Thank you," she whispered, knowing the kind spirit was there and it sounded like she'd brought friends.

Aini and Thane weren't alone.

And that was enough for now.

She breathed deeply as a warmth suffused her tight joints and straining muscles, as her own weight lifted a fraction off the ropes.

Spirits were lifting her—not a lot, but enough to help her breathe, to make it through this moment.

"Thank you," she whispered again. Then she realized she'd only thought the words instead of saying them aloud.

Thane's gaze on her held so much. A wish for a future. An apology he didn't need to give. Pain. Terror. Love. His face blurred.

"I'm fine." This time she was fairly certain she'd said the words aloud.

CHAPTER 11

SPILLING BLOOD

※

"I can't do it, Nathair. I won't. Aini wouldn't want me to. I'm not going to get onto a stage and put on some show while you poison Edinburgh." Seething and raw from worrying about Aini, Thane stood beside Nathair, outside the front doors of the Signet Library.

Workers crawled over Mercat Cross, carrying pine boards and hammers. The stage would be ready too soon.

Nathair nodded, face reddening. "Let's go check on your Seer, shall we?" he whispered. "A surprise peek on what my man has been up to."

Thane struggled against his emotions and kept his words monotone. "Fine. But why are you leading me downstairs?"

"Oh, I had her moved. I suppose I forgot to tell you. My apologies, your Highness."

"Stop. I'm not the king."

"You are in all but ceremony. King of Scotland. It is a mighty thing."

Thane wasn't about to give him the pleasure of rising to the tease. Of course it wasn't a mighty thing. Not the way Nathair had it set up. Nathair would be mighty. The new Scotland would be even worse with him in power.

The carpeted hallways gave way to concrete steps leading to what looked like a solid, brick wall. Nathair slipped his fingers into a crack hidden where the facing wall met the side wall. He pressed three buttons Thane knew very well were there and a grinding noise sounded from behind the wall. The brick barrier swung back slowly, dust rising in small plumes as they entered the hidden cells that had held sixth-sensers for years.

Thane's mind screamed *Why is Aini down here? What have you done with her?* But he bit his questions back and followed Nathair quietly.

The first five cells were empty.

The sixth held Aini.

Thane froze. Thick ropes screwed into the walls secured Aini's wrists, ankles, and neck. She was spread out like a dissection subject, her boots three feet off the floor. Her hair hung lank against her cheeks and her jacket was ripped down the left side, exposing the spot where she'd been shot. But there was no bandage. No blood. Somehow her bullet wound had already healed. Impossible.

Her eyes found his, and a rush of love and fear crashed over him like beautiful, deadly, unstoppable ocean waves.

"I'm fine." Aini's voice was a rasp. She licked her cracked lips, blackened blood making lines down her chin. "I have my own power here." His brave Seer grinned then. Grinned like a poker player holding a secret Ace. Her gaze swiveled to the corner of her cell, but Thane couldn't see anything. Then Aini made a noise, a little moan of pain as she adjusted herself in her bindings.

Thane saw red. Suddenly he was on Nathair, arm circling and

choking. He'd used this move consistently since his fourth job when he was only a kid still. Was it irony that Nathair had taught him this very technique? Thane wasn't sure. Irony was a slippery thing. Maybe it was predestined or darkly humorous. Thane gritted his teeth and held on, feeling like he was in danger of dying too. Death never shifted more than a few steps away these days.

"You promised you would leave her alone if I came with you willingly," he said, his voice low and dangerous. Nathair must've recognized the quiet fury that had come over Thane because he didn't call out for help to the men who were surely just a room away. "You swore to me," Thane whispered. "I don't know why I hoped, why I thought you would keep a promise."

Nathair's skin was red and splotchy. Only another second or two and he'd be out. Then, if Thane held on past the point of unconsciousness, Nathair would be dead. Could he kill his own father? It wasn't a choice. He had to. He strengthened his grip, his own heart stuttering and crying out that this was wrong.

Nathair's men streamed from a side room and took hold of Thane with expert hands. Nathair dragged a breath in and braced himself on his knees. He croaked something that sounded like "son" but Thane ignored it.

Heaving and sweating, Thane fought them. "You have stripped the Campbell name of all honor and it will take more than terror to win the people to our cause. You have ruined it all."

He swallowed the pain in his throat, then ignored everyone but Aini. Every clever thought, every strategy fled his mind. He simply echoed what his heart said with each beat.

"I love you, Aini MacGregor." She smiled for him, and he knew very well it took a Herculean attempt to accomplish it. "I will do everything in my power to set you free."

With the men holding Thane, Nathair wiped blood from his lip and rubbed his throat. Swallowing, he opened the cell's lock with a massive skeleton key. He stared up at Aini.

"If I thought for a moment you would come to your senses and support your Heir and his father here," Nathair said to Aini, "I'd free you myself. We would win against King John easily. We're only asking for Scotland. With you and your command of the spirits and Thane's power to raise the best of them, we'd win in a minute. But no."

Nathair ran a hand over the red-gold stubble on his chin and Thane hated the fact that he knew what that stubble felt like on his cheek and how as a child he had longed for hugs from this beast of a man.

Senga's face blinked through Thane's mind. What did she know? Had the rebels informed her of everything so far? Did they even know Aini had been shot? What were they planning?

Spinning to face Thane, Nathair put the key back on his belt and pulled out a knife. "Heir, you claim I have no honor, but you are mistaken. Technically, I did not break my promise. I didn't take Aini down. She came to Edinburgh of her own accord and Jack Shaw took her freedom. Not me."

"On your orders," Thane said very, very quietly.

Nathair shrugged. "Jackie interprets my orders as he sees fit. He is a clever man with none of the emotional baggage I have with you. It's best this way. My honor won't get in our way."

Thane laughed without any humor. "So why are you flipping that knife around like you have some further darkness to throw at this scene?"

He glanced at Aini, wanting to see her strength. It was there, in her unblinking eyes and fisted hands. Chill air wrapped around Thane's middle and flew up the back of his head, ruffling his hair.

Jackie strolled into the cell, smoking yet again and wearing just a white button-down shirt, a flat cap, and a vest boasting a fine, gold pocket watch. Thane hadn't even heard him open the door. "I told you, Earl Nathair, this Heir of ours is a warrior poet. *Further darkness...*" The man chuckled.

Nathair smiled and there was a true sadness there that surprised Thane. He'd thought Nathair was now only made up of hate and drive and mad energy. But the grief in Nathair's eyes fled quickly and Thane wondered if it had been there at all.

Nathair lobbed his knife into the air and Jack caught it neatly, cigarette still burning between his lips. "Do as you see fit with her," Nathair said and the wind went out of Thane's lungs like he'd been hit by a train. "Our Heir needs motivation. I must keep my promise not to touch her." He left through the secret door, not looking back once at Thane.

Thane thrashed against the hands holding him. They slammed him against the brick wall and stars floated through his field of vision. He blinked and saw Jack approaching Aini.

"Heir, I do hope you don't hold this against me. It's you making this happen, you know. If you'd simply put on the clothing they'd had ready for you and practiced your fine speech," he said, throwing his cigarette to the ground and twisting it under his heel, "even adding your own warrior poet spin to it, we wouldn't be in this position. Aini would still be in the upper rooms having tea."

Thane spat blood from his mouth and tried to pull away. He was yanked back, the wall smacking his skull again. "You don't seem like the type to care about tea, Jackie."

Jackie's eyebrows lifted. "No? I like tea. I appreciate the simple things in life." He set the edge of Nathair's knife against Aini's calf, just above her boot.

"Go ahead and cut me." Aini hissed as the knife pressed into her skin. Blood welled over the steel.

"Really? Hmm." Jackie glanced at Thane and shrugged. "Does she not know what these things do? I'd have thought a rebel leader would have a good awareness of knives."

Aini looked at the cell's corner. "You can't hurt me."

Jackie tipped his head and removed his cap. He tossed it to one of the men holding Thane. "Now that is a lie. I see the pain in your face. See?" He dragged the blade across her leg.

Thane bucked. One man lost his grip and Thane launched himself forward, then there was a gun in Jackie's hand, faster than anyone could've drawn a gun. Jackie pointed the weapon at Thane's head. "This is growing dull. This whole, you fight, I draw a gun thing. More pain for you and her." He looked at his men. "Take him upstairs and see he does as he must." He looked back at Aini's bloody leg.

The blood stopped flowing, and the wound began to mend itself. Thane locked eyes with her. What was this? How was she doing that?

She glanced at the air around her. Jackie made a cut along her other calf. Aini stared Jackie down, then coughed, her body contorting from the struggle of being tied to a wall.

"My Heir," Jackie said, "I will continue to cut her and watch her heal with this strange ability she has. It does hurt, as you can plainly see. It is up to you how much she hurts today."

Thane asked Aini a question silently. She had her eyes closed though. Decision fell over Thane, heavy and dark. For today, he would obey. Until he figured a way out of this. He would be the Heir in Nathair's game. Today. Just today. Somehow he would find a way to warn Edinburgh of the poisoned water coming their way. Somehow. Some way.

CHAPTER 12

THE CURSE OF HOPE

The gulls shouted to one another as Bran followed Neve, Myles, and Vera onto High Street. The sun was strong enough to warm the scarf twisted around his neck and halfway up his face, but the wind was pure Baltic, so he didn't mind it a bit. Neve tugged her woolen cap lower nearly covering her eyes. Her dyed blond hair was tucked under the edge in a bun-braid sort of situation. Myles had a scarf on like Bran's, but with pink polka dots that Bran wasn't sure was very undercover. His bald head and huge sunglasses reflected the mid-morning light as he faced Vera.

"I think I should get one of those blue signal flags too," Myles whispered.

"Do you, aye?" Vera glared, then glanced up the roadway, most likely looking for the lorry of weapons. "Well, I don't."

"Neve, she is being mean. Do something."

The crowd bumped them into one another. The noise of street musicians, though not as upbeat as they'd once been, blended with loud questions from children and jokes between uni students jostling the stream of people headed the same direction.

"We are in a deadly situation, Myles. Can you please stop goofing?" Vera was whispering, but Bran thought maybe she didn't really need to be. No one would be able to hear or really understand what they were talking about. Not unless one was a kingsman undercover. Which was doubtful. The people around their unit seemed legitimately regular folk.

"I shall never, ever stop goofing, sweetheart." Myles grinned widely and Neve's own toothy smile echoed it. "I am happy," Myles said.

"Happy?" Bran had thought he was the only one.

He honestly thought he was going mad. They were headed behind enemy lines with no weapons on them and they'd most likely be recognized by a patrolling kingsman and brought to Nathair who would summarily shoot them all. But he couldn't fight this bright spot of hope inside his chest. It made him feel like he could fly without any hard candies. Aini was alive. Thane was alive. That was a good start.

"Because." Myles adjusted his sunglasses. "Our boy is going to wear a crown today. And the yucky old John isn't anywhere around. Nathair can fuss around all he likes, but Thane is going to show off a crown in front of everyone today. A crown. That has to be good."

"I agree," Bran said. "Nathair is in a precarious position. Aini is really his only Ace to play. If we had her, he'd have a tough time turning this his way. Vera, have we heard back from our French spy yet on support from Lady Darnwell?"

"Not yet. But I'm taking that as a good sign. A *No* would've been quickly reported. Negotiations and planning take longer."

Bran nodded.

The crowd milled about the open area behind the

government buildings. Red-striped caution tape marked off an area along the corner where last night's bullets had eaten some old stone away. Holding very large guns, kingsmen stood around a newly finished stage. The scent of pine stirred in the air and mixed with the scent of expensive perfume.

On the stage, a bevy of Scottish nobles sat in cushioned chairs. Their jewelry glittered in the morning sun and declared as loudly as any pronouncement that they supported Nathair's little move here with all the money in their fabulous bank accounts. Banks Nathair controlled. It was odd not to see all the Campbell supporters up there. The nobles that had gone to the rebels' side were in the crowd now, dressed like common folk in less flashy coats, ready to move on the blue flag's signal or Vera's command. Did the nobles on the stage know what had happened last night? That one rebel faction had warred with Nathair's men? Did they realize how tangled this whole rebellion was?

Nathair himself climbed the stage's steps and raised his hands. His usual kingsman jacket had been replaced by a deep blue coat that came down past his knees, swept back to show his Campbell kilt. He didn't wear the king's black coat. He was a kingsman no more.

"Welcome, my countrymen. Today is the most important day in our lives."

More than a few of the nobles seated behind him swallowed and eyed the crowd, fingers touching necklaces or silk ties nervously. They didn't know how the people of Edinburgh and beyond would react to this open display against the king. And they knew very well how King John would eventually respond. A man shifted in his seat and leaned over to whisper to the woman Bran assumed was his wife. She looked toward the stage's steps like she was considering a quick exit. Nathair had his work cut out for him. Well, they all did. Because if they were going to rebel and win, the Dionadair and converted Campbells would have to win those moneyed nobles too. It's not as if King John was going to hand them Scotland. Ammo cost a lot. Ships and tanks and anti-aircraft weapons cost even more.

Nathair's voice rose. "I cannot and will not hold my tongue any longer. None of us can. King John of England is a tyrant."

Families and factory workers traded panicked looks. Some eyed the street as if John was about to tromp down the lane like a giant and squash them all into nothing.

"He takes the money we earn right out of our palms." Nathair's fists shook at his sides. "Taxes to support his obsession with French land."

A few voices rose in agreement.

"We don't need French lands," Nathair said. "Let our old friends keep what is theirs."

The line of nobles behind him nodded. None were from the French court or French landowners as far as Bran could tell—the French always wore a *fleur-de-lis* in some form or fashion—but many of the nobles on stage held French blood in their veins and were torn by the current wars with King John in northern France.

"King John denies our basic freedoms as Scots, refusing to allow us to marry as we please, making it impossible to run our businesses mindfully, and forcing those of us who hate him to do his dirty work."

"Och, that was a smart line there," Vera whispered.

Nathair was talking about himself. Claiming he'd been coerced into shooting sixth-sensers without a trial, chasing rebels down like dogs, and treating his own countrymen like unwanted guests in his house. Bran's face contorted in disgust. What an arse. Would the people buy this little story of poor

Nathair being forced into being a mean, nasty thing by bad King John? It was ludicrous.

Nathair's hands spread wide like he wanted to embrace the whole of the city. "I must atone for all I've done in the king's name." He dropped to his knees and clasped his hands like he was praying. "This is my home. I cannot abuse it any longer. Will not. No matter what punishment King John doles out onto my clan and kin."

The crowd murmured, some nodding and others whispering quickly like they knew more about this and were sharing secret information.

"He gave one hundred thousand to the hospital yesterday," a woman beside Bran said. "That's what my sister told me. And he fought off the king's assassins that were sent in the middle of the night. Did you hear?"

"Aye." Her friend pulled a broadsheet from her bag. The front showed a picture of Nathair with the Saltire, the Scottish flag, behind him. "This tells the whole story. They were handing them out in the pubs this morning, first thing."

Propaganda. That was fast. The Dionadair were working on the same kind of idea, but with the truth instead of lies. But they'd missed this chance. They'd been too slow.

Vera spotted the broadsheet and her eyes about popped from her skull. She swore and pulled out her phone.

Nathair stood, head dipped like a man heavy with guilt. Bran had seen him use this technique against Thane and Senga. It had worked with both of them. He'd claimed his fault in the matter and played on the need people had to forgive the unforgivable in some lost attempt to change the evildoer in question.

"Thankfully, the kings and queens of old have sent us the solution to all of our problems. I know you've heard the stories." Nathair's gaze flicked to somewhere off-stage, then returned to his audience. "Long ago, the rulers of Scotland, of Alba, were crowned upon an ancient rock given to us by God Himself. Strange happenings surrounded this Coronation Stone. It was said to roar when the true Heir to the throne touched its black and glittering surface."

He lowered his voice and leaned toward the crowd, his forearms braced on his legs. Only the gulls dared to interrupt.

"The stories are true. The stone was on Bass Rock. It has been recovered. It named one man as the true Heir of Scotland. This chosen ruler placed a hand upon that ancient stone and the earth…the earth trembled."

Bran's heart beat loudly as everyone whispered and stared.

Where was he going with this?

"And the curse was enacted." Nathair straightened quickly, causing one man to gasp. "Now, if King John of England dares to defy our true Heir his throne and power here in Scotland, the curse of the old kings will strike him dead."

The crowd was putty in his hands.

"All hail my own son as the Heir to Scotland's throne, Thane Campbell."

Thane strode out of the crowd and climbed the stairs. He wore clothing similar to his father's—dark blue long coat, old-style kilt belted and thrown over the shoulder, boots. But on his brow glowed a declaration of who he was now. A golden crown.

Bran felt sick. That crown was as good as a target on a person's head and it was nothing Thane had ever wished for. But Bran remembered that ghostly sword in Thane's hand on the old hill. This was his fate.

"He is glorious." Neve covered her mouth and glanced at Myles.

Myles shrugged one shoulder. "Can't argue, love."

The Scottish nobles on the stage stood as Thane crossed the

pine surface with stately steps. Thane stared into the crowd, eyes narrowed against the sun that flashed over his crown.

"What's he going to do now?" Myles took his sunglasses off and squinted at Nathair. "He has to let him have the necklace and make this real to these people. But then Nathair will be toast, right? I don't get his angle on this."

Bran plucked the sunglasses from Myles's fingers and slapped the things back onto the colonial's daft face. "Keep them on, fool."

Nathair's new men had surrounded the stage, but their guns weren't aimed at Thane. They were gently tilted toward the crowd to defend the Heir. One man stood on the stage near the earl. He flipped his long, gray coat back to show a red silk lining and a set of serious revolvers. With a confident gaze, he scanned the area like he was keeping an eye out for threats. Bran had the sneaking suspicion this was the man who'd tipped his hat to him as the rebels fled.

Nathair bowed at the waist and kissed Thane's knuckles.

Stomach roiling, Bran bristled. "What a charlatan."

Myles laughed. "You sound like Aini."

"Good," Bran said. "Come. Let's find a place we can talk without all these ears around."

Vera nodded and pushed past him, leading them toward a closed Subject Identification Card check-in shed beside the road, a good stone's throw from the stage. The shed's one window reflected their faces.

Bran huddled the group together, but they all kept an eye on Thane. "I'm wondering what the curse will do if this bunch feels fully devoted to Thane as Heir. Villains are the heroes of their own stories and all that."

"Oh, you're thinking the curse won't work?" Neve bit her lip, her eyes darting side to side.

That's exactly what Bran was thinking.

Nathair, still bowing low, slipped the Coronation Stone necklace from his head, opened Thane's palm, and curled his son's fingers around the piece of ancient stone.

The effect was immediate.

Wind rose and twisted Thane's kilt and lifted his hair, tangling it in the gold spires of his coronet. The ground under their feet shook like madness. People shouted and called out. Two of the nobles on the stage bowed low like Nathair as the blue light of the ghost kings began to gather in the air around Thane.

Thane's gaze found Bran on the outskirts of the crowd. He wanted to shout some encouragement to his friend. Thane's eyes showed pain, grief.

"Is she alive?" Bran spoke the words in the midst of the stone's roar, knowing Thane wouldn't hear him, but hoping he'd understand.

A woman with flushed cheeks fell into Myles, breaking Bran's view of Thane, and the roaring ceased. The woman shoved something into the colonial's hand.

On the stage, Bran noticed Nathair's man bump into Thane and knock the Coronation Stone necklace from his hand. Nathair scooped it up before anyone seemed to notice.

Bran exhaled, frustrated beyond belief. "We are in a bad spot, friends. A bad one." The curse hadn't worked against Nathair because of his show of humility. Were the ancients so easily fooled or was there more to this?

While a mass of common folk and nobles queued up to swear fealty to Thane in the messiest, most desperate way in history, Myles unfolded the paper the woman had given him.

It was filled with numbers.

Vera ripped it from Myles's hand. "It's code. It's from him." She looked toward Thane.

"Can you read it?" If Thane had sent this, they needed to read it and read it now.

Neve touched the paper tentatively, then frowned at something behind them. "Does it say anything about Aini?"

"Hold your wheescht." Vera waved her hands for them to get quiet. "Aini is indeed alive. They're going to hurt her if we don't do as they say. Thane has to obey them." Her gaze tore across the page. "He says to hand out vision-inducing gum when he raises his hands. Something about water supplies here, and in Inverness and Glasgow. Ah, Nathair is going to poison the water."

"What?" Myles and Neve spoke in unison.

Thane's voice carried over the noise. "I am your Heir. I accept my role. I hope to drive the scourge of King John's influence out of our country. My father and I have mended our broken relationship. We want everyone—factory workers, teachers, fathers, mothers, Dionadair, all manner of rebels, kingsmen loyal to the Campbells— to come together and rise up. The French support us in our fight for freedom. They've sent weapons. Ammunition. Ships are on their way. We can win this for ourselves, for Scotland."

The people cried out and many crossed their thumbs over their heads. They curtseyed and bowed to Thane and began milling around, talking excitedly. Some were crying as they hurried home, most likely to fill loved ones in on the news.

The French had promised support. Really? Truly? They'd sent guns? This was big. This was very big.

Nathair clasped his hands together, looking for all the world like an earnest man. "I welcome the Dionadair and all who call themselves rebels to this very spot at sundown tonight to discuss strategy. We are one now. All of us. I trust you will not fire on me and please trust I will not fire on you. Our Heir needs everyone to fight King John. Our country needs all of us. Today marks the beginning of our new Scotland!"

The people erupted into chanting and cheers.

"The fountain." Neve frowned. "It stuttered. Now it's stopped completely."

Bran's chest caved in. "The water. They're getting ready to do something to the city's water. Now."

Thane raised his hands, stretching them wide. "People of Edinburgh."

It was the signal. "He wants us to cause a distraction," Bran said, "then find a way to stop the poisoning. But we must be careful. If they think Thane warned us, Aini will suffer."

Vera spoke into her phone. "Give out vision-inducing gum to everyone you can. Distract the populace. Find a unit close to the waterworks. Nathair is plotting to poison the water."

"Why can't we just tell everyone?" Neve hissed. "Maybe they'll rise up and we can get Aini and Thane out of here."

"That will ruin our own chances against the king. He will come and we need to be united. The French are key. We have to keep this carefully balanced or we will all end up cold in the ground."

Bran had a handful of the gum. He pulled out a piece, ran up to the nearest man, and rammed the gum into his mouth. The man's wife shouted and shoved Bran back as her husband choked, then appeared to swallow the gum.

One of Nathair's new men spotted Bran and started toward them.

"What are you doing?" Myles grabbed Bran.

"He's distracting people. Weren't you listening?" Neve took some more of the gum from Bran's outstretched hand. She ran off and offered the gum to a group of teens who took it willingly between chants of "Thane the Heir! Take down John! Thane the Heir!"

Then the visions started and the screaming began.

"A big snake!" One lass pointed at the sky, her face losing all its blood.

The man Bran had assaulted staggered and held onto his wife. "Lacey. I see...it's a great tree. And a monkey. A monkey and we're in the jungle!" Laughing like a maniac, he looked around like he might be searching for Bran. "You need some of this gum, dear. It's wonderful! What a day. What a bizarre day!"

Vera gripped Bran's elbow. Her red lips were a line. "It's time to move."

Myles, Vera, Neve, and Bran ran from the square. Thane spoke to the nobles onstage, most of him blocked by a circle of men in peaked flat caps and coats.

Bran and the rest pushed through the people watching those who'd chewed the gum. Woolen coats raked across the back of Bran's hands as he wove through the crowd, Vera's patchwork winter cap bright against the gray backdrop of Edinburgh's Old Town. She was chattering into her phone every step of the way. The lorry that held all their guns was parked in front of a noodle shop, quiet and unassuming with its false advert about multi-colored false teeth Myles had painted on the side.

The waterworks building with its towering pumps and churning wheels was eerily silent.

"That's a good sign." Neve trailed Bran inside the even more eerily unguarded front entrance. "The water isn't running so no one is dead yet."

Vera ate a speed caramel, handed one of the candies to each of them, then cocked her gun and held it up. "This isn't going to be a clean job. Get ready."

Chewing his caramel, Bran took out two grenades and held them carefully.

But when Bran rounded the corner, he didn't find kingsmen with tubes of vile-looking, bubbling poison cackling over water pipes. He found a group of men in overalls, each with a pint and evidence of several more glasses already enjoyed.

"Oh!" A man with a freckled forehead waved to Bran. "Here to bring us another celebratory drink? I can't hardly believe Earl Nathair has changed so much!"

His associates laughed and shook their heads as Bran lowered his grenades and put out a hand to keep Vera, Myles, and Neve out of sight, still behind the wall.

Vera put her guns on her hips and whispered to Bran. "Gave them high octane brew so they'd be pissed, aye? That's not overly clever, but I suppose it's done its job. The poisoners will have already moved into the main room of the facility."

Bran did his best to hide his explosives with his position, but he was fairly sure the waterworkers wouldn't have noticed if he'd wheeled in a cannon.

Proving his point, the freckled man fell onto his arse and set his cohorts to laughing.

"Eh," Bran said to the drunks, "there's a lassie that needs directions at the side door. Just there." He jerked his chin across the room and winked.

The men traded jokes and wandered to where Bran had indicated.

Bran, Vera, Myles, and Neve took off in a flash of speed before the workers had any idea they'd been duped. Hopefully, they wouldn't remember Bran if it came to questioning down the road.

A steely corridor led to a cavernous room with a huge

container at its peak and gurgling pipes coming from everywhere.

"There." Bran pointed at a woman in plain clothing standing by a valve. A bucket sat beside her feet and she was talking into a phone.

"We need Thane," Myles said. "He could talk her out of this with that face of his."

"Not every woman is just waiting for a handsome man to influence them, you know." Vera glared.

"Not every man is like that either." Myles crossed his arms. "But I'd guess the percentage is fairly high on both sides of the game. All sides of the game."

"Quiet." Bran's head was aching. "We have to do this so, so carefully. It has to seem like the plan to poison the water simply didn't work. That is wasn't due to Dionadair rebels. We have to keep the woman from doing as she's been ordered and make it look like there was some other reason for it."

"An accident." Neve wrapped her arms around herself, her gun tucked under an elbow awkwardly.

Sweat beaded on Bran's temples. "Yes. We could grab her and dose her heavily with the Bismian. She might not remember our attack."

"Not good enough." Vera clicked her tongue. "If she does remember and describes us, it's over for our Seer. And probably our Heir too."

"So we take the bucket." Neve eyed the metal container. "She'll be too embarrassed to tell anyone the inanimate object took off on her, and she'll disappear into the countryside to live with her spinster aunt."

"What a story." Vera raised her eyebrows.

Myles holstered his gun, flexed his hands, then shook them out. "What if she isn't too shy to admit her mistake?"

"It won't make a difference really." Neve's nose scrunched as she peered around the piping to see the woman. "She won't see us. The drunks won't have a good description on Bran. There's not enough to point it at the rebels. Nathair has it in his head that we're all violence-crazed like he is. He won't consider a subtle maneuver."

Myles kissed Neve hard on the mouth. "You are the sexiest thing."

Neve fought a grin, then punched his arm.

Bran nodded. "The idea has merit. Now, who thinks they're the fastest of us?"

"Not me," Vera said. "Plus these boots make too much noise. We need the most quiet and the speediest of us."

"I'm too clumsy by half," Neve said, looking unashamed.

"I'll do it," Bran said.

"Nah. It's me, man. I'll go. I can be sneaky." Myles began stripping off his gun belt. Bran took it from him and the colonial sped off.

Myles made it to a large vertical pipe right behind the woman. She pocketed her phone and turned away from the valve. It was now or never.

In a blur of movement, Myles ran to the bucket, lifted it, and rushed back. Then they all zipped into the corridor and paused, listening for the woman's reaction.

She made a sound like a hiss and mumbled something Bran didn't catch.

Myles made a face. "Son of a monkey and a donkey? Is that what she said? I don't think that's even plausible."

"Go." Vera pushed Bran and Neve forward.

Bran took the lead, and they didn't stop running, bucket of Bismian in hand, until they'd reached a large bin outside the Bluefoot. He took the poison and hefted it gently into the rubbish container. But it could leak. Leaking would be very bad. "I'm going to wrap it in something."

Looking around, he spotted a plastic tub beside the back wall, near a busted tire. Perhaps the place used the tub for bringing in meat joints. Vera helped him settle the bucket inside the tub and he screwed the lid on tight.

Out of the bin, he dusted his hands and nodded toward the Bluefoot. "I know the men who do the rubbish pick up here. They both cheat on their spouses and have hidden at least one body. I don't think anyone will miss them if they accidentally get into that."

## CHAPTER 13
## GHOSTLY

Aini's body screamed as Jack helped her from the cell's wall and out of those horrible ropes. Every noise echoed loud as a shout against the hard surfaces of the underground prison.

Flicking his cigarette, Jack said, "Behave, and we won't have to do that again."

Aini had never wanted to kick someone in the groin so much in her life. But she could barely lift her feet to follow him out of the cell. "Where are you taking me?"

Her legs crumpled, and her knee hit the gritty floor. With no emotion on his face, Jack helped her up. She braced herself on the wall and shook off his hold on her.

The hidden brick wall entrance slid open with a quiet groan.

"Your lad is dressing for the role he'll play soon, so you've been promoted to a guest room."

The passageway's concrete stairs seemed to wind on forever like some abstract pencil drawing without color or depth. Aini's stomach rolled and every bit of her hurt.

"A guest room, hm?" She commanded her mouth to give Jack a sarcastic grin. He may have seen her body break down, but he would never see her spirit crumble. "With a turn-down service? How about those little mints they put on pillows?"

Glancing over his shoulder, he scratched his chin. That ruby ring of his reflected the light at Aini. A plan blossomed in her head.

"You think you're funny, do you?" Jack led her up the wooden stairs that smelled like rotting lemons.

Aini's leg muscles spasmed and she fought to stay upright. "No. I just have a funny friend. He's rubbed off on me, I suppose."

For a second, she forgot where she was. A memory of Myles's chalk adverts littering the old lab swallowed her. She remembered Father coming into the room, all pressed clothing and shiny shoes. Thane and Neve had been there too. They'd been knocking the moody mixer around and trying to get it to work. It was odd how a regular day could become an important memory. She could still smell the sugar heating in Father's copper pot.

Jack was snapping his fingers in front of her nose. "Eh, girl. Don't pass out on me. We're almost there. I don't wish to carry you. You're all kinds of filthy."

Aini blinked. She was tired. More than that. She was near exhaustion. "I think I need water. And food."

"You do. You'll get it. If you behave."

The hallway led to another hallway and Aini could hardly take one step after another. Her plan. What was her idea? She'd already forgotten it. She definitely wasn't operating properly.

Jack's hands swung by his sides.

Ah. That ring.

If she keeled over, he'd have to lift her. She'd have a chance to touch the ring and maybe, just maybe, see a vision. And maybe it would give her an edge in dealing with this thug.

She dropped like a rock.

The carpet hit her cheek, and she had the briefest sensation of not really caring if she ever moved again at all. Then Jack's hands were under her and lifting. She fought a shudder and tried to focus. Which hand? Which finger had the ring?

Her room from earlier was getting closer and closer. The door was a mere few steps away. It was now or never.

Blindly, she reached under her ribs and took hold of Jack's hand. He glanced down at her, confusion washing his cold features, but before he could say anything, a memory embedded in his ring swept Aini into another country, another time, another life.

*In a dark room, two very young boys with dirty faces stood beside a row of flour sacks. One boy had Jack's too tidy dark hair.*

*The other boy stared up at the ceiling. "Don't tell them, Jack. We can't tell them where my da is."*

*Jack's gaze slid to the front door and five kingsmen burst through.*

*"Robin!" The first kingsman began trolling the store's aisles. "Robin Smithstone. You can't hide from us forever. We'll burn it down if you don't show yourself, then where will your son be?"*

*The boy beside Jack was shaking. Jack was not.*

*One of the kingsmen bent to look the boys in the face. He produced a very shiny penny. Greed—a strange color somewhere between gold and green—glowed around Jack's fingers and suffused the dim shadows of the store. Jack had never seen a new coin.*

*"Now," the kingsman said, "tell me where the man is hiding and you can have this penny. Hmm?"*

*The red stripes running down the kingsman's black jacket reminded Jack of the blood on Henry's cheek after their fight the first time they'd met. He'd won that fight. And he'd win this too.*

*"He's up there." Jack pointed at the hidden attic door, then held out his palm.*

*The other boy sucked in a breath and covered his mouth.*

*The lovely copper penny was warm in Jack's palm.*

*Robin Smithstone yowled like a cat as they dragged him from the attic and toward the front door. Jack smiled and ran up to his friend's da. Grabbed the man's thin fingers. Smiled and whispered, "Sorry." Confusion tangled the old man's face as Jack jerked Robin's ruby ring from his pinky and slid it onto his own small thumb. Jack watched Henry wipe tears and snot from his face.*

*"It's good you said sorry." Henry sniffed. "They'll kill him now, you know. My da. They'll kill him."*

*Jack shut the door with his filthy little boot and grinned, his eyes chilling.*

Aini dropped Jack's hand, sick to her stomach. There was no goodness in this man.

"Getting fresh with me, are you?" Jack dumped her onto the bed and turned to leave.

"I feel bad for you."

Jack rolled his eyes. "Oh, let me guess. You saw some sad memory in my ring. My abusive da and my absent mother. And you think if you just listen to the evil man tell you about his childhood, he'll come around. Cliché. Try again." He leaned out the door and spoke to someone Aini couldn't see. "Get a fire going in here or she's going to die before we're finished using her."

Aini pulled the bed's duvet around her shoulders. Her teeth chattered. "The only thing I saw was your true self. Greed."

Jack stared at the half open door, jaw tensing. Without a word, he disappeared down the hallway.

Another of his men came in, built up the fire, and brought

her a tray. He sat the tray on the side table and shut the door behind him. The lock snapped into place, and Aini jumped.

After downing a glass of tepid water and nibbling a piece of buttered toast, she lay on her side and gave herself some time to simply cry. There was no shame in it. No weakness. She simply had to let the sadness out so she could be strong again. A deep, dark sleep crept over her bruised body and struggling mind. Her nap's dreams were filled with hands made of light, of warmth and cold twisting into something solid she could lean against, something from which she could take comfort.

When she woke, the sun was still shining. She hadn't slept for long. Blinking she looked around the room, then gasped. The sixth-senser ghost—the one who'd helped her—floated, faintly visible, beside the bed. Another spirit filled the space to her right. This ghost was a woman wearing a high, lacy Elizabethan collar that highlighted her throat's dark bruises. She'd been killed on the gallows, it seemed.

There was no guard in the room so Aini spoke freely. "I want to thank you for delivering my message. Did you get to the rebels? And I should know your name. I'm sorry if I've been rude."

The younger ghost smiled. "Bathilda. And this is Lady Margaret."

"Pleased to meet you." Aini sat up and pulled the duvet back. She rotated her feet and stretched her hands above her head. Her head wasn't pounding and her arms and legs were actually working properly. "You healed me again."

"We did." Bathilda's gaze shifted to Margaret. "I reported to the rebels. They are on their way here. Secretly, it seems. They were mourning you, Seer."

Aini touched her chest, feeling her heart beat through her

shirt. She wished she could hold all her friends in her arms. "Thank you."

Lady Margaret cleared her throat. "The Heir has taken to the stage, Seer. We can...show you, if you like." Her lips pursed like she hadn't wanted to make the suggestion. Like the "showing" was something distasteful.

"What do you mean? Thane is out there and you can..." Aini blinked, confused.

Bathilda came close. The scent of magic—sage and something like charcoal—curled around her. Her light illuminated the seams in the duvet and the dried blood on Aini's ankles. "If you take my hand, we will create a chain of spirits to Mercat Cross and an image of the goings-on outside will appear in your mind."

Aini's mouth fell open. She could see Thane? Maybe she could figure out what to do to free them both. "Please. Yes."

She held out her hands. Bathilda took them in hers and that strange cold-hot feeling surged through Aini's flesh. Lady Margaret disappeared, then reappeared a moment later. She took hold of Bathilda's fingers and held out a hand—through the wall. A grimace twisted her face and she spoke to the ghost who must've stood in the corridor.

"Cease that at once, you cur, or I'll haunt your sad cell until midsummer!" Lady Margaret looked back at Aini. "Forgive me. Simon really is a tiresome flirt."

A laugh almost broke through Aini's ripe fear and heavy sadness. She squeezed Bathilda's hand, but passed through the ghostly fingers to find her own thumb.

"Not quite solid, Seer. Apologies." Bathilda grinned sheepishly.

"Don't apologize. I've just...I've never held hands with a ghost."

"You've fought on our side though. You're fighting for all of us sixth-sensers. And you will again."

"I hope so." Aini's heart lifted. She started to say more, but Bathilda's face and the room's television and papered walls fizzed like carbonated water. Another scene played out in front of her eyes.

Under a blue sky, a pine wood stage stretched in front of hundreds of men, women, and children. Nobles sat in chairs along the back of the structure, fine clothes shimmering in the sunlight. Below a flapping banner that simply said *Scotland Forever*, Nathair spoke with arms raised. The breeze lifted a length of his hair out of place and he deftly smoothed it behind an ear.

As she watched Nathair work the crowd in this unbelievable production he'd arranged, she stood, her heart in her throat. Where was Thane? She squinted as if that would help her see a ghost-induced vision, then rolled her eyes at herself. Her pulse beat frantically. He had to be there somewhere. Maybe she had missed him. He'd already appeared and was gone and now she'd never see him again. She swallowed her panic and forced herself to breathe evenly.

And then he appeared. Walking up the stage's side stairs, gaze downcast, Thane entered the carefully orchestrated scene. Crowned. Bruised. The king of grief.

The look in his eyes as he saw Nathair spoke of such sadness that it was all Aini could do not to fling herself out the window just to try to see him, to comfort him. His kilt stirred around his knees as he approached the earl. His aura sparkled like a cloak made of sunlight and stars.

She watched it all—the necklace, the roaring, the clever way Nathair got the necklace back again quickly.

Her hand went to her mouth. "The curse. It didn't protect

him. Why? Do you know why?" Bathilda's face blurred behind the image of the stage.

Lady Margaret dissolved, eyes wide, then Bathilda faded too.

Aini was truly alone.

Why hadn't the curse worked? She replayed the presentation over and over in her head. Wringing her hands, she drummed up every detail she could. Jack and the rest had been armed. They had hurt Thane inside and out. So why didn't the ghost rulers take them out? They were Thane's enemies, standing against the Heir.

"Not right then, though, maybe?" a voice said into Aini's ear.

Aini frowned, confused. "Is that you, Bathilda? What do you mean?"

"I can't materialize," Bathilda said. "Too weak now. Nathair and Jack didn't have guns on the Heir. They bowed to him. They weren't against him during the roaring."

Aini chewed the inside of her cheek and went to the window. Did Nathair and Jack truly fool the curse? A line of men and women—kingsmen and Jack's crew too—streamed across the inner courtyard. The presentation was over then.

Out of an archway, Thane appeared.

Aini splayed her fingers on the window's glass, willing him to look up.

One of Thane's hands held his crown and the other ran through his tangled hair. Jack was hissing in his ear. Thane suddenly stopped, his head snapped around, and he threw words Aini couldn't hear at Jack. Jack's chin lifted, then he pointed one finger at Aini's window.

She held her breath.

Thane's gaze met hers. The world faded at the edges. Her fingers bunched against the cold glass. She stepped closer. The sun and clouds took turns painting Thane in shades of gold and blue. His lips parted, and his chest moved like he wanted to say something. Aini's whole body flamed to life.

"Thane," she whispered. He was her heart, her home, her love. A tightness spread over her throat.

Jack's lips moved as he adjusted his cap.

Thane's mouth became a straight line. He slammed his crown onto his head and held Aini's stare. Fingers shaking, she traced his outline in the window's condensation and imagined his warm skin and the feel of his muscles moving under his jacket as he held her against him.

A hand snaked around her throat, taking her breath. "I won't hurt you," one of Nathair's men said into her ear. She hadn't even heard him unlock the door. "Just show your man there you're being cared for."

Snorting, Aini threw an elbow back, into the man's stomach. "*Cared for* right into the grave."

The man pressed her cheek against the window. Her condensation outline of Thane smeared and ran in wet rivulets past her chin. Straining to see Thane, she glimpsed his movement. Three steps toward her. He'd lifted his head higher to see her better, but he squeezed his eyes shut like the sight hurt him. When he opened his eyes again, she fought her captor's grip, swallowing painfully, and gave Thane a fierce smile and a nod.

"My Heir," she said, moving her mouth so he might discern her words.

His head fell for a moment, then he stared up at her again, fingers gripping the tartan over his heart. "My Seer," he mouthed.

A sob choked Aini worse than the hand on her throat. Tears bled down her face as Thane spun to follow Jack through a side door. Before Thane disappeared under the overhang, Nathair came up behind him and touched his back. Thane glared at his father—betrayal and a boy's longing for love washing over his features. Aini's stomach twisted. Nathair said something, and Thane shook his head and sped up.

"Let me go." She pushed her captor's wrist away. "You've done your job."

The man relented and locked her up, alone.

A soft light blinked beside Aini, the glimmer of a ghost reflecting in the window. "Bathilda? Lady Margaret?"

The light faded and the room was silent. Outside noise—vehicles, people, gulls—streamed in faintly, but the strong quiet in Aini's prison hummed in her ears. She sat on the bed, then lay back and closed her eyes. A list. That's what she needed. A list of what she knew.

1. *Thane is being coerced into doing as Nathair wished (I'm going to annihilate that man some day)*
2. *Bathilda and the other spirits can't help us escape (physically)*
3. *The ghosts can show me pretty much anything (not sure what to do with that honestly)*
4. *They can also heal me (And others? Need to ask.)*
5. *The rebels know the situation here because Bathilda told them (Is Bathilda stuck in this life? I should be concerned about her wellbeing and not so focused on my own problems.)*
6. *Curse not working because Nathair and his rats truly believe they are all for the Heir (eye roll)*
7. *French are supporting Nathair against King John and everything is sticky and tangled as a bad batch of taffy (and far less delicious)*
8. *I can send more messages. (What do I say and how will that help?)*

"I hate to interrupt your pondering, Seer, but—"

Aini shot out of bed, and Bathilda whooshed backward. The sixth-senser ghost was only a shadow of pale blue light with a few darker details here and there. The taffy had completely worn off. "What? No. You're not interrupting."

"We found something." Bathilda glanced at a slip of light in the faint form of Lady Margaret. The spirit raised her chin with fabulous disdain.

Lady Margaret seemed to cough, but the action made no noise. Aini couldn't be sure, but she thought maybe the lady's mouth moved. No sound came out. She was almost totally invisible.

Bathilda held a hand out to her. "I'll handle it, my lady." She faced Aini. "Lady Margaret has been trapped in Edinburgh for a very long time. The...viewing earlier taxed her a good bit."

"Are you trapped in the city too?"

Bathilda's cheeks flushed a deep blue. They were the most visible parts of her since the Cone5 taffy had fled Aini's blood. "I have more freedom. I wish I could explain, but I'm not sure how it works. And I haven't met any others who understand it either."

"But not everyone becomes a ghost. I've never seen my mother." Aini swallowed.

"No, I think there is an element that Lady Margaret and I share...I could perhaps call it anger? We both want revenge on the bloodlines who ended our lives. Our deaths were unjust. More than that, I think. We refuse to move on. Not until we've seen a change. This is where our strength lies. I think...I think those of us who are ghosts were meant to live as ghosts. Fate, I think."

Aini gave her a sad smile. "I am honored to be a part of the change you impart on this world. I hope we can see it through, then you can move on to peace."

Bathilda's grin lit her up like a candle. "Thank you, Seer." Lady Margaret slapped the back of Bathilda's head. Rubbing the spot, Bathilda floated close. Her chiming voice echoed in Aini's ears, unlike any living person's voice. "She wants me to tell you our news. We believe the enemy holds the Coronation Stone in a compartment not far from this room. Would it not be in your best interest to move that ancient stone and its magic so yours and yours alone would have access to its power?"

Aini stood, head spinning around her list of knowledge. "How did you find it? Is it a large piece like this?" She held out her hands to represent the approximate size of the larger chunk of the stone, the piece Nathair had taken from Inveraray along with the smaller one on Thane's necklace.

The spirits nodded. "I saw the thread connection from it to Thane and you," Bathilda said.

"If you take Thane to the stone, and he calls up the ghosts with his touch, maybe I can command them to attack Nathair and Jack despite what lies they're telling themselves and everyone else."

Bathilda shrugged, and Lady Margaret began talking again, still with no sound. "She thinks it will be nigh impossible to help our good Heir escape with that foul-tempered beast hounding his steps."

Aini had to smile. "You quote the lady well."

Bathilda giggled. "I can at least talk to the Heir. He heard me in the wash room."

"The wash room?"

"Aye. I found him there alone."

"Well I should hope so." Aini raised an eyebrow.

"He wasn't sure he'd heard me, but he decided he had." Bathilda clasped her hands excitedly.

"How did he react to a girl's voice in his ear while he was in the toilet?"

Bathilda snorted a little. "He wasn't actually *in* the toilet."

Then they were both laughing, and it felt wonderful even though the world was cracking apart.

"Where are they keeping the stone?" Aini rolled Mother's ring around her finger.

"In a cabinet. Behind Earl Nathair's desk."

"Do you think I'll have to be there when Thane calls up the ghost kings? Or can I command them through you and your mental link—something like what you did for me during the presentation outside?"

"That I don't know, Seer."

"I will try to get there then. Will you go to Thane now? Will you tell him where it is? And if he makes it there, will you tell me?"

She paced the floor like Thane, wishing Thane, Bran, and all their cohorts were there to help her plan. Neve could've given some anecdote from history, some ruse that worked in a plot long ago. Myles would've doled out a ridiculous idea that somehow sparked an idea that would actually work. Vera, well, Vera would've just ran right into Jack Shaw, had her way with him, then been cut down on her mad dash to the stone.

Aini said a silent prayer for each of those wonderful, crazy people she loved, then went back to making mental lists of why one move would work and another would not.

## CHAPTER 14
## QUELLE SURPRISE

Thane stood across from Nathair's desk, listening, plotting, planning. Something about this room made his blood shiver. It was almost the feeling he had when he touched the stone, but not quite. Why he was feeling it here, he had no idea. He put on a poker face, but truth be told he was shaken by what had happened today. Shaken to the soul.

Nathair leaned over the expanse of mahogany and spoke low. "My Heir, you did well."

Thane ignored him. His mind was on Aini and the rebels. At least they seemed to have received his warning about the water. There hadn't been any reports of sickness or death in the poor quarter of the city.

"Get your head out of the clouds, Heir." Nathair's brow knitted fiercely—the same way it did when he used to lecture Thane about bloodlines, legends, and enemies. "The king didn't poison the water and I do wonder what happened with that... plot. But I believe our city, our people are behind us nonetheless."

Thane held a straight face. "Amazing that you can persuade a group of people without terrorizing them, hm?"

Nathair ignored the cut. "My men tell me the king is on the move. He stopped to rest, but will be here by tomorrow night."

A chill seeped into Thane's limbs. "With an army?"

"Aye."

Thane's throat went dry. "Good. I'm ready to fight."

Nathair's mouth broke into a grin. "Are you now?" He glanced at a cabinet behind his desk, then back at Thane. "I am glad to hear it. Do you think your Seer might be as well?"

"I do." She had to be. Somehow, he had to persuade her to side with Nathair for now, then they could deal with him after the battle with the king. *If* they lived to see that day. "I need to speak to her."

"I agree. It's time we move past this and prepare ourselves to take Scotland from John's greedy, English hands. I wish I would've know years ago what I know now. That you are the Heir. That sixth-sensers could be used for good, to free Scotland."

"John is not the only one motivated by greed."

"I want power, Heir. Not money. That isn't nearly enough. Power is the only true currency for men like you and me."

"But you're willing to accept shared power with the rebels who fight alongside the Dionadair? You weren't lying to them today? You won't shoot Vera of the Dionadair on site when she arrives for your little tête-à-tête?"

Nathair rubbed his nose. "Of course not. Why would I strip us of a strong contingent of fighters? Why won't you believe me when I say *We are on the same side?*"

There were thousands of reasons. Only one mattered right now. "Because you shot our Seer."

Nathair waved him off. "Jack's man only wounded her to get

you to come around." He poured a glass of whisky and drank it down in one swallow. "And it worked, aye? You can't argue that."

"Who exactly posed as me?" Thane had figured that much out. Aini had only run to the enemy because she'd thought it was him. The truth of it tied him in knots.

The whisky glass clinked as Nathair set it on the tray. A trace of amber liquid remained and caught the window's light. "You don't need to know that."

"Tell me."

"No orders for you yet, Heir."

Thane lifted his crown and held it in front of Nathair's nose. "Oh aye? Then what's this about then?" He was shaken by the fact that the ghost kings hadn't attacked Nathair or Jack or any of them. If he didn't have them, what power *did* he have here? He flexed his fingers around the crown's smooth, golden edges. "Just something that brings out the highlights in my hair?"

Nathair bowed his head. "No, my Heir. Of course not. But you must remember I have your best interest at heart and I have a lifetime of experience with this world of power and struggle."

"I know exactly what you have experience with, Father."

"Let's go to our rooms and ready for the meeting, aye?" Nathair slipped around the desk and said something to one of his new men at the door.

Thane stayed right where he was. Breathe in. Breathe out. He could handle this. Somehow. Some way.

"Your luncheon is ready, Heir," the guard at the door said, holding the doorknob. His flat cap covered his eyes.

Thane slammed the crown on the desk. He felt impotent. Chained. A pointless figurehead.

A voice rang lightly in his ear. "The Coronation Stone is here, Heir."

He spun. "What?" Gooseflesh spilled over his arms. Ah. A spirit. He would never get used to this.

"The Stone. It is here." The voice faded, but a small brush of wind blew past his leg and rattled a low cabinet below the dark green curtains.

Thane dropped his hold on the crown and eyed the door guard. The man hadn't seemed to notice anything. He was looking down the hallway, listening to some other flunkie moan about the crowds being wild.

"...and claimed she'd seen a dragon. Idiots," the voice said.

Thane grinned. Vision-inducing gum. Myles had used the stuff to cause a distraction while they worked on the problem of Nathair poisoning the water.

Moving quickly, Thane shut the door on the guard and wedged a chair under the handle.

"You can't do this, Heir." The doorknob jiggled. "With all respect, you must open this door. Why are you fighting this? I...I don't understand."

"Je ne parle pas l'anglais, pine d'huître." Let the fool work on understanding that.

Thane hurried to the cabinet the ghost had indicated. He knelt and slid the bolt.

And there it was.

The chunk of the Coronation Stone Nathair had tossed beside Thane in the back of the lorry on their way here from Inveraray. No wonder Thane had felt strange in this room. All along, it had been the stone. *I'm an idiot.*

But what would happen when he brought the kings? Aini wasn't here to command them. They'd simply rise up and fade again. They might go after the daft lad at the door. But that wasn't enough.

A tapping sound came from the windows, behind the partly closed curtains. Thane tugged one back. The sight beyond the glass took his breath.

## CHAPTER 15
## OLD MAGIC

Aini knocked on the door keeping her inside the room. "I need to use the wash room, please."

A Glaswegian voice came through in answer. She thought maybe Jack had called him Michael. "All right. Move away from the door, then."

She stepped back, feeling the chill of both Lady Margaret and Bathilda at her sides. They were invisible, both from her lack of Cone5 taffy and the spirits' own waning strength, but Aini knew they were there. The feel of them reminded her of a trip she took with Father to Ireland. They'd gone swimming in a river-fed lake and every once in a while her toes would find a spot under the water that was cold as glacier run-off. That was what the air felt like now with her ghostly associates populating the room. There was also the herby, dusky scent that spoke of old magic.

A sudden thought occurred to her and she nearly forgot her current plan. What if she smelled like that now? Thane had a bit of it. Ever since he'd made the Coronation Stone roar on Bass

Rock Island. Maybe she had enough magic of her own to hold the aroma of the supernatural? She wasn't sure how she felt about it. All she could do was shake her head at the impossibility of the entire situation.

Here was a girl who wanted nothing more than to help her father run a boutique altered sweets business. Lists and ingredients. Timetables and sales calls. That had been her life's trajectory. Or so she'd thought. Now, it was ghosts and prophecy. Spies and blood. Love and rebellion.

The door opened a crack and Michael moved away so she could go into the hallway. He kept a gun at her back as she walked toward the wash room, beside the stairwell that could take her to the floor where the stone hid.

She glanced at the stairs and wished she hadn't.

Michael frowned. "Don't get any ideas now. I have my orders and you are expendable. Most already believe you're dead. Let's not make it true, hm?"

The door to the toilets squeaked terribly as she pushed inside. The place was lit with chandeliers. What a waste. Aini stood in the first stall and crossed her arms, thinking. Now what? Michael wasn't going to just let her waltz downstairs. She couldn't beat him up. Hurt him, yes, but she wouldn't win against a person obviously trained in violence. Kicking him between the legs would only serve to make life more difficult for her and wouldn't get her to Nathair's office unnoticed. Maybe he could be called away. She cocked her head at the toilet bowl. If there was a leak, he'd have to call it in. Maybe that would distract him enough to give her a minute to run? No. That was stupid. They'd have her again in minutes. She needed to be stealthy in this or she wouldn't have any time in Nathair's office to wait for Thane or to command anyone, ghost kings or otherwise.

"Ideas, ladies? I'm open to anything." She studied the air for glimpses of Bathilda or Lady Margaret.

"Window," a voice said in her ear. "Roof." It was Bathilda. Her voice was the tiniest bell, the softest whisper. And even though Aini was beginning to think of this ghost as a friend, the sounds still gave her a distinct shiver right up the spine. The window. But there wasn't a—

Ah. Above the row of toilets, on the same side of the building as her room and Nathair's office, a rectangular window was covered, mostly, by a sheet of thin, painted plywood. They'd boarded it up and tried to hide it. A sliver of light leaked through a spot where wet weather had bowed the wood.

Aini cracked her knuckles. "Good try, boys. Good try."

She hefted her split skirt and stepped onto the last toilet's lid.

"If only I had Thane's height," she muttered, lifting up onto the tips of her boots.

The edge of the wood left splinters in her palm as she pried it up and popped it off the window.

Michael knocked on the door to the hallway. "Quickly now."

Sweating, Aini lowered the window's temporary cover to the tiled floor. Then with a foot, she flushed the toilet as she cranked the window as far open as it would go. The rushing water mostly covered the squeaky window hinges and she began to pull herself up and out of the wash room.

The inner courtyard was a long way down. Aini blinked at the distance, going a little dizzy. She wasn't fully recovered from her wound. Her head felt like it might float away and an ache with claws dug at the spot the bullet had passed through. She wasn't complaining though. Better to be hurting than dead and Bathilda had done a really fine job of healing.

Scooting to the end of the window's ledge, she reached out

and up to grab the gutter. Using those tree-climbing skills from her childhood, she twisted and managed to get her feet under her before clambering up to the roof. In a crouch, she hurried toward the room where Nathair had the stone. At what she hoped was the right spot, she knelt and leaned over the gutter to peer in the windows. A green curtain blocked her view. She scooted over a bit to see through the slim part between the thick fabric, her knee catching against a tiny rock painfully. Ignoring all her physical problems, she squinted and tried to see inside the office. The partly cloudy sky threw reflections off the glass, making it really tough.

"If Bathilda or Margaret were here, they could help me out..." She looked around hopefully, but no ghosts appeared.

A shadow moved inside. Aini's heart stopped. No. No. No. If she was caught, that would be the end of it. They'd torture her again. She could already feel the knife like it was in her skin. She could imagine Jack Shaw's cold eyes and Nathair's sneer.

But when the curtains moved, neither of those faces appeared at the window.

Thane's mouth hung open, his hands loose at his sides and his sleeves rolled to his elbows.

With a start, he glanced over his shoulder, then opened the window. "What in God's name, hen? My girl. My love. What are you doing?"

He was already partially climbing out and reaching high to help her inside the building. His hands were warm and steady. It nearly made Aini weep with relief. She'd thought maybe she'd never feel his touch again.

Aini tumbled into the office, a tangle of limbs on top of Thane. Taking a breath, she smiled. "You're here. You're really here."

He ran a hand over her cheek and down the back of her head

like he was trying to understand how they had managed this too. "I am." He spread his fingers over the sides of her face and his full lips broke into a sideways grin. Unshed tears made his storm-gray eyes glisten. "And I'm so blessed to have you in my arms."

He brought his mouth to hers and kissed her well. She inhaled his clean and herby scent and gripped his hair so he wouldn't stop. She felt him breathe under her, the muscles in his chest rising to meet her body. He found the spot below her ear. When he dragged his lips over the tender skin, she nearly cried out, completely forgetting where they were and what they should've been doing. She unbuttoned his shirt just enough to slip her hand over his collarbone. The wool of his tartan brushed the back of her fingers as she did the same on his other side. Her hands found his shoulders under his jacket and shirt and she curled her thumbs at the place where tendons and bone and muscle met. She drew her mouth over his throat and he made a deep, rumbling noise. Her cheeks and chest flushed hot. The power of his presence, as well as his body, surged through her, sparking through her skin and blood and making her lightheaded. He was here. Alive. Loving her. It was a treasure and she would savor it for as long as she could.

He kissed her again, more serious now, breaking now and then to look her in the eye or to sweep her back with strong fingers, to pull her closer. Shivers fell across her legs and she wanted to drink him in like water. The coiled power in his limbs. The heat of his chest on hers. Maybe it didn't matter so much if they died after this moment. The perfection of this moment was worth it all. A glimpse of pure happiness.

A loud knock sounded at the door.

Aini gripped Thane tightly. Panic rose into her throat. "I won't go back. I'm done with this. We do it our way."

Jack Shaw's voice filtered through the air. "I'm sure you can wrap up your current meeting, my Heir, to see a very important, surprise guest, hm?"

A string of polite-sounding French words came from a woman out there with Jack.

Thane's eyes grew. "Oui, mais bien sur."

"Who is it?" Aini stood and straightened her skirt. It was a ridiculous thing considering there was still a bullet hole in her shirt. "The stone is here. Did you know? Did Bathilda tell you?"

"Who?" Thane reorganized his kilt and Aini didn't even pretend not to watch that very carefully.

"The spirit."

"Aye. She told me. That's why I'm here."

"Then let's get it. Let's see what we can do with me here. Against him." She glared in the direction of Jack's voice. He kept knocking.

"Our Heir is in love, you see. Yes, I'm sure you understand." His tone spelled out his hatred of the French and whoever was out there with him had to be pretty thick not to notice.

Wait. Jack said "in love" so he knew Aini was there. That was the only way his comment made sense. How did he know? Michael must've noticed Aini was taking too long in the wash room and found out she'd gone through the window. Why wasn't Jack barging in here with that revolver and red silk coat of his to ruin the world?

"Why isn't he shooting at the door hinges right now?" Aini glanced at Thane whose gaze went from her, to the door, to the cabinet.

"Because that's the French queen's sister out there. If she's heard you pulled through—recovered from whatever fatal injury Nathair claimed you suffered in place of the truth—I don't think she'd take you being shot that well. You are the leader of this rebellion they're funding. Jack and Nathair know they need you to lie right at this moment. To cover all that up."

Aini rubbed her temples. Jack knocked. Again.

"The earl will be with us shortly. I apologize sincerely for the interruption. I'm sure you'll have ample time to catch up later on, eh?"

"So calling up killer ghosts right now would be a bad thing," Aini whispered. She took a seat at Nathair's desk.

"I'm thinking so." Thane removed the chair keeping the door handle from moving and opened it up.

A woman with honey-blond hair and a tiny nose smiled. "Enchante, Mademoiselle MacGregor."

It was indeed Lady Darnwell. Aini's smile tugged at her cheeks. "It's so good to see a familiar face."

The woman brought back memories of the simple life she'd had not so long ago. Of parties attended alongside Father. Meetings with Lord and Lady Darnwell near the fire at home. Teas taken in London.

Jack Shaw's gaze flicked from Aini to the Lady Darnwell. "Know one another quite well, do you?"

"We do." Aini moved a chair and gestured for Lady Darnwell to sit. The woman had to be curious about Aini's scratched up knee and disheveled clothing, not to mention her miraculous rising from the dead.

She swept into the room, nodded respectfully to Aini and to Thane, then settled herself. "As you know my husband and I are at your service. I am so glad to see you alive and well, Miss MacGregor."

Aini wanted to say *Funny story, that. See this handsome incarnation of evil here rigged a plan to trick me using this man I love, the one who is supposed to be king. Complicated, eh?* but she knew that wouldn't really help matters. She contented herself with a simple "Thank you" instead.

Lady Darnwell looked like she wanted to know the back story on that, but she had impeccable manners and moved on. "No one except him knows I am here right now," she said. "The French queen must not show her support of your rebellion against King John outright. This must be done with a subtle hand."

"Aye. We understand that." Thane stood beside Aini. It was so good to have him by her side. "And we are so grateful for the aid."

Lady Darnwell nodded. She studied Aini's face. "I am so very glad the news about your death was false." She glanced at Jack, who guarded the half-open door and ordered someone to get tea.

Would it be smart to tell her everything? That Nathair's men had shot and tortured her? That Thane hadn't truly reunited with his father and the rebels were in two very opposing factions?

A man brought in a tray and poured tea for everyone. "Earl Nathair will be here shortly," he added.

Thane was staring at Aini and she thought perhaps he was wondering the same thing: whether or not to tell Lady Darnwell everything. But if the French were nervous about supporting the rebels, such news would make them only more worried. They might pull back. No, it was better to seem a united front while Lady Darnwell was present. Aini sipped her tea with shaking fingers. Good thing she and Thane hadn't used the stone. What a mess that might've been.

Nathair blew into the room like a storm, reddish hair wild and eyes like a predator who'd cornered his prey. He recovered quickly, his features smoothing into a false blandness. "What's this now? What a wonderful surprise. Lady Darnwell." He bent at the waist and kissed her hand, then his gaze snapped to Thane, Aini, then the open window behind them.

Thane's nostrils flared. Aini knew very well Thane was fighting the sudden urge to throw the Nathair out the open window behind them. It would've been so easy.

"Father," he said through gritted teeth, "we were discussing the upcoming meeting with the Dionadair and Lady Darnwell arrived. It's good to have her here. For the meeting. Although I worry for your safety, Lady Darnwell."

What was he talking about? "Why?"

Lady Darnwell frowned.

Thane looked at the stack of messages on Nathair's desk. "Because we have word King John is on his way here. Now."

Aini grasped Thane's hand, not caring what anyone thought about it. John was on his way here? The war was going to happen. "As in tonight? Or tomorrow? What is the timing? Do you know? And does he know what we're planning?"

"Mon Dieu." Lady Darnwell crossed herself.

Nathair poured a drink of whisky and offered it to the French queen's sister. She took it and downed it in one swallow. "King John has a sizeable force. He obviously knows we are set to declare our independence from his tyranny. He stopped to rest and will most likely make it to Edinburgh by sundown tomorrow."

Aini chewed the inside of her cheek and Thane paced the tiny space between Nathair's desk and the window. Several times, his gaze went to the stone in the cabinet.

"But with the Coronation Stone and your...abilities..." Lady Darnwell's eyes were as big as dark moons.

Who knew if the curse would work against King John? It hadn't worked against Nathair or Jack. Was it simply because they'd truly believed they were helping him gain the throne?

Or was the curse a one-time event they'd spent on Bass Rock?

Well, Aini wanted to appear strong and capable to this ally. It would do no good to make her doubt the risk she'd taken to support them. "Yes," Aini said. "We do have power. Power the world has never seen. But we aren't infallible. Undefeatable. We must prepare for this sudden attack, if that's what this is."

"King John will commence negotiation first, I'm sure," Lady Darnwell said. "He is a horrible man, but he has always tried to avoid war. It costs him great bushels of his beloved money." She smiled sardonically.

"She speaks truth." Nathair spun his glass on its edge, then stopped it with a quick hand. "What weapons do the Dionadair rebels have on hand?" His eyes zeroed in on Aini.

She wanted to throw her chair at his face. But for now, they were allies. What a world. "Three hundred automatics. Two hundred grenades. A slew of lesser guns and explosives. Three-hundred-eighty Dionadair." She left off the number of converted Campbells and their kin. He would know that number already. They'd been his until recently.

He nodded. "And we—the units here in Edinburgh—have twice that. Approximately. And the anti-aircraft the French so kindly gave."

Thane locked eyes with Aini, his aura burning, and a sizzle of heat ran over her body. Behave, body, she scolded herself. There was a war to fight. He pushed his glasses into place. "The Seer and I will go to the Dionadair and meet with them at their hideout, as planned."

That wasn't Nathair's plan. They were supposed to come here. But Aini knew what Thane was attempting. If he pretended the plan was for Aini and him to leave, it would be difficult to argue it in front of Lady Darnwell. It would show division. Nathair should fold to his unspoken demand and approve of this move in the best interest of all parties involved.

Nathair and Jack both stared at Thane. "Aye," Nathair said, rubbing his lip with his thumb. "Gilmerton Cove is a fine place for a discussion of war."

Aini sucked in a breath. He knew the location of the hideout. When had he found out?

"We await your orders, Heir," Nathair said.

Thane took Aini's hand, and started toward the door, but Aini had a sudden thought and stopped him.

"Oh," she said over her shoulder. "The Heir will of course need his Coronation Stone." Palm outstretched and flat, she eyed the necklace sitting under the scar on Nathair's neck.

A grin twitched the corner of Thane's mouth.

Nathair's throat moved in a swallow and his eyes were coals. "Of course." He lifted the leather strap, then paused. "But shouldn't we keep this safe here, just in case?"

"In case of what exactly?" Aini kept her hand out. "We are fully allied. We share the same goal." She parroted the words he'd used during Thane's presentation as Heir.

"Is there a problem?" Lady Darnwell tilted her chin and studied Nathair.

Jack smiled at her, firing all the good-looks guns he had. Aini was almost sure Lady Darnwell sighed. He was far too fine for a devil. "A protective father is still a protective father," Jack said, "even when the son is set to be king."

Lady Darnwell smiled sadly. "Ah, that is true, I'm sure."

Nathair glanced at Jack, then removed the necklace and set it in Aini's palm.

She curtseyed to the lady, then led Thane out of Nathair's hold and into relative freedom.

## CHAPTER 16
## REUNION

The sun had dropped well below its zenith while Bran waited outside Gilmerton Cove in the icy cold, wet grass for Viola. She emerged from the trees where she'd been listening for the ghost who'd given them the news that Aini wasn't dead.

"Any luck?" he asked.

"No." She stopped and picked something off Bran's shoulder. "No visitors at all. It's odd, really. Normally I hear them off and on all day. But now, now there's not a voice out there."

Viola was a stranger. He had no business appreciating the way the day's light played over her long nose and smooth cheeks. But the fact that he'd only just met her didn't seem to matter. A powerful longing to hold this woman and chase the shiver out of his bones poured over him. Fighting the pull, he crossed his arms.

"Could it have anything to do with Thane and the stone?"

She shrugged. The afternoon light caught in her pale hair like sun on snow. "Why are you staring at me?"

"I'm sorry. It's because you're beautiful."

"I'm not."

He laughed. "Aye, you are."

"I'm pale and skinny. I don't exactly have men lined up."

"You've got one."

She blushed and looked away. "Are you going to be part of the elders' talk?"

Taking a step back so he wasn't coming on too strong, he nodded and breathed in the chilly air. He felt a little bit like a man who'd thought he would die yesterday, but had been granted a reprieve. The whole world was more lovely than it ever had been.

"I will be in on that talk. Whether they want me or not. They need to know every detail of that message our Heir sent when we were in town."

"Telling on me, are you, you wee clipe?" A very familiar voice echoed from the forest.

Bran thought he was seeing things. "Thane? Aini?"

The two walked out of the dappled shadows like they'd simply been on a nice stroll instead of being held captive in a prison. Three of Nathair's corbies skulked in their wake.

Bran's heart soared as he and Viola ran to meet them. Bran grabbed Thane and hugged him tightly. "My friend. My dear, good friend." He wasn't even ashamed of the tears leaking from his eyes. "I'm so glad to see you, lad."

Thane slapped Bran's shoulder. "And I, you."

The lad's smile was something to behold, Aini's too. She hugged Bran, then shook Viola's hand.

"I'm the Ghost Talker who caught the message from the spirit you sent," Viola said.

"Bathilda is that spirit's name. She is a mighty soul."

"I haven't heard a ghost at all in over an hour. Maybe more. Have you?"

A wrinkle appeared between Aini's black eyebrows. "No, come to think of it. Maybe it's because of this somehow." She held up the Coronation Stone necklace that they'd made for Thane.

Bran raised an eyebrow at Thane. "She holds all your power now, aye? There is a joke in there somewhere."

"Shut your gob, man." Thane shoved Bran gently. "The thing hums like madness when it's near to touching me. I can't stand it really. I'll wear it in battle, but for now, she is welcome to it."

In battle. The phrase made Bran's stomach roil. "How did you get out of there?" He had to be dreaming. This changed everything.

Aini glanced at the mouth of the cave behind Bran. "Bathilda and Lady Margaret—she is another ghost that helped me—found the larger piece of the Coronation Stone in Nathair's office. They told Thane and me about it and we both managed to sneak into the office."

"I didn't sneak. I simply stayed when my father left and slammed the door on one of Jack Shaw's unsuspecting men."

Bran kept an eye on Jack's men. They were keeping their distance, thankfully. "I'm surprised one of Nathair's new hires could be surprised. The man I met was nothing short of a professional gang member." The man in the room at the Signet Library had shot the floor at his feet and told him to run along. Not an amateur maneuver.

"They are that," Thane said. "He found Jack Shaw running one whole side of Birmingham and wanting more. Nathair provided the opportunity for some real purpose and more money and Jackie jumped on it. They also rounded up some roughs from Glasgow. The lot of them make quite an imposing unit. Their fighting skills are fine-tuned and pure deadly."

Thane did have several new bruises. He was favoring one side too. What had he gone through there? Poor lad.

Aini touched Thane's shoulder gently. "We were both in Nathair's office when someone knocked on the door. It was Jack Shaw escorting Lady Darnwell." She looked at Viola.

"She's kin to the French queen," Thane added.

"And a kind friend of my father's."

Viola's eyes widened. "Nice friends."

Aini smiled. "Thane and I wanted to see if the stone's curse would work on Jack and Nathair and the rest, but with the lady there and ready to support us, we held back."

"I don't understand," Viola said.

"The French don't realize we're a rebellion split into two groups who want to kill one another." Thane's eyebrows knitted. "And we don't think that would be a selling point."

"If we killed everyone around Lady Darnwell, she might tell her fellow French that this rebellion is doomed. In truth, if we don't stick together for now, we are doomed. King John is almost here."

Bran fisted his hands. "When?"

"Tomorrow." Thane rubbed his lip with a thumb, a habit he shared with Nathair.

The necklace hanging near Aini's throat caught the sun. "With that," he nodded at the tiny stone, "and the altered sweets we have, I hope we'll have a chance."

Viola's gaze strayed to the cave's mouth. "We need to tell Vera."

Viola needed to tell Thane she was his half-sister. But that wasn't his business. It didn't actually hurt Thane not to know.

Bran would leave it alone. Viola could tell him when she felt the time was right.

"The French sent anti-aircraft weapons and more," Thane said. "They are also sending ships—coming down from the North to avoid capture—to support us from the water, but I doubt they'll arrive soon enough to be of help."

Whistling preceded Myles out of the cave. He jerked to a stop, then bounded over like a big, silly dog. Hugging Thane and Aini with an arm each, he shouted, "This is the best day ever. Neve! Get your adorable self out here. I have two presents for you."

"Less shouting might be a good idea," Aini said into Myles's arm, but the happy tears in her eyes lessened the sting of her bossy tone.

"It's so great to see you both alive." Myles broke away and shook his head. "It's a shame though, Lord of the Highlands. I was getting used to being the best looking guy in the cave."

Viola laughed, light and airy at Myles. "Oh, I like him."

Thane narrowed his eyes at Myles. "Then you've more patience than me."

Neve came running out. "What is the—Aini!" The two ladies embraced and Bran's heart squeezed. "Och, I never thought I'd see you again, friend." Neve hugged her again, tears freely flowing.

Aini whispered something to Neve that made her laugh. Neve wiped her tears on her sleeve.

Thane greeted Neve with a hug and Neve's cheeks went red. "I'm hugging the Heir," she whispered to Myles over his shoulder.

Myles grinned. "I know, sweetie. Try to remember I exist, okay?

Neve shooed him away, smiling.

Thane turned to Viola. "What did you say your name was?"

She stuck out a hand. "I'm Viola Campbell. I'm your half-sister."

Well, guess it was time. Bran had to smile at her unexpected revelation.

Thane blinked.

Aini looked from Viola to Bran and back again. "Really?"

"Aye," Thane answered for her. "I've heard of you. This is... wow. It's great to finally meet. I have to say I'm glad you don't look a thing like our father." He held his arms out, asking for an embrace rather than a handshake. It made Bran proud.

Viola took him up on it and hugged her brother. "You're tall."

"I am," Thane said, a laugh in his voice. "I want to learn all about you, but I think you'd agree we need to deal with emergency matters first."

"Agreed." Viola smiled at Aini and Bran led them all into the cave.

Nathair's men hung back and talked stiffly to the Dionadair guards at the entrance.

Inside, the rebels were of course thrilled to see their leaders. There were chants of "Scotland's saviors! Our Heir and Seer!" and "We will rise!" as Thane and Aini wove through the crowd to reach Vera, Rob, and the others gathered to hear the news and make some decisions on what to do next. Aini filled them in on the situation in the city, Thane adding details.

"This is where they cut me." Aini pushed her sock lower to show lines of reddened skin.

Thane tensed and Bran put a hand on his shoulder. "We're going to get them for that, friend."

Thane nodded and gave Bran a grateful look.

Aini pulled her sock back up and straightened. "I'm not telling you this to get sympathy or fire your need for vengeance

—although vengeance is just fine with me—you need to know the possible advantages of working with ghosts. They can heal. Immediately. That's no small thing."

"Will they heal any of us?" Vera asked. "Or just you because you're the Seer?"

"I should've asked them that."

Viola stepped forward. "Why don't you ask now?" She held out a piece of the Cone5 taffy. "If they can heal us all as we fight, that would be a game changer."

Neve joined Viola. "We have plenty of altered sweets, Aini. So don't worry about using them up. Because of the work we did at Inveraray, we have enough to supply this whole force and then some."

"We must be careful not to double dose." Thane pushed his glasses higher on his nose. "Or to eat the candies too often. It could turn your fine brains to mush, friends."

"We need to clean up first. I can't possibly do anything when I'm like this." Aini gestured to her torn clothes and the dried blood on her legs.

"Agreed. We have time to gather ourselves a bit first, aye?" Thane's eyebrows rose.

They certainly deserved that. Bran herded the crowd away and led the couple toward the side room the rebels had been using for cleaning and washing.

The poor things couldn't keep their eyes off one another as they removed all but their underthings to rinse off with wooden buckets and rough cloths. The old woman running the wash area, keeping fresh water stocked and what not, barked at them several times, reminding them not to linger because the rebellion was underway. She didn't realize who they were and Thane and Aini didn't seem to want to tell her and embarrass her despite the way she hounded them. Bran didn't want to leave them alone with the woman. Finally, the old woman put up two screens—only God Himself knew where she found those in the middle of a revolution—and Seer and Heir finished their bathing quite separate.

After Bran made sure they'd had time to down some bread, cheese, and tea, he brought them back to the crowd.

Neve met them and handed Aini a piece of taffy. Aini chewed it demurely. It was obvious this girl had grown up around nobility. She had the manners of a duchess when she wasn't fighting off kingsmen. Bran had to smile.

"So the king is on his way," Thane said too casually. "He will arrive tomorrow. We must prepare for our big brawl." He cracked his knuckles and glanced at Bran. "You ready for a fight?"

"Very." Since the day Bran met Nathair, he was ready for this damn fight.

"The king is on his way? Already?" Rob looked panicked.

Vera glanced at him, frowning. "Course he is. This is what we want. He comes to us and we do with him as we please. With our altered sweets and the Coronation Stone, we will give him a fight to end all fights. He'll leave our land in a wooden box."

Shouts of agreement went up.

Blinking, Aini raised her hands. "Hello, spirits." She cocked her wee head, listening to words and sounds Bran couldn't hear. She asked them about the healing, then waited, nodding. Facing Thane, she explained. "They can only heal me. I have... something in my blood. I'm not sure how it works."

"You are chosen. Fated. It is a special thing," Vera said reverently.

Several Dionadair raised their crossed thumbs over their heads.

"They said..." Aini rolled her mother's ring around her finger.

"They said I can maybe heal someone else. But only if it is meant to be? Or if I'm tied to them? Something like that. The ghosts I'm talking to—"

"They aren't even speaking English," Viola said, interrupting. She watched what Bran presumed were the spirits, her head going side to side. "How can you understand them?"

"They are speaking English." Aini frowned.

"No, they're not, my Seer." Viola's tone held respect despite the disagreement. "I believe that young man with the axe is speaking in maybe Old Norse? And that woman with the thumb-sucking child is clearly speaking in Latin. Do you know those languages?"

"There were Viking forces in this area during the ninth century," Neve added. "And most people don't know that a wall older than Hadrian's—Antonine's to be exact—extended past this area and included many lowland tribes that were friendly with the Romans."

The woman knew her history, Bran would give her that.

Aini gave Neve another hug. "You are amazing. I didn't know that. Nor do I know either of those languages." She extended her arms, eyes wide. "And I seriously doubt anyone here does either, unfortunately, or we could get an exact translation. Bizarre." She studied the air around her, then shut her eyes. "I can hear sounds from their time periods too. That happened with Bathilda and Lady Margaret—the ghosts I told you about, from the Signet building." Pointing to the right, she said, "When I focus on him, I hear the wind in the trees and shouts that might be battle commands or sailing orders. With her and the child," she said, gesturing left, "cart wheels on stone and braying cattle echo in my ears."

She inclined her head as if the ghost speaking Latin was

saying something. "Oh, I know. I won't waste it. I promise." Her cheeks reddened.

"I am so jealous right now," Neve said.

Thane rubbed his face, shoving his glasses into his hair. "This is mad." His hands fell to show a stunned smile. "My Seer. You are a wonder."

"What did that Roman ghost just say to make you blush red as a cherry drop, sweetheart?" Myles elbowed Aini.

Aini's eyebrow slanted like a spear about to be thrown. "It's none of your business, Myles."

Myles held out his hands and laughed. "Yes, ma'am." He hid behind Neve who snorted and grinned. "Don't sic the MacGregor eyebrow on me!"

Neve pinched Myles backside. "Incorrigible."

"The king isn't the only one headed our way," Thane said. "Nathair is set to arrive here at sundown for the meeting."

"Here?" Myles dramatically pulled at his collar. "Yikes. Will he bring that super scary Jackie Shaw you mentioned, Seer?"

"Definitely." Aini shuddered. Bran didn't blame her. Not after he'd seen those cuts on her ankles.

The light coming in from the outside was waning. "It's nearly sundown now," Bran said. "What are we going to say at the meeting? Are we making any demands? Any assurances? Because you know that man will have all his ducks in a row. We need to know what we refuse to bend on and how we can handle this. We can't trust that he won't turn on us. Even if it makes little sense to do so. I've seen that man turn on everyone he loves. Seen him pull off the most clever political moves, then shoot himself in the foot just out of arrogance and rage. Callum was the one who could calm him and we don't have him here."

"He's right." Thane crossed his arms. "Nathair is unpredictable. Especially now. If we seem to be winning against

John, Nathair might turn on us to gain the upper hand when he's finished using us. We must be prepared for that." He began pacing a line.

Aini clasped her hands behind her back and talked strategy as she walked back and forth in front of the rebel leaders.

Did she get these ideas from ghost generals of the past? Bran didn't think so. This was all her. Seer and general. Merlin and friend. A wonder to behold.

"That sounds like a fine plan," a voice said from closer to the front of the cave.

In his typical tweed and owlish glasses, Owen—this generation's Dionadair leader—broke through the crowd. "Is it all right for me to join back up, sister?"

Vera ran at him. "Brother!"

Dodie came up beside him, smiling for once. "We brought a couple other fighters too."

Owen returned Vera's violent hug, then held out a hand. "Senga and Lewis couldn't stand being cooped up in that shambles of a home you have up there, my Heir."

Thane's face lit up, and he went to his mother and the man who was for all purposes his adoptive father.

Aini embraced her father and Senga too. "I wish you weren't here and that you were safe far away, but I'm also so happy to see you both. Now, did you hear anything more about the king?"

Senga shook her head. "It seems you have the same information we do. What we didn't know is that Nathair is on his way here?"

Lewis grimaced and ran a hand over the place his ring finger used to be. Anger twisted Aini's features. Bran was very, very glad she was on his side.

Thane filled them in on retrieving the stone necklace and Lady Darnwell's arrival.

Owen stood on a chair—must be a family trait, Bran supposed—and opened his arms wide to address the gathered rebels. "I am sorry for my tardy arrival. I applaud you for all you've accomplished thus far. You are gaining advantages left and right," he gestured to the necklace Aini wore, "and we are fully prepared to meet with our less than ideal allies. Tomorrow we battle the king for our country, for our people, for our freedom. For centuries, our land has thirsted for this moment and we will not fail her."

The cheers that rose up shook the ground almost as much as Thane's Coronation Stone. Hope rushed over Bran and washed away his fear if only for a second. He would help Thane stand up to that ogre of a father. This time, he'd be right there next to Senga and Thane. And Viola too. He refused to allow that man another moment of hurting the ones he loved most.

He blinked, realizing what he'd just thought about Viola. The willowy sixth-senser was talking to Aini about enlisting ghosts and strategy, her fair face animated and her lips moving a mile a minute.

A laugh popped out of his mouth. He loved Viola, God help him. She was a stranger, but he loved her and there was no use denying it.

She glanced at him and his heart stuttered. "What is it, Bran?"

Closing the space between them, he cupped her face with his chilly hands. "May I kiss you?"

Shock painted her features, but she smiled. "I would love that, if our Seer doesn't mind."

Aini pushed them closer gently, then slipped away.

Bran pressed his lips to Viola's and he was flying, floating, on a cloud, a star—all of that romantic nonsense suddenly wasn't so daft. This is what people meant when they used those wild phrases and silly terms. With every sweep of her mouth on his, every touch of her fingers at the back of his neck, he was undone and soaring.

Myles's clapping slowly brought Bran back to earth. "This has been such a fine day, folks. Too bad those two-faced, donkey—"

"Myles." Thane glared, then nodded toward Senga and Aini. "Please."

"Oh yes. Thane Campbell, the gentleman with the dark past, has returned and thou shalt not be coarse around the women of his heart." Myles put a hand to the side of his mouth. "He doesn't realize they love all my creative comments." He cleared his throat and took on the nasal tone of a noble. "What I was trying to say was: too bad those less-than-lovely gentlemen are here to ruin the mood." He pointed to the cave entrance.

Nathair and his gray-garbed corbies stood in the dying sunlight, arguing with a mess of rebel guards.

Bran's hands fell away from Viola. She grabbed them and curled her fingers around his. "I'm glad we settled this, then," he said to Viola. "I'll be back for more of you, if you like, after I speak to these two-faced donkey arses."

"I was not going to say arse," Myles corrected.

Neve smacked the back of Myles's head.

Viola squeezed Bran's hands once, then released him. Bran followed his Heir and Seer to the mouth of the cave. It was time to befriend his demons so his friends could beat the Devil.

# CHAPTER 17
# THE WORLD BURNS BRIGHT

Thane felt like a faded version of himself as he walked into the light to meet Nathair and Jack and all their hired hands. At least he had the power of his friends. Aini's glare might end up melting someone's face clean off so there was that. Vera, Owen, and Dodie looked to have grown a foot since their reunion—a family unit, strong and ready again. Bran was steady as the tides, urging Thane to keep on. They would have to talk about Viola very soon. When they weren't busy trying to overthrow every government in their paths. Myles and Neve walked hand-in-hand, faces stoic, not a trace of fear showing.

Aini nudged Thane. "I'm going to rattle them up a little, okay?" She eyed Nathair.

"What? Uh, sure?" What was she planning?

"Also," she whispered, "when this is all through, we will pick up where we left off in Nathair's office." She grinned, cheeks red.

Thane hadn't thought it possible to be roused in the middle of an extremely stressful situation, but Aini proved him wrong over and over again. "Aye, that we will." He gave a look that he hoped told her how much he cared for her and looked forward to that moment, then he pushed those lovely thoughts to the back of his mind and focused on the task at hand.

The two factions of the rebel force lined up across from one another.

No one spoke.

Nathair wore that smirk Thane knew Aini hated. Thane just thought of it as Nathair's face. His hate ran so deeply, he couldn't properly process Nathair's expressions. Jack looked bored. Thane truly wanted to punch him. A lot.

Myles eyed Thane, then Nathair. "So are we going to play Red Rover, Red Rover here or are we planning a king's death? I'm up for either one, really."

Neve had gone a bit pale. "Did you know the origins of that game—sometimes called Octopus Tag or British Bulldogs—is unknown. There is a Norwegian word that sounds like *Rover* which means *robber* and that an argument with that country may have—"

Nathair cleared his throat loudly and stepped forward. "It gives me great pleasure to see us all here like this. No guns. No fanfare. Just Scots and a few Brits joined together to fight injustice and raise my son, the Heir, to Scotland's long forgotten throne."

"And colonials!" Myles waved.

Thane knew he should've wanted Myles and Neve to keep quiet for their own well-bring, but he couldn't want that. It was wonderful listening to their dafty humor and misplaced historical tidbits. For a while, with Nathair twisting him up and Jackie beating him down, Thane had thought he might never hear their voices again.

Aini might've felt the same, but she erred on the side of

caution and gave Myles and Neve a decidedly Aini-style, schoolmaster look that clearly said *Shut it, darlings.*

Nathair walked toward Myles and extended his hand. Myles shook it, but when Nathair rotated a fraction, Myles wiped his hand on his trousers.

"He is right to bring up the colonials," Nathair said. "It is my belief that this man's mother—a powerful woman in the colonies—sold her cotton plantation and joined with a number of other wealthy colonials who would benefit from the fall of King John in Scotland. She sent a vast sum to us, and we used the monies to buy off more of John's men, to purchase rocket launchers from a quiet source not far from our coast, and to fully stock Edinburgh for a siege if it should come to that. Our local farmers and those beyond this region have been fully paid for their produce and meat. The colonial support is a huge factor in our strategy, as is the quiet support of the French."

All the joking had left Myles's face. He looked like he'd tasted something bitter and was rubbing his stomach. Nathair's news had pure given him the boak.

"Myles's mother gave up her foul business there?" Thane knew it would matter to Myles if she'd stopped running her plantation with hired men and women who were treated little better than slaves.

"Aye," Nathair said. "It's to become part of a conglomerate with minimum wage held up since it's now a public company."

It was surprising Nathair took the time to explain that. Thane took the offered olive branch of peace. "Good. Myles should have a request granted since his existence offered so much aid to the cause."

Myles blinked. "Me? Uh. Okay."

Nathair whispered in Jack's ear, but they didn't interrupt Myles.

"I, uh, I request..." Myles rubbed his hands and he looked a little green. "...that our Heir and Seer are never again separated from one another or from a Dionadair leader such as Vera or Owen."

Thane smiled. A fine demand.

Nathair's jaw tensed. Jack's men weren't holding guns, but they definitely had them stowed within reach, tucked into their waistbands under those coats of theirs. Nathair could give the order to kill them all with one word. Of course, the rebels here had guns too and the whole thing would end up as a mess of death if a gunfight broke out, so hopefully Nathair would keep a tight hold on the reins of his temper.

Thane's pulse rate increased like he'd eaten a speed caramel. The muscles in his arms and legs twitched with the need to fight. Aini traded a heavy look with him. She looked at the purple of the sunset, then at an empty space beside Jack.

"Now," she whispered, so, so quietly.

A tiny grin tugged at one side of her gorgeous lips as Nathair's hair blew back. Jack startled as a wind rose. Nathair lunged back, and Jack's hand went to the gun Thane had guessed was hiding there.

"No guns, now, Jackie," Thane hissed, coming up at his right.

Owen nodded at some of the Dionadair and Thane heard the click of guns readied.

"What was that?" Nathair eyed the air around him, lips pale.

Thane didn't think he wasn't talking about guns. Aini had done something with her sixth sense.

Jack crossed himself and spit on the ground. "Ghosts. That was a mess of ghosts."

Viola wiggled her eyebrows at Aini, who winked. Bran covered a laugh with a cough.

"Fine." Nathair dusted his jacket off like the spirits had left some of themselves on him. "Fine. We agree to the colonial's request."

Thane thought of something though. If he and Aini and a Dionadair leader were in the same place at the end of the battle—win or lose—Nathair could easily take them all out. If they weren't looking or were injured or distracted. "I have an addendum to this request. It is non-negotiable."

"Oh aye?" Some of Nathair's old swagger returned.

Aini touched the Coronation Stone necklace at her throat and put a hand on Thane's shoulder. Good girl.

"I mean," Nathair sputtered, "of course. As you will it, my Heir."

Thane fought an eye roll. "You and Jack both will be at our sides too. The entire time. If you wander off, your lives are forfeit."

That would keep them from bombing the stars out of wherever Thane, Aini, and the Dionadair leaders were fighting if Nathair decided it was in his best interest to off them. Surely the curse would keep Thane and Aini safe, but it hadn't behaved like they'd originally believed, so this was insurance.

A shout came from the forest that led to Edinburgh. "They're here. The king's nearly here!"

Thane dragged Aini to him on instinct. She gripped his jacket and whispered a prayer.

A Dionadair scout Thane had met at the safe house in Greenock ran up to Vera and Owen. "I saw a line of military vehicles north of Berwick and trailed them, tracking and checking their pace. I tried to tune my radio to their signal. I managed to hear them talk of a quick attack on Edinburgh to squash the rebellion before the French hit the coast to the south."

"Nice work, man." Owen gripped the scout's shoulder.

Jack and Nathair traded words and two of their men hurried away.

Nathair raised his head. "It seems we have no more time for talk except for those details that are immediately necessary. I need your plans so we can tie ours into them and do the best we can with what we have."

Inside the cave, Aini went over the strategy. Jack added comments and suggestions along the way, and with Owen and Vera's final polish, Thane felt as good as a person could about rising up against one of the most powerful men in the world.

Vera slid around the gathering and pulled Thane into a relatively private spot between two carved-out rooms. "Our other scout reported back too. Do you know who takes over if we shove John into the dirt where he belongs?"

"His daughter?"

"Aye. And she met with our scout."

"What? You can't keep this kind of thing to yourself."

"I didn't think the wee thing would even get an audience. He posed as a tech genius ready to bring the royal company into the next age. I thought it was a daft thing to try, honestly. But it worked so here I am telling you now, my Heir."

Thane gave her a look, knowing there was a hint of attitude hiding inside her words. Vera respected Thane and Aini as Heir and Seer, but she also knew them as friends and human beings who were fallible. It probably wasn't a bad thing that she worked around them from time to time. But this was Vera. Her plans went from a bit risky to downright bananas in a blink.

"So what did this dafty, secret agent find out?" Thane glanced at General Aini over there, pointing and making lists to her heart's content. The candlelight gleamed over her dark hair and in her wide eyes. No one spoke over her. None would dare. She was magnificent.

Vera snapped at Thane's nose. "Over here, lover. Focus. Now, John's heir—Elizabeth—said she wants nothing to do with war. She signed a pact with our agent."

"No." That would be amazing news.

Vera unrolled a tiny sheet of fine paper. The calligraphy showed a peace agreement between Elizabeth, Heir to the British Empire, and Aini MacGregor and Thane Campbell, MacBeth's Seer and Heir to the Scottish throne respectively.

Thane's heart beat fast in his chest. "This says she'll call off the war here and in France. That she doesn't want our country or French land either." He put a hand to his head, shocked.

"Why do you think the French are being so supportive?"

"I'd thought it was only because we provided a nice distraction while they made their next move in Calais."

"If we assassinate John, the French will get everything they want and they won't be in trouble with the United World Federation. No embargoes for assassinating a leader. No fees or reprimands. If we keep their support secret and we, as rebels, do their dirty work, it'll be roses all day long for our old friends." Vera dusted her hands like it was all said and done.

Across the room, Aini leaned over a map Nathair had spread over the long table in the center of the cave's main room.

"This is the weakest spot in Edinburgh's city walls." Nathair jabbed a finger on the map. "The old part of the Flodden Wall in Greyfriars Kirkyard."

Aini's voice carried across the room's damp rock. "But we have Talfer's Wall beyond that over in that direction, right?"

"Right." Thane rubbed his lip. An idea sprouted in his brain. "Aini and I will sneak into King John's camp. We will take him out. The fact that we publicly announced we would stick with Nathair and Jack is actually perfect. Not for the reason I originally suggested, but for a new reason. We'll dress in dark, hooded clothing and dress another two the same, sending them with Nathair and Jack. Our people will gravitate toward the two they believe are their Seer and Heir and it will distract from what we're up to. Plus, if we have any information leaks, this at least will remain secret."

Vera shook her head and some of her hair fell out of its pins. "It's the most dangerous mission though. Why would I let my two most valuable people head right into the lion's mouth?"

"Because we are prepared for it. And no one else is. It will take supernatural means to take down John. He'll be surrounded by very loyal guards—the core group who will give their lives to protect him. This is how we will use the curse. If it works..."

"It will." Vera thumped a fist against her chest.

He nodded, wishing he felt as sure. "It will. And you can bet Aini won't let anyone else take this risk. It'll be her or no one."

Vera grinned in Aini's direction. "It's true. She's become everything my brothers and I ever dreamt of."

"Aini?" Thane raised a hand.

Aini's forehead wrinkled as she moved to see him better. He waved her over. She said something to Jack, a fierce loathing clear in her look, then pushed past him to get to Thane.

"Vera here," Thane said when Aini walked up, "just told me something very interesting and I think we should consider a new plan."

A wrinkle appeared between her eyebrows. "Why don't you tell the group?"

"This is going to be a very secret plan no one knows about except Vera, Owen, you, and me."

He explained everything.

She tapped a foot on the ground, gaze roaming. "Okay. Okay. But we have to include Myles, Neve, and Bran."

"Why?"

"There is no way they'd let us go off without them. Plus, the colonial group who sent the funds has a mole in John's inner circle. Myles can be the contact for that mole and we can use the help when we get inside his camp. Jack just told us about the woman."

"I don't trust him." Vera glared toward the group.

"I don't either, but why would he lie?"

"For the fun of it," Vera said.

Thane didn't trust Jack Shaw any further than he could throw him, but Aini was making good sense. "So there is a man inside John's camp that supports us. A colonial contact."

"Yes." Aini chewed the inside of her cheek, always thinking, planning.

"He can help us infiltrate the camp possibly." Thane let out a breath. That was a good thing. Hopefully. Unless Jack was lying. "So we head into Edinburgh proper with the rest of the forces, but at the walls, our small unit breaks from the rest secretly. We head wherever John sets up his little court. Do we have this contact's name or number?"

"They call him Walker. His family has a stake in this new conglomerate Myles's mother created. He is a lowland Scot. Not an Englishman."

"Small blessings." Vera snorted.

Aini almost smiled. "Nathair believes the king will begin a basic siege. No food or goods into the city. Make the city sweat and hope we give up."

"I don't know." Thane pictured all those French ships in the channel. "He'll be pressured to get this over with quick. He has another war going on."

"Why would he waste money on cannon and ammo if he can simply scare the place into submission by starving the place for a few days?" Aini said.

Thane shrugged, a chill going through him. "I don't know. It's just what I'm feeling."

Aini touched his arm, and an electric warmth replaced the shiver. "Did you Dream it?"

"No. No, I didn't. But I want us to be prepared if this thing doesn't start quietly. All right?"

Vera pinched Thane's cheek. "Smart and gorgeous."

Aini lightly slapped her fingers away. "Respect your Heir."

Vera laughed as she sauntered away. "Oh I respect him. I respect him every night in my own kind of dream."

Smile slipping, Aini started toward Vera, but Thane held her back. "Hen. Save it for the fight. The real fight."

Shrugging his hold off, Aini grinned. "Fine. But I'm the only one who gets to dream about you, okay?" Her gaze burned its way from his toes to his head and he felt every fiery inch of its intent.

Body humming, he pressed her gently against the cave wall. Her chest moved in time with his. "Okay," he said in his best colonial accent.

She broke into laughter. "That was terrible."

"Oh shut your gob or I'll shut it for you."

With a smirk, she leaned close. Her lips met his. They were warm and soft and lovely and absolutely made Thane so glad they had this one moment before the worst came crashing down.

His hand found the small of her back and he pulled her to him. She smelled like coconut shampoo and salt. The feel of her breath on his neck and her fingers climbing his back worked his heart into a bit of frenzy.

"Aini. Let's find a quiet spot, aye?"

While the rest of the rebels gathered weapons and broke into units for their instructions, Thane led Aini down a carved-out passageway and into a room with low benches chipped from the walls. Three tall candles lit the space and a small table held maps of Edinburgh. It must've been where some of the elders met earlier.

Aini didn't wait for Thane to start the kissing again. She held his head between her hands and dusted her lips over his. A feeling like electricity sizzled down his middle. He lowered her onto a bench. With her body flush against his, all the fatigue and stress flew away in a rush.

He dropped a kiss behind her ear and eased his weight onto her. She moaned lightly and he whispered her name. "You're all right with this?"

"Yes." Her eyes blazed. She drew her fingers across his forehead, then along his jawline. A sudden smile broke over her face. "Do you see our light?" Her gaze went from his head to her own fingers, their breath mingling. "Our auras are mixing. Your blue. My blue. It's dark, but somehow illuminated. It's beautiful."

"I can't see it. But what I do see is you, and that is more than enough."

She locked eyes with him, and suddenly he acutely felt the limited amount of time before they had to leave. He wanted to enjoy every breath he had in this room with her.

He jerked her weapons belt off and set it on the ground. Kissing her throat, he felt her body soft under his, rising and falling. He shifted to run his mouth across the fragile skin over her chest. With trembling fingers, she unpinned his tartan and helped him rip his jacket off. Shirt mostly unbuttoned, he lifted her with one hand and helped her remove her jacket too. As smoothly as he could, he fell onto her and she ran her warm hands under his shirt, along the waistband of his kilt. He shivered hard. Her fingers danced over the muscles in his lower back, urging him to come closer. He couldn't seem to catch his breath, but he didn't care one bit.

"Thane Campbell, I love you."

"And I you, Aini MacGregor."

She leaned forward to press her mouth to his chest and her hips moved under his and all the blood ran away from his head, making him dizzy. He pressed against her, and she exhaled in his ear and ran a greedy hand over his thigh, knocking up his kilt a bit. Sparks lit down his legs and back up again. He couldn't get enough of her taste, scent, skin, her soul. It was like they'd starved for one another their entire lives. The room buzzed with their power and suddenly a light glanced off the walls. It was them. Their magic blending. Thane couldn't tell where one of them ended and the other began. Her joy was his joy and only now did Thane realize the strength of the physical demonstration of a soul-filling, true love. No one could defeat this, break this apart, ruin this power they had together. No one.

## CHAPTER 18
## TO THE SKY

❦

Dressed in her clothing for the night's operation—dark trousers, suspenders, a charcoal shirt, and a hooded cloak someone had made—Aini lined up her fellow Ghost Talkers and handed out Cone5 taffy. "Keep some on you at all times. First thing when you see a spirit, you must question them."

A woman in green and blue raised a hand. "We'll actually be able to see them like you do? Like when they choose to be seen, or even if they don't want to be seen? Even though you're the Seer? That's not a special thing?"

She smiled, trying to be patient. "I think they still have to want to be seen for any of it to work. But with the taffy, if they choose to be...physically present, you'll see them quite clearly. It's not a Seer thing. It's a Cone5 thing. You'll see other colors too and not just on the ghosts. You'll see energy and energy imprints all around you. It can be distracting, so you must do your best to focus on the task at hand."

There were whispers and traded looks of worry.

Aini walked calmly around the group, listing the steps they had to take to be the integral part of this battle she knew they could be.

"Now, ask the spirits politely if they know what is happening with King John. If they are a weaker ghost, they may not have any idea about the goings-on in the present time. They may be stuck in their own memories. Be gentle with them. Don't make them angry and don't tell them any details about our strategies, positions in the city, or allies until you feel strongly they are supportive to our cause. Although we all know John kills any sixth-senser he finds, there may well be some hiding in his ranks. There is always the possibility that some ghosts may support the king and England. You can also draw on their clothing, the sounds you hear when you see them, and perhaps their shackles or cage." She told them about Bathilda and Lady Margaret.

"If you find some willing spirits, see if they can shake up the enemy camp. They can send a chill down a back and make a finger miss a trigger. Some may be able to even bump a soldier or throw one off with a strong gust of the wind they seem able to summon. We can ask them to keep John's men up at night with that deeply cold air they hold around them. They can whisper to those who can hear, but pretend not to. Anything they can do to give us an edge is great."

"Time to go." Bran and his explosives team joined the Ghost Talker group.

Aini gave the gathered men and women a nod and what she hoped was an encouraging smile. Her own stomach was flipping unpleasantly, and it most likely showed on her face, but Neve and Vera and Myles—standing at the sidelines—looked positive enough so she guessed she'd done the job all right.

Thane joined her at the mouth of the cave, dressed similarly to her. He held out his arm, looking every inch a king in that medieval-looking cloak. The stars breaking through the clouds glimmered over high cheekbones and proud nose. His serious gray eyes regarded her with a confidence she could lean in to.

"You truly believe we can do this, don't you?" she asked.

"Strangely enough, I do."

She took his arm, and after checking she had Macbeth's knife, the brooch, and a revolver securely in her belt, she accompanied him to a flatbed truck where the rest of their group waited.

All the rebels loaded into some type of vehicle—lorries, cars, and some motorbikes. It was a managed sort of chaos and the air was ripe with fear. John was closing in and they needed to get inside the city walls for protection or they'd be taken down before they had a chance to defend Edinburgh.

JUST PAST AN OLD GATE INTO THE CITY, AINI HOPPED FROM the back of the truck. Thane, Myles, Neve, Bran, and Vera followed, each of them still chewing their strength chocolate. Owen had told them about an old secret passage through Telfer's Wall. They'd found it on a crumbling map and sketched out a route without letting anyone outside their little group hear a word about it.

For now though, Aini's boots pounded the cobblestones and smacked through wet grass as the group traveled the route Nathair and Owen had decided on for the larger group, the unit they pretended they would stay with. The night grew darker, the dove-white moon struggling to be seen through black, talon-shaped clouds.

"Now," Aini whispered, eating another piece of Cone5 taffy.

She and the others broke off from the main assembly as a shout erupted from the city walls. Two kingsmen had climbed the wall, early to the fight. Maybe scouts. But now they'd been spotted.

The unit following Jack's commands—coming up just beside the large unit—had eaten speed caramels. Five of them ran at King John's men and had them down before Aini could cross the next street.

The Ghost Talker group moved like cats, skulking through Old Town and toward the secondary headquarters that Senga and Lewis were running. Sprits swirled around the team in streams of red, green, ocean blue, and sparkling white. Aini said a silent prayer for them.

The moon—shades of silver, pearl, and the palest pink—beat back the wispy clouds. The time-worn road glistened, weaving through rented flats, stores, and petrol pumps. The city was oddly silent, and the hairs on Aini's arms lifted. Ice filled her stomach. A cat screeched and toppled a rubbish bin in an alley. She jumped and heard Myles yelp behind her. Thane started to whisper something as they ran, but a blast shook the ground. Smoke rose like a lost cloak in the wind beyond the walls. Fear grabbed Aini's throat.

John had arrived.

A volley of gunfire rattled against the city walls. A voice called out over a speaker.

"Surrender now, rebels, and you might be allowed to live. Send someone out with a white flag."

It wasn't John's voice. What if he didn't come here at all? What if he sent his generals to fight this battle? If he wasn't here and they couldn't attempt to take him down, this whole plan would go awry.

Thane's hand warmed Aini's back as they shuffled through a tight passage between buildings. She saw Bran's dark eyes over his shoulder. Moss fell from the old bricks onto Aini's dirty fingernails as she braced herself to keep from slipping. The scent of mud and sulfur strangled the night's cold breath.

They couldn't be too far from the spot in the walls where the secret passage hid. It had to be just around the corner. But would they make it in time?

Shouts and another blast sounded toward Edinburgh Castle. Then another on the far side of the Royal Mile, near Holyrood.

A smoking haze filled Aini's nose, acrid and terrifying. This was war.

Thane and the rest on her heels, she jumped over a tangled mess of wires and a metal box that was probably once a public telephone box. Rushing past a gaping hole in the city wall, she caught a glimpse of dark clouds rolling along faraway hills and the flash of gunfire.

A blast sounded above. Aini's ears rang. Thane shouted behind her and Myles called out. A deep crack echoed from the stone building to Aini's right, and she twisted to look up awkwardly as she ran. From the building's top edge, stones tumbled down and hit the first window ledge, then the ground between her and Thane.

"Aini!" Thane was suddenly beside her and pulling her out of the way.

The foundation rumbled, and the whole place began tearing apart. Myles, Vera, and Neve were going to be buried.

"Stop. Go back!" She held her hands out, waving, trying to get their attention amid the artillery noise.

The entire building collapsed into a heap and foul dust mushroomed into the air. Neve's wide brown eyes was the last thing she saw as the debris clogged Aini's vision and her throat too. She coughed and tried to shout for Neve.

Thane gripped her and hugged her tight. "They're all right. Just stuck on the other side of this. Should we go around?"

Aini didn't bother answering, she just took off in the direction he'd indicated. A dying street lamp flickered through the clouds of dust.

"We're here. Over here." Neve was coughing and running through the polluted air.

Aini caught her in a quick, fierce hug, feeling her friend's heart beat against her own for a blessed moment. Myles and Vera appeared too. A thick line of blood ran through the dust on Vera's face.

"It's just a cut," she said, noticing Aini's worry. But Vera stumbled over a rock and Myles caught her arm.

"Just a cut, my rear end." Aini smoothed Vera's hair away from the injury. Blood pooled over her fingers and Vera made a little hissing noise.

"Such language, Seer," Myles said.

Thane and Bran cleared away one of the larger chunks of rubble so Vera could have a small place to sit. Neve gave Vera a sip from her canteen.

Aini scanned the courtyard. A sea-green plume of energy drifted by.

But Aini struggled to focus. The buzzing in her ears and the effects of the taffy were disorienting. The blood on Vera wasn't simply red. It had a thousand shades to it and Aini fought to stop staring and focus on the task at hand.

Finding a ghost.

Another column of what she was beginning to think of as "spirit smoke" curled high above the fallen building, high enough to blend in with the rubble's dust if one wasn't a Ghost Talker who'd eaten the taffy. The spirit's smoke was a dusky pink and had the same other unnameable color to it that the ghost from Callum's hometown had possessed.

"Please, could you help me?" she asked the spirit.

The slightly transparent man zipped over, bringing a vicious chill with him. "This is a terrible thing, this war in my city."

The blue-white shades of his light grew stronger. Everyone around Aini gasped as he made himself visible to all, Ghost Talkers and those with no sixth sense.

"It is," Aini said. "Can you give me some of your energy and help me heal this woman?"

"Can I do that?"

"I think maybe you can do it through me."

"Just tell me what to do," the spirit said, words drifting like leaves in water. "She has a lot of energy herself. Surprised anyone could hurt one like that, Seer."

Adjusting Vera in Myles's arms, Aini coughed at the smell of gunpowder and blood.

Neve edged closer. "I can see him. Just barely. Ask him if he knows who you are."

"I'm dead not stupid," the spirit said.

Aini cut her eyes to Neve, a wry grin tugging at her lips. "He knows."

"We need to move, Aini." Thane's aura flashed blue and gold as he watched the distant fighting under the moon's watery light. He looked very kingly. More so every minute.

The boom of heavy artillery shook the city. Nathair and Jack were firing back with French weapons. Never in her life did Aini think she'd be on the side of men like that. She swallowed bile and took a breath.

"Yes, we do. Just a minute," she said to Thane. They had to take a minute or Vera was going to die of blood loss before she could even have a chance to die of infection.

Aini took the ghost's hand—well, she entwined her fingers in the wispy memory of flesh and bone—then moved it to her shoulder. "Try imagining a light and a warmth flowing from you to me."

The ghost pulled his hand back. "I can't do this. I haven't felt warmth since my death."

"You can do this. I've done it with other spirits. One named Bathilda. Trust me."

Nodding tentatively, the ghost set his hand on her shoulder. Immediately a wave of that strange cold-hot sensation she'd felt when Bathilda healed her gunshot wound flowed through her body. She closed her eyes and envisioned the flesh knitting together as Bathilda had taught. A bright white light glowed behind her eyelids and she imagined it floating from her shoulder, through her own core, then into Vera. The scent of sage permeated the cold.

Vera gasped.

Aini blinked her eyes open. "Feel any better?"

The wound had closed. Crusted blood marred the area and Vera winced as she touched it, but then she smiled. The ghost flitted above their heads in a cloud of blue-green as he eyed Vera curiously. Bran, Vera, Myles, and Neve whispered together, Bran guarding the group with his gun. The side of Thane's mouth lifted and he brushed Aini's hand with his.

"It worked, my Seer." Vera stood on her own. She looked to the East. A Saltire flapped in the icy wind above a row of shops that leaked black smoke. "Now, let's get going."

The moon peered between the clouds and lit the path in front of them. Stones, dust, and rubbish all of kinds—torn paper, dropped plastic cups, even a child's dirty sweater—littered the ground. Aini lifted her hood and led them over the debris and back toward the opening in the Flodden Wall. They followed her like silent shadows, the spirits of long-dead Scots trailing the party in shimmering streams of blue, white, pink, and green.

She glanced at the spirits as they ran. "Please don't make yourself visible. It will give away our position."

Several nodded and their colors dulled. Nearly all became invisible.

In Greyfriars kirkyard, the old city wall held true all along its original lines, except for one spot where a hole the size of a car gaped wide. The whole place smelled sickly sweet. Aini crossed through, very glad the moon was shrouded for the moment. Thane moved past her, holding his gun ready and watching their right as Bran kept an eye on their left. Vera and Neve rushed between them, then hurried to catch up with Aini who was already climbing the small hill that hid a secret passageway through the Telfer Wall. At the top of the rise, Aini looked back to see the giant Saltire flag—the rebel's symbol—flutter down and out of sight. Screams pealed from distant streets.

They were losing the fight.

If John won this, he would put every single one of them to death. Thane. Neve. Myles. Bran. Vera. Forcing panic down, Aini slipped down the hill and found the rectangle of rusted metal, about three feet long, that lined the bottom of the wall.

"Here." Aini knelt on the wet grass and mud, and pulled at the metal's lip. It creaked and cracked, but wouldn't open.

"Owen said there might be a lock somewhere." Vera bent down and pushed the growth away from the metal, searching.

Aini blindly ran her fingers over the cold, flaking rust, then a vision swept her away in a tide of fear.

*They're coming. They'll know.*

*A woman—circled in the bright hue of an emotion that could only be called abject horror—crouched beside the wall. Her fingers were black. She shivered and lost hold of her shawl. A dog barked far off and she jumped. Voices came and her world dropped into nothing.*

Aini panted as the vision slid off her mind.

Thane grabbed her and forced her into a flat position on the ground. His mouth rested on her ear. "I'm sorry. Quiet now."

Everyone else was lying down too. What was going on?

A group of kingsmen wearing the king's personal seal poured over the wall and into Edinburgh, taking off at a run.

When they were gone, Aini sat up and realized the group had opened the lock and the secret passage while she was seeing the vision of that poor diseased woman. She'd been a plague victim. A shudder tried to keep Aini from crawling through the passage behind Thane, but she fought it and won, coming up on King John's side of the wall to join the rest.

Moonlight reflected off the wet ground in Edinburgh's outer villages and streets. But one dark, square shape blotted the light. It was a large military tent.

"He's there. It has to be him."

Aini felt the familiar surge of anger the king's presence always brought out in her. The man who had killed so many innocents. Taken mothers from sons. Fathers from daughters. Sisters from brothers. He taxed the people to the point where they had to choose who would eat and who would die. John ripped lives apart to keep his hands on the crown and his pockets full of gold. He used his birthright to step on Scotland's neck, to abuse and take, take, take. Because of him, Nathair had gained power and taken her father's finger and nearly his life.

She couldn't wait to shove John's face in the dirt right where it belonged.

With so many soldiers and military vehicles surrounding the place, it was impossible to see which path to the king's tent was the least dangerous.

A massive oak towered beside Thane and covered him in darkness the stars couldn't touch. If she could climb it, she could see the camp's layout and find a way to John. But none of the limbs were less than ten feet off the ground. With a gravity-reducing hard candy, she could reach the high shadows of the oak and see the enemy in whole and find a way to infiltrate John's tent. She opened one of her inner pockets and took out one of the lavender flavored sweets.

"What are you doing?" Thane grabbed her wrist, his gray eyes flashing and his aura beaming.

"If I get up high in those branches, I can see which is the best way to do this, to get into John's tent."

"You already ate the taffy. This," he took the candy and held it up, "could kill you."

"Mixing stuff made me puke my brains out at the safe house, remember?" Myles said.

"Can't we just climb it?" Neve asked.

Vera was already trying and getting nowhere. She stepped back and cocked her gun at the tree.

"No," Neve hissed, grabbing her wrist. "Keep your head. Don't get wild."

Vera snorted and put the gun away. "Little spit telling a woman raised in the Dionadair to keep her wits in the heat of battle. Let me just tell you that if we don't get *wild* right now, none of us are going to live long enough to get *anything* ever again."

Myles stood between them, a hand on each. "I don't know what you meant for sure there, Vera, but I feel you. What do we do, Bran? You seem to have good ideas about things."

"I was going to suggest I take the hard candy because all I took was the strength chocolate and I don't think it really works too well on me anyway plus I'm expendable."

"You are not expendable." Thane shoved him hard.

Bran almost smiled and Aini wanted to cry and scream at the unfairness of the world at large. "No, Bran," Aini said. "I love you for being the brave man you are, but no one has worked with the gravity-reducing stuff like I have. It's not easy to use. You could end up on the moon for all we know."

Thane raised his eyebrows. "I don't think that's possible. The ratio of—"

"Shhhh." Vera put a finger to Thane's lips, and he nodded, sighing and rubbing his hands through his hair.

Aini watched the spirits around them. They were nothing more than a shimmer here and a curl of smoke there, but many were present. She could sense them as clearly as her own arms and legs.

"I'm not going to die. And if I start having trouble, the ghosts will help me live through it. I am the Seer after all."

Thane's jaw tensed, and he gripped the candy so hard that his bones pressed against the skin on his knuckles. "After all of this, I can't lose you."

He crossed the wet earth and put his forehead against hers. A hot electricity snapped between them and the Coronation Stone necklace resting on his shirt neck hummed so loudly that it almost hurt Aini's ears. She placed a kiss on each of his closed eyelids. He tasted like magic.

"You won't lose me. I can do this."

He swallowed, then handed the candy over. It was sticky from his palm. She chewed it quickly, the lavender-sugar taste rocketing over her tongue. It took effect faster than she'd guessed. Her head felt like as a bag of feathers, and a tingling sensation bloomed between and above her eyes.

Thane watched her closely. "You all right?"

She nodded, then as the chemicals took hold, she focused on the highest branch of the tree. Drawing on an invisible, imaginary line between her and the oak's limb, she pushed out from that tingling spot between her eyebrows. She began to fly.

The night air streamed over her cheeks and a tickle danced through her stomach as she rose. Thane's fingers trailed away from her boot as she cleared his head. Her toes brushed one of the lower branches and a clutch of leaves snagged her sleeve. She untangled it, her height slipping a bit.

"You all right, sweetheart?" Myles whispered, leaning into the trunk and looking up.

"Good. I'm good."

Focusing, heart pounding, she floated higher, higher, higher. Thane and Neve were nothing more than small areas of shadow. Myles had completely disappeared under the cover of leaves beneath Aini's feet and only the side of Vera's red mouth was visible in a patch of moonlight. Bran hooked his thumbs in his weapons belt, looking grim.

Aini found the limb she'd been aiming for and landed light as a bird. The leaves touched the back of her hand and one had managed to tangle itself in her hair. She left it where it was, studying the landscape laid out like a living map below her. The night's silver glow showed a solid unit of kingsmen with guns ready on three sides of King John's personal tent. Milky, electric illumination leaked from the canvas walls and the silhouettes of more than five people shifted inside. Aini squinted at the seemingly unguarded back entrance. There were shapes in the dark...something with wide plates of metal and...

A chill ran over Aini's back.

"Flyers," she whispered to herself.

If her eyes weren't deceiving her, there were only two. But the night swallowed the rest of the field in that direction, outbuildings and a rise of land blocking the moon's efforts. Using the power of the hard candy, she skipped over some smaller tree branches attached to the limb and hooked a boot around the tree's very last little arm, straining to see. She wished she could call on a spirit to discover how many flyers there were and whether or not any pilots were readying them for takeoff. But if she asked for assistance, a ghost might make itself visible and draw a kingman's attention her way. Doubtful, but possible. And she wasn't out of range for some of those guns in their hands.

Leaving the lofty heights of the old tree, Aini locked eyes with Thane and drew herself down into his arms.

He hugged her tight and quick. "I like it when you're here. Right here." His heart hammered wildly against her cheek before she pulled away.

Bran glanced in the direction of the city, and Aini had the suspicion he was thinking of Viola.

Aini touched Thane's cheek briefly, soaking up the look in his stormy eyes. "Me too. I have bad news."

Neve gathered the group up close to the tree trunk like a mother hen. "What is it?" She nibbled her bottom lip and stood a fraction closer to Myles. Myles's throat moved in a nervous swallow.

"Flyers."

Thane's eyes shuttered closed. "I knew they'd bring them. I just knew it."

"I wonder why they are still grounded?" Bran frowned.

Vera held up her hands. "We need to get into that tent and take King John down before they do deploy those nasty birds. We need to take the wind out of this attack before it has a chance to really get going."

Myles snorted. "I'd say it's already going pretty strong." There was zero humor in his voice as he looked back at the smoke flying from Edinburgh like black pennants. A scream and two blasts punctuated the air.

Bran stared at the ground.

Thane put an arm around him for a second, then dropped back. "She's strong. She'll fight hard."

He was talking about his half-sister, Viola.

Aini suddenly ached for a time when she could talk to Viola and take her to the market for spices with Neve and Myles while Bran and Thane played poker at some terrible pub. She saw a flash of sunlight and heard laughter. Pain thrashed across her chest because it was only a wish, and there was little to no chance they would all survive this and experience a day like that.

"The side where the flyers are seems unguarded. I'm sure there are kingsmen there somewhere, but maybe because it faces away from the city, they have a setup we could infiltrate. I'm going to send some spirits out front for a diversion and ask one to check the back and report to us. I say we go ahead and run that way, sticking to the shadows, and see if we can slip in."

"Spirits, if you are here, please stay hidden, but please listen. Bathilda, I would love to know if you are here." Aini pressed herself to the tree trunk, on the side away from the king's camp.

The temperature dropped, and Myles shivered. The air twinkled around the group and a haze of blue-green spirit smoke fizzled in and out of view.

"I am here, Seer." It was Bathilda.

Aini sighed in relief. "I'm so glad to hear your voice. Would you go around the back of the king's tent over there and see if there are guards there? I'm headed that way regardless, so just let me know what you see, please." She faced the other shimmering shadows floating beside her. She felt like a ghost herself, half hidden in the tree's dark domain and her feet a good five inches off the ground because of the candy. Dizziness swept over her and she gripped her head.

"Seer?" Vera took her elbow.

"It's that double dose of candy." Thane's voice was sharp. "Aini. Talk to us. What are you feeling?"

She blinked up at him and the world tipped to the side. He took her in his arms. "I'm taking you back. We can regroup. I'll... I'll think of something."

She pushed away from the lovely warmth of his body. "No. It's just some lightheadedness. It's already fading. Bathilda?"

Just Bathilda's face emerged from the lightly shimmering air. "Seer?"

"A little help?"

Bathilda's hands materialized on Aini's shoulders, then the spirit looked back at another ghost. "You too, Liam. Place your hands on my back. Thank you."

Heat flooded through Aini's body like she'd stepped into a hot bath. It was wonderful. She let out a sigh as the weakness left her completely. She broke away from Bathilda.

"Thank you. That's enough. I don't want you to use all your strength. I need you now. I need all of you," she said to the night and all the spirits crowding the spot beneath the ancient tree. "Do what you can to attack the kingsmen around the tent with cold, wind—anything you can do. Disrupt their weapons if you are capable."

She didn't bother asking who was on her side. The respect these spirits sent toward her, their energy, their presence, it was as clear as a resounding *We are here for you*. She wondered if the rest of the Ghost Talkers were having similar experiences inside the city.

"Go now, please." She unsheathed MacBeth's knife and held it high. "I am your Seer and I will do all that I can to see your grievances laid to rest with the death of this horrible king and the reinstitution of a Scottish government that cares for its people and those who love its land."

"We will go, Seer," Bathilda whispered reverently. She inclined her head, the bars of her eternal sixth-senser cage just barely visible, then blinked into nothing.

The night warmed a fraction as the ghosts sped away.

Thane's eyes flashed as his fingers drifted close to the Coronation Stone hanging from his neck. "Aini, I need to tell you about a Dream I had."

"Now?"

A sadness tugged at his eyes and the edges of his fine lips. "If this fight comes down to one of us choosing mercy or death for our enemies, we must choose death."

Aini's stomach knotted. "Because you saw what happens if we don't."

His throat moved in a slow swallow. "Aye. Our people will be forced to fight this over and over again. We must not hesitate in dealing out death."

She could feel the truth of it, the shining, hard steel truth of it. "I understand." Holding him close for a blessed moment, she realized he was the Seer in these situations. "You know," she said quietly, seriously, "you are as much Seer as I am."

He took her chin in his warm fingertips. "And you are Heir. We are in this together. Completely together."

Heart beating steady and strong in her chest, Aini kissed his soft mouth quickly, then took off toward the king's tent. Thane and her fierce friends trailed just behind, and her feet never once touched the earth.

## CHAPTER 19
## BANISHED

Bran was hot on Thane's heels. The ground dipped and he nearly tripped over his own feet, catching himself on Myles's shoulder. The colonial gave him a wink, the moon lighting his bald head.

"You should pull your hood up," Bran said, huffing as they sped into the dark, toward the king's tent.

Myles did as told and for once didn't add a little comment. More than anything that made Bran worry. And it was enough to distract him and cause him to pretty much run straight into a kingsman on patrol. Myles grimaced and sidled into the shadows to follow Aini, Vera, Neve, and Thane who were already far enough away not to notice.

Bran's fight training clicked in. Without thinking about it, he kicked the man below the navel to throw him off balance. Bran drove a knee forward and dropped the kingsman. He was sure someone had heard.

"Come on," Myles whispered. He crouched beside a military truck.

The faint outline of Aini and the rest of them showed just outside the king's tent. Aini was looking around like she was trying to find Bathilda or one of the other ghosts.

"Go on. I'll catch up." Bran uncapped a smoke bomb and threw it as far as he could in the opposite direction.

Two hundred thousand thoughts were flying through his head, but one specific fear gnawed at him with very, very sharp teeth as he sped toward what was most likely death in the form of a royal command and a quick shot to the head. He dialed Viola's number as he ran.

"You alive?" Her voice was wispy but steady, like a constant stream of incense smoke.

"I am. How is it coming along over there?" He stubbed a toe against a row of metal boxes labeled in pale military-style numbers.

"Nathair and this Jack Shaw fellow are killing as many of our own as the king's. They just ordered an entire unit into what was clearly pure suicide."

Bran breathed out and rounded the tent's corner. The group had collected outside the door beside one of the king's flyers. Aini and Thane were having a heated but whispered discussion.

"You stay out of that, aye?" Bran said to Viola.

"I'm liking you, Bran, but you can't start telling me what to do now."

Bran almost laughed. "I like you too. Can you please stay alive so we can discuss this further?"

"That I will agree to. Fare well, my good knight."

"Fare well, my lady." Bran tucked the phone away. The ground at his right boot sparkled oddly. He bent to check it out. Something like sand ran in a line as far as he could see in the dark.

He gathered some in his hand and met the group. "I found this on the ground. I don't think it's explosive..."

Thane frowned at the tiny grains in Bran's palm.

Aini frowned. "The ghosts aren't communicating with me. I don't know what waits for us in there." She floated a foot off the ground, her face drawn and worried.

"We can't just stand out here," Vera said. "We'll just have to go for it."

"Heir and Seer," a voice said from the dark.

Vera had a gun aimed at him fast. "Who is it?"

"Walker and Sandoe," another voice said.

Relief loosened the vice that had grabbed Bran's chest. Ah. He recognized that first name. "It's the colonial contact."

Thane took a deep breath. "Och. Good."

Walker and Sandoe came closer, the moon lighting on a man with silvery black hair and a woman with bright red locks, both in kingsmen jackets and armed to the teeth.

"How many are inside?" Vera asked the woman.

Sandoe's mouth bunched. "We don't know. They won't let anyone but their closest go in. We've just been patrolling this entrance for the last hour."

"You were supposed to be in that inner circle," Aini said.

Walker shrugged, but the movement was tight like he braced for a sudden attack. Being a mole in King John's camp was nothing Bran envied, that was certain. "I thought I was," Walker said. "Just before he sent Sandoe and me on patrol, the king told me the order of attack had altered and that he was waiting on a message from inside the city."

"Did he say anything else?" Thane eyed the tent behind them.

"No, but I do know he sent three flyers over the Firth of Forth to land near Arthur's Seat. Said something about *back up*."

Bran didn't like this one bit. He gave Thane a look that said as much.

Thane raised his eyebrows. "Aye, friend." He put a hand on Bran's shoulder. "I agree with that face you're making, but we're in it, good or bad. We can't pull back now."

"What about this?" Bran held up his grainy fingers.

"We need to go. Before this change or whatever it is happens and we lose this chance to surprise John," Vera hissed. "He has someone, possibly more than that, inside the walls. We must move now."

"Agreed." Thane gave the group one last encouraging nod, then pushed into the king's tent beside Aini.

All hell broke loose.

Thane went down fast, glasses flying, four men on him and stretching his hands and feet wide so he couldn't grab the stone necklace or a gun or anything. He struggled hard, the chocolate giving him superhuman strength, but there were just too many against him.

The kingsmen must have heard them coming.

Aini was treated likewise, face slammed into the earth, eyes blinking back tears.

Bran put a hand to an explosive, but before he could even finish the thought, he was on the ground alongside Myles, Vera, and Neve. Why hadn't Bathilda warned them about all the kingsmen in here? Where were all the ghosts?

A figure in all black walked out of the tent's second room. Gold rimmed the edges of his jacket and boots. His shoulder-length curls were oiled to a shine.

King John was here. In the flesh. On the battlefield.

Bran's mouth went very dry. He tried to swallow and ending up making a ridiculous choking noise that had Thane doing his level best to twist and check on him despite the huge men holding him down.

King John leaned down toward Aini and put his hand on his knees. "I bet I can guess what you're thinking. Even though I'm not an abomination like you and your people."

Aini's glare could've melted steel.

The king just smiled. "You're wondering where your ghosts are. I bet you thought you could slip in here and have all the Dead on your side, hm?" He shuddered, then straightened obviously trying to hide his own fear of the paranormal. "We consulted some old tomes and discovered the key to unlocking this problem was very simple."

"It's salt, isn't it?" Neve's voice came from Aini's right.

Salt. It hadn't been sand near Bran's boot outside. It had been salt. Suddenly he remembered Nathair talking at a gathering about his great-grandmother and how she'd banished a mean spirit from a barn at Inveraray with salt. The story had been one of a million and easy to forget among the others that were filled with seemingly more poignant information about clan loyalty and politics throughout the British Empire.

Bran locked eyes with Aini. Was John right? Did the salt keep the spirits out? Her eyes closed in defeat. Yes. The salt erased their key advantage. Now all that remained was the manner in which King John would kill them all.

"Pull back the roof, the walls." John waved his fingers—heavy with gold rings—at the surrounding canvas. "I want to see my city. My Edinburgh. She is in chaos, and I will rectify this situation as a true king. I will show these rebels what royal blood can accomplish."

Bran said a quiet *Fare well* to Viola and prepared to die.

## CHAPTER 20

## DESTINED

Thane watched the king's boots shift in front of his nose. The smell of dirt rose through the fine carpet on the tent's floor as Thane twisted to try to see Aini. Rage scorched his bones, his flesh. They had her pinned like a beautiful butterfly, wings trapped, no chance of flying now. She couldn't move. He couldn't move. The ghosts couldn't pass the ring of salted earth. They were ruined.

"Thane," Bran whispered. "Remember Moot Hill?"

What had he said? Moot Hill? That was the place where the old kings had been crowned. Thane had gone there with Bran during their stay with Callum. Thane had felt welcomed there—strong, powerful, and at peace. But what good was that memory now?

The kingsman who held Bran pushed his face into the ground with the sole of his shoe. Bran grunted in pain.

Thane spat blood from a deep cut inside his cheek. "Your earl and his men are still fighting out there. You haven't won yet."

The King John laughed as two figures were escorted by kingsmen to bow before the king. Thane frowned, trying to make out their faces. When the guard beside the king shifted his weight, Thane caught a clear view of both new arrivals. His stomach dropped like lead through water.

Nathair. Jack Shaw.

They stood like physical embodiments of the lives Thane could've led. Earl, fanatic. Gangster, opportunist.

He'd rather die.

"Offering surrender are you?" Thane shouted. This was the possible change that Walker and Sandoe had heard about.

His heart squeezed until he thought it might burst. Would he never be free of his father and the unique pain the man injected into his soul with every sick smile, loaded turn of phrase, and false promise? He hated the blood he shared with the man. Hated it.

And Jackie. Thane swallowed bile. He'd put steel to Aini's flesh. He'd made her hurt. Being imprisoned injured a person so much more than a simple cut.

Anger flashed through Thane's chest and down his arms as he stared at his two closest enemies, his two temporary allies. He'd held onto it, but now, now that they would surely give Thane and Aini up if King John offered terms, the blaze of righteous fury would no longer be ignored.

"What's it to be then, Your Majesty?" Nathair asked. "Do we have an accord?"

King John raised his big nose into the air. "Call the French ships off right here. Now. And then we will talk."

Jackie shook his phone jauntily, flipping his coat back and flashing the blood-red silk lining. "I'm the only one with the password to do so and I won't call off our allies unless you declare your ceasefire over the loudspeaker for all to hear."

Where did this man get his confidence? It was like he had some unending stash of it in that ridiculous coat.

John's eyebrows lifted to meet his hairline. He looked utterly calm except for the angry flush sneaking up his neck. "I'll just keep blasting until the French ships come closer then. Your choice."

As if pressing his point, a flyer came to life behind them. The propellers thudded away like war drums and tossed dirt and salt into the air, flapping coats and hair riotously. A flash lit the night, and Thane knew more had died and more of the city was in ruins. His stomach lurched. So much damage that could not be undone. So many dead and dying. It was disgusting that Nathair and Jack would treat the rebels' deaths like nothing. If they came to an agreement with King John, those who were dying right now would have died for no reason. Thane wanted to tear the world open and throw Nathair, Jack, and John in and watch them burn.

"None of us wants Edinburgh to become a pile of stone, Your Majesty," Nathair said. "Would you agree? It has made you quite a lot of gold these past years."

Thane realized his hands were shaking with the anger and determination flowing through him. If he could just move enough so that the Coronation Stone touched the skin of his chest or neck, he could call up the curse. He could win. Maybe. If the ghost rulers were stronger than the salt. Inching a shoulder forward over the carpet, he rolled a small fraction and attempted to shift his shirt lower. One of the men holding him rammed his boot harder into his neck. Thane's muscles spasmed, sending pain shooting through his upper back and head.

"Most of which you skimmed away into your own coffers, Earl." The king's voice was low and dangerous. "You call off the French ships now. You give me the Seer and the...Heir," he said, his tone slick and toxic, "to do with as I please. Then you both walk free. I will call the ceasefire only when you make the call."

Thane couldn't let this happen. After all the work and all the terror, this couldn't be the end of all they'd worked toward. He refused to believe Aini's father Lewis, his mother Senga, Aini herself, and so many more had suffered for nothing. His teeth ground together and his pulse pounded behind his eyes.

Nathair was whispering to Jack. Vipers hissing at one another.

Invisible fire erupted along Thane's shoulders. The man holding him down leaped back. The heat zipped down Thane's arm and into his hand and a flickering sword materialized. He gasped and jumped to his feet, everyone else standing, open-mouthed, except Bran who wore a knowing grin. In shock, Thane stared down at the flaming, ghostly sword.

Clenching his jaw and arcing the sword he'd seen just once, on Moot Hill, Thane advanced on his father. He was sick with it, but he knew what he had to do. The image from his Dream haunted him.

"I don't want to do this," he said, "but I can't let you hurt people anymore."

The sword vanished and Nathair blinked—the only movement beyond Thane himself. Now, the room would erupt into gunfire and they would all be lost.

"I must do it," Thane whispered, no idea who he was talking to. Maybe himself. Maybe the ghost kings. Time seemed suspended.

A shiver rolled down his body and the sword blazed into being.

Tears burned down Thane's cheeks.

He ran the ghostly sword through Nathair's chest.

Thane fell to his knees as his father's body dropped beside

Jack Shaw's black boots. The world hummed and warped and Thane was outside of time, beyond pain and anger. This was justice and though it was horrible, it had to be done.

"Thane!" Aini's voice broke through the haze and woke him.

Jack yanked a gun from a kingsman and made to aim at Thane's head.

There was a shout and a noise like a strange wind instrument and then MacBeth's knife was sticking out of Jack's throat. Blood cloaked the man's shirt and he crumpled to the carpet beside Nathair.

Aini was standing, panting, her stance wide. The hand that had thrown the dagger shook. "Your Dream. I remembered what you said, about bringing Death to them. To protect our people."

Thane stood beside Aini, two beings draped in magic and prophecy, spinning the future.

None of the kingsmen or King John himself had moved. Shock, and perhaps a spell, had them all tied tight.

CHAPTER 21

KINGS AND QUEENS

※

Before the king could shake himself from whatever magic Thane had worked, Aini grabbed Thane and dragged him outside the salt circle.

She stood face-to-face with him, as an ally, a partner. Her heart drummed louder than any flyer as she stared into Thane's silver eyes. "Claim your right."

His aura fluttered, then brightened. He gripped the Coronation Stone at his neck.

Her own power flared to life, a shock of heat, a flood of possibility. At that moment, she was unstoppable.

The wind rose to a deafening roar. The ground shook like the very world tilted on its axis. Blue-white shapes curled from the earth in great, shimmering columns to become bearded kings, crowned queens, cloaked rulers from ages long forgotten. The aroma of sage, pine forests, and dark caves whirled into the air and whipped through Aini's wild hair.

She grinned at the queens especially, fire in her veins.

Thane—stone in one hand and ghostly sword in the other—nodded. "It is time."

Three kingsmen opened fire on Thane.

"Protect your Heir," Aini called to the shimmering kings and queens.

Thane spun, his sword weaving through the air to create a glimmering, blue and white web of protection around him. Bullets fell from the weapon's shielding like drops of rain.

A flyer lifted into the air and pointed its guns at Aini. She focused on the flyer's cockpit, and with the gravity-reducing chemicals still riding her bloodstream, she soared toward the big, metal beast. Her outstretched hands blazed with supernatural light. The ghost rulers bolstered and fortified her. Their wall of otherworldly energy sang in her ears.

She smiled like a vengeful angel and threw all her own energy forward. "Take them down," she commanded.

The crowned spirits enveloped the flyer. With a great crunching sound, the metal crumpled like it was made of sand.

Bran, Neve, Vera, and Myles fought the kingsmen inside the salt circle, their strength from the chocolates making them nearly impossible to defeat.

"Leave the salt circle!" Aini drifted toward them. The ghostly army flanked her and more spirits blossomed beyond Thane, ready to join in.

Bran glanced at Aini as he used a dagger's hilt to crush a kingsman's nose. "Here!" he said to Myles. "Out of the circle!"

Neve, Myles, and Vera followed him out of the sparkling ring, still fighting.

In the distance, the colored plumes of spirits shifted up, down, and around the city.

Leaping and slicing with his glowing sword, Thane cut down five kingsmen. Sweat darkened the hair at his brow as he fought for Scotland, for Aini, for all of them. The web around him pulsed in time with the ghost rulers' light, fed by their magic. Aini had never been so proud.

Rising toward the stars, above Thane's head, Aini threw her hands toward a mass of kingsmen with rocket launchers. The ghost queens raced to obey her, leaving the ghost kings to aid Thane. The queens twined their light around bodies and left the deadly kingsmen—those that had already murdered hundreds of innocent men, women, and children—unmoving in the cold mud.

Bran shrieked.

Aini looked down to see Bran jump between Thane's back and King John's sword. The king's blade drove down through Bran's arm and severed the limb completely.

Aini's heart plummeted.

"Claim that man." She pointed at King John.

Thane whirled to see Bran, to realize what his friend had done. With a fierce shout, Thane thrust his sword forward. The steel pierced John's chest. Twenty of the brightest ghost queens and kings spun around the evil king, then dragged him screaming and bleeding to the ground.

"Stop his army and destroy his weapons," Aini commanded the rest of the ghost rulers, watching them spread over the field. A deadly silence followed in their wake.

Aini rushed through the air to where Thane held Bran's head in his lap. There was blood everywhere. The dark fluid stained Thane and Bran and the ground black. Myles, Neve, and Vera crowded around, all at a loss for words.

"Bathilda! Please! Anyone!" Aini studied the skies for help.

Bran coughed up a mouthful of blood and reached a hand toward Thane's chest. Bran's skin turned a dim shade of gray.

Thane pressed his forehead into Bran's hair, eyes tightly shut.

Aini's heart refused to beat. "Please!" She put her hands on Bran's shoulder, right above the horrible wound Neve had stuffed with a strip of cloth. Pouring her energy into Bran, Aini tried to imagine the blood vessels closing and the skin mending, but her mind refused to lock into place. She couldn't focus.

"We're going to lose him." Neve sniffed and put her hands on Bran's ankle. Her face was a mess of dirt and blood specks.

Vera and Myles arranged themselves at each side of Thane, as if to hold him up. Aini choked on a cry for help. Where were the ghosts? There was no time.

In the distance, flyers rose, then crashed over Arthur's Seat, like birds shot down from the clouds. A shout came from the city—so many voices joined. But the words were lost in the cacophony of the ghosts' vengeance on those who had hurt this land and its people. Bran's body felt like a hollowed shell. His spirit was about to leave this life. She could feel it tugging at the strings of this world.

The ghosts weren't coming to save this one man. He would die. Bran, Thane's dearest friend. Aini took Thane's hand in hers. It was cold. Thane bent low over Bran's head and spoke into his ear. The night air blew over Aini's cheeks and tried to dry her tears.

Then a warmth like one thousand hearth fires, one thousand summer breezes, one thousand embraces cocooned Aini.

"Thane. Wait."

Could it be true? What was this?

Night became day as energy surged from Aini's palm and into Bran's dying body.

Thane stared at Aini, the raw hope in his eyes like firebrands.

Bran's mouth opened wide and he breathed in deep and strong. The bleeding ceased. The exposed flesh near the torn fabric of Bran's jacket and shirt smoothed into a scar that seemed years old. The severed limb, not far from where he'd fallen, disappeared. Bran's arm didn't materialize on his arm, but the shoulder seemed healed, and Bran was breathing. Opening his eyes, blinking, he glanced at Aini, then fell into what appeared to be a calm sleep, chest rising and falling regularly as darkness fell like blanket over the field.

Aini cried out in joy.

Thane's watery eyes locked on her. His aura flickered like moonlight touched by fire. "Thank you, hen. Thank you. Thank you. Thank you." His cheekbones reflected the colored light and a length of his hair fell over his forehead. "You are a wonder, Aini MacGregor. I am blessed indeed to have your heart."

Gently, careful of Bran, she leaned over and pressed a simple kiss onto Thane's lips.

Neve hugged Myles, and Vera began barking orders into her phone.

The pink haze of sunrise suffused the sky over the spires and blocky stones of the wounded city. A cheer rose from Edinburgh. The wind carried it across the hills.

"Heir! Seer! Scotland forever!"

Every muscle in Aini's body ached. A shiver buzzed through her when she thought about what they might find inside Edinburgh's walls. Her father Lewis might be dead. Thane's mother Senga too. Viola. Hawes. There were so many.

Bathilda materialized above Aini. She smiled, then faded, too quickly for Aini to say a word. The spirit had accomplished her goal then. Now she was gone, moved on.

"Godspeed, Bathilda. We are in your debt."

Neve, Vera, and Myles gathered around Aini and Thane, who stood guard over Bran's sleeping form. All their faces wore smiles that outshone the blood and dirt marring their cheeks and chins. There was still work to do and grief to fight through, but Aini would take the happiness here in front of her for now and hold it against her soul to steel herself for the future.

CHAPTER 22

FIRE

Aini handed a twist of dark, rose-colored taffy to Thane. The fire in the townhouse's hearth painted his hair gold. The light played on his cheekbones and strong jaw. Busy with setting up Parliament, seeing to the city's wounded, and arranging the coming coronation, they hadn't been alone since before the battle. Aini felt it was high time for an evening alone, but she couldn't bring herself to ask her father, Neve, and Myles to give them a moment. It was still such a joy to have them here, well and happy.

"Haven't seen this shade." Thane examined the candy, its reflection showing in his glasses. "What's it do?" After unwrapping it, he popped the sugary treat between his lips, then licked a finger.

Myles whistled. "You trust her an awful lot. You don't even know what that batch is going to do to you." His music tripped out of his room and down the hall. Banjos and drums vied for attention and it was amazing neither Thane nor Father had demanded he shut it off.

"I trust her with all my heart." Thane dropped a kiss on Aini's nose. His breath smelled like sugar and mint and she wanted very much to kiss that neck of his.

"Of course you do." Neve pulled her legs under her skirt and shifted so she was practically sitting on Myles's lap.

Aini ate a piece of taffy. "It's simply taffy. No chemicals. No hormones. No special effects."

"Boring." Myles stuck out his bottom lip.

Father cleared his throat. His gaze caught on the patched spot in the wall beside his office door, evidence of the vicious fighting that had taken place right on their street. "I think I'm ready for some boring, thank you very much." He held up his well-worn book of Robert Burns. "Should I go on with the poetry?"

"At least finish the one you started," Aini said.

"All right, squirrel. I will do that.

*'Till a' the seas gang dry, my dear,*
*And the rocks melt wi' the sun:*
*I will luve thee still, my dear,*
*While the sands o'life shall run.*"

Myles and Neve were doing some sort of interpretive dance to the poem that was equal parts horribly ridiculous and terribly funny. With a hideous grimace, Myles stood over the couch pillows—Aini assumed those were the poem's rocks—and wiggled his fingers like they were the sun's rays melting away the stones. He put a hand over his heart and knelt at Neve's feet. She spun and sighed so loudly Aini missed the start of the next stanza.

"*...fare thee weel, my only luve!*
*And fare thee weel a-while!*
*And I will come again, my luve,*
*Tho' it were ten thousand mile.*"

Myles ran in place, wiping his head of imagined sweat. "Ten thousand is a lot of miles," he whispered.

Neve laughed and shoved him into the chair beside Father.

The phone on the side table rang and Father picked it up. "Ah, Senga. Thane is right here." He nodded as if she could see him. "Fine. I'll show him when it comes through."

Senga had been injured during the battle with King John. A ceiling had crashed onto her and a few others, but thankfully, all they'd suffered were concussions and minor cuts and bruises. As soon as Thane had been declared King of Scotland with Aini as his Chief Advisor, peace had returned in Edinburgh under Owen's direction, and the new English ruler had signed the treaty, Senga had returned to Inveraray to recover properly. Aini suspected Senga wasn't resting nearly enough though, seeing as there were repairs to be done all around the estate.

"Good bye." Father clicked the phone off, then turned it and showed the screen to Thane. "This is a sketch she's done of the new wing."

The drawing showed detailed alcoves and five new rooms for visiting dignitaries, one of which Vera had claimed since her appointment to the Parliament. "Senga is definitely not resting."

Thane smiled and handed the phone back. "I'm glad she is having a good time up there. Are you going up for the wedding?" Bran and Viola were set to wed at Christmas, but that wasn't the real reason Father wanted to head back to Inveraray.

Aini fought a grin as Father's ears reddened.

"Yes. Of course. For the wedding. We all are and you know it." He set the book down and stood. "Now, it's time I'm off to bed. Myles, Neve, could you please tidy up the lab? And please turn off that music. Thank you."

Thane chuckled. He approved of the budding friendship between their parents.

Father wished everyone *good night* and disappeared down the corridor.

Myles held out a hand to Aini. "I want a piece of that boring taffy. I think it *does* do something fantastic and you're just lying." He took a piece and chewed it noisily.

Aini raised an eyebrow. "I only lie for good reasons."

"Maybe it'll make you hate banjos as much as I do," Thane said, "and the townhouse will finally be at peace."

Neve steered Myles down the hallway toward the sound of his speakers.

"Never!" Myles punched the air.

And finally Aini had Thane to herself.

The fire snapped and he put a new log on. Woodsmoke scented the room. Here was the next ruler of this country, tending the fire for her. Bizarre.

"I suppose I'll have to kneel to you when you're king," she said wryly, teasing him as she finished her drink and set the glass on the table.

Thane, on his knees, faced her, looking up. The fire silhouetted his powerful frame and mixed with the blue and gold of his aura. It was lovely. "You'll never kneel to anyone unless you wish it, hen."

He wrapped a hand around her calf. His thumb drew circles and threw chills across her skin. He pressed a kiss into her thigh, then broke away slowly, very slowly, his breath dancing over the inside of her leg. She tangled her fingers in his hair as his hands slid over her knees. When he tilted his chin up to look at her, his black lashes framed his stormy eyes and his lips parted. His tongue moved like he was about to say something, but before he could utter a word, heat rushed over Aini's body and she went to her knees to meet him. Her stomach brushed his as his fingers found the waistband of her skirt and tugged her closer. She leaned into him. His muscles tensed. His lips lighted on her chin and he whispered into her neck.

"Aini. My Aini."

She ran her hands over his shoulders and along the lines of his upper back as he traced her collarbone with a gentle finger. Her body melted into his, and he pulled her on top of him, the fire crackling beside them. Sitting up, she took a moment to appreciate the view. The heart inside this strong body of his was the finest. Brave. True. A survivor. With his hair and glasses askew, one hand on her waist and the other hovering above her leg, he grinned. His dimples showed in his cheeks. Her own body responded rather strongly to those dimples, heart pounding in approval.

"Enjoying yourself, hen?"

Her eyebrow lifted. "Aye," she said before proceeding to kiss the new king into oblivion.

*For a complimentary prequel to The Edinburgh Seer, visit http://www.alishaklapheke.com/free-prequel-1*
*If you enjoyed this book, please consider leaving a review. Reviews are very important for all readers.*

## Scots Slang Dictionary
## (Thane approved)

**aye**—yes

**baltic**—cold

**bampot**—a fool who is sometimes amusing

**bairn**—baby

**beamer**—red face from embarrassment usually

**ben**—mountain

**bide**—wait, live, stay (depends on context)

**blether**—(sometimes spelled blather) talking on and on, chatting

**boak**—(sometimes spelled boke) vomit

**boggin'**—dirty, no good, smelly

**bonnie**—beautiful

**bowfin**—dirty, smelly

**braw**—beautiful or brilliant

**canny**—clever, shrewd

**clipe/clype**—(varied spellings and usages) a tattletale, a rat, to tell on someone

**close**—a covered alley

**coo**—cow, usually a Highland cow (they are adorable so google that)

**crabbit**—grouchy, mean tempered

**daft**—stupid but usually harmless

**dinnae teach yer Granny tae suck eggs**—Don't try to teach someone something they most likely already know

**doister**—big storm, rain big time

**dreich**—wet and cold weather

## SCOTS SLANG DICTIONARY

**feartie**—coward
**geggie**—mouth
**glaikit**—dumb, foolish
**Glasgow kiss**—headbutt
**gob**—mouth
**hackit**—ugly
**haud yer wheesht**—hold your wheesht (varied spellings) Be quiet
**keek**—a quick look at something
**ken**—know
**kip**—nap
**manky**—smelly
**mawkit**—dirty
**muckle**—a good amount
**numpty**—stupid person
**pure**—very, exceptionally
**skelp**—slap
**skinny malinky longlegs**—skinny person
**sleekit**—clever, sly (negative connotation)
**stramash**—a scuffle, a chaotic tangle of a bother
**tattie**—potato
**tidy**—lovely, good, beautiful
**wean**—child

*Keep turning pages to read a sample of Waters of Salt and Sin, the first book in Alisha's epic fantasy series!*

# WATERS OF SALT AND SIN (A SAMPLE)

A BREATH BEFORE SUNRISE, THE sea was a half-lidded eye, pale blue and white beyond the town walls and lemon orchards. The sea and me, the only two awake this early.

Or so it seemed when I climbed to the roof of the tavern. The streets were only dark mud and shuttered windows. I should've been out scouring too, looking for a fallen dumpling or a bit of orange-spiced chicken. But I couldn't help myself. The glimmering saltwater winked at me and I gave it a lazy smile.

"Soon," I whispered before heading back down.

I had to finish the rope I'd labored on all night, because though magic was good for a lot of things, unfortunately, twisting coconut fibers wasn't one of them.

My hands used to bleed when I did this kind of work. Not now. Now my palms were like moving stones, pressing, rolling over the two sections and twining them around one another until they were long enough to tie off a sail.

My younger sister Avi snored lightly on our straw mat in the port tavern's undercroft. I opened her hand. Someday—if I managed to keep her alive until someday—those angry blisters would disappear and she'd have rocks for hands too. I touched the area around the worst of them gently. Though she was fourteen, I rubbed her arm like Mother used to do when we were little. Soon enough, she'd be beside me on the sea, rushing to finish our day's work before night fell and the salt wraiths came. But she didn't love the risk, the delicious challenge, or the waters like I did.

"Kinneret?" Avi's eyes opened, red and bleary.

"No. I'm Amir Mamluk," I joked, pretending to be the steel-eyed woman who held the town in her ruthless grip, only a few steps below the kyros in power. "I am in disguise as your sister so I can enjoy the pleasures of low-caste life. What's first? Prying barnacles off the hull or watching my hard-earned silver disappear into rich men's pockets?" I clapped my hands like an idiot as Avi bent over laughing.

"You're a madwoman, Sister." She looked past me to the light. "You should've shaken me awake sooner. Did you get your sailing papers stamped?"

I waved her off. "I will. Tomorrow."

"All right." A black spot marred the edge of her grin. She'd lost a tooth last week. The empty place looked wrong next to the pretty yellow-brown hair she'd inherited from Father.

Avi leaned over to touch the shells she hid under her side of the mat. She didn't know I knew about them, so I stood and turned away, giving her a moment. It was her own ritual and whatever gave her peace was fine with me.

Gathering the fibers I hadn't used last night and the new rope, I forced a worthless tear back inside my eye and tried not to hear her little whispers.

"Mother. Father. The kitten. The cat. My broken bird."

She'd found a shell for each of the ones she'd lost. A curving one with ridges, as dark brown as our mother's skin had been. A spotted one for Father. He would've liked that. He'd loved the unusual.

As I tied on my sash, the tiny bells jingling, she drank from the bucket and wiped her mouth with the back of her hand.

"Eat that bread there." I jerked my chin at the stool that served as our table.

"What about you?"

"I ate with Oron late last night," I lied. I was a great liar, but I didn't rejoice in it. Lying was the skill of the desperate, something I intended to stop being as soon as possible.

"He actually ate?" Avi said around the nub of bread. "I thought he was on an all stolen wine diet."

"He wishes. Said so right before he went down to the boat." This time of year, depending on the crowd at the dock, my first mate sometimes slept onboard to protect our only real possession. Harvest brought a lot of strangers who wouldn't worry about consequences.

Smiling, Avi shook her head and handed me the bag of salt I kept tied to my sash. I shook it, felt its soft bottom. There was enough for some Salt Magic if we ended up needing it today.

"What shipments do we have?" Avi asked. "None. We're scouting new port locations again."

"Hope it goes better than last time. Is Calev going to predict our weather for the trip?" Avi grinned.

As a member of the native community of Old Farm—and the chairman's son to boot—Calev was born high-caste, raised to oversee his people's lemon orchards and barley fields, and basically treated like a kyros around town. The brat, I thought, a grin tugging at me.

But despite his powerful family and his position, he had the hardest time predicting weather, a child's first lesson on a farm or at sea. He just couldn't seem to gather the clues hidden in the thrush's song, the clouds' sudden curl, or the moisture in a breeze. Seriously, he was rubbish at it. His eyebrow twitched when it frustrated him and it was—

"You're the prettiest when you smile like that, Kin."

I shoved her gently. "Shut up, you. Come on. We need to go." My relationship with Calev was complicated. And dangerous now that we neared the age of adulthood. Avi really did need to shut up about it. At least until I found some way to snake my way into a higher caste.

I unlocked the door and held it open for her, pretending there wasn't a pile of both human and animal waste we had to step over. Soon, the middle-caste merchants would open their booths in these dirty streets to trade goods and gossip under the white-hot sun.

Ugh. There was the sailmaker's son.

He was still burned over the deal his father gave me when Calev came along to buy our new sail.

"Kinneret Raza the Magnificent, friend to high-castes." He pretended to whisper, but his words were plenty loud. "But only if you have eyes and a backside like that Old Farm boy Calev. For him, she pretends that bag of salt at her sash is for seasoning food. It's a miracle he doesn't see you for what you are. Witch."

A ringing filled my ears. If the wrong people heard him, we'd wish our only problem was finding something to eat today. "The real miracle is that pest birds haven't nested in your continuously open mouth, between your rotting teeth."

His gaze lashed out at Avi. "Soon I won't be the only one with an Outcast's mouth, witches."

I raged toward him and he lifted his leg to kick me off, but

Avi jumped in the way. The tip of his sandal struck her leg, and she winced.

"You better stop it," Avi shouted. "Or you'll be sorry." He laughed and went on as I bent to check Avi's leg. "It's a scratch," she said. "It's nothing."

"That horse's back end is going to be nothing if he ever touches you again. You should keep quiet when he is around."

"Oh, like you do, Sister?" She raised both eyebrows.

I snorted. "Well, I'm Kinneret the Magnificent, remember?" The ridiculousness of the title burned like a brand.

Avi put a hand on my arm and pulled me to standing. "You are magnificent to me."

I hugged her and felt her shoulder bones like driftwood under my arms. My temples throbbed. She was little more than a skeleton. A chill slithered down my back. How long could we live like this?